D0059257

"At times brilliant. . . . Wroblewski's literary skill is most apparent in his intoxicating descriptions of the bucolic setting . . . he handles his task with impressive subtlety." —*New York Times Book Review*

"This debut novel by David Wroblewski is one of the most stunning, elegant books I have ever read. . . . With *The Story of Edgar Sawtelle*, Wroblewski achieves the iconic dream of so many writers, that of bursting forth (after, of course, years of brutal and anonymous work weaving straw into gold) with what can deservedly be called a great American novel." —*Houston Chronicle*

"The literary sensation of the season. . . . You may want to trust me and get the book right now. . . . Fresh and unpredictable to the end. Wroblewski has an uncanny ability to make palpable for us the bones and muscles of his characters." —*Books & Culture*

"It all culminates in a finale that is as gripping as anything you'll read this year—just try to put the book down during its last 100 pages or so." —*Santa Fe New Mexican*

"An audacious retelling of *Hamlet*. . . . Wroblewski brings it off with flair. . . . *The Story of Edgar Sawtelle* is, all at once, a mystery, a thriller, a ghost story, and a literary tour de force. . . . An authentic epic, long and lush, full of backstory and observed detail. . . . Once the reader has fallen under his spell . . . the author exercises a certain magic that catches and holds our attention, a magic that is undeniably his own." —*Los Angeles Times Book Review*

"As do most resonant and powerful novels, *The Story of Edgar Sawtelle* mimics life. . . . Wroblewski's writing is leisurely and lovely, often separated into graceful vignettes. . . . A gripping novel." —*Buffalo News*

"With its taproot in *Hamlet*, this novel spins an engrossing tale of power struggles within a family of Wisconsin dog breeders. . . . Whatever its author produces next will definitely be a book to watch out for." —*Salon*

"In this debut novel, Wroblewski illustrates the relationship between man and canine (at times, from the dog's point of view) in a way that is both lyrical and unsentimental, and demonstrates an ability to create a coherent, captivating fictional world in which even supernatural elements feel entirely persuasive."

—*The New Yorker*

"A passionate first novel. . . . Reading it is like entering a long dream that won't let you out until it's ready. Expect storms; expect a ghost and mysterious events, a riveting trip into the wild with Edgar and three dogs; expect losses and, like Edgar, go where this wonderful novel takes you."

—*Chicago Sun-Times*

"Wroblewski's evocation of this enhanced canine consciousness produces his best writing. . . . We come to love the Sawtelle dogs, to cherish our time with them. . . . The novel is gripping . . . in these moments, Wroblewski steers clear of the sentimentality that often mars writing about dogs, allowing a stoic wisdom to emerge instead."

—*Charlotte Observer*

"It's the must-read of the summer: an enthralling literary saga about a mute Wisconsin teen and his eerily intelligent dogs on the run after a death in the family. All that, plus echoes of *Hamlet*."

—*People*

"The boy-and-his-dog tale at the heart of David Wroblewski's debut novel, *The Story of Edgar Sawtelle*, is deeply observed, as symbolically deep as any epic, and most surprising of all, devoid of easy sentiment."

—*Washington City Paper*

"The book is poised to be one of the breakout titles of the summer."

—*Wall Street Journal*

"If you're looking for a new novel to occupy your summer, or a good part of it, look no further. *The Story of Edgar Sawtelle*, all 566 pages, is surprising and rewarding. It's worth savoring, both its story and its storytelling."

—*USA Today*

"David Wroblewski's rite-of-passage novel sets the standard for fiction about dogs. . . . With David Wroblewski's meaty, masterly debut novel, *The Story of Edgar Sawtelle*, easily the best work of fiction ever written about dogs (as well as the longest), such works are rendered not just moot, but moribund."

—*Chicago Tribune*

"The most enchanting debut novel of the summer. Written over a decade by the heretofore unknown David Wroblewski and arriving as a bolt from the blue, this is a great, big, mesmerizing read, audaciously envisioned as classic Americana. . . . The voice heard in *The Story of Edgar Sawtelle* sounds like no one else's as this book creates its enthralling, warmly idiosyncratic story. . . . One of the great pleasures of *The Story of Edgar Sawtelle* is its free-roaming, unhurried progress, enlivened by the author's inability to write anything but guilelessly captivating prose."

—*New York Times*

"Whether you read for the beauty of language or for the intricacies of plot, you will easily fall in love with David Wroblewski's generous, almost transcendentally lovely debut novel, *The Story of Edgar Sawtelle*. This is a tale set in rural Wisconsin in the first half of the twentieth century, on a farm where the Sawtelles raise a fictional breed of dog. The dogs function like spirits in Shakespeare, or the chorus in Greek tragedy: They color the text with larger meaning yet remain tangibly real, deeply believable as dogs. Edgar is the mute boy who raises them, a mesmerizing fictional hero, primitive and wise. There are passages of language here ('A pair of does sprang over the fence on the north side of the field—two leaps each, nonchalant, long-sustained, falling earthward only as an afterthought . . . ') that make you pause and read again with luxuriant pleasure. Wroblewski's plot is dynamic—page-by-page compelling—and classical, evoking *Hamlet*, *Antigone*, *Electra*, and *Orestes*, as Edgar tries to avenge his father's death and his paternal uncle's new place in the affections of his mother. The scope of this book, its psychological insight, and lyrical mastery, make it one of the best novels of the year, and a perfect, comforting joy of a book for summer."

—*O, The Oprah Magazine*

"Here is a big-hearted novel you can fall into, get lost in, and finally emerge from reluctantly, a little surprised that the real world went on spinning while you were absorbed. You haven't heard of the author. David Wroblewski is a forty-eight-year-old software developer in Colorado, and this is his first novel. It's being released with the kind of hoopla once reserved for the publishing world's most established authors. No wonder: *The Story of Edgar Sawtelle* is an enormous but effortless read, trimmed down to the elements of a captivating story about a mute boy and his dogs. That sets off alarm bells, I know: Handicapped kids and pets can make a toxic mix of sentimentality. But Wroblewski writes with such grace and energy that *Edgar Sawtelle* never succumbs to that danger. Inspired improbably by the plot of Shakespeare's *Hamlet*, this Midwestern tale manages to be both tender and suspenseful. . . . Most of the story comes to us through a masterful, transparent voice: The author, the narrator, the pages—everything fades away as we're drawn into this engrossing tale. . . . The final section gathers like a furious storm of hope and retribution that brings young Edgar to a destiny he doesn't deserve but never resists. It's a devastating finale, shocking though foretold, that transforms the story of this little family into something grand and unforgettable."   —*Washington Post Book World*

"Edgar Sawtelle is the utterly disarming teenage hero at the center of David Wroblewski's wonderful debut novel of the same name. Set on a small farm in rural Wisconsin, *The Story of Edgar Sawtelle* takes all kinds of risks. The hero is mute, a few chapters are narrated from a dog's point of view, and there are all kinds of ways the novel could have dissolved into a syrupy mess. Instead, Wroblewski creates a tender coming-of-age story and grafts onto it a literary thriller with strong echoes of Shakespeare and *The Jungle Book*. The result is the most hauntingly impressive debut I've read all year. . . . Edgar might be silent, but his story will echo with readers for a long time."   —*Christian Science Monitor*

"Young Edgar, born mute, lives with his parents on a remote Wisconsin farm, where they raise a rare breed of dog, and has an unusual rapport with a dog named Almondine (who hears baby Edgar wailing even though he makes no sound). Shortly after Edgar's uncle arrives, his father dies suspiciously, leading to the boy's hasty flight from home, three dogs in tow. What follows is a harrowing quest for survival in the woods, one in which no words are spoken—and none needed. Don't let the book's massive size fool you: This is a good old-fashioned coming-of-age yarn. Grade: A."   —*Entertainment Weekly*

"A stunning first novel . . . a ranging story that is part coming-of-age, part mystery, and part tragedy on the order of *Hamlet*. . . . Wroblewski executes with élan, building an addicting tale peopled by fully dimensional characters. He carries the reader, with authority and confidence, on a thought-provoking ride."
                          —*Denver Post*

"A stunningly well-written novel."   —*Pittsburgh Tribune*

"Colorado-based writer David Wroblewski has been at work at his sprawling debut novel for more than a decade, and the results of his painstaking care are evident in the fascinating world that he's created. His story, filled with fluid, descriptive prose, quickly transports the reader into its timeless setting and rich atmosphere, making the pages fly by. . . . *The Story of Edgar Sawtelle* is a winning debut that will make a great read for the coming—forgive me—dog days of summer. Grade: A-"   —*Rocky Mountain News*

"The Great American Novel is something like a unicorn—rare and wonderful, and maybe no more than just a notion. Yet every few years or so, we trip across some semblance of one. Oof! What's this? Why, it's *The Story of Edgar Sawtelle*, a sprawling skein of a yarn about a farm nestled up against the forest primeval, aka the Chequamegon in northern Wisconsin, a place where the drama of nature unfolds daily, ceaselessly—recorded here with preternatural awareness, as if witnessed for the very first time. It's a story about a stoic husband, Gar; his quietly heroic wife, Trudy; and their loyal, stouthearted son, Edgar, who lacks only a voice, having been born mute. The farm is nothing much—a humble apple orchard, a hay field, and a barn that houses the family's third-generation vocation: a breeding kennel whose dogs are of legendary quality, if obscure pedigree. Into this idyll, however, drifts Gar's prodigal brother, Claude, a spreading human stain of alcohol, tobacco, and the occasional firearm, who has returned home after several decades involving military service and, it seems, some hard time. Gar dies suddenly, incomprehensibly. Edgar suspects that something's rotten in Denmark—but then, he would, seeing how his mother, a shrewd judge of character and a supremely practical woman, soon enough takes up with Claude. The story's both more complicated than it sounds and yet boldly, bald-facedly what it is. How Edgar in time goes about breaking this domestic impasse and strikes out into the wide world will carry you through this novel's 560-odd pellucid, mythos-riddled pages and leave you crying for more. Fortunately, David Wroblewski seems on the evidence of this extraordinary debut to be the sort of fellow who will oblige us much, much more."   —*Elle*

"It isn't every day that big-name authors like Stephen King and Richard Russo rave about a first-time novel months before publication. And it's even less often that critics from industry publications such as *Publishers Weekly* agree wholeheartedly, breathlessly proclaiming that a book is 'bound to be a bestseller.' Put *Sawtelle* on your summer reading list."   —*Rocky Mountain News*

"A literary thriller with commercial legs, this stunning debut is bound to be a bestseller. . . . After another gut-wrenching tragedy, Edgar goes on the run, accompanied by three loyal dogs. His quest for safety and succor provides a classic coming-of-age story with an ironic twist. Sustained by a momentum that has the crushing inevitability of fate, the propulsive narrative will have readers sucked in all the way through the breathtaking final scenes."

—Publishers Weekly (starred review)

"A stately, wonderfully written debut novel. . . . Wroblewski takes an intense interest in his characters; takes pains to invest emotion and rough understanding in them; and sets them in motion with graceful language. . . . The novel succeeds admirably . . . an auspicious debut: a boon for dog lovers, and for fans of storytelling that eschews flash. Highly recommended."

—Kirkus Reviews (starred review)

"Set in Wisconsin, this deeply nuanced epic tells the story of a boy, his dog, and much more. . . . The rich depiction of Edgar's family, who are breeders of unique dogs, creates a warm glow that contrasts sharply with the cold evil that their family contains. This tension . . . makes this an excruciatingly captivating read. . . . Ultimately liberating, though tragic and heart-wrenching, this book is unforgettable; overwhelmingly recommended for all libraries."

—Library Journal (starred review)

"I flat-out loved The Story of Edgar Sawtelle. I thought of Hamlet when I was reading it, and Watership Down, and The Night of the Hunter, and The Life of Pi—but halfway through, I put all comparisons aside and let it just be itself. I closed the book with that regret readers feel only after experiencing the best stories: It's over, you think, and I won't read another one this good for a long, long time. Wonderful, mysterious, long, and satisfying. . . . I don't reread many books, because life is too short. I will be rereading this one."   —Stephen King

"I doubt we'll see a finer literary debut this year than The Story of Edgar Sawtelle. David Wroblewski's got storytelling talent to burn and a big, generous heart to go with it."   —Richard Russo, Pulitzer Prize–winning author of Empire Falls

"In this beautifully written novel, David Wroblewski creates a remarkable hero who lives in a world populated as much by dogs as by humans, governed as much by the past as by the present. The Story of Edgar Sawtelle is a passionate, absorbing, and deeply surprising debut."

—Margot Livesey, author of The House on Fortune Street

"Edgar Sawtelle is a boy without a voice, but his world, populated by the dogs his family breeds, is anything but silent. This is a remarkable story about the language of friendship—a language that transcends words."

—Dalia Sofer, bestselling author of *The Septembers of Shiraz*

"This remarkable hybrid seems like an impossibility: an American *Hamlet*, both ghost story and melodrama, a coming-of-age tale, a hymn to the land—and, central to it all, some of the best writing about the inner lives of dogs anywhere. *The Story of Edgar Sawtelle* is a woolly, unlikely, daring book, and wildly satisfying."

—Mark Doty, *New York Times* bestselling author of *Dog Years*

"This luminescent story has the kind of sprawling, wide-lens focus that readers think of when they talk about the so-called great American novel."

—*Capital Times* (Madison, WI)

"Who says *Hamlet* and canines don't mix? Get thee to a kennel! It's the Prince of Denmark himself who bequeathed to us the phrase 'Every dog will have its day.' And yet David Wroblewski is surely the first novelist to locate a reworking of Shakespeare's tragedy in a family of dog breeders in rural Wisconsin—with a mute boy, Edgar, as his hero. (The soliloquies are silent.) A long, powerfully felt novel, *The Story of Edgar Sawtelle* is far better than it has any right to be, especially given the rapturous Stephen King blurb on the back and the banner praise bestowed by the *New York Times*, which declared it 'the most enchanting debut novel of the summer'—harbingers, I assumed, of disappointment. But Mr. Wroblewski knows how to make use of a good story (thanks, Will!), and his characters (on two legs and four) grab the reader and won't let go."

—*New York Observer*

"David Wroblewski's big tale gets a big telling in his first novel, *The Story of Edgar Sawtelle*, which should come stamped with the cover label 'This Summer's Good Old-Fashioned Read.'" —*New York Daily News*

"For every success like Jane Smiley's *A Thousand Acres*, the Pulitzer Prize–winning update of *King Lear*, there are scores of failed attempts to channel William Shakespeare in fiction or on screen. The arresting prologue of *The Story of Edgar Sawtelle* is the first indication that David Wroblewski might make it work. And by the time readers reach the book's can't-turn-the-pages-fast-enough final chapters, it's clear that *Edgar Sawtelle* merits a place on the short list of novels that do the sixteenth-century writer proud."   —*St. Louis Post-Dispatch*

"Sawtelle is a compelling ride."   —*The Oregonian*

"The cast is small, the story simple, and Wroblewski spins it out masterfully. . . . I've already recommended this 'Story' to my Edgar-age daughter and a colleague on the far side of fifty. I don't know if it's *Snow Falling on Cedars* but I can imagine that sort of ubiquity. I can see it sitting in lake cabins and beach cottages and on countless tables that flank the comfy chairs of confirmed readers from Wisconsin to Westchester."   —*Bloomberg News*

"'It's the story of a modern-day Hamlet in northern Wisconsin,' East Village Books owner Teri Wood TeBockhorst said. 'It's a significant read, but it's getting an incredible amount of praise. All of the reviewers just love it.'"
                                          —*Des Moines Register*

"Debut novels are seldom this ambitious—or this praised."
                                          —*Seattle Post-Intelligencer*

"A stunning novel . . . an epic tale of language, love, loss, survival, and reprisal. But above all, it's a story of family, both human and animal, and the bonds we share."   —*Clarion-Ledger* (Jackson, MS)

"This spellbinding debut novel set in the north woods of Wisconsin resonates with the reader on many levels. . . . *The Story of Edgar Sawtelle* is an unforgettable debut—one to savor, to share, and even, despite its length, to reread."
                                          —*BookPage*

The Story of

EDGAR

SAWTELLE

The Story of

EDGAR

SAWTELLE

a novel

DAVID
WROBLEWSKI

An Imprint of HarperCollinsPublishers

A hardcover edition of this book was published in 2008 by Ecco, an imprint of Harper-Collins Publishers.

P.S.™ is a trademark of HarperCollins Publishers.

THE STORY OF EDGAR SAWTELLE. Copyright © 2008 by David Wroblewski. All rights reserved. Printed in the United States of America. No part of this book may be used or reproduced in any manner whatsoever without written permission except in the case of brief quotations embodied in critical articles and reviews. For information, address HarperCollins Publishers, 10 East 53rd Street, New York, NY 10022.

HarperCollins books may be purchased for educational, business, or sales promotional use. For information, please write: Special Markets Department, HarperCollins Publishers, 10 East 53rd Street, New York, NY 10022.

Grateful acknowledgment is made for permission to reprint from the following: "Bewitched, Bothered and Bewildered" (from *Pal Joey*), words by Lorenz Hart, music by Richard Rodgers, © 1941 (renewed) Chappell & Co., Inc. All rights for Extended Renewal Term in U.S. controlled by WB Music Corp. and Williamson Music. All rights reserved. Used by permission of Alfred Publishing Co., Inc.

"Bewitched" by Richard Rodgers and Lorenz Hart, copyright © 1941 by Chappell & Co., Inc. Copyright renewed. Copyright assigned to Williamson Music for the Extended Renewal Period of copyright for the Richard Rodgers interest in the USA. International copyright secured. All rights reserved.

FIRST ECCO EDITION PUBLISHED 2009.

Designed by Jessica Shatan Heslin/Studio Shatan, Inc.

Library of Congress Cataloging-in-Publication Data is available upon request.

ISBN: 978-0-06-137423-4 (pbk.)

09 10 11 12 13   ID/RRD   10 9 8 7 6 5 4 3 2 1

For Arthur and Ann Wroblewski

There is grandeur in this view of life, with its several powers, having been originally breathed into a few forms or into one; and that, whilst this planet has gone cycling on according to the fixed law of gravity, from so simple a beginning endless forms most beautiful and most wonderful have been, and are being, evolved.

—CHARLES DARWIN, *The Origin of Species*

The Story of

EDGAR

SAWTELLE

Prologue

Pusan, South Korea, 1952

After dark the rain began to fall again, but he had already made up his mind to go and anyway it had been raining for weeks. He waved off the rickshaw coolies clustered near the dock and walked all the way from the naval base, following the scant directions he'd been given, through the crowds in the Kweng Li market square, past the vendors selling roosters in crude rattan crates and pigs' heads and poisonous-looking fish lying blue and gutted and gaping on racks, past gray octopi in glass jars, past old women hawking kimchee and bulgoki, until he crossed the Tong Gang on the Bridge of Woes, the last landmark he knew.

In the bar district the puddled water shimmered red and green beneath banners strung rooftop to rooftop. There were no other servicemen and no MPs and he walked for a long time, looking for a sign depicting a turtle with two snakes. The streets had no end and he saw no such sign and none of the corners were square and after a while the rain turned to a frayed and raveling mist. But he walked along, methodically turning right twice then left twice, persevering with his search even after he'd lost his bearings many times over. It was past midnight before he gave up. He was retracing his route, walking down a street he'd traversed twice before, when he finally saw the sign, small and yellow and mounted high on the corner of a bar. One of the snakes curled back to bite the turtle's tail. As Pak had said it would.

He'd been told to look for an alley opposite the sign, and it was there too—narrow, wet, half-cobbled, sloping toward the harbor, lit only by the signs opposite and the glow of windows scattered down its length. He walked away from the street, his shadow leading the way. Now there should be a doorway with a lantern—a red lantern. An herbalist's shop. He looked at the tops of the buildings, took in the underlit clouds streaming over the rooftops. Through the window of a shabby bathhouse came a woman's shriek, a man's laughter. The needle dropped on a record and Doris Day's voice quavered into the alley:

> I'm wild again, beguiled again,
> A simpering, whimpering child again.
> Bewitched, bothered, and bewildered am I.

Ahead, the alley crooked to the right. Past the turn he spotted the lantern, a gourd of ruby glass envined in black wire, the flame within a rose that sprang and licked at the throat of the glass, skewing rib-shadows across the door. A shallow porch roof was gabled over the entrance. Through the single, pale window he saw only a smoke-stained silk curtain embroidered with animal figures crossing a river in a skiff. He peered down the alley then back the way he'd come. Then he rapped on the door and waited, turning up the collar of his pea coat and stamping his feet as if chilled, though it was not cold, only wet.

The door swung open. An old man stepped out, dressed in raw cotton pants and a plain vestment made from some rough fabric just shy of burlap. His face was weathered and brown, his eyes set in origami creases of skin. Inside the shop, row upon row of milky ginseng root hung by lengths of twine, swaying pendulously, as if recently caressed.

The man in the pea coat looked at him. "Pak said you know English."

"Some. You speak slow."

The old man pulled the door shut behind him. The mist had turned to rain again. It wasn't clear when that had happened, but by then rain had been falling for days, weeks, and the sound of running water was so much a part of the world he could not hear it anymore. To be dry was temporary; the world was a place that shed water.

"You have medicine?" the old man asked. "I have money to pay."

"I'm not looking for money. Pak told you that, didn't he?"

The old man sighed and shook his head impatiently. "He should not have spoke of it. Tell me what you want."

Behind the man in the pea coat, a stray dog hobbled down the alley, making its way gamely on three legs and eyeing the men. Its wet coat shone like a seal's.

"Suppose we have rats," the man said. "Difficult ones."

"Your navy can kill some few rats. Even poorest junk captain does this every day. Use arsenic."

"No. I—we—want a method. What Pak described. Something that works at once. No stomachache for the rat. No headache. The other rats should think the one rat went to sleep and didn't wake up."

"As if God take him in instant."

"Exactly. So the other rats don't think what happened to the one rat as unnatural."

The old man shook his head. "Many have wished for this. But what you ask—if such thing exist—then whoever possess this second only to God."

"What do you mean?"

"God grant life and death, yes? Who calls another to God in instant has half this power."

"No. We all have that power. Only the method is different."

"When method looks like true call of God, then is something else," the herbalist said. "More than method. Such things should be brutal and obvious. It is why we live together in peace."

The old man lifted his hand and pointed into the alley behind his visitor. "Your dog?"

"Never seen it before."

The herbalist retreated into his shop, leaving the door standing open. Past the ginseng, a tangled pile of antlers lay beneath a rack of decanters. He returned carrying a small clay soup pot in one hand and in the other an even smaller bamboo box. He set the pot on the cobblestones. From inside the box he withdrew a glass bottle, shaped as if for perfume or maybe ink. The glass was crude and warped. The top was stoppered and the irregular lip sealed with wax. Inside, a liquid was visible, clear as rainwater but slick and oily. The herbalist picked away the wax with his fingernail and pinched the stopper between thumb and index finger and produced from somewhere a long, thin reed whose end was cut on the oblique and sharpened to a needle's point. He dipped the reed into the bottle. When it emerged, a minute quantity of the liquid had wicked into the reed and a drop shimmered on the point. The herbalist leaned into the alleyway and whistled sharply. When nothing happened, he made a kissing noise in the air that made the man's skin crawl. The three-legged dog limped toward them through the rain, swinging its tail, and sniffed the clay pot and began to lap.

"That's not necessary," the man said.

"How otherwise will you know what you have?" the herbalist said. His tone was not kindly. He lowered the sharpened tip of the reed until it hovered a palm's width above the dog's withers and then he performed a delicate downward gesture with his wrist. The tip of the reed fell and pierced the dog and rose again. The animal seemed not to notice at first.

"I said that wasn't necessary. For Christ's sake."

To this the herbalist made no reply. Then there was nothing to do but stand and watch while the rain fell, its passing almost invisible except where the wind folded it over itself.

When the dog lay still, the herbalist replaced the stopper in the bottle and twisted it tight. For the first time, the man noticed the small green ribbon encircling the bottle's neck, and on the ribbon, a line of black Hangul letters. The man could not read Hangul but that did not matter. He knew the meaning anyway.

The herbalist slipped the bottle into the bamboo box. Then he flicked the reed into the alley and kicked the soup pot after. It shattered against the cobbles and the rain began to wash its contents away.

"No one must eat from that. A small risk, but still risk. Better to break than bring inside. You understand?"

"Yes."

"Tonight I soak hands in lye. This you understand?"

The man nodded. He retrieved a vial from his pocket. "Penicillin," he said. "It's not a cure. Nothing is guaranteed."

The herbalist took the vial from the man. He held it in the bloody lantern light and rattled the contents.

"So small," he said.

"One pill every four hours. Your grandson must take them all, even if he gets better before they're gone. Do you understand? All of them."

The old man nodded.

"There are no guarantees."

"It will work. I do not believe so much in chance. I think here we trade one life for one life."

The herbalist held out the bamboo box. A palsy shook his hand or perhaps he was overwrought. He had been steady enough with the reed.

The man slid the bamboo box into the pocket of his pea coat. He didn't bother to say good-bye, just turned and strode up the alley past the bathhouse where Doris Day's voice still seeped into the night. Out of habit he slipped his hand into his coat pocket and, though he knew he shouldn't, let his fingertips trace the edges of the box.

When he reached the street he stopped and blinked in the glare of the particolored bar signs, then glanced over his shoulder one last time. Far away, the old herbalist was out in the rain, a bent figure shuffling over the stone and dirt of the half-cobbled alley. He'd taken the dog by the back legs and was dragging it away, to where, the man did not know.

Part I

FORTE'S

CHILDREN

A Handful of Leaves

IN THE YEAR 1919, EDGAR'S GRANDFATHER, WHO WAS BORN WITH an extra share of whimsy, bought their land and all the buildings on it from a man he'd never met, a man named Schultz, who in his turn had walked away from a logging team half a decade earlier after seeing the chains on a fully loaded timber sled let go. Twenty tons of rolling maple buried a man where Schultz had stood the moment before. As he helped unpile logs to extract the wretched man's remains, Schultz remembered a pretty parcel of land he'd spied north and west of Mellen. The morning he signed the papers he rode one of his ponies along the logging road to his new property and picked out a spot in a clearing below a hill and by nightfall a workable pole stable stood on that ground. The next day he fetched the other pony and filled a yoked cart with supplies and the three of them walked back to his crude homestead, Schultz on foot, reins in hand, and the ponies in harness behind as they drew the cart along and listened to the creak of the dry axle. For the first few months he and the ponies slept side by side in the pole shed and quite often in his dreams Schultz heard the snap when the chains on that load of maple broke.

He tried his best to make a living there as a dairy farmer. In the five years he worked the land, he cleared one twenty-five-acre field and drained another, and he used the lumber from the trees he cut to build an outhouse, a barn, and a house, in that order. So that he wouldn't need to go outside to tote water, he dug his well in the hole that would become the basement of the house. He helped raise barns all the way from Tannery Town to Park Falls so there'd be plenty of help when his time came.

And day and night he pulled stumps. That first year he raked and harrowed the south field a dozen times until even his ponies seemed tired of it. He stacked rocks at the edges of the fields in long humped piles and burned stumps in bonfires that could be seen all the way from Popcorn Corners—the closest town, if you called that a town—and even Mellen. He managed to build a small stone-and-concrete silo taller than the barn, but he never got around to capping it. He mixed milk and linseed oil and rust and blood and used the concoction to paint the barn and outhouse red. In the south field he planted hay, and in the west, corn, because the west field was wet and the corn would grow faster there. During his last summer on the farm he even hired two men from town. But when autumn was on the horizon, something happened—no one knew just what—and he took a meager early harvest, auctioned off his livestock and farm implements, and moved away, all in the space of a few weeks.

At the time, John Sawtelle was traveling up north with no thought or intention of buying a farm. In fact, he'd put his fishing tackle into the Kissel and told Mary, his wife, he was delivering a puppy to a man he'd met on his last trip. Which was true, as far as it went. What he didn't mention was that he carried a spare collar in his pocket.

THAT SPRING THEIR DOG, Violet, who was good but wild-hearted, had dug a hole under the fence when she was in heat and run the streets with romance on her mind. They'd ended up chasing a litter of seven around the backyard. He could have given all the pups away to strangers, and he suspected he was going to have to, but the thing was, he *liked* having those pups around. Liked it in a primal, obsessive way. Violet was the first dog he'd ever owned, and the pups were the first pups he'd ever spent time with, and they yapped and chewed on his shoelaces and looked him in the eye. At night he found himself listening to records and sitting on the grass behind the house and teaching the pups odd little tricks they soon forgot while he and Mary talked. They were newlyweds, or almost. They sat there for hours and hours, and it was the finest time so far in his life. On those nights, he felt connected to something ancient and important that he couldn't name.

But he didn't like the idea of a stranger neglecting one of Vi's pups. The best thing would be if he could place them all in the neighborhood so he could keep tabs on them, watch them grow up, even if from a distance. Surely there were half a dozen kids within an easy walk who wanted a dog. People might think it peculiar, but they wouldn't mind if he asked to see the pups once in a while.

Then he and a buddy had gone up to the Chequamegon, a long drive but worth it for the fishing. Plus, the Anti-Saloon League hadn't yet penetrated the north woods, and wasn't likely to, which was another thing he admired about the area. They'd stopped at The Hollow, in Mellen, and ordered a beer, and as they talked a man walked in followed by a dog, a big dog, gray and white with brown patches, some mix of husky and shepherd or something of that kind, a deep-chested beast with a regal bearing and a joyful, jaunty carriage. Every person in the bar seemed to know the dog, who trotted around greeting the patrons.

"That's a fine looking animal," John Sawtelle remarked, watching it work the crowd for peanuts and jerky. He offered to buy the dog's owner a beer for the pleasure of an introduction.

"Name's Captain," the man said, flagging down the bartender to collect. With beer in hand he gave a quick whistle and the dog trotted over. "Cappy, say hello to the man."

Captain looked up. He lifted a paw to shake.

That he was a massive dog was the first thing that impressed Edgar's grandfather. The second thing was less tangible—something about his eyes, the way the dog met his gaze. And, gripping Captain's paw, John Sawtelle was visited by an idea. A vision. He'd spent so much time with pups lately he imagined Captain himself as a pup. Then he thought about Vi—who was the best dog he'd ever known until then—and about

Captain and Vi combined into one dog, one pup, which was a crazy thought because he had far too many dogs on his hands already. He released Captain's paw and the dog trotted off and he turned back to the bar and tried to put that vision out of his mind by asking where to find muskie. They weren't hitting out on Clam Lake. And there were so many little lakes around.

The next morning, they drove back into town for breakfast. The diner was situated across the street from the Mellen town hall, a large squarish building with an unlikely looking cupola facing the road. In front stood a white, three-tiered drinking fountain with one bowl at person height, another lower, for horses, and a small dish near the ground whose purpose was not immediately clear. They were about to walk into the diner when a dog rounded the corner and trotted nonchalantly past. It was Captain. He was moving in a strangely light-footed way for such a solidly constructed dog, lifting and dropping his paws as if suspended by invisible strings and merely paddling along for steering. Edgar's grandfather stopped in the diner's doorway and watched. When Captain reached the front of the town hall, he veered to the fountain and lapped from the bowl nearest the ground.

"Come on," his buddy said. "I'm starving."

From along the alley beside the town hall came another dog, trailing a half-dozen pups behind. She and Captain performed an elaborate sashay, sniffing backsides and pressing noses into ruffs, while the pups bumbled about their feet. Captain bent to the little ones and shoved his nose under their bellies and one by one rolled them. Then he dashed down the street and turned and barked. The pups scrambled after him. In a few minutes, he'd coaxed them back to the fountain, spinning around in circles with the youngsters in hot pursuit while the mother dog stretched out on the lawn and watched, panting.

A woman in an apron walked out the door of the diner, squeezed past the two men, and looked on.

"That's Captain and his lady," she said. "They've been meeting there with the kids every morning for the last week. Ever since Violet's babies got old enough to get around."

"*Whose* babies?" Edgar's grandfather said.

"Why, Violet's." The woman looked at him as if he were an idiot. "The mama dog. That dog right there."

"*I've* got a dog named Violet," he said. "And she has a litter about that age right this moment back home."

"Well, what do you know," the woman said, without the slightest note of interest.

"I mean, don't you think that's sort of a coincidence? That I'd run into a dog with my own dog's name, and with a litter the same age?"

"I couldn't say. Could be that sort of thing happens all the time."

"Here's a coincidence happens every morning," his buddy interjected. "I wake up, I get hungry, I eat breakfast. Amazing."

"You go ahead," John Sawtelle said. "I'm not all that hungry anyway." And with that, he stepped into the dusty street and crossed to the town hall.

WHEN HE FINALLY SAT DOWN for breakfast, the waitress appeared at their table with coffee. "If you're so interested in those pups, Billy might sell you one," she said. "He can't hardly give 'em away, there's so many dogs around here."

"Who's Billy?"

She turned and gestured in the direction of the sit-down counter. There, on one of the stools, sat Captain's owner, drinking a cup of coffee and reading the *Sentinel*. Edgar's grandfather invited the man to join them. When they were seated, he asked Billy if the pups were indeed his.

"Some of them," Billy said. "Cappy got old Violet in a fix. I've got to find a place for half the litter. But what I really think I'll do is keep 'em. Cap dotes on 'em, and ever since my Scout ran off last summer I've only had the one dog. He gets lonely."

Edgar's grandfather explained about his own litter, and about Vi, expanding on her qualities, and then he offered to trade a pup for a pup. He told Billy he could have the pick of Vi's litter, and furthermore could pick which of Captain's litter he'd trade for, though a male was preferable if it was all the same. Then he thought for a moment and revised his request: he'd take the *smartest* pup Billy was willing to part with, and he didn't care if it was male or female.

"Isn't the idea to reduce the total number of dogs at your place?" his buddy said.

"I said I'd find the pups a home. That's not exactly the same thing."

"I don't think Mary is going to see it that way. Just a guess there."

Billy sipped his coffee and suggested that, while interested, he had reservations about traveling practically the length of Wisconsin just to pick out a pup. Their table was near the big front window and, from there, John Sawtelle could see Captain and his offspring rolling around on the grass. He watched them awhile, then turned to Billy and promised he'd pick out the best of Vi's litter and drive it up—male or female, Billy's choice. And if Billy didn't like it, then no trade, and that was a fair deal.

Which was how John Sawtelle found himself driving to Mellen that September with a pup in a box and a fishing rod in the back seat, whistling "Shine On, Harvest Moon." He'd already decided to name the new pup Gus if the name fit.

Billy and Captain took to Vi's pup at once. The two men walked into Billy's backyard to discuss the merits of each of the pups in Captain's litter and after a while one came bumbling over and that decided things. John Sawtelle put the spare collar on the pup and they spent the afternoon parked by a lake, shore fishing. Gus ate bits of sunfish roasted on a stick and they slept there in front of a fire, tethered collar to belt by a length of string.

The next day, before heading home, Edgar's grandfather thought he'd drive around a bit. The area was an interesting mix: the logged-off parts were ugly as sin, but the pretty parts were especially pretty. Like the falls. And some of the farm country to the west. Most especially, the hilly woods north of town. Besides, there were few things he liked better than steering the Kissel along those old back roads.

Late in the morning he found himself navigating along a heavily washboarded dirt road. The limbs of the trees meshed overhead. Left and right, thick underbrush obscured everything farther than twenty yards into the woods. When the road finally topped out at a clearing, he was presented with a view of the Penokee range rolling out to the west, and an unbroken emerald forest stretching to the north—all the way, it seemed, to the granite rim of Lake Superior. At the bottom of the hill stood a little white farmhouse and a gigantic red barn. A milk house was huddled up near the front of the barn. An untopped stone silo stood behind. By the road, a crudely lettered sign read, "For Sale."

He pulled into the rutted drive. He parked and got out and peered through the living room windows. No one was home. The house looked barely finished inside. He stomped through the fields with Gus in his arms and when he got back he plunked himself down on the running board of the Kissel and watched the autumn clouds soar above.

John Sawtelle was a tremendous reader and letter writer. He especially loved newspapers from faraway cities. He'd recently happened across an article describing a man named Gregor Mendel—a Czechoslovakian monk, of all things—who had done some very interesting experiments with peas. Had demonstrated, for starters, that he could predict how the offspring of his plants would look—the colors of their flowers and so on. Mendelism, this was being called: the scientific study of heredity. The article had dwelt upon the stupendous implications for the breeding of livestock. Edgar's grandfather had been so fascinated that he'd gone to the library and located a book on Mendel and read it cover to cover. What he'd learned occupied his mind in odd moments. He thought back on the vision (if he could call it that) that had descended upon him as he shook Captain's paw at The Hollow. It was one of those rare days when everything in a person's life feels connected. He was twenty-five years old, but over the course of the last year his hair had turned steely gray. The same thing had happened to his grandfather, yet his father was edging up on seventy with a jet black mane. Nothing of the kind had happened to either of his elder brothers, though one was bald as an egg. Nowadays when John Sawtelle looked into the mirror he felt a little like a Mendelian pea himself.

He sat in the sun and watched Gus, thick-legged and clumsy, pin a grasshopper to the ground, mouth it, then shake his head with disgust and lick his chops. He'd begun smothering the hopper with the side of his neck when he suddenly noticed Edgar's grandfather looking on, heels set in the dirt driveway, toes pointed skyward. The pup bucked in mock surprise, as if he'd never seen this man before. He scrambled forward to investigate, twice going tail over teakettle as he closed the gap.

It was, John Sawtelle thought, a lovely little place.

Explaining Gus to his wife was going to be the least of his worries.

IN FACT, IT DIDN'T TAKE LONG for the fuss to die down. When he wanted to, Edgar's grandfather could radiate a charming enthusiasm, one of the reasons Mary had been attracted to him in the first place. He could tell a good story about the way things were going to be. Besides, they had been living in her parents' house for over a year and she was as eager as he to get out on her own. They completed the purchase of the land by mail and telegram.

This the boy Edgar would come to know because his parents kept their most important documents in an ammunition box at the back of their bedroom closet. The box was military gray, with a big clasp on the side, and it was metal, and therefore mouseproof. When they weren't around he'd sneak it out and dig through the contents. Their birth certificates were in there, along with a marriage certificate and the deed and history of ownership of their land. But the telegram was what interested him most—a thick, yellowing sheet of paper with a Western Union legend across the top, its message consisting of just six words, glued to the backing in strips: OFFER ACCEPTED SEE ADAMSKI RE PAPERS. Adamski was Mr. Schultz's lawyer; his signature appeared on several documents in the box. The glue holding those words to the telegram had dried over the years, and each time Edgar snuck it out, another word dropped off. The first to go was PAPERS, then RE, then SEE. Eventually Edgar stopped taking the telegram out at all, fearing that when ACCEPTED fluttered into his lap, his family's claim to the land would be reversed.

He didn't know what to do with the liberated words. It seemed wrong to throw them away, so he dropped them into the ammo box and hoped no one would notice.

WHAT LITTLE THEY KNEW about Schultz came from living in the buildings he'd made. For instance, because the Sawtelles had done a lot of remodeling, they knew that Schultz worked without levels or squares, and that he didn't know the old carpenter's three-four-five rule for squaring corners. They knew that when he cut lumber he cut it once, making do with shims and extra nails if it was too short, and if it was too long, wedging it in at an angle. They knew he was thrifty because he filled the basement walls with rocks to save on the cost of cement, and every spring, water seeped through the cracks until the basement flooded ankle-deep. And this, Edgar's father said, was how they knew Schultz had never poured a basement before.

They also knew Schultz admired economy—had to admire it to make a life in the woods—because the house he built was a miniature version of the barn, all its dimensions divided by three. To see the similarity, it was best to stand in the south field, near the birch grove with the small white cross at its base. With a little imagination, subtracting out the changes the Sawtelles had made—the expanded kitchen, the extra bedroom, the back porch that ran the length of the west side—you'd notice that the house had the same steep gambrel roof that shed the snow so well in the winter, and that the windows were cut into the house just where the Dutch doors appeared at the end of the barn. The peak of the roof even overhung the driveway like a little hay hood, charming but useless. The buildings looked squat and friendly and plain, like a cow and her calf lying at pasture. Edgar liked looking back at their yard; that was the view Schultz would have seen each day as he worked in the field picking rocks, pulling stumps, gathering his herd for the night.

Innumerable questions couldn't be answered by the facts alone. Was there a dog to herd the cows? That would have been the first dog that ever called the place home, and Edgar would have liked to know its name. What did Schultz do at night without television or radio? Did he teach his dog to blow out candles? Did he pepper his morning eggs with gunpowder, like the voyageurs? Did he raise chickens and ducks? Did he sit up nights with a gun on his lap to shoot foxes? In the middle of winter, did he run howling down the rough track toward town, drunk and bored and driven out of his mind by the endless harmonica chord the wind played through the window sash? A photograph of Schultz was too much to hope for, but the boy, ever inward, imagined him stepping out of the woods as if no time had passed, ready to give farming one last try—a compact, solemn man with a handlebar mustache, thick eyebrows, and sad brown eyes. His gait would swing roundly from so many hours spent astride the ponies and he'd have a certain grace about him. When he stopped to consider something, he'd rest his hands on his hips and kick a foot out on its heel and he'd whistle.

More evidence of Schultz: opening a wall to replace a rotted-out window, they found handwriting on a timber, in pencil:

$$25 \; 1/4 + 3 \; 1/4 = 28 \; 1/2$$

On another beam, a scribbled list:

> lard
> flour
> tar 5 gal
> matches
> coffee
> 2 lb nails

Edgar was shocked to find words inside the walls of his house, scrawled by a man no one had ever seen. It made him want to peel open every wall, see what might be written along the roofline, under the stairs, above the doors. In time, by thought alone, Edgar constructed an image of Schultz so detailed he needn't even squint his eyes to call it up. Most important of all, he understood why Schultz had so mysteriously abandoned the farm: he'd grown lonely. After the fourth winter, Schultz couldn't stand it anymore, alone with the ponies and the cows and no one to talk to, no one to see what he had done or listen to what had happened—no one to witness his life at all. In Schultz's time, as in Edgar's, no neighbors lived within sight. The nights must have been eerie.

And so Schultz moved away, maybe south to Milwaukee or west to St. Paul, hoping to find a wife to return with him, help clear the rest of the land, start a family. Yet something kept him away. Perhaps his bride abhorred farm life. Perhaps someone fell sick. Impossible to know any of it, yet Edgar felt sure Schultz had accepted his grandfather's offer with misgivings. And that, he imagined, was the real reason the words kept falling off the telegram.

Of course, there was no reason to worry, and Edgar knew that, too. All that had happened forty years before he was born. His grandfather and grandmother moved to the farm without incident, and by Edgar's time it had been the Sawtelle place for as long as anyone could remember. John Sawtelle got work at the veneer mill in town and rented out the fields Schultz had cleared. Whenever he came across a dog he admired, he made a point to get down and look it in the eye. Sometimes he cut a deal with the owner. He converted the giant barn into a kennel, and there Edgar's grandfather honed his gift for breeding dogs, dogs so unlike the shepherds and hounds and retrievers and sled dogs he used as foundation stock they became known simply as Sawtelle dogs.

And John and Mary Sawtelle raised two boys as different from one another as night and day. One son stayed on the land after Edgar's grandfather retired to town a widower, and the other son left, they thought, for good.

The one that stayed was Edgar's father, Gar Sawtelle.

HIS PARENTS MARRIED LATE in life. Gar was over thirty, Trudy, a few years younger, and the story of how they met changed depending on whom Edgar asked and who was within earshot.

"It was love at first sight," his mother would tell him, loudly. "He couldn't take his eyes off me. It was embarrassing, really. I married him out of a sense of mercy."

"Don't you believe it," his father would shout from another room. "She chased me like a madwoman! She threw herself at my feet every chance she got. Her doctors said she could be a danger to herself unless I agreed to take her in."

On this topic, Edgar never got the same story twice. Once, they'd met at a dance in Park Falls. Another time, she'd stopped to help him fix a flat on his truck.

No, really, Edgar had pleaded.

The truth was, they were longtime pen pals. They'd met in a doctor's office, both of them dotted with measles. They'd met in a department store at Christmas, grabbing for the last toy on the shelf. They'd met while Gar was placing a dog in Wausau. Always, they played off each other, building the story into some fantastic adventure in which they shot their way out of danger, on the run to Dillinger's hideout in the north woods. Edgar knew his mother had grown up across the Minnesota border from Superior, handed from one foster family to another, but that was about all. She had no sisters or brothers, and no one from her side of the family came to visit. Letters addressed to her sometimes arrived, but she didn't hurry to open them.

On the living room wall hung a picture of his parents taken the day a judge in Ashland married them, Gar in a gray suit, Trudy in a knee-length white dress. They held a bouquet of flowers between them and bore expressions so solemn Edgar almost couldn't recognize them. His father asked Doctor Papineau, the veterinarian, to watch the dogs while he and Trudy honeymooned in Door County. Edgar had seen snapshots taken with his father's Brownie camera: the two of them sitting on a pier, Lake Michigan in the background. That was it, all the evidence: a marriage license in the ammo box, a few pictures with wavy edges.

When they returned, Trudy began to share in the work of the kennel. Gar concentrated on the breeding and whelping and placing while Trudy took charge of the training—something that, no matter how they'd met, she shined at. Edgar's father freely admitted his limitations as a trainer. He was too kindhearted, too willing to let the dogs get close to performing a command without getting it right. The dogs he trained never learned the difference between a *sit* and a *down* and a *stay*—they'd get the idea that they ought to remain approximately where they were, but sometimes they'd slide to the floor, or take a few steps and then sit, or sit up when they should have stayed down, or sit down when they should have stood still. Always, Edgar's father was more interested in what the dogs *chose* to do, a predilection he'd acquired from his own father.

Trudy changed all that. As a trainer, she was relentless and precise, moving with the same crisp economy Edgar had noticed in teachers and nurses. And she had singular reflexes—she could correct a dog on lead so fast you'd burst out laughing to see it. Her hands would fly up and drop to her waist again in a flash, and the dog's collar would tighten with a quiet *chink* and fall slack again, just that fast, like watching a sleight-of-hand trick. The dog was left with a surprised look and no idea who'd hit the lead. In the winter they used the front of the cavernous hay mow for training, straw bales arranged as barriers, working the dogs in an enclosed world bounded by the loose scatter of straw underfoot and the roughhewn ridge beam above, the knotty roof planks a dark dome shot through with shingling nails and pinpoints of daylight and the crisscross of rafters hovering in the middle heights and the whole back half of the mow stacked ten, eleven, twelve high with yellow bales of straw. The open space was still enormous. Working there with the dogs, Trudy was at her most charismatic and imperious. Edgar had seen her cross the mow at a dead run, grab the collar of a dog who refused to down, and bring it to the floor, all in a single balletic arc. Even the dog had been impressed: it capered and spun and licked her face as though she had performed a miracle on its behalf.

Even if Edgar's parents remained playfully evasive on the subject of how they'd met, other questions they answered directly. Sometimes they lapsed into stories about Edgar himself, his birth, how they'd worried over his voice, how he and Almondine had played together from before he was out of his crib. Because he worked beside them every day in the kennel—grooming, naming, and handling the dogs while they waited turns for training—he had plenty of chances to sign questions and wait and listen. In quieter moments they even talked about the sad things that had happened. Saddest of all was the story of that cross under the birches in the south field.

THEY WANTED A BABY. This was the fall of 1954 and they'd been married three years. They converted one of the upstairs bedrooms into a nursery and bought a rocking chair and a crib with a mobile and a dresser, all painted white, and they moved their own bedroom upstairs to the room across the hall. That spring Trudy got pregnant. After three months she miscarried. When winter came she was pregnant again, and again she miscarried at three months. They went to a doctor in Marshfield who asked what they ate, what medicines they took, how much they smoked and drank. The doctor tested his mother's blood and declared her perfectly healthy. Some women are prone, the doctor said. Hold off a year. He told her not to exert herself.

Late in 1956 his mother got pregnant for a third time. She waited until she was sure, and then a little longer, in order to break the news on Christmas Day. The baby, she guessed, was due in July.

With the doctor's admonition in mind, they changed the kennel routine. His mother still handled the younger pups herself, but when it came to working the yearlings, willful and strong enough to pull her off balance, his father came up to the mow. It wasn't easy for any of them. Suddenly Trudy was training the dogs *through* Gar, and he was a poor substitute for a leash. She sat on a bale, shouting, "Now! Now!" in frustration whenever he missed a correction, which was quite often. After a while, the dogs cocked an ear toward Trudy even when Gar held the lead. They learned to work the dogs three at a time, two standing beside his mother while his father snapped the lead onto the third and took it through the hurdles, the retrieves, the stays, the balance work. With nothing else to do, his mother started simple bite-and-hold exercises to teach the waiting dogs a soft mouth. Days like that, she left the mow as tired as if she'd worked alone. His father stayed behind to do evening chores. That winter was especially frigid and sometimes it took longer to bundle up than to cross from the kennel to the back porch.

In the evenings they did dishes. She washed, he dried. Sometimes he put the towel over his shoulder and wrapped his arms around her, pressing his hands against her belly and wondering if he would feel the baby.

"Here," she'd say, holding out a steaming plate. "Quit stalling." But reflected in the frosty window over the sink he'd see her smile. One night in February, Gar felt a belly-twitch beneath his palm. A halloo from another world. That night they picked a boy name and a girl name, both counting backward in their heads and thinking that they'd passed the three-month mark but not daring to say it out loud.

In April, gray curtains of rain swept across the field. The snow rotted and dissolved over the course of a single day and a steam of vegetable odors filled the air. Everywhere, the plot-plot of water dripping off eaves. There came a night when his father woke to find the blankets flung back and the bed sodden where his mother had lain. By the lamplight he saw a crimson stain across the sheets.

He found her in the bathroom huddled in the claw-footed tub. In her arms she held a perfectly formed baby boy, his skin like blue wax. Whatever had happened had happened quickly, with little pain, and though she shook as if crying, she was silent. The only sound was the damp suck of her skin against the white porcelain. Edgar's father knelt beside the tub and tried to put his arms around her, but she shivered and shook him off and so he sat at arm's length and waited for her crying to either cease or start in earnest. Instead, she reached forward and turned the faucets and held her fingers in the water until she thought it warm enough. She washed the baby, sitting in the tub. The red stain in her nightgown began to color the water. She asked Gar to get a blanket from the nursery and she swathed the still form and passed it over. When he turned to leave she set her hand on his shoulder, and so he waited, watching when he thought he should watch and looking away at other times, and what he saw was her coming back together, particle by particle, until at last she turned to him with a look that meant she had survived it.

But at what secret cost. Though her foster childhood had sensitized her to familial loss, the need to keep her family whole was in her nature from the start. To explain what happened later by any single event would deny either predisposition or the power of the world to shape. In her mind, where the baby had already lived and breathed (the hopes and dreams, at least, that made up the baby to her) was a place that would not vanish simply because the baby had died. She could neither let the place be empty nor seal it over and turn away as if it had never been. And so it remained, a tiny darkness, a black seed, a void into which a person might forever plunge. That was the cost, and only Trudy knew it, and even she didn't know what it meant or would ultimately come to mean.

She stayed in the living room with the baby while Gar led Almondine to the workshop. Up and down the aisle the dogs stood in their pens. He turned on the lights and tried to sketch out a plan on a piece of paper, but his hands shook and the dimensions wouldn't come out right. He cut himself with the saw, peeling back the skin across two knuckles, and he bandaged them with the kit in the barn rather than walk back to the house. It took until midmorning to build a box and a cross. He didn't paint them because in that wet weather it would have taken days for the paint to dry. He carried a shovel through the south field to the little grove of birches, their spring bark gleaming brilliant white, and there he dug a grave.

In the house they put two blankets in the bottom of the casket and laid the swaddled baby inside. It wasn't until then that he thought about sealing the casket. He looked at Trudy.

"I've got to nail it shut," he said. "Let me take it out to the barn."

"No," she said. "Do it here."

He walked to the barn and got a hammer and eight nails and the whole way back to the house he brooded over what he was about to do. They'd set the casket in the middle of the living room. He knelt in front of it. It had turned out looking like a crate, he saw, though he had done the best he could. He drove a nail into each corner and he was going to put one in the center of each side but all at once he couldn't. He apologized for the violence of it. He laid his head against the rough wood of the casket. Trudy ran her hand down his back without a word.

He picked up the casket and carried it to the birch grove and they lowered it into the hole and shoveled dirt over it. Almondine, just a pup at the time, stood beside them in the rain. Gar cut a crescent in the sod with the spade and pounded the cross into the ground with the flat side of the hammer. When he looked up, Trudy lay unconscious in the newly greened hay.

She woke as they sped along the blacktop north of Mellen. Outside the truck window the wind whipped the falling rain into half-shapes that flickered and twirled over the ditches. She closed her eyes, unable to watch without growing dizzy. She stayed in the Ashland hospital that night and when they returned the following afternoon, the rain still fell, the shapes still danced.

IT SO HAPPENED THAT their back property line lay exactly along the course of a creek that ran south through the Chequamegon forest. Most of the year, the creek was only two or three feet wide and so shallow you could snatch a rock from the bottom without getting your wrist wet. When Schultz had erected a barbed-wire fence, he dutifully set his posts down the center of the stream.

Edgar and his father walked there sometimes in the winter, when only the tops of the fence posts poked through the snowdrifts and the water made trickling, marble-clicking sounds, for though the creek wasn't wide enough or fast enough to dissolve the snow that blanketed it, neither did it freeze. One time Almondine tipped her head at the sound, fixed the source, then plunged her front feet through the snow and into the icy water. When Edgar laughed, even his silent laugh, her ears dropped. She lifted one paw after the other into the air while he rubbed them dry with his hat and gloves, and they walked back, hands and paws alike stinging.

For a few weeks each spring, the creek was transformed into a sluggish, clay-colored river that swept along the forest floor for ten feet on either side of the fence posts. Any sort of thing might float past in flood season—soup cans, baseball cards, pencils—their origins a mystery, since nothing but forest lay upstream. The sticks and chunks of rotten wood Edgar tossed into the syrupy current bobbed and floated off, all the way to the Mississippi, he hoped, while his father leaned against a tree and gazed at the line of posts.

They saw an otter once, floating belly up in the floodwater, feet pointed downstream, grooming the fur on its chest—a little self-contained canoe of an animal. As it passed, the otter realized it was being watched and raised its head. Round eyes, oily and black. The current swept it away while their gazes were locked in mutual surprise.

FOR DAYS AFTER HER RETURN from the hospital, Trudy lay in bed watching raindrops pattern the window. Gar cooked meals and carried them to her. She spoke just enough to reassure him, then turned to stare out the window. After three days the rain let up but gray clouds blanketed the earth. Neither sun nor moon had appeared since the stillbirth. At night Gar put his arms around her and whispered to her until he fell into a sleep of exhaustion and disappointment.

Then one morning Trudy got out of bed and came downstairs and washed and sat to eat breakfast in the kitchen. She was pale but not entirely withdrawn. The weather had turned warm and after breakfast Gar talked her into sitting in a big overstuffed chair that he moved out to the porch. He brought her a blanket and coffee. She told him, as gently as she could, to leave her be, that she was fine, that she wanted to be alone. And so he stayed Almondine on the porch and walked to the kennel.

After morning chores he carried a brush and a can of white paint to the birches. When he finished painting the cross he used his hands to turn the dirt where paint had dripped. The slow strokes of the brush on the wood had been all right but the touch of the earth filled him with misery. He didn't want Trudy to see him like that. Instead of returning to the kennel he followed the south fence line through the woods. Long days of rain had swelled the creek until it topped the second strand of barbed wire. He found a tree to lean against and absently counted the whirlpools curling behind the fence posts. The sight provided him some solace, though he couldn't have said why. After a while he caught sight of what he took to be a clump of leaf litter twisting along, brown against the brown water. Then, with a little shock, he saw it wasn't leaf litter at all, but an animal, struggling and sputtering. It drifted into an eddy and bobbed under the water and when it came to the surface again he heard a faint but unmistakable cry.

By the time he reached the fence, the creek water was over his knees—warmer than he expected, but what surprised him most was the strength of the current. He was forced to grab a fence post to keep his balance. When the thing swept close, he reached across and scooped it from the water and held it in the air to get a good look. Then he tucked it into his coat, keeping his hand inside to warm the thing, and walked straight up through the woods and into the field below the house.

TRUDY, SITTING ON THE PORCH, watched Gar emerge from the woods. As he passed through a stand of aspen saplings he seemed to shimmer into place between their trunks like a ghost, hand cradled to his chest. At first she thought he'd been hurt but she wasn't strong enough to walk out to meet him and so she waited and watched.

On the porch, he knelt and held out the thing for her to see. He knew it was still alive because all the long walk through the field it had been biting weakly on his fingers. What he held was a pup of some kind—a wolf, perhaps, though no one had seen one around for years. It was wet and shivering, the color of a handful of leaves and barely bigger than his palm. The pup had revived enough to be scared. It arched its back and yowled and huffed and scrabbled its hind feet against Gar's callused hands. Almondine pressed her muzzle around Gar's arm, wild to see the thing, but Trudy downed her sternly and took the pup and held it for a minute to look it over, then pressed it to her neck. "Quiet now," she said, "shush now." She offered her littlest finger for it to suckle.

The pup was a male, maybe three weeks old, though they knew little about wolves and could only judge its age as if it were a dog. Gar tried to explain what had happened but before he could finish the pup began to convulse. They carried it inside and dried it with a towel and afterward it lay looking at them. They made a bed out of a cardboard box and set the box on the floor near the furnace register. Almondine poked her nose over the side. She wasn't even a yearling yet, still clumsy and often foolish. They were afraid she would step on the pup or press him with her nose and scare the life out of him, and so, after a time, they put the box on the kitchen table.

Trudy tried formula, but the pup took a drop and pushed the nipple away with forepaws not much bigger than her thumbs. She tried cow's milk and then honey in water, letting the drops hang off her fingertips. She found an apron with a broad front pocket and carried the pup that way, thinking he might sit up, look around, but he just lay on his back and peered gravely at her. The sight made her smile. When she ran a finger along his belly fur he squirmed to keep sight of her eyes.

At dinnertime they sat and talked about what to do. They'd seen mothers reject babies in the whelping room even when nothing seemed wrong. Sometimes, Gar said, it worked to put orphans with another nursing mother. As soon as the words were out, they left the dishes on the table and carried the pup to the kennel. One of the mothers growled at the pup's scent. Another pushed him away and nosed straw over his body. In response, the pup lay utterly still. There was no point in getting mad but Trudy did anyway. She stalked to the house, pup clasped between her hands. She rolled a tiny piece of cheese between her fingers until it was warm and soft. She offered a shred of roast beef from her plate. The pup accepted none of these.

Near midnight, exhausted, they took the foundling upstairs and set it in the crib with a saucer of formula. Almondine pressed her nose through the bars and sniffed. The pup crawled toward the sound and shut his eyes and lay with hind legs outstretched, pads up, while the bells in the mobile chimed.

Trudy woke that night to find Almondine pacing the bedroom floor. The pup lay glassy-eyed in the crib, without the strength to lift his head. She pulled the rocking chair to the window and set the pup in her lap. The clouds had passed and in the light of the half-moon the pup's fur was silver-tipped. Almondine slid her muzzle along Trudy's thigh. She drew the pup's scent for a long time, then lay down, and the shadow of the rocking chair drifted back and forth over her.

In the pup's final hour, Trudy whispered to it about the black seed inside her as though it might somehow understand. She stroked the fuzz on its chest as it turned its eyes to her, and in the dark they made a bargain that one of them would go and one would stay.

When Gar woke, he knew where he would find Trudy. This time it was he who cried. They buried the pup under the birches near the baby's grave—both of them unnamed, but this newest grave unmarked as well—and now, instead of rain, the sun shone down with what little consolation it could give. When they finished, Edgar's parents returned to the kennel and went to work, their work, the work that never ended, for the dogs were hungry, and one of the mothers was sick and her pups would have to be hand-fed and the yearlings, unruly and headstrong, desperately needed training.

EDGAR DIDN'T LEARN THAT story all at once. He assembled it, bit by bit, signing a question and fitting together another piece. Sometimes they declared that they didn't want to talk about it just then, or changed the subject, trying perhaps to protect him from the fact that there was no happy ending to some stories. And yet they didn't want to lie to him either.

There came a day (a terrible day) when the story was almost fully told, when his mother decided to reveal everything, all of it, start to finish, repeating even those parts he knew, leaving out only what she herself had forgotten. Edgar was upset by how unfair it seemed, but he hid his reaction, afraid she would sugar the truth when he asked other questions. Until then, he thought he understood something about those events, about the world in general—that there would be a certain balance to the story, that somehow there was to be compensation for the baby. When his mother told him the pup died that first night, he thought he'd heard her wrong, and made her repeat it. Later, he came to think maybe there had been a certain compensation, though harsh, though it lasted only a day.

His mother became pregnant again, and this time she carried the baby to term. He was that baby, born on the thirteenth of May, 1958, at six o'clock in the morning. They named him Edgar, after his father. And though the pregnancy went smoothly, a complication arose the moment he drew his first breath to cry.

He was five days in the hospital before they finally brought him home.

Almondine

E VENTUALLY, SHE UNDERSTOOD THE HOUSE WAS KEEPING A secret from her.

All that winter and all through the spring, Almondine had known something was going to happen, but no matter where she looked she couldn't find it. Sometimes, when she entered a room, there was the feeling that the thing that was going to happen had just been there, and she would stop and pant and peer around while the feeling seeped away as mysteriously as it had arrived. Weeks might pass without a sign, and then a night would come, when, lying nose to tail beneath the window in the kitchen corner, listening to the murmur of conversation and the slosh and clink of dishes being washed, she felt it in the house again and she whisked her tail across the baseboards in long, pensive strokes and silently collected her feet beneath her and waited. When half an hour passed and nothing appeared, she groaned and sighed and rolled onto her back and waited to see if it was somewhere in her sleep.

She began investigating unlikely crevices: behind the refrigerator, where age-old layers of dust whirled into frantic life under her breath; within the tangle of chair legs and living feet beneath the kitchen table; inside the boots and shoes sagging in a line beside the back porch door—none with any success, though freshly baited mousetraps began to appear behind the appliances, beyond the reach of her delicate, inquisitive nose.

Once, when Edgar's parents left their closet door open, she'd spent an entire morning crouched on the bedroom floor, certain she'd finally cornered the thing among the jumble of shoes and drapes of cloth. She lost patience after a while and walked to the threshold, scenting the musty darkness, and she would have begun her search in earnest, but Trudy called from the yard and she was forced to leave it be. By the time she remembered the closet later that day the thing was gone and there was no telling where it might have gotten to.

Sometimes, after she'd searched and failed to find the thing that was going to happen, she stood beside Edgar's mother or father and waited for them to call it out. But they'd forgotten about it—or more likely, had never known in the first place. There were things like that, she'd learned, obvious things they didn't know. The way they ran their hands down her sides and scratched along her backbone consoled her, but the fact was, she wanted a job to do. By then she'd been in the house for almost a year, away from her littermates, away from the sounds and smells of the kennel, with only the daily training work to occupy her. Now even that had become routine, and she was not the kind of dog who could be idle for long without growing unhappy. If they didn't know about this thing, it was all that much more important that she find it and show them.

In April she began to wake in the night and wander the house, pausing beside the vacant couch and the blowing furnace registers to ask what they knew, but they never answered. Or knew but couldn't say. Always, at the end of those moonlight prowls, she found herself standing in the room with the crib (where, at odd moments, she might discover Trudy rearranging the chest of drawers or brushing her hand through the mobile suspended over it). From the doorway her gaze was drawn to the rocking chair, bathed in the pale night light that filtered through the curtained window. She recalled a time when she'd slept beside that chair while Trudy rocked in the dark. She approached and dropped her nose below the seat and lifted it an inch, encouraging it to remember and tell her what more it knew, but it only tilted back and forth in silence.

It was clear that the bed positively knew the secret, but it wasn't saying, no matter how many times she asked; Edgar's parents awoke one night to find her dragging away the blanket in a moment of spite. In the mornings she poked her nose at the truck—the traveler, as she thought of it—sitting petrified in the driveway, but it too kept all secrets close, and made no reply.

And so, near the end of that time, she could only commiserate with Trudy, who now obviously longed to find the thing as much as Almondine, and who had, for some reason, begun to spend her time lying in bed instead of going to the kennel. The idea, it seemed, was to stop hunting for the thing entirely and let the house yield up its secret on its own.

There came a morning when they woke while it was still dark outside and Gar began to rush around the house, stopping only long enough to make two quick phone calls. He threw some things into a suitcase and carried it out to the truck and then carried it back in again and threw some more things inside, and all the while he did this, Almondine watched Trudy dress slowly and deliberately. When she finished, she sat on the edge of the bed and said, "Relax, Gar, there's plenty of time." They walked down the steps together, and Almondine escorted the two of them to the truck. When Trudy was seated in the cab, Almondine circled back and waited for the tailgate to open, but instead Gar led her to the kennel and opened the door to an empty run.

She stood in the aisle and looked at him, incredulous.

"Go on," he said.

She considered the temptation of the open barn door. Morning light poured in from behind Gar, casting his shadow along the dry, dusty cement floor and over her. In the end she let him take her collar and lead her into the pen, which was the best she could do. Then there was the sound of the truck starting and tires on gravel. Some of the dogs barked out of habit at the noise, but Almondine was too stunned to do anything but stand in the straw and wait for the truck to return and Gar to rush back inside to get her. When she finally lay down, it was so near the door that tufts of her fur pressed through the squares of wire.

Doctor Papineau arrived that evening and dished out food and water and checked on the pups. The next morning Edgar's father returned, but he hurried through the chores, leaving Almondine in the kennel run. That evening it was Papineau again. When the night came on, she stood in the outer kennel run listening to the spring peepers begin their cacophony and the bats flickering overhead and she looked at the frozen oculus of the moon as it rose above the trees and cast its blue radiance across the field. It was just cool enough for her breath to light up, and for a long time she stood there, panting, trying to imagine what it was that was happening. Some of the other dogs pressed through the doors of their runs and stood with her. The old stone silo loomed over them. After a while she gave up and pushed back inside and curled into a corner and set her gaze on the motionless barn doors.

Another day passed, then two more. In the morning Almondine heard the sound of the truck pulling into the yard, followed by a car. When Trudy's voice reached her, Almondine put her paws on the pen door and joined in the barking for the first time since she had been out there. Gar came out to the barn and opened her pen. She whirled in the aisle, then bolted for the back porch steps and turned and panted over her shoulder, waiting for him to catch up.

Trudy sat in her chair in the living room, a white blanket in her arms. Doctor Papineau was on the couch, hat on his lap. Almondine approached, quivering with curiosity. She slid her muzzle carefully along Trudy's shoulder, stopping just inches from the blanket, and she narrowed her eyes and inhaled a dozen short breaths. Faint huffing sounds emanated from the fabric and a delicate pink hand jerked out. Five fingers splayed and relaxed and so managed to express a yawn. That would have been the first time Almondine saw Edgar's hands. In a way, that would have been the first time she saw him make a sign.

That miniature hand was so moist and pink and interesting, the temptation was almost irresistible. She pressed her nose forward another fraction of an inch.

"No licks," Trudy whispered in her ear.

Almondine began to wag her tail, slowly at first, then faster, as if something long held motionless inside her had gained momentum enough to break free. The swing of her tail rocked her chest and shoulders like a counterweight. She withdrew her muzzle from across Trudy's chest and licked at the air, and with that small joke she lost all reserve and she play-bowed and woofed quietly. As a result she was down-stayed, but she didn't mind as long as she was in a place where she could watch.

Doctor Papineau sat with them for an hour or so. Their talk sounded low and serious. Somehow, Almondine concluded that they were worried about the baby, that something wasn't right. And yet, she could see that the baby was fine: he squirmed, he breathed, he slept.

When Doctor Papineau excused himself, Edgar's father went to the barn to do the chores properly for the first time in four days, and his mother, exhausted, looked out the windows while the infant slept. It was mid-afternoon on a spring day, brilliant, green, and cool. The house hunched quietly around them all. And then, sitting upright in her chair, Edgar's mother fell asleep.

Almondine lay on the floor and watched, puzzling over something: as soon as Gar had opened the kennel door, she'd been sure that the house was about to reveal its secret—that now she would find the thing that was going to happen. When she'd seen the blanket and scented the baby, she'd thought maybe that was it. But it seemed to her now that wasn't right either. Whatever the secret was, it had to do with the baby, but it wasn't simply the fact of the baby.

While Almondine pondered this, a sound reached her ears—a whispery rasp, barely audible, even to her. At first she couldn't make sense of it. The moment she'd walked into the room she'd heard the breaths coming from the blanket, the ones that nearly matched his mother's breathing, and so it took her a moment to understand that in this new sound, she was hearing distress—to realize that this near-silence was the sound of him *wailing*. She waited for the sound to stop, but it went on and on, as quiet as the rustle of the new leaves on the apple trees.

That was what the concern had been about, she realized.

The baby had no voice. It couldn't make a sound.

Almondine began to pant. She shifted her weight from one hip to the other, and as she looked on—and saw his mother continue to sleep—she finally understood: the thing that was going to happen was that her time for training was over, and now, at last, she had a job to do.

And so Almondine gathered her legs beneath her and broke her stay.

She crossed the room and paused beside the chair, and she became in that moment, and was ever after, a cautious dog, for suddenly it seemed important that she be right in this; and looking at the two of them there, one silently bawling, one slumped in graceful exhaustion, certainty unfolded in her the way morning light fills a north room. She drew her tongue along his mother's face, just once, very deliberately, then stepped back. His mother startled awake. After a moment, she shifted the blanket and its contents and adjusted her blouse and soon enough the whispery sounds the baby had been making were replaced by other sounds Almondine recognized, equally quiet, but these carrying no note of distress.

Almondine walked back to where she had been stayed. All of this had happened in the space of a moment or two, and through the pads of her feet she could feel how her body had warmed a place on the rug. She stood for a long time looking at the two of them. Then she lay down and tucked her nose under the tip of her tail and she slept.

Signs

WHAT WAS THERE TO DO WITH SUCH AN INFANT CHILD BUT worry over him? Gar and Trudy worried that he would never have a voice. His doctors worried that he didn't cough. And Almondine simply worried whenever the boy was out of her sight, though he never was for long.

Quickly enough they discovered that no one understood a case like Edgar's. Such children existed only in textbooks, and even those were different in a thousand particulars from this baby, whose lips worked when he wanted to nurse, whose hands paddled the air when his parents diapered him, who smelled faintly like fresh flour and tasted like the sea, who slept in their arms and woke and compared in puzzlement their faces with the ether of some distant world, silent in contentment and silent in distress.

The doctors shone their lights into him and made their guesses. But who lived with him morning and evening? Who set their alarm to check him by moonlight? Who snuck in each morning to find a wide-eyed grub peering up from the crib, skin translucent as onion paper? The doctors made their guesses, but every day Trudy and Gar saw proof of normalcy and strangeness and drew their own conclusions. And all infants need the same simple things, pup or child, squalling or mute. They clung to that certainty: for a while, at least, it didn't matter what in him was special and what ordinary. He was alive. What mattered was that he opened his eyes every single morning. Compared to that, silence was nothing.

BY SEPTEMBER, TRUDY HAD had enough of waiting rooms and charts and tests, not to mention the expense and time away from the kennel. All summer she'd told herself to wait, that any day her baby would begin to cry and jabber like other children. Yet the question seemed increasingly dire. Some nights she could hardly sleep for wondering. And if medical science couldn't supply an answer, there might be other ways to know. One evening she told Gar they needed formula and she bundled up Edgar and put him in the truck and drove to Popcorn Corners. The leaves on the trees were every shade of red and yellow, and crinkled brown discards covered the dirt of Town Line Road, swirling in the vortex of the pickup as it passed along.

She parked in front of the rickety old grocery and sat looking at the neon OPEN sign glowing orange in the front window. The interior of the place was brightly lit but vacant save for a gray-haired old woman, cranelike, countenance ancient, sitting behind the counter. Ida Paine, the proprietor. Inside, a radio played quietly. A fiddle melody was just audible over the rustle of leaves in the night breeze. Trudy had brought the truck to a halt directly before the big plate glass window fronting the store, and Ida Paine had to know Trudy was out there, but the old woman sat like a fixture, her hands folded in her lap, a cigarette burning somewhere out of sight. If Trudy hadn't been afraid someone would come along, she might have waited a very long time in the truck, but she took a breath and tucked Edgar into her arms and walked into the store. Then she didn't know quite what to do. When she realized that the radio had stopped playing, she temporarily lost the ability to speak. Ida Paine looked at her from her perch. She wore oversize glasses that magnified her eyes, and behind the lenses those eyes blinked and blinked again.

Trudy looked at Edgar, cradled in her arms, and decided that coming in had been a bad idea. She was turning to leave when Ida Paine broke the silence.

"Let me see," she said.

Ida didn't hold out her hands or come around the counter, nor was there a grandmotherly note in her voice. If anything her tone was incurious and weary, though benign. Trudy stepped forward and laid Edgar on the counter between them, where the wooden surface was worn velvety from an eternity's caress of tin cans and pickle jars. When she let go, Edgar bicycled his legs and grasped the air as if it were made of some elastic matter none of them could feel. Ida leaned forward and examined him with dilated eyes. Two gray streams of cigarette smoke whistled from her nostrils. Then she lifted one blue-veined hand and extended a pinkie that reminded Trudy of nothing so much as the plucked wingtip of a chicken and she poked the flesh of Edgar's thigh. His eyes widened. Tears welled in them. From his mouth came the faintest huff.

Trudy had watched a dozen doctors prod her son, feeling hardly a tremor, but this she couldn't bear. She reached forward, meaning to reclaim her baby.

"Wait," Ida said. She bent lower and tipped her head and pressed that avian pinkie into the infant's palm. His tiny fingers spasmed closed around it. Ida Paine stood like that for what seemed hours. Trudy stopped breathing entirely. Then she let out a gasp and scooped Edgar into her arms and stepped back from the counter.

Outside, at the four-way stop, a pair of headlights appeared. Neither Trudy nor Ida moved. The neon OPEN sign darkened and an instant later the ceiling fluorescents winked out. In the dark Trudy could make out Ida's crone's silhouette and her hand raised before her, considering her pinkie. The headlights resolved into a station wagon and the station wagon rolled into the dirt parking lot and paused and accelerated back onto the blacktop.

"No," Ida Paine grunted, with some finality.

"Not ever?"

"He can use his hands."

By then the whine of car tires had faded into the night. Orange worms of plasma began to flux and crawl in the tubes of the OPEN sign. Overhead, the ballasts hummed and the fluorescents flickered and lit. Trudy waited for some elaboration from Ida, but understood soon enough that she stood in the presence of a terse oracle indeed.

"That it?" was all the more Ida Paine had to say. "Anything else?"

A MONTH LATER A WOMAN came to visit. Trudy was in the kitchen fixing a late lunch while Gar tended a newly whelped litter in the kennel. When the knock came, Trudy walked to the porch, where a stout woman waited, dressed in a flowered skirt and a white blouse, her steel gray hair done up in a tightly wound permanent. She gripped her handbag and looked over her shoulder at the kennel dogs raising the alarm.

"Hello," the woman said with an uncertain smile. "I'm afraid you're going to think this very inappropriate. Your dogs certainly do." She smoothed down the front of her skirt. "My name is Louisa Wilkes," she continued, "and I—well, the fact is, I don't exactly know why I'm here."

Trudy asked her to come inside, if she didn't mind Almondine. She didn't mind dogs at all, Louisa Wilkes said. Not in ones and twos. Mrs. Wilkes settled on the couch and Almondine curled up in front of the bassinet where Edgar slept. Something about the prim way she walked and folded her hands when she sat made Trudy think she was a southerner, though she had no accent Trudy could detect.

"What can I do for you?" Trudy said.

"Well, as I said, I'm not sure. I'm here visiting my nephew and his wife—John and Eleanor Wilkes?"

"Oh yes, of course." Trudy said. She had thought the name Wilkes sounded familiar, but hadn't been able to place it. "We see Eleanor in town once in a while. She and John look after one of our dogs."

"Yes, that was the very first thing I noticed, your dogs. Their Ben is a wonderful animal. Very bright eyes," she said, looking at Almondine, "like this one. Same way of peering at you, too. In any case, I talked them into lending me their car for the morning so I could see the countryside.

I know it's odd, but I like the quiet of a car when I'm alone in it. A ways back I found myself at a little store, practically in the middle of nowhere. I'd hoped they sold sandwiches, but they didn't. I bought some crackers instead, and a soda. The store is run by the strangest woman."

"You must be talking about Popcorn Corners," Trudy said. "That's Ida Paine's store. Ida can be a little spooky."

"So I discovered. After I paid the woman she told me I wanted to follow the highway a bit farther and take this side road and look for the dogs. It was strange. I hadn't asked for directions. And that's the way she put it, too: not that I should, or could, but that I *wanted* to. She said it through the window screen as I was walking to my car. I asked her what she meant but she just sat there. I intended to turn back the way I came, but then I was curious. I found the road just where she said it would be. When I saw your dogs, I—" She broke off. "Well, that's all there is to tell. I parked on the road and now here I am, feeling loony for having walked in."

Louisa Wilkes looked around the living room, fidgeting with her purse. "But I do have the feeling we should talk some more. You're a new mother," she said. She walked to the bassinet and Trudy joined her.

"His name is Edgar."

The baby was wide awake. He scrunched his eyebrows at the unhappy sight of a woman not his mother leaning over him and he stretched his mouth wide, making silence. The woman frowned and looked at Trudy.

"Yes. He doesn't use his voice—the equipment is all there, but when he cries, there's no sound. We don't know why."

At this, Louisa Wilkes stood up straight. "And how old is he?"

"Just shy of six months."

"Is there a chance he's deaf? It's very simple to test for, even in infants. You just—"

"—clap your hands and see if they flinch. Yes, we've known from the start that his hearing is fine. When he's in his bassinet and I start to talk, he looks around. Why do you ask? Do you know of another case like his?"

"I'm sure I don't, Mrs. Sawtelle. I've never heard of anything like it.

What I *do* know about—well, first of all, I'm not a nurse, much less a doctor."

"I'm glad to hear that. I'm out of patience with doctors. All they've told us is what isn't wrong with Edgar, and that amounts to everything besides his voice. They've tested how fast his pupils dilate. They've tested his saliva. They've drawn blood. They've even taken EKGs. It's amazing what they can rule out on a newborn, but I've finally had to draw the line—I won't have my baby tormented all through his infancy. And all you have to do is spend a few minutes with him to know he's a perfectly normal baby."

Almondine was up now, scenting the bassinet and their visitor with equal concern. Mrs. Wilkes looked down at her. "Benny is such an extraordinary animal," she said. "I've never seen a dog quite so aware of conversation. I could swear he turns toward me when he thinks it is my turn to speak."

"Yes," Trudy said. "They understand more than we give them credit for."

"Oh, it's more than that. I've been around plenty of dogs—dogs that lie on your lap and fall asleep, dogs that bark at every stranger who walks past, dogs that crouch on the floor and watch you like a long-lost beau. But I've never seen a dog behave that way."

Louisa Wilkes looked at Edgar in the bassinet. Then she turned and lifted her hands and moved them through the air, looking intently at Trudy. Her motions were fluid and expressive and entirely silent. She paused long enough to be sure that Trudy realized what she had seen, even if she hadn't understood its meaning.

"What I just said is, 'I am the child of two profoundly deaf parents.'" Another swift flight of hands.

"I am not deaf myself, but I teach sign at a school for the deaf. And I'm wondering, Mrs. Sawtelle, what will happen if it turns out that your boy lacks the power of speech but nothing else."

Trudy noticed how deftly Louisa Wilkes phrased her questions, a steeliness that emerged the moment she signed. Something almost fierce. Trudy liked that—Louisa Wilkes wasn't beating around the bush. And

Trudy could hardly have forgotten Ida Paine's pronouncement that autumn night: *He can use his hands.* At the time, Trudy thought Ida Paine had meant that Edgar would *only* be able to use his hands, that he was destined for menial work, which Trudy knew was wrong. The whole episode had made her angry, and she'd chalked it up to foolishness—her own. She'd never mentioned the incident to Gar. Now Trudy began to suspect she'd misunderstood Ida Paine.

"He'll make do, Mrs. Wilkes. I think we'll find out that there's nothing else different about Edgar. Perhaps, as he grows, his voice will come. Since we don't know why it's gone in the first place, there's no way to tell if this is temporary."

"He's never uttered a sound? Not even once?"

"No, never."

"And the doctors—what did they tell you to do while you're waiting to find out if your son might or might not find a voice?"

"That's been so discouraging. They've told me only the most obvious things. To talk to him, which I do, so if he has a choice, he'll imitate his mother."

"Did they suggest any exercises? Anything you might do with him?"

"None, really. They speculated on what we might do in a few years if nothing changes, but for now, just watch him. If—when something changes, we go from there."

Hearing this, Mrs. Wilkes's reserve, rapidly diminishing ever since the topic had turned to deafness, dropped away entirely.

"Mrs. Sawtelle, listen to me now. I don't mean to presume anything, and for all I know what I'm about to tell you you've already read or been told—though from the sound of it, the doctors you've seen have been woefully ignorant, which would not surprise me at all. You *cannot* begin too early to bring the power of language to children whose grasp may be precarious. No one can say for sure when children begin to learn language—that is, we do not know how early in their lives they understand that they *can* talk and *should* talk, that through speech they will lead fulfilling lives. There is, on the other hand, evidence that by the age of one year the gift of language begins slipping away unless it is nurtured. This has happened to deaf children throughout history, and it is quite a terrible thing—children considered retarded and left to fend for themselves—I'm talking about perfectly intelligent, capable children abandoned because they did not know that *sound* existed. How could they! By the time someone recognized that they lacked only hearing, they were handicapped forever."

"But everything you say applies to children who can't hear, not to children who can't make sound. And there's no doubt that Edgar can hear."

"But what about speech? A person communicates by giving as well as taking, by expressing what is inside. Infants learn this by crying—they learn that drawing attention to themselves in even the most primitive way gains them warmth and food and comfort. I worry about your child, Mrs. Sawtelle. I wonder how he'll learn these things. Let me tell you about myself for a moment. When I was born, my own parents were faced with a dilemma: how could they teach me to speak? They had not learned until it was far too late—in their teens—and so they mastered everything but the production of intelligible speech. And now they had a daughter who they wanted more than anything in the world to speak normally."

"What did they do?"

"They assumed that I was learning even when I seemed to be doing nothing. They played records with conversations, though they couldn't hear anything themselves. They bought a radio, and asked their hearing friends to tell them which stations to tune in, and when. They watched my mouth to see if I was making sounds. They arranged for me to spend time with people who could play with me and speak to me. In short, Mrs. Sawtelle, they made sure that verbal language was available to me in every way they could imagine."

"But there must have been more to it than that. How did they respond when you spoke your first words? How did they encourage you when they couldn't hear you speak?"

Mrs. Wilkes talked then about the readiness of babies to learn language, how impossible it was to prevent, so long as examples were available. How isolated twins sometimes invented private languages. She went on for quite some time. She had worked with both deaf children and the hearing children of deaf parents, she said, and there was a simple principle: the baby *wanted* to communicate. It would learn whatever was given as an example, whether English, French, German, Chinese, or sign. As a child, she had learned to sign as well as speak, almost effortlessly. This last point, she said, was most significant for the Sawtelle baby.

"But how can I teach him to sign?" Trudy said. "I don't know how myself."

"Then you will learn, together," Mrs. Wilkes said. "At first, you only need to know enough to talk with Edgar in the simplest ways."

"Which are?"

"Which are to tell him you love him. To say, here is food. To name things: Dog. Bird. Daddy. Mama. Sky. Cloud. Just like any child. Show him how to ask for things he wants by moving his hands in that sign. Show him how to ask for *more* of whatever he wants"—and here she bounced the fingertips of both hands together as she talked, to demonstrate—"and later, when the time comes to make sentences, you'll already have learned how to do that."

Their conversation went on late into the evening. When Gar came in from the kennel, Mrs. Wilkes began demonstrating the basics. She said she could explain a few signs and straightforward syntax in an evening, and she began with simple words and simple sentences. She showed them a subject-verb-object sentence: "Trudy loves Gar." She explained the miraculous way in which pronouns are used. She demonstrated an adjective.

Trudy was mesmerized, repeating the signs and following Mrs. Wilkes's corrections studiously. Gar tried as well, though he lacked Trudy's coordination and grace. It was near midnight before the woman left—far past the time when they usually went to sleep. Edgar had roused several times during the evening, and when they took him up, Mrs. Wilkes demonstrated how to say "food" and move Edgar's hands. This was harder, since it required performing the sign backward. But it was possible. And Trudy understood the enormous leverage that practice gives the determined trainer.

Edgar

THIS WILL BE HIS EARLIEST MEMORY.

Red light, morning light. High ceiling canted overhead. Lazy click of toenails on wood. Between the honey-colored slats of the crib a whiskery muzzle slides forward until its cheeks pull back and a row of dainty front teeth bare themselves in a ridiculous grin.

The nose quivers. The velvet snout dimples.

All the house is quiet. Be still. Stay still.

Fine, dark muzzle fur. Black nose, leather of lacework creases, comma of nostrils flexing with each breath. A breeze shushes up the field and pillows the curtains inward. The apple tree near the kitchen window caresses the house with a tick-tickety-tick-tick. As slowly as he can, he exhales, feigning sleep, but despite himself his breath hitches. At once, the muzzle knows he is awake. It snorts. Angles right and left. Withdraws. Outside the crib, Almondine's forequarters appear. Her head is reared back, her ears cocked forward.

A cherry-brindled eye peers back at him.

Whoosh of her tail.

Be still. Stay still.

The muzzle comes hunting again, tunnels beneath his blanket, below the farmers and pigs and chicks and cows dyed into that cotton world. His hand rises on fingers and spider-walks across the surprised farmyard residents to challenge the intruder. It becomes a bird, hovering before their eyes. Thumb and index finger squeeze the crinkled black nose. The pink of her tongue darts out but the bird flies away before Almondine can lick it. Her tail is switching harder now. Her body sways, her breath envelops him. He tugs the blackest whisker on her chin and this time her tongue catches the palm of his hand ever so slightly. He pitches to his side, rubs his hand across the blanket, blows a breath in her face. Her ears flick back. She stomps a foot. He blows again and she withdraws and bows and woofs, low in her chest, quiet and deep, the boom of an uncontainable heartbeat. Hearing it, he forgets and presses his face against the rails to see her, all of her, take her inside him with his eyes, and before he can move, she smears her tongue across his nose and forehead! He claps a hand to his face but it's too late—she's away, spinning, biting her tail, dancing in the moted sunlight that spills through the window glass.

BOUNCING ON HIS MOTHER'S HIP as she walks down the aisle of the kennel. Dogs rush through the canvas flaps in the barn wall, look at him, take his scent. Her voice singsong as she calls to them.

HIS FATHER, SITTING AT THE KITCHEN table, papers strewn before them. Pictures of dogs. His father's voice quiet in his ear, talking through a line cross. The corner of a pedigree pinched between his fingers.

RUNNING THROUGH THE YARD, past the milk house, throwing the fence gate closed before Almondine can catch him. He crouches in the tall weeds and watches. She loves to jump. Her stride draws up and she sails over the fence. In a moment, she's next to him, panting. He clenches his fist and mock-scowls. When she looks away, he bolts again. The weeds rush together behind him and then he's in the orchard, monkey-crawling along a branch, the one place she cannot follow, dangling a hand to taunt her. All at once, the world spins. When he hits the ground, a thump sounds in his chest. He begins to cry, but the only sound is Almondine's barking—and, after a moment, the kennel dogs.

ON THE FARTHEST APPLE TREE hangs a tire, its rope hairy and moth brown. He's been told to stay away but forgotten why. He worms his shoulders through both circles of the rubber rim, twists, pumps his legs. The apple trees tilt crazily around him. It takes a minute for the bees to condense from shadow and sunlight, then he is trapped in the careening tire, and they sting him once on his neck, once on his arm. Hot points of light. Almondine snaps at the air, yelps, brushes a paw across her face. Then they are running to the house. The porch door slams behind. They wait to see if the bees will keep coming, grow thick against the screen. For a moment, Edgar almost believes the bees never existed. Then the stings begin to throb.

WANDERING THROUGH THE KENNEL, holding a book: *Winnie-the-Pooh*. He opens a whelping pen, sits. The puppies surge through the underbrush of loose straw, kicking up fine white dust as they come along. He captures them between his legs and reads to them, hands in motion before their upturned muzzles. The mother comes over and they peep like chicks when they see her. One by one she carries them back to the whelping box; they hang black and bean-shaped from her mouth. When she has finished, she stands over them, looking at Edgar in reproach.

They *wanted* to hear, he signs at her, but the mother won't settle with her pups until he leaves.

Winnie-the-Pooh is a good story for puppies.

If only she would let him tell it.

HIS FATHER, READING TO HIM at bedtime, voice quiet, lamplight yellow on the lenses of his glasses. The story is *The Jungle Book*. Edgar wants to fall asleep with Mowgli and Bagheera still in his mind, for the story to cross from the lamplight into his dreams. His father's voice stops. He sits up.

More, he signs, fingertips together.

His father starts the next page. He lies back and moves his hands through the air to the sound of his father's voice. Thinking about words. The shapes of words.

HE IS SITTING ON THE GRAY leatherette cushion of the doctor's bench and holding his mouth wide open. The doctor's face is close, looking into him.

Then the doctor puts alphabet tiles on a table. The doctor asks him to spell "apple," but there is only one *p* and he can't do it right. The doctor turns to a notepad and writes something down while he tries to turn the *b* upside down so it will be right.

"I'd like him to stay for a few days," the doctor says. His mother shakes her head and frowns.

The doctor presses a buzzing, flashlight-shaped thing against his throat. "Breathe out," he says. "Pull your lips back. Touch your tongue to the roof of your mouth. Make a circle with your lips."

Edgar follows his instructions and a word floats out of his mouth: "Ellooooo." But the sound is hideous, flies against a pane of glass.

Don't do that.

The doctor doesn't understand at first. Edgar uses the letterboard and goes slow for him. On the way home, they drink black cows at the Dog'N'Suds. On his mother's face, an expression: Sorrow? Anger?

SITTING IN THE WHELPING PEN, watching a new litter of puppies squirm. At five days old, they are too young to name, but this has become his job.

One of the pups is trying to climb over the others, pushing them aside to nurse. He is a bully. His name will be Hector, Edgar decides. Choosing names is hard. At night he discusses it with his mother and father. He is very young, and has only now begun using his dictionary to find names and note them in the margins.

THE DOCTOR BRINGS IN SOMEONE NEW, a man with a beard and black hair that falls to his shoulders. The man signs hello to him, a flick of his hand off his forehead, then asks him something, signing faster than Edgar has ever seen, one sign melting into another.

Too fast, he signs.

He grabs the man's wrists and makes him do it again.

The man turns to the doctor, speaks a few words, and the doctor nods.

You sound funny, Edgar signs. The man laughs, and even that is odd.

Do I? he signs. I'm deaf. I've never heard my voice.

Edgar stares at him as if he didn't know a deaf person would look just the same. From behind the man, his mother frowns and shakes her head.

How old are you? the man signs.

Almost four, he says. He holds up four fingers, with his thumb tucked in, bumps the *I*-hand twice against his heart.

You're very good. I couldn't sign like you when I was four.

I'm backward from you. I can hear okay.

Yes. It's good we both sign.

Can you sign with your dogs? Mine don't always understand.

My dog *never* understands, the man signs, smiling.

Almondine understands when I say *this*. And Edgar signs something that only he and Almondine know. They watch Almondine approach.

The man pauses and looks at the doctor.

STANDING IN THE AISLE OF THE BARN. His father sits in one of the pens with a mother, stroking her ears. The mother is so old even her tail shows gray. She lies on her side, panting. His father points to the ceiling beams running crossways to the main aisle and tells him they came from trees Schultz felled in the woods behind the barn.

"The first spring, leaves sprouted from those beams," he says, and Edgar sees for the first time the knots and scrapes, sees the tree hidden in each beam and sees as well Schultz and his ponies heaving them up through the field. A string of bare lightbulbs runs the length of the aisle, one descending from every other beam.

"Hang on, gorgeous," his father says, turning back to the mother.

When Doctor Papineau arrives, Edgar leads him into the barn.

"Over here, Page," Edgar's father says.

Doctor Papineau enters the pen and kneels. He runs his hands over the mother's belly and presses the coined tip of a stethoscope to her chest. Then he walks to his car and fetches a satchel.

Edgar's father turns to him.

"Go up to the house now," he says.

From the satchel, Doctor Papineau lifts a bottle and a syringe.

TWO ROLLING HILLS SPAN the south field, one near their yard, one farther out. There's a rock pile in the middle, and a small grove of birches, and a cross. Waves of hay lie over in the August breeze. Edgar plunges through the field, trying to lose Almondine. Always their game. He cuts around the rocks, dives under a birch and lies as quietly as he can. He peers at the white cross, standing alone between him and the yard, and he wonders again what it means. It is so simple, straight, and square, and sometime not too long before, it has taken on a fresh, brilliant white coat of paint.

Then the stalks of hay part and Almondine trots up, panting. She flops down and presses a paw to his chest as if to say, don't do that again. It's too hot for these games. But he jumps up and races away, and she's there beside him, mouth open in a smile.

So often, she runs ahead.

So often, he finds her waiting when he arrives.

A LATE SPRING AFTERNOON. Edgar and his mother sit on the living room couch. The television shows gray static, and the speakers hiss. All the shades are raised. Clouds like bruises scud over the fields. Outside, a sizzle-flash. There's a snap from the kitchen as sparks fly from the electric sockets. He counts one, two, three, until the thunder rolls back at them from the hills.

"It's the iron in the ground, it draws the lightning," his father has said. "See how red the dirt is? This is where the Iron Range begins."

The pines flap their branches in the gusts, swimmers in the wind. He walks to the window to see if the treetops actually pierce the clouds. A tatter of white steam passes over the thrashing treetops, sliding counter to the motion of the storm.

"Come away from the window," his mother says.

Splats of rain hit the glass. Outside, an instant of brilliant light, and sparks leap from the kitchen outlets again. Thunder never arrives, and the extended silence is eerie.

Was that cold lightning?

"Probably."

There's hot lightning and cold lightning, she has told him. Only hot lightning makes thunder. The difference is important: a person hit by hot lightning is fried on the spot. A person struck by cold lightning walks away without a mark.

His mother sits on the chair and watches the clouds. "I wish your father would come in here."

I'll get him.

"No you won't. You'll stay right here with me." She gives him a look that means no kidding around.

I'm taller than you now, he signs, trying to make her relax. Lately, he's begun to tease her about being the shortest in the family. She gives him a tight-lipped smile and turns back to the television. He doesn't quite know what they should be looking for, just that it will be obvious. From a *Reader's Digest* article she's learned about the Weller Method, which they are now performing. The television is tuned to Channel 2 and dimmed until the static is nearly black.

"We just keep watching," she'd explained. "If a tornado comes near, the screen turns white from the electrical field."

They divide their attention between the jitter on the tube and the advancing shelf of cloud. His mother has an endless store of meteorological anecdotes: ball lightning, tornadoes, hurricanes. But today, as during all the worst storms, a haunted look occupies her face, and he knows those stories roil inside her like the clouds in the sky. The television fizzles and crackles. Still, she is okay until Almondine comes over and leans against her for reassurance.

"That's it," she says. "Down we go."

The basement stairs are on the back porch. Through the screen door they see his father standing in the doorway of the barn, his hair tousled by the wind. He's leaning against the jamb, almost casually, his face turned skyward.

"Gar!" his mother shouts. "Come in. We're going to the basement."

"I'll stay here," he calls back. The wind makes his voice tinny and small. "It's going to be a wild one. You go on."

She shakes her head and ushers them down the stairs. "Shoo, shoo," she says. "Let's go."

Almondine plunges down the steps before them. There's a latched door at the bottom and she waits with nose pressed to the crack, sniffing. Once inside, they squint at the clouds through the dusty basement transom windows. No rain is falling—only drips and blobs of water blown sideways through the air.

"What does he think he'll accomplish out there?" she says, fuming. "All he wants to do is watch the storm."

You're right. He just stands in the doorway like that.

"The dogs can take care of themselves. It's having him out there that stirs them up. As if he could protect the barn. It's ridiculous."

Lightning plunges into the field nearby. Thunder shakes the house.

"Oh, God," his mother says.

This last strike has started Edgar's heart smashing, too. He dashes up the cement stairs for a look. As he reaches the top, there's a blue-white flash, dazzlingly bright, and a bomb sound, then he's flying down the stairs again, but not before he's seen for himself: his father, still standing with one hand on the barn door, braced as if daring the storm to touch him.

And it is clear then that everything so far has been a prelude. The wind blows not in fits and gusts but with a sustained howl that makes Edgar wonder when the windows will shatter from the pressure. Almondine whines and he draws his hand along her back and croup. A timber groans from inside the walls. His mother has herded them to the southwest corner of the basement, anecdotally the safest if a tornado lifts the house off its foundation *Wizard of Oz*–style. The wind blows for a long time, so long it becomes laughable. And strangely: with the gale at full force, sunlight begins to stream through the transom windows. That is the first sign the storm will pass. Only later does the solid roar of air slacken in descending octaves until all that remains is an ironic summer breeze.

"Sit tight," his mother says.

Edgar can see her thinking, eye of the storm, but his father's voice echoes across the yard: "That was a doozy!" Outside, it is impossible not to look first at the sky, where a field of summer cumulus, innocuous and white, stretches westward. The storm clouds glower above the treetops across the road. The house and barn seem untouched. The pine trees stand quiet and whole, the apple trees intact at first glance, until he notices that every blossom has been stripped bare, every petal swept away by the wind. Hardly a drop of rain has fallen, and the air is dusty and choking. Edgar and Almondine circulate through the house, plugging in the stove, the toaster, the dryer, the air-conditioner in the living room window. The mailman pauses his car beside the mailbox and drives off with a wave. Edgar jogs up the driveway to fetch the contents, a single letter, hand-addressed to his father. The postmark says, Portsmouth, Virginia.

He is reaching for the handle on the porch door when his father's shout rises from behind the barn.

THE FOUR OF THEM STAND in the weeds behind the barn, gazing upward. A ragged patch of shingles the size of the living room floor hangs from the eaves like a flap of crusty skin, thick with nails. A third of the roof lies exposed, gray and bare. Before their eyes the barn has become the weathered hull of a ship, upturned.

But what astonishes them, what makes them stand with jaws agape, is this: near the peak, a dozen roofing boards have detached from the rafters and curled back in long, crazy-looking hoops that stop just short of making a circle. The most spectacular corkscrew up and away, as if a giant hand had reached down and rolled them between its fingers. Where the boards have peeled back, the ribs of the barn show through, roughly joined and mortised by Schultz so long ago. The breeze rattles the roofing boards like bones. A thin alphabet of yellow straw dust escapes from the mow and flies over the barn's long spine.

After a while, Edgar remembers the letter.

Lifts it, absently.

Holds it out to his father.

Every Nook and Cranny

EARLY MORNING, A WEEK AFTER THE STORM HAD INFLICTED ITS peculiar damage on the barn roof. Edgar and Almondine stood atop the bedroom stairs, boy and dog surveying twelve descending treads, their surfaces crested by smooth-sanded knots and shot with cracks wide enough to stand a nickel in and varnished so thickly by Schultz that all but the well-worn centers shone with a maroon gloss. Treacherous for people in stockinged feet and unnerving to the four-legged. What most impressed Edgar was not their appearance but their gift for vocalization—everything from groans to nail-squeals and many novelties besides, depending on the day of the week or the humidity or what book you happened to be carrying. The challenge that morning was to descend in silence—not just Edgar, but Edgar and Almondine together.

He knew the pattern of quiet spots by heart. Far right on the twelfth and eleventh step, tenth and ninth safe anywhere, the eighth, good on the left, the sixth and fifth, quiet in the middle, a tricky switch from the far right of the fourth to left-of-middle on the third, and so on. But the seventh step had never let them by without a grunt or a rifle-shot crack. He'd lost interest in the riddle of it for a long time, but the sight of the barn's demented roofing planks had reminded him that wood in all shapes could be mysterious and he'd resolved to try again.

He negotiated the first four steps and turned. Here, he signed, pointing to a place on the tread for Almondine. Here. Here. Each time she placed a broad padded foot where his fingers touched the tread, and silence ensued. Then he stood on the eighth step, the brink, with Almondine nosing his back and waiting.

He swung his foot over the seventh tread like a dowser looking for water. Toward the right side, he knew, the thing creaked. In the middle, it let out a sound like a rust-seized door hinge. His foot hovered and drifted over the wood. Finally, it came to a stop above an owl-eyed swirl of grain near the wall on the left. He carefully settled his weight onto the tread.

Silence.

He stepped quickly down to the sixth and fifth and turned back and picked up Almondine's foot and stroked it.

He tapped the owl-eye. Here.

She stepped down.

Yes, good girl.

In time they stood at the base of the stairs together, having arrived without a sound. A quiet moment of exaltation passed between them and they headed for the kitchen. He didn't intend to tell anyone he'd found the way down. They were a small family living in a small farmhouse, with no neighbors and hardly any time or space to themselves. If he managed to share one secret with his father and a different one with his mother and yet another with Almondine the world felt that much larger.

THEY DIDN'T SAY WHERE HIS FATHER was going, only that it was a long day's drive before he would return with Claude. It was late May and school was in session, though barely, and when he asked to go along he knew the answer would be no. That morning he and Almondine and his mother watched the truck top the hill on Town Line Road and then they walked to the barn for morning chores. A pile of secondhand LPs and an old suitcase-style record player occupied a lower shelf of the workshop. Two pennies had been taped to the needle arm, covering the lightning-bolt Z in the "Zenith" embossed in the fluted metal. Through the speaker grill a person could make out the filaments glowing igneous orange in their silver-nippled tubes. His mother unsleeved one of her favorite records and set it on the turntable. Edgar cleaned the kennel to the sound of Patsy Cline's voice. When he finished he found his mother in the whelping room. She was holding a pup in the air in front of her, examining it and singing under her breath how she was crazy for tryin', crazy for cryin', crazy for loving it.

The truck was still gone when he got off the school bus that afternoon. His mother enlisted his help retrieving sheets from the clothesline.

"Don't they smell great?" she said, holding the fabric to her face. "It's so nice to hang them out again."

They tramped up the stairs to the spare room, located across the hallway from Edgar's bedroom. That morning it had been brimming with stacks of *Dog World* and *Field and Stream* and a menagerie of castoff furniture and broken appliances and many other familiars. A rollaway bed with a pinstriped mattress closed up clam-style. A set of seat-split kitchen chairs. Two brass floor lamps, teetering like long-legged birds. And most of all, innumerable cross-flapped cardboard boxes, which he'd spent long afternoons digging through hoping to unearth an old photo album. They had photographs of every dog they'd ever raised but none of themselves. Perhaps, he'd thought, one of those boxes held some faded image that would reveal how his mother and father had met.

His mother swung the door open with a flourish.

"What do you think?" she asked. "I'll give you a hint. Personally, I can't believe the difference."

She was right. The room was transformed. The boxes were gone. The window glass sparkled. The wooden floor had been swept and mopped and the foldaway bed had been laid out flat and at its head a little table he had never seen before acted as a nightstand. A warm breeze sucked the freshly laundered curtains against the screen and blew them out again and somehow the whole room smelled like a lemon orchard.

Great, he signed. It's never looked this good.

"Of course not, it's been filled with junk! Know what the best part is? Your father says that this used to be Claude's room when he was growing up. Can you imagine that? Here, you get that side." She billowed a sheet over the mattress and they tucked their way up from the foot of the bed. Each of them stuffed a pillow into a pillowcase. His mother kept looking at him as they worked. Finally she stopped and stood up.

"What's bothering you?"

Nothing. I don't know. He paused and looked around. What did you do with everything?

"I found some nooks and crannies. A lot of it I put in the basement. I thought you and your father could cart those old chairs to the dump this weekend."

Then she slipped into sign, which she performed unhurriedly and with great precision.

Did you want to ask me something about Claude?

Have I ever met him? When I was little?

No. I've only met him once myself. He enlisted in the navy the year before I met your father, and he's only been back once, for your grandfather's funeral.

Why did he join the navy?

I don't know. Sometimes people enlist to see more of the world. Your father says Claude didn't always get along with your grandfather. That's another reason people enlist. Or maybe none of those things.

How long is he staying?

A while. Until he finds a place of his own. He's been gone a long time. He might not stay at all. This might be too small of a place for him now.

Does he know about the dogs?

She laughed. He grew up here. He probably doesn't know them like your father does, not anymore. He sold his share of the kennel to your father when your grandfather died.

Edgar nodded. After they were finished he waited until his mother was occupied and then carried the lamps up from the basement to his room. He set them on opposite ends of his bookshelves, and he and Almondine spent the afternoon pulling books off the shelves and leafing through them.

IT WAS LONG AFTER DARK when the headlights of the truck swept the living room walls. Edgar and his mother and Almondine waited on the back porch while his father turned the truck around by the barn. The porch light glinted off the glass of the windshield and the truck rolled to a stop. His father got out of the cab, his expression serious, even cross, though it softened when he looked up at them. He gave a small, silent wave, then walked to the rear of the truck and opened the topper and lifted out a lone suitcase. At first Claude stayed inside the cab, visible only in silhouette. He craned his neck to look around. Then the passenger door swung open and he stepped out and Edgar's father walked up beside him.

It was impossible not to make comparisons. His father's brother wore an ill-fitting serge suit, in which he looked uneasy and shabbily formal. From the way it hung on him, he was the thinner of the two. Claude's hair was black where his father's was peppered. He stood with a slightly stooped posture, perhaps from the long drive, which made it hard to tell who was taller. And Claude didn't wear glasses. In all, Edgar's first impression was of someone quite different from his father, but then Claude turned to look at the barn and in profile the similarities jumped out—the shapes of their noses and chins and foreheads. And when they walked into the side yard, their gaits were identical, as if their bodies were hinged in precisely the same way. Edgar had a sudden, strange thought: *that's what it's like to have a brother.*

"Looks about the same," Claude was saying. His voice was deeper than Edgar's father's, and gravelly. "I guess I expected things to have changed some."

"There's more difference than you think," his father said. Edgar could hear the irritation in his tone from across the yard. "We repainted a couple of years back, but we stayed with white. The sashes on the two front windows rotted out so we replaced them with that big picture window—you'll see when we get inside. And a lot of the wiring and plumbing has been fixed, stuff you can't see."

"That's new," Claude said, nodding at the pale green LP gas cylinder beside the house.

"We got rid of the coal furnace almost ten years ago," his father said. He put his hand lightly on Claude's back and his voice sounded friendly again. "Come on, let's go in. We can look around later."

He steered Claude toward the porch. When they reached the steps, Claude went up first. Edgar's mother held the door, and Claude stepped through and turned.

"Hello, Trudy," he said.

"Hello, Claude," she said. "Welcome home. It's nice to have you here." She hugged him briefly, squeezing up her shoulders in an embrace that was both friendly and slightly formal. Then she stepped back, and Edgar felt her hand on his shoulder.

"Claude, meet Edgar," she said.

Claude shifted his gaze from Trudy and held out his hand. Edgar shook it, though awkwardly. He was surprised at how hard Claude squeezed, how it made him aware of the bones in his hands, and how callused Claude's palms were. Edgar felt like he was gripping a hand made of wood. Claude looked him up and down.

"Pretty good sized, aren't you?"

It wasn't exactly what Edgar expected him to say. Before he could reply, Claude's gaze shifted again, this time to Almondine, who stood swinging her tail in anticipation.

"And this is?"

"Almondine."

Claude knelt, and it was clear at once that he had been around dogs a long time. Instead of petting Almondine or scratching her ruff, he held out his hand, knuckle first, for her to sniff. Then he puckered his lips and whistled a quietly hummed tweedle, high and low at the same time. Almondine sat up straight and cocked her head left and right. Then she stepped forward and scented Claude thoroughly. When Edgar looked up, his father had a look of shocked recollection on his face.

"Hey, girl," Claude said. "What a beauty." Only after Almondine had finished taking his scent did Claude touch her. He stroked her withers and scratched her on the chest behind her elbow and ran his hand along her belly. She closed up her mouth and arched her back in a gesture of tolerant satisfaction.

"Man, it's been—" Claude seemed at a loss for words. He kept stroking Almondine's coat. He swallowed and took a breath and stood up. "I'd forgotten what they're like," he said. "It's been a long time since I could just run my hand over a dog like that."

There was an awkward silence and then Edgar's father led Claude up to the revitalized spare room. They'd waited dinner and Edgar set the table while his mother pulled ham out of the refrigerator and cut up leftover potatoes to fry. They worked in silence, listening to the talk. As though to make up for his earlier comment, Claude pointed out differences, large and small, between the way things looked and the way he remembered them. When they came downstairs, the two men stood in the wide passageway between the kitchen and the living room.

"How about dinner?" his mother asked.

"That'd be fine," Claude said. He looked pale, suddenly, like someone troubled by something he'd seen, or some memory newly dredged up, and not a happy one. No one spoke for a time. Edgar's mother glanced over at them.

"Just a second," she said. "Hold it. You two stay there. Edgar, go stand by your father. Go. *Go!*"

He walked to the doorway. She stepped away from the frying pan and let the potatoes sizzle and put her hands on her hips and squinted as if eyeing a litter of pups to pick out the troublemaker.

"Good God, Sawtelle men look alike," she said, shaking her head. "You three were stamped out of the same mold."

Evidently, she saw three self-conscious smiles in return, for she burst out laughing, and for the first time since Claude arrived, things began to feel relaxed.

By the time the meal was finished, Claude's haunted look had softened. Twice, he stepped onto the porch and lit a cigarette and blew smoke through the screen. Edgar sat at the table and listened to the talk until late in the night: about the kennel, the house, even stories about Edgar himself. He taught Claude a couple of signs, which Claude promptly forgot. Almondine began to lean against the newcomer when he scratched her, and Edgar was glad to see it. He knew how much the gesture relaxed people. He sat and listened for a long time until his mother pressed her hand on his forehead and told him that he was asleep.

Vague recollection of stumbling upstairs. In his dreams that night he'd stayed at the table. Claude spoke in a voice low and quiet, his face divided by a rippling line of cigarette smoke, his words a senseless jumble. But when Edgar looked down, he found himself standing in a whelping pen surrounded by a dozen pups, wrestling and chewing one another; and then, just as he lapsed into deep, blank sleep, they stood by the creek and one by one the pups waded into the shallow water and were swept away.

EDGAR OPENED HIS EYES in the dark. Almondine stood silhouetted near the window, drawing the deep breaths that meant she was fixated on something fascinating or alarming. He clambered out of bed and knelt beside her and crossed his forearms on the windowsill. Almondine swept her tail and nosed him and turned back to the view.

At first he saw nothing out of the ordinary. The maple tree stood freshly leafed out just beyond the porch, its foliage black under the yellow glow of the yard light high in the orchard. No commotion had erupted in the kennel; the dogs weren't barking in their runs. The shadow of the house blanketed the garden. He half expected to see a deer there, poaching seedlings—a common trespass in summer, and one Almondine regularly woke him for. Not until Claude moved did Edgar realize his uncle had been leaning against the trunk of the maple. He wore jeans and a flannel shirt that belonged to Edgar's father and in his hand a bottle glittered. He lifted it to his mouth and swallowed. The way he held it in front of him afterward suggested contents both precious and rare.

Then Claude walked to the double doors fronting the barn. A heavy metal bar was tipped against them, their custom whenever a storm might come through. Claude stood considering this arrangement. Instead of opening the doors, he rounded the silo and disappeared. From the back runs a volley of barks rose then quieted. A few moments later Claude appeared at the south end of the barn, hunkered down beside the farthest run. His tweedling whistle floated through the night. One of the mothers pressed through a canvas flap and trotted forward. Claude scratched her neck through the wire. He moved down the line of runs until he had visited every dog and then he returned to the front and set the brace bar aside and opened the door. Had he walked in directly, a stranger, the dogs would have made a ruckus, but now when the kennel lights came on there were a few querulous woofs and then silence. The door swung shut, and Edgar and Almondine were left watching a yard devoid of all but shadow.

The small workroom window began to glow. A moment later Patsy Cline's voice echoed from inside. After a few bars, the melody warbled and stopped. Roger Miller launched into "King of the Road." He had just begun to describe what two hours of pushing broom bought when he, too, was cut off. There followed a swell of orchestral music. Then some big band number. The progression continued, each song playing just long enough to get rolling before it was silenced. Then the music stopped.

Almondine huffed at the quiet.

Edgar pulled on his jeans and picked up his tennis shoes. The lamp in the spare room cast a dim glow into the hall and he swung the door back and looked inside. The line-dried sheets were firmly tucked under the mattress. The pillows lay plumped at the head of the rollaway bed. The only signs Claude had been there at all were his battered suitcase splayed open on the floor and his suit pooled beside it. The suitcase was nearly empty.

They descended the stairs. Edgar had to guess at the position of the owl eye in the dark, but they reached the bottom in perfect silence and slipped out the back porch door and trotted to the barn. He pressed an eye to the crack between the double doors. When he saw no movement, he turned the latch and slipped through the doors and into the barn, with Almondine close behind.

A few dogs stood in their pens. Most lay curled in the straw. All of them watching. Nearby, the workshop door stood open. At the distant end of the kennel, the lights in the medicine room blazed. It was as if Claude had inspected everything and left. Edgar walked to the whelping rooms and cracked open the door and looked inside. Then he and Almondine climbed, again silently, the stairs along the back wall of the workshop. At the top was an unlit plywood vestibule with a door that prevented winter drafts from rushing down. They stood in the shadows and looked into the mow. Four bare bulbs glowed in their sockets among the rafters. The massive stack of straw bales at the rear of the mow—directly beneath the hole in the roof—was covered with tarps in case it rained. Loose straw and a scattering of yellow bales covered the mow floor. Fly-lines ran from cleats in the front wall through pulleys in the rafters and ended in snaps that dangled a few feet above the floor.

Claude lay in the middle of it all on a hastily improvised bed of bales, one hand hanging slackly to the floor, palm up, fingers half curled beside a liquor bottle. Between each of his breaths, a long pause.

Edgar almost turned and led Almondine down the stairs again, but at that moment Claude let out a quiet snore and Edgar decided, as long as Claude was asleep anyway, they could work their way along the front wall to get a better look at him. They edged out. Edgar sat on a bale of straw. Claude's chest rose and fell. He snorted and scratched his nose and mumbled. They moved one bale closer. Another snore, loud enough to echo in the cavernous space. Then Edgar and Almondine stood over Claude.

The black hair. The face so deeply lined.

Edgar was pondering again the differences between his father and his uncle when, without opening his eyes, Claude spoke.

"You people know you got a hole in your roof here?" he said.

Edgar wasn't sure what startled him more—the fact that Claude was awake, or that he'd begun to smile before he opened his eyes. Almondine bolted with a quiet woof. Edgar sprawled backward, encountered a bale of straw, and plopped down.

Claude yawned and sat up. He set his feet on the mow floor and noticed the liquor bottle. An expression of pleasant surprise crossed his features. He picked it up and looked at the two of them and shrugged.

"Going-away present from some friends," he said. "Don't ask me how they got it. Supposed to be impossible."

He lifted the bottle to his mouth for a long, languorous drink. He seemed to be in no rush to say more, and Edgar sat and tried not to stare. After a while, Claude looked back at him.

"It's pretty late. Your parents know you're out here?"

Edgar shook his head.

"I didn't think so. But on the other hand, I can understand it. I mean, some joker shows up and wanders out to your kennel in the middle of the night, you want to know what's what, right? I'd've done the same thing. In fact, your father and I used to be pretty good at sneaking out of the house. Regular Houdinis."

Claude mused on this for a second.

"Getting back in used to be a whole lot harder. Did you use the window or go through the—oh, never mind," he said, breaking off when his gaze shifted to Almondine. "I guess you snuck out the back. The old tried and true. You figured out the way off the porch roof yet?"

No.

"Your dad didn't show you?"

No.

"Well, he wouldn't. You'll figure it out on your own anyway. And when you do, remember that your old dad and I blazed that particular trail."

Claude looked around at the mow. "Maybe a lot else is different, but this barn is just how I remembered it. Your dad and I knew every nook and cranny in this place. We hid cigarettes up here, liquor even—we used to sneak up for a belt in the middle of summer days. The old man knew it was here somewhere, but he was too proud to look. I bet if I tried I could find half a dozen loose boards right now."

Some people got uncomfortable talking with Edgar, imagining they would have to turn everything into a question—something he could answer by shrugging, nodding, or shaking his head. The same people tended to be unnerved by the way Edgar watched them. Claude didn't seem to mind in the least.

"Did you have something you wanted to ask," he said, "or was this purely a spy mission?"

Edgar walked to the work bench at the front of the mow and returned with a scrap of paper and a pencil.

What are you doing up here? he wrote.

Claude glanced at the paper and let it drop to the floor.

"Not sure I can explain it. That is, I can *explain* it, but I'm not sure I can explain it to *you*. If you know what I mean."

Edgar must have given Claude a blank look.

"Okay, your father asked me not to get into too much detail here, but, uh, let's just say I've been inside a lot. I got *really* tired of being inside all the time. Little room, not much sun, that sort of thing. So when I got in that room tonight, even trimmed out and fancy like your mom made it, it occurred to me that it wasn't much bigger than the room I'd *been* in. And that didn't seem like the right way to spend my first . . . ." A bemused look crossed his face. "My first night home. I started thinking maybe I'd sleep on the lawn, or even the back of the truck. Watch the sun rise. Thing is, the outside is awfully big. That make any sense? Spend a long time cooped up, you go outside and it feels almost bad at first?"

Edgar nodded. He set two fingers on the palm of one hand and swept them over his head.

"Exactly right. Whoosh." Claude swept his hand over his head too. "Know what Scotch is?" he asked.

Edgar pointed at his bottle.

"Good man. Seems like most people get interested in liquor eventually, and they're either going to try it on their own . . ."

The bottle of Scotch tipped itself toward him invitingly. Edgar shook his head.

"Not interested, eh? Good man again. Not that I'd have let you have much. Just wanted to see if you were curious."

Claude unscrewed the bottle cap, took a sip, and looked squarely back at Edgar.

"Still, it would be a big favor to me if you'd keep this between us. I'm not doing any harm up here, right? Just relaxing and thinking, enjoying this place. Your folks would probably end up all worried for no reason. This way, they don't know you're sneaking out at night, and they don't know I went for a stroll, either."

Claude's smile, Edgar decided, looked only a little like his father's.

"You'd better get back to the house now. If I know your dad, he wakes everybody up at the crack of dawn to start work."

Edgar nodded and stood. He was about to clap Almondine over when he realized she was already standing in the vestibule, looking down the stairs. He walked over to join her.

"Here's a trick that might come in handy," Claude said to his back. "You know that stair that squeaks? About halfway up? Try it over by the left. There's a quiet spot, not easy to find, but it's there. If you get in the door without slamming it, you're home free."

Edgar turned and looked back into the mow.

I know that spot, he signed. We found it this morning.

But Claude didn't see him. He'd sprawled backward across the bale, fingers meshed behind his head, looking through the gap in the roofing boards and into the night sky. He didn't look drowsy, more like a man lost in thought. It came to Edgar that Claude hadn't really been asleep at all as they'd worked their way along to get a better look at him. He'd been teasing them, or maybe testing them, though for what reason Edgar could not imagine.

The next morning, Edgar came downstairs to find his uncle seated at the kitchen table, eyes bloodshot, voice croaking. He didn't mention their late-night encounter; instead, he asked Edgar to teach him the sign for coffee. Edgar rowed one fist atop the other as if turning the crank of a grinder. Then his father walked out to the porch and Claude joined him and they talked about the barn roof.

"I can start on it," Claude said.

"You ever reroofed a barn?"

"No. Or a house. How hard can it be?"

"I don't know. That's why I'm asking."

"I'll figure it out."

That afternoon, Edgar's father and Claude returned from the building supply in Park Falls with a new ladder tied to the truck topper and the truck bed filled with pine planks, tar paper, and long, flat boxes of asphalt shingles. They stacked the supplies in the grass behind the back runs and over it all they spread a new brown tarpaulin.

The Stray

Mornings, Claude stood on the porch sipping coffee, breakfast plate balanced on his palm. After dinner, he sat on the steps and smoked. Sometimes he unwrapped a bar of soap and turned it over and after a while began to shave away curls with a pocketknife. One morning, not long after Claude moved in, Edgar picked up the bathroom soap and discovered the head of a turtle emerging from the end.

For a long time, Edgar and his father had had a ritual of walking the fence line after first chores, before the sun had cooked the water out of the grass and the air had thickened with dust and pollen. Almondine came along sometimes, but she was getting older, and just as often when Edgar told her they were going, she rolled on her back and held her feet prayerfully above her breastbone. His father never invited Claude, not even those first weeks of summer, before the arguments between them overshadowed everything else.

Their route started behind the garden, where the fence stood just inside the woods' edge. Then they followed the fencepost-riddled creek to the far corner of their property, where an ancient, dying oak stood, so thick-branched and massive its bare black limbs threw full shade on the root-crossed ground. A small clearing surrounded the tree, as if the forest had stepped back to make room for it to perish. From there they bore east, the land sweeping upward and passing through sumac and wild blackberry and sheets of lime-colored hay. The last quarter mile they walked the road. It wasn't unusual for Edgar's father to go the whole way in silence, and when he was quiet, each step became the step of some earlier walk (spray of water from laurel branches; the musty scent of rotting leaves rising from their footfalls; crows and flickers scolding one another across the field), until Edgar could draw up a memory—maybe an invention—of being carried along the creek as an infant while Almondine bounded ahead, man and boy and dog pressing through the woods like voyageurs.

It was on a dark morning that summer, on one of these walks, when they first saw the stray. During the night a white tide had swallowed the earth. At sunrise the near corner of the milk house shouldered through the fog, but the barn and the silo had disappeared, and the woods were a country of the only-near, where the things Edgar saw at all he saw in extraordinary detail and the rest had ceased to exist. The creek ran from nowhere to nowhere. The limbs of the dying oak hung like shadows overhead. In the sky, the sun was reduced to a minuscule gray disk.

They were almost home, walking the road, the world cottoned out ahead, when something caught Edgar's eye. He stopped near the narrow grove of trees that projected into the south field atop the hill. A granite ledge swelled from the ground there, gray and narrow and barnacled with moss, cresting among the trees and submerging near the road like the hump of a whale breaking the surface of the earth. As his father walked along, Edgar stepped into the wild mustard and Johnson grass and waited to see if the ground might ripple and seal over as the thing passed. Instead, a shadow floated into view at the ledge's far end. Then the shadow became a dog, nose lowered to the mossy back of the leviathan as though scenting an old trail. When the dog reached the crest of the rock, it looked up, forepaw aloft, and froze.

They stood looking at each other. The animal stepped forward to get a better look, as if it hoped to recognize him. At first Edgar thought it was a kennel dog enjoying a stolen hunt. It was the right size, with a familiar topline, and its blond chest, dark muzzle, and saddle of black weren't unusual for a Sawtelle dog. But its ears were too large and its tail too sabered, and there was something else—its proportions were wrong somehow, more angular than Edgar was used to seeing. And if it had been one of theirs, all but the most contrary would have bounded forward.

His father had nearly vanished down the road but by chance he looked back and Edgar lifted his arm to point. Seeing Edgar hadn't spooked the animal, but the motion of his arm did. The dog wheeled and retreated into the field, growing grayer and more spectral with each step, until at last the fog closed around it and it was gone.

Edgar trotted down the road to his father.

There was a dog back there, he signed.

In the kennel, every dog was accounted for. They cut back through the field to the finger of woods, hoping to sight it again. They were standing on the road where Edgar had first seen it when his father noticed its stool.

"Look at that," he said, poking the meager pile with a stick. It was the same rusty orange as the road. Only then did Edgar understand why its lines had looked wrong as it walked the spine of the whale-rock. He'd never seen a starving dog before.

THEY TOLD HIS MOTHER they'd spotted a stray and that it was eating gravel. She just shook her head. It wasn't much of a surprise. People were always pulling into their driveway, hoping the Sawtelles would adopt the pups that scrambled across their back seats, maybe even train them along with their own dogs. Edgar's father would explain that they didn't work that way, but at least once every year a car would crunch to a halt by the orchard and a cardboard box would drop to the gravel. More often, pups were abandoned out of sight, on the far side of the hill, and these they would discover in the mornings huddled against the barn doors, exhausted and frightened and wagging their stumpy tails. His father never let them near the other dogs. He'd pen them in the yard and after chores drive them to the shelter in Park Falls, returning grim and silent, and Edgar had long since learned to leave him alone then.

And so they expected to see the stray appear in the yard soon, maybe even that morning. In fact it didn't appear for days and then only a glimpse. Almondine and Edgar and his father were walking the fence line. As they approached the old oak, something dark bolted through the sumac and leapt the creek and crashed through the underbrush. Edgar threw his arms around Almondine to stop her from chasing. It was like holding back a tornado—her breath roared in her chest and she surged in his arms and that night she barked and twitched in her sleep.

His father placed several telephone calls. No one was looking for a lost dog, not that Doctor Papineau knew about. Likewise with the animal shelter and with George Geary at the post office and with the telephone operators. For the next few days, they left Almondine behind on their walks, hoping to coax the stray along. When they came to the old oak, Edgar's father produced a plastic bag and shook out dinner scraps near the twisted roots of the tree.

On the fourth day, the animal stood waiting near the oak. Edgar's father saw it first. His hand dropped on Edgar's shoulder and Edgar looked up. He recognized at once its blond chest and dark face, its black saddle and tail. Most of all its bony physique. Its hind legs quaked out of fear or weakness or both. After a time it turned sideways to them, flattened its ears against its skull, lowered its head, and slunk back toward the bole of the oak tree.

Edgar's father retrieved a scrap of meat from his pocket. His hand swung past and a chunk of meat came to rest on the ground between them. The dog bolted back, then stood looking at the offering.

"Step back," Edgar's father said quietly. "Three steps."

They backed slowly away. The dog lifted its nose and shivered, whether from the scent of food or of people, Edgar couldn't tell. His own knees began to jitter. The dog trotted forward as if to grab the meat, but at the last minute it whirled and retreated, watching over its shoulder. They stood regarding one another from across the greater distance.

"Yawn," Edgar's father whispered.

Edgar raised his hands to sign as slowly as he could.

What?

"Yawn. Real big," his father said. "Like you're bored. Don't look at the food."

So they gaped their mouths and gazed at the sparrows flicking from branch to branch in the crown of the dying oak. After a while the stray sat and scratched its shoulder and yawned as well. Whenever it looked at the meat, Edgar and his father became entranced all over again by the movement of the sparrows. Finally the stray stood and walked up the path, quickening at the last instant to snatch the meat and plunge into the underbrush.

They let out their breaths.

"That's a purebred German Shepherd," his father said.

Edgar nodded.

"How old, would you guess?"

A yearling.

"I was thinking less."

No, it's a yearling, he signed. Look at its chest.

His father nodded and walked to the base of the tree and dumped out the rest of the dinner scraps. He looked into the underbrush on the far side of the creek.

"Nice structure," he mused. "Not so dumb, either."

And beautiful, Edgar signed, sweeping his hands wide.

"Yeah," his father said. "Give him a little food and he'd be that, too."

CLAUDE HAD BEGUN WORKING on the storm damage on the back pitch of the barn roof—hammer strikes echoing against the woods, the scream of nails pulled from old wood, a grunt when he gouged himself.

"They just peel right off," he said at dinner, pinching two fingers and daintily lifting an imaginary shingle from his plate. His face was sunburnt, and his hand was bandaged where he'd driven a toothpick-sized splinter into it. "Some of the roofing boards are in okay shape, considering the shingles have been letting so much water through. But there's plenty of rot."

Claude led them to the mow and pointed out the blackened boards, then climbed the ladder in the dusk and tossed shingles down. If they didn't reshingle the whole thing, he said, they would be reroofing it, timber and all, a couple of years down the line. And any way you sliced things, it would take him a good part of the summer. They closed up the kennel and walked to the house. After Edgar went inside, his parents stayed in the yard with Claude. Their voices, pitched low, came through the porch screen as they talked, and Edgar stood in the kitchen and listened, carefully out of sight.

"That's no good," Claude was saying. "It'll end up in the yard some night, and get into the barn and pick a fight with one of the dogs."

"It'll come in on its own soon enough."

"Out this long and still running? Whoever dumped it probably beat it. Probably it's crazy as hell. If that dog was going to come in, it would have run up to you peeing on itself by now."

"Just give it time."

"They starve out there, you know that. They don't know how to hunt, and it'd be worse if they did. Better to shoot it."

Silence. Then his mother said quietly, "He's right, Gar. We have three mothers coming into heat in the next month."

"You know I won't do it."

"We *all* know," said Claude. "No one has ever been as stubborn as Gar Sawtelle. Strychnine, then." Claude glanced up toward the porch. His expression almost but not quite hid a grin, and what he said next had the sound of a taunt, though Edgar did not understand what it meant.

"You've done it before, Gar. You've done it before with a stray."

There was a pause, long enough that Edgar ventured a look out the window. Though his father stood in profile, half turned toward the field, Edgar could see the anger in his face. But his voice, when he replied, was even.

"So I'm told," he said. Then, with finality, "We take them into Park Falls now." He walked up the porch steps and into the kitchen, face flushed. He took a stack of breeding records from the top of the freezer and set them on the table, and he worked there for the rest of the evening. Claude sauntered into the living room and paged through a magazine, then climbed the stairs, and all the while a silence occupied the house so

profound that when the lead snapped in his father's pencil, Edgar heard
him swear under his breath and throw it across the room.

THEN, FOR DAYS, NO SIGN of the stray. Almondine would stop and
stare across the creek, but neither Edgar nor his father saw anything, and
after a few moments he'd clap her along. He liked to think she'd caught
the stray's scent, but Almondine often stared into the bushes like that,
drawn by exotic scents unknown to people.

Edgar woke one night to the sound of a howl echoing across the
field, a long, lonely *ooooooooooohr-ohr-ooooh* that finished in a high-pitched
chatter. He sat in the dark and listened, wondering if it had only been
in his dreams. There was a long silence, then another howl, this time
farther away.

What happens if he comes in? he asked his father the next morning.

"He's gone, Edgar. If he was going to come in, he would have already."

But I heard him last night. He was howling.

"If he comes in, we'll take him to Park Falls," his father said. Then he
glanced up and saw Edgar's expression, and added, "Probably."

That evening Edgar pulled two yearlings into the kennel aisle and got
the grooming tackle. By the time he'd finished, the setting sun bathed
the back of the house in crimson. Claude stood on the porch smoking. As
Edgar mounted the porch steps, Claude lifted his cigarette to his mouth
and drew on it and pointed its incandescent tip toward the field.

"Look there," he said.

Edgar turned. Down near the edge of the forest, three deer sprang
across the field in parabolic leaps. Behind them, in grim pursuit, the
small, earthbound figure of the stray. When the deer vanished into the
aspen the stray stopped and circulated as if winded, or confused. Then it
too passed into the trees. Claude stubbed out his cigarette in the bowl of
an ashtray as the sun dropped below the horizon.

"There's how it's staying alive," he said. The light had gone gray
around them and Claude turned and walked into the kitchen.

Late that night, an argument. Edgar made out only some of it from
his bedroom. Claude said now there was no choice—it would never come

in on its own once it started chasing deer. His father said that he wasn't about to shoot it if there was any other way. They'd seen no downed deer. Then something else Edgar couldn't make out.

"What happens if it goes onto someone else's property?" his mother said. "We'll be blamed for it, even if it isn't one of ours. You know we will."

Around it went among them, their voices faint and sibilant through the floorboards. Then silence without agreement. The spring on the porch door creaked. Footsteps along the driveway. The barn doors rattled on their old hinges.

The next morning, his father handed Edgar a steel food bowl with a hole drilled in the rim and a section of light chain. He dumped two handfuls of kibble into the bowl. They looped the chain around the trunk of the old oak and snapped it. The next day the bowl was empty. They moved it twenty yards up the trail, refilled it, and chained it to a birch.

FIXING THE BARN ROOF, it turned out, was a perfect job for Claude. It hadn't taken long to see how ferociously solitary the man was. A day spent alone climbing the ladder and ripping tarpapered shingles from old planking left him whistling and jaunty. Sometimes he balanced himself on the long axis of the barn's peak and watched them working the dogs. He might have been earning his keep, but the barn roof was also a convenient surveyor's point, a perch from which their entire, insular little kingdom was revealed. Time and again when Edgar looked up, he found Claude in the process of turning back to work.

As soon as the situation required him to work with Edgar's father, however, arguments arose, puzzling and disconcerting. Though the details differed each time, Edgar got the idea that Claude and his father had slipped without their knowing it into some irresistible rhythm of taunt and reply whose references were too subtle or too private to decipher. Whatever the dynamic, it wasn't Claude's only aversion. Group conversations left him looking bored or trapped. He found reasons to dodge the dinner table, and when he did join them, he seemed to lean away as if ready to walk off if things took an unpleasant turn. Yet he never actually left. He just sat, responding to questions with a word or a nod and watching and listening.

It wasn't that he disliked talk. He just preferred conversations one on one, and then he liked to tell stories about odd things he'd seen happen, though he himself was seldom the story's subject. One evening, after Edgar had coaxed a new mother out of her whelping pen for grooming, Claude slipped through the barn doors and ambled over. He knelt and stroked the dog's ear between his thumb and forefinger.

"Your dad had a dog once," he said. "Named him Forte. He ever tell you about that?"

Edgar shook his head.

"We were just out of high school, before I went into the navy. Your grandpa came up with the name, because of his size. That one was a stray, too, and only ever half tame because of the time he spent in the woods. But he was a *dog*, you know? Smart as any we'd seen. Good build, good bones, ran a hundred-twenty, hundred-thirty pounds once he was fed right. Your grandfather had no qualms about using him for breeding stock when he saw what he had." Claude talked about how strong Forte was, how quick, how the only bad thing about him was how he liked to fight, and how his grandfather made Forte his father's responsibility, because, Claude said, "that dog was so much like Gar."

This last comment made Edgar look up in surprise.

"Oh, yes. Once upon a time your father was a hell-raiser. Come home drunk, or sometimes not at all. Those two were made for each other. Your dad taught him a trick where he'd whistle and the dog would jump into his arms, all hundred-twenty pounds of him. They'd go into Park Falls and your father would let Forte fight somebody else's dog and of course Forte would win, and as often as not the other guy'd pick an argument, and there they'd be, man and dog fighting side by side. They'd come home bloody and sleep so late the next morning your grandpa would get mad and kick them out of bed."

Edgar had never seen his father lift his hand in anger, not against a dog and not against a person. He couldn't imagine him letting a dogfight happen. But Claude just grinned and shook his head as if reading Edgar's thoughts.

"Hard to believe, right? Just like from looking at me you wouldn't necessarily think I was the one patching things up all the time, but that's true, too. Anyway, your father fell in love with that dog, even though he wouldn't listen worth a damn. One night he grabs me and Forte and we drive to The Hollow. He downs a fair number of beers and pretty soon some guy says he's heard of Forte and next thing I know, we're bouncing along a back road in the dust of this guy's truck. Your father's at the wheel, weaving all over, but it doesn't matter because we're so far back in the woods there's nobody else on the road.

"He stops in the driveway outside the man's house, which turns out to be just a shack. There's no lights. Your father leaves the headlights on, and as we watch, the guy walks to a shed and a minute later out comes the biggest, blackest mastiff I've ever seen in my life. The thing puts its front feet on the hood of the truck and looks in at us, slavering like a bear. Your father pushes open the passenger-side door, but Forte's seen this monster and thinks he's got no chance, so all of a sudden he's sitting in your father's lap. The mastiff gets off the hood and comes around by the open door. I'm sitting closest to that side, and I go to shut the door, but the mastiff's head is between me and the handle. Next thing I know, it's hunching backward and then I'm not in the truck anymore—I'm being dragged through the grass by one boot. I've got a free foot, but I'm afraid if I kick it, it'll start in on my leg, so all I can do is holler for your dad.

"In the meantime, this guy's standing in the headlights. He's got a rifle over his shoulder, and he's doubled over laughing. Your father's struggling to get out of the truck, but he's too drunk to move fast, and he's got a grown dog cowering in his lap. He throws Forte out of the truck. The dog no sooner touches the ground than he's back in the cab, and they start all over again. Meanwhile, the mastiff is pulling me back toward its pen to gnaw on me for a good long while.

"Well, your dad finally gives up on Forte and falls out of the driver's-side door, which would have been funny in any other situation, but right then I'm screaming for help. He gets up and grabs the gun out of the guy's hand and runs over, jams the barrel of the rifle into the mastiff's ribs, but it pays no mind. So he jabs it again. It finally notices him and it drops my leg. By the time I get on my feet, it's got him backed up against the side of the shack and he's shouting, 'How do you call it off? How do you call it off?' The man is still laughing. 'I got *no* idea!' he says, and then there's a lunge and the gun goes off and before any of us know what's happening, the mastiff is laid out on the ground."

Edgar led the dog he'd been grooming back to the whelping room. When he returned, Claude stood waiting for him.

"So the guy's mad now," he continued. "He takes the gun from your father and says, 'Get your dog out of that truck or I'll shoot it where it sits,' and it's clear that he means it. Your father goes to the truck and pulls Forte out. You have to understand how angry he was at Forte for cowering in there. The man lifts up the rifle but your father says, 'Wait.' And here's the strange part: he takes the gun away from the guy, easy as anything. They're both real drunk, see, swaying in the headlights of the truck. But instead of punching the guy and pitching his gun into the weeds, he calls Forte out and shoots him himself. *He shoots his own dog.* And *then* he tosses the gun down and cold-cocks the guy."

No, Edgar signed. I don't believe you.

"I put Forte in the back of the truck and drove us out of there. I buried him in the woods across the road, right over there. Then I told your grandfather that Forte ran away, because your father was too sick from the drinking to come downstairs, much less explain what happened. Besides, he didn't even *remember*. I had to tell him. He asked some questions at first—like, why didn't he do this or that, but I think it finally came back. Then he just rolled over in bed and stopped talking. Stayed there for the better part of three days before he could finally face anyone."

Edgar shook his head and pushed past Claude.

"So you see how it is?" Claude said to his back. "There's no way he can do it now, even when it has to be done."

Almondine followed Edgar to his room and they lay on the floor, paw-boxing. He tried to put Claude's story out of his mind. It was a lie, though he couldn't have said how he knew, or why Claude would tell him such a thing. When Almondine tired of their game, he looked out the window. Claude was sitting alone on the porch steps, smoking his cigarette and looking at the stars.

THEY COAXED THE STRAY up the path each day by refilling the bowl and moving it closer to the yard, just a few feet at first and then, as the days wore on, much farther. At least, they *hoped* it was the stray: the bowl was always licked clean. Finally, they staked it close enough to the house that Edgar could see the glint of metal behind the garden, and the next morning, for the first time, the kibble was untouched. At dinner, he suggested they add a generous portion of the roast they were eating, but his mother said they weren't throwing away any more table food, that the time had come to stop the handouts.

In the morning he found a half-dozen black-fingered manikins sitting around the bowl, rolling chunks of kibble in their paws. He shooed them away and stalked to the workshop carrying the desecrated food. His father stood by the cabinets, filing breeding records he'd taken to the house.

Squirrels are getting the food, he signed, indignantly.

His father pushed his glasses up his nose and peered into the bowl. "I wondered when that would happen," he said. "There's no point in putting that out anymore. Once they've found it, they'll never let it alone."

The idea made Edgar wild with frustration. Isn't there some way we could trap him? he signed. Trick him into a pen? He'd settle down once we worked with him, I know he would. I could do that.

His father gave him a long look. "We might, I suppose. But if we tricked him, he'd just run off again. You know that." He sighed and ran a hand through his hair. "Every time I think about that dog, something your grandfather used to say comes to mind. He hated placing pups, really hated it. That's why he started keeping them until they were yearlings—said most people had no idea how to handle a pup. Wrecked their dogs before they were six months old. I remember him taking the truck one night after he'd heard about a new owner holding back food to punish a pup. The next morning the pup was in the kennel again."

Didn't they argue with him about it?

His father grinned. "They thought it had run away. And that wasn't the first one he took back, either. If they cared enough to call, he'd tell them it showed up out of nowhere, give them what for, and *maybe* let them have the dog back. Most of the time he just sent them a check and told them to get a beagle. Anyway, what I mean is, he hated having to *choose* where the dogs went. He thought it was pure guesswork. 'We'll know we've got it right when they choose for themselves,' he used to say."

That doesn't make sense.

"That's what I thought, too. I asked him what he meant, but he just shrugged. I don't think he knew himself. But I keep thinking maybe that stray is making exactly the kind of choice he talked about. We're talking about an adult dog, a dog that's been out in the woods for a long time, trying to decide whether or not we can be trusted. Whether this is his place. And it *matters* to him—he'd rather starve than make the wrong decision."

He's just scared.

"No question about that. But he's smart enough to get past that if he wants to."

What if he does come in?

"Well, if he *chooses* to, then—maybe—we'd have a dog on our hands worth keeping. Even worth bringing into the line."

You'd breed him if he came in?

"I don't know. We'd have a lot of work to do first. Understand his temperament. See how he takes to training. Get to know him."

But he's not one of ours.

"How do you suppose our dogs got to be *our dogs* in the first place, Edgar?" his father said, grinning wickedly. "Your grandfather didn't care about *breeds*. He always thought there was a better dog out there some-where. The only place he was sure he *wasn't* going to find it was in the show ring, so he spent most of his life talking with people about their dogs. Whenever he found one he liked—and it didn't matter whether it was a dog he saw every day or one he heard about halfway across the state—he'd cut a deal to cross it into the line in exchange for one of the litter. He wasn't above cheating a little now and then, either."

Cheating? Like how?

Instead of answering, his father turned to the filing cabinets and began fingering through the records.

"Another time. Your grandfather had already stopped that kind of thing when I was a kid, but I do remember one or two new dogs. All I'm trying to say is, we've got to be patient. That dog's going to have to decide on his own what he wants to do."

Edgar nodded as if he agreed. But something his father had said had given him an idea.

THAT EVENING HE CARRIED a sleeping bag out to the porch along with a flashlight and a book. He had untied and unrolled the sleeping bag in front of the screen door and was settling down to read when Almondine, as if she knew his plan and didn't like it, stepped into the narrow space between Edgar and the screen door and lay down. He poked her in the flank where she was ticklish and she stood with a harrumph, then stepped over him and lay down again, this time draping her tail across his face.

Okay, I get the point, he signed, aggravated but smiling. He coaxed her into standing, this time more gently, cupping his hand under her belly, and he rearranged the sleeping bag. When he was done, there was space enough for them both to look through the screen, though Edgar had to crane his neck to see the spot behind the garden where the bowl sat. Almondine lay with her head on her paws, panting contentedly and watching Edgar with her flecked brown eyes. He drew his fingers along the soft fur of her ears and through her mane, and soon her eyes drifted shut and her breaths deepened on the exhale. He watched her and shook his head. She could be so vehement at times and, yet, when everything had been put her way, so gentle and accommodating and radiating certainty that the world was in order. After a while he propped himself up on his elbows. Under the glow of the flashlight, he paged through *The Jungle Book* until he found the passage that had come to his mind over and over that day.

> Mowgli put up his strong brown hand, and just under Ba-
> gheera's silky chin, where the giant rolling muscles were all
> hid by the glossy hair, he came upon a little bald spot.

"There is no one in the jungle that knows that I, Bagheera, carry that mark—the mark of the collar; and yet, Little Brother, I was born among men, and it was among men that my mother died—in the cages of the King's Palace at Oodeypore. It was because of this that I paid the price for thee at the Council when thou wast a little naked cub. Yes, I too was born among men. I had never seen the jungle. They fed me behind bars from an iron pan till one night I felt that I was Bagheera—the Panther—and no man's plaything, and I broke the silly lock with one blow of my paw and came away; and because I had learned the ways of men, I became more terrible in the jungle than Shere Khan. Is it not so?"

"Yes," said Mowgli; "all the jungle fear Bagheera—all except Mowgli."

He switched off the flashlight and laid his head next to Almondine's. He wondered if it was like that somehow with the stray, whether it had decided after some terrible moment that it was no man's plaything, or whether it was some combination of frightened and crazy, like Claude said. In time the television went silent. Claude walked upstairs. His mother leaned out from the doorway.

"Good night, Edgar," she said.

Good night, he signed—drowsily, he hoped. He could feel her sizing up the arrangement.

"What are you up to?"

It's hot upstairs. We want to sleep where there is a breeze.

When the house had been silent for as long as he could stand it, he sat up, unlatched the door, and slipped outside. Almondine tried to follow, but he shut the door between them. She could open it, sometimes, by catching her claws at the bottom—but he hushed her, holding her gaze until he knew she understood. He walked to the flower bed beneath the kitchen window, and there he lifted a bread bag from among the green straps of the irises and crossed the garden and filled the dish with the kibble he'd packed into the top of the bag. Then he sat on the porch steps, leaning against the door's cross brace, and waited. Eventually, his gaze lifted to the stars.

He woke to the sound of Almondine, behind the screen door, breathing hoarsely at his shoulder. The yard was flush with moonlight. It didn't come to him at once why he was sitting there. His gaze wandered along the clothesline sagging from the house to where it vanished into the shadow of the maple tree. The rattle of kibble against the steel pan finally shook him out of his reverie. He jerked upright. Across the expanse of stakes and seedlings, the stray stood, eating greedily and watching Edgar, its chest silver in the moonlight.

He stood, slowly, and carried the bread bag, heavy and cold, into the shadow of the maple and knelt. The iron scent of blood wafted upward as he opened the bag—ground beef, stolen that afternoon from the freezer. He squeezed a portion into a ball and let out a soft whistle. The dog lifted its head and looked at Edgar. Then it turned back to the bowl to lick up the last dots of kibble and stood on three legs and scratched its chest with its hind fourth.

Edgar pitched the meat underhand, just as his father had done on the trail. The pale mirrors of the dog's eyes glinted. It stepped out of the weeds and pressed its nose into the night air. Another chunk of ground beef sailed out and rattled the leaves of a tomato plant. The animal began to pick its way through the rows of vines and seedlings and foot-high corn stalks, pausing at one offering, then the other.

Edgar divided the remaining meat into two greasy lumps. One came to rest midway between them, no more than ten yards away. The dog went to it, sniffed, and swallowed the meat in a single gulp, then lifted its head and ran its tongue along its chops. The other lump of meat Edgar held in his hands. For a long time neither moved. Edgar leaned forward and set the meat on the grass. The dog walked forward and took the meat and swallowed and stood panting and looking at Edgar. A slash of matted fur crossed its forehead and burrs were twisted into its coat. When Edgar held out his hand, the dog stepped closer and at last licked the blood and grease from his fingers. Edgar ran his free hand through the dog's ruff. He knew then it was possible to bring the dog in the rest of the way. Not that it would happen that night, but it *could* happen. The dog wasn't crazy. Not all its trust was gone. It was undecided, that was all. It had watched them and what it had seen was not enough to make it stay or go. As his father had thought.

Edgar was trying to decide what to do next when Almondine began to whine and tear at the porch door. In four bounds the stray crossed the garden and disappeared. By the time Edgar got to the porch, one of the kennel dogs had pushed into its run, baying, and another was following. Edgar settled Almondine and turned toward the barn.

Quiet, he signed.

The dogs stopped and yawned, but nearly ten minutes passed before they ceased their pacing and bedded down again.

WHEN HE OPENED HIS EYES the next morning, a fluted circle of dirty white lay just beyond the porch steps. He sat on his sleeping bag and rubbed his eyes. What he saw looked like a coffee filter—a soggy paper coffee filter, stained brown. When he walked outside to investigate, Almondine pushed past and, to his surprise, urinated on the thing. Then she rounded the corner of the house with her nose to the ground.

A black plastic trash bag lay in the front yard, chewed open, its contents strewn about—empty soup cans, a Wheaties box, bits of packages, newspapers, a milk carton. When he bent to peer at one of the papers, he saw his own handwriting in the crossword puzzle. The date on the newspaper was three days past. They had taken it to the dump the day before.

Over breakfast, they speculated over how the trash had gotten there. Claude said it was a prank, some kids out drinking. Edgar's mother was the first to conclude that it must have been the stray. The dump was about a quarter of a mile down Town Line Road, up a narrow dirt drive that dead-ended in a semicircle of rubbish and the carcasses of stoves and refrigerators.

"Why would it drag garbage all the way back from the dump, for Christ sake?" Claude said.

His mother looked thoughtful. "Maybe it's retrieving," she said.

"Retrieving? Why?"

"I don't know," she said. "Grateful for the food? 'Here's something you lost, thought you'd want it back'—that sort of thing."

She was right, Edgar knew it at once, but he was the only one who understood the full significance of the dog's labors. He considered telling them what had happened the night before, but that meant explaining how a pound of ground beef had disappeared.

The next morning a long-discarded pair of his jeans lay neatly unfolded in the front yard, as if a boy had evaporated from within them. The morning after that, a single tennis shoe, mangled and gray. His father laughed, but Claude was incensed. He stalked away to his roofing work.

"Imagine if that dog had spread garbage around the living room," Edgar's mother said, when Edgar asked her about it. "That's how Claude feels. To him, the dog's a trespasser."

Then, perhaps sensing its efforts were underappreciated, the dog stopped bringing gifts, but by then Claude had begun his campaign. Bitter arguments erupted, Claude adamant that the stray be shot, Edgar's father steadfastly refusing. His mother tried to make peace, but she, too, thought the stray needed to be dealt with. Two nights later there was an uproar in the kennel that had all four of them out in pajamas trying to calm the dogs. They couldn't find anything wrong. What had happened was obvious, Claude said. The stray had tried to climb into one of the pens. At the idea, some pure form of anxiety inhabited Edgar. He didn't want the dog caught, not if it meant loading it into the truck and driving it away. Yet, if it was getting bolder, something bad was bound to happen.

The problem was, he'd begun thinking of names. It was his job, he couldn't help it, even if he knew it was a bad idea. And only one name seemed right. As if the original Forte had come back.

ON SATURDAY, HIS PARENTS took a trio of yearlings to Phillips for Ice Age Days to proof them around crowds. At first Claude planned to go along, then decided to work on the barn while the good weather held.

Edgar and Almondine spent the morning with a litter of three-month-olds. After the crazywalking, which taught them that people were unpredictable and must be watched, Edgar put them in stays and tossed tennis balls to Almondine in front of them. She was an old hand at distraction training, and she chewed the prizes ferociously, whipping her head from side to side. When the pups held their stay for a ten count, he motioned them free, and there was a mad scramble. Now and then Claude hoisted himself up onto the ridge beam of the barn and sat, shoulders brown and slick with sweat.

After lunch, Edgar fell asleep on the couch while watching television and reading. Distantly, he heard Claude come into the house and leave again, but he thought nothing of it. When he woke, the apple trees seethed in the wind. Outside he found Almondine standing beside the silo, tail down and peering into the western field.

Two deer and a fawn grazed in the hay, small dun figures at that distance. Downwind of them, Forte crouched, stock still, and Claude, in turn, stood downwind of Forte near the wind-lashed tree line. In his arms, loosely cradled, the long black form of a rifle.

The deer flicked their tails uneasily and cantered along the woods' edge. As soon as they moved, Forte trotted forward, hips low, but instead of charging the deer, he slunk into the woods and disappeared. When the deer began grazing, Claude also retreated into the trees, taking steps so slow Edgar could hardly see the motion.

He turned and ran Almondine to the porch, then closed the door and bolted for the trail behind the garden. At the rock pile, halfway down-field, the path curved around a patch of dogwood, and there he found Claude standing in a small clearing, looking over the raised barrel of the rifle. Thirty yards farther, just inside the forest's edge, stood Forte. Edgar hadn't seen the dog in daylight since he'd faced them at the old oak. His ribs showed through his coat and his belly drew up in a steep arc against his backbone. The dog's ears were peaked forward, and he was drawing fast, deep breaths.

When Edgar reached Claude, he put his hand on the rifle stock. Claude knocked Edgar's hand away.

"Get out of here," he muttered. "Get back to the house."

He's almost come in twice, he signed, knowing that at best Claude would only gist it. He can't catch them, not by himself.

He reached for the rifle again. This time Claude turned and grasped the front of his shirt and Edgar found himself sprawling backward into the dry leaves and undergrowth, fighting for balance and then hoping he might make enough racket to get Forte's attention. But the wind was gusting through the treetops, and the stray was intent on the motions of the fawn.

He didn't hear Almondine coming. Suddenly, there was a huffing beside him and she stood there, panting furiously, gaze riveted on the stray.

Edgar swept an open hand in front of her face.

Stay.

She saw the command coming and tried to look away, but he got her attention and repeated it. She dropped into a sit. When he turned, Claude had settled the rifle against his shoulder. Edgar watched his finger tighten over the trigger, but there was no kick, no roar. Claude fumbled along the stock, searching for the safety.

From the time they were pups, Sawtelle dogs learned that *stay* meant remaining not just still but quiet—that whining and barking were a kind of following. And Almondine was in a stay.

Edgar turned to her and touched a hand to his temple.

Watch me.

Her great head swiveled to face him.

Release.

He meant to catch her before she moved, but her hindquarters came off the ground before he'd even completed the sign. All he could do was lunge and clamp his fingers around the hock of her back leg. She sprawled out in the path with a loud yelp.

It was enough to make Claude glance away from the rifle sights. Then Almondine was up again, forging ahead, half dragging Edgar along the path. He finally got in front of her and put his hand around her muzzle and forced her to look him in the eye.

Speak, he signed.

And then Almondine began to bay.

This time Forte couldn't mistake the sounds behind him for wind. He turned and saw them and leapt away all in a single motion. Claude swung the muzzle of the rifle to track the fleeing dog, but there was nothing left to sight on but swinging branches.

Edgar didn't realize he'd loosened his grip on Almondine's collar until she was already away, bounding down the path. She crossed in front of Claude. For a moment, the muzzle of the rifle dropped and tracked her, and then, without pause, Claude pivoted to the field and shot the smaller of the two deer as it stretched its neck, wide-eyed and preparing for flight. The other deer shrieked, executed three springing leaps, then vanished into the woods with the fawn close behind.

Edgar scrambled into the field. The doe lay kicking convulsively. Blood arced from the wound in her neck. Her eye rolled to look at him. Claude walked up beside Edgar and lowered the muzzle of the rifle to the animal's chest and pulled the trigger. Even before the report finished coming back off the hills, Claude had turned and begun walking toward the house, rifle grasped loosely by his leg like a stick of lumber.

For a long time Edgar stood looking at the deer—her brown hide, her black-tipped ears. Crimson blood seeped from her wounds and then stopped. Almondine appeared at the edge of the field, panting. She trotted over, then froze and approached the animal step by step. The moment when Almondine had passed in front of the rifle's muzzle kept replaying in Edgar's mind.

Come on, he signed. Get away from that.

They met Claude walking back into the field carrying a hunting knife and a spade.

"Hold on a second," he said.

Edgar stopped, then began to walk again.

"Okay, but you're gonna have to make a decision in a while," Claude said to his back. "We can help each other here if we want to."

He spent the evening in the barn, Almondine close by, grooming dogs until his hands ached. Claude approached him once, but Edgar turned away. The sun had set and the stars were coming into sight overhead when the truck pulled into the driveway.

The carcass of the deer hung by one back leg from a low branch of the maple tree. His father was asking questions even before he was out of the cab. Claude walked over to meet them. Forte had finally downed a deer, he said. He'd watched it from the barn roof, but by the time he'd gotten the rifle the deer was down and the stray was working on it, and he'd fired a shot to scare it off.

"The doe was still alive but tore up pretty bad. No choice but to shoot it. I didn't want to leave it, so I dressed it out and took off the one leg he'd chewed up and brought it back here," he said.

The lie didn't surprise Edgar, but what Claude said next did. He expected Claude to return to the old argument, insist they bait Forte and shoot him, or poison him. And this time it was an argument he would probably win. Instead, he suggested they forget Forte.

"As far as that dog goes," Claude said, "I don't think I hit it, but I know I scared the hell out of it. Took off so fast I never had time to take a second shot. We're never going to see it again."

He looked at Edgar as he spoke, and at first Edgar didn't understand. His mother caught Claude's gaze and turned to look at him.

"Where were you during all this?" she asked.

Lit by the porch light, flies penciled their shadows against the carcass of the deer. Edgar's father turned to face him as well. Claude stood behind and between them, and the resolute expression on his face lifted. The corners of his mouth edged up into a smile.

Claude was presenting Edgar with a choice. He saw that. All his talk of scaring off Forte had just been making the terms of the deal clear. He was offering to forget the stray, let him come or go. The price was silence. Edgar looked at the carcass of the deer and then at his parents.

I was asleep in the living room, he signed. I missed everything.

IF HE AND CLAUDE HAD struck a pact that night, it remained a silent one. Claude never again suggested they try to find or kill Forte and Edgar never told his father the truth about the deer. When he could be surreptitious about it, Edgar filled the steel dish with kibble and set it behind the garden. It was empty by morning, though whether licked clean by Forte or plundered by the squirrels he couldn't tell.

One evening, as Edgar was crossing the lawn, in that dilated moment after sunset when the sky holds all the light, he saw Forte watching from the far side of the garden and he stopped, hoping the dog would finally trot into the yard. Instead, he edged back. Edgar returned to the barn. He filled the steel dish with kibble and walked up the carefully weeded rows of sweet peas and corn and musk melon until he stood a single pace away. Even then the dog would not come forward. It was Edgar who took the final step, out of the garden and into the wild grass growing at the tree line. There, Forte ate the kibble from Edgar's hand, trembling. Afterward, he let Edgar lay a hand on his shoulder. Thus began a ritual that would last all that summer and into the fall. A week might pass before the stray appeared again. Edgar would carry food out and the dog would eat while Edgar worked burrs from his coat. Always, before Edgar had finished, Forte would begin to pant and then he would turn and walk away and bed down at the forest's edge, where the lights of the house glittered in his eyes. And if Edgar came closer then, the dog would rise and wheel and trot into the woods without pausing to look back or making a sound.

The Litter

H E WOKE THAT DAY TO AN EMPTY BEDROOM AND THE DISTANT
recollection of Almondine jumping off the bed in the gray morning light. He'd meant to follow her but then he lay back, and when he opened his eyes again the sun was bright and the curtains billowing inward, carrying with them a volley of echo-doubled hammer strikes— Claude at work on the field side of the barn roof. He kicked off the covers and dressed and descended the stairs, sneakers in hand. Almondine lay sprawled in a parallelogram of sunlight on the porch. His father and mother were at the kitchen table sharing pages from the *Mellen Weekly Record*. Morning chores had been done and the two kennel dogs, brought to the house on the nightly rotation, were back in their runs.

Edgar ate toast on the porch, looking out at the field. Almondine rolled onto her back, splayed and crocodilian, and stared at his plate. He looked down at her and grinned.

Too bad, he signed, munching.

Almondine swabbed her tongue across her chops and swallowed.

"Edgar, when is school over?" his father called from the kitchen.

Edgar inspected the remaining square inch of his toast. Butter on the edges, the top heaped with red raspberry jam. He nibbled from the crust and smacked his lips. Almondine flexed on her backbone to get a better look. Finally he held the toast out, pinched between thumb and forefinger so her whiskers would brush his palm, an ancient habit. She scrambled to her feet and sniffed his offering, pretending to be unsure whether it would suit her, then lifted the toast daintily away with her small front teeth.

Edgar walked into the kitchen and set his plate on the table.

Friday is the last day, he signed.

"I checked Iris this morning. She's carrying her pups pretty low," his father said. Edgar looked at his father looking solemnly back at him. Was there a problem? Was this too early for Iris? He tried to remember if he had groomed her the day before, or even touched her.

"What would you think of making this litter yours?"

It took a second to register what his father was saying. He blinked and looked out at the barn. The lines in the red siding pulsed through a wave in the porch window glass. "You'd do the birth work. I'd be there, but it would be your responsibility. And you'd look after the pups," his father said. "Every day. If any get sick, you'd take care of them, no matter what else you'd rather do. And you'd do the training, right up to placement, even when school starts."

Edgar nodded. He was smiling, stupidly, but he couldn't stop.

"With my help," his mother said. "If you want it."

She laughed a little and touched his arm and sat back. His father held the newspaper folded in his lap. They looked so satisfied just then, and suddenly he knew they'd been discussing this for a long time, watching him, trying to gauge whose litter would be best. He hadn't asked for any such thing. Ordinarily his father oversaw the whelping. When the pups were old enough, they became his mother's charges. While she trained them, his father arranged placements. Edgar already had endless chores around the kennel, divided between the two of them. He fed and watered the dogs, cleaned their pens, and groomed them—his specialty. He helped with training, too, crazywalking the pups, performing the shared-gaze exercises, creating distractions when his mother wanted to proof the dogs. But this was different. They wanted Edgar to handle a single litter from birth through placement.

"With a little luck, she'll hold off whelping until school is out," his father said. "We have to keep an eye on her, though. You never know." He picked up his paper and folded it in the middle, then glanced over. "You look like *you're* about to have puppies," he said.

Then Edgar started laughing. Almondine came in from the porch to see what was happening, fanning her tail and holding her ears flat. She walked around the table pressing her nose into their hands.

Thank you, Edgar signed. He dropped his hands and lifted them again and put them down when he couldn't think of anything else to say. He went to the refrigerator and poured milk into his glass and drank it with the door open. From the back of the refrigerator he retrieved a package of cheese curds. He ate one in plain sight, palmed the rest, and walked out into the brilliant summer daylight.

THE WHELPING ROOM, set near the back of the barn and enclosed by thick plank walls, was a warmer, darker, quieter place than any other in the kennel. The wood of the walls reeked with birth odors: blood, placenta, milk, sweat. The pens were half-sized, with no outside access, to keep the temperature steady. His father had to stoop under the dropped ceiling. Low-wattage bulbs cast a pale light that made puppies' eyes glimmer, and an old-time wall thermometer hung in each pen—one backed by a Pepsi bottle, another a blue-and-white Valvoline label, both marked with a thick black line at eighty degrees. In the passageway, a battery wall clock with a sweep second hand ticked away quietly.

A mother and her month-old litter occupied the first pen, the pups just old enough to escape the whelping box. They tumbled over one another and pressed their blunt black muzzles through the wire and nibbled Edgar's fingers, and then, for no reason he could see, spooked and scrambled away.

In the farthest pen, Iris lay quietly panting, her back to the whelping box in the corner. He knelt beside her while she tongue-stroked the back of his wrist. He placed one hand on the hot crepe of her belly and in the other a cheese curd appeared. Iris tongued it off his palm. She sniffed her belly where he'd touched her.

You're going to have to work real hard soon, he signed. You know that, don't you?

Iris swallowed and looked at him, eyes wet in the cave light. He reached into his pocket and held out another curd.

HE DREAMED HE WAS RUNNING, feet pounding beneath him, breath coming in gasps. Always he arrived too late. The third night he woke in a fit of anxiety and he was at the kitchen door, on his way to check Iris, before he decided it was a bad idea. At breakfast he peeled an egg and he and his father walked to the barn. He rehearsed in his mind the case for skipping school, but before his father even touched Iris, he said, "It won't be today."

Edgar squatted and stroked her face and broke the egg into pieces and fed it to her while his father tried to explain how he knew.

"Look at her eyes," he said. "Are they teary? Is she walking in circles?" He felt the curve of Iris's huge belly, her hindquarters, looked at her gums, took her temperature. He always had an explanation, but the truth, Edgar suspected, was that his father just *knew*, and didn't know how he knew. They looked up Iris's birthing history; she'd whelped on her sixty-second day with her first litter of six and at sixty-four days with her second litter of five. Friday would be day sixty-two.

When they were finished, Edgar collared Iris and snapped on a lead and let her walk wherever she liked. She headed for the tall grass behind the barn, then the Wolf River apple trees at the top of the orchard. Her hind legs rowed out to her sides when she walked. When Almondine approached, serious and respectful, Iris stood for inspection.

Edgar boarded the school bus in despair. Ten thousand hours later, it ground to a halt in front of their driveway. He felt weightless as he opened the whelping room door. Iris lay sleeping, solitary, enormous. When Friday passed, he barely noticed that school was over. It was just another day when Iris would surely whelp while he was away.

WHEN HE LOOKED IN on Saturday morning, the bedding in the whelping box had been scratched up into a pile. Instead of lying outstretched in her usual gestative pose, Iris was pacing and panting. She came forward with her ponderous gait. Once outside, she forged into the hayfield, aiming for the hazel stand.

"That sounds interesting," his father said, noncommittally, when Edgar found him in the workshop. They walked to the nursery. Iris had settled herself back in the whelping box.

"How's it going, girl? Today the day?"

She looked back and bumped her tail against the slats. His father put his hands in his pockets and leaned against the wall and watched her. "Not right this minute," he said after a while, "but it's going to be sometime today. I want you to check her every half hour from now on. But stay out of this pen—we just want to know if she is sleeping, walking, or what."

I'll stay and wait.

"No. Don't spend any more time here than you have to. When you come in, be quiet and slow. She's worried now and she's wondering how to protect her babies. If we bother her too much, she could panic. Understand? She could try to eat her pups to keep them safe."

Okay, he signed. It wasn't what he wanted to hear, though he understood the reasoning.

"The next thing to watch for is when she starts licking herself or walking around the whelping box. Once that starts, we've got work to do."

NOW TIME THICKENED LIKE wet cement. From his dresser he dug out a pocket watch he'd gotten for Christmas many years before and wound it and set it and shook it to make sure it was running.

He and Almondine walked the path to the creek, but before they'd gone more than halfway he turned and ran back, slapping through the ferns. They arrived five minutes early for the next check. He sat with his back against the narrow front wheels of the tractor while Almondine dozed, annoyingly relaxed, in the cool grass. When the time had passed, he found Iris lying in her box, muzzle atop folded forelegs; she caught his eye and raised her head. In the other whelping pen, a litter charged the door and tried to bite through the rubber toe of his sneaker when he pressed it to the wire. He went to the house, looked at the watch, compared it with the time on the kitchen clock. He fetched *The New Webster Encyclopedic Dictionary of the English Language* and opened it at random. His eyes jittered over the words. *Intake. Intangible. Intarsia.* He flipped a hunk of pages. *Perilous. Perimeter. Perimorph.* Ridiculous, impossible names for dogs. His toes twitched, his heels rattled against the floor. He slapped the dictionary shut and knelt in front of the television, twisting the channel knob to Wausau, Eau Claire, Ashland.

His father parceled out small jobs, concocting them, Edgar suspected, more out of mercy than necessity: pile newspapers outside the pen door; lay towels on the newspapers; straighten the bedding in the whelping box; wash the steel pan in the workshop, fill it with water, and put it on the stove; put scissors and hemostat in the pan and boil the water; put a bottle of Phisohex on the towels; set out thread and iodine; get a short lead.

After dinner, when the next half hour had passed, he excused himself and walked to the barn. They always seem to start at dinnertime, his father had said. The dogs were standing in their pens, muzzles slowly turning to track his progress down the aisle.

All it took was one glance. For fear of making a commotion, he forced himself to walk the whole length of the barn, but as soon as the evening sky opened overhead, his legs made the decision on their own and he bolted for the house.

"REMEMBER WHAT I SAID about her getting nervous? She'll be calm if she knows we're calm, so move slow. She's an old hand at this. Our job is to watch and help just a little. That's all. Iris is going to be doing all the work. We're just keeping her company."

Edgar was waddling along behind his father, a basin of warm water sloshing in his arms.

Okay, he nodded. He took a breath, let it out. The setting sun cast his father's shadow back along the driveway.

"Now," Gar said, "let's find out how she's doing."

Iris stood in her whelping box, head down, digging frantically. She paused briefly when they entered the whelping room, glanced at them, then turned back to her work.

"Go ahead," his father said, gesturing at the door.

Edgar stepped inside the pen, carrying the pan, and set it down in the corner. His father handed him the newspapers, the towels, and all the paraphernalia he'd collected during the afternoon. Iris stopped digging and walked to the door. His father squatted down and stroked her face and chest; he ran the tip of his finger along her gum line and put his palm against her swollen belly; in return, she pressed forward until one of her feet was outside the threshold of the pen door. His father placed his hands on her shoulders and eased her back. He had Edgar latch the hook and eye on the inside of the door and Iris returned to the whelping box and lay down.

Now what? Edgar signed.

"Now we wait."

After twenty minutes or so, Iris stood and circled inside the whelping box. She whined and panted, then sat. After a few more minutes, she stood again. She shivered, turned her head all the way back to her hindquarters, and licked at her hip. She shivered again.

Shouldn't she be lying down? Edgar signed.

"Sit tight," his father said. "She's doing just fine."

Iris lowered herself nearly to the floor, hips suspended above the bedding. A spasm shook her body. She whined quietly, grunted, then raised her hips and turned to look behind her. A newborn pup, dark and shiny in its embryonic sac, lay on the gray bedding.

"Wash your hands," his father said. He'd closed his eyes and tipped his head back against the wall. "Use the Phisohex."

As Edgar rubbed his hands together in the water, he heard a squeak from the whelping box. Iris had already torn the birth membrane away and had turned the new pup on its back. She was running her tongue along its head then its belly and hind legs. Its fur glistened and it kicked its hind legs and squeaked again.

"Has she chewed through the cord?" his father asked.

Edgar nodded.

"Wet one of the small towels and take a dry one and a couple of sheets of newspaper. Kneel over to the whelping box. Go slow. Use the wet towel to clean off the pup. Hold it right near Iris so she can see what you're doing. That's right. She's just checking you; it's okay if the pup cries a little. Make sure its nose and mouth are clear. Hold it in your left hand and get the dry towel with your other hand and dry it off. You can rub a little. Go ahead. That's good, you want to dry it off as much as you can. Now set it down in front of her."

Edgar performed each step as instructed. His father sat with his back against the wall, eyes closed, his voice quiet and even, as if describing a dream in which the pups were born. When Edgar set the pup down, Iris began to lick it again. Edgar took a deep breath and listened to his father's voice as he walked him through tying the umbilical with thread and dabbing the stub with iodine.

"Now look for the afterbirth. Do you see what I mean by the afterbirth? Is it all the way out of her? Trace the umbilical cord to find out. Put it into the newspaper and roll it up and set it by the door. Don't move fast. Now go back to the pup. Pick it up. Use both hands. Remember to praise Iris when we're done, she's being very good about all this. Very gracious. Don't be scared if she grabs your hand; it just means she's not ready to let you touch her pup yet. While you're holding it, she's going to be watching you; try not to take it out of her reach, and never out of her sight. Look it over. Does it look normal? Look at its face. Is it okay? Good. Now set it down so its head is near a nipple. Good. Watch for a minute. Is it taking the nipple? Move the pup a little closer. How about now? Is it taking the nipple? Good."

Iris lay with her neck flat on the bedding, eyes half shut. Breaths like sighs lifted her chest. Edgar discovered he could hear the faint suckling of the pup over the thunderous pounding in his ears. He scooted backward until he could lean against the wall. He took a long, quavering breath and looked over at his father.

"You forgot to praise her," his father said, his voice so quiet Edgar barely heard it. He'd opened his eyes again and he was smiling. "But wait awhile now. She wants to rest."

THE PUPS ARRIVED about a half an hour apart. When the third was nursing, Edgar's father gathered up the newspapers piled by the door and walked out of the whelping room. He came back carrying a pan of warm milk. Edgar held it while Iris lapped, then ran his fingers into the bowl and let her lick the last drops, and then he held her water bowl. She turned to her pups, rolling them and licking them until they cried, and then, satisfied, lowered her muzzle to the bedding.

The fourth pup looked normal in every way, yet it sagged in Edgar's hand when he lifted it. His father pressed the limp shape to his ear and held his breath. He swung the pup high into the air and quickly down to the floor, listened, and did it again. Then he shook his head and lay the stillborn pup aside.

Did I do something wrong? Edgar signed.

"No," his father said. "Sometimes a pup just isn't strong enough to survive whelping. It doesn't mean you did anything wrong and it doesn't mean that there's any problem with the rest of the litter. But now would be a good time to walk her. She'll relax for the rest of the whelping." Edgar nodded and collected the short lead and gently slapped his thigh to coax Iris out of the whelping box. She bent her head to her pups and licked them away from her. They began to peep like chicks. She allowed Edgar to lead her into the yard. The night was cloudless and Almondine watched them from the porch, whining quietly.

Not yet, he signed. Soon.

Iris made for the top of the orchard, urinated, then pulled heavily toward the barn. As he closed the barn doors, and the swath of yellow light narrowed against the woods opposite, he saw a flash of eyeshine, two pale green disks that vanished and appeared again. *Forte*, he thought. He wished he could take the time to walk out and be sure but instead he turned and led Iris to the whelping room. The pen door stood open. His father was gone, along with the stillborn pup. Iris stood over her pups, methodically licking them, then lay and nudged them into the circle of her legs.

Four more pups came that night. Edgar washed and inspected each, offering Iris water and food when he thought she would take it. His father sat against the wall, elbows propped on his knees, watching. After the eighth pup, his father palpated Iris's belly. There were probably no more, he said, but they should wait. Edgar cleaned the fur on Iris's legs and all of her back parts, and he dried her with a fresh towel. He coaxed her into the warm night once again. When they returned, Iris went directly to the whelping box and urged her pups against her teats as she had before.

She's a good mother, Edgar signed.

"She is indeed," his father said. He guided Edgar out of the whelping room. The bright kennel lights cast circles under his father's eyes and Edgar wondered if he himself looked equally weary.

"I want you to stay in the barn tonight, but keep out of her pen unless she's having problems. First, though, I want you to come back into the house and clean up."

They walked into the dark kitchen together. The kitchen clock read 2:25. Almondine lay near the porch door. She sauntered drowsily over and scented Edgar's legs and hands, then leaned against his knee. Edgar's mother appeared in the bedroom doorway wearing her bathrobe.

"Well?" she said.

Three females, four males, he signed. He made the sign for "beautiful," a wide, sweeping gesture.

She smiled and walked around the table and hugged him.

"Edgar," she murmured.

He fixed himself a ham sandwich and told her everything. Some of it was already jumbled in his mind; he could not remember whether the stillborn puppy was the fourth or fifth. Then, all at once, he could think of nothing else to say.

Can I go back out now?

"Yes," she said. "Go."

His father stood and laid a hand on Edgar's shoulder and looked at him. After a time Edgar felt embarrassed and looked down.

Thank you, he signed.

His father raised his fingertips to his mouth and held them there. He drew a breath and tipped his hands outward.

You're welcome.

Almondine squeezed through the porch door ahead of him and plunged down the steps. There were no clouds to obscure the stars overhead or the crescent moon reclined at the horizon. The longer he looked, the more stars he saw. No end to them. He thought of Claude and how he'd been overwhelmed by the sky his first night home.

Whoosh, he'd said. As if a person might fall into something that large.

In the barn, he stopped to collect a clean towel from the medicine room and *The New Webster Encyclopedic Dictionary of the English Language* from its place atop the file cabinets and went into the nursery. Iris lay on her side in the whelping box, breaths tidal, her pups chirping and grunting as they nursed.

He would need names now, particularly good names. He stretched out along the passageway floor, using the towel for a pillow, and opened the dictionary. Almondine scented the air and peered into the pen, tail low. Iris opened her eyes and raised her head. Then Almondine stepped over Edgar and lay beside him. He pulled her onto her side and she pawed the air and gave out a little gasp and they looked through the pen wire together. The low barrier of the whelping box hid the pups, but when Edgar closed his eyes, he saw them anyway, shining black crescents tucked against the down of their mother's belly.

Essence

OCTOBER. DRY LEAVES CHATTERED BENEATH THE APPLE TREES. For three nights running, pearl flakes of snow materialized around Edgar and Almondine as they walked from the kennel to the house. Almondine poked her nose into the apparition of her own breath while Edgar watched a snowflake dissolve in midair, one and then another. Those that made it to the ground quivered atop blades of grass, then wilted into ink drops. At the porch, they turned to look at their footsteps, a pair of dark trails through the lawn.

The four of them played intricate games of canasta until late in the night. Edgar partnered with his mother—they both liked to freeze the deck, slow things down, let the tension rise with the height of the discard pile. Soon enough you got an idea of which cards a player needed and which they hoarded. Sometimes a person was forced to make an impossible choice. His father scavenged the low-point cards, arranging meld after meld on the table. Claude preferred to hold his cards, fanning them, rearranging them, walking them with his fingers until, without warning, he would complete two or three canastas and go out. They harassed one another as they played.

"Your turn, Claude," Edgar's father said.

"Hold on, I'm plotting a revolution."

"Hey, no table talk."

"That's not table talk. I'm trying to get my partner off my back."

"Well, Edgar and I don't like it. There's no telling what sort of signals you two have cooked up."

"All right, here's a discard. Take it."

"Ugh. Does your trash never end? Here's one for my dear husband."

His father looked at the discard and peered around his tract of melds.

"Jesus, Gar. You play like a farmer."

"What's wrong with that? You should thank me. It's your crop, too."

"What's the score again?"

"Thirty-two thirty to twenty-eight sixty. You're behind."

"That's only one natural's difference."

"Now that was table talk for sure."

"I'm just saying what's true. Every time Edgar scratches his ear he's probably telling you all the cards in his hand. Look at that devious expression. What's it mean when he yawns? 'I've got jacks and I'm going out next round'?"

"You wish. I think we're stuck in this one to the bitter end."

"You're the one who froze the pile. Come on, Edgar, what's it gonna be?"

Wait, he signed, one-handed.

"See there. Now, what's that mean?"

"It means he can't decide what to discard."

Edgar pondered. He slapped his thigh and Almondine sauntered over and he held out his two cards, facedown. Could be either one of these, he signed. She scented one, then the other. She nosed the first. He placed a ten of hearts on the discard pile.

"Okay, nice. You've got the dog scouting cards. Remind me to lower my cards when she's behind me. Pass the popcorn. I need to think."

Claude chewed a kernel and looked across the table at Edgar's father. On the wall, the telephone buzzed quietly, the sound like a june bug at a window screen.

"What was that?" Claude said.

"Oh, I don't even hear that anymore. When they converted us off the party line it half-rings like that once in a while, but when you pick it up, it's just dial tone. We call, they say it's fixed, then it buzzes again."

"Hmmm. You ever going to put a phone in the barn?"

"No. Quit stalling."

Claude counted his cards.

"Oh lord, here we go," his mother said.

"Next game I want to switch partners. My brother's run out of luck. All he knows how to do is start melds. Besides, with Edgar on my team, I get two for one."

"You can't have him. Edgar and I are always partners. Another black three? How many of those do you have?"

"That's what you're going to find out. All good things come to those who wait, and I intend to make you wait. Edgar, listen to your poor old uncle Claude. You can get anything you want in this world if you're willing to go slow enough. Remember that. Words of wisdom."

"Did you just call yourself slow?"

"A smart kind of slow."

His father discarded a queen of clubs and looked at Edgar over his glasses. "If you're the good son I raised you to be, you won't pick that up."

Edgar held two cards, neither of them queens. He smiled and pulled a queen off the deck and flipped the new card back onto the discard pile. Claude drew off the deck and tapped the new card on the table and then it disappeared into the mass of cards feathered out in his hand. He looked at Edgar's father.

"If I'm so slow, then how could I know that's the sixth queen in that pile? Which is why I can drop this lovely lady and break Trudy's heart."

He snapped another queen onto the discards and grinned.

Edgar's mother pulled out a pair of queens and laid them on the table.

"I'll be god-damned," Claude said.

"We don't use that kind of language around here," she said, mock-primly, while raking the discard pile over.

"It was for cause. I guess I might as well stretch my legs."

She parceled out the bounty, folding up two of her melds and tossing a set of cards over to Edgar.

"Partner, may I go out?" she said.

"Look at that. Your own wife did that."

"It did seem unnecessary, didn't it?" his father said, but he was grinning.

His mother looked back and forth between them. "All's fair in love and canasta," she said.

Claude counted his cards.

"You were holding two hundred twenty points?" his father said.

"Yep."

"Doesn't seem like it paid off, does it?"

"You just play your old farmer way and I'll be in charge of showing some style."

"A fine proposition if you weren't my partner."

"I'll make it up to you, brother. Haven't I always?"

To this his father said nothing. He counted out cards from his melds to offset Claude's loss, then picked up the pad of paper and noted the results. The phone buzzed again. Claude shook his head and shoveled the cards together and began to shuffle.

EDGAR TOOK ALMONDINE with him to the kennel. At four months old, his pups were clumsy, happy beasts with overlong legs and narrow chests. Their ears flopped over except when they looked intently at something. It had taken Edgar almost two weeks to select names from the dictionary, sampling and rejecting possibilities, sleeping with them held in his mind, and still, the morning after deciding, he'd woken filled with regrets. Now it was as though the pups had been born with names already cast and all he'd done was thrash about until they were revealed.

baboo, babu, *n.* A Hindu title of respect paid to gentlemen, equivalent to master, sir.—**babu.** Babu-English. The broken English of Bengal.

essay, *v.t.* [Fr. *Essayer.* ASSAY.] To exert one's power or facilities on; to make an effort to perform; to try; to attempt; to endeavor to do;

to make experiment of. —*n.* An effort made for the performance of anything; a trial, attempt, or endeavor; a test or experiment; a literary composition intended to prove some particular point or illustrate a particular subject, not having the importance of a regular treatise; a short disquisition on a subject of taste, philosophy, or common life.

finch, *n.* [A. Sax. *finc* = G. Dan. And Sw. *fink, finke,* Gr. *spiza.*] A large family (Fringillidae) of small song-birds, including the bunting, sparrow, and goldfinch, having a small conical beak adapted to cracking seeds.

pout, *v.i.* [From W. *pwtiaw,* to push, or from dial Fr. *pout, potte,* Pr. *pot,* the lip.] To thrust out the lips, as in sullenness, contempt, or displeasure; hence, to look sullen; to swell out, as the lips; to be prominent.

opal, *n.* [L. *opalus,* Gr. *opallios,* an opal; comp. Skr. *upala,* a precious stone.] A precious stone of various colors and varieties, the finest characterized by its iridescent reflection of light, and formerly believed to possess magical virtues.

tinder, *n.* [A. Sax. *tynder, tender,* from *tyndan, tendan,* to kindle (Dan. *taende,* G. *züden*) = Sw. and L. G. tunder, Icel. Tundr, D. tonder, G. zunder, tinder.] An inflammable substance generally composed of partially burned linen, used for kindling fire from a spark struck with a steel and flint.

umbra, *n.* [L., a shadow.] The total shadow of the earth or moon in an eclipse, or the dark cone projected from a planet or satellite on the side opposite to the sun, as contrasted with the *penumbra*; the dark, central portion of a sunspot surrounded by a brighter, annular portion.

After deciding, he'd turned to each entry in *The New Webster Encyclopedic Dictionary of the English Language* and penciled the dog's number, litter number, and birth date in the margin:

D 1114
L 171
6/3/72

The margins were small and filled with annotations, and he had to write carefully, sideways when the word appeared in the middle of the three columns of definitions. After he'd finished, he'd returned the dictionary to its place on the filing cabinets next to the master litter book.

Baboo was the largest of the litter. He could set his front paws on Edgar's shoulders and lick his face with ease. Essay, the wild one, and the leader, liked to play tricks. Tinder flung himself on any sibling he found asleep, growling them into a wrestling match; only Opal could back him into a corner. Pout was thoughtful, sober, and cautious, Finch, a study in earnest impulsiveness. Umbra, black from head to toe, was a watcher, a retreater to corners. They were all ferociously undisciplined and forgetful, but good-natured, too, and sweet to look at. And—for short periods, at least—they reveled in the training.

THE BARN ROOF HAD LONG been completed and another litter whelped and named. As part of his work as the medicine man of the kennel (as Trudy started calling him), Claude took the newest litters of pups under his care. Edgar's father used the extra time to place yearlings and plan litters, spending days on the telephone and writing letters and poring over records. But no sooner did this arrangement seem comfortable than arguments between his father and Claude began to erupt.

"I'm not some fucking stray you lured in," Claude said, during one particularly acrimonious exchange over his casual adherence to the pups' schedules.

"Of course not," Edgar's father replied. "You know me. I'd shoot you if you were."

When things were easiest between them, it was his mother's doing: she mocked their arguments, laughingly, or interposed herself and flirted; when a discussion threatened to slide from fervent to angry, she'd lay a hand on Edgar's father's wrist and he'd look at her, startled, as if he had just remembered something. Then, days of amicable banter, visits from Doctor Papineau, evenings watching television. But Edgar knew the moment he walked in the door when there had been another incident. He'd find his father at the kitchen table, shoulders hunched, glowering at his paperwork. If one of them walked into a room, the other found a reason to leave, and Edgar's mother would sigh in exasperation. And yet, two mornings later, they would be talking again at breakfast and that would be that.

One morning, his father announced that they'd better collect firewood before they got a snow that stuck. This was work they did each fall, cutting the aspen and birch cordwood they'd stacked in the spring alongside the old logging road that cut through their woods.

Can I drive? Edgar asked.

He meant Alice, their old orange Allis-Chalmers C tractor, with its curved fenders and half-moon drawbar. In place of a bucket seat, Alice had a flat padded bench upon which two could ride, though the passenger had to put his arm around the driver and hold one of the uprights. Over the years, Edgar had graduated from running the throttle to steering with his father's hand resting on the wheel, to shifting, and lately, to clutching and braking.

He met his father behind the barn and they walked to Alice together. Edgar settled himself behind the wheel and his father took the crank to the front and slotted it into the hole beneath the radiator grill and hauled the crank over. There was a muffled pop from inside the engine and a belch of sooty smoke escaped the stack, but afterward the engine sat inert. He tried again. Then he walked to the milk house and returned with a can of starter fluid in his hand and he tipped up a hinged plate inside Alice's carburetor and emptied a long spray into its gullet. He walked to the front of the tractor again. He touched the bill of his cap and rubbed his hands together and hauled the crank over. There was a gunshot sound and the handle bucked wildly backward. "Ho!" he said. "We've got her attention now. Give it another notch." Edgar nodded and ratcheted up the throttle lever. This time Alice gave out a roar and from her stack poured a black cloud of exhaust.

The day was warm. A gray cloud ceiling stretched from horizon to horizon and the light coming through cast no shadows on the ground. Edgar backed the tractor up to the ancient iron-wheeled wagon parked at the edge of the south field. His father swung the yoke into place and dropped the hitch pin through and slid onto the seat beside him. They chugged around to the front of the barn, where Claude set the chainsaw and gasoline in the wagon and stepped onto the yoke.

"Haw!" he shouted, and they set off. At the bottom of the slope behind the barn his father reached over and goosed the throttle lever three notches. Edgar gulped and gripped the steering wheel and they shot past the woodchucks in the rock pile, all standing in a line, hands prayerful against fat bellies. His father tipped his hat to each animal in turn, shouting, "Ma'am. Ma'am. Ladies." Then Claude snagged a passing clod of dirt and pitched it overhand, sending the matrons scampering into the rocky crevices.

They crossed the field. Two tremendous birches marked the entrance to the logging road at the edge of the woods. Their leaves blanketed the ground brown and yellow, and their white trunks were decorated with speckled curls of paper. Edgar throttled back, ready to turn the driving over to his father, but his father motioned Edgar ahead. Claude hung out from behind the seat and looked up the trail. When he saw what was coming, he hopped off the yoke and walked alongside. Edgar notched the throttle down and guided Alice through the pools of frost-brown fern cascading over the path. He jackknifed the wagon trying to back it up to the first eight-foot cordwood stack. Then he killed the engine trying to straighten it out.

You do it, Edgar signed.

"Try again," his father said. He walked to Alice's front end and cranked it back to life. Edgar ground the shift level into reverse and sweated and listened as his father and uncle shouted instructions.

"Left. Go left and it'll straighten out."

"Not left, right."

"His left, not mine."

"Far enough. Whoa. Whoa there."

"Okay, a little more. Stop. Little more. Stop. Good."

Edgar flipped the toggle to kill the engine and hopped down. Claude reached into the wagon and pulled out the chainsaw and the red gasoline can. They began to work their way through the pile. The work was monotonous but pleasant. Edgar heaved a log out and Claude sawed off a fireplace-size chunk and Edgar heaved the log again. Sawdust sweetened the air. Edgar daydreamed and looked around and wondered if Schultz had ever cut wood in that part of the forest, and what part of the house or barn might be built from it. Whenever the cut wood piled up, Claude stood with the saw idling while Edgar and his father tossed the chunks into the wagon.

Halfway through the first pile, light rain began to fall, hardly more than a tickle on the back of their necks. When it didn't let up, his father shouted to Claude. Claude glanced over, then returned to cutting while Edgar advanced the log. When he stopped again, the air was filled with a fine, cool mist cut by drops of condensation falling from the skyward branches.

"Let's load and head back," Edgar's father said. He began to loft cut pieces into the wagon, making it rattle and boom. Edgar and Claude joined him, but when they had finished, Claude looked up through the treetops and wiped his face with his shirtsleeve.

"It's letting up," he said. "We don't need to stop."

And all at once, the lightheartedness that had made them joke and wave at the woodchucks vanished. His father's jaw was set. When he spoke next, it was as though some argument had already taken place, with positions staked out and a deadlock reached, all in some sphere invisible to Edgar. "This wood is wet and slippery," his father said. "So is that saw. We can come back tomorrow when it's dry and we won't have to worry about anybody getting hurt."

For a moment the three of them gazed at the stacked cordwood, shiny with moisture. Claude shrugged. "Suit yourself," he said and he braced the chainsaw against a log and yanked the rope starter. The engine sputtered for a moment and caught.

His father shouted something at Claude, who mouthed, "What?" and revved the chainsaw until it was impossible to hear his father's reply. Then he shouted, *"What?"* again. When his father took the bait, Claude squeezed the throttle until the chainsaw howled in his hands. His father paled with anger. A grin spread across Claude's face and he turned and dropped the chain bar into a log and a wake of wet wood chips sprayed onto the ground.

His father stalked over to Edgar and cupped his mouth by his ear.

"Get up on the tractor."

Edgar clambered into the tractor seat and flipped the ignition switch up. His father cranked the starter, swung up onto the driver's side of the seat, gunned the engine, and they bounced their way out of the woods, logs rattling and flying off the back of the wagon. At the house, they stacked the wood in the inside corner by the porch while the whine of the chainsaw pierced the drizzle, reduced by distance to an insect sound. When they finished, Edgar parked Alice beside the barn. Almondine greeted him at the door and chaperoned him up the stairs. He listened to his mother and father talk while he changed out of his wet clothes.

"So what if he wants to cut wood in the rain," she said. "Let him."

"And if he drives the chainsaw into his leg, what then? And if the saw rusts up over the winter from getting wet?"

"Gar, you're right. But you can't ride him like that. He's a grown man."

"That's just it. He's *not* a grown man. He's got no more sense than he had twenty years ago! He gets things into his head, and whatever I say, he'll do the opposite."

"He's a grown man," his mother repeated. "You can't make decisions for him. You couldn't back then and you can't now."

Footsteps, and the click of the coffee pot lid. When Edgar and Almondine walked into the kitchen, Edgar's mother was standing behind his father with her arms crossed around his neck. His father sipped his coffee and handed the cup up to his mother and looked out the window toward the woods.

"You didn't see him down there, gunning the saw whenever I tried to explain to him. It was childish," he said. "It was dangerous."

Edgar's mother didn't respond. She rubbed his father's shoulders and said they needed some things from the store. By the time they returned, Claude had carried everything up from the woods, cleaned and oiled the saw, and lay asleep in his room.

A WEEK BEFORE THANKSGIVING, Claude took the truck into town. When he returned, late that night, even the cold gust of wind that followed him inside couldn't disguise the smell of cigarette smoke and beer. He dumped a bag of groceries on the table and looked at Edgar's father.

"Oh dear, His Eminence is much displeased." He trudged drunkenly into the living room, then turned back. "Look on his works, ye mighty, and despair!" he cried in a booming voice, arms outswept, bowing until he nearly tipped over.

When the days were warm, Edgar stayed away from the house, scouring the woods with Almondine for puffball mushrooms and arrowheads. Looking as well for signs of Forte, who hadn't appeared since late September. One day they would find his bones, he thought, sadly. They walked to the whale-rock and sat at the edge of the peninsula of woods and watched smoke curl out of the chimney. Almondine fell into a half-sleep. Brown leaves drifted down from the trees and her pelt twitched when they landed on her. After dinner, he snuck out to practice stays with Tinder, who wanted more than anything to jump up and run.

He bolted the barn doors from the inside and let the pups run loose up and down the kennel aisle while he sat on a straw bale. Baboo sat with him. Essay started looking for trouble at once. They rolled on their backs and paw-boxed at Almondine, who examined and dismissed them. He fetched half a dozen tennis balls from the workshop and threw them against the doors until the aisle was a mass of surging, raucous animals, and when they tired, he led them into the mow and read to them, signing under the yellow nova of the bulbs in the rafters.

EDGAR FIRST HEARD OF Starchild Colony that fall, and of Alexandra Honeywell, whose long, straight hair was indeed the color of honey. The television news carried the stories of the commune, located on the Canadian side of Lake Superior, near Thunder Bay. Reporters stood beside Alexandra Honeywell on the outskirts of a woody glade, a house framed out behind them, the autumn leaves brilliant yellow. Sometimes she answered the reporter's question directly, and other times she looked into the television and exhorted people to come and help. "This is a place for peace! Come to Starchild! We need people with skills; people who want to work! We don't care if you are a student, a musician, or a soldier. Leave it behind! We need strong hands and brave hearts!"

Alexandra Honeywell was beautiful. Edgar knew this was why she showed up on television so often. If he was in his room and overheard a news teaser about Starchild, he'd come downstairs and sit in the living room and gaze at her while his parents exchanged glances. Claude let out a low whistle at the sight of her.

THANKSGIVING CAME AND PASSED. Edgar woke one night to a sound like a gunshot, though even as he threw off his blankets he understood it was the porch door slamming back against the house. Almondine scrambled up from her place by the door and together they looked out the window. The porch light was shining. The ground was thinly covered in snow and the wind blew hoary gray flakes across the glass. At the base of the porch steps, he saw his father and Claude. Their arms were crooked around each other's necks like wrestlers, shadows cast black and elongate toward the field. Claude had hold of his father's closed fist, as if trying to force it open, and they grunted and pushed wordlessly against each other, counterbalanced and shaking with effort as snow settled on their shoulders and hair.

The clench broke and they stepped apart, breath gray in the cold air. Edgar's father raised a hand and pointed at Claude, but before he could speak, Claude charged, pulling them both to the ground. Edgar's father's glasses glittered in the air. He brought his hands down on Claude's back and hard on the side of his head. Claude's grip loosened. Edgar's father climbed to his feet. Claude scrambled up after him but he slipped and fell heavily down, and before he could get up, Edgar's father was there, foot drawn back. Claude curled his arms over his face convulsively and a shriek filled the yard.

For a time the two men were perfectly still, and the falling snow itself froze in the air. Then Edgar's father drew a breath. He set his foot down. With a disdainful gesture, he tossed what he'd held into the snow. The keys to the truck. Then he turned and walked into the house, and the porch light flicked off.

Edgar and Almondine panted in unison, their breaths congealing on the window. Almondine had been growling low in her chest, but Edgar only heard it now and he reached over and smoothed her hackles. He wiped a watery path across the fogged glass. Claude clambered to his feet and stooped to pick up the truck keys. The feeble cab light glowed briefly over him as he opened the truck door and pulled himself inside and slammed the door shut. The starter grumbled. The taillights flared and flared as if he were stomping on the brake. The truck sat wreathed in clouds of exhaust. Finally it rolled toward the barn and backed around. The headlights swept the yard where Edgar's father and Claude had fought, their struggle drawn in snow that glowed white, then red, then darkened again as the truck roared past the house and away down Town Line Road.

A Thin Sigh

HE KNELT BY THE WINDOW AND LET THE IMAGES REPLAY themselves. The snow lay jaundiced under the yard light and the shadow of the house lampblack across the snow, unbroken save for a single skewed rectangle glowing at its core. Light from the kitchen window. Flakes of snow were captured there, drifting earthward like ash. Up through the furnace register his father's voice rang, tinny and fractured. Edgar walked to his bed and slapped the mattress for Almondine, but she lay in the doorway and would not come. At last he dragged his blanket over to her and arranged himself on the slatted floor. She rolled onto her side and braced her feet straight-legged against him.

Then all the voices fell silent. The light at the bottom of the stairs dimmed. They lay together on the dusty-smelling floor, listening to the timbers of the house groan and pop. Formless light seethed when Edgar closed his eyes. Then he was awake. He put his hand under Almondine's belly and she stood and stretched her feet out front and bowed her spine until a high whine escaped her, and they crept down the stairs, feeling their way in the dark. In the living room, the tiny candlestick lamp cast just enough light to outline the chairs.

He thought the kitchen would be a shambles, but the table stood level, the chairs snugged evenly beneath. All shadow and silhouette. He walked around the table and touched the chairs in turn, points of the compass. The freezer compressor ticked and engaged and murmured a low electric throb; the blower sighed warm air across his stockinged foot as he passed the register. A silver bead of water blossomed at the threaded end of the tap and fell into the void. He twisted down the faucets.

His mother whispered to him from the doorway of their bedroom.

"Edgar, what are you looking for?"

He turned and signed, but in the dark she couldn't read it. He walked to the living room and stood near the candlestick lamp and she followed behind, cinching up the belt around her robe. She sat on the edge of her chair and looked at him. Almondine stood beside her until his mother ran her hand along the dog's flanks, then she downed between them on the floor. Their shadows moved enormous across the walls and windows of the living room as they signed.

Is he all right?

His lip is cut. He lost his glasses. He feels ashamed.

What happened?

It's . . . She thought for a moment, then started again. It's hard to say.

Is he coming back?

She shook her head. Of course not. Not after this.

What about the truck?

I don't know.

Edgar stood and gestured at the door. I saw where his glasses fell. I was going to get them.

Will you still know in the morning?

I think so.

Then wait until tomorrow. He'll wake if he hears the door.

Okay.

Edgar stood and walked to the stairway.

"Edgar?" his mother whispered.

He looked back at her.

"This thing between your father and Claude. It's old, from since they were children. I don't think they even understand it. I know I don't. The thing to remember is that it is over. We tried to help Claude and it didn't work out."

He nodded.

"And, Edgar?"

He turned to look back at her. What?

"I don't think your father is going to want to answer a lot of questions about what happened."

She smiled a little, and that made him smile. He felt some unnamable tenderness toward his father, talking about him in the dark like that. A laugh came up from inside him, like a hiccup. He nodded and clapped his leg and he and Almondine mounted the stairs, the top floor solely theirs once more. And that night, he dreamt of a jumbled world, color and sound without substance, and in the dreaming everything fitted together perfectly, mosaic pieces interlocked in a stately, exquisite dance.

DOCTOR PAPINEAU DROVE THEIR truck back out to their house the next day. Edgar's father packed Claude's things in the truck—not much more than the suitcase he had arrived with: a box of magazines, his shirts and pants, a pair of work boots, and a well-worn navy pea coat. In time, they heard that Claude had picked up part-time work at the veneer mill and odd jobs on the side. He worked for Doctor Papineau, in fact. Later on they put the rollaway bed into the truck, along with the little table and the lamp, and drove them into town, too.

THE SNOW HELD OFF until December that year, but once loosed, it seemed never to stop. Edgar and his father shoveled the driveway while flakes covered their caps. Edgar's father knew the trick of skimming the snow without picking up gravel.

"Leave some on the driveway, would you?" he'd say, reminding Edgar how the stones in the grass shot like bullets across the lawn on the first mowing.

Edgar took his litter into the snow in pairs or trios, Tinder and Essay and Finch, then Pout and Baboo, then Umbra and Opal. They chased one another, sliding on their front paws, reversing, backpedaling, running with their noses against the ground, trenching pale lines in the powder, stopping only to sneeze it out. Those early snows didn't pack. When Edgar managed to squeeze together a snowball, he tossed it at Tinder. It disintegrated in the dog's mouth and he licked his chops and looked on the ground for it.

The Saturday before Christmas they planned to go shopping in Ashland but it was snowing so hard his mother thought they wouldn't be able to get back. They stayed home and watched the astronauts driving around on the moon in their buggy. His father said it looked like they were getting ready to plant corn. And every week there was a news story about Alexandra Honeywell and Starchild Colony. It was cold; people were leaving, she admitted, but the inspired would take their place. She stood in the snow reading poetry to the camera and talked about the voyageurs. Often, those segments played after the weather report. He never failed to be in the living room when the forecast was announced.

ON NEW YEAR'S EVE his mother roasted a duck. Near midnight, they poured three glasses of champagne and clinked. The television counted down to midnight and when Auld Lang Syne began to play, his mother jumped up and held out her hand and asked him to dance.

I don't know how, he signed.

"Then it's time you learned," she said, pulling him up off the couch. Though they were staying home, she wore a black-and-white dress and black shoes with straps across the back, and nylons. She showed him how to put his arm around her waist and hold out his other hand and she put her hand in his.

"This is how the girls will look at you when you dance with them," she said, and she looked into his eyes until he blushed. He didn't know how to move his feet. He couldn't even explain the problem since she was holding his hands, but she knew anyway.

"Here, like a box," she said. She stopped and made him put his hands out, palm down, and she moved them to demonstrate what his feet should do. Then she stepped up to him again. The room was dark, and the lights from the Christmas tree sparkled in the windows. When she put her head against his shoulder, the air grew warm. The sweet cider taste of the champagne was in his mouth, mingled with his mother's perfume, and he knew even then that the sensation would be with him for the rest of his life.

When the song stopped, his mother whispered, "Happy new year." His father had been leaning against the kitchen doorway. When the orchestra started in again, he walked up and said, "Pardon me, may I cut in?" His mother slipped away from Edgar and into his father's arms. Edgar watched them dance, music ringing through the house, and then he opened the refrigerator and took a package of curds and pulled on his shoes and coat. He tried to tell them where he was going. Though the song had ended, they stood there, swaying, silhouetted against the lights of the Christmas tree.

He and Almondine ran through a night black and sharp-edged with cold. In the barn, he switched on the lights and set Patti Page singing "The Tennessee Waltz" on the old record player. Then he used up the curds, handing them out to the dogs, even the puppies, and signing to each in turn a happy new year.

JANUARY THAW. THE ASH they spread along the driveway melted the snow into gray puddles, candied with ice in the morning. He sat in their living room wearing a coat and boots, watching for the yellow caterpillar of the school bus through the bare trees. In the afternoons, the sun was up barely long enough to take his litter into the yard before suppertime to proof them on come-fors and stays in the snow. They learned quickly now. He led three of them at a time to the birches in the south field, then ran to the yard and released them with a sweeping gesture they could see against the sky, and they sliced across the field like a trio of wolves, bodies stretched over the white snowdrifts.

He was getting better, too. With a single dog, he could make leash corrections as well as his mother, catching them in the middle of their first step out of a stay, when they had barely made up their mind to break;

when he did it right, they settled back before lifting their hindquarters all the way off the ground. But he didn't make it look easy like she did. It took every bit of his concentration. He learned to toss a collar chain at their hindquarters if they didn't come on the long-line recalls, though his accuracy was a problem. Plus, he moved his arm so much they saw it coming. He practiced against a bale of straw. His mother could flick her wrist and catch a dog loafing halfway across the mow. When he wasn't expecting it, she threw one against his own backside. The shock of it, the jingle and the impact, made him jump.

"Like that," she said, smiling. "Works pretty well, doesn't it?"

And all the while his dogs grew smarter—caught on to the corrections and found ways to beat them. They would be seven months old soon, and their coats were sleek and winter-thickened. They'd grown as tall as they were going to get, but his father said their chests wouldn't fill out until the summer.

Doctor Papineau, when he visited, could never keep them straight, but to Edgar they were so different it was hard to believe they came from the same litter. He could tell them apart by their movements alone, the sound of their footfalls. Essay always pushed to see what she could get away with, waiting until he looked away to bolt. Tinder, the most rambunctious, would break a stay just because one of his littermates looked at him with a certain glint in his eye. Baboo was the opposite: once in a stay, he would sit forever. He made up for his delay coming off the long line with his love of retrieves. He trotted back to Edgar again and again with the target in his mouth, an aw-shucks swagger rocking his hindquarters.

They were, each of them, brilliant, frustrating, stubborn, petulant. And Edgar could watch them move—just move—all day.

ICY GRAINS, DRY AND WHITE, were falling from low, flannelled clouds. The wind gathered and swept the grains across the yard like a surf. When Edgar opened the barn door, a tendril of snow scorpioned along the cement floor and dispersed at Almondine's feet. His father was kneeling in the farthest whelping pen, where a pup squirmed and mewled on the silver pan of the scale, its ears folded and otterlike. As Edgar watched, his father cradled the pup in his hands and set it back with its mother.

"Giants," he said, writing a note on the log sheet. "And ornery. They haven't opened their eyes yet and they're already pushing each other around. You should be grateful you didn't end up with this batch."

I'm taking mine upstairs, Edgar signed.

His father nodded and turned back to the pup. "I want to clean out those buckets in the workshop before your mother gets back from town. When you finish, find me, okay?"

Okay, he signed. He knew which buckets his father meant—a whole row of them under the workshop stairs, all different sizes, some not buckets at all but battered old lidless ten-gallon milk cans filled to the brim with scrap metal, old nails, hinges, screws, bolts. His father had been threatening to either sort through them or pitch them into the silo for as long as he could remember.

Edgar pulled Finch and Essay out of their runs to practice long-distance downs. The dogs bounded to the workshop and up the stairs, tussling and growling in the straw as he and Almondine followed. In the mow, he could see his breath in the air. He closed the vestibule door. Almondine, without immediate training duties, found a comfortable corner to watch from. Edgar stayed one dog and let it rest while he snapped a long line to the other's collar and put it in a standing stay. On each trial, he lifted his hand overhead to signal a down, rewarding them with a scrub of their ruff, or correcting with a sharp tug on the long line, which he'd threaded through an eye bolt in the floor to direct the force down and not forward. As soon as they'd mastered one distance, he retreated a pace farther.

Essay understood the exercise at once, and how to confound it. She waited until Edgar was walking toward her—when it was hardest to give a correction—then stood up before she was released, panting merrily. Or she would lie down but immediately roll over. Twice, while she was supposed to be waiting her turn, he discovered her poking at the bales of straw, contemplating a climb. Finch, on the other hand, never took his eyes off Edgar. The problem was he just kept standing there, watching, when Edgar signed the down. After Edgar had repeated the command

three times, Finch began to look concerned. Edgar scolded himself for repeating commands and walked over, but the sight of Edgar approaching
struck Finch like a bolt of inspiration, and the dog slid to the floor.

For a break, Edgar flung tennis balls and whirled coffee can lids into
the farthest corners of the mow for the dogs to chase. The pounding
of their feet on the mow floor provoked the kennel dogs below into a
chorus of muffled barks. He'd started the two of them holding retrieval
targets—just taking them in their mouths for a second or two—when
he noticed that the kennel dogs were still barking. Odd, since both his
dogs were now sitting quietly. Edgar opened the vestibule door and listened, then started down the stairs. Finch and Essay, nails clicking on the
wooden treads, crowded past him.

Got to work on that, he thought.

He was almost to the bottom tread before he saw his father, sprawled
and motionless on the floor near the workshop entrance. He was wearing
his winter coat, as if heading outside. And he lay face down.

For a moment, Edgar stood paralyzed. Then he bolted down the steps
and was on his knees beside his father while Essay and Finch stomped and
plunged around them. He shook his father and dug his fingers into the heavy
fabric of his coat and rolled him onto his back and peered into his face.

What happened? What happened?

Behind the lenses of his glasses, his father blinked. How slowly his eyes
tracked Edgar's hands. He strained to lift his head, raising it no more than
an inch off the floor. He stopped and took a breath. Edgar slipped his hand
beneath his father's head before it could fall back against the cement.

And then he was frantic. He withdrew his hand as gently as he could
and checked his fingers for blood, but there was none. He tore his sweater
off and bunched it up beneath his father's head.

His father's mouth had fallen open.

Can you see me? he signed. He yanked down the zipper of his father's
coat and looked at the checkered work shirt beneath. He patted him
from throat to belt. No blood, no injury.

What happened? Did you fall? Can you see me?

His father didn't answer. Nor was he looking back.

Then Edgar was running through the cold, the house jerking in his vision. Wisps of snow coiled around the porch steps. He burst into the kitchen and yanked the phone off its hook. He stood for a moment, unsure of what to do. He pulled the zero around on the dial and waited. Almondine was in the kitchen with him; he couldn't remember her running alongside to the house or even following him down from the mow.

After the second ring a woman's voice came on the line.

"Operator."

He was already trying to make the words. He moved his lips. A sigh came out of him, thin and dry.

"This is the operator. How may I help you?"

His heart surged in his chest. He tried to force sound from his mouth, but there was only the gasp of exhaled breath. He swung his hand wide, then struck his chest with all the force he could muster, mouthing the words.

"Is this an emergency?" the operator said.

He struck his chest again. Again. Each blow drove a single note from his body.

"A-n-a-a-a."

"Can you tell me where you are?" the operator said.

Almondine retreated a step and began a deep, throaty barking, smashing her tail from side to side and dashing toward the door and back.

"I can't understand you. Can you tell me where you are?"

He stood panting. He beat the receiver against the countertop until it was in fragments and left it hanging and ran out the door and up the driveway and onto the road, hoping to see his mother arriving in their truck, or a car passing, any car. Almondine was beside him now. The woods were lost in the falling snow, the apple trees blanched. Beyond a hundred yards everything faded into a featureless blank so white it hurt to stare into it. A car would not be passing in such a storm. When he looked back at the barn, Essay and Finch were crossing the yard toward them. The four of them stood while he looked up and back along the road. Then he ran to the house again. A voice was coming out of the shattered handset.

"—need to stay where you are. I am—"

The dogs pranced in his path as he crossed to the barn. He'd left the door open and all the time cold air had been pouring in. He flung the door shut and threw the latch and knelt beside his father.

Are you okay are you okay are you okay.

His father wouldn't look at him.

Wouldn't look at him.

He ran to the medicine room at the back of the barn and tore his hands across the shelves. Gauze and pills scattered around his feet as he pawed through the supplies. He returned empty-handed. Just keep him warm, he thought. He pulled a spare coat off the hook inside the workshop and draped it across his father's chest.

A wrack of shivers came over Edgar. Almondine walked up and put her nose to his father's cheek. Her hind legs shook, as if scenting something fearful and strange. The sight made Edgar angry and he got his legs beneath him and flew at her. She bolted to the far end of the barn and watched as he staggered back to the workshop. He knelt and looked into his father's face. He pressed his hands against his chest. He thought he would feel breath being drawn, but instead there was a single long exhalation. Through his father's open mouth came a groan, expressionless and mechanical, in a falling note. After that, nothing at all—no movement, no in-suck of breath, no twitch of an eyelid. Just that collapse, like a wax figure melting.

He ran down the line of pens, beating on the wire. The dogs stood on their hind legs and wailed and bayed, the roar of them like an anthem. Yet through it all he heard the whisper of snow seeping beneath the doors, seething along the floor toward his father lying there on the concrete, motionless, looking nowhere and breathing nothing. The floor jolted as if something had struck the earth. Edgar realized he was sitting. He pulled himself upright, square by square along the wire of a pen door. Then he was beside his father again, and the dogs were quiet. Almondine crept over and nosed his hand and sat beside him. The others stayed hidden at the far end of the kennel, panting and watching.

And so they waited.

Storm

WHEN HE CLOSED HIS EYES SOMETHING HORRID BLOOMED there, a black-petaled shape boiling endlessly outward. In his body, he stayed beside his father, but in his mind he stood and walked through the barn door. Outside, it was a summer evening. The sun set, the earth dark. He crossed the yard and entered the house and inside he lifted an undamaged telephone receiver and spoke. No one replied. He was outside again. A windless rain began to fall, carrying down the night. He walked along the road, clothes drenched and hanging, and all was quiet and he walked that way for hours.

He heard a sound: the muffled crunch of tires on the icy driveway. The dogs began to bark. Some threw themselves at the closed drop-gates to their outer runs. A man's voice shouting. The porch door slamming. The sounds drew him back until he was sitting beside his father once more.

He tried to stand, but failed. At the last minute, he threw his weight to the side and scrambled along the barn floor in order not to touch his father. He lay panting. Almondine came from somewhere—near the file cabinets—and nosed his hand until he forced himself up. He went to the barn doors and threw them open. Blue snow. Shadows bluer yet. He was almost to the house when Doctor Papineau appeared at the back porch door.

"Edgar, your door was swinging wide—" he began, and then stopped. His gaze moved to the barn. "What's going on?" he said. "Where are your folks?"

All Edgar could do was stand before the old man, trembling. His teeth chattered and the muscles in his face began jerking all out of control. Then one of his legs buckled and he sank into the snow and the last thing he saw was Doctor Papineau rushing forward.

HE WOKE IN HIS PARENTS' bedroom. He was lying on his side, facing the doorway, Almondine beside him. Doctor Papineau was leaning heavily against the kitchen cabinets, his back to Edgar, talking on the battered phone.

"—yes," he was saying. "Of *course*. For God's sake, Glen, Gar Sawtelle's lying out there in his barn, and his son is in some sort of shock. No. No. I don't know. His hands are bruised and cut up. All right. Okay. Yes, that must have been him. It was busted to pieces and hanging off the hook when I got here. I'm surprised it even works."

There was a pause. "The feed mill," he said. "Maybe the grocery store. If she's not on the way back already. Try to get a hold of her before . . . She has the truck. It's a brown . . . uh, Chevy with a topper. Uh-huh. Uh-huh." Then he said, "No." The word had an air of finality to it.

When he hung up the phone he ran his hands through his white hair and heaved himself upright and turned and walked to the bedroom.

"Son?" he said. "Edgar?"

Edgar looked at him and tried to sit up. The old man put a hand on his shoulder.

"Just lie back," he said. "Do you know what's happening here?"

I shouldn't have left him. He won't stay warm out there.

"Edgar, I can't understand when you sign." Doctor Papineau stood and turned back to the kitchen. "I'll get you a pencil and paper." As soon as he was out of the room, Edgar was up running through the kitchen, but his sense of balance had gone awry. He crashed into the table and fell. By the time he got up and opened the porch door, Doctor Papineau had him by the arm. For a moment he hung suspended, in mid-stride, above the back steps. Then Doctor Papineau couldn't hold on and Edgar fell into the snow just beyond the stoop. Before he could move, Doctor Papineau was on top of him.

"Hold on," he said. "I don't want you going out there. There's nothing you can do right now, and seeing him like that is going to make it worse later. Come inside and wait with me, okay?"

For an old man, Doctor Papineau was surprisingly strong. He lifted Edgar out of the snow by the back of his shirt. Edgar felt the buttons in front straining to pop as he got his feet beneath him.

"Can you walk okay?"

He nodded. The snow where he had fallen was stained red from the cuts and gashes on his hands. They walked into the house, Papineau's hand firmly on Edgar's shoulder. Edgar sat at the table and looked at the veterinarian until the old man looked away, then stood and began to make coffee. Edgar walked to the corner of the kitchen and sat on the floor near the heat vent, letting the air blow across his feet. He clapped for Almondine. She came and stood beside him and breathed and leaned against him. The cuts on his hands stung as if they had burst into flame.

"There's coffee," Doctor Papineau said after a while.

When he didn't answer, Doctor Papineau took a cup from the cupboard and filled it and sat back down at the table. He looked at the phone and the clock and the boy.

"I'm sorry about all this, Edgar," he said at last. "But one thing I've learned from all these years of veterinary has been to attend to the living. Your dad's out there, and I'm sorry there's nothing we can do for him, but it isn't going to do anyone any good for you to go out there and drive yourself crazy. I know that's hard, but in time you'll see it's true. Everyone loses people. You understand? It's terrible. It's a tragedy for a boy like you to have to deal with this, but there's nothing you or I or anyone else can do now but wait until people get here who know how to handle this."

Doctor Papineau's voice was calm, but his thumb was twitching and thumping on the table and he'd put one hand over the other to steady it. Edgar closed his eyes and let the black-petaled thing twist before him. After a while he was walking along the dark road again and the rain was falling, and the longer he walked, the narrower and more overgrown the road became, until at last it was almost a comfort.

WHEN ALMONDINE LIFTED her head, he heard the siren, faint at first, then louder as it topped the hill. He looked at his hands. There were windings of white gauze around each palm, neatly secured with medical tape. Doctor Papineau must have dressed them with bandages, but he didn't recall it. He walked into the living room and found the veterinarian standing at the window. They watched the ambulance pull into the driveway, and then the truck. Edgar's mother sat on the passenger side. She turned to look through the window as the truck passed the house, her face blank with shock.

Edgar walked to the kitchen and sat by the register again. Doctor Papineau opened the kitchen door and went outside. Edgar heard men's voices. In a few moments his mother knelt beside him.

"Look at me," she said, hoarsely.

He turned, but couldn't meet her gaze for long.

"Edgar," she said. "How long were you out there?" When he didn't answer, she said, "The operator got a call around two o'clock, but no one spoke. That was you?"

He nodded. He watched her face to see if she already guessed how much he was to blame, but she only bent her head to touch his and wrapped her arms around his shoulders. At her touch, a flame rose in him and ate him alive, and when it was gone he was left sitting hollowed out in her arms.

"I know what you're thinking, Edgar," she whispered. "Look at me. This wasn't because of you. I don't know what happened, but you're going to have to tell me, no matter how bad it was. Do you understand? I'll wait all night if you need me to, and we'll just sit together, but before we go to sleep, you have to tell me what happened."

It wasn't until she pulled his head up that he realized he had crossed his arms over his head. Her hands were warm against his face. He wanted to tell her everything, right then, and he wanted to say nothing, ever. He lifted his hands to sign, then realized he didn't know what he wanted to say. He tried again.

It won't be true if I don't say it.

She looked down at his bandaged hands and took them into hers.

"But you know that's wrong, don't you? There's nothing we can do to bring him back." Her face crumpled and she started to cry. He put his arms around her and squeezed.

Then a man appeared in the doorway, an enormous broad man, a giant, youthful projection of Doctor Papineau. Glen Papineau, the Mellen sheriff. Edgar's mother stood. Glen put his hand on her arm and guided her to the table and pulled out a chair.

"Why don't you sit down," he said. Glen Papineau pulled out a chair and sat, too, his parka rustling as he moved, the chair creaking under his weight.

"From the way things look out there, he was carrying something heavy, a bucket of scrap metal, when it happened," Glen said. "It's possible he had a stroke, Trudy."

There was a long silence.

"Is there somebody I can call for you?"

Before she could answer, Doctor Papineau spoke up.

"I'm going to spend the night here, Glen. If there's someone to call, I'll do it."

The sheriff looked from his father's earnest, elderly face to Trudy, who nodded absently.

"I'm going to need to talk, uh, with your son, eventually, for my report, Trudy. I know this isn't the best time, but it has to be soon. Now would be best."

"No," she said. "Not today."

"Okay. Tomorrow at the latest. I guess I'll need you, too. He only signs. Is that right?"

"Of course. You know that, Glen."

"I just mean, if you don't feel up to it I could see if we could arrange an interpreter," Glen said. He sounded taken aback at his mother's tone, which was a mixture of weariness and pain and impatience.

"It has to be me."

"Why's that?"

"What Edgar signs is a sort of . . . half his own invention. Gar and I can read it. Could. Can. A conventional signer wouldn't make much sense of it. He could write things out, or we can bring in his old letter board, but that would take a long time. Besides, I wouldn't let you question my son without being there."

"All right, all right," Glen said. "I just thought it might make things easier on you. When you feel up to it in the morning, call the office."

He turned and stepped onto the porch. Doctor Papineau followed him out of the house. They talked outside, on the stoop, voices low. Suddenly, Edgar's mother stood up and strode to the door.

"God *damn* it, Glen!" she shouted, her voice so loud Edgar could hear an echo off the side of the barn. "If something needs taking care of, you talk to me. *Me*, do you understand? Page, thank you for being here. But I won't have you and your son making decisions for us. This is our place. Glen, you'll talk to me."

"Trudy," said Glen, "I, uh, guess I was just telling Dad here that I asked John and Al to take Gar to Brentson's. And that you or he, somebody, should call and talk to Burt about the arrangements. If you want someone else to handle things, he'll help get that squared away. That's all. We weren't trying to hide anything from you. We were trying to ease things up on you."

"I know you're doing what seems right. But I'm not helpless. I don't expect this to be easy, and I don't expect I'll have to go through it alone, but I do expect that whatever decisions have to be made will be made by *me* and no one else. Understood? When I need help I'll ask for it. Brentson's, by the way, will be fine. Glen, if you could let Mr. Brentson know I'll call him in the morning, I would appreciate that. I'll call you in the morning, too. Now, Page, come inside before you catch pneumonia."

There was silence, and then the three of them exchanged brief good-byes. Doctor Papineau came inside, and Edgar's mother walked into the living room and watched the ambulance and the squad car maneuver up the driveway and onto the snow-packed hill toward Mellen.

AFTER THE TAILLIGHTS HAD disappeared, Trudy walked into the kitchen.

"Page, would you mind making some dinner? Anything you'd like. We need to go out to the kennel and—"

"Hold it a second," Doctor Papineau said, gently. "Are you sure you wouldn't rather I took on the chores? That way you and Edgar could spend some time talking?"

"No, we need dinner, and that's much too quiet a thing for either one of us to be doing. Edgar's going to come out to the barn, and when we come back, the best thing in the world would be if dinner was ready. Assuming we can find any appetite."

She turned to Edgar.

"Edgar? Can you come out to the kennel and help with chores?"

Though the idea of going into the barn made him dizzy, Edgar stood. His coat lay on the bedroom floor. By the time they walked out the door, Almondine at their side, Doctor Papineau had taken a white package of butcher-wrapped meat from the refrigerator and was standing and looking into the cupboards.

OUTSIDE, TRUDY STOPPED AND took Edgar by the shoulders and wrapped her arms around him. She whispered in his ear, "Edgar, if we want to keep this place, we have to look like we can do it, right from the start. I don't know if I should ask you to do this, but I'm going to anyway. Listen to me, honey. Can you walk back into that barn with me now? We'll do it together—I know it will be bad, and if you just can't then we won't, okay? But believe me when I say that the sooner you go in there, the better it will be."

She leaned back and looked at him. He nodded.

"Sure?"

No. He smiled a little, and so did she, and her eyes grew wet all of a sudden.

I couldn't without you, I know that.

"You won't have to go there without me for as long as you need."

When they came to the barn she unlatched the doors without a pause and threw them open wide; the aisle lights, so feeble in the daytime, now fanned across the snow, casting Edgar's and his mother's shadows back along the snowdrifts. Almondine trotted in ahead of them. Without stopping to think about it, Edgar walked inside and turned and pulled the doors closed, concentrating on the dimming light against the trees opposite as the doors came together.

Then the three of them stood in the kennel aisle. The dogs were so quiet he could hear his breaths and his mother's. The door to the workshop was open. Inside, the first thing he noticed was the tarnished gray milk can, tipped over, and the scrap of small bolts, nuts, hinges, nails, and washers fanned out across the floor, all coated with an orange powder of rust. He had only the vaguest memory of seeing the milk can before. His mother grasped the lip of the canister and leaned back. He helped her, and it whomped upright. They collected the scrap with their hands and dumped it into the canister. The rust left an orange stain on the gauze bandages on Edgar's palms. When they had collected all the scrap, they took out the broom and dustpan and swept and dumped the dust into the milk can, and together they wrestled the thing back under the mow steps. He thought they had swept up something unnamable and put it in that canister and it was understood between them that they would never move it, never empty it, never touch it again.

They fed and watered the dogs and cleaned the pens and tossed in fresh straw. Edgar scooped a coffee can full of quicklime from the bag by the back door and wheeled the manure down the path. After he'd dumped the manure, he dusted it with the quicklime. He found his mother in a whelping pen when he returned. One of the newborn pups had died, perhaps in fright from all the noise. Perhaps the mother had panicked and stepped on it. Trudy stroked it two-fingered. She and Edgar took it to the medicine room and put it in one of the thick plastic bags they kept there. Edgar took it from her and set it outside it in the snow. The pup's body was still warm through the plastic, as though the mother had lain next to it even after it had died.

When he came back inside, his mother was waiting for him. Her voice shook, and she put her hands on his arms so he couldn't turn away. "I want you to tell me what happened," she said. "Now, if you can. Before we go back."

He began to sign. He told her most of it—how he'd found his father lying there, how he'd dialed the phone and left the receiver hanging. But he didn't tell her how he'd nearly knocked himself down trying to drum a voice out of his chest. He didn't tell her about the thing that boiled and turned when he closed his eyes or the road he'd walked down or the rain. When he finished, she was quietly crying. They stood, arms around each other. At last, they pulled on their coats and extinguished the lights. The snow had stopped falling but the wind rushed against the barn, whirling the dry snowflakes into frigid galaxies. Clouds hung low over the trees, the sky barricaded and gray.

They crossed to the house. Almondine huffed along beside them. Behind the steamed, translucent kitchen window Doctor Papineau appeared for a moment at the sink, then stepped out of sight. When they reached the porch they paused to kick the snow off their boots and they climbed the steps and walked inside.

Part II

THREE

GRIEFS

Funeral

DOCTOR PAPINEAU SAT AT THE KITCHEN TABLE, ONCE MORE the white-haired, narrow-shouldered old man Edgar had known all his life, looking as shocked and hollowed out as Edgar felt. Hard to believe such a frail figure had lifted him out of the snow by his shirt back. But then it was hard to believe almost anything that had happened that afternoon.

Two pans simmered on the stove, lids clicking to release puffs of steam. Edgar shucked off his coat. His mother, resting a hand on his shoulder to steady herself, bent down to unlace her boots. Then they stood looking at one another. Papineau finally broke the silence. "It's nothing much," he said, waving a hand at the plates and bowls populating the table. "Soup and potatoes. I'm not much of a cook, but I know how to open cans and boil water."

Edgar's mother crossed the room and embraced the old man.

"That's fine, Page," she said. "It's all we need tonight."

Edgar pulled out a chair and sat. Almondine stepped between his knees and pressed her head against his belly and leaned in and he set his head in his hands and inhaled the dusty scent of her mane. For a long time, the room canted around them. When he lifted his head, a bowl of soup steamed at his place and Doctor Papineau was sliding a pan of quartered and skinned potatoes from the oven. He dished them around the table then seated himself.

Edgar looked at the food.

If you can eat, you should, Trudy signed.

Okay. It doesn't feel right to be hungry.

Are you?

Yes. I don't know. It feels like someone else being hungry.

She looked at the bandages on his hands.

Do they hurt?

His palms jangled and his left thumb throbbed, though he couldn't remember how he'd sprained it. Facts too trivial to repeat.

Take aspirin.

I know. I will.

She dipped her spoon into her soup and lifted it to her mouth and swallowed and looked back at him. He saw the resolve behind it, and out of solidarity he rolled a chunk of potato into his soup and began to break it up.

Doctor Papineau cleared his throat. "I've closed my office for the morning."

Edgar's mother nodded. "You can sleep in the spare room—the sheets are in the bathroom. I'll make the bed after dinner."

"I'll make my own bed. Don't worry about that."

Then it was quiet, just the tick of silverware. After a while, Edgar's bowl was empty, though he could not have said what the soup tasted like. His mother had given up any pretense of eating.

"These things are a great shock," Doctor Papineau said. It was apropos of nothing, and there was nothing else to say. "When Rose died, I thought I was fine. Heartbroken, but okay. But those first couple of days, I didn't know what I was doing. You two need to be careful now, you hear me? I almost burned my house down that first night. I put the electric coffee pot on the stove and turned on the burner."

"It's true, Page. Thank you for reminding us."

The vet looked at Edgar, then his mother. His expression was grave. "There's some things we should talk about tonight."

His voice trailed off.

"It's okay, Page," Edgar's mother said. "Edgar is a part of everything that happens now, whether any of us like it or not. You don't have to talk around anything."

"I was going to offer to make some phone calls. Edgar will need to be out of school for a few days. I wondered if you wanted to speak to Claude, let him know what happened. And if there were other people you wanted to call. Relatives or whatnot. I could help you make a list."

Edgar's mother looked at Doctor Papineau and nodded. "Yes. But I would rather make the calls. Would the two of you clear the table?"

They all pushed back from their places. Doctor Papineau put the left-overs in the refrigerator and Edgar piled the dishes in the sink, relieved to be moving. He ran water and watched the suds grow over the plates. Doctor Papineau handed him a towel and said he was better off drying, with his hands like that.

Edgar's mother walked to the counter and opened the telephone book and jotted some numbers on a scrap of paper. She looked at the shattered receiver dangling on the hook, cord end up, like a broken-necked bird, then set the apparatus on the counter and dialed. She held the receiver to her face two-handed and asked if she was speaking with the principal. She said that Edgar's father had died.

"Thank you," she said. "No. I appreciate that. Yes. Thank you. Goodbye."

She laid the receiver on the counter, put both hands down, and took a breath. The speaker inside began to bleat from being off-hook and she pressed the hook to make it stop, then dialed again.

"Claude?" she said. "There's some news. I thought you should know. It's about Gar. Yes. He was working in the kennel this afternoon and he had . . . he had some sort of problem. An attack of some kind. He . . . No. No. We don't know. Yes. Yes. Yes."

There was a long silence. "I'm sorry, Claude. I don't feel like that would be right just now. There's nothing . . . Yes. Page is here. Yes. Thank goodness for him. All right. Okay. Goodbye."

Then she dialed a third number and asked for Glen, speaking in a monotone. She arranged to meet at his office the next morning and then she was quiet, listening to Glen talk. Edgar could only make out the moth-buzz voice from the cracked receiver, not the words. But his mother began to fold over the counter like wax softened in the sun until her forehead almost touched the papers.

"Is that absolutely required?" she whispered. "Isn't there another . . .? Yes. Yes, of course, I know. But . . ."

More moth sounds.

"All right," she said. Something in the sound of her voice made Edgar's legs go weak. Doctor Papineau asked him a question. He shook his head without understanding. The vet crossed to his mother and set his hand on her shoulder. She pushed herself upright again.

"Stop now," Doctor Papineau said, when she'd finished. He took the receiver from her hands and set it upside down on the hook. "That's enough for one night."

She looked back at the old man, corners of her mouth tucked, eyes shining.

"Okay," she said. "That was . . . harder than I expected."

She walked around the table to where Edgar sat and put her arms over his shoulders, letting her hands sign in front of him.

Are you okay?

He tried to reply and found he couldn't.

I want you to go to sleep now.

What about you?

I'm going to sit quiet for a minute. Go. There's nothing else to do.

She was right, he knew. His mother was a pragmatist, maybe from years spent training the dogs. Maybe she was born that way. He squeezed her forearms until he felt her pulse beneath his fingertips, then raised a hand to Doctor Papineau in silent good night.

AS THOUGH AGREED UPON beforehand, though it was not, he and Trudy slept in the living room. He'd carried a blanket and pillow downstairs and when he sat on the couch the power to go up again and change clothes deserted him. He pulled the hem of the blanket to his shoulders and drew up his knees and closed his eyes. A ringing began in his ears—perhaps lurking there all along but apparent only when the weight of the blanket dulled his senses. Half-slumber took him. His mother and Doctor Papineau turned out the lights and all was quiet and then a succession of images came forward, resurrected by some crow-eyed part of his mind that would neither wake nor sleep. Fragmentary emotions possessed and released him, drawn like garments from a wardrobe and discarded, one after another. Below that chaos of image and memory, something so powerfully suppressed he would barely remember it: the idea that everything once true in the world was now past, and a thousand new possibilities had been loosed. And, following that, a clap of overwhelming shame.

Sometime later he opened his eyes. His mother had drawn a blanket around her in her chair. She was tucked up into one corner. He had a faint memory of her kneeling beside him and running her hand, warm and smooth, across his forehead, palm touching his brow and ending with fingertips entwined in his hair. He had not opened his eyes in the moment. Her touch had released some tiny increment of the poison bound up in him that would, days to come, ripen into sorrow. And by the time he thought all this he could no longer tell if her caress had truly happened or whether he'd manufactured it out of necessity.

The sleep that followed was black, nothing at all contained in it. Every rasp of snow against the windows roused him up on one elbow only to have him collapse again into sleep, sawing between one world and the other. Papineau snored upstairs in the room they had once prepared for Claude. The sound penetrated the living room ceiling like the lowing of distant cattle: *Moo. Moo.* He woke again when he sensed Almondine walking away from him. In the dark he watched her press her nose against the blanket wrapped around his mother, scenting her as carefully as she must have scented Edgar the moment before. She stood for a time, panting softly, then returned to the center of the room. She circled and downed and their gazes met. Her ears shifted forward. After a while her eyes narrowed, then opened wide, then narrowed more, the liquid glint of them waxing and waning in the darkness. Finally, she sighed and slept.

Come morning, his memory would be of a night spent watching over them all. And each of them—dog and boy, mother and old man—would feel the same.

THEY WALKED TO THE BARN at first light. The cold was fearsome, the sky above dilute and punctured by stars. Inside the kennel, he saw they needed more straw, and he walked through the workshop and climbed the steps to the mow and flipped on the lights. The wall of bales stood tiered like a ziggurat. It was still early in winter—some bales still reached the rafters. A red-handled hay hook hung on a nail on the front wall. He dragged two bales to the center of the mow, lifted a hatch in the floor by a small ring, and looked down. Trudy stood below, waiting. "Go ahead," she said. He pushed the bales through and watched them fall with a half-turn and whomp against the dusty cement.

He cleaned pens with a pitchfork and a wheelbarrow and dashed out fans of quicklime on the bare floors. When he cut the twine, the straw bales opened into golden sheaves. He pulled a slicker brush from his back pocket and hastily brushed the dogs. Doctor Papineau walked in while he was working, declared that he might as well look in on the pups, and disappeared through the door to the whelping room. Edgar went to his litter. Finch and Baboo, the least excitable, leaned on him from opposite sides. Essay tried to climb his front. He calmed them by cupping their bellies and muzzles and asked them to sit and do other small things in lieu of real training.

When they were done, Edgar and Trudy and the veterinarian walked up the driveway together. Doctor Papineau promised to call later and kept walking to his car and drove off. When Edgar came downstairs in fresh clothes, his mother was standing at the counter, broken receiver in her hands. He waited in the living room while she talked to someone at the telephone company about fixing the telephone. When she was finished, she came into the living room.

"You don't have to go," she said. "'I'll call Glen and say you're not ready.'"

You're not going to Brentson's alone.

"Page can come with me."

No.

She started to reply, then nodded. Almondine stood by the kitchen door while Edgar donned his coat, then trotted down the steps and stood by the truck. It was somehow even colder inside the cab. The vinyl seats flexed like tin. Trudy put the truck in gear and navigated up the long slope of the driveway and they drove along without conversation, listening to the crunch of ice beneath the tires. The world glowed translucent blue. Telephone poles rushed forward and fell away, wires swelling and dropping in the intervals. In Mellen, Trudy parked the truck in front of the cupolaed town hall and the three of them followed the arrows painted on the hallway until they reached the sheriff's office. Even inside, their breath steamed. A burnt-hair smell permeated the building. A white-blond girl sat at a desk wearing a winter coat and mittens. At the center of her desk a microphone rested on a stand. She looked at them and stood and peered over the counter at Almondine.

"I'll get Glen. You'll want to keep your coats on," she said. "Something happened to the heat. We're waiting for the repair guy from Ashland."

The girl walked to the office door behind her desk and knocked. A moment later Glen Papineau emerged wearing his blue patrol jacket and hat, diminishing the room instantly. His hands, even ungloved, were like dinner plates. Edgar wondered, briefly, if Doctor Papineau had once been that big, then dismissed the idea. Old men got smaller as they aged, he knew, but no one could shrink that much.

"Trudy, Edgar, come on back. Sorry about the cold—boiler problems. You don't want to know. I've been here since six. It's a miracle we didn't burst any pipes. Coffee, either of you? Hot chocolate?"

Trudy looked at Edgar. He shook his head.

"That's okay, Glen," she said.

"Well, bring 'em anyway, Annie—maybe they'll heat the office a little. Cream and sugar in mine."

He led them into an office somehow both spare and cluttered. Papers and notebooks mounded over his desk, but the walls were unadorned except for a framed certificate and a photograph of a youthful Glen in his Mellen High wrestler's uniform, pinning some unknown behemoth in a fetal curl. In the picture Glen was up on his toes, almost parallel to the floor, body rigid as a log, veined thighs thick as a draft horse's. The referee's arm a blur as he slapped the mat.

Glen had arranged three folding chairs in front of his desk, and he motioned for Trudy and Edgar to sit down, then settled himself. Almondine approached and sniffed his knee and boot. "Hey, girl," he said, then, "Aha," as Annie walked in carrying three paper cups. With his forearm he cleared a swath on the desk. A stack of papers plunged off the other side.

He grinned, wryly. "My New Year's resolution. Every year."

"This one here's hot chocolate," Annie said. She set the cups in the cleared space and piled the fallen papers on the desk with an expression of despair.

"They're here if you want 'em," Glen said, gesturing at the steaming cups. He made a production of opening his notebook and clicking the end of his pencil. "Okay," he said. "What we've got to do here is record what happened. That's just procedure. We want to do this fast before anyone forgets anything. I apologize about this. I know it won't be pleasant. The fact is, Pop came in this morning and gave me hell." He paused as if suddenly embarrassed, Edgar thought, to have referred to his father as "Pop."

"It's okay, Glen," Trudy said. "Just ask whatever you need to. Edgar will sign his answer to me."

"Okay then. Trudy, when did you go into town?"

"It was eleven thirty or so when I left."

Glen scribbled in his notebook. "And Edgar, you were home all day?" He nodded.

"When did you first think something was wrong?"

Edgar signed his answer. "He was working in the mow and he noticed the dogs barking," his mother said. "When he came downstairs, Gar was . . . lying on the floor."

"You were in the mow?"

"We train up there when it gets cold," Trudy said impatiently, before Edgar could reply. "You know that. You've been up there yourself."

"Yeah, I have. I'm just asking to be complete. You were up there with some dogs?"

Yes. Two dogs from my litter.

"The dogs that were barking were downstairs?"

Yes.

"How long had you been in the mow?"

An hour. Maybe longer.

"You wear a watch?"

I have a pocket watch. I didn't have it with me.

"Is there a clock in the mow?"

Yes.

"Do you remember about what time this happened?"

"You must know that from the telephone operator," Trudy said.

"Yes. There's a record of that. But I think it would be good to get it all down as long as we're doing this."

I wasn't paying attention. It was after one o'clock, I know that.

"What sorts of things were you doing with your dogs?"

Come-fors. Proofing stays. Stay-aways. I had a hurdle set up.

"Do those things make a lot of noise?"

Not really.

"I mean, would your father have heard you upstairs?"

He would have heard the dogs running. And my footsteps.

"Could you have heard him downstairs?"

What do you mean?

"If he yelled something, would you have heard him?"

"He would have heard a shout," Trudy said, interceding again. "We call up there all the time. With the door closed, you have to try a few times. Otherwise it's easy to hear someone."

Glen looked at Edgar. "And the door was closed?"

Yes.

"How about something spoken in an ordinary voice?"

"Not with the door closed," Trudy said. "With the door open, you can hear someone talking in the workshop."

"But you didn't hear a shout or anything? Just the dogs?"

Edgar paused. He shook his head.

Glen made a note and turned the page over. "Okay, now I'm going to ask you a hard question, but it's important you tell me as much as you can remember. You were working up in the mow with some dogs. You heard barking, you opened the door, you came downstairs. What did you see?"

Edgar thought about it for a moment.

I don't remember, he signed.

His mother looked at him. You don't remember?

No.

But you told me about it last night.

I mean, I know when I came downstairs I saw him lying there, but I don't *remember* it. I just know he was lying there. It's like I know it because someone else told me about it, not because I can see it.

She turned to the sheriff. "Glen, he doesn't remember it much. Just that Gar was on the floor."

"Well, that's okay. Sometimes that happens. What's the first thing you do remember?"

Running to the house.

"Is that when you called the operator?"

Yes.

"But that didn't work."

No.

"Then what?"

I ran back to the barn. No, wait. I ran up to the road. I thought I might see someone driving by who could talk on the phone. But there was nobody.

His mother repeated this.

"That was after you went into the house?"

I think so.

"You don't remember for sure?"

No. But I think I went back into the house.

"How did the phone get broken?"

He paused again. I don't remember.

"Pop says it was hanging in pieces when he got there."

Yes. I think I broke it, but I don't know when.

"Okay, okay. You had them on the line and couldn't say what was wrong. Trudy, did you ever discuss with Edgar a plan for how he might call for help if he needed to?"

"No, not really. The assumption was that Gar or I would always be there. The main thing we worried about was Edgar getting hurt when he was in the field or the woods. But he always had Almondine with him, and she's been watching him since he was born. So . . . no." Her eyes started to glisten, and she looked down. "We thought through so many possibilities. As soon as we could, we taught him how to write his name, address, and telephone number in case he got lost. We were always worried about . . . always thinking, 'what if' . . . ."

She tipped her face down and closed her eyes. Glen produced a box of tissues and she crumpled one in her hand and drew in a breath.

"We worried about Edgar getting separated from us. Especially when he was little. But it never happened. And he was so *smart*. We're talking about a kid that started reading at three years old. The last couple of years, it just wasn't a concern. He knows how to handle himself with people who can't sign—no, more than just handle himself: half his class knows how to read his sign. All his life he's been teaching people. He's good at it. *Good* at it. And besides, if there was ever any problem, he could just write out what he wanted to say. Nothing like this ever entered our minds."

She stopped and wrapped her arms around her sides. Watching her do it—collect herself that way—made Edgar shudder. He could almost see her reaching inside herself to steady something, catch some falling piece of crockery. Almondine stood and poked her nose against Trudy's hand, and she stroked the dog's back.

"I'm sorry," Glen said. He looked abashed. "I didn't mean to imply you did something wrong. All I'm trying to do is get down what happened as Edgar saw it. We're going to be done here in a couple of minutes, and then we're done for good, I promise. Believe me, I wish we didn't have to talk about this, but I don't have a choice. Edgar, how you doing?"

Edgar nodded.

Glen sat back and clapped his palms on his broad knees.

"All right, let me ask you both a question: had Gar mentioned anything that might indicate he was sick? A headache? Feeling tired? Anything unusual?"

"No, nothing," his mother said, and Edgar nodded in agreement. "I thought a lot about that last night. If he wasn't feeling well, he didn't say anything."

"Would he have?"

"Maybe not. He hated going to the doctor. He says"—she paused a second and corrected herself—"*said*, I mean, they never fix things. They only make you feel worse."

"Who's your doctor?"

"Jim Frost. Same as everyone else around here, I suppose."

"He can fill me in on Gar's medical history?"

"He can. There's nothing much. The only thing that even remotely resembled a medical problem was needing glasses."

"Uh-huh. Okay." This, too, Glen noted.

"All right. Edgar, I'm going to ask you to tell me what you remember about your father when you went back into that barn. I want to understand if he was conscious, whether you talked to him, or what."

He was awake when I came back.

"Did you talk to him?"

No. But he was breathing.

"Could he talk?"

No.

"What did you think had happened?"

I didn't know. He wanted to clear the scrap buckets from under the workshop stairs. When I came downstairs, he was lying in the middle of the workshop. I thought he'd hit his head, but he hadn't. I opened up his coat. I couldn't see anything wrong.

"Then what happened?"

Then he stopped breathing.

There was silence in the office. Glen looked at Edgar and grunted sympathetically. "That's all?"

Yes.

"And then Pop showed up."

I guess.

"You don't remember?"

No.

"What's the next thing you do remember?"

Waking up in the house. Doctor Papineau talking on the telephone.

"You don't remember walking back to the house?"

No.

"Do you remember doing anything after you went back to the barn besides being with your father?"

No.

"Your hands are beat up. Did that happen when the phone got smashed?"

No. I was banging on the pen doors to make the dogs bark.

"Why?"

To make noise.

"In case someone drove by?"

So if an ambulance came they would know to look in the kennel.

"Right." He wrote for a minute in his notebook. "Smart. Just so you know, the operator was still on the line when you did that. She reported hearing what sounded like dogs barking."

Just then there was a knock on the door, and Annie's muffled voice. "Glen, boiler repair is here."

"Okay," he said, loudly. "Send them downstairs, would you? I'll be there in a few minutes."

He turned back to them. "Among my glorious duties, I supervise certain aspects of maintenance." He grinned. "They haven't asked me to wash dishes yet, though."

He wrote something in his notes, then looked up. "Well, I know you two have a lot on your minds. There are some formalities to take care of, and then we're done. Trudy, I'd like to talk to you alone before we finish up."

She looked at Edgar. "Will you be okay waiting outside?"

He nodded. He and Almondine walked into the empty foyer. From the depths of the building came the banging of hammers on pipe and the long *creeeeeee* of rusted threads being turned. He looked at Annie's neatly arranged desk—the microphone, the plant, the canister of pencils, the trays of forms—but when he tried to focus on anything his gaze kept skittering away.

Almondine ambled into the hallway and down to the entrance and he followed. On the street, a truck with the words "LaForge Heating and Repair, Ashland, WI" was parked behind their pickup. The day had warmed, and the street was filled with a soup of brown slush. Pale icicles dispensed a procession of water drops from the diner's eaves. He opened the truck door and climbed in beside Almondine.

Doctor Frost rounded the corner. He entered the town hall through the door they'd just exited. Edgar tipped his head back and closed his eyes and pulled off his gloves so that his aching hands might go numb in the cold.

HIS MOTHER CLIMBED INTO the truck and keyed the ignition and they sat there while the truck idled. A semi passed on Main Street, slush flying in its wake. Further on, the little white spire of the Presbyterian church rose against the blue sky. She put her hands on the steering wheel and straightened her elbows.

"Doctor Frost—" she began, then stopped and drew a shaky breath.

Tell me.

"It's the law that when someone dies unexpectedly, they have to do an autopsy to find out what happened. You know what an autopsy is, right?"

Edgar nodded. One happened practically every night on the detective shows.

His mother sighed. He could see she had been afraid she would have to explain it.

"The main thing to know is that your father wasn't in pain. Doctor Frost said that it didn't hurt. What happened is, there's a place in a person's head called the Circle of Willis. It's in their brain, way down inside. Your father had an aneurysm near there. That means one of his blood vessels was weak and it just broke. And that place where it was weak was so important, that he . . . he couldn't live after that."

Edgar nodded again. He didn't know what else to say; it was so definitive. There was even a name for the place where things had gone wrong: the Circle of Willis.

"Doctor Frost said everyone is born with little flaws in their arteries and veins. Weak spots. Most people go through their whole life and never know. The flaws aren't in places that matter: their arms, their legs. For a few people, the flaws are in bad places, and even then, those people can go their whole lives and nothing happens. But in some people, people who have a weak spot in an important place, that weak spot breaks. Sometimes they die from it. Nobody knows why it happens to some people and not others."

His mother sat there and looked out the windshield. She laid her hand on Almondine's neck and smoothed her fur down, and then slid her hand over to Edgar's shoulder.

Thank you for telling me, he signed.

She turned and looked at him, really focused on him, for the first time since they'd left the house.

"I'm so sorry," she said. She didn't look like she was going to cry, only slack and exhausted and determined. "I think it's better to know what happened than not," she said. "Don't you?"

Yes.

"And it doesn't mean anything like that is going to happen to you or me. We have those flaws, just like everyone, but they aren't in important places." This, with an air of finality.

Yes.

"I have to go to Brentson's now. Are you sure you want to come along?"

He had told her yes, and he meant it. He wasn't scared of the funeral preparations. What scared him was sitting at home, alone, knowing he wouldn't have the energy or the concentration to do anything but look out the window and think. He didn't want to see the thing bloom in front of him again. What scared him was letting his mother do things by herself; he thought they ought to do everything together, for a while at least, no matter how bad. He thought that sometime later they would probably try being apart. He didn't say any of that, he only nodded, and Trudy put the truck in gear and drove them to Brentson's Funeral Home, where he sat beside her and listened as she explained what she wanted.

IN THE HALF-LIGHT, his mother laid her hand on his shoulder.

"Breakfast," she said.

He sat up from the sofa and rubbed his eyes.

How much did you sleep? he signed.

"A little. Come on."

Almondine stood and stretched and followed Edgar's mother into the kitchen. Edgar climbed the stairs to his room and dressed and looked out the window at Almondine, wandering the yard looking for a place to urinate. He walked down the stairs and stepped onto the frigid porch in his socks and pushed the door open. Overhead, a vault of watery blue, Venus and the north star captured within. Almondine backhanded a paw of powdery snow and stood three-legged, looking at him, jaw hanging gaily.

Come on, he signed. It's too cold.

She looked around while he shivered, then mounted the wooden steps. He dropped his hand onto her back as she passed. In the kitchen, she shook the cold from her fur and devoted herself to drinking water in loud slurps. The thermostat clicked and the furnace began to blow.

Edgar took a cup from the cupboard and walked to the Mr. Coffee sitting by the stove. He poured until the cup was half full and lifted it to his mouth. He must have made a face.

"Fill it with milk," Trudy said. "Use lots of sugar at first."

Okay.

He sat and they waited for the sun to rise further. After a while Trudy scrambled eggs and made toast.

"Will you cut the fence this morning?" she asked over her shoulder. "Where we talked about? We need a path to the birches so they know where to plow. Do it first thing. I don't know when they'll be here."

In the workshop he tested the fencing pliers on a nail, squeezing the handles until the halves clinked to the floor. He hooked a training collar over his gloved fingers and pulled Tinder out of his pen. He slipped the loop over the dog's head and heeled him onto a dusting of new snow so weightless it flew from beneath their feet.

The road had been plowed in the night. There were no cars coming. They would have seen them or heard them in the distance anyway, but there never were. At the top of the hill he stopped and gave Tinder a chance to finish in a sit. When the dog walked past, intent on something in the distance, he reversed. They did this twice before Tinder sat by Edgar's knee. Then he released the dog and they waded to the fence. He pulled the pliers from his pocket and cut the barbed wire and spiraled the ends back along the fence and they broke a path through the calf-deep snow. The sun-glaze on the drifts cracked into plates underfoot. On the way back to the road Tinder threw himself down and pedaled with his legs and dug his snout beneath the snow, turning a daft eye on Edgar.

What is it about this weather? Edgar signed. It's making all of you crazy.

In the end he had to kneel and set his mouth by the dog's ear and make words with his lips before Tinder would let himself be guided to his feet. Once up, the dog reared back and did a little canter in place and bit the lead and tossed his head. Edgar sighed and waited. Ten steps farther, Tinder began all over again. This time Edgar gave up and unsnapped the lead and halfheartedly pitched chunks of snow for Tinder to leap at while the dog dashed through figure eights in the field with ears laid back on his skull and tail straight behind, turning so madly his hindquarters slung to the ground. When he'd run out his lunacy, he trotted back. By the time they'd returned to the barn, Tinder was heeling without flaw, and when Edgar stopped before the Dutch doors, the dog dropped into a perfect sit at his knee.

A SNOW-BLADED TRUCK passed their driveway, paused, backed up, and turned in. In the cab sat two men, knit caps on their heads and collars turned up. The driver stepped half out of the cab and leaned over the top of the door while Trudy explained what she wanted.

"Shut the door, for crying out loud," the man in the passenger seat said. He was much older than the driver, who waved his hand as if to shoo something away and kept talking. The older man leaned over and pushed the driver out and slammed the door.

The men backed their truck up the driveway, gearbox whining. The older man was giving directions, much to the other's annoyance. Up on the road, Edgar and Trudy climbed into the truck's bed. When they reached the spot where Edgar had cut the fence, Trudy tapped on the cab's back window. The driver put the truck sideways in the road and the two men produced a pair of snow shovels to clear the plow mound, and then they drove through the cut fence, exposing a swath of honey-colored hay.

The truck rounded the birches and turned back up the hill. Halfway to the road its chained tires lost purchase and they backed down and tried again. They made a second pass and then stopped the truck and stood stamping their feet and clapping their hands while Edgar's mother explained what was to be done next.

The two men worked that morning with picks and shovels. Their argument carried over the field like the squawking of geese. In the afternoon the truck trundled down the driveway again and the men came onto the porch, bickering in hoarse whispers. Trudy opened the door. The men walked into the kitchen.

"Ma'am, there's a problem," the older man said.

"What is it?"

"That ground is harder than concrete. We can't dig in it with the tools we've got."

"Of course it's hard," his mother said. "It's the middle of winter. It's frozen. When we talked, you said you'd done this before."

"Not in the winter. Not in ground frozen that solid."

"You've never done this in the winter?"

"Fact is, we mostly do plowing. The occasional odd job, but mainly plowing. We've only serviced a few, uh, home burials, and those were in the summer."

"Then why on earth did you say you could do this?"

The older man nodded as if this question were exactly his.

"I didn't. My idiot son did." He glared at the younger man, who raised his hands speechlessly. "I'm real sorry. I wanted him to call you when I found out, but I let him talk me into trying. Said we could break through the frost. I was stupid enough to go along. But it's like digging into an iron plate."

"So what do we do?"

The two men stood and looked at her.

"We have a burial tomorrow," she said. Edgar could see she was getting angry. "We are going to bury my *husband*. This isn't a problem I want to have to solve. Do you understand that? Did either of you spend a *second* thinking about what would happen if you couldn't do this?"

The older man shook his head and said, "Ma'am, I can't apologize enough. Whatever kind of equipment it takes to break ground like that, we don't have it."

They stood there for some time. Edgar stood behind the men and he could see his mother's face as she appeared to them, frightening and regal at the same time.

We could build a fire, he signed.

She frowned, then looked back at the men.

"You can't do it."

"No ma'am. The folks at the cemetery must have something. Maybe they could help out."

"Okay," she said. "Follow me." She tore her coat from the hook and walked out the door and in the waning afternoon light led them around the corner to the woodpile.

"Here," she said. "I want you to load this into your truck and take it out to the field. Every stick. Edgar will show you where the wheelbarrow is. Then I want you to go into town and go to Gordy Howe's place and get another truckload and bring that back. I'll call him now."

The old man scratched his head and looked at her.

"Will it be enough?" she said.

"Yes, ma'am, I think it will be. It might take some time, even then, but I believe that will do it."

"And will you help?"

The old man smiled and nodded.

"Oh, we'll help all right. We'll be here until the ground is thawed." He turned to the younger man. "Won't we?" he said. "Son?"

ALL NIGHT THE FIRE BURNED in the snowy field. Streamers of sparks rose every time the men tossed another log onto the blaze. The birches towered orange over it all. Even the barn was painted by the light. Edgar and his mother watched from the living room. Edgar thought of the bonfires Schultz had lit to incinerate the great piles of stumps and roots.

Twice they carried food and coffee out to the men. His mother had to knock on the fogged truck window to get their attention. They refused her invitation to warm up inside the house but took the offering. On the second trip they brought the men blankets and pillows. The cordwood was heaped between the truck and the fire and the blaze occupied a rectangle at the base of the birches. Bare, wet grass surrounded the flames. Edgar's mother walked to the fire and peered into the embers. He joined her. Heat scalded his face. When the smoke drifted back, his mother coughed but stood her ground. Edgar breathed it in, feeling not the slightest tickle.

They made beds in the living room for the third night and watched the glow from the field. Neither could sleep. They talked between long pauses.

I'll take the chair tonight. You have the couch.

"No, I like it here."

What were you looking for back there?

"Where?"

In the fire. It seemed like you were looking for something.

"I don't know. I wasn't looking for anything." She changed to sign. Can I ask you a question?

Yes.

Are you scared?

Because of the funeral?

Because of everything.

No. Not scared. But I didn't know it would be like this.

Neither did I.

They watched the orange firelight play against the limbs of the apple trees.

Do you think it will work?

Yes.

I like that the ground will be warm.

She looked at him. I'm very proud of you, you know.

Aren't you supposed to tell me everything is going to be okay?

She laughed quietly. Is that what you want me to say?

I don't think so. I don't know if I would believe you if you did.

Lots of people are going to say it. I'll say it too, if you want me to.

No. Don't.

They were quiet, just looking out the windows.

Do you remember anything about your father? Your real father, I mean.

No, not a lot. He wasn't around much. She paused, then shifted in her chair to face him. What are you thinking? You aren't worried about going into a foster home, are you?

No.

Good. Because that's not going to happen. Nothing is going to happen to me, or you, for that matter.

Anything can happen, though.

Anything *can* happen. But almost always, just normal things happen, and people have happy lives.

Were you happy before you met him?

She thought about that a moment.

I don't know. Sometimes I was happy. As soon as we met I knew I was unhappy without him.

How was it you met again?

She smiled. In a good way. You'd only be disappointed in the details.

You aren't ever going to tell me, are you?

I will, if you have to know.

He thought then about all the stories his parents had drawn out, how his father, usually so serious, had enjoyed the game of it and how that made him enjoy it, too. To know that one story was truer than all the rest might make it as if those moments had never happened. And perhaps it was better if they'd met many times, in many circumstances.

No, he signed after a while. Don't tell me. He motioned toward the orange blaze in the field. Should we take anything else out?

I think they're getting on just fine.

Good night, then.

"Good night," his mother whispered. After that they were quiet.

IN THE CHAPEL, THERE WAS the casket in the front, and from the moment he saw it Edgar stopped remembering things in order. The drone of the minister's sermon. Candles burning. Doctor Papineau sitting with them up front. At one point, he turned to view the mourners, thirty or forty scattered throughout the pews. Claude's was not among the faces he saw. Afterward, they sat in Doctor Papineau's car and followed the hearse along the main highway, onto County C, turning at last up Town Line Road and passing through the overhang of trees. They stopped where Edgar had cut the fence. Glen Papineau was one of the pallbearers, as was one of the men from the feed store. In all, a dozen of them walked across the field. Graveside, the man from the funeral home began to speak. Snatches rang back from the barn, as if endorsing only a fraction of his words.

Then a pair of headlights flickered through the bare trees. A car came to a stop and Claude appeared at the path entrance. More cars and pickups began to appear in a long line. The proceedings stopped and everyone turned. Doors opened, slammed, voices rang tinny in the cold air. Claude waved someone along. A man leading a dog. It was Art Granger and Yonder, both limping with arthritis. Then Mr. and Mrs. McCullough, with Haze, the third Sawtelle dog their family had owned. Then Mrs. Santone, with Deary. Then a lone woman with her dog, a curve of slack in its leash. A young couple with a boy and their dog. The dogs' exhalations plumed whitely over their heads as they came down the field. For a long time people kept appearing at the top of the path—trainers who had adopted yearlings, men whose voices had sped across the telephone lines in conversation with Edgar's father—and Claude directed them along. There was a man Edgar recognized from Wyoming; another from Chicago. But most were from around that countryside from homes that looked after Sawtelle dogs. Claude stayed on the road and directed them all down the path until the last of them had passed and they all stood in long arced rows around the birches.

Edgar looked at the dogs and then across the field at the house. Trudy wrapped her arms around him and whispered, "No, please stay," as if she thought he meant to run from it all. But she misunderstood and he could not explain. He twisted away and crashed through the snowdrifts toward the house. No sound but the roaring in his ears. Twice he fell and pushed to his feet without looking back.

When he swung the kitchen door open, Almondine stood waiting for him. He knelt and let her chest fill over and over in the circle of his arms and together they returned to the birches, Almondine stepping along in the path he'd broken through the crusted snow. When they reached the rows of people and dogs, Almondine pushed ahead, passing through the ranks until she stood graveside. Then Edgar walked up and put his arms around his mother and they surrendered to whatever unearthly wind it was that howled over them and only them and Almondine sat her wise haunches down beneath the birches and together they watched the casket descend.

THEY'D BROUGHT WITH THEM pies and casseroles, sliced cheese and ham, bowls of black and green olives and sweet pickles, miniature slices of bread fanned like playing cards next to saucers of mustard and mayonnaise. People milled around Edgar and Trudy, murmuring reassurances, pressing hands on their shoulders. Almondine passed through the crowd, quietly presenting herself. Many of the owners stayed outside with their dogs. Claude and Doctor Papineau held leashes so the owners might come in to fill their coffee cups and speak with Trudy. To those who had traveled far, she offered room to stay, but no one accepted. They wrapped gloved hands around coffee cups and walked back outside, stopping to settle their hats before opening the door. Claude took those who wanted into the barn to see the kennel.

Husbands began to come in to let their wives know the car was running. The last of the women washed and dried dishes while cars turned around in the driveway, headlights sweeping the living room walls. Someone came asking for jumper cables. The women patted their hands on dishtowels and took their coats from the pile on the bed. And then only three visitors remained: Doctor Papineau, Glen, and Claude. They stood on the back porch in the bluing dusk. Doctor Papineau opened the kitchen door.

"We'll take care of the dogs," he said. "Don't argue. Go lie down."

Trudy nodded. "When you're done, come get some food," she said. "There's so much left." But afterward the trio walked up the drive. Two pairs of headlights brightened. Edgar watched the cars pull away. He mounted the stairs and pulled off his clothes and fell into bed with barely the strength to thump the mattress for Almondine. As soon as she'd settled herself beside him, he was asleep.

The Letters from Fortunate Fields

THERE FOLLOWED, FOR EACH OF THEM, GOOD DAYS AND BAD, and often Edgar's best moments coincided with his mother's worst. She could be cheerful and determinedly energetic for days on end and then one morning he would walk downstairs and find her hunched at the kitchen table, haggard and red-eyed. Once lapsed, nothing could deliver her. It worked the same with him. Just when normal life felt almost possible—when the world held some kind of order, meaning, even loveliness (the prismatic spray of light through an icicle; the stillness of a sunrise), some small thing would go awry and the veil of optimism was torn away, the barren world revealed. They learned, somehow, to wait those times out. There was no cure, no answer, no reparation.

He returned from school one day in March to find his mother working in her bedroom, her hair a sweaty tangle about her head, her breath coming in ragged gasps. She'd already closed up the flaps on a tall stack of boxes and was folding a pair of his father's trousers and placing them in another box. Her gaze barely paused on Edgar when he walked in. Later, he searched to see what had been lost. The drawer that once held his father's belts and ties was filled with his mother's gloves and scarves.

On top of the dresser, only her sparse jewelry collection remained, and the wind-up alarm clock. She'd even packed away the photograph of her and his father, newlyweds, sitting on the pier in Door County.

HE WOKE ONE MORNING tantalized by an idea: if he could catch the orchard trees motionless for one second—for *half* of one second—if they stood wholly at rest for the briefest moment—then none of it would have happened. The kitchen door would bang open and in his father would walk, red-faced and slapping his hands and exclaiming about some newly whelped pup. Childish, Edgar knew, but he didn't care. The trick was to not focus on any single part of any tree, but to look through them all toward a point in the air. But how insidious a bargain he'd made. Even in the quietest moment some small thing quivered and the tableau was destroyed.

How many afternoons slipped away like that? How many midnights standing in the spare room, watching the trees shiver in the moonlight? Still he watched, transfixed. Then, blushing because it was futile and silly, he forced himself to walk away.

When he blinked, an afterimage of perfect stillness.

To think it might happen when he wasn't watching.

He turned back before he reached the door. Through the window glass, a dozen trees strummed by the winter wind, skeletons dancing pair-wise, fingers raised to heaven.

Stop it, he told himself. Just stop.

And watched some more.

THE WORK TO BE DONE was staggering.

Simplest was the maintenance of the kennel: cleaning the pens, feeding and watering the dogs, shoveling snow from the runs, and the infinity of minor repairs on the kennel's mechanical workings. Then there was nursery duty: checking the pregnant mothers, washing the teats of the nursing and weaning mothers, taking the temperature and weights of newborns. For the blind and deaf neonates there were touch and scent regimes to be followed, neatly penciled in Gar's hand on a yellowing paper tacked to the whelping room wall. For the newly open-eyed, there was a schedule of experiences, from the jingling of car keys to the appearance of an old bicycle horn, which they might sniff until Edgar squeezed the rubber bulb and timed how long before they crept back. A patch of carpet to walk on. A tube. A block. Sandpaper. Ice. The weekly roll-and-hold until they kicked and yipped, keeping one eye on the second hand of the clock. The sessions with aunts and uncles, learning manners, while the mother rested. For everything there were entries on log sheets, milestones checked off, reactions recorded, charts updated, the compiled story of each life. Photographs at four, six, eight, and twelve weeks, and then six and nine and twelve and eighteen months: frontal, lateral, rear, and orodental on Tri-X, the dogs positioned in front of the painted calibration grid on the medicine room wall. At night, there was the house rotation schedule, bringing in pairs or trios, and the pedigree research, and visits by stud dogs, and the heat schedules of the mothers, and the practice placements and negotiations with potential owners.

But it was the training that consumed them. The infants needed to learn the simplest things: to look, to listen, to watch, to wait. The eighteen-month-olds needed finish work and evaluation. And the adolescents—those robbers, thieves, muggers, and bullies, who knew exactly what you wanted and devoted themselves to the opposite—needed every spare minute and more.

One evening after they had come in from the kennel, Edgar's mother asked him to sit at the table. On a sheet of paper, she'd drawn a schedule with columns labeled "Edgar" and "Trudy."

"We need to divide up the work," she said. "We're both doing everything right now. I'm not so worried about the nursery—Pearl's an experienced mother, and she won't need much watching. But I am worried about placing them. Your father spent so much time on the telephone. I have a lot of catching up to do."

She paused and took a deep breath.

"And all that is going to detract from the training. The only bright side to the whole thing is that oldest litter is completely placed. That gives us a few months of breathing room. Then the next litter to go is yours. I don't think they've been spoken for."

She looked at him to double-check this. He nodded. His father hadn't broached the issue of placing Edgar's litter and it wasn't something Edgar had been eager to hurry along.

"We have a few months then. I need to go over the contacts. For all I know, Gar had spoken agreements with people. I hope I won't need to travel—I don't know how we'll manage if I do."

She was thinking out loud. He let her go on and sat listening. Then she stopped short and turned to him.

"There is another option, Edgar, and we need to talk about it. We can sell the breeding stock and shut down the kennel. After these litters are placed, we would be done. We could probably place them all by the end of summer if we wanted to. We would have to move into town. I'm sure I could—"

He was already shaking his head.

"No, listen. We have to consider it. We're going to have to work so hard there'll be no time for anything else. Have you thought about what that will be like? In a year or so you'll want to go out for track or football. You might not think so now, but when other boys are doing those things you're going to resent being stuck out here handling dogs morning and night. What I'm afraid of is that there'll come a time when you hate getting on the bus to come home. And I'll know it when it happens."

It won't happen, he signed. I don't want to live somewhere else.

"That's the other thing. This isn't always going to be your home. In four years, you graduate. I can't possibly run this kennel alone, and even if I could, I'm not going to live out here by myself. Five years one way or another doesn't matter much, Edgar."

It matters to *me*. Besides, how do you know I'm going to leave?

"Don't be ridiculous. You're going to college."

I'm not. I haven't even thought about college.

"You will," his mother said. "You need to understand that there are alternatives. You're being closed-minded. Staying here and working dogs might be the hardest thing, not the easiest. Or the best. As a trainer, you're no great shakes, Edgar. Sleeping with them in the mow doesn't accomplish much, no matter how nice it feels."

Edgar felt himself blushing.

"It's not so hard to guess what's going on when there's silence up there for hours and you come stumbling down with straw in your hair. I know how tempting it is. I've done it myself."

You sleep in the mow?

She shrugged, refusing to be drawn off track. "My point is, maybe that's not where your aptitudes lie," she said. "Oh, of *course* you're good with the dogs—quit looking so punctured. Your worst quality as a trainer is your pride, Edgar. If we're going to make a go of this kennel you're going to have to learn so much more. And you're going to have to take it *seriously*. You only understand the basics. Until now you've been training pups and helping your father. Training yearlings is much more exacting. I can't handle them and do all the rest, too. It's impossible."

But I *want* to learn! I can help.

"What if I said I wasn't sure I could teach you what you need to know?"

You can. I know you can. I've been watching you all my life.

"Yes, you have. So why, at the age of nine months, does Tinder bolt whenever he gets a chance?"

That's not fair!

"Who said anything about *fair*?" His mother's voice cracked a little on the word. He could guess her thoughts: how exactly might the word "fair" apply to any part of their situation? Furthermore, what she'd said about his training skills was true. He was lazy and indulgent; what he liked was the attention of the pups, not the training. He was inconsistent. He worked them on skills they already knew and avoided more difficult things. Worst of all, he understood there was more he should be doing, but he had no idea what it *was*, and that made him feel ashamed.

"You need to realize that this is a business, like a grocery store or a gas station. You're going to find out that's an awfully cold-blooded view. You're asking to be a partner in it. You'll have to think of this place as a business first and a playground with dogs second."

You're talking down to me, he signed. I know what we do.

"Do you? What do you think we sell?"

He must have looked at her as if she were insane.

Dogs. Dogs, of course.

"Wrong. You see, Edgar? It's not as obvious as you think. Anyone can sell dogs. People give them away. Do you know what we charge for each dog?"

He didn't. His father had negotiated these things, and it wasn't something he'd talked much about.

"One thousand five hundred dollars for a trained, eighteen-month-old dog."

One thousand five hundred dollars?

"Yes," she said. "Your litter could be worth between nine and ten thousand dollars. It's not now, but it could be."

How come we aren't rich?

She laughed. "Because most of that money goes toward food, medicine, and expenses. We reimburse people who take care of the older dogs. If we place twenty dogs a year, which is about what we average, we squeak by. And it's not easy to find twenty people willing to pay that much for an adult dog. Most people want pups, you know."

He nodded. Do other dogs cost that much?

"Some. A few cost more—litters out of *show ring* champions." She rolled her eyes when she said "show ring"—her attitude about the dog fancy was just shy of total contempt. "Almost all dogs cost less, though. Much less."

How can we charge so much?

"That's exactly what you need to learn, Edgar. When you know the answer to that question, you'll know why we can place our dogs *at all*, much less at that price. You'll also understand what it is we're selling."

Can't you just tell me?

"I could try, but there are no words for some things, Edgar. Let me ask you a question. You've been around plenty of dogs in town. Do they seem just like ours? Different color, different breed, but otherwise the same?"

Not exactly.

"Kind of scatterbrained, right?"

Yes. But they aren't trained, most of them.

"Do you think that's the only difference? Our pups mature more slowly, do you understand that? They don't have their first heat until

they are two years old. And when they are little . . . you know how frustrating they can be. Look at Essay. We were still working on simple obedience with her when she was six months old, long after any mutt would
have that stuff down pat. But try doing a shared-gaze exercise with one
of those town dogs and see what happens."

But that's easy!

She laughed and stood and turned on the radio to the country-western
station she liked and they cleared the table. She hummed under her
breath as they did the dishes, but it was not joyful—more like a person
singing to keep her mind off something else. Before Edgar went to bed,
his mother said one last thing.

"Edgar, think about what we discussed. Give it a while. Then we need
to do one of two things. Either we stay and make this kennel work—and
that is going to require you to learn finish training—or we begin dis-
mantling the kennel. There's no point in anything halfway."

Edgar nodded. It sounded so rational, the alternatives so clear. He
knew what he wanted the moment his mother posed her question, and
he knew what she *wanted* him to want, despite her attempt at objectiv-
ity. Another life was inconceivable. It would be much later before he'd
realize they'd seduced themselves that night—seduced themselves into
believing they understood all the costs and consequences of what they
wanted. That no mistake they might make could equal what had already
happened. That their calm wasn't simply a veneer.

SINCE THEY WERE IN TOWN ALREADY, Trudy decided they would
eat lunch at the Mellen Diner. As soon as they were seated, Doctor Papineau hailed from across the room and Trudy walked over to him. Edgar
sat listening to the lunchtime chatter and looking out the window. In
the corner booth, a little girl was staring at him. A moment later she
marched past, whispering in a quiet singsong, and disappeared into the
bathroom. When he glanced back from the window he discovered her
standing beside his booth.

"Hi," she said. She was maybe five years old, dressed in a blue jump-
suit with a rainbow-colored elephant across the bib, her hair a yellow

tangle of ringlets. She leaned toward him confidentially.

"Mama says you can't talk," she lisped. "Is that really true?"

He looked at her and nodded.

"Not even a whisper?"

He shook his head.

She drew back and gave him an appraising look.

"How come?" she said.

He shook his head and shrugged. The little girl glanced back at her family—oblivious to her absence—and narrowed her eyes.

"Mama says I should learn some of that from you, but I can't. I tried, but things just come out of me! I said a person who *can* talk *ought* to talk. Don't you think that's true?"

He nodded.

"My gramma's like me. Wanna know what my gramma says?"

Now he was *sure* he didn't know this little girl, and he didn't know her mother or grandmother, either. Yet the more he looked at her face, the more familiar it became, as if he'd seen it often, but at a distance. He glanced back at the corner booth. Her family didn't have one of their dogs—he would have recognized them at once if they had.

"Well, do you want to know or not?" the girl asked, stamping her foot on the linoleum.

He shrugged again. Okay. Sure.

"She says that before you were born, God told you a secret he didn't want anyone else to know."

He looked at her. There wasn't much a person could say in response to a thing like that. He considered scribbling out a note to the little girl: *I could just write it down.* But he thought that was not her point, and she was probably too young to read anyway. He particularly wanted to tell her she didn't have to whisper. People made mistakes like that—talking extra loud or getting nervous. But the little girl wasn't nervous, not in the least. She acted as if she had known him all her life.

She crooked her finger at him. He leaned down and she cupped her hand by his ear.

"You could tell *me* the secret," she whispered. "I wouldn't tell. I promise. Sometimes it makes it easier if just one other person knows."

At first the little girl stood wide-eyed and placid. He sat back and looked at her. Then her eyes squinted into crescents and her lips drew together into an angry little circle.

"You don't remember, do you?" she scolded, and now she wasn't whispering. *"You forgot!"*

Edgar's mother, on the far side of the dining room, stopped talking with Doctor Papineau and turned.

Don't look at *me*, he signed. I don't even know who she is.

Abruptly, the little girl turned and stormed off. She'd taken five or six steps before she whirled to face him again. She was a terribly dramatic child, and Edgar had a glimpse of what it must be like in her house. She was probably staging little scenes like this all the time over eating her vegetables and watching television.

She scrunched up her face as though thinking through a knotty problem.

"Would you tell me if you *did* remember?" she asked, finally.

Yes.

Her expression brightened into a smile. Her face was still oddly familiar, still impossible to place.

"Oh," she said. "Okay!" Then she skipped away. Before she reached the corner booth her attention was caught by a baby in a high chair and she stopped to poke the baby and ask questions when it started to cry.

"What was that about?" Trudy said when she slipped into the booth.

I don't know.

"Maybe you have an admirer," she said.

And for the third time since they'd walked into the diner, he could think of no better reply than a shrug.

THEY WORKED HARD TO distract one another whenever they recognized bleakness descending. Edgar pulled Trudy to the kitchen table to play checkers and eat popcorn. One night she snuck his entire litter into the house without waking him. In the morning, when he opened his eyes, eight dogs lifted their heads to look at him.

Edgar opened *The Jungle Book* and discovered that, for the first time since the funeral, he could concentrate enough to read. And reading was more comfort than anything else. "Kaa's Hunting." "Tales of the Bander-Log." It didn't matter. It touched the old life, the life before. He watched the television for news of Alexandra Honeywell and Starchild Colony, and that too provided a comfort. Yet, in the mornings, the front of his rib-cage ached as if someone had dropped an anvil on his chest in the night.

The whelping rooms consoled him. Also the workshop, despite what had happened there. But it was the row of paint-chipped file cabinets, standing like sentinels against the back wall of the workshop, that drew him most. Atop the cabinets sat a small reference library. *Working Dogs*, by Humphrey, Warner, and Brooks. *Genetics in Relation to Agriculture*, by Babcock and Clausen. *Veterinary Techniques for the Farm*, by Wilson and Bobrow. *Genetics and the Social Behavior of Dogs*, by Scott and Fuller. And of course, *The New Webster Encyclopedic Dictionary of the English Language*. The master litter book was there, too—row upon row of ledgered names and litter numbers, one line for every Sawtelle dog, all the way back to his grandfather's time. A thousand times he must have watched his father run a finger along a page, then snatch an overstuffed folder out of a drawer. Generations of dogs filled those metal drawers. If ever a folder turned up missing, his father said it was as if they had lost the dog itself, and he would search and search, saying, "These records are *it*. Without them, we wouldn't know how to plan the next litter. We wouldn't know what a dog *meant*."

The bottom drawers of the oldest cabinets contained a hash of newspaper articles and letters, most addressed to Edgar's grandfather. There was a letter from a man in Ohio whose dog had rescued him from drowning. Another, from a woman in Washington State, described how her dogs had interceded when she'd been attacked by a mountain lion. Some letters were paper-clipped to newspaper articles from faraway cities. *The Boston Globe*. *The New York Times*. Even the London *Times*. The pattern was clear: his grandfather had been writing to people because their dogs had done something remarkable, something reported in the newspaper.

One letter in particular caught Edgar's attention. It was postmarked New Jersey, and the name, Brooks, sounded familiar. He'd read the first few lines before he stood and double-checked the spine of *Working Dogs*, and then turned back to the letter:

May 2nd, 1934
Morristown, New Jersey

Dear Mr. Sawtelle,

Thank you for your interest in our work. I am gratified that *Working Dogs* is of some assistance, and not a futile documentary effort. Unfortunately, I have no plans that would take me to Wisconsin in the near future, as our work demands my presence here. As one who works with dogs, I trust you understand.

First, to your questions. We do not attempt to train our dogs to make complex choices between training objectives. Of course, the dogs make substantial judgments many times a day, both in training and in service, but a command's intent is always unambiguously clear. For example, when recalled, the dog should always come. When told to stay, it should always stay. I can think of no benefit in asking a dog to *possibly* come when recalled. Scent tracking requires a high level of choice-making, but not the kind you've asked about. We are eminently practical in these matters. Our goal is to produce the best possible working dogs, and consequently we emphasize predictability. I would not like to guess whether the choice-making behavior you asked about can be trained for or tested accurately, or whether it is heritable. And I have no more efficacious proofing procedures in mind than those you suggest. This whole question of choice between objectives has been a cause for idle speculation on my part the last few nights, and I have even gone as far as discussing it with my colleagues. The consensus seems to be that even if it were possible, there would be little utility in it for service dogs.

Second, for reasons I suspect you already understand, we cannot consider an exchange of dogs. The six strains that comprise the Fortunate Fields breeding program represent thoroughly researched bloodlines. In order to select a foundation

stock of just twenty-one animals, we examined the pedigree data
of hundreds of candidates, cross-indexed against their show and
working titles. As a result, all of our dogs have a proven ancestry
that has produced both excellent conformation and great success
at work. Introducing an unknown into the bloodlines is out of
the question.

I should also like to offer two observations. First, by beginning
your breeding program with dogs you found "excellent in
temperament and structure" but of unpedigreed stock, you
have made attaining your objective—and I admit I don't fully
understand it—immeasurably harder. While it is true that our
selection of German Shepherd Dogs was essentially accidental,
the choice to begin with a well-documented lineage was not.
We know, for example, that our dogs have been structurally
sound for at least five generations. When questions arise about
the heritability of some trait, we can contact the owners of
ancestors two and sometimes three generations back. For the goal
of producing a scientifically constructed working dog, this is
invaluable. Without such information, one might expect that the
first dozen generations would exhibit extreme variability in type;
to bring order from that chaos, one would have to aggressively
inbreed, with the predictable amplification of undesirable as well
as desirable traits.

I also feel compelled to say that it is breathtakingly naïve to
imagine creating a breed of dog in the first place. To do so by
selecting what you arbitrarily think are outstanding examples—
whatever dogs happen to catch your fancy—and crossing them
into your line will only result in a jumble, and might well
create unhealthy or unviable offspring. I warn you against this
course. You seem to grasp the principles of heredity, and thus I
am astonished at what you think you might accomplish. You,
the canine species, and our society would be better served if you
accepted the realities of animal husbandry. Yours is a common
vanity, one that every breeder has indulged during a weak

moment—but the best of them put such thoughts aside and ask
what is right for the breed. I hope you soon do so as well. What
you are attempting is, in essence, the opposite of our endeavor,
and I cannot recommend it.

A blank space appeared in the text, and then the letter continued:

Mr. Sawtelle,

    After finishing the last passage, I set this letter aside for some
days, too upset to finish it. I felt I should either write it again
with a more civil tone or simply not post it. Though I am no
less adamant today, in the interim I've found I will be traveling
to Minneapolis. This is unusual and unexpected, but if I've read
my map correctly, I may have time for a brief side trip on my
return, the purpose of which will be to convince you, in person,
of your folly. In addition, as a scientist, I feel some obligation to
review your stock, on the remote chance it might be of use to us.
I should be traveling about six weeks hence, and done with my
business in Minneapolis around June 15.

                                                        Signed,
                                                        AB

The letter was a curiosity. Edgar had read *Working Dogs* years before
and knew that Brooks was one of the original breeders on the Fortunate
Fields project. The makeshift library atop the file cabinets held several
books on that subject, as well as articles about Buddy, the most famous of
those dogs. Fortunate Fields had originated through the philanthropy of
a woman named Dorothy Eustice, whose idea was to breed dogs to help
humanity—in particular, as guide dogs for the blind. An institution
called The Seeing Eye had been established to carry that work forward.
    Fortunate Fields was interesting because guide dogs for the blind
needed to be of a special temperament: unflappable, easy to train, and
happiest at work. This ruled out dogs that were, for example, unnerved
by new surroundings or too laconic to be relied upon for steady work.

The Sawtelle family legend—myth, Edgar had always supposed—was that his grandfather had contacted the Fortunate Fields breeders in the early days and that one of them had taken pains to advise him on breeding and training. The story went that the Sawtelle dogs even carried the blood of Buddy.

Edgar fingered through the letters. There were several more from Brooks. The next was dated two months later.

> July 2nd, 1934
> Morristown, New Jersey
>
> Mr. Sawtelle,
>
> I apologize for rushing off. Your hospitality was more than I should have hoped for—indeed, more than I should have indulged in. After seeing your dogs, I understand your enthusiasm. However, I must repeat that there is no possibility that we could use them as Fortunate Fields stock.
>
> Having also seen your records, I understand that the difference between our approaches is one of philosophy, not technique. You are as selective, in your way, as we at Fortunate Fields. (If I am repeating what I already said while visiting, I apologize—some of it is unclear to me now.) I do not think you have much chance of success, though your definition of success is less precise than ours. That may be more sensible, as you've argued, but it is not scientific, and in science, progress is necessarily slow.
>
> I also cannot let you ship a bitch here to be bred. Although I am on your side in this matter, my colleagues are unconvinced.
>
> However, I tell you the following in confidence: a gentleman named Conrad McCalister has been living with a dog of ours, Amos, just outside of Minneapolis, for two years now. Amos is a sibling of Buddy's, and every bit the dog she is. We consider Amos to be among our greatest successes, though Buddy gets all the publicity. With my endorsement, I believe Conrad would permit Amos to sire a litter with a bitch of your choosing. I could make

sure you had the advantage of our full documentation on Amos, since you would be in a position to appreciate what it meant.

Finally, I would like to mention a personal matter, with the desire that it need never be discussed again. Our night at "The Hollow" (as I believe the establishment was called) culminated in a rather unfortunate—indeed, foolish— incident. The young lady you introduced me to has mailed several letters to my home address since then, indicating that she would rather not put the event into the proper perspective. Rest assured, I have determined that this is only a matter of misplaced affection and not something medical in nature. I believe you know her, if my memory of that night was not completely destroyed by whatever was in those shot glasses. (I shall never again hear the name "Leinenkugel" without some degree of nausea. I am grateful the beverage isn't sold here.)

In any case, I've suggested to her that the best thing might be a subtle remembrance in the form of a puppy related to the famous "Buddy," which she would acquire from you. I've explained to her that this would be Buddy's paternal nephew or niece, but as you well know, those not involved in animal husbandry have little interest in exact filial relationships, and no appreciation of their significance. In any event, if you would agree to make that possible, I would be happy to send Conrad a letter endorsing the mating. And you would have my deepest gratitude.

I believe you have undertaken a particularly interesting project, Mr. Sawtelle. If my prior letter seemed harsh, please accept my apologies.

Most anxiously awaiting your reply,
Alvin Brooks

Postscript: As for naming, I see no reason to call them anything other than "Sawtelle Dogs," or perhaps just "Sawtelles." If they amount to anything besides well-trained mongrels, they will, after all, have been the product of your vision.

And then a third letter, postmarked almost five years later:

> November 18, 1938
> Morristown, New Jersey

John,

I do not share this desire to wax philosophical about the nature of men and dogs. It leads to discussions that are unscientific at best and a waste of intellectual force at worst. You are talking religion, not science.

One part of your letter intrigued me, however—your discussion of *Canis posterus*—the "next dogs," as you call them. I am familiar with the theory of the dire wolf, that gigantic ancestor of wolves that trod the prehistoric earth. I, like you, believe that our modern dogs are descended from the wolves of antiquity, perhaps one hundred thousand years past. As you say, that gives us three points—more than enough to plot a trajectory—*if they belong to the same evolutionary branch of the species*. That is, the dire wolf may have been something entirely separate from *Canis lupus*, an alternative form that natural selection toyed with and discarded.

I must make something clear before I go on. You speak of natural selection and evolution as if they were one and the same, but natural selection—the undirected survival of an individual or individuals—is merely one mechanism of evolution, and not the only one. Mutation, for example, is another mechanism— one way in which novelty gets introduced. As you well know, conscientious animal husbandry serves the same function in domesticated animals that natural selection serves in the wild.

Yet, in geometry, given two points, a line may be drawn. Perhaps the same is true in biology. Suppose those two points we take are the wolf and the domestic dog. That does imply something else farther along the same line—the "next dog," as you like to phrase it.

But this is where your thinking goes awry, for along any such biological line, the farther points are not more advanced than the earlier points, they are only better adapted. That is, evolution and sophistication are not necessarily one and the same. And so your endless speculation on the nature of *Canis posterus*, and hence the next small change that will make them better workers (which is my dream) or companions (yours) is futile, since the forces of selection would either have to know *in advance* what small change is desired, or be able to recognize it when it happens by pure accident. The latter is not a realistic possibility—mutations occur at an extremely low rate in any population, and of course the chance of a specific mutation that would better adapt a dog for companionship . . . well, it is possible, but statistically unlikely.

Which leaves you in the uncomfortable position of speculating on a change that cannot happen unless you already know what it will be (or have the sort of time on your hands that natural selection has). That is the crux of the layman's trouble in understanding evolution: it works on a time scale so far beyond personal experience that one must train oneself to think in eons, not decades. Here at Fortunate Fields, we have carefully defined objective criteria *known in advance* by which our animals may be measured for fitness; we know exactly which behaviors to select for. Therefore, though our progress must be slow, we are confident it will also be steady.

Since you insist on speculating, however, I will say this much. There are limits to what even the most rigorously scientific breeding program can accomplish—based not only on the foundation stock and the limits of precision we have for measuring the dogs, but on limits that come from within *us*—limits, in other words, of our own imagination, and of ourselves as conscientious human beings. In the end, to create better dogs, we will have to become better people.

And that, sir, is the last speculation you will hear from me
along these lines.

There was more in the letter, an exchange of kennel techniques, clar-
ification of older letters. What interested Edgar was how Alvin Brooks
had signed the letter. To move such a formal man from that first out-
raged letter to one in which he closed with "Affectionately" must have
taken dozens if not hundreds of exchanges. Why had these, of all the
letters, been kept? Probably chance, he knew. But he dug back into the
file cabinets to see what else he could find, opening letter after letter
and setting it aside.

It all made him think about their records. The paperwork on a dog
didn't end when it left the kennel. At his father's request, new owners
sent back letters every few months describing how the dog they'd adopted was getting along. When a dog reached five years of age, his father
had contacted the owners to fill out another form. And when the dog
died, yet another form was filled out, recording the age, cause of death,
behavior late in life, and so on. Edgar's father sometimes even called the
dog's veterinarian. As a result, the file for every dog expanded over time
until it was stuffed with notes, letters, photographs.

"A litter," Edgar's father once told him, "is like an x-ray of its parents and
its parents' parents, but an x-ray that takes years to develop, and even then
it's faint. The more x-rays you have, the better the picture you get."

This made sense. A dog might sire half a dozen litters, each with six
or seven pups. That meant forty or more pups who reflected the qualities
of the sire. If, for an extreme example, cleft palates showed up in every
litter—meaning pups that had to be put down—you knew that the sire
carried a propensity toward cleft palate. (Of course, if a sire produced
cleft palates more than once, they stopped breeding him, and a red slash
was drawn across the dog's folder.)

Just before a dog left the kennel, it was evaluated one last time. They
called this "the finish." There were no special tests in the finish, just the
same things they'd always tested for, the same exercises, the same measurements. The difference was, this time the results were rolled up into

a numerical score representing the dog in maturity. That finish score was the best indication of what its ancestors had passed on—the best x-ray.

Once a finish score was assigned, Edgar's father recalculated all its ancestors' finish scores, going back five generations. This was how evidence accumulated about how true the dog bred, how reliably it passed on its qualities, good or bad, to succeeding generations. A second number told them how many of a dog's progeny had contributed to the master score— an index of confidence. When planning litters, the choice between two dogs with nearly identical finish scores favored the dog with the highest index of confidence—the one who had been tested most thoroughly. This was a system Edgar's grandfather had worked out and refined, apparently in long discussions with Brooks, and which his father had practiced, modified, and improved.

It wasn't a perfect scheme, of course. While the finish score gave an idea of how well a dog fared in testing, there were intangibles to consider. Not temperament, which they broke down into individual behaviors and assessed, and not physical qualities, which were easily measured, but how the dog *combined* all these things, for the whole of every dog was always greater than the sum of its parts. Some, for example, seemed capable of inspiration: they clued in on a new way of doing things more often than others. There was no way to measure this. And there was the dog's personality, which was distinct from its temperament. A dog with a keen sense of humor would find ways to make jokes with you, and could be a joy to work with. Others were serious and contemplative, and they were good for other reasons.

Edgar's father had sometimes grumbled that all he did was keep track of a dog's faults, though what he meant was, even the best records in the world couldn't capture the whole of the dog. They could record only what could be measured. And the measuring and testing of the dogs, the follow-up calls and letters, the reassessment of the ancestors of a placed dog, all served to remind his father of a dog's total character. When it came time to plan a litter, the scores and numbers were only a guide. It hadn't been unusual for him to select against the numbers based on intuition.

But his father's complaint also pointed to the fact that the records mainly prevented bad pairings—breeding, say, two dogs that tended to produce weak fronts. That was the interesting thing about planning a cross. Two brilliant dogs couldn't be bred if it risked a litter full of stifles so straight the dogs would be crippled by the time they were five years old. And so the first question about any potential pairing was not how great the offspring would be, but what problems it might produce.

Thinking about all this, Edgar began to understand what his mother meant when she'd claimed not to have the words to describe what made their dogs valuable. Partly it was the training. They spent long hours doing crazywalking, stays, releases, shared-gaze drills, and all the rest until the pups paid attention to where they were going and where they were looking; they learned that a certain expression on a person's face meant that something interesting lay behind them, or in another room. He'd taken that for granted, but now that his mother had pointed it out, he saw how uncommon this was.

So a dog's value came from the training *and* the breeding. And by breeding, Edgar supposed he meant both the bloodlines—the particular dogs in their ancestry—and all the information in the file cabinets. Because the files, with their photographs, measurements, notes, charts, cross-references, and scores, told them the *story* of the dog—what a dog *meant*, as his father put it.

Sometimes when Edgar got an idea, a whole series of other ideas clicked into place right behind it, as if they had logjammed somewhere in his mind, waiting for the way to clear. Suddenly, he saw how the training, the breeding, and the record-keeping worked together, how the training tested the dogs for their qualities, their ability to learn different kinds of work. That explained the training notes and why the Sawtelles had to raise the dogs to maturity: if they placed a pup, they wouldn't know what kind of dog it became. But the Sawtelles could compare them because they trained every dog. So it made sense that a dog's finish score could alter the scores of its ancestors, which in turn influenced the dogs used for the next mating. As if every dog had a voice in selecting the following generations.

Edgar closed his eyes and waited until he could hold it all in his mind, and once that happened, he wanted so badly to ask his father about it, to be sure he'd understood things correctly, that it nearly made him cry. But the only way left to him was through the records. And yet—he felt this, but couldn't find the words for it—something else made the dogs valuable, too, something that hadn't been among this sudden cascade of ideas. He wished he could read his grandfather's side of the correspondence to understand what he'd meant by "the next dogs."

No matter how naïve or wild-eyed his grandfather might have sounded to Brooks, Edgar thought John Sawtelle's vision might not have been so quixotic.

He had a feeling, in fact, it might already have come to pass.

Lessons and Dreams

A FEW WEEKS AFTER THE FUNERAL, AFTER THE SHOCK HAD WORN off and some of the kennel routines were established again, Edgar's dreams began. In them, his father did the most ordinary things—walking along the driveway to fetch the mail, reading in his armchair, lifting a puppy in the dim light of the whelping room to take a closer look. Edgar looked for some connection between his last waking thoughts and what he saw when he fell asleep. One night he found himself walking creekside with his father, the sumac and chokecherry green and jungle lush, though he knew, even in the dream, that outside his window the fields lay buried under thick drifts of snow. Then his father turned and said something, something important. When Edgar woke he lay still, trying to fix those words in his mind, but by the time he shuffled into the kitchen, he couldn't even remember whether his father had signed or spoken.

Trudy peered at him over her coffee cup.

"What's wrong?" she said.

Nothing.

"Was it a dream?" she asked. "Your father?"

Her guess surprised him. He didn't know how to answer. Was she having dreams, too? It seemed possible—some mornings she looked as fragile as a baby bird. She was trying to shield him from whatever bad feelings she had, he could see that. She stayed up late sitting at the kitchen table and pretending to work. Half the time he cooked dinner for her because she seemed to have forgotten to eat. She only pushed the food around on her plate, then stood and began to wash dishes. When she talked with people in town she was calm and poised (though tired-looking), but beneath it Edgar saw something fractured.

And there was, he discovered, a kind of selfishness in him about those dreams. They might have been false memories, but they were memories nonetheless, stolen time. In the end he just shrugged and headed out to start the morning chores. He hadn't fooled her, but they didn't talk about it, either, which, for the time being, was good enough.

HIS MOTHER HAD HIM set up a low barrier in the mow—a pair of up-rights with dowels sticking out, like a track-and-field hurdle. A rough curtain of red ribbon hung from the rod. She asked Edgar to bring up one of the dogs. At first he intended to use Essay, who loved to climb and jump. Then he remembered his mother's admonition about training the dogs on exercises they had already mastered, so he chose Finch instead. He stayed the dog on the far side of the barrier, then walked to his mother's side.

"Have him jump the barrier," she said.

She wasn't asking for a stupendous feat: the rod was on the lowest set of dowels, six inches above the floor. Finch could step over it. When Edgar signaled a recall, Finch wandered forward. He sniffed the uprights then skirted them without stepping over the rod. He trotted the remaining distance and finished in front of Edgar, swishing his tail and glancing back and forth between the two of them.

"What did you think of that?" his mother asked.

He did it wrong, Edgar signed.

"All right, let me put it another way. What did *you* do wrong?"

Nothing. He knew exactly what I wanted. He had to go out of his way to avoid it.

"Is that so?"

Edgar looked at Finch, whose mouth was hanging open slightly, ears erect, eyes shining with mischief. Of *course* Finch knew he was supposed to jump the barrier—not only had Finch seen other dogs do the same thing, but Finch himself had jumped that barrier many times, even when it was set much higher (though never reliably, Edgar had to admit). Certainly, Finch wasn't scared of the barrier, as some dogs were. And on top of all that, it was obviously the shortest path between them.

Yes, he signed. You saw him.

"Okay," his mother said. "We'll forget for a moment that when Finch finally got here, you didn't acknowledge it. He's still waiting for that, by the way, but he's a patient dog. He knows you'll get around to it. There's even a chance he won't have forgotten what you're praising him for by then. In the meantime, why don't you take him back around? Maybe we can do this over and figure out what the trouble is."

Abashed, Edgar scratched Finch's chest and smoothed the fur over the dog's forehead. He looped his fingers through his collar, but before he could take a step, his mother said, "Stop!"

He turned to look at her.

"Why did you just praise Finch?"

He laughed, silently, shoulders shaking. His mother seemed determined to ask absurd questions.

Because he came when called.

"Really?" She looked puzzled. "Okay. Well." She raised an arm and signaled them forward with a limp hand, a queen dismissing courtiers. "Proceed."

He led Finch across the mow, giving the uprights a wide berth so as not to accidentally reinforce the incorrect path. When they'd gotten halfway back to the starting position, his mother again shouted, "Stop!"

They stopped. The barrier was within reach of Edgar's left hand. Far away, near the mow door, his mother stood with her fingers woven into her hair like a madwoman, as if she couldn't believe what she was seeing.

"What in the *world* do you think you're doing?" she said.

This was an act, he knew, and it made him laugh all over again.

Taking Finch to his stay-spot.

"But you didn't go over the barrier!"

You didn't ask me to go over the barrier.

"Exactly," she said. "You see? You can't train a dog to do something if you don't know what you want him to do. When you recalled Finch, you didn't know what you wanted. How can I tell? Because you said one thing to him and expected something else, just like I did. If I had *known* what I wanted from you I would have *asked* for it. But I didn't know until you were already past the barrier. *Now* I know what I want. Come back here. You've taught me what I want."

Dutifully, he led Finch back to her side.

"Thank you," she said, bowing a little.

You're welcome, he signed, bowing in return. He was having a hard time keeping the grin off his face.

"Who was the teacher in that exchange?"

He pointed at her.

"Oh really?"

Oh. I taught you.

"So who was the teacher?"

I was.

"Right. What do you say when someone goes out of their way to teach you something?"

Thank you?

"Exactly. Why did you praise Finch before?"

Because he taught me something?

"Are you asking me or telling me?"

Telling. Because he taught me something.

"Exactly."

When his mother dropped her theatrical stance and smiled he wasn't sure where his tears came from. He didn't feel sad—in fact, he was laughing—but his vision suddenly blurred up. Tears of shock, he supposed, at discovering he'd spent his entire life on the kennel and yet still misunderstood something so elementary. And the force of her personality could be overwhelming. He turned away and passed a sleeve over his face before something even more embarrassing could happen.

She watched for a moment. "Oh Edgar," she said. "I don't mean to be hard on you. I'm just trying to make a point. Remember what I said about not being able to explain what people pay us for? I wasn't being coy. One of the things you need to learn is that training is almost never about *words*. I could try to explain these things, but the words wouldn't mean much. It's like what just happened here: I told you the words for this idea right when we started, but that didn't mean you understood them. But maybe now you see why someone would pay for a 'trained' dog instead of a pup?"

He thought about this, then nodded.

"Especially another trainer?"

He nodded again.

"So why don't you take this fabulous teacher named Finch back *over the barrier* and stay him, and let's try again."

This time she had him stand across the mow beside Finch with a short lead attached to his collar, and she performed the recall. Edgar ran alongside Finch and made sure he jumped the barrier—he only needed one correction in three trials. Then they switched and she ran alongside him for three more trials, while Edgar did the recall.

He thanked Finch each time for teaching him something. In return, the dog's eyes glinted, and he tried to put his feet on Edgar's chest and lick his face. Quite happily, Edgar let him.

DOCTOR PAPINEAU CAME for dinner several nights later.

"Here it is," he announced, as he walked in. He was accompanied by a blast of cold air and a white bakery box, held aloft like a prize. A longtime widower, Doctor Papineau patronized the cafés and bakeries between Park Falls and Ashland. He held strong opinions on who served the best of his favorite foods, from eggs over easy to strawberry cheese-cake.

"Lemon meringue," he declared. "I bought it by hand." This joke was part of the tradition as well. "I told Betsy down at the Mellen Bakery to set aside the best she had. She did, too—she's got a little crush on me, I think, ever since I heroically removed her cat's kidney stones."

Edgar's mother lifted the box from Papineau's hand. "Well, she'll have to get in line behind the waitresses down in Park Falls," she said, smiling. "Cold enough for you, Page?"

"Nope," he said cheerfully. "I'd like to see it colder than this."

"Oh, really?" she said. "Why's that?"

"Because, when I'm soaking in the Florida sun I like to read the newspaper and check the weather here. If I don't see solid minus signs, I feel cheated."

"Ah yes. The annual migration."

"Ah yes. I enjoy it more every year."

They spent dinner talking about the kennel. Edgar's mother had taken one of the older dogs to see Doctor Papineau that week and he had diagnosed hypothyroid. They talked about the medication. Then he inquired about how she and Edgar were holding up, commenting obliquely on how tired they looked. Trudy put him off. Things had been hard, she said, but they were under control. They had a schedule worked out.

Edgar's mother embroidered their success a bit. While it was true that things were slowly returning to normal, it also wasn't unusual for her to be in the barn until nine o'clock, with another hour spent over paperwork at the kitchen table. Edgar worked evenings as well, pulling out dogs for grooming and training. He'd negotiated for two hours with them each night; Trudy said there had to be time for schoolwork, and if he was efficient, an hour and a half would be plenty for training. Saturdays were the exception—they slept as late as they wanted and ran errands in town. But even then, if Edgar happened to wake first, he'd sneak out to the barn and start the chores, hoping that, just once, his mother would open her eyes and realize there was nothing to do. Often, before he'd worked even twenty minutes, the barn doors would open and she would walk in, puffy-eyed, weary, and looking thinner every week. On top of it all, there was the cough she'd developed. It doubled her over sometimes.

"You two are doing an amazing job," Doctor Papineau said. "I can't believe how fast you've got back on your feet. I remember what it was like when Rose died. I wasn't fit for anything for months." He looked thoughtful. "I'm just wondering if you can keep up the pace."

"Why couldn't we?" his mother said. "It won't be long before the weather turns, and things get so much easier when we can train outdoors. Then school lets out for the summer. That's going to make a big difference."

"And a couple of months later, it'll start up again," Papineau said. He knew where the plates and silverware were and he had dished out slices of pie—he liked to serve the desserts he brought.

"Well, what else can we do?" his mother said, looking cross. "There's only the two of us here. Maybe we'll have to skip a litter in the fall. That would make things tight, but I've been going over our finances and we could make ends meet. I'm sorry if that means your share is going to be a little smaller, but it's the best we can do for now."

Papineau waved her comment aside with his fork.

"What I'm wondering is, have you considered that maybe the real solution involves three people?"

"Meaning?"

"Meaning there's a Sawtelle boy in town who knows this kennel inside and out."

"Claude is hardly a boy," his mother said. "And you know how things ended between him and Gar."

"Water under the bridge, isn't it? He's been helping me out at the office, Trudy, and I have to tell you that he still has a gift. I remember what he was like twenty years ago."

"And we both know how he learned all that. You don't get good at ministering to torn-up dogs unless you're around them a lot."

"Okay, okay. I didn't come here to debate Claude's past. The thing is, where is the slack in your schedule, Trudy? There's no room for anything to go wrong, and eventually something always does. Look at the last year. How many things that happened could you have planned for? I'm not talking about Gar, I mean in the kennel. Your barn was hit by a tornado. Did you plan for that? I seem to recall at least one nursing mother last year with mastitis, and we both know how much time bottle-feeding takes. Have you planned for that?"

"All right, Page, here's a question: suppose we hired someone to help out. How would I pay them? The money isn't there. We make ends meet.

We pay our bills. We have a little savings. Period. That truck isn't going to last much longer and when it's time to buy a new one I don't want to be firing hired help to do it. I won't even start down that road."

"It was just an idea, Trudy," Doctor Papineau said. "I'm trying to help."

"It was a *bad* idea," she said. "Is that why you're here? To protect your *investment?*"

It finally began to dawn on Edgar what the references to Doctor Papineau's "share" meant. He signed a question at his mother, but she shook her head angrily and stood and stalked around the table. She ended up standing by the counter where Doctor Papineau had left the pie tin, and in a single swift motion pitched it into the trash.

"I may not have been born here, but that doesn't mean I don't know how this place operates after twenty years. Twenty years, let me remind you, during which Claude was most definitely *not* here."

Edgar's mother was forty-one years old at that moment. He knew she could mask her feelings perfectly when she wanted to because there were dogs who misbehaved expressly to get a reaction, not caring whether it was pleasure or anger. Oftentimes it wasn't until much later that he understood a dog had gotten under her skin. She was certainly capable of that same self-control during a dinner conversation, and yet there she stood, giving herself over to her anger, almost reveling in it. The dark circles under her eyes had disappeared; her shoulders had dropped into a relaxed readiness, her posture suddenly sinuous and limber, like a dancer or a lioness. She looked as if she might as easily spring onto the table as curl up to sleep. Partly calculated, he supposed, to look as far from helpless as possible, wholly in control of their fate, but partly also a surrender to her own willfulness. He thought he ought to be scared by such a magisterial fit of temper, but in truth, he'd never felt safer in his life.

Doctor Papineau, however, was entirely daunted. He tipped his chair back onto its rear legs and held his hands out. "Whoa," he said. "Your decision. I'm not suggesting you do anything that doesn't feel right. But think about this: eventually, something *will* go wrong. What are you going to do then? That's all I'm saying. What are you going to do then?"

"YES," TRUDY SAID, after Doctor Papineau had left. "He has a stake in the kennel. Ten percent."

Are there others? Edgar asked.

"No. Years ago, when we were strapped for money, Page helped us out. Back then, it was impossible to get a loan, so he paid us five thousand dollars in exchange for a share in the kennel. He has obligations, though."

That's why you never pay him for vet work.

"Right."

What about Claude?

"Claude sold your father his share in the kennel when your grandfather died."

Edgar had more questions, but suddenly his mother looked exhausted, and there would be plenty of chances to ask in the morning.

TIME AND AGAIN EDGAR REREAD the letters from Brooks. They were like a puzzle to be solved. Brooks was given to proclamations and dire warnings. Pitched arguments were made for or against the importance of gait, hocks, flanks, the function of the tail; the optimum angle of the pasterns, how much this might vary between the Fortunate Fields lines and the Sawtelle dogs; whether one could ever discriminate between willingness to work and more general intelligence; whether body sensitivity was learned or inherited. The arguments often ascended into theory. Brooks sounded like a man dragging John Sawtelle into the age of science.

"I have the advantage of knowing," he wrote, "that long after I am gone my work will provide a foundation upon which future generations of dogs, breeders, and trainers may build. Skill and talent alone are not enough. If these are bound up in you and you alone, and not in data and precisely recorded procedures, what will your efforts amount to? A few dogs—a few successes—then nothing. Only the briefest flash of light in the darkness."

There had been some setback in 1935, though Edgar couldn't tell what it was—some illness had flashed through the kennel, perhaps, or some spectacular training failure. In any case, it was serious enough for Brooks to shift from debate to encouragement. "There is nothing to do now but take stock of your accomplishments," he wrote. "Now your records must serve *you* instead of the dogs. Study them. Look at how many of your dogs have succeeded in the world. Your records are a history of your accomplishments, John. They will show you why you undertook this work in the first place."

Edgar had never seen his father capriciously select a dog for breeding, but in those early days, there was nothing yet to call a Sawtelle Dog—just John Sawtelle's dogs. What drove Brooks mad was Edgar's grandfather's habit of spotting a dog on the street and deciding it carried some essential quality. The replies from New Jersey sometimes rose to a shriek: "How many times have we argued about this, John? Each time you do this, you introduce more variability into your bloodlines than you will ever profit by. *Why* do you place your trust in chance?"

Edgar arranged the letters from Brooks in chronological order. The last of them seemed to close the argument forever.

December 16, 1944
Morristown, New Jersey

John,

You may be the most stubborn man I've ever met. Let me rebut your points one last time, though I fear no one will ever change your mind on this. At least we are in agreement that by careful documentation of phenotype, one can increase or decrease the preponderance of a quality if one measures it objectively and reinforces it for many generations through selective breeding. The poorest farmer knows this can be done, and benefits from it: he chooses Herefords, Holsteins, or Guernseys depending on his needs. He has definite opinions on whether a Percheron or a Belgian should stand in the traces.

Likewise, we apply the scientific principles of heredity toward the perfection of a breed, so that instead of only one dog out of two litters being suitable for service, 90 percent make the grade. How are we doing this? By defining and measuring those qualities that make a good working dog. And this is where we differ. You feel less need to choose specific traits *a priori*, believing instead that excellent traits will simply emerge if the finest individuals, taken as a whole, are brought into the line.

Let us employ the metaphor of salt. We can't see the salt in a glass of water, but we can taste it. Combining two slightly salty glasses and reducing them gives us a saltier result. Done enough, the invisible becomes visible: salt crystals. We may not have set out to create salt crystals, but now we have them. This is analogous to what you propose. You have cleverly arranged to work with strong brine. You don't know what you will find if you continue to distill it, only that "this tastes ever so slightly saltier than that." And so, by the seat of your pants, you choose one cross over another.

At Fortunate Fields, on the other hand, we not only know we are trying to produce salt crystals, we know the desired size, shape, and color of those crystals and we have carefully documented the salinity of the sire and dam of every litter, as well as their offspring.

Yet I have seen your records and you are nearly as rigorous as Fortunate Fields. I confess, our rigor and precision wearies me at times. I don't claim our process is easy. Quite the opposite—if this were easy it would have been done long ago. But I do claim that it is the only way to obtain reliable results.

In the end, the difference between you and me comes down to the difference between the artist and the factory man. The artist does not know what he wants, but looks for good paint, good brushes, and good canvas. He trusts that talent will produce a desirable result. Sadly, for most people, it does not. The factory man says, what can I make that I can *rely* on? It may not be the ideal, but I must be able to tell my customers that each time they buy, they will receive the same product. The factory man values predictability above "mere" excellence for good reason—

would you frequent a bakery where one cake in ten was inspired, but the other nine inedible?

I realize this portrays you as the romantic figure and me as the plodder. Perhaps you think that diminishes me. I do not. Change the analogy from bread to medicine, and you will feel the same urgency I do. You might be willing to gamble on the odd cake, but if your infant is sick, you will choose the medicine with predictable results every time. I sacrifice brilliance to make a good medicine available to mankind.

No one can say if you are that person who, given good paint, good brushes, and a fine canvas, can produce something better than the factory man. That is, and has always been, beyond the realm of science. You do have the attitude of the dreamer about you. For that reason, I haven't the heart to argue anymore about this—it is a hopeless task. And for a simple factory man like me, an effort must be abandoned once its hopelessness is exposed. Only the artist perseveres in such circumstances.

However, I'll leave you with a question. Suppose, guided only by intuition, you capture the greatness you seek. Never mind that you cannot define "greatness" scientifically. What makes you think you will even *recognize* it when it appears? Some believe that gross animal behavior may be reducible to a set of simple, indivisible traits and that only the multiplicity of ways in which those traits combine creates the illusion of complexity. Suppose you stumble across one small change with dozens of ramifications in the gross behavior of the animal? How will you know what you've done? How will you ever achieve it again?

The painter who creates one masterpiece, never to produce another, is well known. If you have a success, it will most likely be singular. Can you be satisfied with that, John?

Almondine

To her, the scent and the memory of him were one. Where it lay strongest, the distant past came to her as if that morning: Taking a dead sparrow from her jaws, before she knew to hide such things. Guiding her to the floor, bending her knee until the arthritis made it stick, his palm hotsided on her ribs to measure her breaths and know where the pain began. And to comfort her. That had been the week before he went away.

He was gone, she knew this, but something of him clung to the baseboards. At times the floor quivered under his footstep. She stood then and nosed into the kitchen and the bathroom and the bedroom—especially the closet—her intention to press her ruff against his hand, run it along his thigh, feel the heat of his body through the fabric.

Places, times, weather—all these drew him up inside her. Rain, especially, falling past the double doors of the kennel, where he'd waited through so many storms, each drop throwing a dozen replicas into the air as it struck the waterlogged earth. And where the rising and falling water met, something like an expectation formed, a place where he might appear and pass in long strides, silent and gestureless. For she was not without her own selfish desires: to hold things motionless, to measure herself against them and find herself present, to know that she was alive precisely because he needn't acknowledge her in casual passing; that utter constancy might prevail if she attended the world so carefully. And if not constancy, then only those changes she desired, not those that sapped her, undefined her.

And so she searched. She'd watched his casket lowered into the ground, a box, man-made, no more like him than the trees that swayed under the winter wind. To assign him an identity outside the world was not in her thinking. The fence line where he walked and the bed where he slept—that was where he lived, and they remembered him.

Yet he was gone. She knew it most keenly in the diminishment of her own self. In her life, she'd been nourished and sustained by certain things, him being one of them, Trudy another, and Edgar, the third and most important, but it was really the three of them together, intersecting in her, for each of them powered her heart a different way. Each of them bore different responsibilities to her and with her and required different things from her, and her day was the fulfillment of those responsibilities. She could not imagine that portion of her would never return. With her it was not hope, or wistful thoughts—it was her sense of being alive that thinned by the proportion of her spirit devoted to him.

As spring came on, his scent about the place began to fade. She stopped looking for him. Whole days she slept beside his chair, as the sunlight drifted from eastern-slant to western-slant, moving only to ease the weight of her bones against the floor.

And Trudy and Edgar, encapsulated in mourning, somehow forgot to care for one another, let alone her. Or if they knew, their grief and heartache overwhelmed them. Anyway, there was so little they might have done, save to bring out a shirt of his to lie on, perhaps walk with her along the fence line, where fragments of time had snagged and hung. But if they noticed her grief, they hardly knew to do those things. And she without the language to ask.

The Fight

HIS MOTHER'S COUGH WAS BAD IN THE MORNINGS, THOUGH IT was gone by the time they'd finished chores. At school one afternoon, he was called to the office. His mother had telephoned. She would pick him up in the circle drive fronting the school. At first he thought nothing of it; sometimes errands coincided with the end of the school day. He waited under the long-roofed entryway as the buses revved their engines and lumbered forward. He didn't see the pickup until they were gone. His mother sat in the cab, head tipped back, until a coughing fit curled her forward. He trotted up the sidewalk, watching the truck rock on its springs. When he opened the door, the heater was blasting.

What happened? he signed. You look terrible.

"I'm not sure. I got dizzy working in the mow and went to the house to lie down. This thing has gotten—"

She thumped her chest lightly, which triggered a spasm of coughing. She crossed her fists over her chest and doubled up, then rested her hands on the steering wheel. When she looked over at him, her face was shining with sweat.

"I called—" she began, then switched to sign. I called Doctor Frost.

When can you see him?

She looked at her watch. Ten minutes ago.

Then go, he signed. Go!

DOCTOR FROST PRACTICED OUT OF a converted house east of town. His waiting room contained a half dozen chairs and a coffee table covered with ancient *National Geographic* magazines. A tall, narrow window had been cut into the back wall for his receptionist. Before they could sit down, the doctor appeared, sandy-haired, with wire-rimmed glasses, and led Edgar's mother to an examination room. Edgar sat on the couch and looked out the windows. The sun was sinking below the treetops. A pair of jays screamed at each other from the pine trees, launching themselves into loopy, tumbling flights. From inside the exam room came an indistinct conversation.

"Again, please," he heard Doctor Frost say, and another fit of coughing.

A moment later, the doctor appeared at the receptionist's window.

"Edgar," he said. "Why don't you come back and join the party?"

In the examination room, Trudy sat in the corner on a chair. Doctor Frost patted the black exam bench and asked Edgar to untuck his shirt and he pressed a stethoscope against his ribs.

"Cough," he said.

Edgar exhaled a quiet gasp.

"Clear," the doctor murmured. He jotted a note on his pad and turned and pressed his thumbs into the soft skin under Edgar's jaw, looking absently into space, then looked down Edgar's throat with a small, lighted examination scope.

"Say 'Ah.'"

A-H-H-H-H, he fingerspelled.

Doctor Frost glanced at his mother.

"He just said 'ah' for you," she said weakly, and smiling.

"Okay, sense of humor intact," the doctor said. "Try anyway."

Then he clapped Edgar's shoulder and told him to button up. He folded his arms across his clipboard and looked at them.

"Edgar's lungs are clear. He hasn't picked up what you have, Trudy, which is pneumonia. I need to run a lab test on that sputum sample, but there's really not much doubt—the crackle in your right lung is

pronounced. I'm tempted to send you up to Ashland for chest x-rays, but
I'm going to hold off and maybe save you a little money. Right now this
is mild, and you're a young woman, and we're catching it early. We're
going to get you on antibiotics and knock it out quick. There's a catch,
though—"

"This is mild?" his mother interjected.

"Relatively, though I wish you'd come in three or four days ago. This
stuff is nothing to fool with. I'm not trying to alarm you, but I want you
to understand that pneumonia is *dangerous*. People die from it. Any worse
and I'd have you in the hospital."

His mother shook her head and started to say something, but before
she could speak a coughing fit took her. Doctor Frost waved his hand.

"I know, I know—a possibility we want to avoid. So you're going to
have to do what I say. All right?"

She nodded. Doctor Frost looked at Edgar until he nodded, too.

"Here's my concern. Edgar's cough reflex is abnormal. Coughing involves constricting the vocal cords, which, as we know, is difficult for
him. With pneumonia, coughing is good and bad. It's bad because it
wears you out. But it's good because it gets the crud out of your lungs.
If Edgar catches this, he'll naturally be less inclined to cough, and the
bad stuff will accumulate in his lungs. That would be worse than for the
ordinary person. *Much* worse. Understand?"

Again, they both nodded. Doctor Frost looked at Edgar's mother.

"It would be ideal if Edgar stayed somewhere else for a week."

She shook her head. "There's nowhere else."

"Nowhere? How about with Claude?"

She laughed wheezily and rolled her eyes, but there was a flash of anger in her expression as well. Edgar could see her thinking: *small-town
busybodies!*

"Absolutely not."

"All right, then we have to minimize contact between you two for the
next ten days. No meals together, no sitting around in the living room
watching television, no hugs and kisses. Can you quarantine a portion of
your house? Someplace you can sleep and keep the doors closed?"

"Not perfectly. I can close my bedroom door. But it opens onto the kitchen, and there's only one bathroom."

"I don't like that, but I suppose it'll have to do. I realize I'm suggesting extraordinary measures here, but this is an unusual situation." He turned back to the chart and scribbled. When he finished he looked up. "There's one other thing, Trudy. You need bed rest—don't cheat on that."

"How long?"

"A week. Ten days would be better. You're going to sleep as much as you can for the next week."

"You're joking."

"Not in the least. I'm telling you, Trudy, don't push this thing. Antibiotics aren't miracle drugs. If you run yourself down, they won't help."

He turned to Edgar.

"Edgar, if you start feeling like you have a chest cold, if your chest gets tight, let Trudy know. Sometimes people don't want to admit they're getting sick. But if you play that game, it's going to be tough. Understood?"

Doctor Frost led them to the waiting room. He appeared in a few minutes at the receptionist's window with a prescription and a vial of pills, handed Edgar's mother a Dixie cup filled with water, and had her swallow the first dose on the spot.

IN THE TRUCK, EDGAR sat listening to the whistle in his mother's breath. She frowned and turned on the radio.

"I'll be fine," she said. "Quit worrying."

They drove on, music crackling over the truck's speaker.

"You're going to have to do the kennel by yourself."

I know.

When they got home, Trudy went to her bedroom, pulled off her shoes, and dragged the blankets over her shoulders. Edgar stood in the doorway and watched her.

"Is spring break next week?"

Yes.

"I'll call the school and have you excused until then."

Okay.

"Maybe your teachers can send assignments home on the school bus."

Okay.

"About the kennel. Just get the chores done. Check the pups every morning and night. Don't worry about training."

I can do some training.

"Then work your litter the most. Nothing fancy. One dog in motion at a time. Remember that."

Okay, okay.

"Spend as much time as you can in the kennel. Take books. Stay out of the house unless you need to eat, sleep, or—" Before she could finish, a cough wracked her shoulders off the bed. When she stopped, she was propped up on one arm, panting.

What if you need something?

"I won't need anything. I can make soup and toast for myself. I'm going to be sleeping anyway. Now close the door, please."

He stood memorizing her features under the yellow lamplight.

She pointed at the door. "Out," she mouthed.

WHEN HE AND ALMONDINE returned to the house that night, the bedroom door was closed and his mother's wind-up alarm clock sat on the kitchen table. He turned off the kitchen light and held the clock to his ear and looked at the green radium dots on the tips of the hands. A glow shone yellow beneath the bedroom door. He eased the door open. On the bed, his mother lay in a fetal curl, her eyes closed. Her exhalations sounded ever so slightly easier than they had that afternoon. He stood watching and listening for a long time. Almondine pushed past him into the room and scented his mother's thin hand, resting lax and upturned on the sheet, and returned to his side. He closed the bedroom door and stood thinking, turning the wind-up alarm over and over in his hands. Then he walked upstairs. He pulled the blankets off his bed and squeezed his pillow under his elbow and carried them out to the barn. He pushed together four bales of straw in the aisle between the pens and he spread the blankets over the bales and sat and unlaced his shoes and looked at the row of lightbulbs shining over the aisle. He trotted barefoot to the front doors and flipped the light switch. A clap of dark filled the kennel. He flipped the switch up again and took a galvanized pail from the workshop and worked his way along the aisle, stepping onto the upturned pail and licking his fingertips against the heat of the bulbs. He unscrewed all but one, and that far down near the whelping rooms. In the semidark he twisted the knob on the back of the clock until the alarm hand pointed to five then set the clock on the bales beside the pillow and lay back.

Almondine stood on the cement, watching him doubtfully.

Come on, he signed, patting the bales. It's just like in the house.

She circled the setup then climbed aboard and lay with her muzzle near his face. Wind rattled the doors. A pup yipped from the whelping rooms. He pressed his hand into the plush on Almondine's chest, feeling its rise and fall, rise and fall.

He was genuinely terrified of getting sick. It was going to be hard enough keeping his mother in bed; if she thought he was sick, she would do the kennel work anyway, and then she *would* end up hospitalized. And yet, despite his apprehensions, the prospect of running the kennel alone excited him. He wanted to prove he could do it, that nothing would go wrong. And now that he'd begun to see the real problems in training, he felt so many possibilities whenever he worked his dogs.

There was another feeling as well, something darker and harder to think through, because there was a part of him that *wanted* to be away from her. Ever since the funeral, they'd depended on each other so heavily that it was a relief to be alone, self-reliant. Perhaps he thought distancing himself from his mother might distance the fact of his father's death. He understood that might be part of it, and if so, it was an illusion, but that didn't change how he felt. He lay under the gaze of the kennel dogs, his hand on Almondine's side, and thought about being alone.

WHILE HE WAS EATING BREAKFAST, his mother talked to him through the closed door, pausing to catch her breath at disturbing intervals.

"Have you been to the barn yet?"

He swung the bedroom door halfway open. She looked at him glassy-eyed.

Everything is okay. Are *you* okay?

"About the same. Real tired."

Have you taken those pills?

"Yes," she said. "I mean, not yet. I will when I eat breakfast."

I'll make it for you.

He expected her to say no, but she nodded.

"Just toast and strawberry jam. And orange juice. Just set it on the table before you go."

He closed the bedroom door. He mixed up the orange juice, toasted the toast, and covered it with plenty of jam, his heart pounding all the while. When he looked in again, she was asleep. He waited a moment, trying to decide what the right thing to do was, then knocked on the door.

"I'm up," she said groggily.

Breakfast is ready, he signed. I'll check back at noon.

FOR THE NEXT THREE DAYS HE KNEW she'd been awake only because the breakfasts he prepared were gone at lunchtime and the soup eaten when he checked at night. She must have called the school, because the bus didn't slow down at their driveway. Invariably, she was asleep when he looked in on her, a book splayed out on the covers beyond her fingertips. Whenever he woke her she seemed startled; it took a minute for her to make sense of his questions. He asked how she felt; she said she could tell the antibiotics were working. She asked if there were problems in the kennel; he said no.

They both lied.

Each night Edgar lay awake, ridiculously tormented by the windup clock, which, along with its ticking, issued a ratcheting, grinding noise he'd never noticed before. When he finally managed to sleep, his father appeared beside his makeshift bed, so close and real Edgar didn't believe he was dreaming until he found himself sitting up and Almondine licking his face. The fourth morning, he fumbled the jangling alarm into silence and promptly fell back into slumber, worrying even then that he might dream of his father again. And worrying equally that he might not. Instead, he dreamed he could breathe words effortlessly into the air.

The ability hadn't just appeared, it had *returned*, as if he'd had a voice in the womb but lost it when he'd entered the world. And in his dream, he had *chosen* not to speak into the telephone, not to summon the ambulance that would have saved his father's life.

He woke frantic, sobbing. It took a moment before he could marshal the courage to draw a breath, shape his lips, and exhale.

Silence.

The awful thing was, his voice sounded all wrong in his dream—low, like his father's, and gravelly. But *any* voice coming from inside him would have sounded wrong, no less than the buzzing-fly noise from the flashlight-shaped thing the doctors had pressed against his neck. That had given him a voice, but it hadn't been worth it. Unless, of course, he'd had it the day his father fell down in the barn.

He began to take shortcuts with the kennel routine. In order to train all the dogs, he raced through the chores. He found he could clean three or four pens while he fed the dogs if he dumped a pile of food on the cement. Something told him this was a bad idea, but it worked. At night the dogs seemed edgy but that was because the schedule had changed— no one slept in the kennel night after night, much less ran down the aisle and threw open their pen doors to let them race after tennis balls. The late-night training, he told himself, was excellent proofing practice.

It was past midnight on the fourth day when he finally stretched out on the bales and pulled the blankets over him. He'd turned out all the lights and settled himself beside Almondine when he heard his name spoken in a distinct, feminine voice. He sat up and listened. It had only been the squeak of the heater fan, he decided. A few minutes later, a thought began to nag at him: What if it hadn't been the heater fan at all? What if his mother was standing on the back porch, calling? He cast off his blanket and threw open the barn doors but all he saw was a barren yard and the porch standing dark and empty.

IN SOME WAYS, TRUDY THOUGHT, it would have been better if the antibiotics had made her downright sick. As it was, she lay in bed, chilled one moment, boiling the next. She was indifferent to food, though she forced herself to eat. On the third day she'd called Doctor Frost's office as promised, hoping she was saying what he wanted to hear. She was tired, she told him, but not feverish. She was sleeping a lot. That was normal, Frost said. She should beware of dehydration, be careful not to skip doses of the antibiotics. They talked briefly about Edgar. She told the doctor he showed no sign of a cough. Did she think she could drive into town at the end of the week? Was her cough still productive? And so on. She didn't mention that she grew sickeningly dizzy whenever she stood, or that she'd been so foggy-minded she'd forgotten his phone number twice while dialing. And she might have stretched the truth about the fever. But she kept focused long enough to maintain the conversation, which felt like a triumph.

Afterward she fell back into bed. Was it time for her next set of pills? Or had she taken them? One late afternoon had begun to look much like the next, but she was sure she had taken the pills before she called Frost. The antibiotics made her terribly sleepy. She recalled Edgar standing in the bedroom doorway, telling her that things were going smoothly in the kennel. He'd grown so serious since his father's death.

She rolled over. Sleep was the important thing. The way these things worked, tomorrow she would wake up on the other side of it. The fever would have broken, and she would sit up, read a bit, make some phone calls. Get on top of the paperwork.

She took the vial of pills from the dresser and shook them onto the blanket and counted them. It was surprising. So many left.

ON THE FIFTH EVENING, Edgar slipped into the house, checked on his mother, and ate dinner. After washing dishes, he and Almondine walked to the barn to do the chores, but when they got there, exhaustion settled on him like a lead blanket. The straw bales felt luxurious, the pillow soft as a cloud, and for the first night in a long time, there were no dreams. He awoke with Almondine breathing in his face. The windup alarm clock said two o'clock. He sat up and rubbed a hand across his face. There was something wrong with that. He hadn't done the evening chores.

He could get away with leaving everything else until morning, but he didn't like the idea of leaving the dogs without water, and as long as he was going to do that, he could feed them, too. He scooped a mound of kibble into the middle of the aisle and filled a bucket of water from the tap in the medicine room. When he threw open their doors, his litter bounded into the aisle, bumping his legs and dashing for the food. He'd piled up enough for *all* the dogs, not just three or four pens' worth, and he needed to get them out fast so that the first ones didn't gorge themselves and leave the last ones hungry. By the time he'd gone down the aisle, eighteen dogs were scrambling over the cement floor, jockeying for position. Edgar stepped into a pen and began to fill the water trough.

He never saw what started the fight. There was a yelp, and from the corner of his eye he saw a dog leap into the air. Finch. He dropped the pail of water and stepped into the aisle and that was all the time it took for him to realize the enormity of his mistake. *One dog in motion at a time*, his mother had said. It was one of many rules in the kennel, rules that didn't always make sense, or even seem important, until some situation drew the lesson out.

Finch landed and nosed his right hind leg and turned back to the mass of dogs, head lowered, grimacing nastily to show his teeth. He spun to face one of the older females, a dog named Epi, dominant in her litter, bigger than Finch, and not in the least fearful.

In all his life, Edgar had seen only one real dog fight. That had been broken up when his parents sprayed water on the antagonists, hauling them away by their tails. Later, his father said a person never, *ever* reached between fighting dogs. To make his point, he'd pulled up his sleeve and shown Edgar the puckered scar running along the axis of his forearm, jagged and shiny. A dog in a fight will bite before it realizes what it's doing, he'd said. It won't mean to hurt you, but it will see motion and react.

Some of the dogs were backing away from Finch and Epi, hackles raised. Edgar clapped his hands, grabbed two dogs, and hauled them into the nearest pen. Then another two. The noise had grown instantly deafening. He kenneled Tinder, Essay, and Pout. Baboo had already retreated to his run; Edgar shoved Opal and Umbra in after him and ran down the aisle wrestling dogs into their pens one after another and slinging shut the doors.

When he turned, only three dogs remained in the kennel aisle: Finch, Epi, and Almondine. Finch lay on his back. Epi stood over him, jaws buried in the fur at the base of his throat. On her muzzle there was a smear of red. Finch alternately lay limp and struggled to escape. A pace away, Almondine stood with her lips raised, growling, but the moment she stepped forward, Epi released Finch and lashed her muzzle toward Almondine, ears flattened. Almondine jerked her head away but stood her ground.

The important thing was to separate them. Edgar ran forward, coming at Epi from behind. He thought briefly of kicking her to force her away, but he'd have to kick *hard*, maybe hard enough to injure her, and he wouldn't do that. Anyway, he was too close and running too fast. When he reached Epi's hindquarters, he simply threw himself at her.

Later, he would try to understand it all from Epi's point of view. Someone had appeared over her shoulder. A dog's eyes are oriented along the axis of their muzzle, with less peripheral vision than a human being. Edgar intended to thread his fingers through her collar and pin her to the ground using the momentum of his fall, like his mother sometimes did when a dog refused to down. Done right, a dog would be flattened before it had time to resist. If you had enough surprise. If you used enough force. If you got a solid grip on its collar.

Edgar wound up with none of these.

Epi threw her body sideways until her hind feet skidded out on the smooth cement. She could have turned and fled, but her mind was geared toward engagement, and by the time Edgar rolled onto his side, she towered over him. All he could do was loop two fingers through her collar, but without his hands free, he couldn't issue a command, and Epi wouldn't have obeyed anyway.

If it was idiotic to step into a dogfight, it was suicidal to fall into one. He lay on his back, Epi's body suspended over him, all arcs of muscle and fur, and before he could move, she stepped back, arched her neck, and bit him.

In fact, she bit him twice, lightning fast. The first time, her teeth barely touched his skin, as if she were taking bearings, but the second time was for real and by then he was resigned to it, even felt she had the right. The surprise was that she restrained herself, suppressed the bite pressure that could have crushed the bones in his forearm, checked the upward jerk that could have sliced across tendon, muscle, and vein from wrist to elbow in a track just like his father's. Instead, a flicker of recognition appeared in her amber eyes. She was a good dog, just besieged and confused, and when the point of her canine tooth penetrated his arm, she froze.

Then Almondine's muzzle entered his field of vision from the right. She was taking no chances. Epi was younger and stronger, and if Almondine had ever been in a dogfight, it was so long past that Edgar could not recall it. But Almondine didn't want to fight. She wanted Epi *off* him, off her boy. She didn't bark or growl, she didn't try to bite Epi's neck or harry Epi into releasing Edgar's arm.

At that moment, Almondine had one idea: to blind Epi.

TRUDY SAT UP IN BED, annoyed and confused. In her dream, Gar had been on the television, talking to her, so it was terrible enough to wake up at all, and doubly bad when she understood that what had woken her was the dogs, barking and crying, every one of them. Her first thought was that an animal had gotten into the barn. This happened every so often, though God knew why, since the place surely reeked of dog. But once inside, the sounds either paralyzed the animal or drove it into a mindless panic. One time it had been a raccoon; another, unbelievably, a cat. The uproar that had ensued sounded alarmingly like what she now heard coming from the barn.

She tried to stand but lost her balance and began to cough. A yellow haze spread across her vision. Pain shot along her ribs. She sat down on the corner of the bed. The house was pitch dark. She tried calling to Edgar, but she couldn't raise her voice above a whisper. When she felt strong enough to stand again she made her way slowly to the bottom of the stairs.

"Edgar?" she said. "Edgar?"

She waited for a light to come on in his room, or for Almondine to appear. When neither happened, she walked up the stairs. At the top of the stairs, she paused for breath. His bedroom door was open. She walked to the doorway and turned on the overhead light.

The sheets had been carelessly pulled off, the pillow and blankets gone. She made her way down the stairs again, her movements slow and cautious. Something bad was happening in the barn. She pulled on a pair of slacks and a shirt over her nightgown, slipped her feet into unlaced boots, and opened the door.

EDGAR'S EYES WERE FIXED on the sight of Epi's jaws on his forearm, how his skin had rucked up around her canine tooth like a loose stocking. There was no blood yet, and no pain, only a pulling sensation in the skin of his arm.

And so, lying there on the floor, all he saw was a blur and then a gash opened near Epi's eye. Then Almondine's muzzle was stretched wide next to Epi's face and a sound came from her he'd never before heard from a dog—not a bark, but a *scream*, so raw and ferocious and bloody that, for all the baying and howling of the dogs until that moment, the kennel might as well have been silent.

Epi released his arm and scrambled backward. Before he could move, Almondine had straddled him and when he tried to sit up, she thumped him with her hip hard enough to knock him over, as if he were a pup. He had to scoot from beneath her to climb to his feet. Her pelt contracted when he touched her.

Epi had retreated to the front of the barn, alternately growling and nosing the door. A trail of black drops led across the cement. She pawed at her muzzle and shook her head. Edgar led Almondine to the medicine room and flashed his hands over her. She wasn't cut or bleeding. He stayed her, firmly, and turned to Finch. He led the dog to the center of the aisle where the light was brightest. He wouldn't take any weight on his left front foot. When Edgar tried to examine him, Finch jerked his leg away, but not before Edgar saw the gash near the dog's left elbow, and a flash of white through the dog's blood-matted coat. He ran his hands along Finch's muzzle and throat. His fingers came back wet, but not bloody.

Kennel up, he signed. Finch hobbled to his pen. Once the latch was closed, he turned to Epi, pacing near the front door. Whenever he made eye contact with her, she flattened her ears against her skull and lifted her hackles. Her cheek looked like it had been opened with a knife. The sight made his heart thud.

He'd knelt and begun to coax Epi forward when the door swung open and his mother stood illuminated against the night. Instantly, Epi bolted, forcing his mother to step back and grab the door to keep her balance. She watched Epi flee into the darkness, then turned to Edgar.

What are you *doing* here? he signed, frantically.

"What's going on?"

There was a problem. A fight.

"But it's the middle of the night. Your arm—are you hurt?"

He looked down. Blood was smeared across his shirtsleeve. He couldn't tell if it was his or Finch's. He pushed it flat against his side, hoping to conceal the gash on his forearm.

I don't think so. Not much. But Epi's face is cut. She's going to need stitches. Almondine bit her. Finch is lame. I can't tell how bad.

His mother teetered and corrected herself.

You shouldn't be outside, he signed. Go back to the house.

He tried to turn her around.

"Oh my God," she said. "Look at your arm."

Go back to the house. First let's do that.

"Edgar, I'm here already. I might as well stay."

No! Doctor Frost said you could end up in the hospital! He said you could *die!*

She started to respond, but a coughing fit doubled her over. When it passed, he steered her into the night. It wasn't especially cold for spring, but neither was it warm, and he wanted to get her to the house. Then he remembered Almondine. She sat near the medicine room, watching them from the aisle. He clapped his leg, but she wouldn't budge.

Come on, he signed. Come on! We don't have time to screw around.

She took a few steps forward, then faltered and sank to the cement.

He turned to his mother. Just go, he signed. Please.

Almondine was up again by the time he reached her, walking unsteadily toward the door. He hovered alongside.

What is it? he signed. What? What?

By the time he'd slung the kennel doors closed after her, she'd regained some equilibrium and she trotted behind his mother. He shooed them all up the porch steps. Once inside, Almondine lay down again, panting. He dropped to his knees beside her.

Something's wrong, he signed. She stumbled, back in the barn.

"Was she bitten?"

No. I checked.

He slid his hand under her belly and motioned her up. He lifted her feet and flexed her joints, watching for a wince. His mother made him describe Finch's injuries and Epi's; she didn't ask how any of it had happened, or how Almondine had been involved. She just looked at Edgar like he wasn't making sense.

We need to call someone, Edgar signed. He kicked the floor in frustration.

His mother began to talk through the options. "Page is in Florida until . . ." She glanced at the calendar on the wall. "It's what? Wednesday? He won't be back until next Monday."

I'm not talking about Doctor Papineau, he signed.

"There's no use calling that vet in Ashland. Not in the middle of the night. He'll never . . ."

But Edgar was shaking his head.

"Well, *what* then?" she said, annoyed. "If we can get them in the truck, I could drive . . ."

He lifted the telephone receiver and set it on the countertop.

Call Claude, he signed. Call him right now.

Epi's Stand

TRUDY SAT AT THE TABLE AND WATCHED EDGAR CLOSE THE kitchen door as he headed out again to find Epi. She'd made coffee, hoping it would clear her head, and a cup sat on the table issuing ribbons of steam. The overhead light starred and sparked in the periphery of her vision. She found it hard not to squint and would have walked to the switch to turn off the lights but she lacked the energy and possibly the balance.

Something had changed. It was difficult to gauge exactly what, but every movement ached. She could draw a deep breath, but when she exhaled there was a wheeze in her right lung, the sound transmitted through her flesh and bones. She shivered and sweated at the same time. *This is the sort of thing that made people believe in possession*, she thought. And she did feel inhabited, taken over, usurped by something blind and ferocious. What had Doctor Frost said about the antibiotics? How long before they took hold? The walls of the kitchen receded alarmingly. She felt a doubling, a sense of being inside her body and floating above herself at the same time.

She closed her eyes to shut it out. After a time, she jerked awake.

Just stay awake, she told herself. But the reason escaped her.

She stood. She made her way toward the bedroom, watching it all from above, her blue and shrunken hands reaching forward, gripping the counter, Almondine, lying on her side by the refrigerator, panting, the kitchen table with the now-cool cup of coffee, the feed store calendar with a picture of a farm hanging by the door. How oddly the veins crawled over the bones of her fingers. She was wearing an old flannel shirt of Gar's over her nightgown. Her hair stood out in a wild tangle.

When she reached the bedroom door she stopped to look at Almondine. She'd had some sort of spell in the barn, Edgar had said, but Almondine was fine. She lay there resting, showing none of the inward look of a dog in pain. She was just *old*. Edgar needed to start babying Almondine, stop expecting her to have the energy she'd had five years ago. Trudy thought of the very first night Almondine spent in that house, a bumbling ten-week-old. There'd been a thunderstorm, she remembered, and Almondine had whined half the night, frightened and lonely for her littermates. Now her muzzle had grayed and she couldn't stand up quickly after a long sleep. But her gaze was as steady and clear as it had ever been. That gaze was what had made them choose her out of all the other pups. Nowadays it seemed to take in more than Almondine could possibly express, and it gave her a sad, pensive look.

Trudy closed the bedroom door behind her. She dragged a twist of linen across her shoulders and lay back. Someone was coming. Page? No, Claude. There'd been a dogfight. She'd tried to get Edgar to explain as he maneuvered her back to the house, but he'd said he would explain later, and she lacked the strength to argue. More and more, he was his father's son, so certain he was right.

In the morning she would call Doctor Frost and tell him the antibiotics weren't working.

There was a chance he would want to send her to the hospital.

Perhaps she'd give it one more day.

CLAUDE ARRIVED IN A SNOUTY, mean-looking car with the letters *SS* overhanging the front grill. Impala, said the insignia on the blue scoop of its front fender. It was a twenty-minute drive from Mellen, and unless Claude had been ready to key the ignition the moment his mother called,

Edgar thought, he'd driven very fast. Claude brought the car to a halt near the barn, where Edgar stood waiting.

"Your mom said there was a fight?" Claude asked. The odor of beer and cigarettes clung to him like a halo.

Edgar handed across the note he had written in advance.

Epi is behind the barn. I can't get near her.

"Where is she hurt?"

He ran his finger along his eyebrow.

Claude cupped his hands in front of his mouth and shivered and looked up at the night sky. His breath whitened in the air. He walked past Edgar and into the barn. In the medicine room he rifled the cabinets. When he was finished, he turned back empty-handed.

"Is there still Prestone in the milk house?" he asked.

Edgar looked at him.

"You know, starter fluid. We used it in the tractor last fall. There was almost a full can back then. Go see how much is left."

Edgar ran to the milk house and pulled the chain on the ceiling bulb. He surveyed the tangle of rakes, shovels, and hoes tilting in the corner. Rototiller. Lawn mower. Chainsaw. He spotted a red-and-yellow aerosol near a row of oil cans on a shelf, grabbed it, and ducked out. Claude met him by the barn door with a collar and a training lead tucked under his arm, and a large plastic bag into which he was putting a rag from the medicine room, neatly folded into a square pad. Edgar handed over the Prestone.

"How much we got?" Claude shook the can. He clamped the bag around his wrist and pressed the nozzle against the rag. The bag puffed out with fog. "Ninety-nine percent ether," he said. He looked suddenly concerned. "You aren't smoking, are you?"

Edgar shook his head before he understood Claude wasn't serious.

"Good thing, too," he said. "Otherwise, there'd be a big flash and you'd be able to tell all your friends about your uncle Claude, the Human Torch."

When the hiss from the aerosol tapered off, Claude extracted his hand and held the bag up. The saturated rag slid greasily inside. He waved the arrangement under Edgar's nose. A sweet tang like sugar and gasoline swept through his sinuses. It made the hairs at the back of his neck crawl upright.

"At least it's cold tonight," Claude said, taking a cursory whiff of his own. "In the summer this would already be half gone. You might want to keep upwind anyway. This isn't exactly airtight."

Then Edgar led Claude behind the barn, quarter lit at best by the occluded yard light and the gooseneck lamp over the kennel doors. Epi heard them coming and backed up defensively until she stood in front of an unused old dog house near the silo. Drops of blood stained the snow around her.

"If we both come up she'll run," Claude said. He was carefully looking at a point on the ground a few feet in front of him. "Go around the other side of the silo."

Edgar hesitated.

"Get going," Claude said. "Before she decides to cut through that way."

Edgar turned and rounded the stony circumference, passing briefly back into the light before he reached the thick cement pier a foot high and three feet wide that connected the barn foundation to the silo. Through the gap he could see the dog house and the kennel runs beyond and the dogs standing in them, watching. Meltwater from the roof had rotted a line into the crystallized snowpack beneath the eaves.

Epi stood stock still, fixated on Claude. Edgar crouched on the cement pier, ready to intercept her if she bolted his way.

HOW IT GOT STARTED even Claude didn't remember. There must have been some first time in the kennel, some formative moment, when a pup had injured itself and backed into a corner, scared and defensive, and Claude had stepped past everyone to somehow enchant it, which was the only word for what he could do. He knew instinctively how to approach, how to touch, how to confuse and distract, so that, fearful or not, the dog found itself acquiescing. Maybe that first time had happened when he was very young. In any case, it was something he'd known how to do all of his life.

In high school, Claude began working afternoons and weekends at Doctor Papineau's shop. At first, it was odd jobs—clean up, repair, filing, walking the convalescent dogs. He liked the antiseptic smell of the place and the rows of prescription drugs on the shelves, like bottles of magic. When animals needed their dressings changed, he helped with that, too, asking many questions, which flattered the veterinarian, and seldom forgetting the answers, which impressed him. In time, Claude persuaded Doctor Papineau to let him assist on minor surgeries. The veterinarian showed him how to administer intramuscular injections of sedative, as well as the older skill—waning even then in veterinary practice—of the ether drip.

Occasionally, a dog came in wild with fright. Doctor Papineau had a noose pole for such situations, but people hated seeing it used, and Claude learned to work without it, crawling into the back of the truck—or wherever the frantic dog hid—and emerging with a docile animal and an empty syringe. He was bitten more than once, but they were fear bites, quick and shallow, and Claude had excellent reflexes. He became a masterful judge of how far a dog could be pushed. And eventually he craved the thrill of those moments more than anything.

On Sunday afternoons, when the shop was closed, Claude cleaned up and administered medications by himself; he knew where to call Doctor Papineau in case of an emergency. And if, on those Sundays, a dog was boarded that Claude had taken a dislike to, when he was done with his work he let it out to run the halls. Then he jimmied Doctor Papineau's desk for the key to the pharmacy room, prepared whichever method of sedation most interested him that day, and began to search. Once the dog was unconscious, he carried it to its pen and checked his watch. Both methods had their uses, he decided, but he was faster and more adept with the needle.

Though not perfect. Doctor Papineau attributed the first dog's death to post-surgical trauma. The second dog, however, puzzled the veterinarian. He'd questioned Claude for a long time about the dog's condition that Sunday. The session had left Claude shaken, and after that, there were no more incidents at the shop.

Late night, autumn 1947. Claude was leaning against the wall at the back of a long-abandoned barn, watching the crowd, all men, disperse into the cool night. A few of the men led dogs muzzled and close-leashed against their thighs. A few more stood cocooned in silence and disappointment. A man counted out money into another's hand. The rough-shod plywood ring had been dismantled already and under the light of two white gas lanterns someone was pitching water across the boards to rinse the blood away. Outside, bitter laughter, black undercurrent of animosity. An argument followed, quickly shouted down.

Then Gar appeared, shouldering his way inside. He blinked at the glare of the lanterns. He was about to leave when he spotted Claude and walked over, glowering.

"Come on," he said. "We're leaving."

"I got myself here. I can get myself home."

"If you leave the house with me, you're damn well going to walk back in with me. The only thing I want to know right now is whether any of our dogs were here."

"No."

"Tell me which dogs."

"I said no. Why do you think I'm here, anyway?"

"I don't know why you're here. That's what we're going to talk about after we leave."

Then a man trotted into the barn. "Hey, Doc," he called, waving Claude forward. Gar looked at Claude and then at the men cleaning the plywood. Claude had kicked the satchel behind him when his brother walked in, but Gar spotted it anyway. He picked it up. He looked at the initials embossed on the top. Then he opened it and looked inside.

"You're kidding me," he said. "You patch them up afterward? Is that the idea?"

The man called again, this time more urgently. Claude started to take the satchel, but Gar pushed him back against the beam.

"Wait here," he said. He walked over to the man. Claude couldn't hear the conversation but he saw Gar shaking his head. The man cradled his arm in front of him and pointed off somewhere. Gar shook his head again. Finally he turned and motioned to Claude and the three of them walked out of the barn, Claude carrying the satchel. Out on the road, motors started and tires rolled over gravel and the beams of headlights swung cross-eyed through the trees. Claude could see the bite punctures in the corded muscles of the man's forearm.

A shaggy shepherd cross with a stocky build and a blunt muzzle was chained to a tree near the road. As they approached, the dog hobbled to its feet and began to bay, one bloody hind leg held off the ground.

"Knock it off!" the man shouted.

The dog licked its chops and limped forward. The owner sidled up to it, but the moment he tried to slip an arm under its flanks, the animal set his muzzle beside the man's ear. Even from where Claude stood, the baleful rumble in the dog's throat was unmistakable.

"See?" the man said, backing away. "He was okay when we first got out here. Now I can't get him in the truck."

Gar looked at Claude. "You can tranquilize him?"

Claude nodded.

Gar guided the man back a few paces. Claude set the satchel on the ground and opened the jawed top and pulled out a bottle and a syringe. He drew fluid into the syringe. Then he walked to a point just beyond the reach of the dog's chain and whistled a warbly double-tone—*tweee, tweee.*

The dog tipped its head, curious.

NOW, IN THE DARK behind the barn, Claude had turned sideways to Epi. He kept his gaze averted, elbows pressed to his sides, knees bent, trying to minimize his profile as he crabbed toward her with a slow side shuffle. He was mumbling a monotone stream of nonsense, the words an endless, senseless flow of noise. "Say, honey," he said. "Such a good girl. Goodness gracious. Such a sweetie pie." He held the plastic bag crumpled against his far hip, and something metallic glinted in his hand. He moved a foot closer, then paused, his delay just long enough that he seemed to be drifting pointlessly inward, every gesture slight and contained and almost accidental so that he hardly seemed to be moving at all, never a direct glance, never a raised voice, but closer, always closer, and always the steady meaningless patter.

Epi retreated toward the empty dog house, looking wide-eyed across her flank. She knew she was trapped, and she turned to look at Edgar. He thought she might decide to come to him, but the howls and the flashing teeth and the desire to flee overwhelmed all else in her mind and she froze. Edgar raised his hand to sign a down. She saw him and turned back to Claude and lowered her head miserably, mouth closed up, ears flattened. The gash on her face was black and wet and she dragged a paw across the cut and sank to the cold snow and tucked her feet up tight beneath her. She sized up ways past Claude. When he was three small side steps away from her, she retreated into the dog house and, shortly, a low growl emanated from inside.

Claude opened the plastic bag. Fumes wavered toward the ground. He pitched the soaked rag far back into the doghouse and quickly turned and sealed the door with his jacketed back.

"Wait," he said to Edgar. He'd stopped the patter and all was quiet. Inside the dog house there was a panicky clomping as Epi positioned herself between the rags and the door. Claude sat looking downfield. A long time passed. Finally, he rose and stepped back.

"Come on, girl," he said. "Come on out."

Epi's muzzle appeared. She blinked and stepped into the night. She tottered and growled uncertainly. Claude closed the distance between them in two quick steps and cuffed her under the chin with his left hand and stepped back. Her jaws snapped shut hollowly.

"None of that," he said.

In her confusion—compounded by the night's events and the ether fumes and now this lightning strike from Claude—Epi let her topline soften and her tail uncurl. For a moment all defiance left her, as if she were letting herself be taken down finally and forever in some fight that still carried on in her mind. Then Claude's arm was looped over her back, his hand against her belly. She flashed her muzzle back at him in surprise, but he already had the needle between her shoulder blades, talking again, low and quiet, and he stayed there even after he'd tossed the syringe away, stroking her and waiting.

"Okay, honey," he said. "Edgar, keep still. If you spook her, I'm the one she'll bite. Time to lie down and rest, sweetie. Been a long night. Such a good girl."

He ran his hand down Epi's back. She sagged and folded herself against the ground and a shudder passed through her.

"Bring that lead over," Claude said. "Slow."

Then: "Put it on her."

"Okay," he said. "Let's find out what we've got here." Claude knelt and slipped one arm under Epi's brisket and the other under her flanks and she came up in his arms, the whites of her eyes showing and her body lax. They rounded the silo and Claude waited under the metal-hooded flood lamp while Edgar fumbled with the door latch.

"There's a bag in the car," Claude said, walking into the kennel. "Front seat. Go get it."

Claude was in the medicine room when Edgar returned. Epi lay stretched out on the examination table, limp but awake, keening feebly as Claude shaved the side of her face with the electric clippers. He stopped periodically to pour antiseptic over the pink skin he'd exposed, flushing loose hairs from her wound. Beneath the velvet fur her skin was freckled. The brown liquid streamed down the fur of her neck and puddled on the table.

Edgar set the weathered satchel he carried near the wall. The initials *PP* were embossed along its top, the curves and arches of the letters abraded over time into a pale felt. Claude laid the clippers aside and rummaged through the bag, producing black suture thread and a needle, both of which he doused with antiseptic. The wound was smaller than Edgar expected, opening just below Epi's eye and ending near the corner of her mouth. Whenever Claude applied pressure, blood seeped from the ragged edges of the laceration and the sight made yellow rings jitter at the edge of Edgar's vision.

You made this happen, he thought. Stop it. Pay attention.

He clenched his hands until they ached, and watched. Twice, Claude dropped the needle into Epi's fur while placing stitches. He cursed under his breath and re-rinsed it with antiseptic.

"Is there another dog hurt?"

Edgar nodded.

"Look in that bag for a bottle of pills marked 'Valium.'"

The bag sat jawed open on the floor. Edgar pulled out bottles and examined them then turned and held one out for Claude to see.

"That's the one. Give it two of those and wait for me."

Claude returned to his suturing. Edgar shook out the pills and walked to Finch's pen. The dog met him, hobbling gamely on three legs. By the time Claude carried Epi out of the medicine room and settled her in her pen, with her head cushioned by a pair of towels, Finch had relaxed into sleep.

The stitches in Epi's face were neat and black and even. Edgar counted twelve, top to bottom. Claude had smeared a glistening salve over the wound. Edgar dipped three fingers into the water dish and let the drops fall on Epi's tongue and listened to the pop and hum of the clippers. By the time Claude carried Finch out, Epi had come awake enough to lift her head and watch. She tried to climb to her feet, but Edgar ran his hand along her back and guided her down again.

Courtship

IN THE HOUSE, CLAUDE WALKED ACROSS THE KITCHEN AND knocked at the closed bedroom door, coat bunched in his hand. Edgar knelt and stroked Almondine's muzzle.

What happened tonight? he signed. Why couldn't you stand?

She dug her nose along his arm and legs, scenting him to divine what had happened after he left the house. Her eyes were bright. She searched his face. When he was satisfied she was okay, he stood and walked to the bedroom door, where Claude was still waiting.

"Trudy?" Claude said, knocking a second time.

The door swung back. Edgar's mother stood there holding the jamb for balance. Her hair was matted with sweat, her eyes set in hollowed circles above chalk-white cheekbones. Claude drew a quick breath at the sight of her.

"Christ, Trudy," he said. "You need a doctor."

She turned and sat on the bed. She looked past Claude as if his presence hadn't registered.

"Edgar?" she said. "Is Epi okay? What time is it?"

Before Edgar could sign an answer, Claude said, "She had a cut near her eye, but it wasn't deep. Finch is going to be limping for a few days, that's all. They looked worse than they actually were."

Edgar's mother nodded.

"Thank you, Gar. You're right, I don't think these antibiotics are working," she said. "Could you drive me to see Doctor Frost?"

They stood in silence for a moment. At first Trudy didn't recognize her mistake but Claude's posture straightened as if he'd laid a hand on some low-voltage wire. Something like embarrassment and fear and another feeling he couldn't name made Edgar's face flush.

"Yes," Claude said. "I can do that."

Trudy passed her hand in front of her face as if clearing cobwebs.

"*Claude*, I mean," she said. "*Claude*. I'm going to lie back down. Wake me at eight, would you? Then I'll call and make an appointment."

"Not a chance," Claude said. "We're going now."

"But he won't even be in his office for another hour and a half."

"He will be after I call him," Claude said.

She insisted Edgar stay behind, that he not get near her. Reluctantly, he agreed to stay and watch Epi and Finch and Almondine. Claude backed his car up the driveway and headed toward town with Edgar's mother huddled against the passenger-side door.

Edgar dragged himself through morning chores, lining the pens with the straw bales he'd slept on before the fight. He checked on the pups in the whelping room and weighed them for the log sheets and sat in the straw in the corner of their pen and dozed. The pups mustered the courage to mount an attack. He brushed them aside, but they charged again, biting his fingers and shoes and the belt loops on his jeans, and then he pushed himself up and went to Epi's pen.

LATER, HE WOULD BLAME himself for not seeing what would happen, as if he could have prevented it, but during the weeks that followed, his preoccupation was above all with his mother's health and the mending of the injured dogs. He cleansed and salved Epi's sutures every morning, and held warm compresses in place until they had cooled in his hands, leaving for school with his fingers stained brown from antiseptic. Her fur began to grow in, but she was distrustful and skittish. Finch's leg healed quickly. Most important of all, Almondine's spell in the kennel was not repeated.

But lying in bed, Edgar would reenact the events of that night, changing the smallest action to stop everything from unraveling.

If I had let fewer dogs out . . .

If I hadn't fallen asleep . . .

If I had fed them the right way . . .

Sometimes he worked himself all the way back to *If she hadn't gotten sick . . . If I could have made a sound . . . If he hadn't died . . .*

The future, when he thought about it at all, held little threat and little promise. When the Impala returned that afternoon, and his mother emerged on steadier feet, new prescription in hand, he thought all their mistakes had finally been made. She needed to recover. His father had died in January; it was only the end of May. They needed to stick to the routine they'd established during the intervening months. In that way, their life would return to its original shape, like a spring stretched in bad times but contracting eventually into happiness. That the world could come permanently unsprung never occurred to him. And so, for the longest time, he was oblivious to what was happening, for where his mother was concerned, some things seemed no more possible than if she might suddenly fly through the air.

THE PACE OF WORK hadn't slackened. The pups came first, then the food, the water, the cleaning, the meds. The rest of their time was devoted to training. While his mother was still recovering, Claude arrived in the morning, unloaded supplies, and helped with chores. Edgar walked Finch up and down the aisle so he could judge the dog's recovery. Afterward, Claude stayed only long enough for a cup of coffee, drinking it standing up, with his jacket on; Edgar's mother talked to Claude about what needed to be done in the kennel, as though they had come to some agreement about his helping out. Then he set his coffee down and walked to his car.

After she was back on her feet, Claude stopped appearing in the mornings. Since he wasn't there when Edgar boarded the school bus, there was no reason to believe he'd been there at all, until one afternoon he came across a pile of white soap shavings on the porch steps. Claude came for dinner the next evening. The moment he entered, Edgar's mother's movements grew slower, more languid. And when the conversation turned to Epi and Finch, Edgar understood that Claude had been out to the kennel many times since Edgar had last seen him, including that day. By then, nearly a month had passed.

After dinner, Edgar went upstairs. He listened to their footsteps, their murmured talk not quite covered by the noise of the television. Her words filtered up to him lying in his bed.

"Oh, Claude. What are we going to do?"

Her question ended with a sigh.

Edgar rolled over and waited for sleep. Listening and not listening.

If she hadn't been gone that day . . .

If I hadn't been in the mow . . .

If I'd been able to speak . . .

Sometime in the night, the Impala started with a throaty rumble. In the morning, when Edgar stood beside his bed, fiery spikes radiated from the center of his chest.

IT WAS WARM NOW, at least on some nights. One evening he walked out onto the porch and straddled an old kitchen chair to watch the sun set. Days of sunshine had melted the snow in the field, and a brief rain had rinsed everything clean. Almondine found a spot on the old rug and began chewing a bone, her mouth propped open against the hollow end. Shortly, the kitchen door opened and his mother's hands came to rest on his shoulders. They listened to the water drip from the trees.

"I like that sound," she said, "I used to sit here and listen to water run off the roof like that before you were born."

I know, he signed. You're very old.

He felt rather than heard her laugh. She dug her fingers lightly into his shoulders. "This is the time of year your father found that wolf pup. Do you remember us telling you about that?"

Parts of it.

"See those aspens down there?" She reached over his shoulder, and he closed an eye and sighted along her arm at a stand of trees occupying the lower corner of the field. "When he came up from the woods that day, those were only saplings. You could wrap your fingers around the trunks of most of them. They'd just begun to leaf out. I happened to be looking there when your father came through. It was the most amazing thing—he just *shimmered* into place, walking so slow and cautious. At first I thought he'd hurt himself. It made the hairs on the back of my neck stand up to see it."

Because you thought he was hurt? Or because of how it looked?

"Both, I suppose. I should have known he was carrying a pup right away. He was walking the same way he carried a newborn in the kennel."

With his shoulders hunched.

"Yes. But from a distance, I didn't recognize it."

The sound of her voice was pleasant, and Edgar felt like listening, and he supposed she felt like talking. He'd heard bits and pieces of the story as far back as he could remember, but now she told him about the miscarriages that preceded it, the final trip to the hospital, the figures in the rain. By the time she finished, the aspens at the back of the field had dissolved into the gloaming.

Did you ever name the baby?

"No," she said, at length.

Suppose it had lived.

His mother took a deep breath.

"I think I know what you're getting at, Edgar. Please don't ask me to compare different kinds of grief. What I'm trying to tell you is that after the miscarriage, I lost myself for a while. Time passed that I don't remember much about. I can't explain what it was like, exactly, but I remember feeling angry that I'd never had a chance to know that baby before he died, not even for one minute. And I remember thinking I'd found a place where none of it had happened, where I could just rest and sleep."

He nodded. He recalled how, waiting in the barn beside his father that day, something had blossomed before his eyes when he closed them, something dark and forever inward-turning. He recalled how after a time he had found himself walking along a road, how the one Edgar had stayed with his father and the other had kept walking, how all around the road was pitch dark and how rain was falling on him and gently drenching him. And he remembered thinking that as long as he stayed on the road he was safe.

"Do you want to know why that hasn't happened to me now?" she said.

Why?

"Because I *did* have a chance to know your father. It's so unfair he died that I could scream, but I was lucky enough to know him for almost twenty years. That's not enough. I could never have known him enough, not if we both lived to be a hundred. But it is something, and that makes a difference to me." She paused again. "What happened to your father isn't your fault, Edgar."

I know.

"No, Edgar, you *don't* know. Do you think I can't read you? Do you think I can't *see?* You think just because you don't make a sign for something it isn't written all over your body? In how you stand and walk? Do you know you're hitting yourself in your sleep? Why are you doing that?"

It took a moment to sink in. When he stood, the chair clattered to the floor behind him.

What do you mean?

"Unbutton your shirt."

He tried to walk away, but she laid a hand on his shoulder. "Do it, Edgar. Please."

He unfastened the line of buttons and let his shirt fall open. A bruise, mottled with sickly blue and green, covered the center of his chest.

Somewhere, an icy tuning fork struck a bar of silver and rang and rang. He walked to the bathroom and stood before the mirror and pressed a fingertip into the bruise. An ache pulsed outward along his ribs.

How long had he been waking with that feeling of an anvil having been dropped on his chest? A week? A month?

"What is that?" Trudy said, when he walked into the kitchen. "God-*damn* it, Edgar. What's going on with you? You're so closed up around your sadness you've left me here alone. You can't do that. You can't shut me out. As if you're the only one who lost someone." She put her hands on his shoulders. "In the mornings when you walk into the kitchen, I'll see you out of the corner of my eye and think you're *him*—"

That's crazy. I don't look anything like him.

"Yes you *do*, Edgar. You *move* like him. You *walk* like him. I've watched you in the whelping room and you even carry the pups like him, just the way you described, with your shoulders hunched up, taking those careful steps. Do you realize that there are times when I need to leave the house, when it's just you and me, because I look at you and I feel like he isn't gone? I come back from the barn some nights and I can't help myself. I go up to your room to watch you. It's the only time you let me near. It's the only way I can get close. To you or him."

I'm not him. I'm not half who he was.

Then a wrack of shivers ran through him. He pushed past Trudy onto the porch, buttoning his shirt. There was something else he'd wanted to say, but discovering the bruise on his chest had swept everything else from his mind.

"Edgar, I know what it's like to disappear into bad feelings. I know how tempting it is. You think by going further into it you'll finally come out the other side and everything will be okay, but it doesn't work that way. You need to *talk* to me. I can't shake the feeling you haven't told me everything that happened."

I *did*. I told you. I came down from the mow and *there he was*. I had to wait for someone to show up.

"The handset on the phone was shattered."

I got mad and hit it on the countertop. I told you that.

"What else, Edgar? What else happened?"

Nothing!

"Then what is *that*?" she said, pointing at his chest.

I don't know! I must have fallen against something. I just don't remember.

"Edgar, I've watched you do it in your sleep. You're hitting your chest. You're trying to sign something. What is it?"

He couldn't reply, paralyzed by the memory of throwing his fist against his body. Every time he thought of it he almost shook with the blow. He stood on the porch, his ragged exhalation matching hers, until at last he remembered what he'd wanted to say.

Claude isn't like him, either.

Now it was his mother's turn to be silent. She looked past him into the field and sighed. "After that last miscarriage, I wanted to have an operation to make it impossible for me to get pregnant. I liked that idea—that way I could be sure I'd never feel that bad ever again. But your father said I was only imagining the worst case. One more time, he said. Not because it won't be terrible if it happens again, but because it will be wonderful if it doesn't. And he was *right*, Edgar. The next time, we had *you*. I can't imagine what our lives would have been like if your father hadn't believed so strongly in fresh starts."

He turned and stared out into the night.

"Edgar, there's a difference between missing him and wanting nothing to change," she said. "They aren't the same things at all. And we can't do anything about either one. Things always change. Things would be changing right now if your father were alive, Edgar. That's just life. You can fight it or you accept it. The only difference is, if you accept it, you get to do other things. If you fight it, you're stuck in the same spot forever. Does that make sense?"

But aren't some changes worth fighting?

"You know that's true."

So how do you know which is which?

"I don't know a way to tell for sure," she said. "You ask, 'Why am I really fighting this?' If the answer is 'Because I'm scared of what things will be like,' then, most times, you're fighting for the wrong reason."

And if that's not the answer?

"Then you dig in your heels and you fight and fight and fight. But you have to be absolutely sure you can handle a different kind of change, because in the end, things will change anyway, just not *that* way. In fact, if you get into a fight like that, it pretty much guarantees things are going to change."

He nodded. He knew she was right but he hated what she said. A person could stop a specific thing, but they couldn't stop change in general. Rivers can't run backward. Yet, he felt there must be an alternative, neither willfulness nor resignation. He couldn't put words to it. All he knew was, neither of them had changed their minds and neither of them could find anything more to say. He stood there until his mother turned and went into the kitchen, then he pushed open the porch door and walked to the barn.

THERE WAS PLENTY OF binder twine lying around the mow. With a little trial and error, he fashioned a double loop and a tail that he could knot around the bed frame. The thing was easily hidden beneath the blankets, and if she walked in at night, she wouldn't see it. He passed his wrists through the rabbit ears. All it took was a twist to keep them from slipping free while he slept.

Late at night, the rotary dial on the telephone resonated through the walls, the rip of a digit rolled clockwise, the grind of the dial working backward, loud enough to wake him. Whatever part of her conversation wasn't captured by the handset rode on air currents through that old house, a gray smoke so fine it drifted up the stairs and through the furnace registers, and wherever it brushed a wall, or a curtain, or a lightbulb, it crumbled into a dust that settled over everything.

In the mornings, he tucked the twine into the toe of an old tennis shoe and looked at his chest in the mirror.

It worked surprisingly well.

THE FIRST THUNDERSTORM OF spring came through in the middle of a night, lightning flashing through the sky and thunder rattling the glass in the windows. In the morning, the storm had lapsed into a ceaseless, undramatic rain. Slow, even sheets of water that paused for a minute or an hour, but soon enough returned, along with the splash of water running off the eaves. After two days, the basement began flooding. It was no surprise, and no emergency, either. The legs of the tables had long been set in coffee cans. Edgar watched the water seep through the rocks Schultz had set in the basement walls. The float rose in the sump pit twice an hour and the lights flickered as the motor engaged. Then a thump as the column of water hit the elbow in the vent pipe.

Outside, the world became a riot of vegetable odors, boggy and florid—the waft of old hay, tamarack, algae, moss, sweet sap and rotted leaves, iron and copper and worms—a musky yawn that hung in the yard.

FOR TWO NIGHTS IN a row the dogs woke him.

They'd begun leaving the run doors up at night and the dogs slept with their muzzles propped across the wooden thresholds. From his bedroom window he could make out their black noses and shining eyes. The first night he ignored their barks and rolled over and covered his head with his pillow, but the second night he detected a kind of fervor in their tone that drew him fully awake. He picked out the voices of Essay and Opal over the drumming of falling rain. He and Almondine knelt at the window. The dogs were standing wet in their runs, tails slashing happily behind them.

Deer in the orchard, he thought. Or a raccoon.

He went to the spare bedroom, where the window faced the orchard and the road. There was nothing to see. By the time he'd walked back to his room, the dogs were silent again. It occurred to him that the dogs might have seen Forte, and that idea cheered him. The stray seemed just contrary enough to come back after wintering with some adopted family.

Edgar lay awake in his bed, hoping now the dogs would start up again. Or that he would hear Forte's howl. With his attention so pitched, he began half hearing a voice—the voice he'd heard in the barn when he'd slept there. The voice he'd heard (now he remembered) the night before. Always intertwined with some other sound. He heard his name cried as the bedsprings creaked; a wordless call in a gust of wind against the windowpane. He sat up and pulled books off the shelves, running his eyes over the letters like so many scribbles, until the sky lightened outside his window.

At breakfast he waited for his mother to mention the barking.

Did the dogs wake you last night? he asked, finally.

"No. Were they barking?"

A lot.

"That's okay," she said. "They get restless with the thaw."

By the time he'd finished evening chores that next day he was so tired he staggered up the stairs and fell into bed. It was pitch dark when the sound of his name woke him. This time it had come through the splash of rain in the gutters. He sat up in bed, arms folded, listening. In a minute, the dogs began again. He slipped out of bed without turning on the light, raised the sash, and craned his head out. Everywhere, rain was falling. Directly below his window, Claude's Impala sat parked in the driveway.

In each pen, a dog stood, baying.

He slipped on his jeans and shirt and haphazardly tied his shoes. He crept down the stairs, hand on Almondine's back to slow her. His mother's bedroom was dark. The clock in the kitchen read one thirty.

He knelt before Almondine.

You have to stay. I don't want you getting wet.

He opened the porch door and leaned out. A breeze tousled his hair. There was no lightning, no thunder, just the steady whisper of warm rain, like the murmur of the creek—the sound that had once made Almondine pounce on the snow-covered creek as if something hid there. Silvery sheets of water poured into the gutters around their roof.

Near the door was a light switch. When he flipped it, the goosenecked flood lamp over the barn doors came on, casting a cone of light across the rough planks of the double doors. He half-expected to see a woodchuck or a fox scurrying off but there was only the glint of rain dropping into the light. And yet the dogs kept barking with such a strange mixture of alarm and recognition, wet and shining as they looked into the yard. A flicker danced in the rain before them and was gone. Edgar was about to turn back inside when something caught his attention near the barn door. When he looked closer, there was just rain.

Then, abruptly, the dogs fell silent. They braced themselves four-footed and shook off and one by one trotted to the portals at the back of their runs, where they pushed through the canvas flaps and disappeared.

Whatever was making them bark, Edgar thought, had to be inside the kennel. He was never going to find out what it was standing on the porch. He turned to Almondine one last time and knelt to quiet her. Then he stepped into the rain and began to cross the yard.

In the Rain

HE WAS DRENCHED BEFORE HE REACHED THE CORNER OF THE house. The same rain, warm on his hand, now soaked through his shirt and jeans, chilling him, but it was pointless to go back for a coat. He walked to the Impala and pressed his hand against the hood. The engine was cold as a stone.

He stepped onto the weed-covered hump in the center of the driveway, muddy streams on either side of him. In the pale glow of the yard light, the freshly greened grass looked greasy black. The two tall pines stood shivering like sentries, water cascading down branch by branch. But there were no deer, no streak of red that would be a fox, no shining eyes of a raccoon. He turned and walked to the deserted runs, wiping a streaming hand over his face.

From one of the small doorways, a dog's head and shoulders emerged— Essay, watching him approach, half in and half out. When he squatted down and pushed his fingers through the wire mesh, she bucked along down the run, stepped into his shadow, and licked his fingers, blinking at the rain. Her posture conveyed curiosity without anxiety, anticipation but not fear.

What's going on out here? he signed. Where would you go if I opened this door? What would you chase?

Essay waved her tail and met his gaze as though turning the question back on him. He pulled himself upright along the timber of the door. The waterlogged wood of the frame creaked. He turned to look behind him to see what the dogs might have seen.

The yard light, high atop the pole in the orchard, cast its globe of yellow. The earth mounded away from him, passing beneath the trees of the orchard and leveling near the road. The house sat at the edge of the light, bright along the driveway side, dim where it faced the garden. The shadows of the apple trees lay stretched across the grass. The forest across the road, an undulating scrim of gray. High in the air, raindrops descended into the light, curtained by the breeze into willow shapes that swayed across the yard and back into the night.

When Edgar glanced back, Essay had retreated into the barn and a line of glittering eyes watched him from the canvas flaps. He rounded the milk house and walked through the cone of light beneath the floodlight over the barn doors. When he reached the silo, he tried to look out over the field to the west, but his eyes were dazzled and the dark began just a few yards beyond. He stared into the blackness toward the back runs and saw nothing, just the side of the silo sliding off into the dark and the silhouette of the broad roof. After a moment he turned back to the barn.

And for the second time that night something moved in front of the double doors. It took a moment to make sense of it. A change in the falling of the rain. Something about the way it fell. He stepped forward to look more closely, traced a single drop of water as it passed into the light. Just above his head, the raindrop paused, wobbling in midair like a transparent pearl, and began to fall again. It splashed into the puddle at his feet. He wiped his face and looked up. Another raindrop had taken its place, and then *that* one fell, to be replaced by another, and another. Nothing he could see held them in the air, yet each one hovered for a tick of time, then continued to the ground. He watched it happen a dozen times or more. Despite himself, he reached out to touch the spot, then hesitated at the last moment.

He stepped back and saw the same thing was happening all up and down the space in front of him: hundreds of raindrops—thousands—suspended for a heartbeat in the lamplight. He caught a glimpse of something, then lost it. He squeezed his eyes shut. It was like watching the orchard, trying to catch everything motionless for one instant. When he opened his eyes again, the way to see them all together had clicked into place.

Instead of raindrops, he saw a man.

His head, his torso. Arms held away from his body. All formed by raindrops suspended and instantly replaced. Near the ground, the figure's legs frayed into tattered blue-gray sprays of water. When a gust of wind passed through the yard, the shape flickered and the branches of the apple trees twisted behind it, refracted as through melted glass.

Edgar shook his head and turned away. An endless cascade of raindrops struck his arms and neck and face. The same breeze that shimmered the figure caressed his skin, carrying a swampy, marshy smell. There was the scent of the kennel, and of the water itself.

Suddenly he needed to touch something, something too solid to exist in a dream. He stumbled to the barn. He ran his palm against the planks of siding. A wood sliver snagged his skin and slid into the flesh at the base of his thumb. The pain was brief and hot and unquestionably real.

He glanced around. The figure in the rain had turned to watch.

He attended once more to the barn, his examination now minute and frantic. He traced the rusted iron door hinge with his fingertips, and the jagged crevices between the boards, where the shadows were as sharp as the line dividing the moon. He knew if he waited long enough he would see crazy things—fantastic, inexplicable, dreamlike things—but everywhere he looked he found the ordinary stuff of the world. Painted wood. Pitted iron. Water falling earthward from his face, each droplet's path so foreshortened it seemed motionless and shrinking until it struck the ground. He shut his eyes and listened to his breath blowing.

When he turned, rain fell evenly through the light. He was alone. He looked about, then spotted the figure standing near the corner of the milk house. Having once learned the trick, Edgar could not unsee him.

The figure gestured. His legs blurred into skirts of rain and then he disappeared from view. The dogs began to bark.

Edgar found him standing in front of the pens. All the dogs were out, peering forward, unafraid, excited recognition in their voices. Their tails jerked back and forth, throwing sprays of water. The figure turned to him and his arms moved in sign. Trails of water fell through the air. The distance and the figure's indistinct form made it difficult to read.

Edgar stepped forward. The figure repeated the sign.

Release a dog.

Edgar blinked in the rain.

Why?

You think I'm not real. Open a pen.

Edgar walked to Essay's pen. He flipped up the latch and linked his fingers through the wire mesh and pulled the door open. Essay bounded out at once. She dropped her nose to the ground at the spot where the figure had stood and slid a paw along the grass. She looked at Edgar and then into the yard. Her tail swung happily behind her. The figure gestured a recall, but Essay was already closing the distance at a trot. When she arrived she circled several times, her shape contorting as she passed behind and finished on his left in a sit. The figure stepped forward, a water-shimmer, and turned and signaled a down. Essay dropped onto the wet grass at once. The figure bent down and passed his hand across the side of her face. A stream of water coursed along her already soaked cheek and she panted happily and pulled her lips back in a grin of pleasure and lapped at the figure's hand. Her tongue passed through a stream of water. She closed her mouth reflexively and swallowed and began to pant again.

The figure looked back toward the barn and signaled a broad sit and in unison all seven dogs behind Edgar sat. Then he signaled a release. One by one they stood. They trotted back into the barn. A moment later the canvas flaps parted and seven muzzles appeared.

You see?

At last, the figure signaled Essay to kennel. She trotted to her pen and disappeared into the barn. Before Edgar had latched the door behind her, she had joined the other dogs looking out at them.

He turned back to the rain.

Edgar.

What—what are you doing here?

Don't you recognize me?

I don't want to say. I'm not sure. I might.

How many times have we stood here and looked back at the house together? How many times have we counted the deer in the field from here? How many times did I lift you into the branches of those trees to pick an apple? Look at me Edgar. What do you see?

I don't know.

What do you see?

I know why you're here. I'm so sorry. I tried so hard.

You think you might have saved me.

I couldn't think of what to do. I tried everything.

I would have died anyway.

No. I couldn't tell them. There could have been doctors.

They would have done nothing.

But I was there. I made it *worse!*

The rain-figure bowed his head. A space of perhaps three feet separated them. After a moment the figure looked up and stepped forward and began to raise his hands as if to embrace him.

Edgar couldn't help himself. He stepped back. Instantly, a wave of remorse washed through him.

I'm sorry, he signed. I didn't mean that.

You didn't understand what you were seeing that day.

The figure turned and melted away toward the front of the barn, then rounded the corner of the old milk house. After a moment Edgar followed. He stood before the barn doors. Under the floodlight, his sign was easy to read.

Go inside. Now. Before the rain stops.

And do what?

Search.

For what?

What he lost. What he thinks is lost forever.

Then the figure stepped away from the door. Edgar tipped the old iron bar away and turned the latch handle. Inside, it was dark but dry and the cessation of rain shocked him. He looked out the door, but it was only rain falling again. None of the dogs barked, though a few stood watching from their pens.

He pushed the workshop door open and froze, unable to cross the threshold at first. He reached inside and flipped up the light switch and surveyed the room: workbench to the left, the pegboard covered with tools mounted on the wall above it. Vise twisted open halfway. Except for the filing cabinets, they had barely touched any of it that winter, and a velvet hoar of straw dust lay over the bench. Across from him, the mow stairs led upward, and in front of them, shelves filled with cans of paint and creosote, their labels stained with drips and runners.

He took a breath and stepped inside. He took the paint cans off the shelf and stacked them on the workbench. Though the rest of the workshop was covered in dust, the paint cans were not; only a thin powder covered them, as though they had been recently moved. When he finished, only a pile of old brushes and rollers remained, stacked haphazardly at one end of the shelf, and these he put on the workbench, too.

Beneath the shelves, on the floor, sat the two enormous cans of scrap his father had been trying to move that day, brimming with bent nails, stripped screws, spare machine parts, the iron rusted to a dark brown, the steel parts dull gray. He crouched and tried to tip the nearest one out from the wall. After the third or fourth heave, the welded metal handle snapped off and he tumbled backward. He returned to it on all fours, hugged it, and lunged. The bucket tottered and fell and he quickly rolled it along, leaving a trail of orange scrap. He knelt and swabbed the scrap about.

The second can had lost its handle long before. Another spray of scrap. In the process, something sharp had sliced the tip of his finger. Blood mixed with the rust on his hands and began to drip to the floor. He got down on his knees again, but it was hopeless and he sat back. Under the mow stairs, a jumble of dusty odds and ends lay tucked into the crevice where the stair stringers met the concrete floor—a paintbrush, long ago fallen from behind the shelf, a bunched-up rag, a tin of washers. He scuttled over. One by one he tossed them into the workshop. A maroon drop of blood caught in the cobweb below the last tread and shivered blackly in the air. He reached out and brushed the cobweb away.

There, against the wall, lay a plastic-barreled syringe. He picked it up and blew the dust away and held it to the light. The plunger had been pressed three quarters of the way down; the black double gasket touched the final graduated mark on the barrel. The needle's shaft reflected the light in a long clean line. He shook the thing. Two glassy crystals clicked within the barrel.

He walked into the rain with the syringe in his hand, night-blind from the barn lights. The rain had slackened to a drizzle, and at first he couldn't make out his father and he looked around in a panic before realizing he stood exactly where Edgar had last seen him. The rain had grown so fine his form was barely discernible.

Edgar held out the syringe.

This was under the stairs.

Yes.

What does it mean?

You've seen him use one.

Claude?

Edgar looked at the Impala sitting in the driveway, then the dark house. At his bedroom window, he thought he saw the shine of Almondine's eyes.

He's proposed.

She won't accept.

She laughed at him. But she will. When she's alone, she'll accept.

She won't! She—

Before Edgar could protest again, his father set his hand flat against the center of Edgar's chest. A whispery splash on his skin. At first he thought his father only meant to lay his hand on him in a gesture that meant, *be still and listen*, but then he brought his other hand forward

and Edgar felt something pass into him, and his father made as if to cra-
dle Edgar's heart. The sensation was so strange Edgar thought his heart
would stop. But his father only cupped the thing in his hands as though
it were a newborn pup. On his face Edgar made out regret and anger and
joy and most of all unutterable sorrow.

Any thought to protest or resist left him. The world grayed. Then
memories flooded into Edgar in a cascade, like the drops of rain passing
through his father's figure; images seen by a baby, a toddler, a young
man, an adult. All his father's memories given to him at once.

Standing over a crib looking at a silent baby whose hands move over his chest.
Trudy, a young woman, laughing. Almondine, a wet, blind pup. Vision of a young
boy with a younger boy beside him holding something in the air; something bloody.
And smiling. A thousand ruby-lit dogs. And with the images, a sense of responsi-
bility; the need to put himself between Claude and the world. Dogs fighting. Storms
mounting the field. Trees slipstreaming past the truck windows. Dogs: sleeping, run-
ning, sick, joyful, dying. Always and everywhere, dogs. Then Claude, retreating
from the workshop, searching the floor for something. Darkness. And now, standing
before him, a boy as clear as glass, his heart beating in two cupped hands.

Edgar fell to his knees, gasping. He leaned forward, emptied his stomach into a pool of rainwater. From the corner of his eye he saw the syringe
lying in the mud, light glinting off the shaft of the needle.

He looked up, panting. His father was still there.

Whatever he's wanted, he's taken, ever since he was a child.

I'll tell the police.

They won't believe you.

Edgar began to sob.

You're not real. You can't be real.

Find—

What? Stop! I couldn't read that.

His father signed it again, fingerspelling the last word.

Find H-A-A . . .

He couldn't make it out. It was *H-A-A* and then something else, followed by a very distinct *I*: *H-A-A*-something-*I*.

I still didn't . . .

The mist had lessened further, and his father was barely visible. His hands sprayed away on a gust of wind. Then he vanished entirely. Edgar thought he was gone forever, but when the wind died he reappeared, kneeling now in front of him, his hands so faint Edgar could barely make out the motion.

A touch of the thumb to the forehead.

The *I*-hand held to his chest.

Remember me.

And then his father reached forward a second time.

He thought he would rather die himself than feel that sensation again. He scrabbled along the muddy ground until the barn was against his back and signed furiously into the night, arms crossed over his head.

Don't touch me! Don't touch me! Don't touch me!

After that everything quieted to absolute silence. The mist grew so refined it made no noise as it came to earth, only the drip of water from the eaves. He could not bring himself to look up until it had stopped altogether.

From behind a feathered break of clouds, the moon emerged, a gleaming sickle of bone as pointed as the syringe beside him. The trees at the edge of the forest glowed blue. He walked along the driveway and looked back at the barn. The dogs were at the front of their pens holding sit-stays, coats like mercury. Their muzzles tracked him as he approached. They lowered their brows and ducked their heads, not wanting to be out anymore. But they did not move.

From the moment they opened their eyes the dogs were taught to watch and listen and trust. To think and choose. This was the lesson behind every minute of training. They were taught something beyond simple obedience: that through the training all things could be spoken. Edgar himself believed this—believed they had the right to ask of the dogs certain things. But the more forcefully they asked, the more certain they had to be, for the dogs would obey. Doubtful, uncomfortable, uneasy, frightened: they would obey.

The line of dogs waited for him to signal a release.

The clouds gaped and folded and closed across the moon.

Part III

WHAT

HANDS DO

Awakening

HE CAME UP OUT OF A DARKNESS THAT WAS NOT SLEEP BUT something vaster and more comforting, the black of willful unconsciousness or perhaps the night that precedes the first wakening, which babies know in the womb and forget ever after. There was Essay's breath panting slow and hot against his face. When he cracked an eyelid her jet-whiskered muzzle and curious eye filled his vision and he pushed her away and curled his head to his knees and squeezed his eyelids shut. Even so, he'd glimpsed enough to know he lay inside the run farthest from the doors and nearest the whelping room, and that the bare lights blazed along the kennel aisle. Outside, rain fell, roaring, a torrent against the roof. There was the rustle of the canvas flaps and another dog trotted up, this time Tinder, who dug his muzzle into the crevice between Edgar's chin and chest and snuffled and drew back and cocked his head with a low, puzzled groan.

Bits of straw began to itch along his neck. His shirt clung to his ribs, gelid and damp. A spasm shook his body, then another, and he gasped and despite himself drew a full breath that carried into him the odors of the kennel—sweat and urine, straw and turpentine, blood and defecation and birth and life and death—all of it alien and bitter as if the whole history of the place itself had suddenly blossomed in his chest. And with it, masked until the last instant, the memory of what had happened in the night.

Then Essay and Tinder accosted him together. He could summon only the strength to sit cross-legged against the wooden wall and bury his face in his arms, counting by sound the dogs shuffling through the straw in their pens as rain thundered onto the barn. When he lifted his head again, Essay and Tinder stammered before him and snaked their necks against his palms and shimmied. In time he pushed himself upright. Patches of wet cloth sucked away from his skin. He slipped out of the pen and walked to the Dutch doors and stood with one hand on the latch listening to water sheeting off the eaves.

He drew a breath and swung the door outward. The sapphire sky above floated a small, lone cloud made orange by the sunrise. The new leaves on the maple stirred and quaked; sparrows cartwheeled over the wet field like glazier's points against the sky, and the swallows nesting in the eaves plunged into the morning air. The house burned white against the green of the woods. The Impala, neon blue. But there was no torrent to be seen, not even a drizzle. The sound of falling rain possessed him for one moment more and then vanished.

He was past the milk house before he remembered the syringe and turned and found it crushed in the center of a grassy puddle, needle snapped, barrel broken and awash. He cupped it in his palm and carried the pieces to the old silo where he pitched them through the rusted iron rungs and listened as they struck the far curve of cement and stone with a papery ring. Then he walked up the driveway, faster as he passed the house, the orchard, the mailbox. He started up the road, wheeled and headed the other way, breaking into a run and then dropping into a jerky reined-up step. He turned again. After a time he found himself walking back down the driveway and he began to circle the house in that same halting stride. Five times around, ten, twenty times, looking into the darkness behind the window glass. Each time he passed the old apple tree its lowest branches tugged at him and he brushed them away until he finally came to rest, panting, caught for the umpteenth time, and at last he turned to look at it.

It was an old tree, old already when he was born, maybe older than the house itself. At eye level the trunk split into three thick and nearly horizontal limbs, the longest of which arced toward the house and ended suddenly in a mass of waxy leaves. The branch would have continued through the kitchen window had it not been pruned mid-limb. He was shaking and chilled and his fingers were stiff but he managed to boost himself into the crotch of the tree and from there he worked himself onto the limb. The bark felt greasy from long days of rain. Past halfway it began to buck and wobble under his weight. Rainwater cupped in the new foliage showered him every time he moved. He worked slowly along. When he got to the stump end he steadied himself by gripping a hornlike pair of limbs and settled his sternum against the branch and lay outstretched, a swimmer among the boughs.

The window over the sink was closed, the gingham curtains parted to either side. The thin morning light was not enough to illuminate the interior, and at first only the orange power light at the base of the freezer was visible, its bulb winking and flickering. His breaths made the limb tremble like the string of an instrument wound overtight; it was no wider than his hand and its bark bit into his chest and soon his chest began to ache from it. He did not know why he was in the apple tree or what he was looking for but he lay waiting. In time, the side of the barn glowed red. One of the kennel dogs pressed into its run and looked around and retreated. The morning air was bright and water-laden. From downfield a killdeer chattered *kee-dee, kee-dee.*

Almondine floated into the kitchen, padding along on old legs. She paused beside the stove and circled the table and disappeared. Then Edgar's mother walked into view, robe cinched around her waist. She stood with her back to the window and started the Mr. Coffee. She lifted her hair in a rope and dropped it outside her robe and waited. She filled her cup. She liked coffee black with just a bit of sugar—he'd made it for her many times that winter—and he watched her lift the spoon from her cup and put it wet into the sugar bowl twice and sip the coffee. The corner of the kitchen was windowed on two sides. She stood in profile looking west at the vapor writhing over the field. When Claude appeared he was dressed, as if he had just arrived. He walked up behind her and put one hand on her shoulder and let it rest there. He smoothed the collar of her robe against her neck and walked to the sink and rinsed out a cup. He didn't look out then, just turned and poured his coffee and sat in the chair nearest the sink.

Their murmur penetrated the window glass but not their words. After a few minutes Edgar's mother set her cup on the table and walked to the bathroom. Claude sat watching the mercator of sunlight advance up the field. Wisps of fog swirled and thinned under the new heat of morning. A flock of sparrows lit at the bird feeder at the corner of the house, bickering and flapping one another out of the way, so close Edgar could have snatched one.

He lay in the tree and watched. Claude was leaner than his father and though he was younger and without his father's bookish stoop, his hair was shot with gray. He sat in Edgar's father's chair and pursed his lips and brought the coffee cup to his mouth.

Edgar had been afraid he would see them kiss.

Almondine went up to Claude and raised her face and Claude smoothed his hand over the top of her skull. Edgar's mother emerged from the bathroom, hair turbaned. Incandescent light from the bedroom fell across the kitchen table. Claude stood and went to the sink and rinsed out his coffee cup and finally he looked out that window.

Maybe he didn't know what he'd seen at first. His gaze passed aimlessly across the tree and moved on. Edgar had time to wonder if the new leaves were camouflage enough to hide him, though it didn't seem possible and he didn't care anyway. Claude swabbed the dishcloth in his cup and picked up a towel and began to dry it. But somewhere in the back of his mind there must have been a twinge, a nag, an afterimage, for when he lifted his face again he looked straight at Edgar and then he shuddered and stepped back from the sink.

A STEP BACK — A SMALL MOTION, perfectly natural, if any reaction can be said to be natural when you realize someone has climbed a tree outside the window and has been watching like a panther for God knows how long. Since you woke up, perhaps. You lean forward. The boy's hair is wet and dripping, as if he has been there all night in the rain. He has a frozen, impudent look on his face as if the pane of glass between you could protect him from anything, from everything, and if he blinks you do not see it. After a long stare to be sure you are seeing what you see, you understand that the boy *has* been up there all along—the rustle wouldn't have escaped your attention even if you had been half-asleep and distracted. And the birds would never have battled like they did over the feeder just an arm's length away.

You weigh the idea that this is a prank. You lean back and try to quietly laugh, as if you are in on it. You turn your back and set the coffee mug on the table and then look out the window again and watch with false equanimity as the boy peers back, hands clasped around the bough he is balanced so far out upon. When his mother comes up behind you, you turn and face her and that is when you kiss. You unselfconsciously kiss. Her hand lingers on your shoulder. You stand with your back to the window, saying nothing about what you have seen, as she pulls her coat off its hook. She says one last thing and then she and Almondine are out the door and walking toward the barn.

You turn back to the window. Though you expect him to have looked away to gaze at his mother and the dog as they cross the yard, he has not. His expression is slack and his eyes fill his face. He is all watching, no reacting. And a small voice in the back of your mind says this is a boy that spends his days watching. You're not going to win a staring contest.

And you get to thinking as well (he is still staring from his wet perch) that if this is a contest then you have already lost, because in that moment when you first understood what you were seeing through the window— when your eyes said it was so and your mind replied it was impossible— in that moment, as you think of it from the boy's viewpoint, you know you looked frightened. You stepped back from the window, back from the sight of his foreshortened body, fronted by that face, those eyes, that shock of hair hanging over his forehead, dripping.

You stepped back and looked up and your eyes were wide. Now you glance up again, attempt an insolent grin, but it does not come off easily. It comes off forced and the grin fades as if the muscles of your face have grown paralytic and this is also something the boy can see, who has not once looked away or betrayed an emotion. But your failure to muster a smile isn't what gets to you. What gets to you is that the boy seems to be reading your mind, can hear these thoughts, and this makes you wonder what else he has seen, what else he might know, or guess. And as you lock gazes and you finally force the amused smile you wish had come easily, what unnerves you, what finally makes you turn away, is that without moving a muscle or blinking an eye he begins to smile back.

Smoke

BY THEN THE YARD WAS IN FULL MORNING LIGHT, THE LAWN a beaded pelt of water. Edgar clambered backward along the apple tree branch and dropped to the ground and trotted past the porch steps. His mother had hooked the barn doors open using the eyelets screwed into the red siding. From the doorway he could hear her voice. She was in one of the whelping rooms soothing a mother as she examined her pup. He walked into the workshop where metal scrap described an ocher swath across the floor. From its nail above the bench Edgar took down an old framing hammer, the one Claude had used roofing the barn the previous summer, the same one he'd lost more than once in the tall grass so that now it bore a freckled patina of rust. The thing was heavy in his hand and he meant to walk back to the house with it, but when he turned Almondine stood in the doorway. Her gaze was fixed upon him and her tail swung side to side in an unhurried wingbeat. The sight of her pulled him up short. He tightened his grip on the hammer's handle-shaft and went forward and bent and put his free hand to her forechest to walk her back, but instead of giving way she craned her muzzle up and pressed her nose to his ear and then his neck.

He stood. A quaking breath escaped him. He looked at her peering upward, her irises grained with bay and black, the whorls of fine brown fur contouring her face, the diamond of ebony feathering down from her forehead and between her eyes and along the top of her muzzle. He jammed the claw of the hammer into his pocket and this time he set both hands against her. By the time he'd moved her clear of the doorway, the mash of his hands against her fur had quelled something in him and he wound up on his knees while she scented up and down his wet clothes.

His mother emerged from the whelping room. She had a young pup with her, spinning and biting at its leash. "There you are," she said, then broke off to correct the pup. When she'd finished she was kneeling too and she looked over at him.

"Good grief," she said. "You're soaked. Have you been down in the woods already?"

No. Not—No.

He was still figuring out what to say when he heard the back porch door open and whack shut. It was all the provocation the pup needed to leap up and shake the lead in its mouth as if it were a serpent. Edgar's mother deftly settled it and circled its muzzle with her thumb and forefinger to stop its nipping. "These guys are stir-crazy," she said. "Thank God the rain stopped. Hurry up and get changed. I'm going to need help this morning." She kept her attention on the pup as she spoke, waiting for it to break again. Edgar couldn't tell if she was avoiding his gaze and he waited. When she looked over he saw she was avoiding nothing.

"What's wrong?" she said.

He could have told her then about what he'd seen that night past, but it was as though she knelt in some place visible to him but unreachable by words. He thought if only he waited she might notice the difference in him. Maybe in the world itself. Outside, there was the thud of the Impala's door closing. The starter turned over and the engine roughly idled. He knelt there and looked at the doorway. The hammer's claw bit into his hip. He knew there was still time to walk to the Impala, drag open the door, bring the steel head of the hammer crashing around, but a kind of dislocation passed through him, as though some alternate Edgar had split away to pursue that different future. Then the Impala was rolling along the driveway. On the road it throated up and topped the hill.

He looked up. His mother was still watching him but he didn't answer her. He turned back to the workshop and replaced the hammer and walked to the house. After he'd changed clothes he came downstairs to the living room and looked at the blanket and pillow lying crumpled on the couch. Claude had not been on the couch when Edgar walked through the house the night before and the gesture at pretense left him feeling hollowed out. He sat with a hand in Almondine's ruff and stared at the couch. Finally he stood and walked out the door.

What happened next was impossible, yet it happened anyway: an ordinary morning passed. But ordinary was the very thing Edgar was least prepared for. As soon as he walked out the door, his mother asked him to begin fetching the dogs from the kennel in pairs and triples, youngest first. By the time the sun was halfway to its zenith the ordinariness of the day encroached from every direction, the concrete, tangible, undeniable world insisting that the preceding night had not happened. Those memories that had poured through him, indelible at sunrise, began to fade until all that remained was the finest scrim in his mind. It could have been any warm summer morning except for the fact that whenever Edgar closed his eyes a gloss raindrop hung in the darkness before him, the yard lights captured and inverted within. By noon he felt he was coming apart. What he felt was confusion, though it seemed more complicated than that. When his mother headed in for lunch he said he wasn't hungry and led the last two dogs to the barn and kenneled them and put his head against the pen door and listened as they lapped their water. He found work gloves and scooped up the rubble in the workshop and poured it into the milk can and dragged the can back where it belonged.

When he was done he climbed the mow steps. Almondine stood waiting for him in the midday twilight of pinholes and cracks. He sank onto a pair of straw bales and drew his knees to his chest. Before he could reach out to her, sleep engulfed him. She stood beside his curled body and set a nostril to the finger he'd cut the night before. After a time she circled and downed and lay watching him.

IN HIS DREAM, Edgar sat atop the mow stairs, looking into the workshop. He knew that wasn't possible—the rough timbered wall of the stairwell should have blocked his view—but his sleep had a lucidity that rendered the wall as transparent as glass. Below, his father stood at the workbench, back turned. Edgar could see the black, tousled hair on the top of his head and the temples of his glasses hooked behind his ears. The top of the workbench was covered with leatherworking tools and a tin can of grommets, and his father held a leash whose clasp end had frayed. When Edgar glanced at the file cabinets, his father stood there too, walking his fingers across the overstuffed manila folders of an open drawer and lifting one out and splaying it open. Both of them worked silently, each engrossed and oblivious to the other.

A tendril of white smoke advanced between the ceiling beams. No flames in sight, no fire to extinguish. Edgar descended the stairs and stood in the workshop. The smoke thickened into a gray haze. He inhaled a wisp of it and coughed, but his father, both his fathers, carried on, unaware. Somehow Edgar had grown impossibly tall, his head almost brushing the ceiling beams. He had the power to be ordinary-sized, he knew, but then the figures of his father would vanish and he would be alone in the workshop.

He found the hay hatch by feel alone, running his hands along the ceiling until he could trace the outline. When he pressed upward a ponderous weight resisted—Edgar himself, asleep on the bales. He shifted both hands to one edge of the hatch and pushed again, straining. A crack appeared. Streamers of smoke shot through, sucked into the space above, but the weight of the hatch was too much and he had to set it back. Then a new plume of smoke appeared, dense and black and tasting like hot metal.

The next instant, the ceiling was out of reach and he was alone in the workshop. It was night. Light from the gooseneck lamp over the front doors penetrated the small workshop window, casting a skewed yellow rectangle against the wall. Almondine appeared, leading Claude. A hesitant expression played over Claude's face, but Almondine nosed him forward. He passed Edgar and took up the frayed lead. His hands worked the leather and soon the lead was repaired. Claude nodded and stroked Almondine's back. Then Edgar walked to Almondine's side and he, too, began to draw his hands along her flanks.

THEY COOKED DINNER THAT night standing side by side, Edgar frying sliced potatoes while his mother turned a pair of pork chops in a skillet, reaching over occasionally to add a dab of fat to his potatoes, like an old married couple thinking about the day while the grease spat. She set out silverware and plates and bread and butter and halved a grapefruit and sprinkled some sugar on top and put the halves face up in bowls.

They sat to eat. He pushed his spoon into the skin between the grapefruit sections and looked out the window at a world gone blue. Blue sky, blue earth, blue trees with blue leaves, as if visible through miles of clear water.

"What are you thinking?" she asked, finally.

He wanted desperately to talk about what had happened the night before but old feelings rushed forward from those first few weeks after the funeral when he'd dreamed about his father: speak and you'll forget it all even as the words come out. You won't remember long enough to finish. And he thought, too, about his father signing, *They won't believe you.*

Do you think there is a heaven or hell? he signed.

"I don't know. Not in the Christian way, if that's what you mean. I think people have a right to believe in whatever they want. I just don't."

I don't mean like the Bible. I mean, do you think anything at all happens to a person after they die?

She spooned up a section of grapefruit. "I guess I don't think about those things as much as I should. It's hard to believe it matters when there's the same work to do either way. Lots of people think it's an important question, though, and if they think so, then it is for them. But they have to answer it for themselves."

If someone came in here and gave you positive proof, would you do anything different?

She shook her head. "I think it's just as likely that someone could say that this place, right here, is heaven, hell, and earth all at the same time. And we still wouldn't know what to do differently. Everyone just muddles through, trying not to make too many mistakes."

I like that. This is heaven and hell and earth.

After they cleared the table and washed dishes, they walked to the barn and checked the night rotation schedule and pulled two yearlings to bring up to the house. The dogs roughhoused the length of the barn. When they came up to Almondine they stopped abruptly and presented themselves.

"You know, you need to get that litter named," his mother said. "It's been two weeks."

Her tone was mild, but all of a sudden his head was throbbing and he felt dizzy with some mixture of anger and embarrassment and uncertainty—above all, with the overwhelming effort required to pretend that nothing had changed.

What's the difference? Name them anything you want. Don't name them at all.

She looked at him. "You've been dragging all day. Are you sick?"

Maybe I am, he signed. Maybe I'm getting tired of the smell of perfume.

"Don't take an attitude," she said. Her face flushed. "What's bothering you?"

We train and train and then one day we just hand them over to strangers and it starts all over again. There's never any end to it. There's never any *point*. We don't have any more choice in it than they do.

"Oh, I see. And did you have an alternative in mind?"

I don't know. Something that doesn't involve shoveling out dog pens every morning. Something that doesn't mean we have to spend all day in a barn. Something just the two of us could do.

This last he hadn't known he was going to say and he felt himself blushing.

She searched his face for a long time and ran her hands through her hair, letting it spill over her fingers like strands of dark glass. "This is going to be hard to understand, Edgar. I've put off talking about it with you and now I think that was a mistake. I'm sorry."

You're sorry. For what, exactly?

Then it was her turn to blush. She sat up straight and a kind of leonine recurve came into her posture.

"I know you saw your father and Claude fighting, but what you didn't see is that those were *old* fights. Fights that had been going on all their lives. I don't understand it, probably no one does, not Claude, not even your father if he were here. But I know this: it's possible for two good people to be all wrong when they're around each other. Give Claude a chance. I have, and I've discovered a different person than I expected."

He closed his eyes.

A different person.

"Yes."

After four months.

"Edgar, do you actually think that how long a person grieves is a measure of how much they loved someone? There's no rule book that says how to do this." She laughed, bitterly. "Wouldn't that be great? No decisions to make. Everything laid right out for us. But there's no such thing. You want facts, don't you? Rules. Proof. You're like your father that way. Just because a thing can't be logged, charted, and summarized doesn't mean it isn't real. Half the time we walk around in love with the idea of a thing instead of the reality of it. But sometimes things don't turn out that way. You have to pay attention to what's *real*, what's in the world. Not some imaginary alternative, as if it's a choice we could make."

But he's *not gone*.

His heart pounding as he signed it.

"I know. And all the same, you and I buried him. But he's here, too, isn't he? In this kennel, in the house, everywhere. But unless we walk away from this place and never come back we're going to live with that every day. Do you understand?"

No, he signed. Then: Yes.

"And is that the same as saying he's alive? Do we treat that feeling as if he were really here?"

He found he couldn't answer her. What if he *did* think that the length of a person's grief was a measure of their love? He was as troubled by the simple fact of her asking that question as by his own inability to answer. And something else bothered him, something that had happened during the morning training sessions. One of the pups had been in that contrary mood that came over them sometimes, when they cared more about drama than praise. The pup had been provoking his mother, taunting, goading any way it could, purposefully misunderstanding what she'd asked of it, tackling its littermates—anything to make her angry. But it hadn't worked. The carefully modulated tone of her voice and her equally modulated posture had conveyed only nonchalant indifference. It wasn't until Edgar kenneled the pup that she said, "Next time he pulls that nonsense, I'm going to wring his neck," and he'd realized that in fact she *had* been angry. Furious, in fact. That was part of her skill, wasn't it, not to show any feelings that worked against the training? But if she could fool him about a pup, what might she be concealing when they talked about Claude?

Then his mother said Claude would be coming back in a day or two, and he would be bringing some things to stay. Edgar asked did she love him, and she said, not the way she'd loved his father. He asked if they were going to be married. She said, honey I'm still married, as far as I'm concerned. She said she didn't expect it to make sense to anyone, maybe especially not to him, and that she could see how the two things might not add up and she didn't know how else to explain it except just to say that it did, for her. He knew she was a direct person, with little patience for explanations. Claude was coming back for a while, and though she didn't say it, the implication was it could turn into a long while. Maybe forever.

Perhaps his shrug surprised her. He saw he had no vote in the matter, and didn't bother to ask for one. When his mother chose to be imperial, arguing with her was hopeless. You could disagree with her words all you wanted, but her *bearing* was irrefutable. He said he'd stay out in the kennel a while, and she led the two dogs away. At the doorway she looked back at him as though she were about to add one last thing, then she seemed to think better of it and turned and walked to the house.

AFTER SHE WAS GONE HE hooked the top of the kennel doors back and let the night breeze blow in and opened the pens for his litter to run the aisle. Edgar knelt beside Almondine and set a hand in her ruff and for the first time that day he felt some measure of calm.

I wish you had been out here with me last night. Then at least I could be sure it really happened.

His recollection was vivid enough to make his insides tremble, but there were gaps, too. He'd woken up in the barn, in the pen with Essay and Tinder. He didn't remember going inside or anything that happened after standing in the rain. And in the morning the syringe lay broken in the grass, as if he'd stepped on it, but he didn't remember that happening, either.

He tried to sort out his feelings. There was the desire to run; there was the desire to stay and put himself in front of Claude the moment he returned; there was the desire to take his mother's explanations at face value; above all, there was the desire to forget everything that had happened, an aching desire for everything normal and familiar, for the routine of the kennel and reading at night and making dinners, just the two of them, when he could almost believe that his father had stepped out momentarily to check a new litter and would be right back.

He half expected to be spooked in the barn, but he wasn't, maybe because the night sky was clear. If rain had been falling he wouldn't have had the courage to stay out. He watched Essay put her feet on the front doors and try to peer over the ledge into the yard. When she tired of that she began parading in front of the dogs, whipping a piece of twine back and forth in her mouth and mock-pouncing.

Quit teasing them, he signed. Come here.

He put them in stays and got out the grooming tackle and nail clippers. They were done blowing coat for the spring, and he used the undercoat rake to draw out the last vestiges of downy gray beneath their guard coats. They lay in a circle around him, panting and watching. He brushed out Almondine first, then Opal and Umbra together, then Finch and Baboo. Tinder and Essay he saved for last because they needed to learn patience. Essay disliked being brushed and Edgar didn't understand that. He talked to her about it and listened to her complaints but he didn't stop. They always came to like grooming. He was proud of that. Even if he had a lot to learn as a trainer, he was as good a groom as a person could be.

The stroke of the brush from croup to withers helped him think. What was confusing was his mother's mercurial attitude. One moment she asked him to decide the future of the kennel, the next she dictated their lives. He couldn't tell what she truly felt about anything. An expression he'd read in a book came to him: she was taking up with a man. A dumb, old-fashioned expression. In the book it had been something simple and clear. Taking up with someone. As direct an act as turning on a light or shooting a gun, an indivisible act.

Yet this was complicated beyond any ability he had to express it. He felt he could do nothing until he had the right words, but the ones that came to mind only captured what he *had been* thinking, trailing his real thoughts like the tail of a meteor. To say his mother was taking up with a man: that was an idea that had occurred to him days before, maybe weeks. But only just then had the words bubbled up inside him. As soon as he heard them in his mind he discarded them as fussy and stupid, a remnant of past thought. What he was thinking *that* moment was something entirely else and he didn't know if anyone had ever come up with words for those ideas. He stopped grooming Essay and tried to explain, and for a long time the dogs lay watching as his hands traced his thoughts in the air.

Anyway, he told them, all of that was beside the point after seeing his father. He'd found a syringe in the workshop last night. That was his own memory, he was sure of that much. Then his father had touched him and Edgar had been filled with his father's memories but like some half-made vessel he'd been unable to capture them and they'd vanished, all but a few tattered vestiges. One vestige was the sight of Claude backing out of the barn doors and into a cold, white world.

His father had died from an aneurysm.

A weakness in some place called the Circle of Willis.

Except he didn't believe that now. Claude had been there that day. He would have left tracks in the snow. Had Edgar seen tracks? Yes—his own, his mother's, his father's. The tracks of half a dozen other people might have been there too but he wouldn't have known the difference, because it wasn't anything he'd been looking for. The wind had been blowing steadily, filling every footstep and tire track with a dune of white on its lee side. Would Claude's tracks have led up the driveway? Through the field? Into the woods? He must have gotten there somehow. Edgar remembered running out to the road, but beyond fifty or sixty yards everything had blanked out into a white wall of snow. Claude's Impala could have been parked at the crest of the hill or two miles off; either way it would have been equally concealed. He thought, for the first of many times, about the expression on Claude's face that morning as he'd peered in through the kitchen window. Had he seen surprise? Or guilt?

And if it *had* been guilt, what was Edgar supposed to think about the kiss that followed, so purposeful and defiant? Why go out of your way to bait a person who might know your terrible secret? Unless, he thought, it was better if that person were blinded by anger. Could Claude have concluded so quickly that if Edgar sounded mad with jealousy, anything else he said would be discredited?

He looked at the dogs lying sprawled in various postures of sleep, all except for Almondine, who sat leaning heavily into his thigh.

We're going to have to sit tight, he signed. We're just going to have to wait.

He led the dogs to their pens. He spent a minute squatting in the straw with each, drawing a hand across their muzzles and down the curve of their shoulders, making sure they were settled. Then he turned out the aisle lights, and together he and Almondine walked into the dark.

On the gravel-shot lawn, where the syringe had lain crushed in the rainwater, an oblong of grass and weeds caught his eye. He sat on his heels to look. The spot was maybe the size of his palm and at first glance he thought the grass was dead but it was not. It was lush and thick and there in the watery moonlight it was also as white as a bone.

Hangman

HE LAY IN BED THAT NIGHT WITH ALMONDINE BESIDE HIM, both of them waiting for sleep that would not come. Outside, a night wind was blowing and through the high window of his room the rustle of the apple tree and the maple made a continuous surf. Almondine lay with her forelegs outstretched and her head reared up, looking with suspicion at the movement of the curtains. In time, she gave a long, gaped yawn and he reached over and set a hand on her foreleg. Wind she distrusted. Wind could come into the house and slam doors. He smoothed the fine filamentary whiskers that arched over her eyes. In the morning she would be sleeping on the floor, he thought. If she started the night on the bed she always ended on the floor. If she started on the floor there was a chance he might wake in the morning to find her on the bed but more likely she would be standing at the window or lying in the doorway. There was some notion of propriety in her about this but he had never been able to fully make sense of it.

He was looking at Almondine and trying to think of nothing when the image of his father, fingerspelling, came back to him. He sat up in his bed. What was it his father had said in those final moments? How could he have forgotten it?

Find *H-A-A*-something-*I*.

He squeezed his eyes shut and tried to see again what had happened the previous night. The rain had turned to drizzle. His father's gestures had been vanishingly faint. Edgar sat in a reverie, watching his father's hands, shaped by mist, tracing out the letters, and when he opened his eyes again he thought he'd misread the third letter that night. It seemed to him now to have been a *C*, not an *A*.

Find *H-A-C*-something-*I*.

The knowledge came at some cost. He'd seen his father reaching toward him again and remembered how he'd begged not to be touched, instead of saying what he wished he'd said. He believed, though he couldn't have said why, that his father had been spelling out a name, a dog's name. He turned on the light. On his bedside table he found a scrap of paper and a pencil and he wrote down the letters, leaving a blank for the unknown. Even incomplete, it looked familiar to him. He had no idea what it meant.

Almondine trailed him down the stairs. His mother had turned out the lights in the living room and kitchen and lay in bed reading. It was ten by the kitchen clock.

"Edgar?" she called.

He walked to the door of her bedroom.

"I wish I hadn't been short with you tonight."

He shrugged.

"Do you want to talk more?"

No. I can't sleep. I'm going out to the barn to look for names.

"Don't stay out long. You've got circles under your eyes."

He held the door for Almondine, but she decided it would be better to sleep on the porch. He walked to the workshop and pulled down the master litter book and paged through it. If he could find a name that fit, he would be able to get the dog's number and, from there, its file.

And then?

He didn't know what would happen then.

It took almost an hour to look through the entries, at first scanning the pages, then going more slowly, considering each name for a diminutive. He wound up with nothing—no possibilities, nothing even close. He made a list, filling in the blank with every possible letter and crossing out whatever looked like nonsense: "Hacdi" and "Hacqi" and "Hacwi." It was like playing hangman, where you guessed a word one letter at a time while your opponent filled in the head, body, arms, and legs of a man on a gallows.

But in this case it was surprisingly difficult to eliminate prospects. The possibility that it was a foreign name had occurred to him, and names were more idiosyncratic than regular words. In the end, he simply had to guess. He crossed out all but six possibilities:

Hacai

Hacci

Hachi

Hacki

Hacli

Hacti

He looked up each word in *The New Webster Encyclopedic Dictionary of the English Language*, though, as he suspected, none had entries. He paged through the master litter book one last time, looking for names that could be abbreviated or distorted, but even as he ran his finger down the pages he knew it was hopeless.

Again and again, his eye returned to "Hachi." The missing letter was an *H*, he was sure of it—index and middle finger extended horizontally from a closed hand. He visualized his father's hands, translucent and wind-smeared. The problem was, the wind had gusted and he had barely seen the sign in the first place. In despair, he replaced the master litter book atop the cabinets. He could go through the files one by one, he supposed, though that would take days, weeks even. He leaned his head against a cabinet. He kicked the bottom drawer.

The drawer containing the letters.

Then he got it. Hachi was right, but it was only part of the name. Hachi-something. Hachigo? Hachiru? He'd seen the name in a letter perused and discarded while searching for letters from Brooks. He dropped to his knees and yanked open the drawer. Now that he knew what to look for, it didn't take long. He recognized the handwriting even before he'd spotted the name.

Hachiko.

May 1935
Chicago

John,

Just a note to let you know that my friends in the diplomatic corps have sent some sad news. Hachiko was found dead in Shibuya station on the seventh of March, in the very spot where I met him so many years ago. He was waiting for Ueno, of course. By all accounts, he still made the trek each day unless his arthritis was so bad he couldn't walk.

I have included a photograph, sent to me by my friends, of the monument that was erected for him. He walked past it for the better part of his last year. I suppose he never noticed it at all. Yet another example of our dogs exceeding their so-called masters.

How is it, John, I feel I have lost an old friend, though I met him only twice? Perhaps it is because of our Ouji. He and Charles, Jr., are inseparable companions, and I don't think I exaggerate when I say they have equaled the bond I once had with Lucky.

I take some consolation knowing that a fraction of Hachiko's bloodline is in my care—and yours. I hope the grand experiment is proceeding well. (I know you don't like me calling it that, but I can't help teasing you sometimes.) Last month, while visiting my district in Chicago, I met a family that owned a Sawtelle dog. I saw them walking down the street and bolted from the car like a madman. Perhaps you remember them? The Michaelsons? It is probably my imagination, but I swear I saw a trace of Ouji in their dog. Could it possibly be from one of his matings?

Yours, as always,

Charles Adwin

Eighth Illinois District,

United States House of Representatives

Nothing in the letter seemed significant. Edgar didn't know of anyone named Charles Adwin. Why had his father told him to find Hachiko? Hachiko, whoever that was, was dead, and had been for many years.

He sat back.

Ueno? Ouji?

He turned back to the file cabinet. He had searched one drawer, but there was a second, also filled with old correspondence and miscellany. He began searching it for a letter postmarked from Washington, perhaps Chicago, and thus he almost missed what he was looking for, because it bore international postage. Only Charles Adwin's distinctively broad handwriting made him take a closer look.

October 1928

Tokyo

Dear Mr. Sawtelle,

    With some difficulty, I have contacted the family of Hachiko and discovered, to my amazement, that there is indeed another litter produced from the same sire and dam. I do not know how you knew this, or if this was a spectacularly lucky guess. Nor do I pretend to understand your breeding project. I know little about dogs and simply admire them like most people, ignorantly, I suppose. But admire them I do, and I have known the best of them. As a boy I had a Setter named Lucky that was the moral superior of any man I've known, myself included.

    Hachiko is a phenomenon here in Tokyo, much talked about among the residents. The stories are true. I have stood on the

Shibuya train platform in the afternoon and watched him walk
out of the crowd, alone, and sit and wait for the train to arrive.
He is a regal animal, pale cream in color, and he moves with
great dignity. I have, as well, walked over to him and stroked
his thick pelt and looked into his eyes, and I must say I felt the
presence of a great soul. As we stood there, the train arrived
and the doors opened and Hachiko watched to see if his master,
Professor Ueno, would disembark, but of course he didn't. Ueno
hasn't stepped off that train for nearly three years, since a stroke
felled him at the university. Hachiko must know by now that
he isn't going to appear, but he waited anyway. And so I waited
alongside him. A pair of foolish boys stood off to one side of the
platform, laughing and taunting the dog, and before I knew
what I was doing, I had run over to them and chased them away
in a fury—hardly the behavior of a diplomat. Hachiko was not
so easily distracted. Indeed, so assured in his posture was he,
so patiently did he sit and watch that train, that I felt *we* were
the ones blind to the truth, not Hachiko. After a long wait, he
stood and walked back into the crowd, alone. The next day, he
was there again, waiting for the train. I know, because I returned
as well, drawn to this quiet drama for reasons I cannot easily
explain.

Hachiko's story has become widely enough known that
strangers passing through Shibuya station recognize him at
once. Some have begun to set food out for him. There are stories
of people bursting into tears at the sight of the dog sitting and
waiting. As I have already confessed, I was not without some
emotion myself. I suppose one cannot conceive of such devotion
in man or animal until one has seen it with one's own eyes. There
is already talk of erecting a monument to the dog.

Frankly, I was prepared to dismiss your request, but meeting
Hachiko changed my mind. With some difficulty, I was able to
locate the breeder. This involved following Hachiko through
the streets of Tokyo, to the house where Ueno lived. There the

dog paused, briefly, and I fully expected him to walk to the door.
Instead he turned his gaze up the street and continued to the
home of Professor Ueno's gardener, who now cares for the dog.
(The professor had no family.) The gardener was able to direct me
to the breeder, Osagawa-san. I introduced myself and explained
your request, and that was when I found out there was a litter.
He was adamant that no dog of his could be shipped in the
manner you suggest. He does not believe a pup would survive
such a trip intact in mind and body, and refuses to consider the
idea. He said (after I calmed him) that you are welcome to come
to see the pups yourself, at which time he would discuss whether
you might be a fit owner. I explained that such a trip was not
within your means. Osagawa-san is quite devoted to his dogs.
I think he is right about the pup traveling. Though they have
been used to hunt bear, the dogs seem extraordinarily sensitive,
and even if we found a place for one on a ship to San Francisco
or Seattle, there are thousands more miles to go by train before
he would find his way to you, with no one to look after him. It
simply isn't practical. I'm sure you understand.

However, another avenue may have opened, if you would
consider it. An unexpected result of my visit has been the
opportunity to acquire one of these pups for my own family.
We have named him Ouji, which means, roughly translated,
"Prince." He is a fine specimen. At four months of age, he lacks
the sagacity of Hachiko, but that is to be expected. At times he is
a terror to us, but I believe the day will come when I shall thank
you for bringing us together. I see in him some of the character
I remember in Lucky so many years ago, and though it might be
my imagination, I may have caught a glimmer of what I saw in
Hachiko's gaze on the train platform.

The opportunity I suggest is this. In the next twelve months
I expect to end my assignment here in Japan and return to my
home. I have already announced my intention to resign. Life
in the diplomatic corps has been good, but I cannot deny my

midwestern roots. In the spring my wife, son, and I will board a ship bound for San Francisco, and by fall we should be settled in Chicago again. Ouji will be about eighteen months old then, and if you should want to come and meet him, you would be welcome. If you are interested, and he is suitable, I don't think he would object to siring a litter for you. I've already put the question to him, but he was busy demolishing a corner of my briefcase and did not answer.

I apologize for failing to plead your case with Ogasawa-san; however, I owe you a debt of gratitude for inspiring my visit to Hachiko. It is a moment that may well have changed my life. You see, my decision to come home was finalized during the long walk beside Hachiko as he made his way through the streets of Tokyo. I cannot justify the feeling, but it seemed possible—indeed, likely—that a third presence accompanied us, someone whom only Hachiko could see. And in that moment, I understood that I had been too long away from home.

Before I close, I must voice one final thought. I cannot believe you thought any plan to ship an unaccompanied pup via freightliner and rail would have worked. I have half entertained the notion that you manipulated me from afar into adopting a sire for your project. If that is the case, then you are a genius, sir, and we could use your kind in the diplomatic corps.

Yours,

Charles Adwin

Senior Secretary

United States Ambassador to Japan

Edgar leaned back, letter in hand. He didn't have to puzzle over its significance. His father had been pointing him toward something like evidence, though not of anything Claude had done.

I am no dream, his father had been saying. It's happened before.

A Way to Know for Sure

THE METRONOME OF THE KENNEL TICKED AWAY, SUNRISE AND sunset. A new litter was arranged, a late-summer whelping expected. Four dogs from the oldest litter were placed over the next two weeks, entailing a frantic burst of finish training, evaluation, and paperwork. Doctor Papineau found a reason to drop in whenever the adoptive owners arrived, exuding what seemed to Edgar an increasingly proprietary air. And Edgar found himself drawn between opposed desires: To wait and watch or to run away. To tell his mother what he suspected or to fling himself at Claude. Days, his head rang with fatigue. Nights, he dropped onto the bed and lay for hours as his gaze jittered across the ceiling. Summer storms drew him like a moth to a porch light and he walked aimlessly through the rain, coring his interior with second thoughts, treble thoughts. The strangest kind of curse had been laid upon him: knowledge without hope of evidence. He felt haunted not so much by his father's figure as by his father's memories, poured into him that night only to be lost again. Nothing he did could recall them. *There*—was that a memory of his own or a shred of his father's? Or had his ceaseless inward scrutiny manufactured phantoms that were no one's recollections at all? His mind seemed capable of twisting back along any slithery line of thought, reflecting its own desires like a bead of mercury jiggling before a mirror, recalling anything he wanted, true or false. Whenever the rain stopped he was left disappointed and angry—angry most of all at his father and then aghast at himself for it.

And despite his mother's declaration, Claude did not come to stay all at once. There was never a clear boundary, never a decisive moment to which Edgar could object. If Claude spent the afternoon working in the kennel, he would leave before evening came. The next day he might not show up at all, or might stop by long after dark to leave a bottle of wine while the Impala idled in the driveway, some companion waiting in the passenger seat, features underlit by the dashboard while the radio played. And his mother following Claude to his car.

Sit tight, Edgar told himself. Just wait.

That meant sitting at the dinner table and watching Claude slice and chew and swallow and smile while Edgar's heart vibrated like a hummingbird in his chest. It meant sitting in the living room afterward, pretending indifference. Mornings, it meant looking at the soap shavings scattered about the porch, and the cakes become turtles frozen in the act of hatching—altogether too much like Edgar himself, caught and unable to move as days lapped and receded. It meant, worst of all, being obliged to help Claude in the kennel, where, despite his resolve, Edgar too often replied to Claude in slashing, incomprehensible torrents of sign. But when he could stay calm and watch, he saw not one Claude but many: the quiet one, the jovial one, the confidential one, the one who sat silent in a group. When people came to visit, he watched Claude steer them outside to walk through the apple orchard or into the field or up the road. Anyplace quiet, private. There would be talk and laughter. A gesture of surprise. A head nodded in agreement.

None of which told Edgar what he needed to know. In the end he was certain of only one thing: Claude kept coming back. Whatever Claude wanted, whatever he had done—no matter how nonchalant he acted—he had to keep coming back.

THE WHITE PATCH HAD SPREAD, or so it seemed. A lone dandelion, as bleached and colorless as the grass around it, sprouted in the center, mop half-open. Edgar plucked the albino thing and pressed the scentless mass to his nose. When Almondine began to investigate the spot, he shooed her back and rolled the wheelbarrow over, spade rattling in the bed.

His mother emerged from the depths of the barn and stood watching.

"What are you doing?"

He dug the point of the spade into the white patch.

Does that look normal to you?

"What?"

This right here. This spot.

She looked at the patches of dead grass scattered around the lawn, all withered from the dogs' urine, then back at Edgar with an unhappy expression. When he looked up again she was gone. He dug out a hole until it was below the dandelion's taproot and carted the dirt into the field by the hazels. He filled the hole with quicklime from the bags stacked by the rear barn doors and poured a bucket of water over it all and watched the quicklime slake. When he'd finished, he filled a coffee can with the same chalky powder and walked to the hazels and salted down the dirt.

DUSK. BATS WHICKERED THROUGH the corona of insects around the yard light. The dogs' attention spans were long now and they began to show rare, unnameable talents, which Edgar cultivated for hours in lieu of being in the house. There were long recalls in the field, Baboo and Tinder bounding through lime-colored hay from some far zenith. Finch and Opal, learning to untie simple knots. When asked to clear a leash tangled around her feet, Essay would crouch and leap, avoiding in one adroit move the laborious process of stepping out of the loops. In the mow, he sat the dogs in a circle and knotted a treat into a rag and tethered it to one of the fly lines threaded through a pulley in the rafters. He released a dog by name. If any other dog moved, the treat flew into the air and all the dogs grumbled. When he ran out of ways to proof them, he stood in the doorway of the barn and looked at Claude's Impala and listened to the music playing through the living room windows, waiting for the lights there to go out.

AFTER DINNER ONE EVENING Claude maneuvered Doctor Papineau out to the kennel, unaware, it seemed, that Edgar was there. When he heard them coming, he stepped into the dark outside the rear barn doors and listened. The two men walked into the whelping room, then came out and stood looking into the night.

"Maybe it *is* time," Doctor Papineau was saying. "I've maintained these dogs are a too-well-kept secret for years now."

"Well, you know what I think," Claude said, "but Trudy might appreciate your advice. She respects your opinion something fierce."

"I don't know about that. With Trudy, it's better to wait to be asked than to offer an opinion."

In the dark, Edgar grinned. He wasn't sure what they were talking about, but he remembered well the night Doctor Papineau had provoked his mother and how quickly the old man had backpedaled.

"We'd want to rethink your share if you came in on this. Twenty percent might be more reasonable."

Doctor Papineau grunted, a low *hmmm-hmmm-hmm*. "I never have gotten around to selling that lot on Lake Namekegon. It's just sitting there," he said. "How many does he want to start with?"

"Twelve, for now. A pilot run at Christmas, and then something bigger next year."

"I suppose I could talk to Trudy next time I'm out."

They were quiet for a time.

"You know, Stumpy's is having a fish boil on Saturday. First of the summer."

"Is that right. Lake trout?"

They turned and walked up the kennel aisle.

"Whitefish, I think. Why don't we swing by and pick you up? I could make myself scarce if you wanted to talk to Trudy then."

Edgar watched them go. After Doctor Papineau had driven away, he walked into the house and clapped his leg to call Almondine to go upstairs, all the while feeling Claude's gaze on his back.

WHEN SATURDAY NIGHT CAME, Edgar made it clear he wasn't going anywhere with Claude. His mother feigned indifference, as with a contrary pup, though he knew she felt otherwise. The moment the Impala's taillights disappeared, he rifled the mail drawer, then the kennel files laid on top of the freezer, and the working notebooks. Almondine sat and watched him search. In the closet, he checked the pockets of Claude's coat and trousers. He found nothing to help make sense of that overheard conversation.

Then he turned to more unlikely places—the ammo box with the old telegram, the truck, and finally the spare room. It was almost empty, and had been since Claude moved out, but on the interior wall was a small door. He crouched and opened it and looked into the unfinished rafter space above the kitchen. There, stacked haphazardly across the dusty batts of pink insulation, were a dozen cardboard boxes, the ones his mother had packed that winter day he'd come upon her with her hair wild about her head and so lost in grief she had not even seen him. He knelt on the joists and pulled the boxes into the room. They were printed with logos for canned tomatoes, baked beans, ketchup, their flaps crossed and taped down. The heaviest were jammed with shirts and trousers exuding the faint scent of his father's aftershave. Edgar ran his hands along the insides, feeling for anything not fabric. Two of the boxes held coats and hats, and two more, shoes. Finally, a smaller box of miscellany: his father's spring-banded wristwatch, his razor, his key ring, his empty leather billfold, shiny on the flanks but the corners stretched and pale and the stitching unraveling on one side.

From the bottom Edgar lifted out a Mellen High School yearbook, class of 1948. Tucked inside the front cover was his father's diploma, printed on thick stock with "Mellen High School" crested across the top. He paged through the black-and-white photographs until he found his father among the twenty-five graduates, between Donald Rogers and Marjory Schneider. His father's expression was severe in the style of many of the portraits and his gaze focused on some distant concern. He'd worn glasses even then. Edgar turned to the sophomores. Claude was listed as one of three without a picture.

Edgar scrutinized the posed group shots and candids—the football team, the farm club, the choral group, the crowd in the cafeteria. In the process, two loose photographs slipped from the latter pages. People and places he did not recognize. He shook the yearbook over his lap. Three more photographs fluttered out. In one, his father stood on a lakeshore, fishing. In the other, he sat in a truck, sporting several days' growth of beard. His elbow rested on the open window and his hand was draped over the steering wheel.

The final photograph had been taken in their yard. In it, the barn appeared in the distance, rising darkly above the slope of the side lawn. His father was looking on from near the milk house, a tiny figure. In the foreground stood Claude, dressed in a T-shirt and jeans. A massive, full-grown dog had just leapt into his outstretched arms. He was laughing and staggering backward. And one of his eyes was black.

Edgar sat looking at the photograph. The dog, in motion when the shutter was tripped, appeared mostly as a blur, but it was very big, that much was obvious. It didn't look like one of their dogs, not exactly, a mix of some kind, though predominantly shepherd, with a dark face, high-set ears, and a saber tail. Edgar turned the photograph over. On the back, in his father's draftsman-like handwriting, a caption read: *Claude and Forte, July 1948.*

CLAUDE HAD TAKEN ON the kennel paperwork, an idea Edgar's mother welcomed. Edgar found Claude at the kitchen table often, letters spread about, talking on the telephone for follow-ups and new placements. If Edgar walked in during one of his conversations, Claude would cut his conversation short, as if his brother's work was hard enough without his being under observation as well. The files and records themselves were neatly organized and legible; the problem was mastering the lineage of the dogs available for breeding the next litter and holding all the requisite information in his head. Claude knew the basics, of course. John Sawtelle had drilled the principles of animal husbandry into both his sons. But Claude had been away from the kennel long enough that the complex scoring system, refined by Edgar's father over the years, was now a mystery to him.

On the other hand, Claude's attitude toward any accomplishment was cool indifference, a studious lack of awe. No matter what the feat, whether a pyrotechnic piano solo on a variety show or Kareem Abdul-Jabbar sinking a last-minute skyhook for the Bucks, Claude was unimpressed. He often declared that a person could get anything he wanted if he was willing to go slow enough. The pianist, he would point out, had sacrificed his childhood practicing—of *course* he could tickle the ivories. Jabbar was born tall and he worked at the game five days a week, all year round.

"Everyone gets good at their job," he said. "It's osmosis. The most ordinary thing in the world."

Edgar's mother laughed when Claude started in, having decided it was a form of backhanded compliment, since the more impressive the feat, the more steadfastly Claude held to his position. It wasn't disrespectful, he maintained, because the principle applied to everyone, straight across the board: Trudy, Edgar, and most especially Claude himself. It was never a question of whether Claude could learn to do something, just a question of whether it would be worthwhile and how long it would take. This was his approach to mastering the kennel records (and learning to read sign, for that matter, despite the fact that he walked past the sign dictionary in the living room every day). If he kept his hands in the files long enough, the scoring system would become clear and the merits and flaws of the various lines would sink in without effort. During telephone conversations he idly flipped through whatever folder happened to be in front of him, doodling lineage charts on the newspaper.

His father had been planning a litter for a sweet-natured black and chestnut mother named Olive. He'd spoken of finding a perfect cross, but Claude had searched fruitlessly in Edgar's father's notebook. As Edgar well knew, that notebook was a mess of illegible notes, lists, reminders, and diagrams. The same man who filled out log records with the precision of a penmanship teacher wrote his notes in a madman's scribble. But Olive was coming into heat soon, and Claude sat at the table after dinner behind an avalanche of manila folders. Late one evening, he walked into the living room.

"I have Gar's cross for Olive," he said.

Edgar's mother looked up from the magazine she'd been reading. "Who?"

"Drift," he said. "He's sired three good litters. Healthy as a horse. He's down in Park City."

Edgar's mother nodded. She had intuition on crosses, based on her memory of how past litters behaved, but she had always been indifferent to the detailed research, leaving that to Edgar's father. The pups were what excited her, all their talents as yet unrevealed. But Edgar saw the problem at once, and he was signing a response before he had time for second thoughts.

That's a line cross. A bad one.

Trudy looked back at Claude and interpreted. "A line cross?"

"Let's see," Claude said. "Olive was sired by . . ." He retreated into the kitchen and rummaged through papers. "I'll be damned," they heard him say. "Olive and Drift are both from the same sire, one generation apart. Half Nelson. Sired by Nelson, who was out of Bridger and Azimuth."

"What's the problem with that?" his mother asked.

Remember Half Nelson and Osmo? Edgar signed.

"Oh yes," she said. "Not good."

Claude had returned, but he couldn't read Edgar's sign.

"Meaning?"

"Meaning that a couple of years ago, Half Nelson sired a litter out of Osmo, with three pups stillborn and the rest with straight fronts. Gar decided it was a bad cross."

He had decided more than that, Edgar thought. His father had considered that litter a disaster. He'd paid scant attention to superficial traits like coat color, but bones mattered, and straight fronts, which meant bad angulation in the dog's forelegs, were hard to eliminate from a line. And yet Osmo had borne good litters from other sires. Edgar's father had spent most of a day pulling folders and making notes until he'd tapped his pencil twice and announced he'd found what he was looking for, line crosses with a common ancestor in Nelson. Edgar sat with him while he talked it through, and he could still see the diagrams they'd drawn.

"Would have been nice to know that a couple of days ago," Claude said.

"Edgar didn't know you were considering Drift until just now," his mother said, before Edgar could respond. She turned to him. "Who *would* be good, then? Do you have an opinion?"

Edgar wanted to leave Claude hanging, make him work it out for himself so he would look foolish and slow. Any help he gave Claude would only advance his brainless theory of osmosis, but Edgar wasn't sure Claude wouldn't take a wild guess, and he couldn't stand the idea of the dogs being used clumsily.

Gleam, he signed. Or one of his sibs.

After Trudy translated, Claude pursed his lips and returned to the kitchen while Edgar grinned. His mother gave him a don't-push-it-buster squint and turned back to her magazine. He knew what Claude would find: Gleam was a four-year-old brindle, placed with a farm family east of town. The little boy who lived there sometimes sought out Edgar at school to tell him about the dog. He also knew Claude wouldn't find any problem with the cross; he'd have to go back seven generations before he found any common ancestry, if he bothered to look that far.

When Edgar came downstairs the next morning Claude was sitting at the table, manila folders stacked before him. "We're going with Gleam," he said. He waved a coffee cup over the records. "Did you want to check me on this? I'm going to call the owner this afternoon and arrange it."

Edgar tried to think of a response but his mind seized up. He shrugged and walked to the doorway.

"Look," Claude said. "Is there something in particular you want to say? It's just me and you here. Whatever's on your mind will stay between us."

Edgar stopped.

I bet it will, he signed. He thought how he'd capitulated the night before, how he'd helped Claude though it was the last thing in the world he'd wanted to do. Slowly, and with great precision, so that the gesture was unmistakable, Edgar angled his left hand in front of him and shot his right beneath it, index finger as straight as the knife it was meant to evoke.

Murder. That's what's on my mind.

Claude's eyes tracked Edgar's hands. He looked as if he were searching his memory, nodding all the while noncommittally.

Edgar turned and walked onto the porch.

"I just want you to know," Claude called from the kitchen. "Picking Gleam like that. I was impressed."

Edgar pushed through the screen door and let it slam, blood rising in his cheeks. He'd mustered the resolve to accuse Claude to his face, yet somehow Claude had twisted the moment into a chance to look magnanimous. And to whom? No one had been there to see it. Worst of all, Claude's compliment had elicited in him a flush of pride that made him instantly loathe himself.

The problem—the very troubling problem—was that, when he wanted to, Claude could sound so much like Edgar's father.

NIGHT. HE STOOD IN THE bathroom and crossed his arms at his waist and peeled his shirt over his head and looked in the mirror. Where a story had once been written in mottled blue and green, now only pale and ordinary flesh.

Memory of his father's hands sinking into that spot. How, with the slightest pressure, his heart might have stopped. The stream of memory passing through him like rain, now as faint and undetailed as dreams called back from sleep. He pressed a thumb to his sternum. A familiar ache lit his ribs.

He swung his arm wide, hand curled into a fist.

The sensation, when he brought it to his chest, exquisite.

WARM AFTERNOONS, HE WALKED with Almondine into the woods, where they slept under the dying oak. Sometimes he took Essay or Tinder along to make it look like training. Whenever his mother insisted he spend the night in the house, he waited until she and Claude were asleep, then led Almondine downstairs, bearing all his weight onto the creaking treads. From the bedroom doorway his mother watched him rummage through the refrigerator.

"What are you doing?"

Going to the barn.

"It's eleven o'clock at night!"

So?

"Oh, for God's sake. If you can't sleep, read something."

He slammed the back door and stalked across the yard.

Yet he couldn't oppose them in everything. One problem that irked him especially was naming the newest litter, something he'd delayed for three weeks. But now the pups' eyes were open and their milk teeth were beginning to come through and they had begun exploring. The earliest puppy training would start soon—the playing of unusual sounds, the setting up of miniature stairs and hoops and all those puzzles for infants—and when that began they had to have names. He carried the dark blue *New Webster Encyclopedic Dictionary of the English Language* into the whelping pen and sank cross-legged into the straw. Four pups bumbled to the edge of the whelping box and looked at him.

The spine of the dictionary cracked dryly when he laid it open. He sprayed the pages through his fingers. Annotations flickered past, the oldest in his father's handwriting, but most in his own squarish lettering. Good names had once lived between the dictionary's covers: Butter. Surrey. Pan. Cable. Argo. Sometimes he could even remember the exact place he'd been sitting when the word had risen from the page and declared itself to be a name. At the back of the dictionary was an essay by Alexander McQueen, the editor, entitled, "2,000 Names and Their Meanings: A Practical Guide for Parents and All Others Interested in Better Naming." Edgar knew it by heart. "The naming of an infant is of more than passing importance," McQueen had written. He'd listed seven rules for choosing names, such as "The name should be worthy," "It should be easy to pronounce," and "It should be original." Now, the more Edgar thought about those rules, the more the unclaimed words turned to nonsense: *Spire. Encore. Pretend. Herb.* The mother dog lifted her nose to scent the dry pages, then sighed to acknowledge his difficulties, and he closed the dictionary.

The pups had fallen asleep, except one who fussed at a nipple, nursing then letting go then taking it again. He reached past the pup and rolled the nipple between his fingers and brought his fingers wet to his nose and tongue.

What are you complaining about? he signed.

He set aside the dictionary and shifted the pup back into place, stroking it two-fingered while it nursed and he didn't stop until it, too, lay asleep.

AFTERWARD, HE HERDED HIS LITTER into the workshop and up the narrow steps, stopping only to retrieve the photograph of Claude and Forte from its hiding place, tucked into the envelope with the Hachiko letter. The mow was still warm from the day's heat. He swung open the broad door at the front and let the night air wash in, cool and thick with pollen. The dogs wrestled and plunged across the straw bales at the back, for the once-vast wall of yellow had diminished to a low platform. They would need more straw soon. That meant a day standing at the mow door, waiting at a creaking conveyer for bales and driving in the hay hook and stacking them crosshatched to the rafters. He looked out at the dark woods. He wondered if Schultz had imagined teams of men working where he stood at harvest time, shouting, cursing, taunting those below to bring on the hay as they hauled on the sling ropes.

When the dogs settled down he shut the door and they began to work. He'd forsaken the regular training schedule, instead teaching them playful acts with no point and no purpose. Tagging one another. Carrying scraps of doweling from place to place. Dropping to the floor during a carry. Watching the dogs was the only thing that put him at ease, and he made a game of it, trying variations, setting up barriers, switching the order, testing connotations. A tag, they decided, meant not merely scenting another dog, but a solid nose-push. A carry meant not dropping a thing, even when a tennis ball rolled by. Edgar found a pen and an old spoon and a length of welding rod and he asked the dogs to take those items in their mouths instead of doweling, despite their strange texture and taste.

When they'd agreed on this new meaning of *carry*, an hour had passed and he declared a break. While the dogs lounged in the loose straw, Edgar took out the photograph of Claude and Forte. The stray was on his mind for the first time in a long while. Such a foolish dream to have hoped the dog would come in from the woods. He thought of that day in the field, how swiftly Claude had turned to shoot the doe after the stray bolted. After a while he slid the photograph back into his pocket and he read from *The Jungle Book*, letting his hands swipe through the air.

> So loud did he howl that Tha heard him and said, "What is the sorrow?'" And the First of the Tigers, lifting up his muzzle to the new-made sky, which is now so old, said: "Give me back my power, O Tha. I am made ashamed before all the Jungle, and I have run away from an Hairless One, and he has called me a shameful name." "And why?" said Tha. "Because I am smeared with the mud of the marshes," said the first of the Tigers. "Swim, then, and roll on the wet grass, and if it be mud it will surely wash away," said Tha; and the First of the Tigers swam, and rolled, and rolled, till the Jungle ran round and round before his eyes, but not one little bar upon his hide was changed, and Tha, watching him, laughed. Then the First of the Tigers said, "What have I done that this comes to me?" Tha said, "Thou hast killed the buck, and thou hast let Death loose in the Jungle, and with Death has come Fear, so that the People of the Jungle are afraid one of the other as thou art afraid of the Hairless One." The First of the Tigers said, "They will never fear me, for I knew them since the beginning." Tha said, "Go and see." And the First of the Tigers ran to and fro, calling aloud to the deer and the pig and the *sambhur* and the porcupine and all the Jungle Peoples; but they all ran away from him who had been their Judge, because they were afraid.

He roused the dogs again and began rehearsing two new commands.

He began with *away*, demonstrating in small increments: at first it was enough to look somewhere else without moving. The shared gaze training helped now, and they caught on quickly. Then he coaxed them into taking a step, then several steps, then running all the way across the mow. Finch was the first to get it: no place in particular to go, just *not here*. The dog fairly danced with excitement.

Far more difficult was the idea that *another dog* might convey a command. For example, if he wanted Baboo to down, all Edgar had to do was lift his hand in the air—Sawtelle pups knew that sign when they were three months old. But now he wanted Baboo to down if Finch or Essay nosed him on the hip. They called this linking—teaching a dog that one action automatically followed another. Linking was what made a dog sit when his companion stopped walking. Linking was what made for a clean finish on a recall, when the dog not only returned but circled behind and sat on one's left. And when it came to linking, the Sawtelle dogs were genuinely gifted.

He put Baboo in a stay and stepped one pace back.

Tag, he signed to Essay, indicating Baboo.

The instant Essay touched the dog, Edgar raised his hand. Baboo downed. A moment of revelry. They practiced again, this time with Baboo tagging. After dozens of trials—with breaks to race for a knotted rag thrown into the dark corners of the mow—they'd all gotten the hang of it. He moved them farther apart—five, ten, twenty feet—using a long line threaded through a floor ring for corrections at a distance. After more practice, with just a hint of *down* the dogs dropped when tagged—not every time, but half the time, then two thirds of the time, until finally he could stand motionless and watch while Essay dashed across the mow, nosed Baboo's hindquarters, and Baboo sank to the floor.

Edgar celebrated by rolling them onto their backs and holding their feet against his face. They were fastidious about their pads and when he inhaled against them, an earthy popcorn smell filled his senses. The dogs craned their necks to watch, eyeing him as if astounded, and boxing and writhing to coax him back again. He clapped them to their feet for more practice. Always the same few commands now. He played them again in different orders with different pairings. Different obstacles. Longer or shorter releases.

Roll on your back.

Carry this to the other dog.

Tag that dog.

It was very late, and he was almost tired enough to sleep when he chose a sequence at random and watched them work it out. Opal trotted across the mow holding a dowel in her mouth. She tagged Umbra. Umbra dropped to the floor.

Something about the sight of it brought Edgar to his feet. He had them repeat the sequence.

Carry this to that dog.

Tag that dog.

Down when you are tagged.

All at once blood was roaring in his ears. He understood that an idea had slowly been dawning on him, parceled out over the course of days in bits and pieces from some dim compartment of his mind. They went through the drill again. Each time, he saw more clearly the image of Claude backing out of the barn, looking for something dropped or flung away, the white snowy world behind him.

If that sight brought the memory back for Edgar, might it do the same for Claude?

When he was too tired to run the dogs, he sat and peered at the photograph of Claude and Forte. He closed his eyes and lay on his side, distantly aware that the dogs had gathered around, watching. For so long he'd lurched between one truth and another. Nothing had seemed certain, nothing had even seemed knowable.

But now—perhaps—he'd found a way to know for sure.

Driving Lesson

HE HEARD THE SOUND OF FOOTSTEPS ON THE MOW STAIRS, and his mother ducked around the vestibule door, her dark hair in a loose ponytail that swung sinuously across her shoulders. Essay, Tinder, and Opal were in the mow with Edgar, in sit-stays at the moment, and he was holding a length of thick rope, knotted at both ends, of the kind they used for practicing retrieves. Almondine lay sprawled near the doorway.

"How about a ride into town?" his mother said. "We could stop for lunch."

The three yearlings, excited by his mother's appearance, began to lift their haunches off the floor and Edgar stepped into their line of sight and caught their gazes until they settled back into sits. When he was sure they would stick, he turned to his mother.

I want to keep working Essay, he signed, a half-truth. He'd begun the morning practicing the tag-and-down sequence but they'd fought him on it, playing dumb after being pushed night after night. He wanted more than anything to be left alone to work, for there to be no chance that the sight of Claude near his mother would bring on one of those cramps of anger that could snatch his breath away. The idea of the three of them squeezed into the truck—or worse, the Impala—set off a caw of panic in his mind. His mood, after a night of half-recalled dreams in which he repeatedly slipped from the branches of the apple tree into some formless abyss, was already black and raw.

"Okay," she said, cheerily. "Someday you'll be my son again, I just know it."

He heard their voices in the yard and then the truck started and crunched along the driveway, and Edgar and the dogs went back to work. He clapped up Almondine and they went through a few retrieves while the yearlings watched. When Essay had executed three fetches in a row without a mistake, Edgar rotated Opal through the routine, then Tinder, and then he began with Essay again, this time, lest she grow bored, tossing the rope into a maze of straw bales he had hastily constructed. When Tinder finished, he led them all downstairs.

He decided to eat an early lunch rather than risk their coming back while he was in the house. He walked past the Impala, checking the impulse to mule-kick a dent into its side, and let Almondine up the porch steps ahead of him. When he walked into the kitchen Claude was sitting at the table. He was smoking a cigarette, and the newspaper was quartered in his hand. Edgar's first impulse was to turn and stalk out while the spring on the porch door was still jangling, but he forced himself to cross the kitchen and yank open the refrigerator and pile sandwich fixings on the table. Claude kept reading as Edgar slapped together slices of bread and cheese and pimiento loaf. At last Claude laid aside the newspaper.

"I'm glad you came in," he said. "There's something I want to talk to you about."

Edgar faced the cool depths of the refrigerator and pretended to hunt for something. Then he pulled out a chair across from Claude and sat and began to eat his sandwich.

"You know how to drive that truck?" Claude asked.

Edgar shook his head, which was the truth. His father had let him steer now and then from the passenger side, but only briefly.

"Now, that's a crime," Claude said. "When Gar and I were your age, we'd already been driving for quite a while. It's handy sometimes, you know."

Edgar tore off a corner of his sandwich and handed it down to Almondine.

"I've been trying to talk your mom into the idea we ought to teach you, but she's not convinced. She's in favor of Driver's Ed." He said "Driver's Ed" as if it were the silliest thing in the world. "One day our dad just took us out and showed us how. That's all. After about an afternoon of tooling around, we were all set. Down to Popcorn Corners and back to begin with—a milk run, like they say."

Edgar thought he understood where Claude was heading and he nodded.

"Of course, you and I have an advantage. It was all stick back then, every truck we ever had. But the Impala's automatic. As long as your mom's off in town, I was thinking you and I might have a little fun. Something we could slip off and do, something your mom doesn't necessarily even need to know about. By the time you get into Driver's Ed you'll be the best in your class. Plus, you'll impress the hell out of your mom the first time you two go for a practice drive. What do you say?"

Edgar looked at Claude.

O, he fingerspelled, as he took a bite of his sandwich.

K, he signed.

Claude watched Edgar's hands, then slapped the table. "There you go," he said. "Swallow it down, son, it's time to take the wheel. Your whole life's about to change." He rattled the newspaper together and stood and twirled the car keys around his finger. Edgar set the remains of his sandwich on the table and stood and walked out with Almondine at his heels.

The Impala was parked facing the road, driver's-side wheels resting in the grass. Claude opened the passenger door and prepared to get in, but when he saw Almondine, he tipped the seat forward and said, "Jump in, honey. Your boy's about to amaze you." Then Claude said one thing more. He was looking down the drive with his forearm resting on the roof of the car. He patted the metal with the flat of his hand.

"Right here's something Gar would never have done," he said. "He'd have kept you pinned down as long as he could."

Almondine had jumped into the back seat. Now she was looking out at Edgar, panting. He'd been hearing a ringing in his ears ever since Claude had said the word "son," and now something that had been hanging by a thread inside him seemed to come loose.

He opened the driver's-side door.

Come out, he signed to Almondine. You have to stay home.

She looked at him and panted.

Come, he signed. He stepped back. Almondine maneuvered out of the car again and he led her up the porch steps and into the kitchen. He squatted down in front of her and ran his hand over her head and down her ruff and he took a long look at the sublime pattern of gold and brown in her irises. You're a good girl, he signed. You know that.

Then he closed the door and walked back to the Impala. Claude stood watching him over the flat blue expanse of its roof. The three little vents set into the car's flanks reminded Edgar of shark's gills.

Let's go.

He didn't care if Claude understood his sign. His body language was clear enough.

Claude dropped into the bucket seat on the passenger side. He rolled down his window and Edgar did the same. "You know the gas from the brake, right? Everybody knows that."

Claude handed Edgar his ring of keys. Edgar examined them up in the light and gave the gas pedal an experimental push.

"You don't want to pump the gas," Claude said. "You'll flood it."

The key slid smoothly into the ignition and the Impala's starter whirred and the engine roared to life. Edgar held the key twisted over a moment too long and there was a horrendous grinding noise. He let up, then seeing the expression on Claude's face, twisted it again. He pulled his foot off the gas pedal and set it on the floor and listened to the motor idle.

Claude started talking again, but Edgar wasn't paying attention. He tested the brake pedal experimentally, felt it give under his foot. The shifter was on the column. The orange tip of the gear indicator was under

the speedometer. He'd seen people do this before with automatic trans-
missions; he pulled the shift lever back and dropped it into D.

The car began to roll forward.

"That's right," Claude said. "Nice and easy."

The steering wheel turned with a strange oily smoothness compared
to Alice. Edgar wondered if the Impala had power steering. Stranger yet
was the huge flat hood extending in front of them. He was used to a thin
orange oblong with a smokestack coughing black fumes. This felt like
steering from behind a vast blue table. The engine sounded distant and
muffled. And he couldn't see what the front wheels were doing—he had
to steer by feel alone.

"That's good," Claude said. "Just ease it down the drive and we'll see
what's coming. Take a left, head down toward the Corners so your mom
won't catch us if she's coming back from town."

Edgar looked at him and nodded. He began to press the gas pedal, and
then, without quite realizing he'd made any decision, his foot kept pressing down, a surprisingly long way, until it was flat against the floor.

The Impala bellowed. It fishtailed in place on the dirt and gravel of
the driveway. Edgar had a good grip on the wheel, and he kept the car
more or less straight ahead as it shot forward—maybe a little on the grass
to the right, but that was better than clipping the house.

"Whoa there, son," Claude exclaimed. "You got a tiger by the tail. Let
up! *Whoa!*"

It took no time at all to reach the end of the driveway. Edgar wondered
how fast they were going but he didn't have time to look at the speedometer, so much was happening. For one thing the trees in the orchard
were coming up fast on the right. For another, he had craned around to
watch the barn receding in the back window, and that was difficult to do
with his foot squashed down on the gas. When he faced front again, he
thought a very long time before he decided not to run the car straight
off the road into the woods across the driveway, because he knew they
weren't really going that fast. Out on the road, they'd be able to pick up
a lot more speed. As the last apple tree blurred past the side window he
started turning the wheel.

Claude had stopped shouting "Whoa!" as if they were on a horse-drawn wagon and reached over to throw the wheel to the left. They struggled a little trying to agree on when to return the wheel to center; Edgar thought that should happen when the mailbox was dead square in front of the windshield but Claude wanted to start earlier than that. Together, they worked out a compromise. The Impala's nose heaved left and the car performed a deeply satisfying slide and then they were crossways in the road, or nearly, and there was the deafening sound of gravel being chewed up under the tires and spat at the quarter panels. Claude now had both his hands on the wheel; he had definite ideas about the direction they should be headed.

Okay, Edgar signed, you steer.

He took his hands away, keeping his foot smashed down on the gas pedal. Unburdened of the task of navigating, he could twist around to look through the rear window again; it was exhilarating to see the road shrinking away like a broad brown strip of taffy being pulled out of the trunk. Also, now he had time to check the speedometer. He didn't know if it was right; it didn't seem like they could be climbing past fifty already—they weren't even to the fence line. Maybe it was just the wheels spinning out on the gravel. On the other hand, they *had* started moving pretty fast once Claude got them headed down the center of the road. Claude had once said the car was a four-twenty-something. Edgar thought that was good; he thought that meant it would go very, very fast.

Air began to roar through the open windows.

Don't we get to listen to some music? he signed.

Then Claude was shouting about the gas pedal. Edgar reached past him and turned on the radio. Over the roar of the engine, he heard the steely twang of a guitar.

Country music, he signed. My favorite.

He pressed one of the big black preset buttons to switch channels, then another.

I really don't like it when you call me *son*, he signed. That's not right. I'm not your son.

He turned the radio off again.

"I can't understand you," Claude said. "*Let up on the gas*, for Christ sakes."

In fact, he signed, I really don't like you being in my house at all.

Claude reached over and tried to shift the transmission into neutral, but Edgar put his hands on the steering wheel again and wrenched it to the left. The car slewed across the gravel and a stand of maple trees filled the windshield. Claude let go of the shifter and put both hands back on the wheel and, to Edgar's surprise, was able to square their line of travel with the road again.

Now the speedometer was up to seventy-three. The Impala was jittering around as if it were traveling on a strip of ball bearings. That was the fastest he had ever traveled in a car, Edgar thought, and it was interesting that it was on gravel. The speed really ate up the road; ahead, he could see where the dirt merged onto the broad curve of blacktop that continued north and veered east to Popcorn Corners. There was a little bridge over a creek up ahead, and he wondered if they could get the Impala up to seventy-five by the time they reached it. Before he had a chance to ponder it further, they'd arrived. There was a lurch, and when they landed again, Edgar felt as if his body were still sailing through the air while his eyes had fallen back to earth.

He smiled at Claude and checked the speedometer. They'd made it to seventy-five after all. The hood of the Impala was tarnished, and that was a shame. On a nice day, he bet it would be fine to see the clouds climbing across that blue mirror stretched out in front of them. Like flying into the sky.

"Okay," Claude said. He had quickly gotten the knack of steering from the passenger side. They hardly wobbled at all, which was a good thing, because the road was narrow.

"Okay," Claude repeated. "You're the boss. What do you want?"

Edgar wondered that himself. He didn't really have a plan. In fact, the whole driving thing had been Claude's idea. And there was that clanging in his head. It was driving him batty; he tried hammering the heel of his palm against his forehead to make it stop. It didn't help—though, at least now his head had a reason to ring. He turned and grinned sheepishly at Claude.

Why not go all the way to Popcorn Corners, he signed. A milk run, like they say.

"I don't understand you," Claude said. "You know I can't read—"

P-O-P-C-O-

"Don't fucking fingerspell at me," Claude shouted. "Let up on the *gas*!"

And then, before Edgar could react, Claude reached past him and flipped the transmission lever up into neutral. From where he sat, Claude couldn't have seen the shifter window in the dashboard, so it had to have been a wild guess, and he might easily have thrown it into reverse instead. *That* was an interesting possibility, and one Edgar hadn't considered before. What happened if you dropped into reverse going, what, sixty-four miles an hour? No, make that fifty-eight. Fifty.

The sound of the Impala's engine, roaring while in gear, now rose to a shriek, as if it might leap from its moorings. Claude twisted the key and the engine died. They drifted to a stop. For a while there was just the sound of the two of them panting and a clicking, thumping sound. Edgar looked down and discovered his foot spastically pumping the gas pedal. Their plume of dust caught up with them, then swept past, a dry, brown fog. The cooling engine block made a low ticking sound.

When do I learn to parallel park? Edgar signed. I hear that's tricky.

Claude pulled the keys out of the ignition and sat back in the passenger seat. He couldn't possibly have understood what Edgar had signed, but he started to laugh anyway. Pretty soon he was howling and slapping his knee. Edgar got out of the car and began to walk back up the road toward the house, two or three miles distant. Behind him, he heard the passenger door slam and the crunch of footsteps on gravel. The starter on the Impala whined and stopped, whined and stopped.

Before Edgar had gotten far up the road, Claude had backed the car around and then it was rolling along beside Edgar. The engine made a wounded sound and something was tapping or clicking under the hood. *Wha-ting! Wha-ting! Wha-ting! Tingtingtingtingtingtingtingting!*

"Guess I had it wrong about driving," Claude said. "No hard feelings?"

Edgar walked along.

"While you're enjoying your stroll, you might want to consider that you and I have people in common. Your mother, for instance."

And my father, he signed.

Claude couldn't help trying to read his sign, even when Edgar flashed it out. The Impala rolled alongside him while Claude replayed the gestures in his mind.

"Yeah, likewise," Claude said, taking a wild guess. Then he gave the Impala the gas. It knocked and stuttered down the road. He'd gone about a half mile toward the house before the car slid to a stop again and he climbed out.

"You're *just* like your father! Goddamn it all!" he shouted, kicking the gravel. Then he turned and climbed into the Impala and roared away.

Trudy

IF TRUDY HADN'T BEEN PREOCCUPIED AS SHE DROVE TO MELLEN, she might have felt pleasure in the trip, for it was one of those perfectly warm June days when the sun felt like a voluptuous and reassuring hand pressing down on a person's skin. Ordinarily she liked the radio, but the roar of air past the truck window was best for thinking, and Edgar was on her mind. He was engaged in a rebellion she didn't completely understand. It was over Claude, she knew that much. Three nights in the last week he'd refused to come in from the kennel, sleeping instead in the mow. But whenever she tried to talk to him, he just walked off or stood there and shut her out as only Edgar could.

He had, of course, always been hard to read, even as a little boy, so inward and stoic, beyond anything she'd expected. He had virtually never cried as an infant. Almondine had done his demanding for him, half nursemaid, half courier. His teachers attributed his stoicism to his lost voice, but Trudy knew that wasn't it. In fact, Edgar had started communicating with a desperate urgency when he was only a year old. By the time he was two he had absorbed the clumsily demonstrated basics of sign language and begun, to her amazement, to construct a vocabulary of his own. There'd been a period—memorable but exhausting—when he'd demanded she name things from the moment he woke until his eyes fluttered closed in exhausted sleep. The ferocity with which he applied himself was almost frightening, and though she supposed it could have been a perverse form of motherly pride, she could not believe such obsession was typical. Almost in self defense, they'd handed him the dictionary and started him naming the pups.

He had also been demonstrative and intelligent from the very beginning, his questions startlingly insightful. She would watch him absorb a new idea and wonder what effect it would have on him, because, with Edgar, *everything* came out, eventually, somehow. But the *process*—how he put together a story about the world's workings—that was mysterious beyond all ken. In a way, she thought, it was the only disappointing thing about having a child. She'd imagined he would stay transparent to her, more *part* of her, for so much longer. But despite the proximity of the daily work, Edgar had ceased long before to be an open book. A friend, yes. A son she loved, yes. But when it came to knowing his thoughts, Edgar could be as opaque as a rock.

A perfect example had been the Christmas when he was five. He'd started kindergarten that year. Every morning they stood together at the end of the driveway and she'd watched him board the school bus, and every noon he'd returned, hands upraised to greet Almondine, who almost flattened the boy as soon as he stepped clear of the bus, making such a spectacle that other children called Almondine's name from the bus window. Edgar had been excited to be around other children that fall, but he wouldn't tell her much about school unless she probed him. What had they done that day? Was his teacher nice? Did she read stories? Then she would coax him into telling her the story. Sometimes there was a sign he didn't have yet, and together they would look it up in the sign dictionary, and if that failed, invent one on the spot. When December came, he'd sat at the kitchen table and written out a wish list for Santa and sealed it in an envelope before she could read it. She'd had to wait until he was asleep to steam the envelope open.

At the top of his list he'd written, *Pocket watch WITH A CHAIN*.

It had taken her completely by surprise. He had never once expressed a desire for a watch, and he already knew how to tell time—he'd learned when he was four. For a few long weeks he had included the time in everything he said—At six fifteen we are going to eat dinner. When I get done with my bath it will be eight thirty. That had quickly lost its thrill, but perhaps his obsession with telling time had just been internalized, gone opaque. In any case, it was the *number one thing* on his list and she was determined he would find it under the tree. She and Gar located a watch shop in Ashland whose proprietor rummaged around in back and produced an old pocket watch that a boy might use (and almost certainly break). *And* it came with a long chain. The winding knob was intricately knurled and engraved on the brass cover was a flowery letter *C*. Trudy liked the *C*. They could say it stood for Christmas. The man told them it would run for almost a whole day when fully wound; perhaps it lost five or ten minutes, but that would be okay for a boy—better, in fact, since he would have to wind and set it frequently. They'd wrapped the watch and put it under the tree and made sure that the smallish box in green foil was the last one Edgar opened. He'd looked at the watch in his hand and smiled exactly the smile she'd been hoping for, and then he slipped it neatly into the pocket of his pajamas.

"Aren't you even going to open it?" Trudy cried. "Press the little lever! Look at the hands!"

He took it out of his pocket and let them demonstrate how to wind the works and set the time. He watched intently, but when they'd finished, he closed it up and slipped it back into his pocket. That was the last they saw of it for almost a week, until Trudy walked into the living room and found Almondine in a sit and Edgar swinging the watch back and forth before her eyes. Almondine panted and looked past the swinging timepiece at Edgar. When Edgar understood that someone else was in the room he turned around.

It doesn't work on dogs, he signed.

"You're trying to *hypnotize* her?" Trudy had said. "That's why you wanted a watch?"

He nodded. Come on, he signed to Almondine. It'll work better on puppies. And he pulled on his coat and marched out to the kennel while Trudy stood there, mouth hanging open.

That had been the moment she'd realized how he carried things around inside, things entirely separate from her. Five years old, barely in kindergarten. She had no idea where he'd heard of hypnosis. She couldn't remember seeing anything on TV that might have put it in his head. She didn't think any of his books mentioned it. Wherever he had picked it up, he'd been walking around with that idea for weeks—months, maybe—without mentioning it even once. Just watching, thinking, wondering. That was the kind of boy he was. And she realized that he was, in some sense, already lost to her—had outgrown her in some essential way. He wasn't keeping secrets. If she had known to ask him if he was interested in hypnosis, he would have told her. He just hadn't offered the information because she hadn't asked.

And the obvious question was: What *else* was he thinking about? What else had he already learned that no one even suspected?

Edgar's career as a hypnotist continued for several weeks. At the high point, he mesmerized little Alex Franklin into throwing a snowball into the playground teacher's ear. When Trudy investigated further, it turned out that *Alex Franklin* had made that claim. Edgar had only told the boy, deeply under the influence of his swinging timepiece, to take a bite of a snowball that looked more than a tad yellow. Instead, Alex had extended his arms like Frankenstein's monster and trundled toward the teacher, then wound up and let fly. Edgar hadn't expected that. The whole hypnosis business was unpredictable, he'd confessed.

Which led to a discussion about responsibility. It was like with the dogs, Trudy had told him. If you asked them to do something, you were responsible for what happened next, even if that wasn't what you intended. You were *especially* responsible to the dogs, she said, because they respected you enough to do what you'd asked, even if it seemed like nonsense to them. If you wanted them to trust you, you had better take responsibility, every single time.

And then she'd let him try to hypnotize her, but she didn't get sleepy, sleepy. He'd been disappointed, but she wouldn't lie to him about it. Nor would Gar. Nor would Almondine, nor any of the puppies (who wanted to swat the watch out of his hands and chew it to bits). Then Edgar gave up on the whole idea, though he didn't stop carrying the watch around. Once in a while he opened the cover and checked it against the kitchen clock and wound it, but Trudy suspected he did this only when he was around them. By the time the snow had melted that spring, she found the watch lying buried among his touchingly small, white Fruit of the Loom underwear in his bottom dresser drawer.

IF EDGAR HAD BEEN INWARD and opaque to her at five, now he was a total mystery. Since Gar's death, he'd been sleepwalking through his days, looking angry one minute, then tragic, then thoughtful and happy a moment later. Only working his litter seemed to capture his attention. She told herself she shouldn't worry. After all, he could have been shooting drugs (if a person could even find drugs in Mellen, which she doubted). If he really wanted to spend day and night in the kennel, let him.

Truthfully, this latest obsession hadn't started until long after Gar died, really, the last couple of weeks of school, when he'd taken to running off from his classes. She'd talked with the principal. She wasn't going to have them cracking down on Edgar and ruining his attitude toward school for good when he was muddling through what, she was sure, would turn out to have been the worst period of his life. He was delicate right now—deal with this rebellion wrong, and it would set. She didn't think that the lessons from dog training always transferred to people, but it was just the nature of things that if you punished anyone, dog or boy, when they got close to a thing, they'd get it in their head the thing was bad. She'd seen people ruin dogs too many times by forcing them to repeat a trial that scared the dog or even hurt it. Not finding a variation on the same task, not coming at things from a different angle, not making the dog relish whatever it was that had to be done, was a failure of the imagination.

And in this case, the analogy applied. She'd told the principal she didn't give a damn whether Edgar showed up even one more day that semester after what he'd been through, and if they pushed him any harder, she would withdraw him herself. They knew as well as Trudy that the teachers were coasting the last couple of weeks. Who cared if he sat in class and stared out the window or if he just wasn't there? How many farm kids, she asked, went truant when it was time to show livestock at the county fair? She could use the help around the kennel anyway.

Then there was Claude, whom Edgar objected to. In his position, who wouldn't? After Gar's death, she and Edgar had grown so close it was almost as if they had been a couple themselves, making dinner, curling up together on the couch to watch television, arms wrapped around each other. She'd fallen asleep that way more than once. And on other nights, when he'd been the one to sleep, she'd stroked his brow like he was a baby. After that, of course he would be jealous. Maybe she should have held back from him a little, let him handle his grief his own way, but when you're hurting, and your son is hurting, you do what you need to do.

Besides, Claude wasn't something she'd planned—about the last thing she'd had in mind, particularly after the nasty falling-out between him and Gar. (Not that she understood *that*—a brother thing, buried under too many layers of family history for her to unearth.) Things with Claude had just, well, *happened* one morning—a breakdown on her part, a strange, momentary kindness on his. It hadn't felt wrong; afterward she'd even felt as though some great burden had been lifted—as though she'd been given permission to carry on with a different life. What Edgar didn't understand was that it was all going to be a compromise from then on out. That wasn't something she could say, not to Edgar, not to anyone, but she knew it was true. They'd had the real thing, the golden world, the paradise, the kingdom on earth, and you didn't get that twice. When a second chance came, you took it for what it was worth. Yes, Claude had proposed; that was silly, foolishness, not worth discussing. Not then, anyway, not when there was so much work to be done.

She and Gar had had the predictable discussion about what they'd want the other to do if one of them died. She'd been direct and forthright about his responsibilities: "I want you to spend the rest of your life in abject mourning," she'd said. "Cry in public twice a week. A shrine in the orchard would be nice, but I realize you're going to be busy handling the kennel *and* giving lectures on my divinity, so I won't insist on that."

Gar had been more modest. He'd wanted her to remarry the moment she met someone who made her happy, no sooner and no later. That was Gar in a nutshell, of course—when you asked him a serious question, you got a serious answer, every single time. She'd loved him for that, among many other things. He was passionate in a way that Claude would never be—passionate about principles and passionate about order, which he'd seen as a primary good. Like those file cabinets, filled with records. The kennel had been important when he talked about what should happen if he were to die; he hadn't said it straight out, but he'd clearly expected Trudy would find a way to carry on the work with the dogs.

So Trudy thought Gar wouldn't necessarily object to how things were working out. It looked like the kennel would be back in order by the end of the summer. And what they had both cared most about was that the other person find a way to be happy. Gar might not have liked some of the changes Claude was suggesting, but Gar had envisioned remaining a one-kennel, boutique breeder forever. Claude was less concerned with bloodlines, which freed him up to think more broadly about other things.

In the meantime, it was a matter of seeing into Edgar more clearly, making sure he got through this bad patch. And that's all it was—a bad patch. There wasn't anything seriously wrong.

She'd have known at once if there were.

Popcorn Corners

THE NEXT DAY EDGAR SET OUT AGAIN FOR POPCORN CORNERS— this time alone, by bicycle. Anything to get away from the house while Claude was there, and he was there all the time now. Edgar slipped the picture of Claude and Forte into his back pocket and pedaled away to the north, retracing the route he and Claude had traveled along that thin gravel line cut through the Chequamegon Forest. A county gravel truck roared past, drawing a tawny billow in its wake. The air was still thick with dust when he came to the blacktop and turned onto a small forest road. He passed marshes boiling with frogs and snakes, and later, a turtle, plodding between the ditches like a living hubcap, its beaked mouth open and panting.

A stop sign appeared in the distance. When he reached it, he surveyed the entirety of Popcorn Corners: a tavern, a grocery, three equally decrepit houses, a band of feral chickens that lived in the culverts. He coasted past the tavern, which sported a Hamm's Beer sign, lit to show the beer bear fishing in a shimmering Land of Sky Blue Waters, and halted in front of the grocery, covered with white clapboards that hung slightly off parallel, as if covering some profound skew of the building's timbers.

A pair of colossal ash trees cast their shadows across the storefront and a single antiquated gas pump tilted among the weeds off to the side.

The small parking lot was empty. He lowered his bicycle to the ground and pulled the screen door through its quarter-circle in the dirt. Up front, behind a long, grooved wooden counter, sat Ida Paine, the hawk-nosed, farsighted proprietor of the store. Stacks of cigarette cartons filled the shelves behind her—red-and-white Lucky Strikes, aqua Newports, desert-colored Camels. From somewhere, a radio droned out the news from the AM station in Ashland. Edgar raised a hand in greeting. Ida returned the gesture in silence.

He and Ida had a long, though stilted, acquaintance. He could re-member his father carrying him into the store when he was barely a toddler. Though Ida had never yet said a word to Edgar, he never tired of looking at her. He liked especially to watch her hands as she rang up purchases. They moved with an agile independence that made him think of tiny, hairless monkeys. Her right hand slid dry goods down the counter while her left hand danced across the keys of an ancient adding machine. And Ida, unblinking, looked her customers up and down, her pupils magnified to the size of quarters through dish-lensed spectacles. After each entry, her left hand slammed the adding machine lever down hard enough to stamp the numerals into a piece of oak.

The locals were inured to all this, but strangers sometimes lost their wits. "That it?" she would ask when she'd totaled their items, cocking her head and fixing them with a stare. "Anything else?" The veiny dig-its of her left hand punched the keys of the adding machine and leapt onto the lever. *Thump!* The thump really startled them. Or maybe it was the head-cock. You could see people stop to think, was that *really* it? The question began to reverberate in their minds, a metaphysical conun-drum. Wasn't there *something* else? They began to wonder if this could possibly be their Final Purchase: four cans of beans and franks, a bag of Old Dutch potato chips, and half a dozen bobbers. *Was* that it? Wasn't there something else they ought to get? And for that matter, had they ever accomplished anything of significance in their entire lives? "No," they'd gulp, peering into Ida's depthless black pupils, "that's all," or sometimes, "Um, pack of Luckies?" This last was issued as a question, as if they had begun to suspect that an incorrect answer would get them flung into a chasm. Cigarettes often came to their minds, partly because Ida herself smoked like a fiend, a white curl always streaming from her mouth to rise and merge with the great galaxy of smoke wreathing over her head. But mainly, when the uninitiated stood before Ida Paine, they found themselves thinking that the future was preordained. So why *not* take up cigarettes?

When something Ida didn't know the price of landed on her counter, her right hand would pick it up and twirl it until she spied the white sticker with its purple numerals, and then she would glance at a yellowing index card taped to the counter and say, without emotion, "On sale today." She never declared the price. Edgar listened for these asides. On the drive home he liked to match the stickers with the numbers on the adding machine tape that came with their purchases. Sometimes, the numbers all added up; more often everything was scrambled. He'd once gone through the exercise of totaling up the stickers himself. Though none of the individual numbers was correct, the total had been exactly right.

He walked along the farthest aisle, past the canned milk and SpaghettiOs and the cereal. There was nothing he wanted, really, and he didn't have much money, but he dawdled. The plate-glass window facing the road admitted less light than a person would have guessed, and the gloom only increased farther back. He half expected to find spiders spinning webs in the darker recesses, but that was the thing with the Popcorn Corners grocery—at first glance it seemed disheveled and broken down, but when you looked closer, you found clean and neat. The rear of the store was a butcher shop, the domain of Ida's gaunt, aproned, white-hatted husband. When Edgar was little, he'd entertained the notion that Ida's husband *lived* behind the meat case among the grinders and cutters and the scent of chilled blood and flesh.

Bottles kept catching his eye, especially smaller bottles. He picked up a bottle of fingernail polish remover and carried it for a while. He knew of only two uses for it—the second was to kill butterflies, an act he'd seen performed but had never done himself. The idea reminded him of Claude and Epi and the Prestone. He picked up bottles of saccharine, bottles of syrup, bottles of corn oil, and hefted them and set them down again.

At last, he returned to the front counter. Ida stood with her back turned, twisting the radio's antenna as the speaker hissed and crackled. Then she turned and centered him in her black pupils. He pointed at the soda case outside and she nodded. Her left hand groped toward the adding machine, paused over the keys, and withdrew. He expected her to ask her question, but all she said was, "Nickel for the bottle."

He dropped a quarter and a nickel into her palm. She stopped cold for a moment, blinked, then turned and dropped the coins into the cash drawer. Outside, he lifted a bottle of Coca-Cola from the red cooler and pried off the top using the zinc bucktooth of the opener and watched the soda fizz. Clouds had appeared in the blue sky during his ride and now they'd begun to clot, turn dark. The breeze carried with it a vestige of spring chill.

The window sash by the cash register slid up. Ida Paine's face appeared gray behind the screen.

"You miss your daddy," she said. "He was a good man. He came in about a week before and I got a feeling then. Nothing certain. Happens all the time. Someone hands across corn flakes, soup—nothing. Then they'll hand over some little thing and I'll get a jolt off it, it's so loaded up. It's not a message. People will tell you it's a message, but they're wrong. What it is, you pay attention to it long enough, you can start to *read* it. Read the juice."

Through the screen he could make out the shape of her face, the glint of her glasses, the stream of smoke fluttering up from her nostrils.

"Some juice feels good," she said. "Some juice feels bad."

He nodded. There was hot and cold lightning.

"What can you do?" she said. "No one knows when something like that's going to happen. Weight of a coin can make all the difference. Man came in once, told me how he'd nearly died except for the change in his pocket, change I'd made for him the day before. Something about that dime being just the right size to turn a screw, and without it, he'd've been lost."

She didn't expect a response, he knew that. He stood waiting for her to go on and thought about all the times he'd watched Ida Paine's left hand hop over the keys of her adding machine.

"When your daddy came in that last time he bought milk and eggs. That's all. I rung up the milk same as any day, but with the eggs there was so much juice it was like a *hand* grabbed me when I touched them. I dropped the whole carton on the floor. He went back and got himself another one. I was half afraid to ring it up. And I had this powerful feeling—almost never happens—that I should charge your daddy *more* for those eggs, not less. More, you see? But I can't do that. People get mad. But your daddy, he looked at me and said, 'Here's for both.' I should have taken the money. That would have been the right thing to do. But I said, no, that it was me that dropped them, and I wouldn't charge for both. And that time, the total rang up two dollars, even-steven."

She was silent for a long time.

"Even-steven," she repeated. "That was the last time I saw him. I should've come, but I couldn't. To the funeral, I mean."

Then she tipped her head and looked at Edgar one-eyed, a primeval bird in its cage. "Child," she said from the gloom, "come in here and show me what it is you brought with you."

He almost didn't go back in. He stood and looked at his bicycle and then at the clapboard siding with its crazing paint and thought how, though every individual board looked straight and square, when you took them all together something was cockeyed. But in the end he pulled open the screen door and walked to the counter. From his back pocket he drew out the photograph of Claude and Forte and set it on the scored wood between them.

Ida's right hand scrambled across the counter and lifted it up for her to see.

"That one hasn't been here for a long time," she said. She looked from the photograph to Edgar and back again. "I remember him, though. Those dogfights." Her left hand placed a nickel on the counter. "Take your deposit," she said.

He reached out and set the empty Coke bottle on the counter. Before he could let go of it, Ida's adding machine hand sprung forward. Its fingers encircled his wrist with a surprising might and pinned his hand hard against the counter. At once his fingers cramped closed around the fluted bottle. Then, before he quite understood what was happening, Ida's other hand had pressed the photograph of Claude and Forte against his free palm and she'd somehow curled his fingers closed and locked that hand shut as well. Then she leaned over the counter toward him.

"You think you can find that bottle?" she said. "You need to look for that bottle. Because unless you can lay hands on it, you need to *go*. You understand me? You need to *go*. That's what's in the juice."

He didn't understand her. Not in the least. Her face was dreadfully close to his and her fingers were squeezing his fist until the crushed photograph bit into his palm. The smoke above her head crawled in knots and ropes. Images he didn't understand occupied his mind's eye: a dark, cobbled alleyway, a dog limping through the rain, an elderly Oriental man holding a slender length of cane with great delicacy. Edgar looked at the Coke bottle in his rigor-locked hand and Ida's monkey fingers encasing his wrist like a hot iron manacle and then he saw that the bottle had changed. It had taken the shape of an antique cruet or inkwell, maybe a prescription bottle from olden days. Some oily liquid glazed the inside, prismatic, clear, viscous. The thing was banded with a ribbon, and the ribbon was covered with markings in some foreign alphabet.

"And if you go," she whispered, "don't you come back, not for nothing. Don't you let the wind change your mind. It's just wind, that's all."

Then she cocked her head and looked at him. She blinked. He recognized in her then a wizened version of the little girl with Shirley Temple curls, the one who had confronted him in the Mellen diner and asked for the secret he didn't know.

My gramma's like me. Wanna know what my gramma says?

A slab of a hand appeared on Ida Paine's shoulder, carrying with it the odor of blood and flesh. Then the butcher stood behind the old woman, his white apron smeared with sausage-size lines of red.

"Ida," the man said. "Ida."

"It's just *wind*," she repeated. "It means *nothing*."

Her fingers uncurled from his wrist. Instantly, Edgar felt his grip relax and the bottle was simply a Coke bottle again and not the odd-looking vessel they'd grappled over. Ida snatched it and slumped onto her stool, chin on her chest, drawing great, deep breaths. Smoke issued lazily from her nostrils. When her eyes, magnified through the lenses of her glasses, went momentarily pink, he saw the doll-like face of the little girl again.

She says that before you were born, God told you a secret he didn't want anyone else to know.

The butcher lifted the Coke bottle from Ida's grip and clomped to the rear of the store. There was a clank as he racked the empty. For some time Edgar stood rooted to the unvarnished floor of the Popcorn Corners grocery while the radio hissed out pork futures.

The next thing he knew he was pedaling like a maniac over the gravel of Town Line Road, halfway home.

FOREWARNED WAS NOT FOREARMED. The catastrophe, when it came, turned on a vanity of Edgar's so broad and innocent that he would look back on the events of that afternoon and find blame only in himself.

He had nearly arrived home, pedaling the upslope on the last small hill before their field opened greenly to the west, when the shakes came over him, first in his hands, then his shoulders and chest, until he thought he would either be sick or jerk the handlebars sideways and pitch onto the gravel. He ground the coaster brake under his heel and stumbled away to sit in the weeds beside the road.

Whatever had happened under Ida Paine's grip had been frightening enough, but worse, it had brought on a sudden, suffocating desire to recall his father's memories, those memories he'd held so briefly. He closed his eyes, pressed his palms to his head. He heard the hiss of rain striking the new grass and he felt the thousand soft impressions of it falling coldly on his skin. He remembered his father's hands passing into his chest. The sensation of his beating heart cradled. The images sieving through him. The dogfights. The desire to stand between Claude and the world. A whole history he couldn't know. But their substance was again lost to him, as fugitive as the shape of a candle's flame.

I have to go back, he thought. She can help me remember. She knows something about Claude—what had she said about dogfights? And who was the old man he'd seen in the alleyway? What was he holding? But he thought of how Ida looked afterward, slumped on her chair like the empty shell of an old woman, and he wondered if she would even remember talking to him. If he asked her about the old man in the alley, he felt sure she wouldn't know what he was talking about. And anyway, he didn't have the courage to face her again. Not for a long time. Maybe not ever.

When he remembered the photograph, he clapped his shirt pocket. Empty. Sweat broke out across his forehead. At first he thought he'd left it at the grocery. If so, he'd *have* to go back. He lay in the grass and frantically searched his pants pockets until he found it, bent in half and roughly jammed in the back right. The photograph was in bad shape after being crushed in his convulsed fist under Ida's fingers. The emulsion was shot through by white cracks half a dozen ways. He pressed it flat. It puckered into meaningless, geometric bas-relief, dividing the image into triangles and trapezoids. But Claude and Forte were still unmistakably the subjects. Edgar propped his arm on his knee and held the photograph out and looked at it. When his hand stopped quaking he remounted the bicycle.

He topped the hill and coasted up their driveway. It was mid-afternoon. The Impala was parked behind the tractor and Edgar's mother was crossing from the barn to the house with a set of training notes in hand. As he rolled past, she called to him.

"Edgar! Could you unload the truck? I was at the feed mill yesterday."

He walked his bike into the milk house, wishing he could have gotten home unseen, to go somewhere with Almondine and think before he had to face his mother or Claude. At least his mother had been preoccupied; by the time he shut the milk house door, she had disappeared into the house. He turned the corner into the barn to get the wheelbarrow. As he passed the workshop, he glanced through the doorway out of habit. He wasn't looking for anything in particular. He didn't even know anyone was there.

Claude stood before the workbench, bent over something small, perhaps a jammed spring latch for a lead, tinkering with it like a watchmaker. Almondine lay on the floor, hips tilted, peering up at Claude, relaxed and complacent, her mouth hanging open in a quiet pant. A wedge of light streamed from the high workshop window. Motes of straw dust hung suspended in the air. Everything there was lit in degrees of light and shadow—Claude's shoulders and head, the chaff on his shoes, the saws and hammers hanging from the pegboard, the outscooped curve of Almondine's chest, the contour of her head and ears, the scythe of her tail trailing along the dusty floor. Almondine turned to look at Edgar, sleepy-eyed and relaxed, and then back at Claude. All of this was framed in the doorway, like some sort of painting, but it was the accident of a moment, something unpracticed and undesigned.

And, to Edgar's eye, beautiful.

His breath stopped as if he'd had the wind knocked out of him. Suddenly nothing at all about the situation seemed tolerable. He saw with absolute clarity that he'd lulled himself into acquiescence and complicity. But now some last thing gave way inside him, something with no name. Perhaps it could be called the hope of redemption. For him. For Claude. For all of them. When it was gone, he felt that he had become someone else, that the Edgar who had split away that first morning after the rain had at last returned, and in that new state, as that new person, he believed Almondine had acted unforgivably, her pose so lovely and serene, completing that homely tableau as if Claude belonged right where he stood, when in fact he belonged anywhere else. In jail. Or worse.

He managed to keep walking. He grabbed the wheelbarrow from the far side of the barn and hurled it before him along the aisle and onto the driveway. Then Almondine trotted up beside him. He flung the handles forward and turned and raised his hand above his head to down her.

She looked at him for a moment, then dropped to the ground.

He turned and kicked the wheelbarrow ahead, runners raking clouds of dust from the driveway. Almondine broke and came forward and this time he whirled and lifted her by the ruff until her front feet came off the ground and he shook her and shook her and shook her. Then he let go and downed her again and turned away. He loaded the heavy sacks of quicklime into the wheelbarrow and piled the bags of food on top crosswise and walked around to the handles and backed the wheelbarrow away from the truck. He meant simply to walk away without another word to her but at the last minute he turned and knelt, his arms and shoulders trembling so violently he almost lost his balance.

I'm sorry, he signed. I'm sorry. But you have to stay. Stay.

He rolled the overloaded wheelbarrow up the driveway, staggering. When he tried to turn it toward the barn the thing tipped and the feed bags spilled onto the ground. One of them split and its contents poured out and he kicked it over and over until kibble was spread out in a brown swath across the ground. He reached down and threw fistfuls toward the woods until he couldn't breathe. After a while he righted the wheelbarrow and loaded all the bags of food that had not split into the wheelbarrow's bed and bore it heavily forward. He emerged from the barn with a rake clattering inside. He made a pile of the loose food and shoveled it into the wheelbarrow with his hands. It took a long time. Spots danced before his eyes as if he had stared into the sun.

Almondine was holding her down-stay behind the truck when he walked out of the barn. He passed her on his way to the house, stride halting and overbalanced as though his spine had fused into a column of stone, and then he threw his hands into the sign for a release.

At the porch steps, he turned back. Almondine stood in the sun panting and looking at him, tail uncurled behind her.

Go away, he signed. Release. Go away. Get *away*!

And before she could move, he walked up the porch steps and into the house.

The Texan

THE INSOMNIA THAT NIGHT WAS BEYOND ANYTHING EDGAR HAD experienced, a goblin presence in his room, goading him between self-recrimination one minute and white anger the next. The sight of Almondine lying at Claude's feet like an idiot puppy had wounded something in Edgar so close to his center, so bright, so painful, he couldn't bear to look at it. He sat flinging out arguments, rebuttals, accusations, his heart firing like a piston in his chest, his thoughts whirling like flies around some phosphorescent blaze. He should have acted that morning, so long ago, the moment he'd understood what Claude had done. The hammer had been in his hand. Instead he'd faltered and doubted, and the flame in him had choked to embers. But one breath of pure air had drawn it up again. That had been Almondine. None of it was her fault, he knew. And yet he couldn't forgive her.

When his mother saw how he'd been treating Almondine, late in the evening, she'd dropped any pretense of patience. He would stop immediately, and while he was at it, she said, he was going to rejoin the household and quit the nonsense about sleeping in the kennel. He'd stormed upstairs and slammed the door and stood swaying with rage and confusion. The red rays of sunrise were coating the woods before he at last fell into an exhausted slumber. But it was no rest and no balm. When the sound of his mother working a pair of dogs in the yard woke him it was almost a relief.

He sat on the bed and looked at the closed bedroom door. He couldn't recall a morning in his life when he hadn't opened his eyes to the sight of Almondine. When she was younger (when *they* were younger) she'd stood beside his bed and nosed the tender part of his foot to wake him; later, she'd slept beside him, rising while he stretched and yawned. Even if she'd gone downstairs to greet the early risers, no matter how quietly he walked to the stairwell, she was there waiting, front feet on the bottom tread, peering up at him.

He pulled on jeans and a T-shirt. He could hear the scrabble of her nails on the hallway floor. When he turned the knob and swung the door back, she pretended it was a surprise, and she bucked in place and landed with her front feet spread wide, head lowered, ears twisted back. And he meant to forgive her, but at the sight of her, playful and coy, all his arguments from the past night possessed him again: How she pandered. How she was so much like another person he could name that she ought to go find *her* instead. Or even *him*, since she didn't care who gave her the attention she craved. She danced along behind him, catching the cuffs of his jeans. It took her a minute to follow him down the varnished stairs—the headlong plunge of her youth replaced by cautious navigation—but she darted past as he crossed the living room and whirled to face him, making a little yowl and play-bowing again.

He signed a down and stepped over her.

Two empty coffee cups sat on the kitchen table, the chairs pulled out to hold invisible occupants. He swabbed out a cup from the sink and poured himself the dregs from the coffee pot. It tasted like acid on his tongue. He swallowed once and flung the rest down the drain.

His mother was working the two dogs to be placed that day, Singer and Indigo. She would, he knew, be in a terrible mood. On the mornings of placements all she talked about were the qualities that made the dogs unprepared to leave. Edgar knew the litany by heart. All that time spent building their confidence. All that work teaching them a language in which questions could be asked and answered—all of it about to be abandoned and lost. His father had always been more circumspect about placement, but then he had surrendered the pups once already, to training. He was also the one who managed the carefully scheduled mail and telephone correspondence with new owners to keep track of the dogs, so in a sense he never lost them. Edgar's mother, on the other hand, would storm around the house, indignant at the idiocy of owners, their laziness, their lack of compassion, flinging papers, slamming doors.

The irony was, a person wouldn't have known any of that from watching her as she worked the dogs, not even on the day they were placed, because with the dogs, she became a different woman, almost a character she played—the trainer, who was interested only in what the dogs were doing in that moment. The trainer showed no anger when dogs were unruly. The trainer gave instant, forceful guidance. As their time for placement approached, the only difference the dogs might notice was that they got less attention; if they were a bit lonely, it helped them bond with their new owners.

Edgar didn't attempt to help his mother. He did morning chores, then pulled Tinder and Baboo and drilled them on close work—heels, stays, leash tangles, and the things they had been practicing in secret: the tag, the drop, the carrying of small items in their mouths. Claude was bottle-feeding one of the new pups. When he came out of the whelping room, Edgar took the dogs into the field.

And Almondine placed herself along his route wherever he went. If he was behind the barn, she lay near the silo. If he was in the barn, she waited in the shade of the eaves to meet his glance. Each time he refused her. Finally, she lost heart and found a place to sleep. It took a long time for that to happen, but he saw the moment she finally turned away. And he let her go.

JUST BEFORE DINNER Doctor Papineau parked his sedan on the grass behind the Impala. Edgar watched from the barn as the old man clapped a hand on Claude's shoulder and they walked into the house. Shortly, an unfamiliar pickup slowed to a stop at their driveway and turned and trundled past the house. It was a big truck with an elaborate topper and Texas license plates. His mother and Claude and Doctor Papineau walked out of the house with Almondine trailing. There was something about watching Almondine from the barn, thirty yards distant, something in her carriage, tentative and almost frail, that finally made Edgar understand how cruel he'd been. He made a promise in his mind to make things up to her that night, though there was nothing he could do just then—events required him to stay where he was for a little while longer.

Claude walked around to the driver's window and gestured at the turnaround. The pickup backed around and stopped again, facing the road. Then the door opened and a man stepped out. There was a short conversation. Almondine greeted the visitor along with the rest of them. Then Edgar's mother looked over and called, "Edgar, would you bring out Singer and Indigo?"

This was the start of the presentation, in which he'd always played a very specific role. When he'd been little, it had especially impressed new owners to see a child hardly taller than the dogs lead them out of the kennel. Now that he was older, the presentation was less dramatic, but the stagey element remained: after the new owner arrived, after introductions and talk, Edgar emerged with the dog (or dogs, in this case—not uncommon, since they placed many pairs). His father had loved the little choreographed drama of it. After all, he'd said, owners meet their dogs just once. Why not make sure they remember it? It was a small, extra guarantee the dogs would be treated right. Sometimes the owners gasped when Edgar and the dogs appeared; he'd even seen his mother smile, despite her dire predictions, as he measured out steps along the drive, affecting a relaxed, nothing-out-of-the-ordinary expression.

The dogs, excited by a stranger's arrival, raced one another along the lengths of their pens, pushing out through the canvas flaps to get a look and turning and pushing back in again. Edgar quieted them and walked to the pen that held the two dogs to be placed. Singer was a gloss russet male with an imposing stance but an easygoing demeanor. Indigo was petite for a Sawtelle dog and as black as if dipped in ink, except for a blaze of cream on her chest and another swirl across her hips. Edgar drew the slicker brush from his back pocket and went over them one last time. Indigo's coat was fine and luxurious when brushed up. The dogs stomped in the straw and panted under his brush. Singer protested the delay with a deep moan.

Hold on, he signed. You'll know soon enough.

He stroked their faces and squatted in front of them. He made them look at him steadily and he put his hands on their chests, seeking the spot that would calm them. Then he put collars on them and brought them into a heel, one on each side, hands on their withers, and they walked up the barn aisle. When they stepped outside, the knot of people by the house shifted. The talking ceased. Edgar paused for a moment with the old gooanecked light fixture overhead. His father had often joked about hearing angels sing when he and the dogs turned that corner.

"Oh my," he heard the man say.

When they were halfway up the drive, Edgar patted each dog lightly on the shoulders. They turned to look at him. He flicked out a release and they arrowed forward, all silken motion, feet thumping softly on the ground as they ran. Then there was chaos and introductions. The new owner was a slight man, leanly built, with brown hair and jug ears and a thick mustache. His accent matched his license plate, a heavy drawl. He knew dogs; he presented the back of his hand rather than his fingers; his touch was confident and slow. Occasionally, the dogs might be skittish with a new owner, but not this man and these dogs.

"They sure do *look* at you, don't they?" he said.

Edgar's mother and Claude explained about the gaze exercises and then they introduced Edgar. The man's name was Benson.

"Pleased to meet you," Mr. Benson said, shaking his hand. They let Mr. Benson get a good look at the dogs, see their structure. Edgar ran them through recalls to get them moving. Mr. Benson knew what to look for. He checked their stifles and hocks and he commented on their gait. By the time they had finished, the sun was almost set and they walked to the house together, the dogs surging ahead to wait by the door.

"Son," Mr. Benson said, "you've got the touch with these dogs, even more so than your mama." He turned to Trudy. "No offense, ma'am. I mean that as the highest compliment. I've never seen like the way they do for him."

"None taken," she said. Edgar could see she was reluctantly charmed by the man, and proud of the dogs' behavior, which had been flawless. "Edgar makes it look effortless."

"It's not even so much *effort*," Mr. Benson said. "It's something else. It don't have a name. They just want to work for him."

Edgar's mother laughed. "Don't be too impressed. They're on their best behavior tonight. We'll go over things more thoroughly tomorrow. Indigo has a couple of bad habits you should know about. But they're good dogs."

"Well, I'm daunted by the prospect of living up to what these dogs have been used to," Mr. Benson said. "I'm not ashamed to admit it. I wonder why they'd listen to a dope like me after working with y'all."

They downed the two dogs, along with Almondine, in the living room and sat down to dinner. Mr. Benson said he lived in the hill country near San Antonio. He wondered if they had ever been there, and they said no, and he told them about it, the live oaks and the pecan trees and the wild mistletoe and the river. They asked about his trip. The drive had been long, he said, but he loved the open highway, that stretch of asphalt opening out before him.

Edgar sat and listened. Mr. Benson had taken a room at Fisher's Paradise, south of town. He was staying for several days. He liked to talk, almost a match for Doctor Papineau, but his thoughts ran to philosophy and religion. "Tell you something I think is curious," he said. "In the Bible there's hardly no mention of dogs. What there is makes them out like vermin. I can't make sense of that, can you?"

"Sure," Edgar's mother said. "Back in those times, for every dog that lived with people, a dozen more ate garbage and ran through the streets. Companion dogs were the exception."

The man nodded and looked at all of them. Edgar got the impression he'd raised this question before at other tables.

"'Give not that which is holy to the dogs, neither cast ye your pearls before the swine'—that's Matthew. It's always bothered me. I'm a heathen nowadays, though. People in my congregation fall faint if I walk in on a Sunday. But a lot of them aren't as holy as a good dog."

Doctor Papineau was inspired to contemplate the population of dogs on the Ark, and from there the conversation turned back to Singer and Indigo. Edgar's mood had lightened, briefly, while he worked the dogs, but as Claude began explaining the history of the kennel, it turned wretched again. Mr. Benson didn't question Claude's authority, though to Edgar every word he spoke marked him as an impostor. Now Claude was explaining about Buddy and the blood tie between the Sawtelle dogs and the Fortunate Fields breeding program. That surprised Edgar—he thought what he'd learned through the letters was a secret, or forgotten, but it wasn't, and there was no reason Claude wouldn't know. Now he was explaining how many dogs they placed each season and how the breeding program established by Edgar's grandfather worked; how half the dogs they placed went to families who had already owned a Sawtelle dog; how the majority of breeding dogs were fostered by farm families nearby. And as Edgar sat and listened to Claude, he wondered why he hadn't plunged the Impala into the trees when he'd had the chance.

When they finished dinner, his mother brought out Doctor Papineau's cheesecake and poured coffee. Mr. Benson commented on the cheesecake, and Doctor Papineau chimed in with his shopworn joke. Something about it made Edgar angry. Whenever he looked at Doctor Papineau he saw that fatherly hand laid on Claude's shoulder and he thought the old man was a fool to let himself be manipulated so transparently. Even the new owner had begun to bother Edgar. Most wanted to get away from the table as soon as possible, to release their dogs from their stays and touch them, but Mr. Benson seemed oddly incurious. The dogs were patiently holding stays; Singer was even dozing. But anyone could see they were waiting to spring up and investigate the man all over again.

Then Mr. Benson turned to Claude.

"Now, I've got something to ask, and you should just say no if I've overstepped. Of course, we'll get to this tomorrow when we work through the branch contract and pick out stock, but I'd be obliged if I might have a look at your kennel. That's a fine barn. I haven't seen many like it since I passed Killeen. And I want to see for myself what sort of magic happens there."

Claude and Doctor Papineau were looking at the man with equally self-satisfied expressions. Edgar turned to his mother.

What is he talking about?

She waved him off with a small gesture. He signed again.

Why is he talking about a branch contract?

She turned to him, her expression calm, but beneath that, flushed with anger.

Not now, she signed. You haven't wanted to talk for weeks. We'll discuss it later.

What does he mean, selecting stock? Breeding stock?

Not now.

Mr. Benson was watching the exchange and he leaned back.

"I don't mean to be rude. It was just itching at me. Maybe that's for tomorrow."

"Not at all," Claude said. "I have to tell you, though, there's nothing magic to be found out there. Just slow, steady work."

Claude led Mr. Benson outside, followed by Edgar's mother and Doctor Papineau. Singer and Indigo loped ahead. Edgar stood on the porch. He recalled that game of canasta they'd played the autumn before. *You can get anything you want in this world if you're willing to go slow enough*, Claude had said. At the time, Edgar had taken it as beer-fueled backwoods munificence, but now he heard it as a perverse taunt.

When did you start wanting this so badly? he wondered, watching Claude walk alongside the stranger, explaining what they did as something to be replicated, capitalized, multiplied. Was it one of those afternoons you spent on the barn roof watching us all? Were you surprised at what your brother had accomplished after you left? Or have you been thinking of this for longer than that? How slow have you been willing to go?

From out in the yard, Mr. Benson's voice rose in reply to some question Claude had asked.

"I have good news for you there," he said. "I talked with the son, James, the night before I left. He's very excited about this idea, calls it a unique opportunity. He keeps saying over and over: a Caruthers dog, a milestone in catalog merchandising—the first time a breed has ever been brand-named. Says he's got a mock-up of the Christmas wish-book on his desk, pups on the inside of the front cover and everything. Course, they're the wrong kind of pups right now, but they can fix that picture in one day flat."

Almondine walked up behind Edgar and stood at the threshold of the kitchen door. He'd wanted to make amends with her all evening, but now he was seething again and in his mind he saw her lying in the workshop, light streaming over her like some kind of painting, and Claude at work. He swung the kitchen door shut and made sure the latch caught. He trotted after the others. The long twilight had faded. A fitful wind shook the maple. To the west, the canopy of the forest shivered against the darkening rim of blue.

"I forget sometimes what it's like to be this far from city light," Mr. Benson was saying. "Our night sky is never this black, with San Antone so close. D'you ever see the northern lights?"

But before anyone could respond to the man's question, something curious happened. A gust of wind passed through the yard, carrying with it a sheet of warm rain, translucent and swift. The drops pelted the roofs of the vehicles and splashed thinly across them all. The dogs snapped at the air. Dust rose from the driveway. Then the rain was gone, returned to the night. Everyone looked up. There was nothing overhead but a field of stars.

"That don't surprise me," Mr. Benson said. "That happens back home. Rain'll fall smack out of a clear sky. That rain could have been in the air in North Dakota and only now touched ground."

They'd come to a stop in front of the barn, near the leaden pock of quicklime where the grass had once turned white. The man squatted down to stroke Indigo's chest. It was the first time he'd touched either of the dogs since dinner, and when he stood again he produced a handkerchief from his pocket and wrung his hands in the cloth and pulled it along each finger.

"It occurs to me every once in a while that it's raining *somewhere*, even when the sky is clear—there's more water in the air than we're apt to think. You took all the water out of the air, there'd be a flood that only Noah would recognize. When I can't make sense of things, I try to think big enough to see rain falling somewhere. Water's always moving—that's the view I try to get. If it's not falling, it's coming up through the ground getting ready to fall again. That comforts me, I can't say why. Sometimes I only need to get above the treetops. Late afternoons where I live, you can see half a dozen big ole bull thunderstorms coming along, shafts of light between them and rain trailing underneath like a jellyfish. Sometimes, though, I have to go up high enough to see most of the whole country—way, way out to California— before I see rain and clear sky both. That's all in my mind, of course. But no matter where I am, if I can get to where I see it raining and where it's clear, that's when I can do my most powerful thinking."

Then Mr. Benson caught himself.

"Good God," he said. "I didn't realize how long I've been sitting alone in a truck."

Edgar's mother laughed and they walked into the kennel. None of them seemed to take more note of the rain, though to Edgar, it had felt like a hand brushing his face. For a moment he was unable to move. When he caught up, the dogs began to bark. His mother hushed them, a small thing that impressed the man greatly. Mr. Benson started asking questions: how long did they let the pups nurse, did they believe in docking dewclaws at birth, why didn't they use sawdust instead of straw, and so on. Claude took down the master litter book and pulled a file at random and talked about the breeding research and the log sheets and the scoring, all with great authority, like a man describing furniture. Edgar's mother led Mr. Benson up to the mow and showed him the fly lines, the floor rings, and all the rest.

"Where does this young man come in?" Mr. Benson said when they came down again. "He earns his meals, I'm sure."

"Well, for one thing, Edgar names the pups," his mother said. "And he's in charge of grooming. And this year, he's training his first litter. I expect they'll be ready by fall."

Mr. Benson asked to see Edgar's litter, and Claude set his hand on Edgar's shoulder and told him to bring them out. Until that moment Edgar hadn't decided to have his litter play out what they'd practiced. He'd always imagined some circumstance with just him and the dogs and Claude, but now he saw it didn't matter who else was there. There was no choice anyway. He had to have an answer. He couldn't stand the knowing-and-not-knowing, the residue of memory without the memory itself, the coming-apart every time he sat across the table from Claude. All he needed was one unguarded moment, like the one when Claude first spotted him watching from the apple tree. An expression had flashed across Claude's face then, shock or guilt or fear, but whichever, it had vanished before Edgar had understood what it might reveal. This time he would be ready. He would see it for what it was. And if he saw guilt, he would not be stopped by anyone's touch, not his mother's, not Almondine's. He would not sink to his knees, shaking like a newborn calf.

"Let's proof them on stays while we're at it," his mother said.

He nodded. He walked past the pens and into the medicine room, where he yanked open the drawer reserved for Doctor Papineau's supplies and stuffed six syringes into the breast pocket of his shirt. It looked strange, he knew, and he tried to act nonchalant as he walked out again. He brought out Opal and Umbra and stayed them in the aisle, then Pout, Baboo, Tinder, Finch, and finally Essay. The seven of them sat, twitchy and excited, forty feet down the aisle from his mother and Mr. Benson and Claude.

"This will just take a moment," his mother said. She shot Edgar a quizzical look and kept talking. "We try to use every opportunity to train them. When a stranger visits, the dogs naturally want to investigate. A lot of our training is just finding ways to test their skills in new situations, like holding a stay when there's a distraction. Here, Edgar, send one of them over."

First, tell them the dogs see everything that happens here, he signed.

What?

Just say it. Say they see everything and they never forget. You'll understand in a minute.

He stood and waited. He thought his mother might ignore his request, but she turned to Mr. Benson and Claude and Doctor Papineau. "Edgar says to tell you that the dogs see"—she faltered for a moment, then continued—"that they see everything that happens here, and they never forget."

Edgar was standing before the dogs, looking down the line to make sure they didn't break. He touched Opal under the chin. She looked at him. He released her and she dashed down the aisle to the four of them standing by the workshop. Then he pulled one of the syringes from his shirt pocket. His hand was shaking and as the syringe came out, it snagged another which went clattering to the floor. He snatched it up and placed it in Baboo's mouth.

Tag, he signed. Then he turned to watch.

Baboo trotted down the aisle with the syringe in his mouth. Edgar kept his eyes on Claude, who had caught sight of the syringe. When Baboo reached them, he pressed his nose into Opal's hip, and Opal looked toward Edgar. He gave a small gesture with his right hand. She dropped to the floor and lay on her side.

"Well, I'll be," Mr. Benson said. He stooped to stroke Baboo's muzzle and came away with a syringe in his palm.

"What's this?" he said. He held the syringe in the light. Before anyone could answer, Edgar sent Pout and Pout tagged Baboo and Baboo went down. Mr. Benson reached over and extracted the second syringe from Pout's mouth.

"This is part of their training? To carry medicine?"

Seeing the expression on Claude's face, Edgar began trembling so violently he had to kneel. Finch went next; he tagged Pout, Pout looked at Edgar, hesitated, and dropped. Then it was Umbra's turn, and Tinder's. Each time there was a syringe and a tag on the hip, and the dog went down.

"Well, I'll be," Mr. Benson said. "It's almost like . . . as if . . . Do they think . . ."

Claude stood watching it all. He glanced at the open door, then back at the dogs, then at Edgar.

Edgar didn't expect the last part to work—it was different from the rest, something he'd worked out with Essay alone. He put the remaining syringe in her mouth and signaled her down the aisle. When she reached Tinder, the only dog standing, she turned to look back at him.

Left, he signed.

Essay veered around Tinder. The barrel of the syringe was sideways in her mouth. She walked up to Claude. The safety sheath was on the needle, but when she pressed the blunt soft tip of her nose into the muscle of Claude's leg, he flinched as if he'd been stung. Edgar was walking down the aisle, neither blinking nor averting his gaze.

"Drop it!" Claude said. "Drop it!" He looked again toward the Dutch doors and then faced into the workshop and then got control of himself and took a breath and looked steadily at Edgar. A muscle under his left eye was jerking.

"What the hell, anyway!" he said, and stalked out of the barn.

Edgar began turning in the aisle, performing a weird, exhilarated dance. He signed a broad release and the downed dogs scrambled to their feet and stirred around Mr. Benson. His mother allowed herself an angry look at him, but when she spoke, her voice was cool and modulated.

"Edgar," she said, "would you put these dogs back in their pens? I think we've seen enough."

Did you see? he signed. Did you see his face?

I certainly did.

"That was extraordinary," Mr. Benson said. "What was that?"

"I haven't seen that before myself," Doctor Papineau said, "and I've watched these dogs do some pretty unusual things."

Edgar's mother turned to Mr. Benson. "It doesn't always make sense when you see it in progress," she said.

"Go," she said to the dogs jostling at their feet. "Kennel up. *Go.*"

The dogs trotted down the aisle. Edgar went to Essay's pen and grabbed her by the ruff and scrubbed her up, then visited all the rest. Good girl. Yes. Good dog. Good girl. Everyone had walked out of the barn, and as he praised his dogs he listened for the Impala starting, but he heard only a hasty parting conversation between his mother and Mr. Benson.

It was full dark outside now. If he went to the house, there would be demands and arguments and he needed quiet to close his eyes and watch everything again—see the look on Claude's face as Essay tagged him, the flush of blood across his cheeks, the muscle tugging his eyelid. He climbed the workshop stairs and flicked on the lights in the mow. As the sound of Mr. Benson's truck faded, his mother stormed in.

"We're going to talk, Edgar. Right here, right now. I want to know what that was about. Do you have *any* idea how embarrassing that was?"

Did you see his face? The look on his face?

"Whose face, Edgar? Mr. Benson's? Who thinks I have a lunatic for a son? Or Claude's? Who, by the way, is in the house right now, royally pissed off?"

He walked between straw bales scattered across the mow floor, then stopped and looked into the rafters. His breath roared in his ears.

It's raining, he signed.

"What?"

Is it raining? Do you hear rain?

He ran to the front of the mow and unlatched the broad loading door and swung it open. He gripped the lintel and hung his body into space and looked into the stars burning in the clear night sky, then out toward the woods.

Remember me.

He pulled himself inside.

Come here, he signed. See for yourself.

"I can see from where I am. There's no rain. Come away from there."

But his patience was spent. He walked to her and tried to pull her forward. When she resisted he clasped his hands around her neck and swung her toward the mow door, his body counterweighted against hers. Bales and rafters spun around them. His mother tried to get her hands under his and pry them away. They'd halved the distance to the mow door when he lost his balance and they crashed to the floor. In the tumult, he knelt over her and pinned her arms. They panted. He let go and began to sign wildly.

Did you help him? Tell me now if you helped him.

"Help him? Help *who*?"

I'll show you who.

He stood again and took his mother's wrist and began to lug her toward the mow door, still hanging open onto the night. When she realized what he was doing, she began to kick along the floor to get to her feet.

From behind them came a hoarse cry. Not speech, not words, just a groan of apprehension. He looked over his shoulder. Inside the vestibule at the top of the stairs stood the chiaroscuro figure of a man. Edgar dropped his mother's wrist and ran toward the door, so grim and ecstatic and oblivious he fell over a bale of straw and went down, legs kicking. When he'd scrambled to his feet again, the hay hook was in his hand. He threw himself at the doorway, hook dragging through the air behind like a great single claw. The figure stepped deeper into the shadows and tried to close the vestibule door, but Edgar struck it headlong before it latched.

The door slammed back with a splintering boom. There was a grunt and then the sound of a body tumbling heavily on the stairs. Then silence. Edgar looked up to find the hay hook driven thumb deep into the timber of the doorframe. He wrenched the thing free and flung it ringing across the mow. His mother had gotten to her feet and was running toward him, saying, "What was that? What did you do?" but he couldn't answer at first. A savage, godish electricity ran through his nerves. From his chest, a spasm rose. His hands snapped open and shut so that he could barely force them into sign.

I should have done it the first night he stayed here.

Only after his mother cried out did he follow her into the vestibule. She was standing halfway down the stairs, the heels of her hands pressed to her temples. At the bottom of the stairwell lay Doctor Papineau, feet askew on a high tread, head on the workshop floor, canted horribly. One of his arms was flung forward, gesturing casually away. Edgar pushed past his mother and stepped over the veterinarian's body. He bent to look. The old man's eyes were skimming over even then.

Tears streamed down his mother's face as she descended the stairs.

Edgar stood. The muscles of his legs were still twitching with what-ever galvanic charge had possessed him in the mow.

Now you cry? You think this is terrible? Don't you have dreams? Isn't he there when you sleep?

"My God, Edgar. This is not your father. This is Doctor Papineau. This is Page."

Edgar looked at the old man lying there, so small and frail. The same man who'd summoned the strength to lift him out of the snow by the back of his shirt.

He wasn't so innocent. I heard them talking.

His mother put her face in her hands. "How are we going to tell Glen?" she said. "I don't understand what's happened with you. We're going to have to . . . have to . . ."

She looked at him. "Wait," she said. "I need to think for a minute. Page fell down the stairs."

She dropped into sign. You need to go.

I'm not going anywhere.

Yes, you are. I want you to run, get out into the field. Find a place to hide until tomorrow.

Why?

Just *go*!

So you can be rid of us both?

He didn't see her hand moving any more than the dogs saw her leash corrections. A hot jolt traveled from his cheek to his spine. He staggered back against the wall to keep from toppling onto Doctor Papineau's body. The side of his face felt like it had been set on fire.

Don't you dare, she signed, and she was Raksha now, Mother Wolf. You're talking to your mother and you'll do as I say. I want you to go. Stay away until you see me standing behind the silo, alone. Watch in the evening. When you see me, it's safe to come back. Until then, disappear. Even if we call, stay away.

He turned and stumbled out of the workshop and into a yard pale and blue in the moonlight. He squinted past the light above the kennel doors. The night sky cloudless. There was no time to fetch tackle. He rounded the barn and unlatched the pen doors and signaled his litter out. Seven dogs bounded into the grass. Together they ran down the slope behind the barn until they reached the rock pile, and there Edgar sat, senseless, while the dogs milled about. He watched Claude cross from the house to the barn and back. He closed his eyes. Time passed, whether a minute or an hour, he couldn't have said. Then his mother was calling, "Edgar! Edgar!" Her voice toylike and shrunken.

The stars wheeled in his vision. Impossible that he had ever lived there.

He stood. He began to run, the dogs beside him. As they reached the woods, a squad car appeared on the road at the top of the hill, blue and red flashers strobing the trees and throwing off a dopplered siren scream. Glen Papineau, come to find his father. Now there was no going back for Almondine, he thought. And having thought it, found it almost impossible not to turn back.

The moonlight was enough to see the two birches marking the entrance to the old logging trail. The dogs crashed through the underbrush in crazy ellipse, all but Baboo, who trailed a few steps behind. The woods were so much darker than the field. He didn't understand how little progress they'd made until the headlights of the squad car, bouncing over the tractor-rutted field, lit the tree trunks in front of him. Spears and creases of white shot between the trees, but Edgar would not turn his dark-adapted eyes back to look. They wouldn't bring the squad car into the woods—it couldn't make headway on the logging path, and there would be no way to turn it around without miring it.

Fifty yards from the creek, the ground began to slope downward. The dogs were cast wide about him now. When he reached the water, he clapped his hands. Baboo had stayed nearby and sat by his leg, panting. Finch materialized from a stand of bracken, followed by Opal and Umbra, like shadows out of shadows. Then Pout and Tinder. In the dark, it took a long time to be sure it was Essay who was missing. He stood again and clapped hard and listened to the water flowing along the creek bed. Then he could wait no longer. When he walked into the creek, the water covered his ankles, cool and slick. He grabbed the first fence post he touched and hauled it back and forth until it came loose, gasping in its hole. The thing was as heavy as a granite pillar and he had to kneel in the water to get it to move. When it finally came up, he balanced the rough end of it on a flat rock in the creek.

Two of the dogs bounded into the water even before he could call them, though in the dark he couldn't tell who. He pushed them under the wire and they stood on the far side and shook off. He clapped for the others. The remaining four dogs paced beside the creek but would come no farther. A flashlight beam began to cut through the air overhead. The dogs whined and looked over their shoulders. Finally Edgar stepped out of the creek and knelt and put his hands in their ruffs and pressed his face against the crowns of their heads. Finch and Pout and Opal and Umbra. Then he stepped back and released them. At first they sat and looked at him uncertainly. Then Finch wheeled and tracked up the slope in the direction they'd come and the other three followed, crashing along his trail.

Edgar walked into the shallow water of the creek and scrambled beneath the barbed wire. He lost his footing trying to reseat the post; the hole had filled with mud and suddenly he found himself lying flat in the water and wet to the sternum. In the end he left the post standing cockeyed in the stream. He'd wanted to set it back the right way but doubted it would make much difference.

He sank to the ground on the far bank of the creek. Not two but three dogs greeted him: Baboo and Tinder and Essay, Essay having crossed elsewhere on her own terms. They jostled and licked his face and danced around him like savages performing some ancient, unnamed ritual. As though they knew exactly what lay ahead. His hands, when he rose, were covered with clay. A paste of it had begun to dry and crack on his face. He cupped his hands in the creek and emptied the water over his head again and again. Then he stood and turned from everything he knew and the four of them began to make their way into the dark Chequamegon.

Part IV

CHEQUAMEGON

Flight

THIN REMNANTS OF MOONLIGHT PERMEATED THE WOODS. SWEET fern arced throat-high over the old logging path, cloaking blackberry canes hidden like saw blades in sheaths. Spray of dark sumac. Shafts of birch and aspen, faintly luminescing. Overhead, a pale and narrowing crack divided the forest canopy, marking their way more clearly than any earthly thing. For fear of jutting branches, he held his hands across his face and let the blackberry thorns rip his clothes. Now and then he stopped and clapped for the dogs. They came and snuffled nose and lip against his palm and vanished again, so sure in the dark. He paused. Peered after them. Shadow upon shadow, all of it. He swung his foot forward and began again. All around, fireflies glowed their radium bellies. The voices calling after them had long since faded into the creak of tree trunks flexing in the night breeze like the timbers of a vast ship. They hadn't circled; he couldn't have said how he knew. The direction of the wind, perhaps, or the westering cast of the moonlight. When a stand of birches glowed blue where he expected a gap he understood the path had fizzled out or they'd lost it.

After a time he came upon the dogs, bunched and waiting. He counted noses, then moved his hands about in the dark, trying to understand why they'd stopped. His fingers brushed a wire, barbed and rusted, and a weather-split fence post. He slid his hands down the knotted wood until he'd located the bottom strand of wire, then he sidestepped away from the fence post, bent over and tracing the barbs loosely with his fingers. He stopped when there was enough slack to haul the wire up. He clapped twice and the dogs came forward. By touch he moved them under the wire—Essay first, he guessed, then Tinder, then Baboo. They were panting and hot as they went. He rolled under last of all and stood and pointlessly brushed off his clothes, wet and hanging on him like sheets of wax. He looked up. Islands of stars in a lake of black. The forest spectral and pathless all around. He set off in a direction he hoped was west. Hours of the night passed.

He stopped when the woods opened onto a glade. The moon was high and bright, and before him the charcoaled skeletons of trees rose from blue marsh grass. He blinked at the excess moonlight in the clearing and clapped for the dogs. High in the crown of a charred tree, an owl revolved its dished face, and one branch down, three small replicas followed. Baboo came at once. Tinder had begun pushing into the tall grass and he turned and trotted back. Edgar clapped again and waited. When Essay did not appear he led Tinder and Baboo into the trees and touched his hand to the ground. The dogs circled and downed. He paced a few steps away and unzipped his pants. His urine seemed to take with it all the warmth in his body. He peeled off his wet shirt and jeans and hung them on a branch and stood there in the night, clad only in underpants. Clammy as they were, he could not bring himself to take them off. He walked back and lay next to Baboo. Baboo raised his head and looked at Edgar's arm draped across his chest and laid his head down again. When they were all settled, Essay stepped out of a deer track in the sedge. She sniffed the three of them and walked to the clearing's edge and peered upward and returned and stood panting until Edgar sat up and set his hand on her croup. She downed and tucked against his back, grunting with what sounded like disapproval. One after another the dogs heaved sighs and pressed their heads tight to their sides.

Edgar lay watching the silhouettes of the owls warp as they scanned the clearing. He wondered if they should have pushed on until they came to water for the dogs, but after so many hours of stilted, cautious movement in the dark, a crashing weariness had come over him. And yet the moment his eyes closed, there lay Doctor Papineau at the bottom of the mow stairs.

Edgar gasped and opened his eyes.

You're a murderer, he said to himself. You get what you get.

The next instant, he was asleep.

WHEN HE WOKE, the dogs were standing above him like nurses puzzling over a patient, sighting along their muzzles and cocking their heads. The ground beside him was still warm from their bodies. He unclasped his hands from between his knees and pushed himself upright. The dogs bucked and wheeled. Essay planted her back feet and walked out her front until the cords quivered in her sides. Baboo and Tinder yawned out soft creaks from gaping mouths. The owls were gone. Across the glade, the treetops glowed carmine where the rising sun touched them. His head throbbed. He thought they couldn't have slept more than two hours.

He sat, arms around his knees, until the unfurling weeds began to tickle his nether parts. He fetched his trousers from the branch where they hung. They were as wet as when he'd taken them off, and now cold. He lifted a foot, then stopped and peered down the leg holes. When he'd finished dressing he thought he might as well have clothed himself in wilted lettuce.

Baboo had stayed beside him, but Essay and Tinder had already slipped into the tall grass, hunting each other. Trails of grass shook and they dove into the clear and wheeled and plunged back in. He stroked Baboo's neck and watched. The dogs had filled out in the last few months. Their chests were thick and deep, their backs broad, and they moved with a powerful, leonine grace. He clapped his hands. The grass stopped moving and Tinder and Essay cantered out. He sat them in a row and paced backward and recalled them one by one. They repeated this three times, then he snapped off a dead tree branch and rolled it between his palms to scent it up and had them each fetch it. They practiced downs and rollovers and crawls while the birds around the edge of the clearing chattered.

They were heated up then, even lackadaisical Baboo. He thought they'd better find water. His nighttime fretting seemed pointless; no creek could be far off in the lower Chequamegon. He looked back along the way they'd come. Then he led them around the perimeter of the clearing and picked a spot and set foot in the forest again.

AFTER HALF AN HOUR they descended a shallow alder-choked ravine that bottomed out in a creek six inches deep and filled with pale green grass laid over in the current like mermaid hair. The dogs began to lap at once. Edgar tossed his shoes and socks across and waded in and scooped up a handful of water that tasted like cold, weak tea. He let the water run over his feet until the dogs climbed out and sprawled near a mossy log, and then they moved on.

The slant of the morning sunlight made it easy to keep his bearings. They were traversing the ridges west of the kennel, ridges he and Almondine had gazed over countless times as they sat on the hill in the south field. He didn't know how far the ridges went or what they gave onto. They'd seldom traveled that direction; that old life, suddenly so remote, had been oriented along the meridian of Highway 13, with Ashland to the north, and everything else—Wausau, Madison, Milwaukee, Chicago—to the south. So he gave himself just two rules: stay off the roads and travel west. Whenever he was forced to detour around an obstacle, he chose the northernmost alternative. Beyond that, he had no specific destination or design, no more than when he'd first begun training the dogs on those odds and ends in the mow. He wanted distance from that prior life. He wanted time, later, to think about what had happened and what to do about it. Until then he wanted to think about the four of them and how they should move. He was already beginning to worry about the dogs. He didn't know what to do about food. He didn't even have a pocketknife.

Despite himself, he wondered what was happening at the kennel. He thought about Almondine, how he hadn't had a chance to make amends with her. He wondered where she'd slept without him in the house. He wondered if his mother was standing behind the silo that morning, signaling him to return. Perhaps they were still walking through the woods shouting his name. The thought gave him twinges of both satisfaction and remorse. The jolt of his mother's slap kept coming back to him, and her furious expression. And Doctor Papineau's eyes, the life dimming in them as he watched.

His resolve wasn't tested until late that morning, when they came to a road cutting through the forest. It was barely more than a dirt track strewn with gravel and overhung on both sides by trees, so desolate he felt no qualms about standing in the middle of it. The sun was almost at its zenith. He squinted both directions for mailboxes or stop signs. There was nothing, not even telephone poles, just washboards ribbed into the dirt. The long, clear line of the road was a surprisingly welcome sight, for the unceasing effort of reading the tangle of underbrush and choosing a path had begun to wear him down.

Plus, mercifully, there was breeze enough in the open to dissipate the mosquitoes, which had progressed from an annoyance to a torment as he and the dogs traveled. Every fern frond and blade of grass they brushed stirred up another cloud of the hateful things. In self-defense, he'd broken into a trot, swinging his hands around his head and slapping his face and neck, but the moment he stopped they descended again, doubly drawn to his overheated skin.

He sat on the dirt, legs crossed, and gathered the dogs. An approaching car would be visible miles away and he wanted to rest for a minute. If the traveling was hard, he thought, at least there was some consolation in watching the dogs. Back at the kennel, Essay had always been the most delinquent, the hardest to train and the first to grow bored, but in the woods she was at ease, scouting, acting the huntress, forging ahead to challenge any oddity she found: a strangely aromatic stump, a chipmunk skittering through the leaves, a drumming grouse. When she was nearly out of sight, she would turn to look back, though not always; sometimes she charged into the underbrush. It made her a flagrantly inefficient traveler, covering twice as much ground as she needed to, but whenever Edgar tried to keep her nearby she whined and dropped her ears. Baboo was the steadfast one. If Edgar told him to wait, Baboo waited like a stone laid upon the earth by God himself, pleased to know his job. That Baboo was charmingly literal had always been clear, but in the woods he was a pragmatist. He trotted along behind Edgar as he broke trail, sometimes sticking close at Edgar's heels, sometimes dropping back. But if more than a few yards came between them, Baboo crashed recklessly forward to close the gap. Of the three, Tinder was the hardest to pin down. He always stayed in sight, neither shadowing Edgar nor launching himself into the underbrush, but whenever Essay reappeared from one of her forays, it was Tinder who met her and dropped back to touch muzzles with Baboo, as if carrying news.

Edgar sat in the sun in the road. To the far side was a deep patch of fern so lush it looked primordial. They ought to get out of the open, he knew. He was still persuading himself to brave the mosquitoes when Essay's ears twitched and she turned her head. He followed her gaze. Far down the road, a tiny cloud of orange dust was rising and a windshield heliographed as it passed in and out of the shade.

He scrambled up into a crouch. The car was far away and at first he felt no rush. If the driver had seen Edgar and the dogs at all he had probably taken them for deer. Edgar clapped his hands, signed *come*, and waded into the overgrown bracken. The dogs thrashed along behind him. He dropped into the green shadow world of grass and fiddleheads and worked his way along on all fours. At the back of the thicket they came to a dense blackberry bramble, the thorns curved and sharp as scalpels. Even if he forced himself through, the dogs would balk. He chided himself for running toward the unfamiliar. He thought there was still time to cross back the way they'd come, retreat into known terrain, though they wouldn't get more than twenty yards into the forest before the car passed.

Baboo and Tinder were close behind, but Essay had already turned and begun to nose her way back toward the road. He stayed the two dogs—Baboo dropped into a sit like a soldier—and duck-walked through the ferns and tapped Essay on the hip. She looked at him across her flank. He led her back. When she was sitting again he raised up into a crouch and peered over the fronds.

The car was closer than he expected, a hundred yards away and slowing down. There was no way to cross without being seen. They were maybe fifteen feet into the ferns and they had broken a path wide enough to see the dirt of the road, but he guessed they would be hidden from a moving car. He got the dogs' attention, then signed *down*, his hand rising briefly into the clear. The dogs eased themselves to the ground. Essay whined and tucked her hind feet under her hips and elevated her nose in a shaft of sunlight, poking it upward in tiny saccades to take the scent.

He laid one arm over Essay and reached back with the other to touch Tinder, hoping that if he could keep two of them steady, he could count on Baboo to follow their lead. The car's bumper appeared through the stems of the ferns, moving slowly. There was the *pong!* of a stone popping from under a tire. Essay quivered beneath his hand. A white front fender passed his line of sight, then a tire. A black-and-white door. Another door. Another tire. The rear bumper. When the car was some distance down the road, he snapped his fingers. The dogs looked at him.

Stay, he signed. He eyeballed Essay and repeated the command.

That's two stays. You better stick.

He finished with one finger warningly in front of her nose. She broke into a pant and tipped her hips to the side. He raised his head out of the ferns. The car was a sheriff's cruiser covered with dust as if it had been trolling roads all night. A lone, massive figure sat behind the wheel, arm outstretched along the top of the seat. The brake lights stuttered. Edgar dropped back down into the ferns.

He counted to one hundred. When the only sound was the heat bugs in the noon sun he released the dogs. They looked at him. He released them a second time to no effect. He understood something was wrong then and he cautiously raised his head out of the ferns a second time. The cruiser was parked two hundred yards farther along. Only then could he hear it idling. The driver's-side door was open and Glen Papineau stood looking down the road, so big he hardly seemed capable of squeezing back in.

Edgar fell down into the ferns.

Stay, stay, he signed.

Essay swiped her tail and tucked her feet and Tinder pressed his muzzle against Edgar's palm with a questioning stare, but in the end both of them stayed put. It was Baboo who began to rise, half in curiosity, half in confusion. Edgar clapped once, overly loud. The dog froze and looked at him through the stalks of the ferns.

Down, he signed frantically. *Stay*.

From up the road, he heard Glen Papineau's voice.

"Edgar?" he called. "Edgar Sawtelle?"

Baboo lowered himself to the ground, eyes wide. They waited. Edgar heard a door slam and then the faint rumble of the engine as the cruiser pulled away. This time they waited until he began to worry that the road was a dead end and that Glen might double back. He left the dogs in stays and crept out to the road.

There was nothing to see, not even a cloud of dust.

He clapped. The dogs bounded out of the ferns and danced about him in a sort of pageant his mother called The End of Down dance. A few yards up the road he found a clear line into the woods, and in another minute the road had disappeared behind them and they passed into the evanescent stipple of the forest at midday.

BY LATE AFTERNOON EDGAR was hungry—had been hungry, in fact, for quite some time. The final vestiges of panic from the night before had been drained by the monotony of breaking trail and he felt light-headed and irritable and his stomach gnawed at him. He wondered if it was the same with the dogs. They didn't seem uneasy. They'd spent all afternoon tramping through underbrush and fording backwoods streams. So far the dogs had only missed their morning feeding, but *he* was used to breakfast, lunch, and dinner, and he didn't even have a match to light a fire, much less a plan to get food.

He did have something in mind, though it wasn't exactly a plan, since it depended largely on chance. The woods were dotted with vacation cabins and fishing shacks. What was called the Chequamegon, as if it were a single block of forest, was in fact a Swiss cheese of government-owned forest and private property, particularly around the dozens of lakes. Sooner or later they were bound to find a cabin stocked with supplies or come across a car with some fisherman's lunch inside. They hadn't seen one yet. He hoped that meant they were due.

The problem with that idea, he thought as they reached another clearing, was that cabins and cars were located on *roads*, not in the middle of the woods. And roads were to be avoided at all costs—the encounter with Glen Papineau had removed any doubt from his mind about whether anyone was searching for them. If they were spotted—even by someone driving along who later called the sheriff's office to report a boy with a bunch of dogs—they would have a good idea where he was. Cutting through the woods, however, meant slow going. He doubted they were covering more than a mile every two or three hours, with all the underbrush and marshes and the dogs to manage and the caution with which he needed to pick his steps. A sprained ankle would be a disaster.

He wondered if someone might try tracking them with dogs. The woods near the kennel would be so soaked with his scent, the fields so crisscrossed with layers of track from his ordinary daily work, that only the purest, most experienced tracking dog had any chance. And every hour that passed, their track blended farther into the general mélange. Then there was the question of where they'd find tracking dogs, anyway. Sawtelle dogs would be useless. Field tracking was an art they didn't practice. He could hear his mother laugh at the idea; she would tell anyone who suggested it that they might as well track him with cows.

But away from the kennel, everything changed. Their scent would be undisguised and distinctive, and between the four of them they were laying a scent track a mile wide, as obvious to a real tracking dog as if the ground had been lit on fire. The only way to break such a trail would be to get into a vehicle, but hitchhiking with three dogs was as good as walking into the sheriff's office in Mellen. Which brought him back again to staying off the roads.

He was thinking about this problem, circling it and drawing out the alternatives in his mind, when through the trees he glimpsed sunlight reflecting off water. The late afternoon had grown cooler and the wind had calmed. When they reached the water—it was a lake—they walked out onto a small peninsula of sedge and cattails. The shoreline was irregular and densely forested. He scanned for cabins, but all he saw were pines making a sawtooth pattern against the sky and birds diving over the lake, sweeping up insects. Mosquitoes, he fervently hoped. The dogs walked to the water's edge. Having spent no time at lakes, they reared and jumped at the small waves that washed up onto their feet.

They would have to go around the lake one way or another. Because he could see most of the shoreline to the north, he chose that direction. In the twilight they came upon a snapping turtle the size of a dinner plate marching toward the water. The dogs gathered around it, rearing as it turned its blunt head, jaws agape and hissing. He rushed over and shooed them away, thinking of the stories he'd heard of turtles' jaws staying locked onto whatever they'd bitten, even after their heads were cut off. He kept his own feet well back from the thing. He didn't want to find out if the stories were true.

As soon as the dogs abandoned the turtle, Tinder wheeled and backtracked along its path, then began to whine and dig. In a moment, the other dogs joined in and dirt was flying through the air. They were gobbling the turtle's eggs, teeth clicking, when Edgar got there. He reached past them and picked up an egg. It was cool and soft in his hand, the size and texture of a leathery Ping-Pong ball. Looking at it, his stomach did a traitorous little flip. Before his mouth could water any more, he took three additional eggs from the rapidly diminishing pile and brushed the dirt off them. When Baboo looked up, he tossed one back. The dog snatched it from the air. Edgar tucked the other three in his shirt pocket.

It bothered him to see them eating like that, but he had nothing better to offer. When they could find no more eggs he slapped his leg and turned to pick a place to sleep while there was still some light. He chose a spot under a stand of ash near the water. The sky overhead was a deep cobalt. Suddenly he was bone tired. He walked the four of them out to the lake and let them drink and slipped off his shoes and rolled up his jeans and waded in. His feet stirred up silt in the water and he had to reach far out, overbalancing himself, to ladle up anything clear. Even then it tasted of algae and muck and left grit between his teeth. He drank again. He led the dogs back, carrying his shoes and socks. They curled up at once. He tried to lie between them, but a rock poked his ribs. His clothes had dried during the day, but they felt greasy and lax and his stomach was bloated with water. He thought he might gag if he dwelt on its taste. Hunger twisted inside him. He got up and found a better position, though he could reach only Essay. Baboo stood, grumbling as if to say, oh all right, and moved over and circled twice and settled with his muzzle near Edgar's face. Shortly, Tinder followed.

HE WOKE SOMETIME IN THE NIGHT. The dogs lay curled about him in circles of slumber and somewhere a nightingale was calling, "Old Sam Peabody, Peabody, Peabody." Whatever had roused him had been in his dreams. Then he remembered. He was in the air above the workshop stairs. And he was falling, falling . . .

SUNRISE. CLAMOR AND SCREECH of birds, as if the sunlight had set them afire. The dogs stretched where they lay. Immediately, he was thinking about food—his belly felt curdled and a coppery tang coated his teeth, as if the minerals in the ground had seeped into him. By the time he sat up, the dogs were snooping in the undergrowth. He called them over one at a time and felt for stickers and burrs, starting with their tails and moving toward their heads. They lay chewing their forelegs as if pulling kernels off a corn cob as he worked. Occasionally, they nuzzled his hands, objecting to some pinch or tug. Then he stayed the dogs and walked each of them out and trotted back and signed a release. When they returned, he reached into his shirt pocket and produced a turtle egg. Tinder first, then Baboo. Essay went last—a vain attempt to teach her patience. Having watched the others get their reward, she streaked toward him through the woods the instant he moved his hands.

Then they set out again, keeping the lake to their left. The underbrush was sparse compared to the previous day's travel and they made good time. The morning air was thick with moisture and the grasses shed water droplets that glistened on the dogs' coats. When they'd rounded the lake halfway, he could see water stretching away in a jagged meander to the south.

He was fretting over the problem of food when he glimpsed the first cabin. The sight of it did nothing to ease his mind. He stayed the dogs and walked forward until he understood it could not possibly be occupied. They walked out of the brush together to inspect it. The little shack had collapsed inward many years before. If it had ever been painted, the paint had long since washed into the earth, and now only the roofing shingles, bright purple, hadn't grayed. A scabrous folding chair stood on what remained of the crude front porch, shedding paint flakes the color of dried mustard as rust worked its way underneath. Inside was a calamity of plywood and mossy bedsprings and vast spider webs hanging like spinnakers between the timbers. The whole thing covered no more ground than a good-size tent, ten feet on a side. The dogs circled and poked their noses into crannies and corners until he called them away for fear of rats and snakes.

An hour later they came to a place at the water's edge where the riotous undergrowth gave way to a small crescent of gravelly sand. Further out, reeds projected through the silver surface. He stripped off his clothes and parted the dogs and waded in. The water was brown with tannin. He was covered with mosquito bites and the cool hug of liquid soothed the itching. He looked down to see a panfish darting between his knees. The dogs stood watching and wagging their tails but wouldn't come in the water.

He emerged naked and knee-deep, splashing the dogs. They dashed away and back again, ears laid low, crouching and scrambling to dodge the spray, remembering, perhaps, games they'd played in the yard with the garden hose. Part of him was glad he'd found something that pleased them, but he quickly stopped. In himself he felt nothing but gloom, and the play seemed false, a pretense that everything was going to be okay. Besides, he began to worry about working them up. That wasn't right, not until they got real food. Already they looked thinner to him, though that was probably his imagination. They were acting a little *too* wild, their hunger making them frantic. They stood panting and watching as he swept beads of water off his legs. In a minute or two the sun had dried him enough to dress. This time he flapped his trousers out and looked down the legs and knocked his shoes against his hand without a second thought.

THE NEXT CABIN LOOKED more promising. It was painted a utilitarian green, but it was sturdy and well maintained. A galvanized smokestack pierced its sloped roof. A pair of small windows were set high off the ground on either side of the door. It was so tidy, in fact, he watched it for a while before he was sure it was unoccupied. Even then his skin tingled as he approached. The door was held shut by a padlock threaded through a heavy metal latch. The padlock had been slathered with grease and wrapped with a plastic bag, presumably to protect it against the elements. He turned the knob and tried a few hard pushes. Then he backed up and took a running start and hit it. He bounced off. He tried again. The structure shook, but the door didn't budge in its frame. And his shoulder began to hurt.

The dogs stood and cocked their heads.

It works on TV, he signed. Shut up.

He looked at the windows again. They were three-paned, top-hinged transom windows, set about six feet off the ground. Big enough to fit through, he thought, and he could easily break the glass, but it seemed unlikely he could heft himself through without cutting himself to ribbons. And, while he'd been throwing himself at the door, it had occurred to him that it would be best to enter without being obvious.

He searched the surrounds for a log or anything that might serve as a boost—to know whether it was worth breaking the window, and help him climb through if it was—but he found nothing useful. He looked for a likely spot to hide a key. Nothing again.

He walked to the front of the cabin and looked at the dogs.

We're going back for that chair, he signed, and they set off the way they'd come.

HE DIDN'T REALIZE HOW far they would have to backtrack. It took over an hour before he glimpsed the purple shingles again. He grabbed a stick and swept the cobwebs from the chair and yanked it off the porch. Half a dozen spiders scrambled away like rotted berries on legs. The web straps that had formed the seat hung in brown tatters, but the frame itself seemed solid, if rusty. Baboo nosed it curiously. Essay and Tinder lay down. All three dogs had kept their noses to the ground on their return, no doubt hoping for more turtle eggs. More than once they had bolted after squirrels gibbering in the underbrush before learning it was a waste of time. Now they were acting dispirited and a stab of anxiety entered his chest.

When they passed the little beach on their return he was so eager he started jogging along. He set the chair frame beneath one of the transom windows and he was about to hoist himself up when he checked the impulse and decided to test the chair first. He planted his rump on the arm. One of the crusty front legs crumpled like a paper soda straw. He looked at it in surprise, then flipped the chair over and pressed both hands onto the joint where the back and the seat came together. Satisfied, he stepped onto the frame and put his fingertips on the windowsill.

During the walk back he had allowed himself to imagine how a fisherman might stock such a neatly kept shack with all sorts of canned goods and tackle, but his view through the window revealed only a bare cot folded against one plywood wall, a prefab fireplace at the base of the galvanized chimney, and a small kerosene stove and a lantern. There was no point trying to get in; it was obvious he'd find no food, and even if the lantern had fuel, which he doubted, it would burn for only a few hours. The camp stove was too unwieldy to carry.

He hopped to the ground. He sat beside the crippled chair and chastised himself. A good fisherman would never leave food to lure animals. He should have known that, but instead he'd talked himself into a fantasy. They'd wasted the better part of the day on a pointless errand. He was so hungry now his insides spasmed. His mouth had watered as soon as the cabin came into view. He'd read somewhere that a person could live for a month without food, but that seemed impossible. Perhaps if the person sat in one place and did nothing, but not if they were crossing miles of unpathed forest.

It was too much. With all that had happened at the kennel, and now the hunger and the worry about the dogs, and suddenly without Almondine there, it felt like some organ had been ripped from his insides. He brought his knees to his chest and lay over on his side. He thought he was going to cry, but instead his mind emptied and he lay staring along the roots and leaves of the forest floor and listened to the far-off sound of the dogs rattling through the underbrush. He stayed like that for a long time. Eventually, the dogs returned—Baboo first, then Tinder and Essay. They panted and licked his face and stretched out around him, grunting and sighing and finally sleeping.

HIS MALAISE DIDN'T ENTIRELY PASS, but it did lighten, and he sat up and looked around. In the distance, a prop plane sputtered. A flock of small, black birds with obsidian beaks cackled warnings at one another from lower branches of the trees. He forced himself to stand and the dogs assembled around him, nuzzling his hands for food. He knelt and stroked their ruffs.

I don't have anything, he signed. I'm sorry. I don't even know when I will.

They walked the lakeshore. In a clearing, he spotted a lone ripe blueberry hanging from a bush. Too early in the season, but there it was. He did not think it was nightshade, but he turned over the leaves to check. The blueberry patch covered a circle of thirty feet or so, and from it he harvested a single handful of ripe berries. He tasted one, then squatted and held them out. The dogs sniffed his bounty and walked away. No, try them, he signed. Come back. But they would not. As soon as he swallowed them his stomach began to churn. For a moment he thought he might vomit, but he didn't.

At dusk he picked a spot to bed down among a grove of maples. They were settled and half asleep when a high, thin whine swelled in the treetops, then hovered downward until it seethed all around them. When he looked at his arm it was covered in undulating gray fur. He swiped a hand from elbow to wrist, leaving behind a mash of blood and crushed mosquitoes. At once, a rapacious new layer appeared in the slime. Mosquitoes began crawling in his nostrils and ears. The dogs leapt up and snapped at the air and Edgar waved his arms and slapped his neck and face, but in the end they ran and ran, the dogs disappearing ahead into the gloom.

After a while he halted, gasping and disoriented. The forest floor was covered with a layer of pine needles thick enough to choke the under-brush. He listened for the mosquitoes, shuddering. A cloud of them had waited in the forest canopy, and he and the dogs had lain willingly be-neath. He'd never heard of such a thing. The dogs trotted out of the gloaming and they made their beds on the pine needles. He lay looking into the treetops. He was hungry, tired, dejected, and now humiliated. The stomachs of the dogs gurgled as they lay around him.

They were going to have to find a road after all, he thought, or they would starve.

By the third day, he was doing the math continually: the dogs had eaten nothing but turtle eggs for two days. He'd eaten maybe thirty blueberries. One moment he told himself it wasn't a disaster to miss six meals. The next moment his stomach pulsed and contracted. Squirrels and birds were everywhere, but he had no idea how to catch one. The lakes were probably brimming with fish, but he didn't have a single inch of monofilament line, much less a hook.

They heard the moan of tires along the blacktop half an hour before they reached the road. From behind a balsam they watched a ragged procession of cars pass, then snuck to the embankment and bolted into the woods on the far side and began following the highway as they'd followed the shoreline the day before, staying well hidden in the forest. Twice, streams too deep or marshy forced them back to the road to wait and dash across a bridge before they could move on.

In the afternoon they came to a field of sedge and chokecherry about a quarter of a mile wide and several hundred yards deep. Halfway to the back tree line, Edgar stopped and looked at the road. On the one hand, they would be exposed if they crossed there, but on the other he was start-ing to tire and it was a significant shortcut. The grass was tall enough to hide the dogs. He could duck if a car appeared. They'd crossed halfway when something chittered through the grass and Tinder leapt after it and the other dogs after Tinder. Edgar caught up with them dancing around a burrow entrance. Out on the road, a car was approaching. He dropped to all fours and waited. For some time the faraway burr of a small airplane had been swelling and fading; when it began to swell again he craned his neck and looked up. He saw nothing against the blue sky. The burr grew louder and then louder still. The moment the car passed he clapped the dogs out of their stays and bolted. By the time he dove into the birch on the far side of the clearing, he could almost hear the individual cylinders firing in the airplane engine. The dogs had stuck close by him for once and he huddled them up beneath a dogwood. When the airplane passed over, it was so low he could read the Forest Service insignia.

Idiot, he thought. You were going to stay in the woods.

They kept hidden there for the better part of an hour, tracking the sound of the airplane as it progressed north and south along its search pattern. After he got the dogs moving again he kept them strictly under tree cover, circling even the smallest glades. Mid-afternoon, they came to a gravel road tightly enclosed by pine forest. There were power lines strung along on creosoted poles. A few hundred yards east the road intersected the blacktop. They tracked it in the opposite direction, staying back in the woods. The dogs had begun moving with their tails down, edgy and wild-looking. Seventy hours, said the counting part of his brain. One turtle egg for every four hours. One blueberry an hour for him. Half a blueberry.

They watched a station wagon rumble by with its backwash of brown dust. They walked to the tree line. Ahead, where the road curved, he saw the first cabin and the lake glittering behind it. Then all the other cabins nestled among the trees. Posts with reflectors marking the driveways. Over the lash of waves against the lakeshore he heard a boat motor sputtering and the cry of sandpipers and inland gulls.

The station wagon had rounded the curve and driven on. He led the dogs along until they were across from the nearest cabin. No car in the grassy drive. The dogs knew something was happening and they circled and poked one another with their muzzles and hopped ticklishly.

Down, he signed. They whined but complied, one after another.

Stay, he signed. *Stay*.

He'd slipped into bad habits already, he thought. Repeating commands was minor. Failing to trust them, far worse. He forced himself not to repeat the stay a third time and walked out to the road and looked back. The dogs lay panting in the forest shade, watching him. He turned and walked up the cabin driveway, trying to look as if he belonged there.

This was no fisherman's shack. A window sash had been raised. Curtains ruffled in the breeze behind the screen. A Formica table sat beneath the window covered with folded newspaper and a scattering of mail. Ceramic cows labeled *S* and *P* curtseyed to one another. Beyond, he saw a kitchen with plain cupboards and an icebox and a stove. The counter was strewn with cellophaned packages. Cookies. Potato chips. Loaves of bread.

His hands were shaking now. He tried the front door but it was locked. He returned to the window. At the back of the cabin was a screen door, latched with a hook and eye. He rattled the door. The hook wouldn't shake loose.

He turned to look around. No one sunbathed on the beach. No one swam off the dock. He trotted into the nearby woods and came back with a short, blunt stick and he punched a neat line of screening away from the center bar of the door and threaded his arm through and popped the hook and swung the door open. He stepped over the jumble of toys on the living room floor and then he was in the kitchen, throwing open the cupboards. Cans of SpaghettiOs and pork and beans stood in neat rows beside Kraft Macaroni and Cheese, Jiffy Pop, hot dog buns, bread. In the icebox he found hot dogs, ketchup, mustard, relish. Two six-packs of beer.

He grabbed all the hot dogs, then, thinking better of it, put one package back. He set out the cans of SpaghettiOs and pork and beans. He rifled the drawers and slipped a can opener into his back pocket. Then he lost patience. He'd gathered up the loot and was heading for the back door when something on the Formica table caught his eye. The pepper cow stood atop a white mimeographed page titled in big blue letters.

He could only see the first half: *RUNA*.

Awkwardly, he set down the food and slipped the sheet from under the newspaper. The pleasant odor of mimeograph fluid rose off the paper. There was a poorly reproduced photograph from the school yearbook and beneath it a short notice:

RUNAWAY

Edgar Sawtelle, disappeared June 18. Age fourteen, height five feet six inches, black hair. Boy cannot speak, though he may use written notes or sign language. He may be accompanied by one or more dogs. Last seen wearing blue jeans, sneakers, and a brown-and-red-checkered short-sleeved shirt near Mellen . . .

Before he could finish reading, he heard a bark from the direction of the woods. He stuffed the notice in his pocket and scooped up the canned goods and wieners. Outside, he had to dump everything on the ground again to reach through the ripped screen and set the hook into the eye. Then he smoothed the screen into place as best he could, gathered up the food, and ran across the gravel road.

Essay stood waiting a few feet inside the edge of the woods, Tinder and Baboo not far behind. He put them all in down-stays, sternly, then turned and fumbled with the can opener. He poured SpaghettiOs into three widely separated piles. The dogs moaned. He signed a release and they pounced, and the SpaghettiOs were *gone*, but he was already ripping open the wieners and stuffing one into his mouth and handing them out to the dogs.

Then he came to his senses. Somewhere he'd read that people who tried to eat after long stretches without food threw it up, though he felt in no danger of that himself, only a comforting sensation in his middle. Probably, that wisdom had been written by the same person who could survive for a month without food. They had lasted three days. But it would be foolish not to wait a few minutes, just to be sure. The dogs scoured the ground where the SpaghettiOs had so briefly lain while Edgar counted out one hundred breaths. The wieners were salty. They made him thirsty, but that was okay. That was just fine.

He picked up the remaining food and retreated to a clearing out of sight of the cabins. It was the friendliest-looking place he'd seen in days. He sat down Indian-style while the dogs gathered around him, transfixed, and like a magician performing sleight-of-hand, he began working the opener over a can of pork and beans.

Pirates

BY THEN THEY'D BEEN GOING FOR TEN DAYS, MAYBE MORE—Edgar had started to lose track—and over that time they'd come to a new set of accommodations for how to be together. He had no tackle with him—no leads, no collars, no long lines, no ground rings—none of the means they'd had at the kennel to agree about what mattered: the ways to stop and start, when to stay close and when to explore, how to attend one another. He had few rewards to give, some days not even food, though that happened less often after the first week—after they learned to work the cabins. And so, by necessity, he began to watch the dogs more closely, stop more often, touch them more sweetly and more carefully than he ever had before.

And the dogs, in turn, discovered that if they waited after he'd asked them to stay and disappeared into a cabin, he would always return. Together they practiced new skills he devised. They had long understood what was being asked of them during a stay, whether in the training yard or in town; now he asked if they would stay in a forest glade when they were hungry and the flickers pounded the ground, thumping up millipedes, or squirrels harassed them, or a rock sailed over their heads and rattled the dead leaves. Several times each day he found a likely spot, shielded by sumac or bracken fern, and he placed them in guard over something small—a stick he'd been carrying that morning, say, or a bit of rag. Then he walked off into the forest, careful not to push them past the breaking point since he had no way to correct them. Later, he tied a length of fishing line to the guarded thing and asked them to move only when it moved, keeping it surrounded. When they got that right, he'd sail back into their midst signing, *release!* and throw himself at them to roll and tickle, toss the thing for them to catch, see to each of them in whatever way he'd learned was the greatest delight for that dog.

He learned, too, the limits of their patience, different for each of them. In a stay, Baboo was as immovable as the hills, and likely to fall asleep. Essay, ever alert, was the most tempted of any of them by the skitter of a rock pitched through the ferns. And Tinder, equally likely to stick or bolt, who twice jumped up when Essay broke her stay and licked her muzzle and coaxed her back into a sit.

They agreed, more slowly, that running away mattered as much as staying. After some time he could ask them to find a spot elsewhere and wait. At first they ventured only a few feet; later, they ran until he couldn't see them anymore. They agreed it was important not to bark when they needed his attention or when they got excited. They practiced these things many times each day, whenever they tired of breaking trail through the underbrush. He began to link the idea of running away and guarding; he put the thing to guard on the ground and walked the dogs away from it, then made them return, watch it, scoot along with it as it jerked through the dead leaves on its string. He spent long evening hours picking through their coats for ticks and burrs. He checked their feet a hundred times each day.

And he compromised his idea of their destiny in order to live. They could make only as much progress as food allowed. What point was there in bolting northward if they starved halfway to wherever he intended to go? They had to pick a route that kept them hidden and let them harvest food. That meant a pace slower and a route more circuitous than he'd imagined.

He became an expert burglar of vacation cottages and fishing shacks. Mornings, while the campers fried bacon and flipped pancakes, he and the dogs lingered in the weeds; later, those same cabins would stand empty, ripe for plundering. He learned to enter without breaking, and always left without taking enough to be noticed. He carried few supplies, and none that would tie him down. A can opener and a jackknife and, later, when their diet made his teeth and gums feel buzzy, a toothbrush. A child's Zebco spin-casting rod, small enough to carry through the woods. A fisherman's satchel with a bobber and some hooks set in a piece of cardboard. With a little skill, he provided for them all—panfish, mainly, but sometimes a bass or a bullhead, too. Plenty of nights they went to sleep hungry, but seldom starving. The cabins yielded Twinkies and Suzie-Q's and Ho Hos by the armful, deviled ham and custard pies and corn chips and peanut butter to eat straight from the jar, handfuls of Wheaties and Cap'n Crunch washed down with soda, and an endless procession of wieners and salami and sardines and Hershey bars. Occasionally he even found dog food, which the dogs gobbled from his palm like the most uncommon delicacy.

And he stole Off!, that balm of peace and contentment, that ambrosia of the skin. Heavenly, wonderful, miraculous Off!—above all, the Deep Woods variety, whose bitter flavor and greasy viscosity came to signify something as essential as food or water: a day unmauled by deerflies, a night of refuge from mosquitoes. He stole it from every cabin he tiptoed through—all of it, remorselessly. Wherever they spent more than a day, he hoarded two or three of the white-and-orange aerosols, and a batch of Bactines as well.

Rainy days were hard. Sometimes there was no better shelter than the base of a thick jack pine, and if the wind blew, that could be no shelter at all. Rainy nights were torture: great, racking storms, with lightning exploding all around. If he looked into the strobed rain too long, he ended up curled and oblivious, for if there was no figure to be seen in the falling drops of water, he felt abandoned, and if he saw anything—a shape, a movement, a form—he screamed, silently, despite all resolution to the contrary.

Other dogs were a problem, idiot dogs that, having scented them, loped into the woods, disregarding the cries of their owners to come back, come home, come play . . . Some trundled along like clowns, others, looking for trouble, like snipers. Baboo, especially, took umbrage, and he led his littermates in savage charges, ignoring Edgar's protests until the marauders ran howling away.

They drifted from lake to lake, like stepping stones across a creek, moving westward through the Chequamegon. Sometimes Edgar learned the names of the lakes from leaflets inside the cabins—Phoebus, Duckhead, Yellow—but usually it was just The Lake. Without maps, they found themselves hemmed in by marshes and forced to backtrack. The dogs had long since grown expert at finding turtle eggs; one or the other would suddenly track down and run along a tangent and start to dig. The eggs ripened and grew ever more disgusting, apparently in equal proportion to their delicacy. But Edgar helped with the digging and pocketed a few for later, as rewards. He tromped along the rushes at shorelines until frogs leapt toward the waiting dogs, who pounced and munched.

He stole matches whenever he spotted them. During the day he wouldn't build fires, wary of smoke-watching rangers in towers, but at night he allowed himself small, yellow cook fires, kindling them with papery curls of birch bark. After he tamped them out with dirt, he and the dogs slept listening to the yips and moans of beavers. At daybreak, loons cried.

THE LAKE WAS NAMED SCOTIA, and the Fourth of July holiday had brought campers in such droves that Edgar and the dogs were forced to retreat far from the cabins and campsites. Though he couldn't be sure exactly which night the Fourth itself would fall on, firecrackers had been popping for three nights running. He'd moved them down near the lake, into the woods across the water from a small campground. He picked a spot well inland and was preparing to light a little pyramid of sticks and birch bark when a barrage of husky whistles came across the water. He turned to see red trailers in the air followed by three loud whomps. He led the dogs to the water and onto a spit of land occupied by a pine grove and they sat. The sky was filled with sculpted clouds, stars blazing in the interstices. A dozen campfires burned in the campground. He heard music and laughter and children's shrieks. Silhouettes ran between the fires and the lake, whipping hairy sparklers through the air. A fiery beetle skittered across the beach, crackling and sparking.

Another round of rockets lifted over the water. A string of firecrackers crackled. Single and double flowers blossomed, big as moons, and in the aftermath red and blue particles showered down, reflections rising from the water to extinguish them in the meeting. The dogs sat on their haunches watching. Essay walked to the lake's edge to nose one of the spirit embers, then turned and nuzzled Edgar for an explanation. He only sat and watched and lifted a hand to cup her belly.

Somewhere a song played on a radio. The campers began to sing, voices quavering over water. A dog howled, followed by a peal of laughter. The dog carried on, voice high and keen. After a while Tinder lifted his muzzle and howled in response. Essay was up at once, licking his face. When he wouldn't stop, she joined in with her own *yike-yike-yow!* and then Baboo completed the trio. The camper's dog listened as if considering some proposition and then yodeled again. Edgar knew he should stop them, but he liked the sound. It was lonesome in the woods that night, more than usual, and he couldn't resist some connection, however tenuous, to those people and their festivities. The dogs chorused in rounds and the campers laughed and joined in until all but Edgar bellowed into the sky.

After a while the dogs fell silent and the campers stopped. For a time it was quiet. Then, from the hillside north of the lake, where no cabins stood and no campfires burned, there came a basso *ooooooooooohr-ohr-ooooh* that ended in a high chatter. Edgar recognized that howl at once, though he'd heard it at the kennel that one night only—a cry of such loneliness it drove the warmth of the July night into the stars. Essay leapt up, hackles raised, then Baboo and Tinder. Edgar set his hands on their backs and guided them down and he walked out on the wind-scoured cobble and waited. A burst of nervous laughter issued from across the lake. Then, slowly, all the sounds of the night crept back: the peepers and the crickets and the swish of the wind in the trees and from farther away the rumble of heat lightning and the eerie calls of owls and nightingales and whippoorwills. But the howl had come only once, and would not again.

HE DREAMED THAT NIGHT of Almondine, her gaze unflinching, seeking the answer to some question. It woke him in the dark. When he returned to sleep she was there again. He woke in the morning desolate and weary, dwelling on the things he missed. He missed the morning chores and the simplicity of breakfast at a table. He missed television—the afternoon movie on WEAU. The softness of their lawn. Second only to Almondine, he missed *words*—the sound of his mother's voice and *The New Webster Encyclopedic Dictionary of the English Language* and reading and signing things out to the pups in the whelping pens.

And he woke hungry. He collected the Zebco and the satchel and kicked leaves over the dead coals of the fire and they traced the lakeshore to a spot he'd fished the day before. From the satchel he pulled one tattered leg of a woman's nylons, rolled up his jeans, and waded barefoot into the lake. He returned with a handful of minnows in his makeshift seine. A few minutes later he popped a sunfish out of the lake, gutted it, set it aside for the dogs, and threaded another minnow onto the hook. He fed the dogs in turns, making sure each of them had their share, scaling and filleting the flesh from the bones and tossing aside the skeletons, and when he finished, he gave them each two heads to take away and crunch. He himself would not eat the fish raw. To the south was a cottage he'd raided once; if he couldn't get into it now, he would have to wait until he could roast himself fish in the evening.

He left the rod and satchel and led the dogs away. When they were close to the cottage, he stayed them and pushed through the undergrowth for a better look. The cottage sat near the lake at the end of a long dirt drive. It was painted bright red with windows neatly trimmed in white. Two families were toting things to a car. He backtracked to the dogs and waited. He heard the chatter of children's voices, the slam-slam-slam of car doors, and a motor starting. When all was quiet again he brought the dogs forward and stayed them at the clearing's edge.

A second car, a brown sedan with a leatherette-covered roof, sat parked in the weedy yard. There was no sound from the cottage except for a pair of gray squirrels bouncing loudly across the roof. He looked in a window, then knocked at the door. When no one answered, he slid the window up and levered himself onto the sill. A few minutes later he slipped out carrying two peanut butter sandwiches, a package of bacon, and a stick of butter. In one back pocket he had a Hershey's candy bar and in the other a bottle of Off!

He was passing the car again when he remembered the car keys he'd seen glinting on the countertop inside the cottage. He looked through the driver's-side window at the stick shift on the floor, an *H* pattern engraved on the knob. He didn't think he could drive it, but for a moment he let himself imagine it anyway: sitting behind the wheel as they sped along a highway, windows down, Essay up front and Baboo and Tinder in back, their heads out the windows in the streaming summer air.

And then what? How far could he get in a stolen car? How would they buy gas? What would they eat? At least the way things were now, though they moved at a crawl, there was food almost every day. With a car, there would be no waiting outside cottages, no stealth. Worst of all, taking a car would destroy the illusion that he and the dogs were long gone. The Forest Service airplane had stopped flying above the treetops a week ago. He hadn't seen police cruisers trolling the roads since that first day. Flyers had stopped appearing in cabins. But someone who steals a car exists. He can be chased, tracked, caught. And even if they took back roads (not that he knew *which* back roads to take) the four of them would be a spectacle. Taking a car meant stepping out of their phantom existence and back into the real world.

He trudged back to where the dogs lay stretched out and panting. He sat and fed them strips of bacon and squeezed the stick of butter into pats they could lick from the platform of his fist. Afterward they hounded him for his peanut butter sandwiches.

Get lost, he signed. He turned around and around, then relented and pinched off a corner for each, requiring each to do some small thing. Lie down. Fetch a stick. Roll over and show their belly to the sky. But he kept the Hershey's bar for himself, broken and softened and melted to pudding by body heat. When he'd licked his fingers clean he set off for a place he had in mind to sleep.

THE FOUR OF THEM WERE ensconced in a clearing near the fishing spot. Edgar had anointed himself with Off! and begun to doze, the dogs stretched out around him alligator-like. Clouds unfolded and unfolded beyond the treetops. Waves passed through the reeds at the water's edge, *hush, hush,* and timbreless voices piped across the water—*Mom, where's that shovel? I thought I told you not to do that!* Laughter. A delighted toddler's long *screeeeeeee. Go fill this up from the lake.* Car doors slamming; dishes clanking, bottles breaking. *Not in the car, you won't.*

Baboo lay whimpering and jerking his leg, dreaming of voles running along weedy tunnels. In his dream, he'd shrunken to their size and bounded after them, blades of grass passing swiftly as he gained, but he was full-size, too, inside and outside the tunnel, big and small at the same time. And likewise with the other dogs, drafting the warm afternoon into their chests and exhaling sighs, dreaming and listening to the whoosh and slosh of water and the wind in the trees.

At first the dogs had thought they'd left home on a lark and would soon return. Now it seemed their world had come unmoored and their home traveled with them while the earth turned beneath their feet. Creek. Forest. Marsh edge. Lake. Moon. Wind. The sun presently baking them through the treetops. Back at the kennel they'd slept near Edgar many times—in the mow, in his room in the house, even in the yard—but it had never been like these recent nights, never curled beside him so intimately that his thrashing drove them to their feet, where they stood and watched him struggle against some unseen threat. It raised their hackles. They dropped their heads beneath their shoulders and grumbled and peered around. So vulnerable he was with his blue skin in the moonlight and his arm twisted over his face and blood pulsing beneath his skin. At such times only Essay wandered off, hunting in the dark.

They worried when he walked off for food. They argued among themselves. He's gone. He'll come back. What if he doesn't, what happens then. He will. Ofttimes, in his absence, the trees bent round, carrying their freight of jays and squirrels engrossed in bitter dispute. Sometimes he returned bearing delicacies unknown before. Sometimes he came empty-handed but ready to play.

That afternoon, they'd set their fretting aside. The place was familiar. There was nothing to do but flick away flies and let the sun pass. Edgar half slept, more hypnotized even by the afternoon sun than they. He didn't catch the scent that drifted into the clearing, nor react to the sounds that, one after another, the dogs heard. It wasn't until they leapt up—Essay first, then Tinder, and then, in a big scramble of leaves, Baboo—that Edgar finally woke and stood and saw what had happened.

BY THE TIME THE YOUNGER of the two girls reached the glade, she and her companion had long since talked themselves out. They came to a driveway cut into the woods that ended at a red cottage. A car was parked in the weeds, but no one seemed to be home. They picked their way through the woods and along the shoreline looking for a sandy spot until they found the spit of land and there the older girl walked out and sat with her back to a tree and looked across the water at the campgrounds. The younger girl dawdled her way along the reeds and sedge. She came upon a fisherman's satchel and a child's fishing rod propped against a tree. She looked around. There was a clearing in the woods penetrated by a shaft of sunlight and she wandered in that direction, hoping to spot the white, three-petaled trillium blossoms that were her favorites.

The boy was already watching her when she looked up. He was standing on the far side of the clearing, tall and limber-looking, with thick shocks of hair hanging across his forehead and over his eyes, all of which suggested youth, though in the bright sun his face seemed lined like an old man's. A heartbeat later she saw the three animals standing around him, one forward and one at either side. *Wolves*, she thought, but of course they weren't. They were dogs—shepherds, maybe, though not any kind she'd seen before. Their coats were chestnut and black and their tails swept down to trace the extension of their hind legs. But what struck her most was the poised stillness of their bodies, and especially their gaze, fixed on her and unwavering.

Then the boy gestured and the dogs were whisking through the clearing. One leapt away into the woods. The other two bounded toward her in an unswerving line, their shoulders rolling lionlike and their backs bowing and stretching. The sight made her gasp. When she looked up, the boy was pointing at her. He pressed an upright finger to his lips, then held the flat of his palm out in a way that clearly meant she should be quiet and stand still.

The two dogs that had crossed the clearing came to a halt in front of her, left and right. They didn't look unfriendly but they didn't look completely benevolent either. She took an instinctive step back, and from behind her came a disquieting rumble. She froze and turned her head. The third dog stood with its muzzle at the back of her knee. It nosed her leg and looked at her. When she put her foot back where it had been, the dogs in front of her stepped closer, and that made her sway a little, as if she were pinched in a slowly tightening vise. Yet as soon as she'd regained her balance and stood still, the dogs stepped back again.

She looked across the clearing. The boy was gone.

Now, from behind her she heard the older girl's voice: "Jess? Let's go. Jess?" The girl wanted to reply, but she couldn't tell what the dogs would do if she starting hollering. Besides, there was something fascinating about the way they had lasered in on her. The way they stood just out of arm's reach. She had the distinct sense that the dogs just wanted to keep her still. And they were beautiful, with furrowed, honey-colored brows over brown eyes that shone with an extraordinary sense of . . . what? Concern? Serene concern. She wondered what would happen if she talked to them. Would they step forward and touch her?

She was about to test this idea when she heard a sharp double clap. Instantly, the dog to her right dropped away, oozing into motion and disappearing into the bushes. A moment later, the dog behind her wheeled and vanished as well. But the third dog didn't move. It stood looking at her, then stepped forward and sniffed the hem of her shorts, quivering. She held out her hand. The dog stepped back with a look of something like guilt on its face. Then it, too, bolted. She craned her neck to watch it move, so graceful and surefooted. A dozen yards away the two other dogs waited beside the boy, who was kneeling and gesturing to draw the last dog toward him. When it arrived, the boy's hands flashed expertly along its sides and down its legs, as if checking out of long habit for injuries. The little fishing rod she'd seen earlier lay on the ground near him, and the satchel was looped over his shoulder. He stood. The dogs looked at her across their flanks one last time and then they were gone and the underbrush had flicked back into place.

She let out her breath.

I should be scared but I'm not, she thought. And, strangely: *Nothing like this will ever happen to me again.*

She waited another moment, then let out a whoop and raced toward the sound of the older girl's voice.

HE KEPT THEM MOVING until it had grown so dark he couldn't see the way. Long ago, on their first night running, the sky had been clear and a full moon had shone directly overhead, but now the moon was a waxing crescent. He chose a spot near a stand of jack pines and scraped together needles, tossing away any resinous clumps. He downed the dogs. They knew it meant no water or food for the night and a chorus of grunts and complaints followed.

Four and a half days at Scotia Lake. They should have been pushing west and north, but instead they'd lingered where the food was easy at the risk of being spotted. He'd known it was a mistake even as they'd done it. The howling had been bad enough the night of the fireworks, but now the little blond girl had gotten a good long look at him and an even better look at the dogs. He'd heard her shout as they were running from the clearing, "Hey, Diane! DIANE! Over here! Oh my *God*! You're *never* going to believe this!"

Whoever Diane was, she'd believe it, all right. She'd believe it, and her parents would believe it, and the county sheriff's office would believe it, too. There was nothing to do but move as far and as fast as possible and always keep away from the roads—the old plan. The only plan he'd ever had. They'd covered maybe two miles as the light waned. If they pushed hard the next day they could cover another three or four straight through the forest.

There was some good news, at least. The Zebco fishing rig, being a stubby affair, had survived their mad dash. Once they'd crossed the forest road, Edgar had cut off the hook and embedded it in the makeshift cardboard hook-book he kept in his back pocket. Afterward, he'd managed to thread the rod through the underbrush by tucking it under his arm. The other good news was how perfectly the dogs had translated the guarding game. It had been lovely to see them move through the sunlight toward the little girl. Part of Edgar had wanted to stand and watch them. Once they had surrounded her, whenever she moved, whenever she even shifted her weight, one of them pressured her back into place. And when it was time to run, they'd kept close and quiet.

Essay lay with her head beside Edgar's knee. He listened to her stomach growl and began the arithmetic again: on foot, breaking a trail and having to sidetrack for food and water, they might advance three solid miles a day. Ninety miles in a month. It was early July. He hoped it wasn't more than one hundred miles to the Canadian border. That put them where he wanted to go by mid-August.

He was going to need a map soon. They were still in the Chequamegon, but if they made steady progress, they wouldn't be for long.

THE NEXT MORNING A MIST began to fall so fine it coalesced in beads on the dogs' fur. By noon the mist had turned to rain, and when a high-skirted pine presented itself, they scuttled beneath to wait out the weather. Half an hour later, the pelting rain was deafening. Sheets of water swept across their knee-high vista. Their adopted tree shed water erratically; without warning, a chilly gush would cascade through the core of the tree and onto their backs. When he was willing to take on more water, Edgar poked his head from beneath the tree's hem to look for a break in the clouds. The dogs alternated between groaned complaints and half-sleep, trotting into the rain to urinate and returning, shaking out at the fringe of the tree, or sometimes—to everyone's displeasure— beneath it. The air beneath the pine began to reek of wet dog. After a while Edgar could find no position that was both comfortable and dry. His bones began to ache. Only Baboo passed the time with equanimity, head on paws, hypnotized by the sight of falling water, sometimes even rolling on his back to watch the proceedings upside down.

At first Edgar's thoughts were practical: they needed to keep moving. He measured his own hunger to gauge how the dogs might feel. He'd gained a sense for how long they could go without. Skipping a day, he thought, would leave them distracted but not in danger. They were used to a little hunger now. In fact, except for the discomfort, there wasn't anything particularly wrong with spending a day sitting under a tree. Hadn't they done pretty much exactly that for the previous three days?

But something in his mind made him fidget as the day passed, something he didn't want to think about. For the first time since they'd crossed the creek at the back of their land he felt genuinely homesick, and once that began, the litany of memories quickly overwhelmed him. His bed. The sound of the creaky stairs. The smell of the kennel (which their time beneath the tree was reminding him of ever more powerfully). The truck. The apple trees, surely heavy with green fruit by now. His mother, despite the tumult of emotions surrounding her in his mind. And most ferociously, he missed Almondine. Her image appeared accompanied by a spasm of pure wretchedness. The dogs with him were fine dogs, astonishing dogs, but they weren't Almondine, who bore his soul. Yet he kept making plans to go farther away from her and he didn't know when he would ever be back. He couldn't go back. His last image of her was that despondent posture, lying in the kitchen, tracking him with her eyes as he turned away. Her muzzle had grayed so in the last year. Once upon a time, she had bounded down the stairs ahead of him and waited at the bottom; lately, there had been mornings when she'd tried to stand but failed, and he'd lifted her hindquarters and walked alongside as she navigated the steps.

But what she'd lost in agility she'd gained in perception—in her capacity to peer into him. How had he forgotten that? How had he forgotten that in the months after his father's death, she alone could console him, nosing him at precisely the instant to break some spiral of despair? How had he forgotten that some days she'd saved him simply by *leaning* against him? She was the only other being in the world who missed his father as much as he did, and he'd walked away from her.

Why hadn't he understood that? What had he been thinking?

He needed only to close his eyes to feel all over again the sensation of his father's hands reaching into him, the certainty that his heart was about to stop. The memory was too dazzling, like the memory of being born—something that, if recalled in full, would destroy a person. He couldn't separate it from the image of his father lying on the kennel floor, mouth agape, and that final exhalation Edgar had pressed from his body. Then he thought of Claude and the look on his face when Essay had trotted up to him with the syringe in her mouth, and of the white dandelion and the patch of white grass that had surrounded it. And he thought of Doctor Papineau, eyes open and head turned at the bottom of the workshop stairs.

He was stumbling through the rain before he knew what he was doing. He didn't care what direction he traveled, only that he moved. When he looked down, the dogs were bounding alongside. His wet clothes had warmed to the temperature of his body, but the rain flushed away the heat. He flung himself through the brush, bursting through thickets, stumbling and standing and running again. For the first time since they'd left home, true meadows appeared. Twice they crossed gravel roads—strange, unbroken lines of rusty mud. All of it washed through him, washed the thoughts away. The rain became a senseless tapping on his skin, neither warm nor cold, and he welcomed it. A July rain should never have stopped them. The danger had been in staying still so long. They encountered many fences now, some downed and rusty and more dangerous because they were difficult to see. He stripped blueberries from their stems wherever he found them and held them out to the dogs, who rolled them in their mouths and reluctantly swallowed. The cardboard holding the fishhooks dissolved in his pocket and the hooks began to poke his skin. He spent an hour standing naked from the waist down, extracting the hooks and wrapping them in layers of birch bark, and when he finished, his fingertips were puckered and raw.

Near twilight the clouds fractured and the rain let up. Tracts of deep blue appeared in the sky. They were within sight of a small hayfield of perhaps fifty acres at the far end of which stood a lone old barn. He stripped off his sodden clothes and bedded them down inside the edge of the woods. Before any but the brightest stars shone, the four of them lay overlapped and sleeping at the rim of the Chequamegon.

When he woke in the morning he didn't understand that the dogs were gone, or even how late it was, only that a thousand pounds of sand covered each of his limbs. He lay on his back, arm draped over his face, letting the radiant sun warm his chest and arms. The absence of the dogs' soft weight against his body meant nothing—there was only the dreamer's logic, wishing a return to the seadreams from which he'd run aground. When his eyes finally came open, he stared at the flattened weeds where Tinder should have been sleeping and pushed himself up-right and looked around. Before him lay a field gone to wild grass and milkweed. It rolled in a long upsweep to the barn he'd seen the evening before. Two hawks glided over the field, hunting and diving.

One of the dogs—Essay?—porpoised out of the weeds in the middle of the field and the others followed, arcing and disappearing into the deep grass. He stood and clapped and they worked their way across the field, zigzagging and leaping, until at last Essay burst into the clear. She carried in her jaws an enormous brown-and-black garter snake, thick in the belly and almost as long as she. She stopped near Edgar and shook it until its lifeless body writhed in the air. Baboo and Tinder whisked past, trying to snatch her prize. She trotted one way then another, until finally Tinder got hold of the snake's tail. After a struggle, the snake separated into two parts with a string of entrails quivering between. Baboo and Tinder repeated the process with the rear half of the snake until each dog retreated with their portion.

Ugh, God, Edgar thought, turning away, not so much disgusted by the idea of their eating a snake (though garter snakes smelled foul) as their eating it *raw*. He wondered if the matches in his pocket were still dry; he could cook the snake for them. But by the time he dressed, noth-ing was going to be left. The dogs had to be ravenous, if his own stomach was any indication. Nothing else felt half as important as finding food.

He dressed in his damp clothes and gathered the dogs and they waded up through quack grass and milkweed and mullein, the dogs skating around him in wild, hooped orbits improvised on the theme of his path. The old barn stood beside a weed-shot blacktop road with no house in sight. It was the first barn they'd seen in their travels and Edgar took it as a sign they'd finally crossed the Chequamegon and were in farmland again. He pressed his eye to one of the thumb-width spaces in the barn's siding boards. Inside sat a disk harrow and a moldboard plow, each with its spooned metal seat, and a dilapidated hay wagon whose framework back sagged like a frowning thespian mask. At the far end, an antique sower made of rusty knives and funnels. Irregular planes of light striped the machinery and the hay-strewn dirt floor as if he were looking through the ribs of a great bird-picked carcass at whatever had eaten it from within and been trapped.

The dogs ignored the barn and poked along the dilapidated barbed-wire fence bordering the road, nosing the fireweed and morning glory twisting up the fence posts. Edgar walked to the pavement. Not even the shadow of a centerline. The dogs were acting downright gay, he thought, watching them run toward him, as if relieved to have returned to the itinerant life after being pinned down in the rain. They crossed a shallow ditch together and passed through a line of trees, where an orderly two-stranded barbed-wire fence stood. The dogs slipped beneath, hardly breaking stride.

Before them stood an up-sloping field of sunflowers taller than Edgar—row upon row of sage trunks topped by hairy, fluted plates, all pointed off angle to the risen sun. They walked the edge of the sunflowers for easy traveling until a car appeared distantly on the blacktop. Edgar turned for one last look at the desiccated barn, then clapped his leg and they ducked into the gap between two infinitely receding rows of sunflower stalks.

Outside Lute

THEY WERE HALFWAY DOWN THE FAR SIDE OF THE FIELD BEFORE the sunflowers dwindled into an open patch and Edgar stopped to look around. At the bottom of the slope the field ended at a tree-filled farmyard. The house was simple and square, with attic dormers and plain brown asphalt shingling. A long driveway hooked around behind the house to stop at a freestanding building that looked like a carriage house or shed. In front of the shed sat a battered old car. No one was walking around, no dogs lay on the back porch, no sound emanated from the small barn at the back of the yard. All he could hear was the collective hum of thousands of bees harvesting the sticky nectar glinting on the sunflower heads. The field itself was long and narrow, an alley bounded on one side by a barbed-wire fence and on the other by a solid stretch of woods. Over the treetops rose a water tower, aquamarine and round-bellied. Wide-spaced cumulus clouds languished above it all in shades of white and blue, their shadows tracing the contoured land. The name of a town was painted on the water tower's barrel in tall white letters: Lute.

He clapped the dogs over and held their muzzles in his hand and ran his fingertips around their gums to see how thirsty they were. It gave him a chance to gauge whether Essay was in the mood to bolt or to stick, whether Tinder or Baboo were fretful. When he was satisfied that they would stay nearby—when the four of them agreed on that—they made their way to the edge of the field.

During his thief's apprenticeship, Edgar had learned not to waste much time speculating on whether a place was unoccupied or just *looked* that way—it was easiest to just walk up and knock. If someone stirred inside, he could always run off. And, too, his hunger made him reckless. He down-stayed the dogs (Essay walked it down inch by inch—they were going to have to practice that) and strode his most innocent walk to the back door. He heard no voices inside, no television, no radio. The sash on the small, square window beside the door was down and latched.

He knocked. When a minute passed (long enough for someone to get out of bed and start walking across the room; long enough for someone to shout, "Who is it?"; long enough for a dog to bark) he opened the screen door and tested the inside knob. To his surprise, the door swung inward and he stood looking into a neat, linoleumed kitchen with a Christmas floor mat just inside. He leaned in and knocked again, louder this time. The only reply was the click of the refrigerator compressor shutting off.

He took one more look around and then it was a mad dash. He threw open the refrigerator. Cans of beer and bottles of Coca-Cola. He grabbed a Coke and rummaged through the cabinet drawers until he found a bottle opener and upended the cold bottle against his lips. From the counter near the door he grabbed a loaf of bread and a bag of potato chips and stepped outside and tried to stroll along, though he knew, in his excitement, he was heel-walking like a dope. A patch of weeds near the edge of the field began to shake. He dove in, awkwardly signing a release before the dogs broke anyway. They weren't idiots; they knew food when they saw it coming.

He ripped open the plastic wrapper on the bread and handed out slices all around; he gobbled one down himself, then another, following it with big washes of Coke. In a minute, half the bread was gone. He tore open the bag of chips and shoveled them in, chip after salty, crunchy chip. The dogs tried to jam their snouts into the bag. He clamped it shut, then parceled out the delights, with the dogs following his hand each time it disappeared. He smiled, bits of potato chip and bread showing in his teeth. The true depth of his hunger had only then become evident. The sight of all that food almost panicked him—he'd needed to take something modest or he'd have fainted right there in the kitchen.

He sat watching the house again, half-expecting someone to barge out of the door at last, shouting and shaking a fist. The dogs panted in his face as if to say, what are you waiting for? Then they broke into a sprint. There was no holding back. Whoever lived there might come back at any moment and the opportunity would be lost.

This was not going to be elegant, he thought.

The dogs had not been inside a house—or any building, for that matter—for many weeks. They circled skittishly at the threshold until he shooed them in. They entered slinking. He filled a big plastic bowl with tap water and put it down. They leapt forward and slobbered up the water, spookiness vanished, while he rifled the cupboards, setting food aside as he discovered it. When he opened the refrigerator his gaze fell on a package wrapped in white butcher paper. The purple-inked label read, "Bratwurst."

They ate like starved kings. They would be gone in a few minutes and never see the place again and he fed them all as much as they could hold. He carried the bratwurst to the back door and tore the paper and spilled the rubbery links across the planks of the stoop. Even before they'd stopped writhing, the dogs were tearing at them. A jar of caramel-colored honey sat on the kitchen table, cloudy with crystallized sugar. Edgar unscrewed the top and ran a finger's-worth out, then topped a bowl of Wheaties extravagantly with it and splashed milk over the top and stood in the doorway and watched the dogs while he shoveled the concoction into his mouth. The bratwurst was gone almost before he started to eat; the dogs licked their chops and looked at him.

Okay, he signed. Stand back.

He set his cereal down and emptied the water bowl and dumped the contents of a half dozen cans of Campbell's Chicken Soup into it and several more of creamed corn. When his cereal was gone, their bowl had been licked clean as well. Then he walked onto the stoop with a bag of marshmallows. Three brilliant white cubes sailed through the air. He mashed one into his cheek, grinning evilly, and began another round. Halfway through the marshmallows he was suddenly done. He gestured the dogs back into the kitchen and began to search the kitchen methodically, sorting the food into what he could take and what he should put back. When he finished, he pulled a brown grocery sack from a mass of them behind the refrigerator and stuffed it with their trash. He put the can opener into the silverware drawer and refilled the plastic bowl with water and let the dogs drink. They pushed lethargically to their feet, stomachs belled out. Suddenly he thought it was stupid to have let them eat so much after a long hungry stretch. That risked bloat. But they also risked starving, came the reply. He rinsed the water dish and put it under the cupboard where he'd found it.

There was precious little they could take along. A bag of jellybeans. A flat, frosty package of bacon from the freezer. While he was looking in the freezer he found a package of stew meat, also butcher-wrapped, but too big to carry. He set it in the refrigerator where the brats had been. A jelly jar with pencils and pens and packs of matches stood on the countertop by the door. Out of habit, he grabbed the matches ("The Lute Bar and Grill") and dropped them into his shirt pocket. Then he searched the small bathroom off the kitchen. The medicine chest contained Bactine (he took it) and iodine and mercurochrome and a scattering of small adhesive bandages in their waxed envelopes (he left them) and gauze, but no Off!

The dogs were milling around the kitchen when he came out. He hustled them out the door and removed his muddy shoes, and then he washed the dishes and rearranged the kitchen and wetted a towel that lay draped over the back of a chair and wiped up the dirt they'd tracked in. When he finished, the kitchen looked reasonably like it had before they'd arrived. The kitchen clock read one-fifteen. He carried the paper bag containing the evidence of their crime to the trash can behind the shed, lifting a fly-strewn bag from on top and jamming his beneath.

They retired to the field. He fetched the Zebco and the satchel and walked along the fence line. Halfway up the slope the Lute water tower was visible again. He heard a rumble and noticed for the first time the railroad tracks at the bottom of the bluff beside the field. A freight train appeared from the south. Out on the road, the crossing bars dropped and the bell clanged. They watched a locomotive and fifteen cars roll along. The tracks appeared to pass by Lute on a tangent. That was good luck, he thought. They might try walking the rails.

But not just then. A postprandial lethargy had taken hold of Edgar and he stumbled to where the dogs lay stretched out in the shade of the lone tree overhanging the fence. Tinder lay on his back, feet raised in a posture of surrender. Baboo and Essay faced the fence, chins on paws, gazes dreamily fixed on the horizon. As Edgar reached them, Essay heaved a roaring burp, licked her lips, and rolled onto her side. Edgar felt just the same. The sunflowers hid them nicely from the house. He sat down beside Baboo and stroked his ruff until the dog's eyes drooped shut. Then Edgar lay back on the grass.

WHEN HE WOKE, enormous cuneiform clouds had rolled across the sky, and between them great slant columns of afternoon sunlight tilted onto the earth. He yawned and sat up. He looked around. Though evening was well along, an hour or two of good light remained, he guessed. If they started at once and the traveling went easily, they might make several miles' progress before bedding down again. His head throbbed from sleep or feast or both. The dogs, too, seemed dazed. They stood and yawned and shook themselves out and somehow slid down to the ground again. He let them lie and snuck downfield for another look at the house.

Someone had recently arrived. A plain-looking sedan sat parked next to the stoop and the trunk was hinged open and a tall, lean man, maybe thirty years old, was hefting grocery bags out of its depths. The man had already been inside the house, for the back door stood open, but he seemed unalarmed. Edgar smiled to himself. He'd begun to take pride in his skill as a burglar. He had turned it into a kind of game—how much could he take before they noticed? How could he rearrange things to hide what was missing? People didn't expect someone to break into their houses to steal a little food; they expected to be *ransacked*—to lose televisions, money, cars, to find their dresser drawers dumped, their mattresses overturned. No one in the cabins (as far as he could tell) had ever done more than scratch their heads at their depleted larder. Who stole *half* a loaf of bread and then cleaned up after himself? Edgar and the dogs had feasted where this man now unpacked his groceries, and there was a chance he wouldn't even notice.

When he returned, Edgar found the dogs sniffing with great interest the package of bacon he'd taken from the kitchen of the little farmhouse. He looked at them and shook his head in disbelief. Edgar himself felt like one of those snakes that swallowed pigs whole; he didn't actually *slosh* as he walked but the idea of putting more food inside his belly was laughable. He shooed them away and they pranced backward and watched him while he stuffed their loot into the satchel. Then he grabbed the Zebco and led the dogs down the bluff.

The railroad tracks veered to the northwest. A person could judge whether a train was coming, he'd read, by pressing an ear to one of the rails, and he tried it: the scored silver bar was warm but silent. The four of them trotted up the track far enough that a passing motorist wouldn't make much of them—a boy and some dogs—and then, as the night came on, he ambled along, tie to tie, feeling content and even swaggering a bit at the thought of their success raiding the farm. Scrub wood paralleled the tracks left and right. Far ahead, a low uncovered bridge waited in the gloaming. Stories came back to him of people struck by trains as they walked the rails, and he wondered how that was possible—wouldn't anyone hear a train thundering toward him long before it arrived? He hoped one would come by just so he could count off the seconds between the first sound of it and when it passed.

These were his thoughts when Tinder first cried out, a yike of surprise and pain that made Edgar's stomach instantly knot in fear. He knew where each of the dogs was—Essay and Baboo had been poking along beside him on the ties, as content and lost in thought as he, but Tinder had trotted down the grade to investigate something in a stand of cattails.

Probably frogs, Edgar had thought. He even recalled seeing, from the corner of his eye, Tinder stiffen and pounce. But his attention had been directed up the tracks, imagining onrushing trains. Tinder's motion had looked unexceptional—the dogs pounced dozens of times each day, on toads, frogs, field mice, grasshoppers, who knew what.

But this time Tinder let out a shrill *ai-ai* and leapt back. Edgar stood watching, unable at first to move, as the dog tried to set his foot down. Tinder shrieked and threw himself down amidst the cattails, holding his right paw in the air and striking at it with his left.

Snake bite, was Edgar's first coherent thought. Somehow that finally broke his paralysis. He crashed through the weeds below the embankment and dropped to his knees beside Tinder, but even before he touched the dog he saw the blue-green shard of glass, muddy and jagged, impaled in the bottom of the dog's foot, and the thin spear protruding from the top. Out of reflex, Edgar grabbed Tinder's muzzle. In days to come he would remember that instinctive motion and think he had at least done one thing right, because Tinder was about to bite the glass and would have gashed his mouth as badly as his foot.

Tinder shook off his grip and tried to scramble up. Edgar threw a leg over the dog and rolled him. Tinder lashed his body side to side, kicking a fine crimson spray over them. Then Edgar felt Tinder's teeth on his forearm, but there was no time to see if he'd been bitten, or how badly. Somehow, he got himself kneeling over the dog. Essay and Baboo had plunged down the embankment alongside him and they danced at Tinder's muzzle, worrying and licking his mouth. For a moment Tinder's body went slack as he looked at the other dogs. *Now*, Edgar thought, knowing he might not get another chance. He gripped Tinder's paw tightly and grasped the crudely serrated wedge of glass between his thumb and forefinger and pulled. There was a horrible sawing as the speared point slid back into Tinder's foot. The glass was slick with blood and mud and Edgar's thumb slipped along the edge. Had Tinder not jerked his foot back, the tearing sensation in Edgar's thumb would have made him release the shard before it was out of the dog's pad. He felt Tinder's teeth on his forearm, this time harder, but by then it was already done. He dropped the piece of glass and rolled and lay on his side, squeezing his hand and looking at the ragged incision that had appeared in the fleshy front of his thumb. The cut burned like acid and he shook his hand to slake it.

Tinder hobbled away and sank to the ground near the embankment. If the sensation in Edgar's thumb was any measure, Tinder must have been in agony. Edgar curled his thumb into his fist and ran to the dog, blood dripping from between his fingers. He sat panting. Essay and Baboo were nosing through the cattails, swiping their tails in curiosity. He stood again and ran to them, panicked at the idea of more broken glass, clapping his hands until blood splashed across his shirt. He hustled the dogs back toward Tinder, where they scented the dog along his legs and sides until they were certain they had located his wound.

The shard of glass lay in the weeds. Edgar picked it up. The broad end had three smooth ridges—threads for a jar cap. A fragment of a jelly jar or something like that, pitched into the weeds from a passing train or by another walker of ties. Bloody dirt packed the threads. He flung it angrily into the cattails and forced his thumb out straight and pulled open the gash to look at it. He felt a thump and then he was sitting. Essay was nosing him and licking his face. When his vision stopped tunneling he pushed himself to his feet, wobbled, and sank to his knees.

Wait, he thought, drawing a breath. Try again.

On his next attempt he was able to stand. He staggered over to Tinder, who lay with his paw curled inward before him, as if cradling some orphaned part of his body, sorrowfully drawing his tongue across the pad. His pelt contracted where Edgar lay a hand on it. Tinder turned away from his injury momentarily to look at Edgar. With his good hand, Edgar stroked the dog from the top of his head down along his backbone. He palpated Tinder's back feet, hoping he would understand what was coming. Then Edgar ran his hand along Tinder's foreleg again, this time all the way to his pad, without a protest from the dog beyond a short rumble of apprehension and a lick.

A crescent-shaped wound lay in the center of the triangular middle pad, oozing blood and dirt. Edgar didn't attempt to touch it, but slowly—very slowly—rotated the paw until he could look at the blood-stained fur on top. He delicately touched the tips of Tinder's claws, one by one, manipulating his toes. When he touched the second toe, Tinder whined and jerked his foot. So that was it. Something in his second toe; maybe not the bone, but there were ligaments, tendons, tiny muscles in there.

He released Tinder's leg and stroked him and tried to think. He bent his thumb experimentally. It didn't hurt more bent than straight, which was a good sign, but they could both probably use stitches. He stood, still wobbly, and retreated a few paces, bringing Essay and Baboo around behind him. Tinder lay watching, ears back, as if he knew what Edgar was about to ask of him.

Come, Edgar signed.

Tinder looked at him. He whined, then stood on three legs and held his damaged forefoot in the air, nosing it like a broken thing.

Edgar knelt.

I'm sorry, he signed. We have to do this. Then he recalled Tinder again.

Tinder set his foot on the ground and jerked it up. He hobbled a step, looked at Edgar, and tried again. When he finally reached Edgar, he dropped to the ground, panting, and refusing to meet Edgar's gaze even when Edgar put his face in front of his.

He might be going into shock, Edgar thought. He ran a fingertip along Tinder's gums. They were moist, which was good, but it was obvious that the dog couldn't walk. Edgar got Tinder to his feet by slipping a hand under his belly. He passed one arm behind the dog's back legs and threaded the other under his chest, careful not to touch his dangling foot. He thought if he did it wrong Tinder might bite him out of panic, and if he dropped the dog, he knew he would not be granted a second try. But Tinder panted in his face and waited and Edgar came smoothly to his feet.

Slowly he made his way up the side of the railroad embankment, digging the toe of each shoe into the gravel before trusting his weight on it. Once on top, he could take only one small step at a time, for fear of tripping on a tie. His thumb throbbed as if it had burst. Tinder hung slack in his arms, as if he'd concluded that this was how things would

have to go. And that, if nothing else, made Edgar realize how badly the
dog's paw had been mangled.

Then he remembered the Zebco and the fisherman's satchel lying beside the tracks. He didn't turn back for them. It would be impossible
to carry them anyway, and the dark was quickly becoming absolute. He
would have to go back later. Far in the distance, headlights glowed then
faded as a car crossed the railroad tracks beneath the bluff they had descended.

He focused on that point and took another step.

BEFORE THEY REACHED THE blacktop, he'd had to set Tinder down
three times to let the knots in his back unkink. The dog was heavy—
ninety pounds or more, over half Edgar's own weight. Each time they
stopped, Tinder tried to walk, managing only to hobble a few yards before lying down. The lucky thing (if that was what it could be called) was
that they had gone only about a mile down the track. Essay and Baboo
had stuck close by—another good thing, since Edgar had no way of signing a recall with his arms full.

He picked up Tinder. They began again.

Then they stood on the deserted blacktop. The only light came from
the windows of the little foursquare house beneath the sunflower field.
The adrenaline that had first powered Edgar had ebbed, and he staggered along with Tinder in his arms. The asphalt was wonderfully flat
and smooth beneath his feet. When they reached the mailbox, Edgar
walked up the driveway, under the row of tall trees in the front yard. The
air around the house was alight with fireflies. A june bug buzzed past.
Essay and Baboo charged ahead and rounded the corner of the house. The
moment they disappeared, Tinder began to squirm and Edgar walked
faster.

Essay and Baboo were milling about on the unlit stoop when he got
there. He knelt and guided Tinder down onto the wooden planks. Then
he clapped softly and led Essay and Baboo a few feet onto the grass and
downed them as well.

When he turned back, a man's face had appeared in the window above the kitchen sink. The porch light flared. Edgar checked the dogs. They lay at attention, watching. The inside door swung open and the man he'd watched carrying groceries from his car that evening looked at him through the screen.

"Can I help you?" the man said. His gaze fell on Tinder, panting on the stoop. He looked at Edgar and saw the blood. "You've been in an accident?"

Edgar shook his head and signed a response. The man wasn't going to understand sign, but there was no better way to get started. With luck, he'd understand he was being signed *at*.

My dog is hurt. We need help.

The man watched Edgar's hands. Edgar waited while he figured it out. "You're deaf," he said.

He shook his head.

"You can hear me?"

Yes.

Then Edgar gestured toward his throat and shook his head. He made as if to write on his palm. The man looked at him blankly, then said, "Oh! Got it. Right. Just a second," and disappeared into the house, leaving Edgar to stare into the kitchen he'd ransacked that morning.

His legs trembled as he waited. He knelt by Tinder and stroked his ruff and watched as the dog tongued his wounded paw in long strokes, eyes glassy and unfocused, as if staring into another world. In the yellow porch light his bloody fur gleamed black. Then Edgar went to Essay and Baboo and set his hands intimately under their jaws, touching them the way he would if everything were okay, and together they watched the doorway.

The man returned. He stood behind the screen holding a pencil and a pad. His gaze went to Tinder, then to Edgar squatting beside the two other dogs. Evidently, he hadn't noticed Essay and Baboo before.

"Whoa," he said. He put his palm forward and patted the air, as if trying to make everything stay still while he took stock of things.

"Okay. Okay. Definitely . . . definitely not an ordinary situation," he said, giving Essay and Baboo a wary gaze. "They're friendly?"

Edgar nodded. For the man's benefit, he turned and stayed them. There was something morose about the man, Edgar thought. It was an odd idea to have about someone he'd just met, but an unmistakable aura of resignation enveloped the man, as though he were one of those people depicted in cartoons who walked around with rain clouds over their heads, people whose change fell out of their pockets when they bent down to pick up a penny. The man's reaction to Essay and Baboo only reinforced this impression—as if he'd somehow been expecting to find a pack of ferocious dogs outside his door one day. He didn't smile—his expression was guarded, though not unfriendly—but he didn't frown, either. If anything, his eyes conveyed a look of benign misgiving, the result of some lifelong despondency.

"Right," he said. "Trained. But friendly? Yes?"

Yes.

He peered into the dark. "Any more out there?"

Edgar shook his head and he'd have smiled if his stomach hadn't been churning with anxiety. The man opened the screen door and stepped out, fixing the dogs with a doubtful look. Edgar took the pencil and the pad.

My dog cut his foot. I need water to clean it and a pan or bucket.

They looked down at Tinder.

"Are any people hurt?"

No.

"I should call a doctor," the man said.

Edgar shook his head vehemently.

"What's wrong with your voice? Did you hurt your throat somehow?"

No.

"You've always been that way?"

Yes.

The man thought for a second.

"Okay, wait, I'll be right back," he said.

He walked inside. Edgar heard some clanking and rattling and then water running in the kitchen sink. In a moment, the man emerged carrying a white enamel pot, water sloshing over the sides. A ratty blue towel was tucked under his arm.

"Here," he said, setting the pot down on the planks of the stoop. "It's warm. You can get started with this. I'll get you a bucket and see what else I've got."

Edgar carried the pot to Tinder and ladled up a handful of water and held it out for the dog to smell. Tinder was panting hard, and he licked the water from his fingers. Edgar dipped the rag into the water and ran his hand down Tinder's foreleg. The dog whined and poked his nose at Edgar anxiously but let him dab at the dirt on his foot. Edgar rinsed the rag. The water clouded and turned brown. He pressed his face to Tinder's muzzle while he soaked the cloth against Tinder's pad again and again. Each time the rag came away covered with a mixture of blood and muck.

The man emerged carrying a metal bucket and walked to a spigot that projected from the house's foundation. It squeaked when he turned it. Fresh water sprayed out. While the bucket was filled, he turned to Edgar.

"If I bring this over, will it spook your dog?"

Edgar had his arm over Tinder's back. He didn't think a stranger's approach would scare him, but it was a good question to ask, and his opinion of the man went up a notch.

No.

The man toted the bucket over and set it a cautious distance away and sat. The water in the small enamel pot was gritty and brown. The man reached over and tipped the dirty water out and dipped it into the bucket and returned it.

Essay and Baboo groaned behind Edgar. It had been a mistake to place them where his back would be turned, making them more likely to break their stays out of curiosity. He sat up straight, keeping one hand on Tinder's withers, and gestured at the man to stay still. The man nodded. Edgar turned and looked at the two dogs, who tucked their feet and locked gazes with him.

Come, he signed.

They bounded forward. Edgar worried that Tinder would forget his wound and rise to meet them but the pressure of his hand between the dog's shoulder blades kept him steady. Essay and Baboo charged around them, heads reared back to get close with their chests while taking the stranger in widely.

"I hope you meant it when you said they were friendly," the man said. He was sitting very straight, trying to look at them both at once. Then he gave up and just looked at whichever dog happened to be in front of him.

"Whoa buddy," he muttered. "Okay. Okay."

When they'd discharged enough of their curiosity, Edgar clapped and gestured to a spot in the grass nearby. At first they refused. Edgar clapped again, and they trotted over, grumbling. He'd selected a spot where they could watch what was going on, and he felt them relax now that they could make eye contact with him. He turned back to cleaning Tinder's paw. The fresh water had dirtied again, though now more bloody than brown.

"You're hurt, too," the man said. Edgar nodded. His thumb blazed each time he dipped it into the wash water, but it reminded him how Tinder felt when he dabbed the cold cloth across his paw.

"What happened?"

Edgar stopped washing Tinder's paw long enough to pantomime spiking the flat of one hand on two fingers of another.

"Uh. Ouch," the man said. He watched in silence for a while.

"Okay," he said at last. "Tell you what. I'm going back inside to see what I've got in my medicine cabinet. Here, let me get that—" He reached over and dumped the pan and refilled it from the bucket again. "I might have mercurochrome or hydrogen peroxide."

Edgar concentrated entirely on Tinder now. He'd cleaned most of the dirt away and he needed to swab between Tinder's toes and around the pad. He maneuvered the dog's paw so that he could submerge it in the small pan entirely. The water turned brown. Tinder yelped and jerked, but Edgar slowly worked his fingers between Tinder's toes again, dumping the water several times while the man was gone.

Then the man was squatting down in front of them. He set down a metal pan wrapped with tin foil, on top of which lay a collection of bottles retrieved from his medicine chest. One of them was Tylenol. He opened the bottle and held out two capsules.

"Maybe you should take a couple of these," he said.

Edgar popped them into the back of Tinder's mouth at once and pointed the dog's muzzle upward and stroked his throat until his tongue swiped his nose. Then he scooped up a handful of clear water from the bucket and let Tinder lap it. The man nodded. He held out two more capsules, which Edgar quickly swallowed.

"Right," the man said. "Also, I've got something *these* guys might be interested in." He folded back the foil and lifted a hunk of browned stew meat between his thumb and forefinger—the meat Edgar had taken from the freezer that morning to replace the stolen bratwurst. "I just made this tonight. It's even a little warm yet."

Edgar nodded and released the two watchers. There was a time, he thought, when the dogs would have checked with him before accepting food from a stranger; they'd been drilled on it in town. But that was a remnant of a life long gone, cast aside by animals who hunted frogs and snakes and ate ripe turtle eggs. Essay and Baboo arranged themselves around the man, ears up, waiting their turn as he flicked hunks of glistening beef onto the grass. The man acted almost bashful under their combined gaze. With trepidation, he allowed Tinder to take the meat directly from his hands. But Edgar was grateful for any distraction that allowed him to more thoroughly wash Tinder's wound. When the meat was gone, the man let Tinder lick the gravy off his fingers and pushed the pan out with his foot for the other dogs to clean up. He had a wry expression on his face. Edgar got the feeling this might be the happiest the man could look.

"Call it what you will," the man said, "but this is *definitely* not ordinary."

Henry

WITH EDGAR'S HANDS OCCUPIED, THE CONVERSATION RE-
mained lopsided. Essay and Baboo lay in the grass, sated, observing the proceedings by the glow of the moth-crossed porch light. Edgar lifted Tinder's paw and examined the flayed wound in the center of his swollen, heart-shaped pad.

"Jeez, that's gruesome," the man said, as Edgar dabbed Tinder's foot. "He'll be lucky ever to use that thing again." After another moment's thought, he added, "Your thumb doesn't look so great, either."

Edgar replaced the water in the enamel pan and went back to washing Tinder's paw. Threads of blood diffused into the water. The outside tap water was icy, but that was okay—he wanted it as cold as possible. If he could barely feel his hands, maybe Tinder would barely feel his injury.

He worked the bones of Tinder's foot, lifting and pressing the toes like piano keys, tracing Tinder's nails with his own, pressing his fingertips into the soft caves between the pads. Gently, gently, he opened the incision, letting the dog tell him where the pain was. When Tinder snatched his paw away, Edgar closed his eyes and pressed his face into Tinder's ruff, stroking his chest and jaw, listening to the rush of blood through the dog's neck, making Tinder realize how important the water was, asking over and over if they could try just once more. After a time Tinder let Edgar lift his foot back into the pan. Edgar waited until his fingers numbed, then began to rock the wound open, let the water flush it clean again.

When he opened his eyes, the pan had been refilled with fresh, cold water.

"That's really something," the man said. "Sometimes I can't tell whether it's you or the dog moving his foot."

Edgar nodded.

"You know him real well, huh?"

Yes.

"Same with the other dogs?"

Yes.

"It's okay that he's got his teeth on your arm like that?"

Edgar nodded. Yes, yes.

He continued to work Tinder's foot. When the water stayed clear, he sorted through the medicines on the stoop. He dumped the hydrogen peroxide into the pan, pouring it over Tinder's paw. It fizzed at Tinder's pad and the pursed white flesh on Edgar's thumb. When the fizzing stopped, he propped Tinder's paw over his leg and padded it dry. The man went inside and returned with a towel and a rag and some scissors.

"I don't have gauze, but if you want you can wrap it in this," he said.

Edgar nodded and took the pencil and paper.

Do you have a sock? he wrote.

"Right," the man said, and disappeared into the house again.

He cut the rag into strips and wrapped Tinder's foot and tied off the ends of the bandages so they wouldn't come loose. The man returned with a white sock in his hand. Edgar secured it with the last strip.

"Okay, look," the man said. "I need sleep. Work tomorrow." He looked doubtfully at the dogs. "I'm guessing you won't go inside without them?"

No.

The man nodded as if accepting another in a long series of humiliations.

"Tell me they're housebroken. Lie if you have to."

Edgar nodded.

"All right, come on. We'll figure out what's next in the morning."

Edgar called Baboo and Essay and hastily washed their feet. The man held the door, bleakly ceremonious, as the dogs trotted over, raising their noses at the threshold to scent the air, and walked into the kitchen. Edgar knelt and arranged Tinder in his arms and staggered sideways through the doorway.

"Left," the man said.

Edgar sidestepped along a short hall. Tinder sniffed at the coats hanging from the hooks as they passed. Then he was standing in a living room with a sofa, an overstuffed chair, bookcases, and a television with a phonograph on top. The floors were beat-up hardwood, deeply grooved and darkened with age. He lowered Tinder to a throw rug in front of the sofa. The dog tried to stand, but Edgar lifted his front feet from under him and set him down again. By the time the man appeared with a pillow and a pair of blankets, he had all the dogs downed and stayed.

"Here," the man said. "I'd appreciate it if you slept with one of those blankets under you, what with the mud and everything."

Edgar looked down at himself and realized that, though he had cleaned up the dogs, he was covered with a mixture of dried blood and dirt.

"Get some sleep—not that I think you need me to tell you. You're swaying, you know that, right? The bad news is, I have to be up early tomorrow for work. There's a bathroom off the kitchen. I put some Band-Aids and some antibiotic goop on the end table, if you want to take care of that thumb."

Edgar nodded.

The man took another long look at the dogs.

"When they start chewing on things, try to steer them over to that chair, would you?" He jerked his thumb at an overstuffed armchair in the corner. It was upholstered in orange and brown. Images of ducks were involved in the pattern. "I hate that chair," he said.

Edgar looked at him, trying to decide if he was making a joke.

"By the way," he said. "My name's Henry Lamb."

He held out his hand. Edgar shook it and then Henry walked to a doorway off the living room and turned and looked back.

"I don't suppose you have people you want called? Family? Someone to come get you?"

No.

"Yup," Henry grunted. "Had to ask."

Edgar was too tired to wash up. He spread the blanket over the couch and lay down. His head ached with fatigue; his thumb just plain ached. He took the Band-Aids and slathered antibiotic ointment over the raw and puckered wound on his thumb. He was still trying to decide if he had the energy to turn out the light when a wave of exhaustion swept him away, the ointment and the Band-Aid wrappers still lying on his chest.

THE SOFA SHOULD HAVE BEEN a rare pleasure. Instead, his sleep was plagued by absences: Why did the night withhold its panoply of sounds? Where were the bodies of the dogs that warmed him in the dark? He drifted near sleep like a buoy off a shore, until sometime in the night the great rock python Kaa materialized and looped his iridescent coils around Edgar's legs and chest. It was comforting to meet a figure he recognized, yet how oddly like cotton Kaa's reptilian skin felt under his fingertips, warm and downy and shot through in places with something almost like a turned hem. The wedge of Kaa's head swayed before him, lisping nonsense, but even that master hypnotist couldn't draw him deeper into sleep. Missing dogs. Smothering quiet. Snake's coils.

When dogs began to bark, Edgar jumped up, electrified by the alarm in their voices. He didn't bother to disentangle himself from what he knew to be a dream figment, but somehow Kaa had passed into the waking world and taken the form of a blanket wrapped tightly around his legs. Considering how briefly he remained vertical, Edgar gleaned an admirable amount of information about the situation: there was Essay and Baboo and Tinder, hackles raised, fixated on something across the room; there was Henry Lamb, the object of their attention, wrapped in a threadbare checkered bathrobe, standing puffy-faced and startled in his bedroom doorway; and beyond the living room window there was a perfectly nice summer morning pouring itself into the yard. Then all Edgar saw were chair legs and carpeting, because he was busy crashing to the floor. The dogs turned to look at him. Their shoulders drooped and they began to sweep the air with their tails, gulping and panting in postures that said, possibly, they'd overreacted. Baboo pressed his nose into Edgar's ear and slobbered to make amends.

Henry slumped against the doorway. He attempted speech, but only a grunt came out. He shuffled past and into the kitchen.

"Coffee if you want it," he croaked after a while.

Edgar settled the dogs and knelt beside Tinder. The bandage was still on his foot, which surprised Edgar and worried him, too. Had Tinder been healthy, he would have chewed it off in the night. With his hand under Tinder's belly, Edgar coaxed the dog into taking a few steps.

Good, Edgar thought, watching Tinder hold his foot aloft. At least he's not going to try walking on it.

When Edgar came into the kitchen with the dogs, Henry was sitting at the table cradling a coffee cup. Edgar tipped open the door and Essay and Baboo began trotting around the weedy lawn between the house and barn. Edgar laid his hand on Tinder's back to guide him outside. The dog hobbled a few steps, urinated, and hobbled back. When he stepped back into the kitchen, the shower was running and Henry's cup sat empty on the counter. Edgar poured himself some coffee. He found milk in the refrigerator and sugar in a little bowl by the window. The result was bitter and thick but it shocked him awake. He sat on the stoop next to Tinder.

Henry walked outside, car keys jingling in one hand, a lunch bucket in the other.

"Had time to think about what you're going to do today?" he said, easing down next to them.

Edgar shook his head. This was a lie. What to do that day was exactly what he'd been worrying about, watching Tinder and trying to guess how long his bandage would last if they started walking. Or if Tinder could walk at all.

"How's your dog?"

Edgar shrugged.

"Right. Probably too soon to tell."

They sat watching Essay and Baboo.

"Okay, here's the thing," Henry said. "While I was showering I tried to figure what most people would do in my place. Like, what's the *ordinary* way to handle this? Call the police, I suppose, tell them I've got a lost kid and three dogs on my hands. That's my first instinct, so I don't trust it—it doesn't show much imagination, you know?"

Edgar nodded.

"So I'm not going to do that. I mean, I don't *think* I'll do that."

Henry turned to give Edgar a look—a meaningful look—though Edgar couldn't be sure exactly what its meaning was. It struck him again how there was something likable about the man's defeatist sincerity. Henry Lamb saw the world as filled with road blocks and difficulties, or so it seemed. He conveyed, somehow, the impression that no bad news would surprise him, that every situation was a double-bind waiting to be discovered.

"Look," Henry said, "I'm telling you right now I'm not trustworthy. I was once, but not anymore. No promises. Nowadays I'm reckless and unpredictable." He said this without a hint of irony in his voice.

Edgar blinked.

"I'm going to leave the house unlocked. You can stay if you want, give your dog's foot time to heal."

Edgar nodded his head. They sat on the edge of the stoop and looked at the sunflowers. It was very early in the morning, and the sun was just preparing to slip over the horizon, but already their enormous dished heads were tipped eastward.

"I don't suppose you're planning to rob me blind."

Edgar shook his head.

"Well, what else could you say? But if I kick you out and lock the door, you could just put a rock through the window, so what good would that do? I've got to either trust you or call the police and take most of the day off to deal with that."

He pushed himself to his feet with a grunt and walked to his car.

"Could be, I'm stupid. Just in case, I'll tell you right now there's hardly any money in there, and nothing much valuable you could carry on foot—no jewelry, nothing like that. No guns. Kitchen's stocked up, though. I just went shopping yesterday. Eat anything you like—you look like you're starving. Stay out of my bedroom. *Don't* mess with this car"— he gestured to the wreck on blocks—"and the TV's busted. Anything else you want to know?"

No.

Henry backed his sedan around. As he pulled up to the house, he leaned over and rolled down the passenger-side window. "If you do leave," he said, "lock the door. But don't, otherwise, unless you want to wait outside until I come back—the only other set of keys is in my desk at work."

He idled down the driveway and then there was the sound of tires on blacktop, fading in the direction of Lute.

EDGAR STAYED ON THE STOOP, sipping Henry Lamb's noxious coffee. The house sat in a pocket of morning shadow behind the sunflower field; the cloudless sky was shot with white rays, as if someone had thrown powdered sugar into the air. A faint turpentine odor drifted off the sunflowers.

Essay and Baboo were snooping along the perimeter of the barn. When Tinder whined, Edgar signed a release and the dog hopped forward. He stopped and solemnly nosed his bandaged foot, then persevered until he reached the other dogs, tapping his foot lightly on the ground as he hitched along. The dogs sniffed one another. Then Tinder limped back to the stoop and lay down, sighing.

Watching the dog move told Edgar it would be two weeks—two, three, even—before they could travel, assuming Tinder's paw didn't get infected, and he hadn't cut a tendon or ligament so vital he would (as Henry had so delicately suggested) be crippled. The irony was that if any of the dogs was going to hurt himself through foolish exploration, it should have been Essay, not Tinder. Tinder had just been unlucky—and hunting frogs, no less, always harmless in the past.

So did they have any choice but to accept Henry's offer? The man didn't seem to know the first thing about dogs. Edgar doubted Henry had any idea how long Tinder's convalescence would last, or what it took to feed three hundred pounds of hungry dog every day. Edgar had no money to pay for food. Without a lake nearby, and no cabins to pilfer, fishing and burglary weren't options.

Plus, to top it all off, Henry was such a strange character. His warning about not being trustworthy—people didn't say things like that. At the same time, Henry clearly liked them. He'd even glimpsed the man smiling after the morning's ruckus. Or maybe that had just been his reaction to the sight of Edgar toppling to the floor. But even if Henry had been sincere in his offer, on his drive to work (wherever that was) he could decide he'd made a mistake—what was he *doing*, turning his house over to a stranger? The next thing Edgar would know, a squad car would be pulling into the yard. After weeks in Chequamegon woods, Edgar felt sure that, able-bodied, they could evade any single pursuer. But with Tinder lame, and so many open fields around, there would be no ducking anyone. Not unless they had a long, long head start.

Of course, that *was* an option. They could leave, right that moment. Tinder's wound would slow them down, but it wouldn't stop them. He'd carried Tinder a mile the night before—true, his back was still aching like the blazes, but he could do it again if he had to. So what if they could go only a mile a day? A mile up the track from Henry's house was as good as the next county, for all anyone knew, and once they got to a lake, they could lay up for a long time. Until now, they'd depended on no one. It was the one plan he knew worked.

He clapped Essay and Baboo back and led them all into the house. He started the water running in the shower and stripped. As the small mirror over the sink fogged, he looked at himself: hawk-thin, face dotted with mosquito bites, hair bleached brown and hanging over his blue eyes. The weeks they'd spent fending for themselves had burned away the softness in him, and he looked like a sight hound, edgy and strung up tight.

Also, he was filthy. The dirt on his sunburnt neck stopped somewhere around his shoulders. He fiddled with the temperature of the water, then

stepped into the shower and pulled the white plastic curtain and lath-
ered up. He let the steaming water course over his body. Despite his
daily doses of Off!, every inch of his skin seemed to have been dinner for
some horsefly, chigger, or mosquito. When the hot water was drained,
he pushed back the curtain. Essay and Baboo stood peering quizzically
through the doorway. He smiled and grabbed a towel and brandished it
like a toreador.

After he'd dressed, he filled a bowl with Wheaties, milk, and honey
and carried it with him as he looked around the house. The hallway was
covered with pictures—an elderly couple posed before a studio backdrop, Henry's parents, he guessed; some pajama'd children holding up
toys beside a glittering Christmas tree; a younger Henry, in the lobby of
a large building, next to his parents, a doubtful expression on his face.
On the end table he noticed a portrait of a cherubic woman, signed in
a loopy swirl, "Love, Belva." The television remained dark when Edgar
switched it on, but there was a record player in working order. On the
bookshelves he found a stack of car repair manuals and some Bell System
handbooks—it looked like Henry worked for the telephone company.

The bedroom door was closed. He considered opening it, but everything in the house was somehow of a piece, and he could easily imagine
the plain bed, the linens rumpled but not too rumpled, the checkered
bathrobe flung down. The dresser. The closet. More family pictures on
the wall. Staying out of there was the only thing Henry had asked. He
hadn't even asked them not to rob him—which they had already done,
gluttonously, and without a shred of remorse.

Edgar walked back to the kitchen and rummaged. He poured four
cans of beef stew into one bowl for Essay and Baboo, and two cans of tur-
key and dumplings into another for Tinder, and set the bowls out. While
they ate he peeled the Band-Aid off his thumb and inspected his wound.
The cut was deep and ugly, but it was clean. He began rolling the sock
off Tinder's foot. His mind's eye conjured the sight of Tinder thrashing
on his back, spear of glass glinting both above and below. He hoped his
imagination had made Tinder's injury worse than it was—that it might
look benign by the light of day.

It did not. A brown stain had formed on the dressings. Tinder licked and pulled at the bandage as Edgar unwound it. With difficulty, he rolled the dog onto his side and turned his foot upward. The pad had swollen to twice its normal size. He forced himself to part the wound and was rewarded with a spine-tingling view of pink and gray meat and a glimpse of a white cord contracting. Then he had to stop, partly because his head was swimming, and partly because Tinder yelped and yanked his foot away, licking it with long, slow swipes and looking reproachfully at Edgar.

The enamel wash pan sat on the counter. He filled it with warm water and metered out four drops of dish soap. Tinder threatened to revolt when Edgar set it on the floor. Edgar wrapped his hand around Tinder's muzzle and looked him in the eye.

Get used to it, he signed. We're going to do a lot of this.

FROM THEIR VANTAGE POINT in the field, Edgar watched Henry's car stop beside the mailbox, then roll along the driveway. It was late afternoon, and he and the dogs had retreated to the spot where they'd slept away the previous afternoon, the best compromise he could think of between staying and going. Although Tinder couldn't put the slightest weight on his foot, when Edgar had tried to carry him, he'd thrashed so mightily Edgar had set him down at once, afraid he might jump and compound his injury. Reluctantly, he'd let the dog pick his way along the fence line, taking half an hour to complete the journey. But once they were settled, Edgar felt much better. He'd taken a chance that morning and down-stayed the dogs in the house and run up the tracks to fetch the Zebco and the satchel from the railroad embankment. Now the fishing equipment was hidden amidst the sunflowers. In a few seconds they could *all* be hidden amidst the sunflowers, even Tinder.

Down below, Henry stepped out of his sedan, a bag of groceries under his arm and lunchbox in hand. He called out and opened the back door, then disappeared inside. They had left the house empty and unlocked, without even a note of thanks. It was rude, but he couldn't leave evidence that he and the dogs had been there, in case Henry arrived accompanied by—well, who knew who might tag along, or follow a few minutes behind?

Henry returned to the stoop, beer in hand. He looked around the yard. Edgar ducked, and when he raised his head again, Henry stood on the road, staring along the blacktop and shaking his head. Then he dragged a round-bellied barbeque grill from the barn to the stoop. He produced a bag of briquettes and a can of lighter fluid and soon flames jumped out of the black hemisphere and heat waves shimmered above.

In short order Henry carried out two kitchen chairs and a card table which he unfolded on the lawn. He set plates on each side of the table and populated the center with a bag of thick brown rolls, bottles of ketchup and mustard, and a dish of something that was either potato or macaroni salad. He used a drinking glass as a weight over a small sheaf of paper and he dropped a pair of yellow pencils into it. Then he unwrapped a package of what could only be fresh bratwurst and arranged them on the grill and opened a can of baked beans and let it heat beside the brats. When everything was cooking to his satisfaction, and a column of smoke rose off the grill, Henry sat in one of the chairs and unfolded a newspaper.

Watching it all made Edgar smile. If they had been spotted, Henry could have just shouted to them without going through this performance. Probably, though, Henry had no idea whether they were nearby, much less watching. It was an interesting act of faith from a man who declared himself reckless and unpredictable. If anything, Henry struck Edgar as wildly dependable—making dinner and acting out this invitation for guests he couldn't even be sure existed.

And though he hated to admit it, Henry's plan was working. After the previous day's orgiastic meal, Edgar had thought he wouldn't eat for a week, but now his mouth was watering. Every time he looked, something new had appeared on the table. Pickles. Root beer. Something wrapped in butcher paper. What looked like lemon meringue pie. Yet they couldn't walk into that yard. Short of waiting, there was no way to be positive the man hadn't told the sheriff's department to stop by around, say, nine o'clock, when he could be sure the kid would be sitting in his house.

When the bratwurst finished cooking, Henry juggled the hot can of beans with an oven mitt and dumped them into a bowl. He stacked the sausages on a plate and set the plate on the card table and casually helped himself, scooping out a mound of potato salad and a dollop of baked beans. Then he quartered the newspaper in a flapping commotion and plucked a pencil from the empty glass across the table and began to work the crossword. Maybe it was Edgar's imagination, but he thought he could smell the spicy aroma of cooked bratwurst all the way up in the field. Baboo certainly could. He sidled up to Edgar and panted anxiously in his ear. Edgar smoothed his hand absently along the dog's topline.

A half-dark had fallen. A handful of stars had emerged in the clear azure sky. He stood and clapped quietly to bring Essay forward. When she didn't appear at his side, he suddenly understood that Baboo hadn't been panting over food. He whirled and clapped more loudly. When he turned back, Essay was already trotting into the circle of the porch light, her gait jaunty, her tail slashing prettily through the air, swinging her front legs in wide circles as she ran, as if greeting a long-lost friend. Henry set down his newspaper. Essay finished before him in a perfect sit, perhaps three inches away.

"Hello, you," Henry said, leaning back. His voice carried up the slope in the still evening air. Even from that distance Edgar could see Essay giving Henry the moocher's eye, sitting up straight, perking her ears, swishing her tail.

Baboo, standing beside Edgar, began to whine and stomp.

Sit, Edgar signed.

With a bitter groan Baboo sat, then sidled to his left for a better view. Then Tinder hobbled forward. The two of them sat scenting the air, heads bobbing and tilting like marionettes whenever Henry spoke.

There's no use now, Edgar thought. He walked to Tinder and knelt. You're not running down there on that foot, he signed. He got the dog up and put his arms underneath him and looked him in the eye. When they understood each other, he released Baboo, then put one arm under Tinder's belly and the other under his chest and stood. Tinder was heavy, but his weight was becoming familiar, and Edgar took slow, careful steps down the hill.

Henry took a swallow of beer and watched them approach. In the last fifty feet, Baboo discarded any shred of reserve and bolted forward, skidding into a sit beside Essay. The two dogs looked back and forth between Edgar and Henry. Then Essay trotted back to meet Edgar and Tinder, oblivious to the look Edgar gave her and tossing her head as if escorting them to a fête, all of it her idea.

Tinder had been patient on the walk down, but now he began to wriggle in Edgar's arms. Edgar lowered him to the ground. The dog nuzzled Essay then hopped across the grass. In a moment, Henry was ringed by dogs. Given all his preparations, Edgar expected Henry to issue a cheerful invitation, but he didn't know Henry very well yet.

"I thought you'd run off," Henry grunted, looking over the dogs' heads at him. He gestured toward the food. "Have a brat. I burned them pretty bad, but I guess they're better than nothing."

AFTER EDGAR STUFFED A BRAT into a bun and scooped potato salad onto his plate, Henry gestured toward the white parcel on the table. Edgar unwrapped it to find three large soup bones with shreds of raw, red meat attached and plenty of marrow.

"Guy at the meat locker told me those were good ones for dogs," he said.

Edgar nodded. He offered the package to Henry so that he could hand them out, but Henry shook his head. "Thanks anyway, but I was planning on using all my fingers tomorrow," he said. By that time the dogs had scented the bones and were waiting when Edgar crouched beside his chair. They trotted off to grind their teeth against the shanks and imagine, with unfocused gazes, the animal from which the bones had come.

Then, as if Edgar's arrival weren't of the least interest, Henry returned to his crossword puzzle. Occasionally he sat back and tapped his pencil and looked into the dark, as lost in thought as the dogs.

Finally, he set the pencil down and opened a fresh beer. "Darn it," he said. "I need a twelve-letter word meaning 'butterfly-like.' Starts with L."

Edgar looked at Henry. He picked up a pencil and wrote, *Lepidopteral*, and pushed the paper across the table.

Henry turned back to the crossword. "Nice," he said. "What can you get for a . . . let's see . . . six-letter word for 'echo.' Ends with R-B."

Edgar thought for a moment and, beneath his previous entry, wrote *reverb*.

"Yep. Yep. That works again," Henry said. "Aha—lentil!" he cried, and filled in another row. "One left. Eight-letter word for 'Formed of fire or light.' Starts with *E*, ends with *L*."

Edgar shook his head.

"All right, forget it. I got close. Thanks for the help." He set the paper down, divided the pie into six slices, passed a plated slice to Edgar, then took one of his own. He pointed his fork at Tinder, who busily gnawed his soup bone. "How's that guy's foot?" he asked.

Bad, Edgar wrote. Swollen.

"His main problem is going to be infection, you know that, right?"

Yes.

"You wash it out again today?"

He held up four fingers.

Henry nodded. "I'm not telling you anything you don't know, am I?"

Edgar shrugged, not wanted to seem ungrateful.

Henry ate a forkful of pie and looked at him. "I don't mean to pry," he said, "but it would make things a little easier if you told me your name."

Edgar sat mortified while Henry finished his pie. In all his thinking and planning throughout the day, this was one detail that hadn't crossed his mind. He couldn't simply write his real name down. After years of naming pups, he thought, it ought to be simple to come up with a name for himself. But he didn't have days or weeks to think this over. He tried to cover his confusion by helping himself to a second slice of pie. He looked at the dogs. Then an idea came to him. He scribbled on the paper and pushed it over to Henry.

"Nathoo?" Henry said, doubtfully. "You don't look much like a 'Nathoo.' Is that Indian or what?"

Call me Nat, Edgar wrote.

Henry looked at him.

"What do you call your dogs?"

The words *Essay, Baboo*, and *Tinder* appeared on the paper. Henry repeated them, pointing to each of the dogs in turn.

Yes.

Then, to get Henry off the subject of names, Edgar decided it was time to clean Tinder's foot once more. He filled the enamel pan with soapy water and carried it out to Tinder.

"This going to take as long as it did last night?" Henry asked.

Edgar nodded.

"Then I'm turning in. Make yourself comfortable when you're done."

Henry gathered up the remains of dinner, as well as the card table and chairs. By the time Edgar rewrapped Tinder's foot, Henry had retired to his bedroom. Edgar led the dogs inside and downed them on the rug in the living room.

He hoped the previous night had been a fluke, but as soon as he stretched out on the sofa it became clear he'd lost the ability to sleep on upholstered furniture. This had not previously seemed to be a skill. Just weeks before he had regularly slept in a bed, under sheets and blankets, with a roof overhead and a single small window through which to view the night. Now his body insisted he was in a chamber. The night sounds came through the half-open window as if down a long pipe. The pliability of the sofa cushions felt all wrong; far more comfortable than twigs gouging his side and bugs biting, but in the forest he and the dogs had slept touching one another—if any of them moved, the others knew it at once. Now he was forced to reach down to touch the dogs at all, and even then it was only with his fingertips. And anyone could walk up to the window before he knew it.

Finally, he stood, blanket wrapped around him, and led the dogs through the kitchen and onto the flat expanse of the stoop. They bedded down in a tangle of canine and human limbs with the house comfortably at their flanks, eight eyes and eight ears facing into the night. One by one the dogs exhaled deep sighs. Overhead, cool white stars arced in the black sky. The moon and the thin corona around the moon shone. It looked to him empyreal—formed of light or fire—the word that would have completed the crossword puzzle. Why hadn't he wanted to tell Henry? He pondered that question while the night sounds eddied around them, but before an answer came, he'd fallen asleep.

Ordinary

Birdsong. Scent of percolating coffee. Henry pushed open the screen door and looked at Edgar and the dogs lying curled and overlapped and shook his head as if they were the most pitiful sight he'd ever seen. Baboo was the first to rise, splaying his front feet and ambling sleep-drunk to Henry. Edgar tightened his grip on Tinder and Essay, but they were awake and panting. Water rang through the pipes in the house and the shower hissed. Edgar pushed himself up and walked into the kitchen and poured himself a cup of coffee and brought it back out on the stoop. Essay remembered her soup bone, which reminded the other dogs, and the sky brightened to the sound of three sets of teeth scraping bone. They barely looked up when Henry walked out, lunch bucket in hand. He dropped a pair of canvas work gloves onto the porch beside Edgar.

"Follow me," Henry said. He walked to the shed and jiggled a bent bolt out of a flap latch and threw open the doors. "Here's the deal. I want to park *that* car"—he gestured at the rusting monolith on the cinder-blocks—"in *this* shed."

Viewed from the outside, Henry's shed was unremarkable if slightly ramshackle. It measured maybe fifteen feet wide and twice that deep, a windowless little structure with a peaked roof and sun-blasted white paint. But inside lay a junkyard in miniature. It took Edgar a moment before he could make his eyes settle on any one thing. The walls were encrusted with hubcaps, spools of wire, license plates, ancient tire irons, hand saws, rakes, hoes, scythes, circular saw blades, and a menagerie of antique iron tools, rusted and strange. Coils of chain link lay heaped around the perimeter like petrified snakes. A length of rain gutter crumpled and folded. An unframed mirror footed by dusty, cracked sheets of plate glass. There was a stack of rusty buckets overflowing with doodads and piece parts. Off to one side, a crumbling pyramid of red bricks topped by a thick rope, shedding fibrous creepers. Plywood sheets, delaminated like picture books fished out of a puddle. There were mounds of tires, stacks of newspaper oatmealing in place, wash pans haphazardly stacked, their enamel crazed like desert mud. A squat brown anvil. Toward the back, a cylindrical wringer washer lurked, and what looked to be either a fire hydrant or part of a truck transmission.

And all that was around the edges. At the center stood—or stooped, rather—an ancient hay wagon. It gave the impression of a broken-backed animal driven to the ground by its burden. Three of its wheels had sprung out to the sides in expressions of shock and exasperation. Its front axle had buckled, tilting the fourth wheel inward, and the whole rotted platform melted diagonally back to front beneath a mountain of timber, shingles, doorframes, rolls of barbed wire, and rust-red stanchions. Had the wagon still been on its wheels, the debris would not have cleared the lintel.

"You see my problem?" Henry said.

Edgar nodded. He looked at the ruined car on its blocks. It definitely belonged in the shed, he thought. Then Henry laid out his plan—what to tackle first, what he wanted Edgar to avoid until both of them were there. It took him a long time to explain—there was a lot to do, and he instructed Edgar in detail. "Carhartts in the closet when you get to the pokey stuff," he said, gesturing toward a nest of barbed wire. Then he took Edgar to the barn and showed him where he could find wire cutters and a wheelbarrow. When they walked back to the house, Edgar scribbled out a request for bandages and Henry produced an old white bedsheet. They made a list of things he needed from town. And then Henry drove off.

Baboo and Essay had followed them to the shed and now stood peering into the kitchen through the screen door. Tinder had joined them, standing on three legs. He met Edgar's gaze with a glint of defiance. Unless Edgar wanted to hold him down, his look said, he was going to start moving.

First we clean that foot, Edgar signed.

Tinder's wound oozed a gray-green pus, odorless but nonetheless frightening. The sight made beads of sweat wick into the hair all over Edgar's scalp. He pressed the back of his hand to the injured pad. It was not overly hot. He began to work it in the water too roughly and Tinder yelped and jerked his paw away.

I'm sorry, Edgar signed. But we can't stop yet. He sat with his hand out. In time Tinder offered Edgar his dripping paw and the next time he went slower. Afterward he washed the old bandages in the sink and strung them up to dry on the clothesline. Tinder began to chew the new dressings.

Stop it, Edgar signed. He put the soup bone in front of Tinder and returned to the clothesline. Out of the corner of his eye, he saw Tinder return to his bandages. He walked back and stopped him again.

We can just do this all day if you want, he signed.

He counted back in his mind: three days since he and the dogs had been through drills. He lined them up in the grass behind the shed. They worked through recalls and come-fors in the morning sun, then fetches, stays, and guarding. It reminded them all of home, he supposed, but back then they'd only been going through motions, answering classroom questions upon which nothing depended. Chasing. Sitting still. Scenting targets. Now the same acts drew up the ties between them, put them back together, as though shaping the world from scratch. As they worked, they put the sky in place above, the trees in the ground. They invented color and air and scent and gravity. Laughter and sadness.

They discovered truth and lies and mock-lies—even then, Essay played the oldest joke there was to play, returning a stick past him as if he were invisible, cantering sideways, tossing it about in her mouth as if to ask, it's all play, really, isn't it? What else matters when there's this to do?

THE FIRST PART OF HENRY'S plan was simple—pull everything onto the dirt and grass and sort it into three piles: junk to burn, junk to haul away, and junk to save. The old lumber would be burned, along with the magazines and papers; the old chair and the stanchions would be hauled away. The category of junk to be saved was largely theoretical, Henry had said. Also, while Henry wasn't aware of anything that called the shed home, it was hard not to imagine a rat nesting inside somewhere. Edgar picked out a whacking stick and before he moved anything big, he whaled on it. A lone garter snake had slithered from behind the plywood, but so far that was it.

In short order he had the stanchions stacked haphazardly on the gravel and a mound of rubbish near the burning barrel. One after another the dogs trotted over to scent what Edgar had pulled out. Baboo and Essay marked the old car seat; when Tinder tried, it turned into a balancing problem, since he had only three good legs. Edgar made as if to stop them, then wondered what the point would be.

At noon he doled out scraps to the dogs and soaked Tinder's foot again, rewrapping it with dry bandages from the clothesline. There was the sound of a car passing along the road. Out of habit, he glanced up to locate the dogs, but there was no real cause for concern. Baboo and Tinder were sleeping in the shade. Essay had selected a spot in the sun from which she could follow his progress. All of them were concealed behind the house. He briefly reconsidered starting down the railroad tracks, then rejected the idea again. Besides the difficulty of traveling with Tinder, and the hydrogen peroxide and other supplies that Henry would be bringing back that evening, Edgar had made a deal with Henry and he already felt more than a twinge of guilt over having burglarized the man. He didn't want to renege. Cleaning out his shed seemed like a small repayment.

Edgar walked back to the shed, letting his mind wander as he worked. Each time he salvaged something interesting—a puckered, moldy globe or an apple-masher with a broken wooden handle—he turned it over in his hands, brushing away the dirt and dust and cobwebs. He wondered about whoever had built the place. How many summers had he clamped that contraption to his kitchen table and worked the now-cracked handle, squashing apple after apple, levering the burst pulp out of the cylinder, straining the juice through cheesecloth? Did the house smell like cider the next morning? Did hornets collect on the window screen as he worked?

He couldn't have pinpointed when, exactly, he knew he wasn't alone. He'd been working slowly, passing in and out of reverie, when his neck hairs began to prickle, as if a rivulet of sweat had been reduced there to salt by the wind, a sensation that at first meant nothing to him. The second time it happened, he glimpsed, from the corner of his eye, a figure standing in the depths of the shed, and he stumbled backward into the sunshine and stared into the gray morass of shadow.

He looked at the dogs sprawled about the yard. He walked around the shed, keeping a good distance away from it. There were no windows to look through and all he could do was trace the runs of clapboard with their paint peeling off like thin, irregular patches of birch bark. When he'd come full circle he stood outside the doorway and shielded his eyes and peered inside. He could see the outline of the old wagon and the rubbish mounded over it, but that was all. He'd tipped his whacking stick into the corner just inside the door and he leaned in and snatched it and rapped the wooden doorframe. After a while he walked back inside and beat the pile of stanchions until a cloud of orange rust dust filled the shed. All else lay inert. He stood nodding to himself. When he turned, the dogs were lined up in the doorway looking at him.

Good idea, he signed. Down. Watch me.

After the dogs were settled, he went cautiously back to work. The next time he felt the prickle along the back of his neck, he forced himself to look at the dogs first. Only Baboo was still awake, lying panting and unalarmed in the sun. Edgar let his gaze drift toward the rear of the shed.

The figure, seen from the corner of his eye, was there, yet when he turned to face it squarely, it was not.

He compiled an impression bit by bit: a slump-shouldered old fellow with a farmer's thick arms and a broad belly. He wore blue jeans and a grease-stained T-shirt and a feed store cap rested high on his graying head of hair. When the man finally spoke, his voice was low, almost a whisper, and he pronounced words with an accent Edgar recognized from many hours spent listening to old farmers at the feed store who said "da" for "the" and "dere" for "there."

It was the wife, the man said. Nothin' could go to waste. Everything had to be saved.

Edgar, wary of what had happened the last time he'd looked, forced himself to concentrate on wrenching a pair of car wheels free.

She wanted to keep every God-darned thing in case we needed it for parts, the man said. I could of used this shed for better, I'll tell you that. I ended up having to put all the real machinery over to the neighbor's.

Edgar stacked the wheels one atop the other and knelt and began sorting through some smaller items to keep his eyes on his hands.

Take that coal furnace there.

Edgar ventured a glance toward a hulking metal form behind the wagon. He didn't dare examine it too closely, for he could feel his gaze drawn toward the old farmer, but it certainly looked like it had once been a furnace. Until that moment he'd only noticed something round and metal and riveted.

We put that into the basement before we even laid the first floorboards. God, it was big! Took three of us all morning. Rained cats and dogs the whole time. That wasn't so bad, though. Gettin' it out was lots worse—had to bust it into pieces with a sledgehammer. "Make sure and save that," she says. "You never know."

From the corner of his eye Edgar saw the man shake his head.

I can't tell you how many ton of coal I shoveled into that thing. Got so I was pretty fond of it. Called it Carl. Gotta go stoke Carl, I'd say, when it got cold. Or, Carl's going to have a hell of a time tonight, when a blizzard come through.

How long did you live here? Edgar signed. But he let himself look, and once again there was no one there. He carried a steering wheel out to the yard and devoted himself to his work until his neck hairs stood again.

Thirty-seven years, the man said. About fifteen years in, nothing fit in the shed no more, so she let me haul some away. She wrung her hands the whole time. Ah, I shouldn't be so hard on her. She was a sweet woman, and she loved our kids like crazy. After she died I found a shoebox full of wire twists from bread bags. *Thousands* of 'em! Probably ever one we ever brought into the house. What was she thinking we would use them for?

Edgar didn't try to respond. He averted his eyes and selected an old crate filled with broken canning jars to carry to the discard pile. Then he pulled a wire cutter from his back pocket and began cutting a snarl of barbed wire and fence posts, bending lengths of wire straight and tossing them into a pile like the stems of iron roses.

When she died, the old farmer continued, I thought, *now* I can clean that shed. I come outside, opened the doors and thought, nope, can't do it. Thirty-seven years of putting in, I can't start taking out now. Would have been like burying her twice. So I sold it all and moved to town. When we had the auction, I told people they could have everything in the shed for twenty bucks if they emptied it out. Not one person took me up on it.

Then, despite Edgar's best efforts, his glance slipped toward the man again and he was gone. Edgar worked and waited. The afternoon passed. Then Henry arrived home, bringing the dog food and other supplies Edgar had requested and several cans of paint and brushes. He'd brought something else, too: phonograph records, which he made a point of taking out of the car immediately so they wouldn't melt in the hot sun.

The dogs sallied excitedly around the yard, letting out creaking yawns to calm themselves until Henry reemerged from the house. Edgar stayed Tinder, who keened quietly. The other two accosted Henry. The man hadn't been around many dogs, that much was obvious. He stood watching, arms in the air like someone wading in a pool. When Baboo sat in front of him, rather than scratching behind the dog's ear or stroking his ruff, to everyone's surprise Henry gripped him by the muzzle and shook it like a hand. The gesture was well meant, and possibly Henry even thought the dog liked it, but Baboo lowered his head tolerantly and cast a sidelong glance Edgar's way. Essay, having witnessed Baboo's fate, danced skittishly away when her turn came. Finally Henry walked over and patted Tinder's head open-handedly, as if tamping down a stubborn cowlick. He sized up the debris piles, which had grown impressively over the course of the day, and walked to the shed and looked in.

"Jesus," Henry said. "There's just as much here as when you started."

This was Edgar's sentiment exactly and he was relieved to hear Henry confirm it. He started to put the work gloves back on, but Henry interrupted him.

"That's enough for one day," he said. "If you keep at it any longer I'll feel obligated to help."

Edgar pulled the shed doors closed and dropped the bent bolt back into the rusty latch. They walked together to Henry's car. Henry fished two sweating six-packs from the floor of the passenger's side. In the back seat lay a forty-pound sack of dog food. Edgar slung it over his shoulder and carried it to the stoop and he sat and fed the dogs straight from the bag, cupping the kibble in his hands.

THAT NIGHT IT WAS A workingman's dinner. Henry sat at the kitchen table and read the newspaper and ate reheated brats and potato salad. He motioned for Edgar to help himself and eyed the dogs as though expecting them to lunge for the food. He started to ask Edgar to put them outside, then seemed to reconsider. Instead, he folded the paper into quarters and pored over the crossword, tapping his pencil on the table and picking off the easy clues. Then he said, "Oh!" and walked into the living room. There was a warm pop from the phonograph speakers. Piano music began to drift through the house.

"They call this one *The Goldberg Variation*," he said when he returned. He was holding a battered album cover in one hand. He looked at it again and, with self-conscious precision, corrected himself: "Varia*tions*." He took up the crossword puzzle again, shifting and fidgeting and touching his forehead as if perturbed by the sound of the piano. He emptied his glass of beer and leaned over to the refrigerator and extracted another, pouring it down the inside curve of the glass while streamers of bubbles tumbled upward.

"Hey, read something, would you?" he said. "When you just sit there it makes it hard to concentrate." He didn't sound angry, just a little dejected. "There's magazines and books in the living room."

Edgar took the dogs outside and began grooming them using the pin brush Henry had bought. It was a cheap plastic brush, but it was better than he could do with his fingers, which were all he'd had to work with for weeks. The dogs' undercoats were terribly matted. Twilight had ended but the kitchen window cast enough light. He worked Essay's tail until she grew impatient, then moved to Tinder and Baboo, and then back to Essay. The piano music drifted out the screen door. When it stopped, scratchily, he listened to Henry's footsteps pass through the living room. In a minute, a new melody began. Henry walked out onto the porch, paper and pencil in one hand, beer glass in the other, and sat with his back against the white clapboards. Baboo walked over to him. Henry tentatively pressed his fingers into the fur under Baboo's jaw, attempting to scratch without getting slobber on his fingers. Baboo endured it for a moment, then turned his head so that Henry's hand slid behind his ear and began to push back against Henry's fingers.

"Nat," Henry said, "what's a ten-letter word for 'Augments vision.' Starts and ends with S."

He slid the paper over to Edgar. "Twenty-three down."

Edgar glanced at the crossword puzzle and set down the brush and penciled in *spectacles* and pushed the paper back.

"Right," Henry said. "Should have got that." He held his beer up to the porch light and looked through it. "Spectacles," he repeated pensively, as if the idea of spectacles had just occurred to him. He tipped his head back against the house. When he stopped scratching Baboo, the dog nosed Henry's hand and laid a paw on his leg.

Watch it, Edgar signed at him.

Baboo withdrew his foot.

"You know," Henry said, "it's probably hard to tell, but I've never had a dog. Not even when I was a kid. Lots of cats—three, four at a time. My best friend in elementary school had a little spotted dog named Bouncer. Maybe a twenty-pounder or so. Pretty smart. He could balance stuff on his nose. He'd follow us everywhere. But these dogs—these dogs are something else. I mean, the way they look at you and all."

They sat in silence for a while. The light from the kitchen was skewed across the boards of the stoop.

"You had them all their lives?"

Yes.

"You trained them?"

Yes.

"How's that one—Tinder. How's Tinder's foot?"

Edgar was working the myriad tangles in Essay's tail and she wasn't enjoying it. When he set the brush down and released her, she leapt and circled, examining her priceless appendage, then bounded over to Henry and Baboo and nosed them both. Edgar joined them. He unwrapped Tinder's bandage and held his paw up to the light.

Henry scooted over. "Oof," he said. "I thought I just imagined that from the other night."

Edgar fetched the rags and the pan and a bottle of hydrogen peroxide.

"That's the biggest bottle I could find. You can probably stretch it if you soak a rag and dab," Henry said.

Edgar nodded. He reached over to the paper.

Why did you plant sunflowers? he wrote in the margin. He sopped up the hydrogen peroxide as Henry suggested. The edges of Tinder's wound were red and weeping, and the hydrogen peroxide sizzled under the cloth.

"Aha. Well, interesting question," Henry said. He sat and looked out at the field. "Call it an experiment. Usually, I plant corn, but I wanted to do something different this year. Something out of the ordinary. So I came up with this idea. Further south sunflower isn't so uncommon, you know, but you don't see it here much."

When Tinder's foot was as clean as he could get it, Edgar retrieved the tattered bandages from the clothesline.

Does it pay better than corn? he wrote.

"Not really," Henry said. "But I don't care. Fifty cents a pound for the seed. I could make more money with corn, but not so much more." He looked out at the field and frowned. "I'm not sure how you harvest it, though. It'll take forever to do it by hand. The man who harvested the corn last year thought he could get a special attachment for his combine. Then again, I might just let them sit there if they look nice. It all depends. Of course, nothing's more depressing than a field full of dead sunflowers." He drank his beer and looked at the stars. "You haven't been able to talk for a long time, huh? With the hand signs and everything?"

Edgar shook his head.

"Was there an accident or something? If you don't mind me asking, I mean."

I was born this way, he wrote. The doctors don't know why. Then he shrugged and wrote, Thank you for buying dog food.

Henry looked at the piles of debris. "What a god-awful mess," he said. He turned his gaze to the car on blocks. "I appreciate the help. I need to get that heap out of the rain before it rusts to pieces. I ought to just sell it, you know."

He stared at the car and produced another bottle of beer from somewhere. "I just can't part with it," he said.

Edgar nodded. He slipped a fresh sock onto Tinder's foot and tied it up again, using his forefinger to warn the dog from chewing. Tinder broke into a pant, as if amazed Edgar had read his mind.

"Nat," Henry said. "Have you ever been called 'ordinary'?"

Edgar looked at him.

"You know—ordinary. Just . . . ordinary. I bet no one has ever accused you of that."

No. Edgar looked at him. Not that I remember.

"Yeah, I wouldn't think so. Running around with trained circus dogs or whatever. Jesus. Want to know something ridiculous? I have. By my own fiancée—*ex*-fiancée, I mean. We were going to get married in March, and then, from out of nowhere, she called it off. Said she loved me, even, but she'd decided I was too ordinary, and that over the years it would destroy our marriage. 'Ordinary *looking* or what?' I said. 'No, just all-around ordinary,' she said. 'Ordinary in the way you do things, ordinary in what you see and think and say. Just ordinary.' Once she got that idea in her head, she said she couldn't shake it. Every time she looked at me she felt love, and she felt ordinariness at the same time."

He took a big swallow of beer. "Now I ask you, does that make sense?"

Edgar shook his head. The fact was, it *didn't* make sense to him. He loved ordinary things, ordinary days, ordinary work. Even as Henry spoke he felt a pang over the routine of the kennel—and if that couldn't be called ordinary, what could? Besides, while Henry didn't strike him as being highly unusual, he didn't see any reason that should be an offense. Or for that matter, what it would even *mean* to be called ordinary.

"Darn right, it doesn't," Henry declared in a sudden burst of indignation. Then he wilted. "She had a point, though. What exactly *have* I done out of the ordinary? Every day I go down to the central office, and at the end of every day I come home. I have a house like everyone else. I plant a crop in a field and harvest it every fall. I have a car on blocks that I tinker with. I like to fish. What isn't ordinary about that?"

Is she ordinary? Edgar wrote.

Henry looked at Edgar as if he hadn't considered the question before.

"Well, I guess you might not pick Belva out of the crowd walking down the street. But she's pretty unusual once you get to know her. For instance, one of her eyes is blue, the other one is brown, so that puts her out of the ordinary right there. Also, she's an atheist. She says if there was a God, both her eyes would be the same color. Myself, I believe in God, but I just don't want to lose an entire morning at church. I figure God doesn't care whether you worship in the church or on your drive to work. Belva says that doesn't count as being either an atheist or a believer; that's just lazy."

Do you believe in ghosts?

"Wouldn't surprise me," Henry said, as if this confirmed his darkest suspicions. But he wanted to talk about Belva; it was as though he could picture her right then, in front of them.

"You should see her ankles—gorgeous, delicate ankles, ankles like the ones on statues. We were engaged for two years." He heaved a sigh. "She's dating some guy at the bank."

Hasn't anything out of the ordinary happened to you?

"Not that I know of," Henry said. Actually, he moaned this. Then he snapped his fingers. "No, wait. You want to know the most unusual thing that ever happened to me? One time last year I went to the supermarket. Middle of the day, hardly anyone there. I'm going down the aisles, buying milk and soup and potatoes, and I remember I need bread. So I go to the bread aisle. There's loaves and loaves of bread sitting on the shelves at the far end of the aisle. I start pushing my cart toward the bread. And what do you think happens?"

Edgar shrugged.

"That's right, you *don't* know," he said. "Because it's not ordinary. What happens is, before I reach the end of the aisle, one of the loaves sort of *unsquashes* itself and falls to the floor. Nobody touched it, it just stretched itself out like an accordion and there it went. Plop. I pick up the loaf and put it back on the shelf. Then I push on over to the condiments. Now, here's the unordinary part: I'm heading to checkout, and I turn down the bread aisle again. And what do I hear from behind me?"

He gave Edgar a significant look.

What? Edgar signed, though he probably could have guessed.

"Plop!" Henry said. "That's right. I turned around and there was the *very same loaf of bread* lying on the floor."

What did you do?

"I'm not an idiot. I bought it, of course. I put my regular brand back."

Was it better?

"Same difference," Henry said, shrugging. "I switched back the next week." He took a long swallow of beer. "So there you have it. That's the peak. The apex. The apogee. That's the exotic life that Belva turned down."

That doesn't happen to everybody, Edgar wrote.

Henry shrugged. "It would be great to see a UFO, but I don't think that's going to happen."

Then the piano music began to skip and Henry walked inside to fix the record. Baboo went to the door and watched through the screen. Baboo, it seemed, had come to some sort of decision about Henry—Edgar had been noticing it all night. When Henry was seated again, Baboo stood next to him, eye to eye, and waited until Henry discovered that he needed to be scratched under the chin or on the top of the head or across his back just in front of his tail. Even sober, Henry might not have been aware of how deftly Baboo placed Henry's hand where he wanted to be scratched.

Henry leaned his head back against the house and, after a time, fell asleep, mumbling. Edgar and the dogs were left looking into the summer night. The music reminded Edgar of New Year's Eve, so long past, when he had danced with his mother; how his father had cut in, how the two them had swayed by the lights of the Christmas tree; how he had stolen curds to give to these same dogs to celebrate. Back then, he'd hardly known them, he thought.

Then the piano music ended and Henry jerked awake. "Now suppose I joined the navy," he said, vehemently replying to some argument in his dreams. "I sail off somewhere. Burma. After a while I stop being ordinary. Okay. *But how's Belva gonna know?* That's the problem. I have to stop being ordinary right here in Lute." He leaned forward and looked blearily at Edgar. Then he must have understood what had happened, because he stood and heaved a dramatic yawn. "Okay," he said. "That's it. I'm done."

Edgar and the dogs followed Henry into the house. Henry might have been amused to find them sleeping on the porch one morning, but he didn't want to try the man's patience. When he came into the living room the dogs had already curled up on the throw rug. He turned off the light on the end table and hung his arm off the sofa and laid a hand on Tinder. In the dark, he thought about the old man in the shed. He checked the blanket to make sure it wasn't wrapped around his legs. In all their days of running through the Chequamegon, he had never once forgotten to look down the legs of his pants for spiders, but his first night indoors he'd been flummoxed by a blanket.

Something had changed, he realized. Settled there on the couch, he felt none of the previous night's trapped sensation, and he thought that part of him had decided to trust Henry, that this was a place they could sleep through the night in peace. Perhaps that had happened only a few minutes before. Perhaps when he was watching Baboo.

Then the counting part of his mind began its litany: Three days in one place. Beginning of August. How much faster would they have to move once Tinder healed? How much longer could they stay? How far could they get before it turned cold? How far away could they get at all? Finally, Edgar eased himself off the sofa, nudging one of the dogs over, and he arranged himself, amidst a chorus of sighs and groans, so that he was touching them all.

Please, he told himself, half warning, half prayer. Don't get used to this.

Engine No. 6615

For six days Edgar had been working in Henry's shed. Mornings he washed and dressed Tinder's foot. The bandages were no longer stained from weeping, but if Edgar worked too hard at cleaning the wound, the wash water turned pink. Despite Edgar's attempts to keep Tinder in quiet down-stays, whenever Essay and Baboo wrestled in the yard, Tinder hobbled along, his foot clubbed by a graying sock. Sometimes he yelped and rolled, but he quickly hopped up again. Evenings, they listened to scratchy library records Henry brought home, music composed by Russian generals: Tchaikovsky, Rimsky-Korsakov, Shostakovich. During dinner Henry swore at the crossword while Edgar read the liner notes. Afterward, Edgar tended to Tinder's foot and taught Henry sign.

Henry had departed on Saturday midmorning with a list of errands to run. He expected to return by early afternoon, he said, though with his luck, it could be evening and the day would be shot. After he left, Edgar stood in the shed deciding what to tackle first. The walls had been stripped of rusted tools and saw blades. The disintegrating wagon was half excavated. As Edgar wrestled with an oval wall mirror, miraculously unbroken, he felt the tingle of evaporating sweat on his neck, the sign that the old farmer had appeared in the shed's farthest recesses.

That mirror, that's one I hate to let go, he said. That was my daughter's the whole time she was growing up. It probably seen her more than me—everything from a baby up to twenty years old. Sometimes I wonder if all that might still be inside it. Got to make an impression on a thing, reflecting the same person every day.

Edgar swiped a rag along the glass and peered in. The mirror's surface was dusty and the silver had been eaten away in islands of black. He waited for ghostly afterimages to form: a baby in its mother's arms, a girl brushing her hair, a young woman twirling blithely in a prom dress. But all he saw was his own reflection leaning up toward him.

There's no one there, he replied.

Oh, said the man. Well, I thought maybe.

The best way to keep the man talking, Edgar had learned, was to stay quiet and wait. He leaned the mirror back against the wagon and began collecting the broken china that lay around it and dropping the pieces into a chipped ceramic pan.

Whole years went by I wasn't so happy here, the old man said. Most of the late 1950s in particular. The Eisenhower years. Bad times.

You were a farmer?

Yup.

Didn't you like farming?

Oh, gosh, I guess I hated it sometimes. Do you know how early you have to get up to milk cows? You get to 'em late, they try to step on your feet. They see you with the stool and the bucket at ten in the morning and you better be walking directly down the center of the aisle, because sure enough a ten-pound hoof is gonna come striking out. They'll kick you squarely in the nuts if they think they got a shot at it. I know one fella it happened to. He quit farming and moved to Chicago soon as he could walk again.

Edgar thought about this.

Was his name Schultz, by any chance?

Naw, one of the Krauss boys, the old man said. Anyway, just out of fear, if nothing else, you get up when it's pitch dark and they're still a little sleepy. You milk until your hands ache. Then you shovel out the stalls, which is no great treat. I was always amazed at just how much poop come out of a cow. Little hay goes in, huge cowpies come out. How does that happen?

I don't know much about cows, Edgar signed, after a long pause.

And that's just the work before breakfast, the man continued. Then there's planting and harvesting. Things breaking down. Calves birthed in big blue placentas with veins thick as your finger. Mastitis. Worms. You ever seen a cow magnet? Unbelievable. Looks like a giant metal bullet. You shove it right down the cow's throat and a year or two later it comes out the other end covered with nails, bolts, hunks of wire. I know a man found his watch that way. We cut silage right up to the time snow flew, wondering if we were going to kill everything by putting it up wet. Fences broken, cows wandering in the woods. Some nights I'd come to the house so tired I didn't know if I could lift a fork to my mouth.

If you didn't like it, why didn't you quit?

To do what? Wasn't anything I knew better than farming. I was cursed, that was the problem. Just because I didn't *like* it didn't mean I wasn't *good* at it. I could call the weather, for instance. I'd walk outside one spring day and think, now we can plant. Down at the feed store they'd say, George, you're going to get frozen out. You put in too early and you're going to lose three quarters of it. But I had a sense. Always got it right, too; even if snow fell, it was a dusting. Farmers around here started planting as soon as they heard I'd bought seed.

That doesn't sound like a curse to me.

It's a curse all right, you're just too young to know about that sort of thing. To be good at something you don't care about? It isn't even unusual. Plenty of doctors hate medicine. Most of your businessmen lose their appetite at the sight of a receipt. It's a common thing. Old Bert down to town, he despises that grocery store. Says the routine bores him out of his mind: ordering, stocking, worrying about produce going bad. One day he told me he dreams about tomatoes more than he dreams about his own wife.

What would you have done if you could have quit?

I'd've been a railroad engineer. Best job in the world. You turn a crank and ten thousand tons of freight starts to move. You ever been inside a locomotive?

No.

I was up in Duluth once and I went to the rail yards just to look at locomotives and I got to talking with a fellow and he knew one of the engineers walking by. He says, Hey Lem, come on over here. And this fellow—he's dressed in overalls and a conductor's cap just like you might see on television—he walks over. This man says, here's a gentleman never seen the inside of a locomotive. Is that right, Lem says, and he walks to a telephone and makes a call to someone. Maybe the trainmaster, I don't know. Then he hangs up. Well, come on, he says. We start walking down the platform, past all the hopper cars and tankers and cabooses and he says over his shoulder, whatcha wanna see? Steamer or diesel? Steamer, I says. And he leads me to engine number six-six-one-five—the number was painted in big letters on the side. It was one of them big ones, cow-catcher like a bushy mustache, covered with bolts the size of your head, drive rods thick as your leg. Black, like it was carved out of a solid block of ore. He just points and names things. Air reservoir. Cylinder. Sandbox. Steam dome. Injectors. Drive wheel. Then he scrambles up a ladder and motions me up, and we stand inside the cab. He keeps naming things off. Firehole. Reverser. Regulator. Throttle. That engine was cold and dead while we was standing in it—Lem said it was in for repairs—but even like that, a person could feel the power in it.

The man's voice took on a wistful note.

If there was ever a moment I was tempted to just walk away from it all it was then. Nineteen fifty-five. I was fifty years old. I stood there for a while, soaking it all up. Then Lem tells me to sit in the engineer's seat and lean out the window. You'd have to wear a cap and goggles if we were really running, he says. There'd be a stream of hot cinders going past the window. You know what happens if you're dumb enough to lean out uncovered, he says. Then he bends down and points to the right side of his face. It's all pocked with little burn scars, like old craters there in his skin. That's what, he says. But he was grinning like anything. I almost expected to see cinders stuck in his teeth. And from the look on his face I could see he was one of the lucky ones, one of those people who like doing what they're good at. That's rare. When you see that in a person, you can't miss it.

Edgar cautiously let his eyes drift over until the old farmer registered in his peripheral vision. He was standing with his chin dropped to his chest, lost in thought.

Now here's the thing, the man said, after a long time had passed. When I sat in that seat and leaned out the window into the rain and imagined that stream of red-hot cinders going past my face like fireflies, watching a bridge coming up, which was my lifelong dream, do you know what I thought about?

Your farm?

That's right. There I was, sitting in a steam locomotive, one of the most beautiful engines ever devised. It was magnificent—big and heavy and it made me think of a giant laid over sleeping. Ever since I was a boy I'd thought running a train'd be the most amazing thing ever—especially out in the open countryside, with the throttle screaming wide open, the whole world split by those two rails you're hurtling down. I could *feel* it—even in that cold, dead engine—I could feel exactly what that would be like. And when I leaned out into the rain, and the engineer told me about the sparks flying and he showed me his face, all I could think about was all the mud in the pasture, what cranky bitches the cows were going to be in the morning if they didn't get to pasture. And whether the mow roof was leaking.

Now, if that isn't a curse, the man said, what is?

Before Edgar could answer, he heard Henry's car pulling up the drive. Edgar took off his gloves and walked into the sunshine. He had to kneel next to Tinder and put his hand against the dog's deep chest to restrain him as Henry climbed out of his car, and he and Tinder watched while Essay and Baboo circled and jumped.

THAT NIGHT HENRY OFFERED to drive them into town. Edgar said no. But Henry had long since deduced that Edgar didn't want to be seen. He pointed out that they could drive around in relative safety after dark. The idea took Edgar by surprise—he was so used to traveling by day and bedding down at night, it hadn't occurred to him, not even when he'd stood looking at the car back at Scotia Lake. When nightfall came, he relented. They loaded the dogs into Henry's car, a brown sedan with a capacious but slippery back seat. Edgar made Tinder sit on the floor up front. Baboo and Essay scrabbled to balance themselves on the back seat.

"How long has it been since you've been in a car?" Henry asked, as he eased down the driveway. Then he looked alarmed. "Wait a second. When's the last time these *dogs* were in a car? Is this going to make them puke?"

Edgar shrugged, grinning.

"Great," Henry said. "You're cleaning it up if they do. Deal? Otherwise I'm turning this thing around right now."

Before he could gripe any more, Baboo leaned forward from the back seat and slobbered in Henry's ear.

"Aw, god," Henry said. "I *hate* it when they do that." But he didn't really hate it. Edgar could see that. Anyone could see that.

Out on the blacktop, they headed toward town. The headlights caught dandelions leaking up through the cracks in the asphalt. They passed a culvert over a creek where the moon's reflection wobbled between the cattails.

Lute was a crossroads town, its one intersection controlled by a stoplight swinging like a lantern from crisscrossed wires. On each corner sat matching two-story brick buildings, like four old-timers crouched around a pan of beans. A Rexall drug, Mike's Bar and Grill, a True Value hardware, and the Lute grocery.

"Closed up tight after five," Henry said, waving a hand at the buildings. "Society life begins at six thirty, when Mike's opens." On that night, society life consisted of the three cars in the tavern's small parking lot, lit by the otherworldly glow of the Pabst Blue Ribbon sign ("finest beer served . . . *anywhere!*".) hanging over the door.

On the far side of town, the pale chambered heart of the Lute water tower hovered in the night sky, tethered to the earth by four metal legs and the central stalk of its drainpipe. Once in the countryside, they drove without destination, wherever Henry wanted to go, and Henry wanted to go north. Henry liked to drive fast. That surprised Edgar, but it pleased him, too. He'd forgotten the weight of acceleration. They coursed along a maze of back roads. Essay and Baboo slid across the slick back seat when Henry powered around curves. Marshes and forests and lakes flashed by. Tinder craned his neck to see out the window. Headlights approached like balls of white flame. Their speed compressed the scent of the night into a dense, algal perfume that roared through the windows. Henry spun the radio dial, looking for distant AM stations—Chicago, Minneapolis, Little Rock. The signal cracked with the heat lightning over Lake Superior.

At the outskirts of Ashland, with its downtown lights and police cars, Henry swung the car onto the shoulder and shot away from town by an entirely different route, past shanties set back from the road. He paused by a bog that glowed eerily when he shut the headlights off. When they arrived at the railroad tracks, Edgar looked at the bluff to his right, and realized they'd made the round trip. They retired to a pair of lawn chairs. Henry drank a beer and then another and then he walked to the old wreck of a car.

"Tell you a secret," he said. "This car was here when I moved in. I may have bought the place just to get the car."

This was certainly news to Edgar. He'd been walking past the vehicle for days without deeming it worthy of a closer look. It sported a broad hood and headlights shaded by exaggerated brow ridges. The front fender sloped toward the rear wheels in a long arc while a compensating ridge developed into a tail fin. But whatever grace of form the car had once possessed was gone. Its body was so thoroughly dented it looked as if someone had beaten it, savagely, with its own tire iron. Rust had consumed major continents from the rear quarter panels. The chrome of the elaborate, two-tiered front bumper was dull as ore. And of course, the vehicle lacked tires—it levitated above the gravel on shadowy cinder blocks. All in all, the car gave the impression of an animal that had crawled to within inches of its lair before expiring.

"The vehicle at which you are now looking, um, at," Henry said, sweeping his arm as if addressing an awestruck crowd, "is a 1957 Ford Fairlane Skyliner, the first retractable hardtop convertible ever made in America. No car looked like it before or since. Even the fifty-eight looks different—Ford messed up this beautiful bumper and grill for no reason. This is one of a kind."

Henry patted the car's side mirror with pride. It fell away and dropped to the ground. "Darn it," he said. He snatched up the mirror and jiggled the bolts back into the corroded holes.

"It's a little dinged up," he said, "but watch this." He opened the driver's-side door and pulled a lever and the trunk popped open, hinged backward, near the rear bumper. Henry wrenched the trunk hood up, casually at first, then applying more effort, grunting and scrabbling his feet against the gravel. He circled the car, unsnapping latches. The metal roof separated from the body. It folded halfway into the trunk and then caught. "This is supposed to be electric," Henry said over his shoulder, "but there's no battery." Then he reached into the back seat, withdrew a hammer, and beat unmercifully on a hinge. The roof dropped into the trunk cavity with a final metallic screech that temporarily silenced the night birds. Henry slammed the trunk shut and turned to Edgar, triumphant but panting.

"So you see why I can't just sell this car. There's so much potential here. Some guy offered to buy it for parts last summer, but I couldn't let it be torn apart. I explained all that to Belva, but it made zero impression. She said it was an eyesore—which, I admit, okay, it is, *now*. But *ordinary*? I don't think you can say that."

Henry had gotten himself wound up talking about the Skyliner, but he stopped and shook off the idea with a shake of his head. "Who am I trying to kid," he said.

No, Edgar signed. You're right. It isn't ordinary.

Henry peered at him, gisting the sign.

"You think?"

Edgar nodded.

"I can never tell anymore," he said. "When my guard is down, I forget. I slide right back to ordinary, and I don't even see it."

He walked to the lawn chairs and together they contemplated the Skyliner.

"I almost took you to the police station tonight, Nat," he said. "You probably should know that."

Edgar shook his head and smiled. No you didn't.

"Oh yes. There was a moment when I thought, 'All I have to do is turn left at the next stop and we'll be at the Ashland police station.'"

The shed's not done.

"Yeah, the shed saved you," Henry said. "This time. Better figure out how to stretch things out, is my advice."

They'd reached the limit of Henry's ability to read sign, and Edgar picked up the newspaper.

You couldn't have forced us inside, he wrote. We'd have just run.

"How could you run with Tinder?"

Edgar didn't know what to say to that. He wouldn't have gotten into the car with Henry if he hadn't trusted him. There were moments when Edgar understood Henry better than Henry understood himself. What Henry couldn't see was that, ordinary or not, he was trustworthy. That much was clear as day.

ON SUNDAY THEY WORKED in the shed side by side, tackling the items that took two people to move, like the wringer washer and the old furnace. Henry connected a hose out to the spigot on the house and started a fire in the burning barrel. They fed it old newspapers, gray split fence posts with stringers of barbed wire that glowed red, busted-up wooden chairs. Henry chopped the wagon's tongue in two with an axe and up-ended the halves, hardware and all, into the barrel. A gout of orange cinders flew into the air. By the time the fire settled, it was late in the day. They sat on the stoop eating potato chips and looking at the remaining debris.

"I know a trailer we can use to haul this stuff away," Henry said. "Maybe I can get it next weekend."

Your car doesn't have a hitch, Edgar wrote on the newspaper. Before he handed it over, he completed 14-down in the crossword puzzle: a ten-letter word for "a short movement connecting the main parts of a composition." The second letter was *N* and it ended with *O*.

Henry looked at the word Edgar had written: *intermezzo*. He squinted over at him.

"You ever think about entering a contest or something?"

Edgar shook his head.

"Well, you ought to. And a person can rent hitches."

Tinder limped over. Henry was a soft touch for treats and as soon as Tinder began crunching a chip, Baboo started working Henry over. Edgar finally told them both to stop. A rapport was developing between Henry, Baboo, and Tinder. Only Essay stayed aloof. She didn't mind Henry, that was just how she was. With Essay, more than with any other dog Edgar had known, trust was something you had to earn.

THAT WEEK HE SCRAPED flakes of paint from the sides of the shed and caulked the holes. Henry had purchased barn-red paint for the outside. Inside, it was to be whitewashed. Applying whitewash was lonely work—the old farmer had stopped appearing as soon as the last of the junk was out. The days were hot and the skies filled with monumental clouds. Late each afternoon, Henry turned his sedan up the driveway. When he got out of the car, he squatted and let the dogs wash his face, then inspected Edgar's progress. "It's a pretty good color," he said, after Edgar finished painting the exterior. "Makes the house look shabby, though."

Nights, they went on careening drives, Henry glowering and accelerating through curves while tree trunks strobed past and the dogs slid across the back seat. When they returned, Henry cracked a beer and gravitated to the Skyliner. Often he ended up sitting behind the wheel. Tinder would limp over and scramble onto the seat alongside him.

And somewhere along the line, between the crossword puzzles and the records from the library and the beer, Henry asked Edgar to teach him about the dogs. They went out after dinner and Edgar taught him a few signs. Then he and Essay demonstrated something simple: guided fetches. He put two sticks on the ground and asked Essay to go to them. It was a variation on the shared-gaze exercises, and all of the dogs knew how it worked. When Essay reached the targets, she looked back at Edgar. When he looked at the stick on the left, she snatched it and brought it to him, tail swinging. Edgar took the stick and ran a hand across Essay's cheek. After another demonstration with Baboo, it was Henry's turn. He chose to work with Tinder, a good choice. Something about the dog's injury and enforced convalescence had taught Tinder an extra measure of patience, which he needed, because at first, Henry was hopeless. And yet the dog persevered, as if he had decided to take on Henry as a personal project. At times, Tinder even forgot about his foot and stopped limping for a few steps.

To begin with, Henry's sign was vague, neither a recall nor a release nor a request to go out, but Tinder got the idea and walked to the sticks. There was no skill involved in the next step, and yet somehow Henry managed to confuse the dog, who patiently did not pick up either target but stood waiting. Then, for some reason, Henry gave the release command again. Tinder's ears dropped. Henry walked forward. He was about to lift the stick up to Tinder's mouth in desperation when Edgar stepped in and gave the command correctly and looked at the rightmost stick. Tinder snatched it off the ground at once.

Edgar forked two fingers sternly at Henry's eyes.

Watch the target. They know the difference.

"Okay, okay." Henry took the stick from Tinder, forgetting to thank him, and set it on the ground. Edgar let this breach of etiquette slide, and they retreated. When Henry started to sign a release instead of a go-out, Edgar grabbed his hands and moved them until the sign had been correctly formed. Henry blushed. But the next time, he signed the request perfectly. Without hesitation, Tinder limped across the lawn, looked at Henry, and brought him the target.

And at that moment, Henry got it, whatever *it* was—the difference between commanding Tinder and working with him. When Henry had signed that go-out, he'd looked at Tinder instead of his hands; when Tinder checked back, he'd trusted the dog to read his face. And then the cascade of revelations began, just as it had for Edgar. He could tell by the expression on Henry's face. Edgar thought of all those letters between

Brooks and his grandfather, the endless argument about companionship and work, how his grandfather had argued that there was never a difference, how Brooks, in exasperation, had refused to discuss it further. He thought, too, of the question his mother had posed to him a million years before: what *were* they selling, if not dogs?

And there stood Henry Lamb, beaming. Until that moment, Edgar had never seen the man smile without some fatalistic reserve that said he knew the joke would ultimately be on him. And though Edgar was no closer to putting it into words, for the first time he was sure he knew the answer to his mother's question.

"WHERE WERE YOU HEADING, anyway?" Henry said. It was later that night, and they sat at the kitchen table. "I'm not trying to pry. Don't answer if you don't want to."

It's okay, Edgar signed. He jotted *Starchild Colony* on a sheet of paper and handed it to Henry. What was interesting was that, before the words had appeared on the paper, he hadn't been sure himself what his answer would be—at least, not to say it so flatly that way. But he'd always been veering northwest, hadn't he, to get past the tip of Lake Superior, and then start the walk along the lakeside to sneak past the Canadian border? Then, somehow, find the place? That had been the plan. Alexandra Honeywell had said they needed people, people who were willing to work hard. He was willing to work hard. So that's where they had been going.

Henry whistled. "The place on the news—Alexandra What's-Her-Name? Up by Thunder Bay?"

Edgar nodded.

"You know somebody there?"

No.

"Anyone know you're coming?"

No.

Henry shook his head. "That's a couple hundred miles. What were you going to do, walk the whole way?"

Edgar shrugged.

"I guess you could. I'm not sure what a person would do for food."

Edgar scuffled his feet at the memory of looting Henry's kitchen.

"Can Tinder make it on that foot?"

And that was the question, wasn't it? Tinder's foot wasn't bandaged anymore, but mornings, the dog gimped badly. Edgar didn't know when Tinder would be ready, if ever.

He shrugged his shoulders. There was no answer except to try.

ON FRIDAY, HENRY ARRIVED home with a trailer hitched to the sedan. He got out and he knelt and, grinning at Edgar, let the dogs accost him. He gestured at the trailer, where four inflated tires lay.

"I had retreads put on the wheels for the Skyliner. Tomorrow, she's gonna roll for the first time in, oh, fifteen years." He pulled a bag of groceries from the passenger seat of his car. "Chicken on the spit and potato salad," he said. "Ordinary or not ordinary?"

Ordinary, Edgar signed. But good.

They started the grill and put the chicken on and sat in the lawn chairs and looked out at the piles of junk.

"I've almost got used to seeing it there," Henry said. "Putting the Skyliner in the shed: ordinary or not ordinary?"

Not ordinary, Edgar signed.

"Just checking," Henry said. He was working a crossword puzzle.

"Six-letter word meaning 'to stamp a coin.' Starts with Q."

Edgar looked at him.

I don't know.

"Gotcha!" he said. "Only joking. It starts with an I." He handed the newspaper over to Edgar.

Incuse, Edgar wrote on the paper and handed it back.

"Jesus," Henry said. "That's just plain scary."

THE NEXT DAY THEY jacked up the Skyliner, mounted the tires, and dragged the cinder blocks away.

"Oh man," Henry said. "Oh boy! Hold on, wait a second." He ran to the barn, returned with a hammer, and folded the car's top into the trunk again. When he finished, they coaxed all three dogs onto the front seat. It took the better part of an hour, laboriously pushing the car back and forth, to align it in front of the shed. The dogs had long since abandoned ship.

"Come back," Henry cried as they fled. "That's an *honor*!"

Then they pushed the car into the shed. Henry ran around front to keep it from rolling into the wall, since the brakes didn't work. "Careful," he said. "Just . . . a little . . . more . . ." And then the Skyliner was inside. They closed the now bright red doors and Henry dropped the bolt through the flap latch.

Henry fetched a beer and began to walk through the piles of junk sitting in the yard, scratching his head. He looked at the mirror and the stanchions. "Jeez, that's a shame," he said. Over a broken porcelain sink he moaned, "Whoa. Just imagine what happened to *that*."

He walked to the stoop and sat down.

"I can't do it," he said.

Can't do what?

"Haul that stuff away. It was here before I was." He took a long swallow from the beer and held it up to the light. "Putting that stuff back in the shed: ordinary or not ordinary?"

Edgar looked at him.

I don't know.

Henry made the decision.

They worked like maniacs. Not everything could go back in, but they rehung the hubcaps and the old tools on the walls. They found space in the rafters to lay the salvageable sheets of plywood. Edgar handed up the old broken sink and the pruning shears and they leaned two of the stanchions in a corner. When they had finished, the mirror graced the front wall of the shed, reflecting the Skyliner's broad front bumper, and two of the wagon wheels leaned against the outside like wreaths of gray wood. The shed was jammed full. The Skyliner could roll out, but with inches to spare.

"That's it," Henry said, stepping back to look at what they'd done. "That feels right."

It *did* feel right, Edgar thought. He watched the dogs sniff the wagon wheels as Henry backed the trailer up to the gravel apron. They hefted the old furnace and the transmission and the wringer washer onto its bed.

"What say we celebrate with a little ride?" Henry said.

Edgar shook his head. Not in the daylight.

"Oh, come on. Lighten up. Nothing bad's going to happen."

Maybe it was the idea of Henry Lamb telling him to lighten up that made the request seem reasonable.

All right, he signed. Okay.

They unhitched the trailer, piled into the car, and barreled through the waves of heat rising over the blacktop. Henry took them daringly through the middle of Ashland, and Edgar felt, if not entirely carefree, more light-hearted than he had in a long time. They were heading back toward the open highway when the light on the railroad crossing started to flash and the thin striped crossing arms levered down. Henry brought the sedan to a stop and a flush of adrenaline went through Edgar. He slid down until he was hidden from the cars around them. That was safe enough, he thought. A man with three dogs in his car wasn't that unusual. The train lumbered past. The crossing lights flashed and the bells pounded. Edgar lifted his head to see if the caboose was visible yet, then ventured a look around.

A young woman sat alone in the car next to them.

Edgar tapped Henry's arm and pointed.

"Holy cow," Henry said. "That's Belva. Act natural."

Edgar wasn't sure what Henry meant by that. Edgar *was* acting natural. The dogs were acting natural. Henry, however, had immediately stopped acting natural. He sat ramrod straight and began whistling a little nervous tooty-toot-toot and drumming his fingers on the steering wheel as if some pounding rock-and-roll ballad were playing on the radio, though in fact it was the weather forecast—partly cloudy today, the announcer droned, chance of severe thunderstorms tomorrow. Harvest weather, Edgar thought.

The woman must have glanced over and noticed Henry, for when Edgar lifted his head to look again, she too was turned forward, looking intently ahead. The train kept rolling along, car after car. There was plenty of time to read the letters and numbers on the sides. Finally, the woman leaned over and rolled down her passenger-side window and shouted, "Henry!"

Henry turned and looked at her, still whistling. Toot-toot-toot.

"Belva," he shouted back.

"I've been meaning to call you!"

"Is that right?" Henry said. He glanced at Edgar and gave a little wink. "I guess you saw the sunflowers!"

"What?"

"The sunflowers! I guess you saw the sunflowers!"

"What sunflowers?"

"Oh," he said. "Never mind!"

"I'm moving," she shouted.

"What?"

"Moving. I'm moving to Madison."

"How come?"

"Why are all those dogs with you?" she shouted, instead of answering his question.

"Oh, I don't know," Henry said, lamely. He pounded a fist on the steering wheel and looked down at Edgar, scooched below the windows.

Ordinary, Edgar signed up at him.

"Right," Henry muttered. He turned back to Belva. "I just decided to get a dog. Uh. Three dogs."

"Wow," she said. "They're really nice."

Very ordinary, Edgar signed, rolling his eyes.

"Actually, they belong to my nephew," he corrected. "I'm just looking after them."

She laughed again. "You don't *have* any nephews, Henry. You're an only child."

He looked stricken for a moment. "What's that? No, no, not 'nephew.' *Nathoo*. They belong to my friend Nathoo. Say hello, Nathoo." He waved Edgar up from the floorboards.

Edgar shook his head.

"Come on," he hissed. "Help me out here."

No.

"Who are you talking to?" Belva shouted.

"Nobody—just the dogs," he said. "Why are you moving to Madison?"

There was a long pause, and Edgar could hear the clank of the joints between the train cars, and the clang-clang of the crossing gates, and even, faintly, radios playing in the cars around them. The dogs were looking out the windows and panting happily. Baboo, in particular, seemed interested in Belva. He pushed his head out the driver's-side window to get a better look.

"Well," she shouted at last, "because Joe is."

"Joe?"

"My fiancé."

"Ah," Henry said. "Aha. Oh."

"You *did* know I was engaged, right?"

"Yes, of course!"

"It was in the paper!"

"Yep, that's where I saw it!" he said. "I bet he's a moron."

"What?"

"I said, I bet you'll love Madison."

"Really, Henry. Who's in the car with you?"

Henry looked over at Edgar. Beads of sweat stood out on his forehead.

"Come on," he hissed. "Just this once."

Then the caboose rattled past and Edgar thought he could probably risk it that one time—the guard arms were already lifting and they were about to drive away. He was being silly, hiding under the dash like that.

He sat up.

He waved hello to Belva.

And that was when he looked through the rear window of Henry's sedan and noticed the State Patrol cruiser.

Glen Papineau

GLEN PAPINEAU SUPPOSED HE WAS IN MOURNING. HE HAD USED that word before, even thought he understood what it meant, but he really hadn't. For one thing, mourning sounded like a formality, a stage a person was required to go through—wearing a black suit and attending a funeral—but *real* mourning didn't end the day after the funeral, or the week after, or even the month after. His pop had died nearly two months earlier, and sometimes Glen felt like he'd just then gotten the call.

In his mind, he called them the day feeling and the night feeling. The day feeling caught up with him before lunch most days, a hot blanket of lethargy so suffocating it made his temples pound. He dragged himself around work as if facing a high wind. Everything took an eternity, became a laborious detail. And Glen hated details. He was built for broad gestures—all a person had to do was look at his hands to know that. A man with hands like Glen's would do certain things, and certain other things would never be in the cards. He'd never be a pianist, for example, or a veterinary surgeon. Not that he wanted those things, it was just that he'd found himself looking at his hands a lot lately, and his hands said they weren't there for detail work.

The day feeling was bad, no question, but the night feeling was the real killer—a bleak sledgehammer to the soul, as if some stranger had whispered a terrible secret in his ear, and that secret was how death was senseless and inevitable. The knowledge made sleep impossible. He sat up watching television, and if he didn't want to be alone, he went to the taverns—not the smartest move for local law enforcement to drink in public, but people understood. Some even bought him beers and told him stories about his pop.

There were moments of acceptance. After all, his pop had been getting up in years, and Glen had contemplated his death more than once, though he'd imagined something long and slow—a tangle with cancer, an unnameable decline. What he hadn't expected was that death's visit would be so sudden. One day he'd been a vigorous sixty-seven-year-old man, running his clinic, flirting with the bakery ladies, blabbering to anyone who would listen about his winter vacation in Florida, and the next he was lying at the bottom of the stairs in the Sawtelles' barn.

Glen, as an only child, had been responsible for the funeral arragements. There had been a detailed will, specifying that his father be buried alongside Glen's mother in Park City. At the shop, as his father called the veterinary clinic, Glen had boxed his father's desk, his books, the jackets hanging on the hooks. Jeannie had called all his father's clients and referred them to Doctor Howe in Ashland. The will specified that the vet school in Madison be contacted and his practice be sold *in toto* rather than auctioned off, but no one seemed terribly interested in a practice in the hinterlands and Glen had gotten no serious calls. The shop stood dark and silent now, pharmacy locked down, plastic sheets thrown over everything as if it were a morgue. The place was a break-in waiting to happen, Glen thought; in fact, someone had already put a rock through one of the back windows, though nothing was missing.

So there was the day feeling and the night feeling, and those were bad, and he was drinking a little more than he used to, but Glen thought he was handling things, if not thriving, until Claude called and said he wanted to talk. Glen offered to come out to the Sawtelle place, but Claude suggested the Kettle, a tavern south of town. The Brewers were playing on the television when Glen walked in. Claude hailed him from the end of the bar. The bartender, Adam, drew him a Leinenkugel and Glen sat down next to Claude.

They watched the game and talked about Pop, how Claude remembered him coming out to the kennel back when he was a kid. Claude said some nice things about his pop. He said that, besides Glen, he thought he was probably the closest thing to family Pop had. Said he thought of Glen's father as an uncle, which meant a lot because the Sawtelles were a small family.

It was much later when they got to Claude's reason for calling. Doctor Howe was incompetent, Claude said. Until they found another vet, Claude intended to do the workaday medicine himself—worming the pups, treating mastitis, and so on. He'd been a medic in the navy and he knew his way around a medicine chest. Glen knew his father had some sort of arrangement with the Sawtelles, since it wasn't practical to be running out there five days a week just to prescribe penicillin. So they had set aside a medicine chest in their barn for the supplies Pop usually locked up in his office. And now Claude wondered if Glen would be willing to sell off some of the meds in the shop pharmacy, seeing as no one was beating down the door to take over.

They were four or five beers in at that point, which wasn't much for someone Glen's size, but he'd also had a couple before he drove down. They watched the Brewers give up another run. Adam swore at the television as a service to the bar patrons.

"You know what I think about when I think about your dad?" Claude said. "The Hot Mix Duck Massacre."

Glen chuckled. "Yup. That first rain—remember all those ducks quacking around the shop?"

When Glen was eight years old, the state had come through and re-paved Main Street and put up street lights, the first significant improvement that Mellen had seen, on its long glide toward oblivion after its lumbering heyday, since Truman was in office. The streets had been so bad the town kids made a game out of riding bicycles down the street without crossing any pothole patches. It wasn't easy. In some places, it hadn't even been *possible*.

But instead of the pebbly tar-and-gravel asphalt that had once covered the street, the state crew had applied a new formula that went down like black, smoking glue and hardened pudding-smooth. This was called "hot mix," presumably because they poured it from a huge wheeled furnace. The hot-mix furnace stank to high heaven for the three weeks it took to resurface the street, but it was a small price to pay; afterward, Mellen's previously pocked Main Street was a pristine strip of smooth, black pavement.

Things were hunky-dory until the first rainy spell. One night, a couple of ducks flew by, looking for a spot to land on the Bad River. With the new street lights shining off the rain-slick hot mix, Main Street must have looked like a placid, fish-filled stream, more inviting than the Bad River had ever been. The first two ducks came in for a water landing, quacking like mad, and broke their necks on impact. Then the main flock came up over the trees, their tiny bird brains unable to figure out why their compatriots looked so odd there in the water. The result had been known ever after as The Hot Mix Duck Massacre.

The luckiest birds tumbled head over heels, shook their bills in confusion, and flapped off, but a half-dozen others became dinner for quick-thinking observers. The rest suffered all manner of injuries. The diner emptied. A strange roundup of the wounded ensued. People herded limping, stunned ducks into boxes, captured them under blankets, even shooed them into cars. A caravan had arrived at Glen's father's shop.

"They got so they limped around behind Pop wherever he went," Glen said.

Claude had forgotten some of the details, but as they'd drank and talked, he'd gone from grinning to laughing out loud at Glen's recollection.

"Yup. What I remember best is him setting them on the receptionist's counter," Claude said, "and talking to people as if he couldn't see them. 'What duck?' he'd say. I used to fall down laughing when he did that."

Glen remembered that, too. That was back when Claude had worked around the shop doing odd jobs. He remembered thinking back then what a striking figure Claude was—a bit of a hero to Glen, in fact. He'd been athletic. (He still looked good for—what, forty?) And another thing: Claude always seemed to have a girlfriend, which, even back when he was eight, Glen suspected might turn out to be a problem for him.

"Did I ever tell you what he did at the diner?" Glen said.

"What's that?"

"One time, when the splints were off and he knew those ducks would do just about anything for him, he put one in an old medicine bag and closed it up and we went to the diner for lunch. He set the bag on the seat in the booth and waited. The duck never made a sound. Pop ordered first, and while the waitress was taking my order, he reached over and opened the bag and out popped the duck's head."

"No," Claude said, laughing.

"When I finished, he said, 'Aren't you going to take *his* order?' and she saw the duck and screamed."

"No."

"Yes! Dropped her order pad and everything. And do you know what the duck did?"

"What?"

"It jumped out of the case and chased her back to the kitchen, gabbling at her heels. She hollered the whole way."

Claude was shaking and holding onto the rim of the bar as if he were about to fall off his stool.

"Pop shouted back that his friend wanted the smelt."

"Oh, God."

"He said he wouldn't put the duck back into the bag until it was done eating, that even ducks had a right to a decent lunch. Especially in Mellen."

"Stop," Claude begged. "Please. Stop." Tears were streaming down his face.

Glen liked being able to make Claude laugh like that. He hadn't quite realized what a funny story it made, but Claude had really given himself over to mirth, and Glen found it impossible not to laugh along with him. When Claude finally wiped his eyes, he ordered another round and they clanked their glasses.

"To Page."

"To Pop."

"What ever happened to those ducks?"

"I don't remember," Glen confessed. "They never could fly again. I think Pop gave them to a farmer down by Prentice."

They watched the game for a bit longer and then Glen bought a six-pack to go and they headed for the shop. Claude followed in his Impala. Glen walked up to the dark side door and pulled out of a set of keys, drunkenly trying one after another. Inside, he flipped a switch and a bank of unearthly fluorescents flickered into service overhead. The pharmacy was nothing more than a neatly organized closet beside his pop's office. Glen unlocked it, swung the door open, and stepped back.

"What were you looking for?"

Claude stepped inside and carefully examined the shelves of bottles and vials, pausing two or three times to look at labels more closely, almost as if window-shopping rather than just looking for the penicillin. When he had finished his detailed scrutiny of the pharmacy's contents, he pulled three containers from the rack. "This," he said, handing one across to Glen. "This. And this." He stepped out and let Glen shut the door. "If you know where the sales slips are, I'll write these up," he said.

"Take 'em. It'd cost more to tell the lawyer than to just give them to you."

"Well, thanks," Claude said. "Maybe I can find a way to make it up to you."

"No need," he said, waving a broad hand at Claude. "Forget it."

They walked outside and locked up and walked to the cars. Glen reached into the back seat and pulled out two beers and they stood looking into the night sky. Then the silence turned clumsy. Glen knew Claude had more on his mind than just medication. The fact was, Glen had been in touch with Claude and Trudy quite a lot over the last two months. The night his father had died, Edgar had run off with a couple of the dogs. It was more than the kid could take, seeing two men die in the same room. At first they thought he was hiding in the woods. Then they expected to spot him hitchhiking. That's what happened to most kids who ran off. Each morning, the Highway Patrol broadcast a list of runaways picked up, but there was never a match. Of course, Glen had worked the grapevine around Mellen: Walt Graves, who delivered RFD mail, made a point to talk to everyone on his route; at the telephone office, Glen had hinted that the switchboard operators might place an anonymous call if they heard something interesting on a party line. The Forest Service had briefly run a search plane. But in the end, Edgar was just another runaway, and there wasn't much to do except wait for him to turn up, then ship him home.

And so, without being asked, Glen said, "You know I'd call right off if something came through."

Claude sipped his beer in silence and looked thoughtful.

"Most runaways—the ones that aren't trying to get away from some sort of bad situation, at least—come home on their own before it gets cold. He'll either get picked up or show up."

"Yup," Claude said. And then, after a while, "Just between you and me, though, I'm not sure that would be such a good thing. Maybe he's better off run away. You can't imagine the torment that boy has put Trudy through in the last nine months. He's got something in him . . . well, he's wild."

"He's getting to be that age. Plus, he must have been awfully shook up about Gar. When I talked with him, he couldn't remember much of what happened."

That got Claude's attention. "Trudy mentioned that, too," he said. "How did that work, anyway? Did he recall anything about the day at all? Or was it just a pure blank?"

"Oh, sure. Lots of stuff. What he was doing with the dogs, what he ate for breakfast. But the closer we got to the moment he found Gar, the sketchier things got."

"Uh-huh," Claude said. Now he was peering at Glen intently. "I always thought that was strange, the way he just . . . *found* him. I haven't wanted to ask Trudy about it, stir up bad feelings. But are you telling me he didn't hear *anything*? Gar calling for help, the dogs barking, anything like that?"

"Not when we talked. That was the next day. Technically, I should have talked with him right away, but Pop got a little mad when I suggested it. He was sure it could wait, and I could see for myself the kid was a wreck." Glen shrugged and took another swallow of beer. "Could be different now, though. People remember things after a while."

"I suppose," Claude said. "But how would you know those memories are for real, you get them months later?"

Glen thought about Claude saying Edgar had something wild in him. He looked over at Claude.

"If I recall the rumors, you were pretty wild yourself once. Maybe it just runs in the family."

Claude nodded. "I had my moments. Not so much at his age, but I know what you're saying. I don't fault him for wildness. But with Edgar, it's different."

Glen looked at him. "Different how?"

"Well, I got wild the way most boys get wild—I wanted to shake things up. I thought everything *needed* shaking up. I never set out to hurt anybody. With Edgar, though . . . I don't know. He can't always control his temper."

Then Claude stopped. He looked like he was searching for words. He took a long swallow of beer.

"I don't know how to tell you this," he said, "but on the other hand, I don't like keeping secrets, either."

"Tell me what?"

"About your pop."

"What about him? I suppose you're going to tell me that he was a hell-raiser, too?" Glen laughed at the idea. If his father hadn't been a veterinarian, he would have been a school teacher—more likely a principal. He liked being an authority figure, the one who told people what was what.

"No, nothing like that," Claude said. "You understand everything I'm going to tell you is secondhand—I wasn't there when it happened, okay? I was in the house, and the first thing I really saw—with my own eyes— was when I walked into the barn and Page was lying there."

And then, though it was a warm summer night, Glen felt a chill.

"Thing is, after Edgar ran off, I found out from Trudy that Page didn't just trip. It sounds like he fell down those stairs because Edgar was coming after him."

There was a long silence during which blood began to pound in Glen's ears.

"Coming after him."

"Yeah."

"You mean, coming after him to hit him?"

"Yeah. That's what I mean."

"Why would he do that?"

"Well, that's the part we don't understand. After Gar died, he clammed up. And when Edgar wants to clam up, there isn't a thing anyone can do about it. That night, we were talking to a breeder interested in operating a branch kennel. Had some interesting ideas about approaching the Carruthers catalog people. That really disturbed Edgar. He opened up that big mow door and dragged Trudy over to it and nearly pushed her out. Who knows what would have happened if he hadn't stopped. Plus, he was none too happy about me spending so much time out there, which I suppose I can understand. Fact is, most nights he slept out in the mow. Like that was his place instead of in the house."

"Claude," Glen said. "For Christ's sake."

"I don't know, Glen. Maybe Trudy got it wrong. It's not my place to tell you this anyway. I've gone over it and over it in my mind, and no matter how you slice it, it was a freak accident. Pick up the *Milwaukee Journal* tomorrow and check the obituaries; I'd bet you fifty dollars you find someone who died in some sort of freak accident. Remember when Odin Kunkler fell out of his apple tree trying to shake a porcupine off a branch? He could have broke his neck instead of both arms. Who knows what made the difference? Even if Trudy had it right, Edgar didn't touch your pop. He just ran at him and Page fell."

"That's still manslaughter," Glen said.

"Besides . . ."

"Besides, what?"

"Well, I didn't know if you were all that close to your dad. Some people are glad when the old man is gone."

"Aw, god. Aw, shit. Jesus fucking Christ, Claude! We had some words sometimes, who doesn't? But he was my *father*." Glen looked at Claude to see if he'd meant to provoke him, but Claude looked genuinely sincere. If anything, a little puzzled by the vehemence of Glen's reaction.

"Aha. Well, it isn't always that way. Between father and son, I mean. I wasn't sure."

"Well, now you know."

"No offense intended, okay? I'm just telling you to be straight. I think a person needs to keep things aboveboard," Claude said. "Look, if you wanted to, you could sue us. After all, your dad *was* on our property, he *did* fall down our stairs. Whether Edgar scared him into falling or not probably wouldn't even come into it; the right lawyer would just argue that we didn't do something we should have, like we didn't have good enough handrails or whatnot. Though there *is* a handrail . . ."

"Don't be ridiculous."

"Maybe, but the point is, I was always taught that, in a case like this, where nothing is black and white, *we'd* have to be the ones to decide what's right. I'm not talking about courts; I mean, the people themselves decide. But if you want legal justice, there it is. You could shut down the kennel if you wanted. No more Sawtelle dogs, ever again. That's got to be your decision, and that's okay. I can't speak for Trudy, of course. She's awfully dependent on those dogs now, especially with Edgar run off. I have to argue with her to place every single one."

"I don't want that and you know it."

"Don't you? Wait and see. Maybe tomorrow you'll wake up discouraged and depressed. That's the way these things work. You won't be angry, not then, just laid out, like all the wind's been taken out of your sails. But the day after that, or the day after *that* you might wake up and before you have a chance to think about it, you'll get dressed and head over to your pop's place, out the door and down the street before you remember your pop is gone for good. And *that's* when it'll hit you. That's when you're going to get angry. It'll be over some little thing that really doesn't matter. So don't tell me what sort of justice you want, Glen. That's a promise you can't keep."

"Well, I can tell you this much: I'm not going to sue you and Trudy for something Edgar did."

"Why the hell not?" Claude said. "He's a minor. Trudy's his mother and I'm his uncle. Trudy raised him. She must have done *something* wrong or he wouldn't have come after Page."

"No, no, it doesn't work that way. Well, maybe it does. I don't know. I mean, think about me—I was a mixed bag at best. But Pop, he did the best he could. There wasn't one time he didn't tell me just how to . . . why I should have . . ."

Then Glen realized he was crying. It was embarrassing, but it just came up out of him, and there was no way to stop it. And that was the moment he'd realized he wasn't done mourning—in fact, maybe he'd hardly begun. A person who was done mourning didn't cry into his beer.

"I was pretty much of a fuckup, if you recall," Glen said, when he could talk without blubbering. "Maybe you don't know what it feels like to *know* what the wrong thing to do is, and just watch yourself do it anyway. Like you don't even control it. But I do. My pop stuck with me through a whole bunch of times when I thought I'd end up in juvie jail."

Claude sipped his beer and nodded.

"Pretty ironic that I ended up as the cop here, don't you think?"

"I think it fits you. I think you do a good job."

"Thanks," Glen said. "I try." There was something else he wanted to say, some other point he'd been trying to make, but the beers had finally added up, and he couldn't remember. His head would have been swimming even if he was sober, and Claude had a way of making things confusingly complex.

"Tell you what," Claude said at last. Glen could see Claude was troubled by the whole thing, maybe more troubled than Glen himself. "You have the power here. You know it and I know it and there's no point in pretending otherwise, or thinking that you know this minute what you want to do about it. That day when you get angry is coming. When it arrives, all I can think to offer is that you call me, and we'll find a place to sit and drink some beers and talk about what to do. That's the least I could do—hear you out."

Glen looked at him. Claude seemed like he might be about to cry himself.

"Way back when, the old guys had all the answers," Claude said. "Your dad. My dad."

"Yup."

"We're the ones, now. We've got to have the answers."

"They're not all gone yet."

"No. Mostly, though."

"Ida Paine is still around."

Claude shuddered. "Ida Paine has *always* been around," he said. "Ida Paine will be around long after you and I are gone."

"I was out to the store just last week. If anything, she's gotten creepier."

"Did she say it?" Claude asked, and Glen didn't need him to explain what he meant by *it*. "Did she look at you through those Coke bottle glasses and say it?"

"Oh, yeah. 'Is that all?'" Glen croaked, a fair imitation of Ida's smoky voice. "'Anything else?'"

It was funny, but neither of them laughed. You didn't laugh at Ida Paine.

Claude pushed himself upright and walked to the Impala.

"Remember what I said."

He fired off a drunken salute. "Okay. Ten-four. Roger. Over and out."

Then Claude drove off, taillights dwindling as he topped the rise south of town. Glen didn't feel like leaving just yet. He leaned on the trunk of his car, swaying in the moonlight, and considered the dark outline of his father's shop. It was a fine summer night, the peepers all around making a melodious racket, the sky above a parade of stars and galaxies. When he was sure no one would see him do anything so maudlin, Glen Papineau raised his bottle of Leiney's to the sky and let the tears come again.

"To you, Pop," he whispered. "To you."

Wind

ALL IT HAD TAKEN WAS ONE PARALYZING LOOK OUT THE REAR window of Henry's sedan to realize their sojourn had ended. As soon as the train passed and the State Patrol cruiser diverted onto a side street, Edgar jumped into the back seat, and for the rest of the drive he'd held Tinder and Baboo in down-stays, ducking and hoping that Essay, up front with Henry, would look unremarkable. He should never have agreed to a joyride in broad daylight. If the State Patrol officer had looked at them a *little* longer, been a *little* less distracted, or had been reminded that morning of the curious bulletin outstanding for a runaway with three dogs, then the flashers atop his cruiser would have started to spin and that would have been the end of it.

By the time they pulled into the driveway, Edgar had resolved to leave at once. Henry stalled him and dug out a map and calculated the distance from Lute to Thunder Bay. It turned out to be over two hundred miles. Henry pointed out the impossibility of Tinder walking that far with a half-healed foot. "And that's if you go straight through Superior. How did you plan to do that if you're so worried about being spotted?"

I don't know, Edgar wrote. We'll figure out something.

"Look," Henry said. "If you're dead set on this, let me drive you as far as the border. I know the back roads around here. We can stay off the main highways. I can even get us around Superior. Then it's a straight shot up the North Shore Highway."

Let me see that map, Edgar signed.

He traced out the route for himself, but there was no real choice. Henry could jump them ahead by weeks in a single day. Once near the border they could choose a likely spot and continue on foot. After that, they both guessed five more days walking to Thunder Bay, ten if he babied Tinder. In truth, accepting Henry's offer looked like the only way Starchild was reachable.

Okay, Edgar signed. But we leave tomorrow.

HE WAITED UNTIL HENRY was asleep that night and walked to the shed and opened the doors. He squeezed his way along the fender of the Skyliner and hiked himself over the door and sat in the driver's seat and rested his palms on the fluted ring of the steering wheel. In the dark, he could barely see his hands.

Are you there? he signed.

He waited. A long silence followed. After a time he decided it was no use and he started to go back to the house. Then he told himself it wouldn't hurt to try anyway. He lifted his hands in the dark.

Did you see that thing in me? he signed. That rare thing?

IN THE MORNING EDGAR calmed the dogs by running exercises in the yard—fetches, come-fors, heels. They had stayed so long with Henry the dogs were lax about sticking near him, and now that they were heading out again they would need those skills. Henry called in sick to work, coughing weakly into the telephone receiver and grinning at Edgar. They left just after ten o'clock, when Henry guessed traffic would be lightest. Tinder sat up front, but Edgar stayed in back with Essay and Baboo and a set of blankets, trying to shake off his jitters. He downed the dogs and drew the blankets over them whenever a car came into view. Henry was quiet. He laid his arm across the front seat and rested a hand on Tinder's shoulder.

After an hour they were west of Brule. Henry cut across Highway 2. He had a spot in mind, he said, where they could stop, give the dogs a break—a little cove he and Belva had discovered while exploring the coastline.

Keep going, Edgar signed. They don't need it.

"Are you kidding?" Henry said. "These dogs are pee machines. I don't want to find out what it's like to wipe that out of the nooks and crannies of my fine vinyl seats."

Essay seemed to sense an opportunity. She peered into Edgar's face and breathed anxiously.

Stop it, he signed. You're going to get us in trouble.

When they'd left Henry's little valley, the sun was shining between sparse white clouds, but as they approached Lake Superior the clouds merged into the solid blue mass of a storm front. By the time Henry arrived at the turnout and killed the engine, the sun had been eclipsed by the advancing storm.

Henry climbed out of the car. Edgar sat in the back seat, looking up and down the road for traffic.

"Relax," Henry said, knocking on the side window. "Don't you want to see the lake? Look around. No one's here."

Henry was right, but the thought of standing in the open with all three dogs made him edgy. He'd spent whatever luck he had. On the other hand, the weather was turning ugly, so there was little chance they'd linger. And it *would* be harder to let the dogs out in the rain.

"See," Henry said. "Nobody for miles. You'll like this. Follow me."

He led them through stands of scrub pine and maple on a faint trail. The trees were slick with green moss and the ground slippery, and made all the more treacherous by the storm gusts that had begun lashing the underbrush. The air was filled with the scent of the lake. Even before Edgar glimpsed water he heard the smashing of waves against the shore.

They emerged near a secluded cove, not much bigger than Henry's yard. At the back stood a sheer rock wall, twenty or thirty feet high, forming an irregular curve covered with gray ledges and pocked with erosion holes, some so big they looked like caves. A colony of water birds squawked and flapped near the top, where a shag of turf and tree roots overhung the rock.

Edgar saw at once why Henry liked the spot. On a sunny day, it would have felt cozy and secluded—a place where Edgar could have relaxed and watched the flat, watery horizon without fear of being spotted. Up and down the coastline all he could see were trees on rocky cliffs. No houses, no roads, not even boats on the water.

As Edgar and Henry picked their way down the last few feet of trail the dogs bounded onto the driftwood-strewn beach. Out on the lake, the water beneath the storm had turned black and choppy. A thread of lightning flickered between the sky and the water.

When Tinder paused to lift his leg against one of the larger chunks of driftwood, Henry gave Edgar one of his significant looks. The dog was only scent marking, but Henry took it as vindication that the dogs indeed needed a break.

"I told you. Don't feel bad. You just have to know how to read them," he said, modestly. "If you were staying around longer, I could teach you how I know these things. People think it takes some special talent, but I tell them—"

Then his mouth dropped open and he lifted his hand to point. Something was happening out on the lake. In the time it had taken them to walk onto the beach, the storm front had lowered, blackened, begun to roll over itself. What looked like a puff of steam jumped off the water, disappeared, then formed again.

"Tornado," Henry said. "Waterspout, I mean. Oh, Jesus Christ, look at that."

Edgar turned and was instantly riveted at the sight. As the funnel drew water up from the lake, it resolved, bottom to top, translucent at first, then white, then gray. Two more funnels appeared behind the first, wooly tubes dropping from the clouds. A chest-rattling thrum reached them. The dogs looked up, hackles raised.

"This is not good," Henry said. "I don't like this."

Somehow the three funnels gave the impression of standing still and hurtling forward at the same time. Edgar felt no impulse to run or hide or do anything but watch. The most distant of the three was nothing more than a sinuous thread coiling over the water. The one nearest to shore, maybe a mile away, had thickened into a sturdy vortex that narrowed to a point at the water's surface. All three were heading east, across the lake; if they kept going, they would pass in front of the cove, though not by much. He stood wondering if the storm that had corkscrewed the boards on their barn roof had birthed funnels like these.

Henry shared no part of Edgar's fascination. He turned to the steep trail leading into the woods, trotted a few feet, slipped, stood, and turned around.

"Uh, no. We ought to find cover. We don't want to be in a car if they come this way," he said. "They say to find a culvert, if you can." He surveyed their surroundings and the rock wall curving behind them. "Let's get into one of those caves," he said. "There's no time for anything else."

The center funnel lifted off the lake. It was close enough that it seemed to *slam* against the water when it came down again. Just moments earlier, it had looked broad and sluggish. Now it was more compact, as though drawing itself inward, spinning faster, and the noise of it was suddenly very loud.

"Nat?" Henry said. "Nat? Are you paying attention? We need to get out of the open. *Now*."

Reluctantly, Edgar tore his gaze away from the water. He clapped and recalled the dogs as the first real blast of wind caught him flat against his back. He stumbled and almost pitched forward. By the time he'd gotten the dogs together, Henry stood waiting at the rock wall.

"Here and here," Henry said, pointing and shouting above the roar. "We have to split up. Nothing's big enough for all of us."

Henry had located two recesses, each a few feet off the ground—alcoves scooped from the rock by thousands of years of waves. Neither was very deep, four or four five feet at most. There were other, deeper, nooks in the wall, but they were either too small or too high to reach without an arduous climb.

Edgar nodded at Henry and trotted forward, Baboo following at his heels, Essay and Tinder hanging back. The alcoves were separated by forty feet or more; the leftmost was larger, but also higher and more difficult to reach. Edgar chose that one for himself and two of the dogs.

He signed Tinder over toward Henry, then turned to Baboo.

Up.

The dog looked at him, trying to make certain what Edgar wanted.

Yes, he signed. Up!

Then Baboo crouched and sprang to the ledge. As soon as the dog landed, Edgar turned to Essay, who was back-pedaling toward the water.

Come, he signed to her. Up.

Essay shook off and retreated again and Edgar ran to her.

No games now, he signed. Come on.

He put his hands under her belly and wheelbarrowed her forward. She twisted and mouthed his arms, then broke free and leapt to the ledge beside Baboo and the two dogs stood side by side looking at him. Behind them, the roof of the alcove was soot-blackened—someone had once built a fire inside. The floor, eye level for Edgar, had been swept clean by wind and water. He backed away, holding the dogs' gaze, then looked over at Henry and Tinder, who were standing together in the sand.

"He won't let me lift him," Henry said. "He won't jump, and there's no other way up."

Edgar looked at the vacant hole in the rock. It was just big enough to fit a man and a dog. And Henry was right; beneath the opening was a ledgeless rock face. There was no way Tinder could climb it.

Edgar walked to Tinder and took the dog's head in his hand.

You're going to have to try.

Henry scrambled onto the ledge while Edgar led Tinder back a few paces. Then Edgar ran forward and slapped his hand against the rock.

"Come on, Tinder!" Henry cried. "Try not to get us all killed."

At first, Tinder just stood there, panting and looking over his shoulder at the funnels roaring on the lake. The sound came from every direction now as the rock wall gathered it and echoed it back over the water. Twice, urged by Edgar and Henry and the barks of the other dogs, Tinder hobbled forward, but each time he drew up short and lowered his ears and looked at Edgar.

Then Essay and Baboo leapt down from their ledge and came running across the sand; Edgar caught Essay two-handed as she passed, but Baboo kept running. When he reached Tinder they touched noses and then without delay Baboo wheeled and ran to the rock wall. Tinder didn't move. Baboo backtracked, barked, and nosed him. And this time they ran forward together, Tinder limping badly.

When they reached the rock wall, Tinder launched himself awkwardly into the air, yelping as he left the ground, his feet pedaling. He landed hard, back leg nearly off the ledge and kicking loose sand into the air, but Henry had him by his front legs, pulling him forward. Baboo had sailed through the air beside him, but there was barely room for the three of them on the tiny ledge and he jumped down at once.

The roar from the lake penetrated every part of Edgar's body. He prodded Essay and Baboo toward the other alcove and they sprang up without hesitation. Edgar scrambled after them.

"Nat?" came Henry's shout. Edgar looked across the rock wall. Henry knelt on the other ledge, hands cupped around his mouth. "There's going to be a lake swell. Stay in the cave." Then there was nothing more to say and nothing Edgar could have heard over the wind. He turned back to the dogs.

They were in a low, shallow scoop that narrowed rapidly into an egg-shaped cavity. Edgar had hoped to block the entrance with his body, but he saw at once that was impossible; at best, he might shield half the opening. He scuttled back, scraping his head on the sooty ceiling, and turned to face the lake. He signed Baboo down across one leg and scissored him with the other. Then he downed Essay—who, to his amazement, complied—and he wrapped both arms around her. That was the best he could do. If they panicked, he could keep them in place, for a while at least, maybe long enough to calm them down.

And then, backed into that cramped hole, they waited and looked out over the lake. Two of the waterspouts were close now, their sound a blast of every octave and pitch as they ground their way through the atmosphere. The closest stood a quarter of a mile out, like a cable dropped from the clouds into a ball of water vapor at the lake's surface. A fragment of cloud revolved along its shaft and vanished. Gobs of water splatted against the rocks, gulped out of Lake Superior and thrown landward.

It made Edgar think of how his father stood in the doorway of the barn during thunderstorms, looking up at the sky. Even as he tried to pull the dogs farther back into the cave, Edgar wondered if his father would be doing the same thing now.

As Henry predicted, the water began to rise; the spot where they first sighted the funnels was already submerged by the waves crashing ashore. The wind entered Edgar's nostrils and mouth, puffed out his cheeks, tried to lift the lids of his eyes. Sand and pebbles pelted them. He thought the sound and the wind might cow the dogs, but it didn't—the dogs permitted his hold on them but never rolled back against him for reassurance. A gray chunk of driftwood began to roll end over end along the beach, come alive now and fleeing for its life; the dogs turned their muzzles to track it.

Then the smallest of the funnels slid by, its bloom of water skimming the lake's surface like an upended rose. A jagged thread of light snaked down, drawn to a tree near the shoreline. The sound that followed was more like an explosion than thunder, but it was instantly swept away by the howling wind. When Edgar looked back at the lake, only the larger funnel remained, so squat and black it looked as if the thing were drawing earth and sky together.

What happened next took maybe ten seconds. The ropy funnel that had just passed out of view reappeared, skipping and twisting across the water like a tentacle, moving back along its line of travel. Then the sinuous gray thread of its body was pulled toward the large funnel. They separated for a moment, then twined, the smaller of the two spiraling around the larger before it was consumed. Or nearly so. A whirling streamer peeled away and flailed over the lake, dipping halfway to the water before evaporating. At the same time, the larger funnel changed from ashen to ghostly white, towering palely over the cove, lunging and retreating.

Unbelievable, Edgar thought, as the wind buffeted them. What he was seeing was unbelievable.

Yet he had seen unbelievable things before, came the answer. And he had run from them.

That was the moment Essay decided to bolt. One instant Edgar's arms were wrapped tightly around her chest, the next she'd slipped away as effortlessly as if greased. She dashed across the cove, her bounds fore-shortened by the wind. Baboo barked and scrabbled his hind feet against the bare rock, but Edgar doubled over and threw his arms around the dog, clamping one hand over his muzzle to stop his thrashing. Almost at once he understood that Baboo didn't intend to follow Essay—he wasn't drawn by her vision, her compulsion, whatever had made her race to meet the pillar that roared at them from out on the water. He was only trying to call Essay back.

The white funnel lurched toward shore, two hundred yards away now, maybe less, the distance from the Sawtelles' house to the middle of the lower field, and there it came to a standstill, swaying over the lake. Essay faced it, barking and snarling, tail dropped like a scimitar. When she turned sideways, the force of the wind blew her hind feet out from under her and she rolled, twice, barrel-wise, before scrambling up and facing the wind squarely again, this time carefully holding her ground.

Something crashed to the beach in front of the rocks and a spray of blood pinked the air—an enormous fish of some kind, guts burst and streaming across the pebbled cove.

Now Essay tried to advance. Each time she lifted a foot from the sand her body wobbled precariously in the gale. Finally, it drove her to the ground. She lay there, ears flattened against her skull, muzzle wrinkled, legs extended like a hieroglyph of a dog, stripped by the roar of the wind, it seemed to Edgar, to her essence, insane and true all at the same time. When the wind abated for an instant, her hackles stood. Then it hit again, harder than ever. The trees along the shore whirled and bent and righted themselves, the breaking of their limbs like rifle cracks.

I should go out there, Edgar thought. She's going to be killed. But then Baboo will bolt.

He had time to debate it in his mind, to weigh the loss of one against the other, and he saw there was no way to decide. *She* had made this choice, he thought—what his grandfather had always wanted, what he'd wished for time and again in his letters. So, in the end, Edgar lay on the floor of the cave as the wind fired stones at them like bullets. He redoubled his grip on Baboo and watched between his fingers as Essay was driven back to the tree line, crouching and retreating, her muzzle moving but no sound reaching them.

And in that moment, he thought: it isn't going to work. I'll never get far enough away. I may as well never have left.

Out on the lake, something changed. The funnel stalled, narrowed, whitened, whitened still more, then lifted off the water. The steam at its base dropped into the lake as if a spell had been broken. The stem of it writhed in the air above them like a snake suspended from the clouds. The wind lessened and the blast of sound abated. Essay's bark came thinly to them and Baboo began to bark in response. From across the cove, Edgar heard Tinder doing the same.

Overhead, the tube of wind slid sickeningly through the air, preparing to crash down again, this time directly onshore, but without pause it revolved up into the clouds and disappeared as if pursuing some tormentor there. A wash of foamy black water swept up from the lake almost to the rock wall, then carried back with it half the water flooding the little cove. The freight train sound vanished; the wind gusted and was still. There was the hiss and boom of waves breaking up and down along the shore.

The moment Edgar loosened his grip, Baboo sprang from the ledge and ran to Essay, who was already trotting triumphantly before the retreating waves. Baboo accompanied her for a few yards then turned and bounded toward the rocks where Tinder and Henry huddled, and he paced there, waiting.

Getting Tinder down was not easy. The rock was wet and slick and Tinder resisted being carried. Henry took him in his arms and slid down, managing just enough grace to maintain his hold and scraping his back across the rocks in the process. When Henry set Tinder down on the wet sand, the dog limped to the wind-thrown fish and sniffed it. Drops of rain—real rain, not flung lake water—began to fall. Out on the lake, a huge mass of driftwood floated in the water like the tangled bones of a sailing ship dredged from the bottom.

They found Henry's car plastered with green leaves. The passenger-side window sported a long white crack. They hustled the dogs inside and sat for a long time breathing and listening to the patternless drum of rain on the roof.

· "There's something wrong with that dog," Henry said. "That wasn't hardly a sensible thing to do."

Edgar nodded. But he thought, how can we know? He closed his eyes and the image of Ida Paine, bending toward him across her counter, filled his mind. *If you go,* she whispered, *don't you come back, not for nothing. It's just wind, that's all. Just wind. It don't mean nothing.*

It don't mean nothing. He tried saying that to himself.

He took up the paper and pencil lying on the seat.

Let's turn around, he wrote.

"Now *that's* more like it," Henry said. He keyed the ignition and wheeled the car onto the road facing the direction they had come. "At least one of you is thinking straight."

Edgar smiled, grimly, his face turned to watch the rain and the passing trees. If Henry knew the alternative, he thought, he'd like it even less.

On the way back, Henry kept the radio off. He drove without comment, except for once, when, apropos of nothing in the moment, he shook his head and muttered, "Christ all Friday."

It was steaming hot that next August afternoon, as Henry's car rolled along the forest road near Scotia Lake, where Edgar and the dogs had passed the Fourth of July in what now seemed to him a time of aimless wandering. The water was hidden by the trees and foliage. From the inside of the car, it all looked unfamiliar. They overshot the driveway before Edgar caught sight of the little red cottage, now boarded up for the season.

Stop, he signed. That was it.

"You sure?"

Edgar looked again and nodded. He recognized the white trim and the front door and the window he had crawled through. He remembered the taste of the chocolate bar he had stolen there, how it had melted in his back pocket while he fed the dogs butter squeezed through his fingers.

Henry nosed his sedan into the weedy drive and killed the engine. "I'm going to say this one last time," he said. "I can take you all the way to wherever you're going. I don't mind."

Thanks, Edgar signed. But no.

He knew Henry wanted him to elaborate, but what he wanted to do there at the lake—whom he hoped to find, what he hoped would result from it—required him to go on foot. He could think of no words to explain his hopes, just as his mother had been unable to find words for the value of their dogs. They got out of the car and he retrieved the fishing satchel and the Zebco from the trunk. He hooked the satchel's strap over his shoulder. The dogs nosed about until their curiosity was satisfied, then trotted back to the car, Tinder first, limping out of the underbrush, followed by Baboo and Essay. Edgar knelt in front of Tinder and stroked his muzzle. He lifted for the last time his injured foot to run his fingertips over the scarred pad. He watched Tinder for a flinch, but the dog only peered back at him. All the swelling was gone now, but his second toe still stood out. He set Tinder's foot down. Tinder lifted and presented it again.

Stay, he signed. He did this out of habit and immediately wished to take it back, for it wasn't what he meant. He started to get up, then knelt again.

Watch Henry. He doesn't know much yet.

Then he stood and held out his hand and Henry shook it.

"All you ever need to do is come back and ask," Henry said. "I'll take good care of him until then."

No. He belongs with you. He chose.

And he had. Edgar could see it as Tinder sat bright-eyed and panting and leaning slightly against Henry's leg. He'd seen it in the car, driving back from Lake Superior, and later that night at Henry's house. It seemed to Edgar that Tinder was still making the leap onto that ledge to join Henry, and in one way or another, he would be making it every day for the rest of his life.

Edgar turned and walked up the cabin driveway with Baboo and Essay beside him. He let himself look back just once. Henry and Tinder stood by the car, watching them go. When they reached the lake, Baboo noticed that Tinder wasn't following. He looked at Edgar, then wheeled and trotted back toward the car. Halfway there, he came to a halt. Edgar stopped and turned and slapped his leg. Baboo came toward him a few steps, then looked over his shoulder at Henry and Tinder by the car and whined unhappily and sat.

Edgar stood looking at the dog. He walked back and knelt in front of him.

You have to be sure, he signed.

Baboo peered at him, panting. He looked past Edgar's shoulder at Essay. After a long time, Baboo stood, and together they trudged to the car. Baboo bounded the last twenty feet and jumped into the back seat to join Tinder.

"It's not about me, is it?" Henry said. "He can't leave Tinder."

No.

"You think I can do right by both of them?"

Edgar nodded.

"It's okay with me. Hell, more than okay."

Edgar stood looking at the two dogs for a long time, trying to fix the memory of them in his mind. Then Essay trotted up and Baboo jumped out to meet her. They circled, end to end, as if they hadn't seen each other for a long time, and Baboo lay his muzzle along her neck.

Edgar turned and walked up the drive. He didn't give a recall or any other command. He couldn't bear to turn around. The underbrush whipped his face but he hardly noticed it over the pounding in his head. He squeezed his eyes down to slits but the tears leaked out anyway. Eventually, Essay appeared by his side. Then she bolted ahead and vanished into the underbrush.

No more commands, he thought. Never again. She knew where they were as well as he and she could run as she pleased.

Behind them, Henry's car groaned to life. Despite himself, Edgar tracked the sound as it rolled along the road until, even standing still, only the forest sounds came to him.

Return

THEY SPENT THAT NIGHT ON THE SPIT OF LAND WHERE THEY had watched the fireworks consumed by their own reflections, where the howling of the dogs had moved another watcher to announce himself. The next day they walked the perimeter of the lake. Shady patches giving onto cattails and vast tracts of water lilies. Leopard frogs bounded into the water wherever they stepped. The fish were plentiful, the campers sparse. Most of the cabins had been shut down for the season, plywood nailed across their windows, and there was no point in forcing his way into them. Henry had supplied him with matches, fishhooks, and a small gnarled brown-handled pocketknife with ivory inlays.

For each of the next three nights they moved their camp a little farther into the low hills north of Scotia Lake. Essay adjusted to the solitary life more quickly than Edgar expected. At night she and Edgar slept spooned together against the chilled air. She understood that they waited for something or someone. At times she stood and paced, scenting for her two missing littermates. The days had grown shorter now. The August dusk began by seven o'clock, night an hour after that.

Late in the evening of the fourth night, when their small fire had burned down to embers, a pair of eyes glinted in the underbrush. Not deer or raccoon, whose eyes reflected the orange firelight as green. These eyes mirrored red when the flame was red, yellow when it was yellow, disappearing for an instant and then flickering back. Their possessor had approached from upwind, a habit, Edgar supposed, after all that time in the woods. He laid an arm across Essay's back. He'd saved a bit of fish and he picked it up now and tossed it across the fire.

Forte stepped out of the shadows. He padded forward to sniff the offering. When Essay saw him, her body tensed, but Edgar asked her to stay with the pressure of his hand. It wasn't a command. He felt he hadn't the right anymore, that he had long ago fallen from grace but only recently understood it. The stray's colors were just as Edgar remembered, amber and black across his back, his chest broad and blond. One of his ears hung tattered from some fight long past. But his body had filled out and his legs were thick and solid.

Essay rumbled a warning in her throat and Forte retreated into the dark. Edgar nursed the fire along late into the night, bent over the coals like a wizened old man, fatigued, though they had hardly done a thing all day. In the morning, Essay, too, was gone. She returned at noon, panting and covered with burrs. Edgar had already amassed a great number of fish. He fried the fish on sticks and they gorged themselves. When Essay turned her nose away, he urged her to eat anyway; it was important she not want it later. He fished some more and cooked the fish and thought of Henry sitting at the card table behind his house, roasting bratwurst while he and the dogs looked on from their hiding place by the sunflowers.

Blue evening reflected in the water. Starshot cirrus veils. Forte appeared again late that evening and this time Essay trotted forward to meet him and scented his flanks while he stood rigidly waiting. Then she posed in return. When Forte left, much later, the pile of fish Edgar had set aside was gone.

HE BEGAN TO FISH AGAIN as soon as he woke the next day. He cooked the fish and stacked them up. Catcalls sounded from the woods around them. When they had eaten their fill, he stuffed the remainder into his satchel and left the Zebco lying on the ground and they set out. The traveling was easy now. He didn't understand why it had taken so long to cross such a meager distance on the way out. In a single day they covered a quarter of their return. Occasionally, he dropped a shred of cooked fish onto the ground as a trail. He'd wondered if he would recognize the route they'd taken all those weeks before. He did.

Essay disappeared for an hour or more at times but always he kept moving. Then there would be a rattle of bracken and she would burst into a clearing and dash over to him, swiping her tail through the air. They came upon a familiar lake late in the day and he built a small fire. He slept beside the dying embers as if trading them for dreams.

He knew for certain that Forte was following as he'd hoped only on the second night. They'd walked all day picking at the fish, a particle for himself, a particle for Essay, a particle tossed on the ground. Essay rooted for turtle eggs, but that season was past. A few stray blueberries hung on bushes, cooked in their skins. They stopped midday along a lake and Edgar stripped and walked into the water and stood until his skin cooled and the fresh mosquito bites stopped itching. An egret lifted out of the reeds near the lake's edge, white and archaic. It glided across the water and settled near the shore a safe distance away and cawed its objection to his scaring the fish. But the egret was wrong. Edgar ate only the fish that remained in the satchel, reheating them over the fire. God, he was tired of eating them.

He set the remainder of their cache near the edge of the firelight. He suspected it was a bad idea. The satchel was greasy from the fat in the bodies of the fish. Perhaps every bear in the region knew where they were by now, but so would Forte, and he was right about that. When he woke in the morning, the stray raised his muzzle and gazed at him over the glowing char of the fire. He lay still. Essay stood and circled to Forte and nosed him and both dogs circled back. Forte extended his neck and scented him, legs trembling. He stroked Essay under the chin, then let his hand pass to Forte.

When he stood, the dog backpedaled. With his one shredded ear, he looked at once comical and cagey. Edgar turned his back and gathered his things. When he looked around, Forte was gone. As was Essay.

Now Almondine occupied his thoughts. He hadn't seen her for two months or more and suddenly it felt like he'd been severed from some fundament of his being. At the end of the next day or the day after that, they would be joined again. Perhaps she would have forgotten his crimes, for which he wanted more than anything to atone. Everything that had happened to him since he'd left made him think of her. Others dreamed of finding a person in the world whose soul was made in their mirror image, but she and Edgar had been conceived nearly together, grown up together, and however strange it might be, she was his other. Much could be endured for that. He also knew that she was old, and he had squandered some portion of their time circling in the woods, blind, confused, stopping and starting with only vague notions of what to do. Without the strangest kind of intercession he might never have seen her again. Perhaps only when he'd become an old man would he realize how reduced he'd been by that decision, how withered he'd become, away from her.

He'd left in confusion, but his return was clarifying. So much of what had been obscure while he faced away was now evident. No sooner had he walked away from that cove by the lake than the need to go home possessed him. He understood the rightness of Tinder's decision, and Baboo's. Henry was a fretful person, filled with doubts and worries, but he was faithful as well. Edgar wondered what would have happened to them if Tinder had injured his foot a mile farther along. So much of the world was governed by chance. If they had left Henry's house a day earlier, they might have been in Canada that very moment, maybe even at Starchild Colony. Life was a swarm of accidents waiting in the treetops, descending upon any living thing that passed, ready to eat them alive. You swam in a river of chance and coincidence. You clung to the happiest accidents—the rest you let float by. You met a good man, in whose care a dog would be safe. You looked around and discovered the most unusual thing in the world sitting there looking at you. Some things were certain—they had already happened—but the future could not be divined. Perhaps by Ida Paine. For everyone else, the future was no ally. A person had only his life to barter with. He felt that way. He could lose himself to Starchild Colony or trade what he held for something he cared about. That rare thing. Either way, his life would be spent.

These were his thoughts as he walked the edge of a marshy clearing. Across the way, Essay bounded and turned and nipped at Forte, who followed her, suddenly awkward and puppylike. At length, from Forte's ineptitude and lurching clumsiness, a fight broke out between them. But it was a mock battle, and soon Essay gallivanted over to Edgar, ignoring the lout.

They slept far from water or any landmark familiar to him. He made a fire for warmth and let it bank. Forte lay watching, curled beneath a chestnut sapling. That night Edgar crossed the lighted circle to sit near the stray and work the burrs out of his coat. When he finished, he stroked the animal along his withers. Forte scented his wrist. He remembered those nights in the garden, Forte silvered in the moonlight and quivering beneath his hands. Then Edgar returned to his side of the fire. His last thought before he slept was that he was glad not to be eating fish, even if it meant going hungry.

The next morning they set off eastward, tracing shadows back to their source again and again. Essay and Forte disappeared. When he saw Essay again, her muzzle was stained red with fresh blood. He knelt beside her and ran his fingers along her gum line and ruff and legs but the blood was not hers. Forte was nowhere to be seen.

They came to the clearing filled with fire-scarred trees where they had stopped the very first night, where the owls had turned to watch them. He began to run. The sumac blazed red where earlier it had stood like green parasols. When he looked down, Essay was by his side.

The old logging trail appeared. They came to the fence line set in the middle of the creek. The water was no more than a trickle and the fence post he'd uprooted sat cockeyed in the silt and dirt. He stepped into the water and lifted the barbed wire. Essay passed beneath almost without breaking stride. On the far side she shook herself needlessly and waited. The creek water slipped over the sand and rocks. He stood waiting for Forte. After a time he decided the dog would find his own way to cross, if he was going to cross at all. He pushed the fence post over and stepped across the wires, not bothering to restore it as he walked back onto their land.

Almondine

WHEN SHE WASN'T SLEEPING ALREADY SHE LAY IN THE SHADE and waited for sleep to return. In slumber everything was as it had once been, when they were whole and he ran beside her, pink and small-limbed and clumsy. Those were nights when the timbers of the house had breathed for them and no sand had yet worked into her joints. No search for him was necessary. In her dreams, he was there, always, waving bachelor's buttons for her to smell, unearthing oddities she was required to dig from his clenched hands for fear he'd found some dangerous thing. Not so in the waking world, which held nothing but an endless search.

All her life she had found whatever she had been asked to find and there had only been one thing ever. Now he was truly lost, gone away, crossed into another world, perhaps, some land unknown to her from which he could not return. The closet was as puzzled as she, the bed silent on the question. It was not out of the question that he had learned the secret of flight, and the window was not too small for him to pass through. There, sleeping on his bed at night, she would be the first to see when he returned. Old as she was, she still had questions to ask him, things to show him. She worried about him. She needed to find him, whole or changed, but know in any case, and she would taste the salt of his neck.

She had learned, in her life, that time lived inside you. You *are* time, you *breathe* time. When she'd been young, she'd had an insatiable hunger for more of it, though she hadn't understood why. Now she held inside her a cacophony of times and lately it drowned out the world. The apple tree was still nice to lie near. The peony, for its scent, also fine. When she walked through the woods (infrequently now) she picked her way along the path, making way for the boy inside to run along before her. It could be hard to choose the time outside over the time within. There was still work to do, of course. The young ones in the barn knew so little and she had taught so many before. It hardly seemed worth trying when she was asked, though she did.

She slowed. The farm danced about her. The apple trees bickered with the wind, clasped limbs in union against it, blackbirds and sparrows and chickadees and owls rimming their crowns. The garden cried out its green infant odor, its mélange the invention of deer or, now it seemed to her, the other way around. The barn swung her fat shadow across the yard, holding it gently by dark wrists and letting it turn, turn, stretch out in the evening upon the ground but never slip. Faster it all revolved around her when she closed her eyes. Clouds rumbled across heaven and she lay beneath, and in the passage of shadow and yellow sunlight, the house murmured secrets to the truck, the traveler, who listened for only so long before its devout empiricism forced it away in wide-eyed panic to test such ideas among its fellows. The maple tree held the wash up to the light in supplication and received (bright flames) yellow jackets each day, its only reply. The mailbox stood soldierly by the road, capturing a man and releasing him, again and again.

Among them, the woman passed, oblivious to it all, leading the pups once more through what they surely must already have learned—the foolish pups who made them all stop and watch, such was their power. Almondine sat and watched them and then, somehow, the boy would be sitting beside her, arm across her withers. The pups had so little time inside them they barely stayed attached to the ground. As it had been with her, she supposed. And then she turned her head and looked and Edgar was missing all over again. Had he really been there? Had it only been some bit of time inside her?

The answer mattered more and more, even as the power in her to find him ebbed. They'd shaped each other under the heat of some more brilliant sun whose light had quietly passed from the world. The towering pines in the front yard knew it; they suffocated one night when an ocean mist drifted into the yard, though no one noticed but she. Three days she lay beneath them, mourning. The squirrels, respectful of nothing, ransacked the carcasses. The nights grew darker, the stars distracted. She slept beside his bed because, if nowhere else, he would return there. He had been tricking her—he had hidden so cleverly! What a reunion they would have when he stepped out of his hiding place, how they would laugh, what joy there would be! The greatest trick of all revealed by him, there all along and watching while she searched! All along! The thought was so startling she rose and panted and shook her head. So many places worthy of another look. But empty, all of them, and all extracting their penalty, impassive, blithe, unconcerned.

And then, midmorning of a day when the sky rang overhead, she reached a decision. She rose from her sleeping spot in the living room. In the kitchen, she set her long soft jaw on the woman's leg and tried to make it clear she would have to look elsewhere. The woman stroked her absently, a hand familiar against her flanks and caressing behind her ears. Almondine was grateful for it. The door stood unlatched. She still had the strength to pull it open. She walked between the rows of trees on the long slope of the orchard and waited near the topmost tree.

Perhaps he traveled. Now she would, too.

From far away, she heard the traveler coming. For as long as she could remember, they'd passed her yard, acquaintances of the truck, exchangers of the empirical, the factual, the mathematical—traders in unknowable quantities. Longitudes and azimuths. Secants and triangulations. She had thought them intruders when she was young, but learned to pay no attention, her alarm foolish. They were benign, careening about for reasons of their own. Unstealthy, broad, and stupid, they were, but they saw a lot of the world.

It was coming up the far side of the hill; its cloud of dust filled the air between the trees. The glint of its frontpiece appeared. She was not scared. One must try new things. Inside, she held the image of him on that first morning, awake in his mother's sleeping arms. She'd thought what had begun then would never end. Yet he'd been too long missing for things to be wholly right. Nothing knew of him in the yard. Nothing in the house. All of it forgetting, slowly, slowly, she could feel it, and one could last only so long separated from the essence.

A quest waited in those circumstances, always.

The traveler was almost there. If this one knew nothing, she would ask the next. And the next. One of them would know. She'd asked the truck her question, but with silence it professed ignorance. It had not carried him lately, though it would not deny it had carried him many times before. She had never thought to ask the other travelers until that morning. The idea had come to her in a whisper.

She stepped onto the sharp red gravel of the road. She was very nearly not there at all, so deeply was she inside her own mind. There was a time in her when he had fallen from an apple tree, a tree she'd just stepped away from. He'd landed with a thump on his back. A time in the winter when he'd piled the snow on her face until the world had gone white and she'd dug for his mittened hand. Inside her were countless mornings watching his eyes flutter open as he woke. Above all, she recalled the language the two of them had invented, a language in which everything important could be said. She did not know how to ask the traveler what she needed to ask, nor what form its reply might take. But it was upon her now, angry and rushed, and it wouldn't be long before she knew the answer. A bloom of dust like a thundercloud chased it down the hill.

She stood broadside in the gravel and turned her head and asked her question.

Asked if it had seen her boy. Her essence. Her soul.

But if the traveler understood, it showed no sign.

Part V

POISON

Edgar

THEY WALKED UP THROUGH THE MANTLE OF TREE SHADOW stretching across the western field. Ahead, the red siding of the barn glowed phosphorescent in the mulled sunset. A pair of does sprang over the fence on the north side of the field—two leaps each, nonchalant, long-sustained, falling earthward only as an afterthought—and crashed through the hazel and sumac. The air was still and hot and the hay rasped dryly at Edgar's legs. Stalks of wild corn dotted the field, leaves frayed and bitten to the cane, and the Indian tobacco was brown and wilted from the heat. All of it brittle and rattling as if folded from sheets of cigarette paper.

By the time Edgar reached the rock pile, Essay had already coursed the yard, whipping the kennel dogs into a frenzy. He perched on a rock and listened. Equal parts of longing and dread washed through him, but the sound of the dogs pleased him the way a lullaby might please an old man. He picked out their voices one by one and named them. From where he sat, he could see only the roof of the house hovering darkly over the yard. He waited for some human figure to appear, but there was only the flash of Essay's body, low and elongate, cutting through the grass as she made another round.

He stood and walked the rest of the way. The house was dark. The Impala sat parked in the grass. In the garden, he could see the green tract of cucumber and pumpkin vines and, far back by the woods, a half dozen sunflowers leaning bent-headed over it all. He peered through the living room windows hoping to see Almondine, knowing all the while that had she been home, she would already have found some way to bolt from the house.

When he entered the barn, the dogs braced their forepaws on their pen doors and greeted him with yodels and roars and howls. He went from pen to pen, letting them jump and claw his shirt, laughing at their mad dashes and play-bows and rolls. He saved Pout and Finch and Opal and Umbra for last. He knelt and mouthed their names into their ears and they washed his face with their tongues. When they had quieted, he found a coffee can and dished kibble into a pile for Essay. She started eating daintily, then leaned into it as if suddenly remembering food.

Two pups greeted him in the nursery—just two, from the litter of eight whelped before he left. They were weaned and fat, shaking their bellies and beating their tails. He squatted and scratched their chins.

What did they name you? Where are the others?

He walked to the workshop. He looked at the file cabinets and the books arranged atop them. *The New Webster Encyclopedic Dictionary of the English Language* weighed so little in his hands. The scent of its pages like road dust. He leaned against the wall and thought of his grandfather and of Brooks's never-ending admonitions, and he thought of Hachiko. Among the mishmash of correspondence he found the letter from Tokyo and withdrew the crumpled photograph he'd hidden there. He looked at Claude and Forte through the webwork of cracks in the emulsion, then slid it into his pocket.

He closed up the kennel and walked to the house. The kitchen door key hung from a nail in the basement. He ate straight from the refrigerator, fog pouring over his feet. Bread and cheese and roast chicken off the bone, then walked through the house cradling a five-quart bucket of vanilla ice cream under his arm, spooning it up and looking around. The kitchen clock. The stove. The candle night-light. The living room furniture sitting petrified and ogrelike in the dusk. The clothes hanging in his mother's closet. He walked up the stairs and sat on his bed. A puff of dust lifted into the air. Across the plank flooring, dead flies lay scattered, dry husks, blue and green, with cellophaned wings. He hadn't imagined everyone would be gone. He hadn't imagined saying hello to the place before seeing his mother. Before seeing Almondine most of all. He *had* imagined sleeping in that bed again, but looking at it now, he didn't know how he could.

He put the ice cream back in the freezer and dropped the spoon into the sink. Essay scratched at the porch door. He walked out and pushed the door open and let her trot through the house, repeating his inspection. He was seated at the table, at his father's place, when she returned. He sat for a long time, waiting. It was hard for him not to think about what things would be like. Finally, he decided to wash up. When he lifted his face from the towel in the bathroom he saw the green soap turtle sitting on the windowsill, complete and perfect except for one shriveled hind foot.

He walked into the kitchen and found a pencil and a scrap of paper and touched the lead to the paper and stopped and looked out the kitchen windows. The windows had been propped open on sticks and a night breeze, hot as an animal exhalation, ruffled the gingham curtains. Dark, ripe apples swung from the branches outside the window. He put the pencil to the paper again. I ate while you were gone, he wrote. I'll come back tomorrow. Then he took the photograph of Claude and Forte from his pocket and set it beside the note.

He gave Essay the option of staying or coming along. She walked down the porch steps, calm now, curiosity satisfied. He pocketed the key and stood trying to decide where to sleep. The mow, on a night that hot, would be stifling. In the milk house he found a pile of burlap sacks. They walked into the field. It was full dark by that time but the faint reach of the yard light cast his shadow before him. At the narrow end of the trees by the whale-rock he snapped the dust from the sacks and threw them down. Essay circled and circled, solving again the everlasting riddle of lying down to sleep. She came to rest with her back to him, muzzle fitted high on her foreleg. Overhead the aurora flew, sheets of wild neon. He focused on the hovering seed of the yard light flickering through the hay and breathed the scent of pollen and decay that infused the night.

They'd slept for some time when the truck crested the hill. The moon was up. The field around them like salt and silver. He sat on the burlap and watched the truck back around and stop by the porch while the kennel dogs barked a frantic greeting. Essay stood and whined. Edgar laid a hand on her hip. She nosed him and turned back to watch.

The truck disgorged the figures of Claude and his mother. Claude lifted the gate on the topper and lifted out two bags of groceries while his mother paused to settle the dogs. The porch door creaked and slapped. The kitchen light appeared dimly through the broad windows in the living room. Twice more Claude walked between the back porch and the truck. On his last trip, he stood looking around the yard, then closed the topper and walked to the porch and turned out the light.

And sitting under the stars and the sky, Edgar waited to see Almondine. She had not jumped down from the bed of the truck. He had watched for that. I just missed her, he said to himself. He closed his eyes to see it again. But she would have scented him at once. He felt himself perfectly drawn and repelled, wishing to be done with that part of his life and wishing never to let it end, knowing that whatever came next would only reduce what had already happened until there was nothing but memory, a story eroded, a dream thinly recalled.

If she wasn't at home, then she must have gone into town with them. It was one or the other. One or the other.

He looked at the stand of birches, alone in the center of the field. It was the middle of August and when he stood, the timothy almost reached his waist. He stumbled through it, striking at the heads with his splayed hands. The trunks of the birches tilted and blurred and the leaves in their canopy quavered whitely. Then he was standing in the broad circle of grass scythed away at the base of the trees. There was the familiar white cross for the stillborn baby and the newer one for his father. And next to them, as yet unmarked, an oblong of fresh, dark ground.

It blew the breath out of him. He fell like a puppet severed from its strings. He lay with his forehead pressed to the ground, the scent of iron and loam filling his nostrils, and he clutched the dirt and poured it out of his hands. An oceanic roar filled his head. All his memory, all his past, rose up to engulf him. Images of Almondine. How she liked peanut butter but not peanuts; how she preferred lima beans to corn but refused peas; how, best of all, she adored honey, any way she could get it, licked from his fingers, from his lips, dabbed on her nose. How she liked to snatch things from his hands and let him take them back. How if he cupped her chin she would lower and lower her head all the way to the ground to stay like that. How different it was to stroke her with his palm than with his fingertips. How he could lay a hand on her side while she slept and she wouldn't open her eyes but nonetheless understood, and her breath came differently.

He remembered a time when he was small, when Almondine was young and rambunctious, more like a wild horse than a dog to him, when she could cross the yard faster than a swallow and catch him running across that same field. He liked to sneak away—make her chase, see her fly. When she reached him, they would turn and sprint into the field, heading for a thicket of raspberry canes, a place he liked simply because he was small enough to move through it unscathed. But when they arrived, something was standing there—an animal he had never seen before, with a broad face and pointed nose and great smooth black claws. They'd run up quickly and surprised it and it turned to face them with a hoarse cough, hissing and slashing the ground, mistaking their headlong rush for a charge. Gouts of dirt sprayed the air behind its haunches. He tried to step back, but the thing bounded equally forward, tethered to him by some unseen force, staring with black marble eyes as though beholding a monster, panting throatily and turning and snapping at its hind legs and whirling to face them again, a beard of gray foam lining its jaw.

How long Almondine stood beside him he didn't know, transfixed by how the thing crabbed forward with each step back he took. Then she glided lengthwise between them, blocking his view and hipping him so hard he nearly fell. She didn't run to do it, used none of the enchantments of play, nothing clever, no dancing grace. She just stepped between them and stood, tail unlashed. Then she turned and licked his face and he was stunned at what he understood her to be doing. If she moved she exposed him, and therefore she would not move. She was asking him to leave, saying it was *he* who could save *her*, not the other way around. She would not even risk a fight with the thing. She would leave only if he were gone and in such a way that it wouldn't chase. She took her eyes off it just that one instant, to make things clear.

He watched her standing there for the longest time as he backed away. When he reached the barn, she crouched and sprang and materialized at his side. And he remembered how they'd seen the thing, dead and fly-strewn, on the road the next day.

There was Almondine, playing their crib game. Dancing for him, light as a dust mote.

He thought of his father standing in the barn doorway peering sky-ward as a thunderstorm approached, while his mother shouted, "Gar, get indoors, for God's sake." That was how it was, sometimes. You put yourself in front of the thing and waited for whatever was going to happen and that was all. It scared you and it didn't matter. You stood and faced it. There was no outwitting anything. When Almondine had been playful, she had been playful in the face of that knowledge, as defiant as before the rabid thing. It was not a morbid thought, just the world as it existed. Sometimes you looked the thing in the eye and it turned away. Sometimes it didn't. Essay might have been taken up in the whirlwind at the lake, but she wasn't, and there was nothing special in that except her certainty that she had driven the thing away.

In the morning, he planned to walk into the house. He didn't know what would happen then. Claude had been the one to find his note. He understood that. If his mother had read it, she would have run out shout-ing his name. But the house was dark and no one had run out.

He rested a hand on Essay's back and they watched the yard. He felt hollow as a gourd. He knew he wouldn't sleep anymore that night. The yard light stood high and brilliant on its pole above the orchard, its glow enveloping the house and yard and all beyond that darkness and the sky black above. After a while Claude stepped from the porch and walked along the driveway. A stripe of light appeared beneath the back barn doors. In a few minutes the stripe winked out and Claude crossed back to the house and mounted the porch steps and without pause was swallowed up in the shadows.

Trudy

TRUDY LAY IN BED, HALF SLEEPING, THINKING ABOUT THE DOGS — that peculiar note of agitation she'd heard in their voices when she'd first stepped out of the truck. Not frenzy, exactly, though something akin to it, and enough to make her stop and look around the yard. She'd seen none of the usual causes for alarm—no deer poaching in the garden, no skunk scuttling into the shadows, no raccoon peering red-eyed from an apple tree. In fact, the moment she'd signed *quiet* the dogs had settled down. She'd decided it was just the lateness of their arrival or the spectacle of a full moon hovering in the treetops. But the edge in their voices nagged at her now. And maybe it nagged at Claude, too; as she was having these thoughts, he sat up and began to dress by the blue moonwash streaming through the window.

"I'm going to check on those pups," he whispered.

"I'll go with you."

"No. Stay and sleep. Back before you know it."

The spring on the porch door gave an iron yawn and then she was alone. The dogs, she suspected, weren't the only reason Claude had gotten up. He was, for reasons she didn't understand, embarrassed about his insomnia, reticent to the point of silence whenever she asked in the mornings how long he'd been awake. The first few times she'd woken to find him missing, she'd stolen out to watch him pace the yard, hands in his pockets, head down, walking until the steady rhythm of step, step, step worked whatever it was out of him. But mostly it was rainy nights that plagued Claude. He'd sit on the porch drawing the tip of his pocketknife across a bar of soap until a facsimile of something or another appeared in his hands and was carved down into something smaller and then something smaller yet until it finally disappeared entirely. The crumbs and curls she found in the trash spoke most eloquently of how long he'd sat in the dark.

Trudy had her own reason for wanting to go outside. It would have been an opportunity, though belated, to stand behind the silo—to make her nightly signal that it was safe for Edgar to come home. But it had been late when they'd parked the truck and carried in the groceries, and full dark. Even so, had she found an inconspicuous reason to go out, she might have tried anyway.

This arrangement between her and Edgar was one fact about that night in the mow she had kept secret from Claude, letting him believe, along with Glen and everyone else, that Edgar had fled, panic-stricken at the sight of Page lying so near where Gar had died. Why she'd withheld this fact from Claude, when she'd told him so much of the rest, she couldn't have said. Partly because she'd thought it would be such a short-lived deception. The very next night she'd walked into the tall grass and stood facing the sunset, expecting to see Edgar emerge from the woods as Gar had, so long ago, shimmering into place between the aspens. Finally, afraid that Claude would ask what she was doing, she'd walked to the house, ignoring the whisper that said Edgar was there, watching, but choosing not to believe her.

So it had gone the next evening. And all the evenings after.

What had possessed her to tell Edgar to leave? Almost instantly she'd realized it was unnecessary and foolish, but by then he'd disappeared. Standing behind the silo had become her daily penance for that mistake, though one that did nothing to ease her mind. Her only consolation was

that the dogs who'd followed Edgar had never turned up, which meant
they were still out there. Which meant he was safe. She drew a ragged
breath, thinking of it: he was all that remained of her family, and he was
somewhere.

But sometimes Trudy couldn't help imagining that Edgar had returned, just once, on an evening when she'd found no excuse to be outside and he'd lost hope and set off for good. What came into her mind at
those times was the image of a black seed, grown now into a vine with
stems and leaves of perfect black—an image from those days long ago
that followed her last miscarriage.

(The night was hot. Her thoughts had begun to drift on a plane between reverie and sleep; circling, eddying. She gave herself over to them,
a lucid passenger in her own mind.)

She and Gar had been so certain everything was okay with the pregnancy. Afterward, there had been in her a void, a raw, sunlight-scraped
center—something atrocious that muttered how simple it would be to
fall down the stairs. To find a quiet place on the river and walk in. Eating
had been like pouring sand into her mouth. Sleep a suffocation. Relief
came only when she turned inward and embraced that place. The decision was indulgent and self-pitying, yes, but time passed there in such
a soothing contraction. When she opened her eyes, it was morning. Gar
was holding a cup of coffee for her. When he walked away she closed her
eyes and then it was another morning, and the day had passed.

Each hour spent like that poisoned her, she'd thought, yet the sensation was irresistible, enthralling, equal parts dread and desire. She'd roused
herself, finally, out of a perversely selfish concern for Gar, because a retreat
to that black center would provide her no peace if he were dragged down
too. She'd forced herself out of bed and gone downstairs. Gar had been
almost giddy. He'd left her alone on the porch and returned cradling that
feral pup, so chilled it barely drew breath, black and gray and brown in
his hands, eyes glittering, feet scuffling against his palm. And that was
the first thing to move her—the first tangible thing—since the stillbirth.
From the moment she touched the nursling she'd known it wouldn't survive, but just as certainly had known they would have to try.

The crib had been ready for weeks. Live or die, she wanted the pup to decide there. For those preparations to have some purpose. When Almondine woke her in the night, she'd leaned over the wooden rails and carried the pup to the rocking chair and set it in the folds of her robe. She'd rocked and watched the pup. Did it have its own black place? she wondered. It wasn't injured. Could it simply choose to live? And if it wanted to die, why did it struggle so? She traced the tines of its ribs, the pinfeather fur of its belly. Somehow a bargain was articulated between them; Trudy was unsure how that had happened, only that it was so. Then the pup closed its eyes and gave a last, infinitesimal sigh.

It was one thing to live in a world where death stood a distant figure, quite another to hold it in your hands, and Trudy had held it now twice within a month. She thought that night she'd made a pact with death itself: she could stay if she allowed death to stay as well. In choosing life, she embraced contradiction. The night passed. By the time Gar found them the next morning, a great swell of sorrow had risen in her and receded and in its wake the black place had been reduced to a grain.

Afterward she poured her life into the few of them there—into Gar, into Almondine, into the dogs and their training. She locked away that shriveled particle, ignoring and submerging it under feverish work. Years passed. Edgar was born, a never-ending mystery to them all, it seemed, except the dogs. Trudy seldom thought about that night. She came to believe that the black place had left her and to remember with the full force of her imagination would only call it back.

She'd been wrong. After Gar's funeral, when the pneumonia was at its peak, that tiny seed appeared again in her sleep. Its hull cracked. From the fissure a thread sprouted, delicate as silk. It vanished like a skittish animal the next morning. But her deepest fever dreams were yet to come, and in them she coaxed that tendril out. It circled her hips, her waist, her breasts. It wove itself through her hair and across her face until it bound her up, every inch of it velvety black. A comfort at first. Then she woke one morning to discover the tendrils had become a cage. There was a moment of panic before she remembered how it worked; and then she drew a breath and turned toward it.

She'd made some decisions during the time that followed, bad decisions, possibly. She'd convinced herself that Edgar's resentment toward Claude would lessen. Now she wondered if that hadn't played a part in Edgar's staying away. She could not look directly at this thought, or the thought that Edgar might never return. Such things could be examined only in the periphery of her mind. Such were the contradictions she'd learned to live with. In July, Claude arranged placements for two of Edgar's litter—Opal and Umbra, the ones Edgar called "the twins"—but when the time came, Trudy balked. Had grown hysterical, in fact, at any diminishment of her son's presence. The placements were canceled. To placate everyone, she agreed to let two pups go instead. Something they had never done before.

(In the bedroom, Claude had returned. He sat on the edge of the mattress, unbuttoning his shirt. She sighed and turned away.)

For weeks after the pneumonia she forced herself out to the kennel, pretending to be recovering. No, not pretending—she *was* recovering, in her body. In the mornings, after Edgar boarded the school bus, the silence in the barn was intolerable. Playing music, even worse. Almondine found her and curled up and slept nearby, a comfort, but the bed called to her so strongly, the weight of her encumbrance was so great that by midmorning most days she was in the house exhausted and asleep.

One day, just after noon, Claude's Impala appeared at the end of the driveway. Trudy watched from the porch as he swung open the barn door and walked inside. She sat in the living room and waited. Finally, she went to the barn. She found him weighing a pup and making notes. He looked at her but said nothing. That entire first week passed almost wordlessly between them except for small questions, immediate problems. Trudy didn't welcome Claude's presence, and she couldn't hide that; she wanted to ask him to leave, but she knew she needed the help. Each day, before Edgar came home, Claude got into his car and drove off, sometimes with no more than a sidelong "G'bye." Twice, when she looked up, he was simply gone.

That Saturday, when Claude didn't show up, all she felt was relief. By midafternoon on Sunday she found herself looking out the window. The Impala appeared again late Monday morning. Trudy lay in bed, unable to rouse herself. Then, anger. What was it he wanted? Silent or not, Claude kept coming for a reason. But she needed to be left alone. What little energy she could muster was spent stumbling through the chores and looking after Edgar. She stalked to the barn. Claude was kneeling on the floor of the medicine room. The drawers and cabinets all stood open. Vials of pills and stainless-steel scissors and packages of gauze and bottles of Phisohex and Betadine surrounded him. She intended to ask him to leave but instead blurted out a question.

"Just tell me this. Do you miss him?"

Claude stood and looked at her and licked his lips. He took a breath deep enough to make his shoulders rise.

"No," he said. And then, after a pause: "I remember him, though. I remember him just like he was."

She had expected some facile lie. She'd *hoped* for that; it would make it easier to tell Claude to leave. But he'd spoken the words as if offering a gift of some kind. A reparation. In the silence that followed, she thought he might even apologize for his answer (that would be false, too), but he simply waited. His posture, and the look in his eyes, said he would go if she asked. She still didn't understand what he was doing, but he wasn't trying to force his presence on her. He was coming, she thought, for some purpose of his own, to assuage some memory or feeling connected with Gar. Or maybe he was making amends for *not* grieving his brother's death.

"If you're going to keep coming out, you could at least ask me what needs to be done," she said.

"What, then?"

The first thing that came to mind was that the medicine room was a disaster, that it needed to be thoroughly cleaned, the expired medicines discarded, reorganized. But they were standing in the middle of it, and he was already engaged in exactly that.

"One of Alice's tires went flat over the winter," she said.

"All right. What else?"

"Nothing. Everything."

"Leave the pens in the morning," he said. "I'll clean them when I come out."

WHAT HAPPENED WAS THIS: when Trudy felt most vulnerable, she had seen in Claude a chance to anchor herself, to stop the backward slide that, alone, she could not check. She asked him to recall something of Gar.

"What do you want to know?"

"Anything. Tell me the first thing you remember about him. Your earliest memory."

His eyes fluttered briefly and he looked away.

"You might not like it," he said. "I knew a different Gar than you."

"That's okay," she said. "Just tell me." But inside, she thought: *I hope so. If you knew the same Gar, we're both lost.*

"If you really want to know, what I remember is a snowstorm," he said. "The start of a blizzard—the first one I'd ever seen. I couldn't have been more than three years old, because seeing that much snow falling was a shock. We were standing in the living room looking out the window, across the backyard and down the field. Everything began to disappear—first the trees at the bottom of the field, then the whole field, and then even the barn. I got the idea that the world had changed forever. It got me so excited I wanted to go outside. I remember wanting to see how many snowflakes I could grab in my hand. Whether I could follow one of them all the way down to the ground and see it land. I wanted to taste one. I didn't understand that it would be cold and I couldn't see why Gar stopped me. Except, now that I think about it, he didn't care about the cold. What he cared was that no one—"

"—put tracks in the snow," she whispered.

Claude looked surprised and nodded.

"That's right. He told me how, if we waited until morning, we'd wake up and be amazed. The truck would have disappeared. The barn would be an igloo. But only if we didn't trample the snow while it was falling. But I'd latched onto the idea that something tremendous was happening—that some force had been let loose, and by morning it would all be back to normal—and I started to run. Next thing I know, he's standing between me and the kitchen door, pushing me back and yelling."

Yes, she thought. All those thunderstorms with Gar standing in the doorway of the barn, watching the sky. A knot inside her relaxed. Claude

hadn't known a different Gar, just a younger one. She laughed. Unbelievably, she *laughed*. Later she'd cried, of course, the way a person cries when
a salve is finally applied to a burn. But most miraculous of all, she'd
rested that night for the first time since Gar had died.

The next day she called to Claude from the porch door and poured
him coffee. She'd asked whether they had ended up going out into the
snow after all, or had they waited until morning. She felt she was tread-
ing some dangerous ground, that if she pulled too hard (and that was
her instinct—to seize the thread of story Claude had offered and yank it
with all her might) it would silence him. A seduction of sorts began. Yes:
sexual. He wanted that more than she, but she wasn't unwilling. They
weren't exactly trading one thing for the other. True, sometimes when
she ran out of questions, she found herself leading him into the bedroom,
and there was always an element of gratitude about the act. But there was
selfishness as well. And at night, she slept. She blissfully slept.

The irony was, the more Claude's memories of Gar released her from
the haunting she felt, the more they'd occupied Claude. By listening
to his stories, Trudy was finally able to say goodbye—goodbye to the
young Gar, the teenaged Gar, the Gar she had never known but had,
somehow, expected to know. Claude spoke about his older brother in a
clear-eyed, unsentimental tone. She learned things that only a brother
could know, particularly a younger brother who had grown up in Gar's
shadow, studying him, copying him, worshipping him, and fighting
horrendously with him.

How could she explain any of that to Edgar? How could she say that she
needed Claude because Claude knew Gar and wasn't destroyed by his death?
How could she say that when she missed Gar most she talked to Claude and
he told her stories and for a moment, she remembered, *really remembered*, that
Gar had existed. How could she explain that she could get out of bed in the
morning if there was a chance she might touch Gar again?

AND SLOWLY, SHE LEARNED about Claude. The great distracter. He
took an almost malevolent pleasure in tempting the dogs while she
trained them. One day, when she was proofing recalls, he walked across

the yard with a cardboard box filled with squirrels—not that she knew it at the time. When the dogs had crossed halfway to her, he yanked open a flap and three gray streaks shot across the lawn. The dogs had wheeled and chased.

"Okay," she said, laughing. "How'd you do *that*?"

"Ah. Ancient Chinee secwet," he said.

Claude's gift—if that's what it could be called—was all the more baffling for its effortlessness. He seemed to know every human recreation within a day's drive. Unsolicited, people bore news to him of celebrations, large or small. Everything from the feed mill codgers' plan to sample the diner's new meat loaf to baseball games and back-alley fights. That very evening they had set out to buy groceries in Park City and ended up at, of all things, a wedding reception in someone's backyard, the friend of a cousin of a man Claude had once met at The Hollow. Just for an hour, Claude had promised, though it had been close to midnight when they'd driven home. As an orphan, handed from relation to relation a half dozen times before she was twelve, Trudy could wield an insular self-reliance, but how could she not be charmed when a group of near-strangers welcomed them—people she'd lived among for all these years but had never met. How could that be?

Comparing Claude and Gar was a bad idea, she knew, but in this way they were such opposites. Gar had, if anything, repelled commotion, even happy commotion, in favor of a passionate orderliness. Those breeding records—so many drawers overflowing with log sheets, photographs, notes, pedigrees—Gar *loved* them. He'd believed as fervently in the power of breeding as she believed in training—that there was nothing in a dog's character that couldn't be adapted to useful work. Not changed, but accommodated and, ultimately, transformed. That was what people didn't understand. Unless they had worked long and hard at it, most people thought training meant forcing their will on a dog. Or that training required some magical gift. Both ideas were wrong. Real training meant watching, listening, diverting a dog's exuberance, not suppressing it. You couldn't change a river into a sea, but you could trace a new channel for it to follow. This was a debate she and Gar had cheerfully never resolved. Gar claimed her training successes proved that his records, properly interpreted, brought each new generation of pups closer to some ideal, even if he could not put that ideal into words. Trudy knew better. The training had, if anything, gotten *more* difficult over the years.

But Claude paid those files scant attention. To him, they were nothing more than a means to an end. He was more interested in catching the eye of the Carruthers catalog people after the branch kennel arrangement fell through with Benson, the man from Texas, who'd witnessed enough the night Edgar had run to be apprehensive instead of enthusiastic.

Perhaps the diversions were no accident. Whenever she began to brood, Claude practically leapt to draw her away, toward wine and music, things immediate and uncomplicated. A movie in Ashland. Back road drives through bosky glades. A walk by the falls, where the Bad River crashed through granite sluices with an engulfing roar. She'd given in to that last idea more than once; standing on the footbridge across that gray chasm, he'd produced a flask of brandy and they'd watched the water clench its fist in the air and drop away. After he'd taken a few turns at the brandy, he'd murmured, "Mid these dancing rocks at once and ever, it flung up momently the sacred river. Five miles meandering with a mazy motion, through wood and dale the sacred river ran, then reached the caverns measureless to man, and sank in tumult to a lifeless ocean."

He moved the old record player from the workshop to the house. He loved music of any kind—Big Band, Elvis, the Rolling Stones. Only classical music bored him with its orderly sterility. Most especially, he adored *voices*—crying, pleading, laughing voices—and the great melodious singers were his favorites, whether they radiated unrestrained longing or sultry indifference. He liked Frank Sinatra for his brute power. He liked Eydie Gormé for her bright untouchability. ("Blame It on the Bossa Nova" got him ridiculously worked up.) But he held a special fondness for crooners—Perry Como for example, or Mel Tormé, whom Trudy despised. Whenever Claude dropped the needle on a Mel Tormé record he'd announce, in a hushed voice, "It's the Velvet Fog!" and give Trudy a wide-eyed stare, as if they'd found themselves trapped in a scene from a horror movie. But that was Claude—tricking her into laughing precisely because she resisted. It made her a little angry, though she ended up wishing he'd do it again, like a girl clapping and crying out for the magician to release another dove from his sleeve. Only with Claude, the dove seemed to come from inside *her*.

(She was in that twilight of quarter-consciousness where notions crack and drift like floes of ice. Claude lay behind her, solid, heavy, hot. She was glad he had checked the kennel. The first news she would have to give Edgar was of Almondine; how vulnerable he would be to it. She must call Glen Papineau tomorrow. But if there'd been news, he would have driven out to tell them in person. And she had to be careful; every time she asked, she chanced making the connection between Edgar and Page's accident stronger in Glen's mind.)

Edgar

H E SAT BY ALMONDINE'S GRAVE AND LOOKED AT THE HOUSE and the oversize barn, wondering if everything that was happening was by dint of his own imagination, though he knew it wasn't so, just as he'd known well enough that night in the rain what was real and what was not. He thought about the first night Claude had stayed with them, how he and Almondine had snuck into the barn. How they'd found Claude asleep in the mow, but not really asleep. Looking up into the rafters.

"This is just how I remembered it," he'd said. "Your dad and I knew every nook and cranny. We hid cigarettes up here, liquor even. The old man knew it was there somewhere but he was too proud to look for it."

One time, they'd opened up a wall in the house and discovered Schultz's writing hidden inside. And once, Edgar had found a loose section of floorboard near the front of the mow that lifted away. Beneath it lay a space big enough for a pack of cigarettes or a flask of whiskey. The only contents had been a lace of cobwebs and a bottle cap and at the time he'd thought nothing of it.

A bottle cap.

Someone had once hidden a bottle there.

My gramma's like me. Wanna know what my gramma says?

He tried to remember if he'd ever looked under that board since that first, strange conversation with Claude.

Do you think you can find that bottle? You need to look for that bottle. Unless you can lay hands on it, you need to go. That's what's in the juice.

He stood. The moon had risen late, haloed and dimming the nearby stars. Essay had trotted off, exploring in the moonlit field, but now he couldn't see her and he began to walk. When he neared the kennel, two dogs began to bay. The noise didn't worry him, so long as it was brief. He even felt a kind of dark thrill, knowing that, that night, it wasn't a deer wandering through the orchard that started them or an owl dropping onto a rabbit in the long grass.

He opened the rear kennel doors. A rectangle of moonlight skewed across the aisle and his shadow in it. Before he'd run off he could have walked into the barn in the dead of night and the dogs wouldn't have uttered a sound, but they were on the verge of an uproar now. He groped his way to the medicine room, felt his irises shrink when he flicked the light switch up. He went down the line, crouching in front of their pens and touching them, looking at the catchlights in their eyes and signing, *quiet*. When they were calm he found a flashlight in the workshop and extinguished the light in the medicine room. He stood at the back doors looking for Essay, but she was nowhere to be seen and he pulled the doors shut.

In the dark he heard a dull electromechanical buzz. He shined the flashlight beam up the aisle until it stopped on a telephone mounted on one of the thick posts. They had put an extension in the barn, but the crosstalk ring was the same as ever. He lifted the receiver to his ear. Beneath the dial tone, a faint conversation, two strange voices, a man and a woman.

He walked to the workshop and climbed the steps, forcing himself past the spot where Doctor Papineau had lain. The mow still trapped the day's heat. The rear third was stacked with fresh straw, bales all the way to the trusses. The smell would have been lovely under different circumstances. It reminded him of all the time he'd spent there, bales shoved into makeshift corrals, rolling pups until their hind legs kicked, teaching them to sit for the slicker brush and the nail clippers, or paging through the dictionary for names.

He started searching near the vestibule doorway, swinging the beam of the flashlight in downward-angled arcs and kicking straw aside until, near the far front corner, he spotted the stub of board he had in mind. One edge had been splintered by a screwdriver or a knife and he squatted and flicked open Henry's jackknife and wedged the blade into the slot before he noticed the nails at either end and the hammer strikes in the wood. He found a pry bar in the workshop. The board tipped up a quarter inch before the old wood gave way and the pry bar popped free. It was enough to raise the nail heads.

The hollow beneath the board was just as he'd remembered, a few inches of clear space floored by one of the broad main timbers, into which a dugout had been chiseled, and as empty as when he'd first discovered it. But the bottle cap and the cobwebs were absent. And there was another difference: a fresh set of chisel marks widened a stretch of the original cavity by half an inch or more on each side. Unlike the older, carefully made depression, whose surfaces were smooth and edges straight, the new indents looked chewed into the timber. He ran his fingers along the splinters. A few amber wood chips lay scattered across the old beam.

He tried to remember how that bottle had looked, clasped between him and Ida Paine. The stopper a crude blob of glass. The ribbon, with its indecipherable lettering. The oily contents licking the insides. He looked at his palm, measured the sensation of it against the chisel marks. He sat back and shone his flashlight against the staggered yellow wall of bales. Chaff drifted through the light. With the barn broom, he swept the straw back from the front wall and crossed the floor, tapping at boards. Dozens of hiding places, Claude had said. Edgar could work until sunrise and still not test them all.

The dogs in the back runs let out a volley of barks. He cracked open the mow door and looked down to find Essay trotting past. He ran down the mow stairs and opened the back doors and clapped for her until she trotted up from the dark. Then he led her to the pen with Finch and Pout and opened the door. Before he could sign anything, she walked in and the three of them settled into the straw.

In the medicine room he sloshed water around a coffee can and tossed the grit at the drain hole and refilled it and took a swallow and carried it with him back up to the mow. He tipped the board into its slot unnailed and kicked the loose straw around until it didn't look swept. The batteries in the flashlight had begun to fail. He flicked it off and shook it and waited and pushed the thumb switch forward again. The filament came on yellow, then dimmed back to ember-orange. It was enough light to climb the stacked bales by. Once on top, he wedged the flashlight into the crook of a rafter and wrestled bales around until he'd created a hollow and he settled in and switched off the flashlight. In the dark, the heat in the rafters congealed around him. He had to force himself to take a breath.

After a long time, swallows began to trill from their nests in the eaves. The first cicadas cried out their complaint. Far away, the porch door creaked and two of the dogs called out. The doors at the front of the barn rattled as they were hooked open. Then Claude's voice, echoing through the kennel. Edgar wondered how long it would take before he discovered Essay. When light began to show through the cracks beneath the eaves he tipped the coffee can to his mouth. The water tasted of iron and dust and blood. Finally he slept, but it was a cursed sleep. Every sound jerked him awake. Chaff covered him like ash. With every movement came some new scratch or bite, and he drifted in and out of consciousness, not knowing what else to do besides wait.

Glen Papineau

IT HADN'T HAPPENED EXACTLY THE WAY CLAUDE PREDICTED, BUT once the seed of the idea was planted, Glen found himself brooding over Edgar Sawtelle.

Claude had worried about him filing a lawsuit, but that was the furthest thing from Glen's mind. The fact was, over the last several months, Claude had turned out to be a pretty nice guy, a fine friend. Dragging them into court wouldn't be right. They were nearly as busted up over his father's death as he was, plus they had a runaway to worry about. Anything bad a person could wish on them had already happened, and worse.

No, the way it worked in his mind was, suppose Edgar did turn up? Suppose Glen walked into his office one morning and a description of the boy *had* come over the wires? Would he call the Sawtelles straight off? Or would he want to check it out first? That seemed like the humane thing—verify it before he got their hopes up. It depended on where Edgar turned up, of course. A lot of runaways stuck surprisingly close to home, which for Edgar meant Ashland, Superior, Eau Claire, or one of the dozens of small towns in between—an easy run to fetch him. Glen could even imagine going as far as Madison, though much beyond that and Edgar might as well be in California.

Yet . . . suppose it was nearby? Suppose the officer who called him was a small-town cop like Glen and Glen could just walk in and say, "Yep, that's him." That would be the right way to do it—identify the kid in person before making calls, avoid any confusion and a bad false alarm for Trudy. He'd make small talk, they'd sign custody over, and after that it would be just Glen and Edgar in the squad car. Of course, he'd deliver Edgar safe and sound, but that didn't mean he couldn't stop to ask a couple of questions. Discuss what had happened in that mow. Find out, one way or another.

It was natural for Glen to imagine that conversation taking place in the squad car because he did his very best thinking there, right behind the wheel, with the trees and fields and houses sliding across the windshield. He liked to let his mind wander a bit. One thing that really bugged him was the notion that other officers—and he used that word with a grain of salt, because it implied a certain dignity and honor they didn't all have—mocked him. He had a nickname, he knew, something hung on him since childhood. Ox. He *hated* it when people called him that. After graduating from Mellen High, he thought he'd left it behind, but somehow the trainees at the academy in Madison had found out. His looks didn't help. People took one glance and thought, "That must be the one they call 'Ox,'" practically mouthing the words. Before long, someone saw him in his blues, and that cemented his fate, that memorable but tenuous connection to Paul Bunyan, or rather, to his beast of burden: Babe the Blue Ox.

The name didn't bother him so much as the implication that he was clumsy or stupid. But most people saw what they wanted to see. Little skinny guys looked smart. Big guys looked dumb. Even police officers, trained to see past appearances, fell into that trap. When they saw Babe the Blue Ox coming, they saw dumb, and any little mistake became emblematic.

For example, the interview with the boy. At a staff meeting in Ashland he'd let slip that Trudy had translated Edgar's answers rather than having the kid write them out, and people had actually guffawed. Like, there goes Ox Papineau, doing the dumbest thing you could imagine. What they didn't understand was that his pop had spent the night with the Sawtelles. He'd stopped by the office that morning ahead of them and said, in no uncertain terms, to make it quick, that Trudy and her son were wrecked, barely functioning. There wasn't any use forcing Edgar to relive the experience and it might very well do damage. So Glen had promised he'd keep it to the point.

Plus, the night before the boiler had gone on the fritz, and he'd spent every spare minute that morning convincing it to work. When the time came for the interview, he maybe hadn't been as prepared as he would have liked. Yes, he'd had Annie type it up and run it out for them to sign, but that didn't stop the wingnuts in Ashland from re-enacting the scene, one of them asking questions, another waving his arms around in reply, a third spewing preposterous interpretations. It had gotten so that any time he asked a question, they launched into mock-sign while some wise guy leaned over and whispered, "He says he didn't do it." Which cracked them all up: stupid old Babe the Blue Ox.

So whenever he dwelt on the idea of questioning Edgar again, his spirits lifted. Not in an entirely nice way. When he was patrolling, with nothing much else going through his mind, he imagined glancing in his rearview mirror and seeing Edgar sitting back there. And then Glen asking, what the hell *did* happen up in that mow, Edgar? This is my father we're talking about. I have a right to know. That's all I want: to hear what happened.

And then, in Glen's imagination, Edgar Sawtelle did something he'd never, ever done before: he replied out loud.

He said, "I'm sorry." That was it, just "I'm sorry."

In Glen's imagination, the boy's voice was as gravelly as an old man's, because it had never been used. The gratifying thing was, Edgar had chosen to speak those first words to Glen because he knew he had contributed to, if not caused, Pop's death. *That* showed true remorse.

Once that little movie got into Glen's head, it stuck like a burr. He began to rehearse it in all kinds of places. Sometimes they were alone on a country road, without a farmhouse or a car for miles; sometimes he had just parked the cruiser in front of the town hall—a last-chance-before-we-go-inside kind of scene. Sometimes they were caught in traffic in Ashland. But wherever it happened to be, Glen always looked up in his mirror and asked his question, and always, Edgar Sawtelle answered out loud.

Glen had even begun to say his own part out loud as he drove.

"What the hell happened up there, Edgar? I'm asking because I'm his son and I have a right to know."

The first time it felt silly and he blushed. Despite himself, he looked to see if the mike key wasn't somehow, freakishly, depressed and he'd been transmitting. (He could see the reenactments of *that* in the locker room in Ashland.) But it was okay, totally private. And cathartic. He did it again. Even picked up the mike, pretended to key it, and asked his question, letting his eyes burn into the mirror. Sometimes he emphasized "son," sometimes "know." He finally settled on a version with emphasis on both, but just a little more on "son," to make it clear he was speaking as a family member and not as a police officer.

All of that was very satisfying.

Less satisfying was that no one answered.

And that was where things stood for a couple weeks. Then, like a man shaking himself out of a dream, he understood he was being compulsive and bizarre and had to stop. It was a little too much like some other activities he could name: you shouldn't do them, even if they felt good. Nobody had to tell you that. You just *knew* it wasn't healthy.

In order to purge himself, he'd decided to talk to Claude. This time Claude had come to Glen's house. They'd sat in the living room and talked until the wee hours. After enough beer (and "enough," for Glen, had come to mean a twelve-pack as the summer went along; he'd stopped going to The Kettle or The Hollow, had even started driving to Ashland to stock up) he'd stammered out the basics of his little scenario.

Confiding in Claude turned out to be the right decision. Claude said two things. First, he was beginning to think that Edgar wasn't going to come back. If he'd been gone that long—almost two months—he must be pretty committed to staying away. By then he could have made it to Canada, Mexico, or either ocean. Second, and more important, he'd thought Glen's response was totally reasonable. After all, did Glen want to hurt Edgar? Certainly not. He just wanted to put the question to him, didn't he? Hadn't they both lost a father in the last year? Wouldn't *Edgar* want to ask the same question if someone knew what had happened to *his* father? Damn right he would. When you looked at it that way, even Edgar could hardly begrudge Glen a single goddamned question when the tables were turned. In fact, the longer they talked, the more it seemed that if Edgar *did* show up, Claude would have no objection to Glen taking the boy for a ride before he came home. If that could be arranged. Which seemed possible, since, if he was coming home, it was probably going to be escorted by a cop.

Of course, he could always hitchhike back home, Glen said.

Even then, Claude mused, maybe something could be arranged. Claude could call, let Glen know Edgar had shown up. They'd installed a phone in the barn that summer—he could just wander out, pick up the handset. And some night when Trudy was out, Glen could swing over. Claude would look the other way. They agreed it wasn't ideal; it would be better if Glen asked his question before Edgar got home. (Because, Glen thought, what if the answer were something more than "I'm sorry?" Then they'd have to take a ride to the tank in Ashland, go through the whole sorry juvenile justice meat grinder, which, by the way, meant that he walked away with a clean record at eighteen, no matter what. Which some people might find a little unfair.)

Glen had fretted over the logistics of it. How exactly would he get the boy into his car if he were already home? He didn't think he could just *talk* Edgar into going for a ride. In fact, he'd probably fight like the dickens to avoid it, and fighting a kid hadn't been part of the movie in his head. Because what those idiots up in Ashland didn't understand was that "Ox" Papineau valued finesse over strength. Even in his wrestling days, lunging against three-hundred-pound behemoths with their hands hooked behind his neck, finesse always won out over simple strength. He'd tied guys into knots with finesse. And those skills hadn't gone to waste, either. Just the other day he'd used them when Mack Holgren, fighting with his wife again, decided to swing on Glen.

Plus, in Glen's imagination, one of the reasons the boy was willing to talk straight—was willing to talk at *all*—was that just being in the car made it clear how explaining himself would get him home. Glen wouldn't say that, of course; that's why it was finesse.

But if the boy was *already* home . . .

Glen had been puzzling aloud on that one when Claude grinned a funny, nasty little grin and held out a freshly uncapped bottle of beer. Something about the gesture set Glen at ease, because if there was one thing Claude Sawtelle understood, it was the nature of camaraderie. Claude leaned back in his chair. He took a long swallow of beer and looked over at Glen.

"Have I ever explained to you," he said, "about Prestone?"

WHEN CLAUDE CALLED THAT NIGHT all he'd said was that Edgar had left a note on their kitchen table. Claude didn't know if the kid had stolen a car or what. Most likely he'd hitchhiked home and was hiding in the woods somewhere. The note said he was coming back the next day, so if Glen was going to ask his question like they'd talked about, he needed to get on the stick.

Then he was faced with it: all those times he'd imagined Edgar sitting in the back of the squad car. During the day. In the country. In town. Now it looked like it was going to be out in the country, and at night.

If he acted on it at all. With the opportunity staring him in the face, Glen wasn't sure it was such a hot idea. Claude had pretty much read his thoughts.

"Sounds kind of dumb now, doesn't it?"

"Yeah," Glen admitted. "Oddball thing to do, at least."

"Well, no one would blame you if you didn't," Claude said. "You're the only one who has to live with it, either way. It's just, I've been thinking, and I don't see how it could work once he's home. If you've ever seen Trudy when she's riled up—"

"—oh, yes."

"Then you know what would happen. When we talked, it seemed like you could just come over and take him, but now I'm thinking we were unrealistic. Could be, if you want a chance to talk with him, this is it."

Glen admitted he probably was right about that as well.

"So. What do you think, then?" Claude asked.

Glen was quiet for a long time. "Did he say where he was going?"

"No. Just, 'I ate while you were gone. I'll be back tomorrow.' I'm looking at the note right now."

"What did you tell Trudy?"

"What do you *think* I told her?"

"Oh. Well, it can't hurt to take a little drive around, I guess."

Then Claude hung up and Glen stood, receiver in hand, listening to the off-hook stutter tone begin. He thought about the Prestone trick that Claude had explained, something he'd never heard of, but of course Prestone was almost pure ether. And Glen knew just where there was a supply of true, medical-grade ether. That made him smile, because he liked the idea of one-upping Claude just a little bit. Somewhere along the line, Glen had acquired a beat-up old whiskey flask, a good-sized one with a pull-off top, and he pocketed that now and headed out the door.

He parked the cruiser in the grass around back of the shop, unlocked the side door, and walked past the shrouded furniture and examination tables. He opened the door to the little closet pharmacy. He didn't have to look around. In his mind's eye he'd already located what he wanted, up on the top shelf: three tins, sitting in a row, each topped by a squat mushroom-shaped cap. The labels were printed in cream and brown:

Ether Squibb

For Anesthesia U. S. P.

1/4 lb.

POISON

Below that, in broad green script, the words "Copper protected!" were inscribed. Glen was a little surprised Claude hadn't commented on those little cans the night he'd perused the pharmacy. They were an oddity, for certain, and Claude didn't miss much. But then, Claude hadn't grown up a veterinarian's son. Perhaps he didn't know what he was seeing.

Glen pulled a can off the shelf and gathered a few other supplies and took them outside, locking the door behind. The stuff was potent—you didn't want to mess with it indoors unless you had the ventilation equipment roaring, or you could knock yourself into outer space. He pulled the whiskey flask from his back pocket, twisted off the cap, then punctured the mushroom cap on the ether with the cruiser's ignition key and began pouring the ether into the flask. It dripped and gulped out, silvery clear as water. He set the tin down and widened the hole, but even then, without a funnel, it took a good long time before he was done.

He wasn't so dumb as to think the whiskey flask wouldn't leak vapor, but he knew a little trick from his pop. He'd snagged a surgical rubber glove on the way out, and now he stretched it over the neck of the flask and twisted the cap down, pinching the material tight. Then he peeled away the excess until just a little skirt of rubber remained below the cap.

He waved the flask under his nose. The good thing about ether was you could smell right away if it got loose on you. But his improvised rubber glove seal worked fine. Only the faintest whiff came to him, the residue of a single drip, quickly evaporating off the warm metal. A flowery petroleum odor that tingled in the back of his sinuses. He pitched the ether tin into the woods and carried the flask two-fingered to the squad car and set it on the passenger side of the broad front seat.

GLEN KNEW THOSE BACK ROADS pretty well. If he kept an eye out, he thought, he might come across the kid walking along the road or cutting through a field. He could also cruise the roads near their place looking for suspiciously parked vehicles. If it wasn't a couple of high school kids necking, it might be Edgar, sleeping in a car he'd stolen.

He tried approaching from the south first, but there was no Edgar walking along, no cars parked in any of the dozen little pull-offs that hunters liked to use. At the hill near the Sawtelles', Glen made a three-point turn and headed back to the highway, then came around from the north. All he saw was Jasper Dillon's truck, broken down near the old Mellen cemetery, where it had sat for the better part of two weeks. He stopped and shone his flashlight across the dusty bed of the truck and through the window, in case Edgar was using the truck as shelter for the night, but the only thing the cab contained was a greasy toolbox and two crushed packages of Marlboros. He walked back to the squad car and pulled away. Then he was coming up on the Sawtelles' yard, close enough to see the light at the top of their orchard. He parked about fifty yards back from where the woods cleared, pocketed the flask, a couple of rags and a flashlight, and set off.

Keeping to the far side of the gravel road, he walked the length of the yard. A dog was running loose, circling the barn in silence. Before it could spot him, he turned and cut down along the fence line north of the house. When he reached the back of their garden he found a little path worn into the woods. In the open, the late moon had given plenty of light, but once in the woods Glen had to flick the slider up on the flashlight and swing the beam to and fro across the tangle of night-black foliage to see where he was going.

Within thirty yards he knew it was pointless. If Edgar were holed up in the woods, Glen would never walk up on him with a flashlight. Maybe if he was sound asleep with a fire blazing. But why would he do that if he planned to come back the next day? Why not just walk in, save himself the trouble? And even supposing he *was* in those woods, the Sawtelle place was, what, ninety acres, a hundred? Glen could search for a week in broad daylight and never find him.

He turned and retraced his route. When he reached the road again, he stood looking at the house. Either he's in that barn, Glen thought, or he's miles from here. And there was no way of getting into the barn without the dogs raising Cain. It wasn't going to work.

He crunched along the gravel toward the squad car. Something told him he shouldn't drive past the Sawtelle place, having already taken so much trouble to avoid it. With the headlights off, he pulled another three-point turn and headed toward Mellen. Maybe he would patrol a few more back roads on the way home.

The moon was bright. The underbrush leaned into the road, green and hypnotic as it flowed past the high beams; red-lanterned eyes looked back from the tangle just often enough to break the pattern, keep him alert. Only after his breath came easier did he realize he'd been panting. To stop, he forced himself to sigh.

When he reached the blacktop, the cruiser picked up enough speed to level out the potholes and float along through the night. Tendrils of fog drifted palely across the road, condensing on the windshield like a kind of dream writing that he let accumulate and then erased with a swipe of the wiper blades. All of that put him at ease. After a while he couldn't help but glance into his rearview mirror.

With great earnestness, almost bashfully, Glen let himself ask his question, out loud, one last time.

Edgar

HE TRACKED THE MORNING KENNEL ROUTINE BY SOUND FROM his hiding place, high in the mow. The August sun beat against the barn roof and the atmosphere near the rafters squeezed beads of sweat from his skin. To pass the time, he counted the points of the roofing nails hammered through the new planking and thought how in days past he had instead counted bright pinholes through the roofing boards. Light seeped around the edges of the mow door, filling the space with a dilute, perpetual dawn. By midmorning his mother had worked the two pups, then the six-month-olds and the yearlings, and rotated back to the pups. Edgar could close his eyes and hear her cajoling them in a low, even voice, see her crazywalk the little ones, ask for retrieves of the others, always testing, proofing, asking what it meant and didn't mean to stay, watch, recall, follow. He drifted into a half-sleep suffused by those sounds, as if he himself had grown to envelop the mow and the barn and the yard. There was the slap of the porch door as Claude went inside. The twinning ring of the telephones both below and in the kitchen. The jays bickering among the ripening apples. A car idling along the road, gravel crunching under its tires as it passed the tree line by the garden.

Near noon there was a restrained clomp of feet on the mow steps, but he didn't fully wake until the vestibule door had already swung open. He flattened himself into the hollow in the bales, sweat streaming from his face. There was a long silence. Then the door closed and there were descending footsteps. Below, the sliding gates banged shut to lock out the dogs while Claude cleaned the pens. Edgar sat up and drank from the coffee can, resisting his body's plea to pour the water over his face. After a while he crawled to where the roofing boards converged with the walls in the corner and rose on his knees and released a stream of urine and watched it disappear into the straw.

When he could no longer endure the heat and cramped quarters, he clambered down the staggered cliff of bales through strata of cooling air, his legs trembling for fear of making noise and from being broiled so long. As soon as he touched the floor, he sank onto a bale. In the rafters above, like a great trapped beast, he could feel the heat he had escaped, waiting for him, and he sucked gulps of the cool, habitable air into his lungs and let his blood cool and the sweat dry on his skin. But before a minute had passed, he grew convinced that he had betrayed his presence somehow, that Claude must be standing below, looking at the ceiling and listening.

Just until sunset, he told himself.

He drew a slick forearm across his face and climbed back into the furnace.

IN THE AFTERNOON THE vestibule door opened and Claude walked into the open space at the front of the mow.

"Edgar?" he said, softly. Then, after a long pause, "Edgar?"

Edgar pressed himself into the hollow in the bales and held his breath. When the pounding in his head was too much to bear, he allowed himself an exhalation so measured he thought he might suffocate. There were footsteps on straw. A tremor shook the stack of bales. Something heavy thumped to the floor. The bales shook again, and there was another thump. For one protracted moment Edgar was sure Claude had begun tearing down the monolith of straw to get at him.

The shaking and thumping continued in a steady rhythm. Though there was barely enough room between the bales and the rafters, Edgar wormed his way forward. Claude was working by the long western wall, his head five or six feet below Edgar's. He wore a pair of canvas work gloves and he was dragging out bale after bale and letting them tumble to the floor. It wasn't easy—the bales were stacked one pair lengthwise over another crosswise so that no column could shear away. He'd already opened a semicircular cavity, deeper at the bottom than at the top, and his shirt was dark with sweat halfway down his back. Edgar could hear him gasping in the heat. When thirty or forty bales lay on the floor, he stopped and pulled the gloves off his hands and picked up a hammer from the floor and knelt in the cavity he'd created, half concealed from Edgar. There was the screech of a nail pulled from dry wood and a board clattering. Claude leaned back and rubbed his hands together as if reconsidering, then fetched his work gloves and put them on and shot his fingers together to seat them.

The thought crossed Edgar's mind to pitch a bale down. Forty or fifty pounds of densely packed straw, dropped from that height, could knock Claude flat. But what would that accomplish? He wouldn't stay down. Besides, Claude was already glancing uneasily toward the vestibule door; in such cramped quarters, long before Edgar could wrestle a bale to the edge and tip it over, Claude would hear and look up.

Then Claude was backing away from the bales. He set something small and glinting on the floor. A bottle, an old-time bottle, with a crude blob of glass for a stopper and a ribbon around the neck with black markings. Claude stood looking at it, as mesmerized as Edgar. Then he moved the bottle against the mow wall with a gloved hand and thrashed up a pile of loose straw to cover it. He began to restack the bales. Edgar retreated. Shortly, there were footsteps on the mow floor, the click of the vestibule door latch, and more footsteps on the stairs. Edgar waited for the sound of Claude's boots on the driveway, but all he heard was his mother's voice as she encouraged the pups in the yard. He elbowed forward. Claude hadn't bothered to wrestle the topmost bales into place. Near the floor, the stacks bulged from the otherwise neat stair step of yellow. Where

Claude had momentarily covered the bottle in straw, Edgar now saw only a stretch of bare planking.

He tipped the coffee can to his mouth and then climbed down, his body oily with sweat. He dragged away the bales Claude had moved. The wood plank was splintered where the nails had been pulled. He pressed the point of Henry's jackknife into the crack and pried it up. He didn't know what he expected to find. The hole was dry and empty, like the one he'd found the night before, though deeper. It could easily accommodate the bottle Claude had set aside—the bottle that had not been a figment of his imagination. Or of Ida Paine's.

It existed. He'd seen it, in daylight, if only for a moment.

He walked to the front wall and cracked open the mow door and pressed one eye to the gap, blinking against the midday brilliance. Fresh air poured across his face, hot from the August sun but soothingly cool after what he'd endured in the rafters. The mow door was hinged on the side nearest the house and he could see only downfield, where grasshoppers leapt like firecrackers ignited under the rays of the run.

Then Claude's footsteps sounded on the gravel. The truck started, idled alongside the barn, and stopped again. Edgar's mother called the pups. She would not keep them out for long in the heat, he thought. He listened for a moment, then shut the mow door and walked to the top of the stairs.

Trudy

WHEN TRUDY REACHED THE SHADE OF THE BARN, SHE TURNED and knelt and recalled the pups, then coaxed them down the long concrete aisle. They were too old to be sleeping in the whelping pens, but keeping four-month-olds there during the heat of August wasn't all bad. Pups that age still had a hard time regulating their body temperature, and didn't always have the sense to get out of the sun. The whelping rooms, sealed from the outside, were often the coolest part of the kennel.

She was latching their pen door when she felt his arms around her. She let out a brief pip of a cry before a hand clamped over her mouth and another was thrust in front of her face, fingerspelling like lightning.

Quiet. Only sign. Okay?

She nodded. He let go and stepped back and she turned to look at Edgar.

He stood holding a finger to his lips. His cheekbones jutted from his face and the line of his jaw swept so sharply toward his throat that he seemed to be made all of sinew and bone. His hair lay matted and sun-browned across his forehead and his ragged clothes reeked as though he'd

spent days in the barn. But his eyes were startlingly, almost preternatu-
rally, clear, looking steadily at her from a face lined by tracks of sweat cut
through dirt. The sight of him raced ahead of her thoughts, condensing
only afterward into distinct, namable feelings, as if her mind were accommodating too slowly the flash of a bright light: overwhelming relief,
knowing her son was safe; fury, for his punishingly long absence; bewil-
derment at his appearance, which spoke of a long, harrowing journey.
Before she could distill any of those thoughts into words, he was looking
past her, through the whelping room door and into the main kennel.

Where's Claude? he signed.

He's changing the oil in the truck. *Where have you been? Are you okay?*

He reached over and pulled the door closed.

I wasn't going to come back. I almost didn't.

But why? I signaled for you the very next morning. I told them you
ran because you were upset after what happened to your father.

They were looking for me.

Of course they were. You were a runaway. But it's all right now. I told
them it was an accident. She paused and corrected herself. It *was* an accident.

Did you find my note?

What note?

You were gone when I got here last night. I left a note on the table.

There was no note.

Claude found it, then.

She had to think for a minute about what that meant.

I need you to do something, he signed.

Just come to the house. Don't go away again.

If you do this, I promise to stay. But I need one night out here, alone.
After dark I need you to keep Claude in the house, no matter what.

Why?

Because he's hiding something here.

Claude?

Yes.

What would he hide?

He stared at her, as though trying to divine something.

What? What is it?

Have you seen him?

Claude?

No. In the rain. Have you seen him?

She blinked. She didn't know what Edgar was talking about. She shook her head. All this time she had imagined him coming back and everything being okay, but instead Almondine was gone and here was Edgar and he was obviously not okay. Not okay at all. He was starved and crazed.

Just come to the house.

I don't want him to know I was here.

You said he already knows.

Yes, but he doesn't know I was out here. Not in the barn.

Okay.

Don't cry. Take a breath.

Okay.

You can't tell him. If you tell him, I'll go away again. I swear it. I'll never come back. You'll never see me again.

She shook her head and signed, No, no.

You know I'll do it.

Yes.

You'll make sure he stays in the house after dark?

I could say I wanted a night away. We could go into town.

No. Keep him in the house.

What if I can't?

You have to. Turn the porch light on if you can't. Turn it on if I should stay away.

All right.

When this is done I'll come back for good, I promise.

Okay.

Then there was the slam of the truck door and Claude's footsteps along the kennel aisle. Edgar stepped into the nearest whelping pen and pressed up against the wall. The pups began to yip and leap.

"Everything good in there?" Claude called.

"You bet," Trudy said, taking a breath and trying to sound breezy. "Just teaching these wild things to sit for a brushing."

"Need a hand?"

"Nope. I'll shout if I do."

"Okay. Done with the truck in twenty minutes," he said. She heard Claude fetch something from the workshop and walk outside.

Edgar slipped out of the whelping pen.

I'll be back after dark, he signed. Remember, if the porch light is on, I'll stay away until tomorrow.

Edgar. There's something I need to tell you. Something bad.

He looked back at her.

I know. I was by the birches last night.

I'm so sorry, Edgar.

He shook his head and wiped his eyes roughly and pushed past her and looked down the barn aisle.

I put Essay in with Pout and Finch.

What?

She's in the run with Pout and Finch. Claude must have found her this morning when he fed them.

No. He would have told me.

He's hoping I'll leave again.

Before she had a chance to ask Edgar anything else, he slipped past and trotted out the rear doors. Trudy followed and stood at the threshold and watched him cut across the field and disappear into the thicket without breaking his stride. When she came back in, she stopped at one of the runs and rapped on the wood frame of the door. Finch and Pout pushed through the passageway from outside. A moment later, Essay joined them. The dogs had been watching Edgar leave as well.

Edgar

WHEN HE REACHED THE CREEK, HE PEELED OFF HIS SHIRT and submerged it in the cool shallows and wiped the sweat and chaff from his skin. It was hot, very hot, and the air was sticky-wet and he stood waiting while the beads of water evaporated. Then he walked to the vast dying oak at the far corner of their land, hoping to find Forte there. The tree stood black and vacant of leaves on all but a few high limbs. The moment he settled himself against its gnarled roots, he understood why the place had once appealed to the stray: from where he sat, Edgar had a clear view down the trail both ways. Neither the creek nor the road was visible, but a person approaching from either direction *would* be, and the trunk of the oak was broad enough to hide behind. But he didn't think he'd have to worry about that. Claude would have no reason to look for him in that spot over any other. He had never been along when Edgar and his father walked the fence line and he knew nothing of the tree's significance.

Edgar lay back and watched the mosaic of sky pass through the naked branches. In his mind the image of Doctor Papineau kept appearing, the old man twisted and dying at the bottom of the mow stairs. After all that had happened, it seemed far too much to wish that Doctor Papineau hadn't fallen, hadn't died, but Edgar thought how he would like to talk to Glen Papineau. He felt he couldn't stay unless he did that, but neither could he think of how to put his feelings into words. Regret was too simple. Woe, perhaps, was the closest thing. But it was a woe mingled with anger, and he didn't know what the word for that would be. And that wasn't right, anyway.

He thought, too, about what he'd said to his mother, and what he hadn't said as well. She had to believe he would run again if she didn't help, so he'd withheld what he knew she'd most wanted to hear—that he'd been so glad to see her; that touching her had nearly overwhelmed him. His memory of her had grown abstract while he'd been gone; the details of her face, the way she smelled, the vast, charismatic aura of *her*. He'd desperately wanted to tell her what he'd learned from living, working, running with the dogs day and night, about Henry Lamb and Tinder and Baboo, about the sunflowers, the fireworks, about the old man who had spoken from the back of Henry's shed. The temptation to return to the house with her had been so powerful he'd finally had to run before his resolve collapsed under the weight of his loneliness.

And loneliness was a big part of it: his proximity to the house and the knowledge that Almondine was gone had swept a desolation through him like he'd never known. He thought of the letters between Brooks and his grandfather, all those debates about the dogs and what they might become, how Brooks had said it would be better to imagine how men might become more suitable for dogs and not the other way around.

After the last night, nearly sleepless in the heat, neither the afternoon sun nor the chatter of the squirrels could keep him awake long. He was thinking about Brooks and the dogs when exhaustion and sorrow combined to press him into unconsciousness. The August sun beat down. The cicadas paused their automaton scream when a cloud passed over the sun. Presently the sky cleared and they took it up again.

He woke when he heard a loud rattle approaching in the underbrush along the creek. Before he had a chance to move, Essay burst into the clearing and ran up to him, panting and scenting him frenetically. Someone had collared her and, near the buckle, a span of the collar was crudely wound with gray duct tape.

He sat Essay and removed the collar and peeled the tape away. There, folded in thirds, he found the photograph he had left on the kitchen table beside his note, the photograph of Claude holding Forte in his arms. Inside that, three one-hundred-dollar bills, a twenty, and a ten.

And a key to the Impala.

Glen Papineau

IT WAS LATE AFTERNOON WHEN CLAUDE CALLED THE OFFICE, WHICH made Glen uneasy. Not good to be having such conversations at work, but he didn't have time to object; Claude's tone was so obviously rushed that Glen understood their conversation would last only a few seconds.

"What happened last night?"

"Nothing. There weren't any cars parked around your place. The yard was empty. I walked your fence line a ways, but there wasn't any point."

"He hasn't shown up here."

"I bet he's in that barn, Claude. Didn't you say he'd been sleeping up in the mow before he ran off?"

"Maybe he was there last night, but not now. It's hot as hell up there during the day."

"Think he'll come back?"

"Yeah."

"To the barn or the house?"

"I don't know. I have a hunch he's planning to take the Impala and run. I just discovered the spare key missing."

Glen thought about that for a second. That would make things easy.

He could pursue in the squad car, say he recognized the vehicle but not the driver.

"Okay. I'll come out tonight."

"Wait until dark. I'll make sure we stay in the house. I might even try to get Trudy away up to Ashland. Anyway, if you see a light in the barn, it's Edgar."

"What if he comes to the house?"

"Then I'll put the porch light on. If you see the porch light, forget it. We'll work something else out."

"Porch light on means he's in the house?"

"Yeah. And if you think he's in the barn, come up from the south field. Use the doors on that end. The dogs are less likely to see you."

And that had been the end of the conversation. When five o'clock rolled around, Glen went back to his house. The day had been blistering and the evening hadn't cooled much. A guy Glen's size had a job staying cool. He sat in his kitchen, drank a beer, and then another. He looked at the whiskey flask standing in the middle of his kitchen table. He'd dumped the ether from the night before onto the lawn when he'd gotten home—the stuff was highly flammable and you didn't leave it standing around, particularly in a poorly sealed vessel. The spot where he'd dumped it was already marked by a kidney-shaped brown patch.

When it was almost sunset he drove the cruiser to the shop. He took a tin of ether, just like the night before, but this time he didn't bother opening it, just set it on the car seat and drove out to Town Line Road. He parked his car in the weeds on the far side of the hill from the Sawtelle place. Then he pocketed the rag and the flask and took the rest of his equipment—a church key and a six-pack with the tin of ether wedged in—and walked up the road. A natural embankment rose on the side opposite the Sawtelle property at the very crest of the hill. Glen scrambled heavily up the rocks and settled himself where he had a view of the house and the huge old barn.

The scene before him was awfully pretty. He could see down into the yard and along the hills rolling to the west. Whoever decided to build a farmhouse there had made a smart decision, he thought, nestling it down in a valley like that, protected from the wind yet flanked by open field on two sides. Both the truck and the Impala were parked in the yard. The porch light was dark, meaning Edgar hadn't gone into the house. It felt like a stakeout, Glen thought, sitting there. He'd never been on one of those—not much need for it around Mellen. The idea tickled him. He cracked a Leiney's as the twilight drained down the western horizon and stars began to volunteer in the evening sky.

For a long time, he watched the field and saw nothing but creation. He rehearsed in his mind how he would put his question to Edgar, how he wanted to emphasize that he was asking as Pop's only child, not as an officer of the law. Behind him, enough of a moon had risen that he could see the leaves shiver on the long, thin stretch of maples that jutted into the field, a slim finger of woodland pointing to where they'd buried Gar, an island of birches in the middle of that shimmering lake of hay.

He thought about what would happen. Once Edgar was groggy he would carry the boy to his car. He couldn't weigh more than one-twenty. Glen could *sprint* across the field carrying that much. And when Edgar came awake again, they would be traveling down some back road.

Faintly, he saw the gray silhouette of a figure wading through the hay, halfway between the road and the woods farther back. A dog accompanied the figure. They paused at the birches. Glen grabbed the tin of ether and scrambled down the embankment and crossed the road, keeping his gaze fixed on the two of them. There wasn't really any doubt about who it was, but he had to be careful now. He waited to see whether a light would go on in the barn, or whether the Impala might suddenly roar to life. The figure disappeared into the darkness behind the barn. There came a brief volley of barks, then silence.

It wasn't until Glen reached around to get the whiskey flask out of his back pocket that he remembered he'd laid it aside at the top of the embankment. The ether tin was too squat to fit in his pocket. He looked at the beer bottle in his hand. He drained it in a gulp and punctured the little mushroom cap on the ether and tipped the vessels together. Vapor curled down the side of the bottle, spilling over his fingers in silvery waves before dissipating into the night air. When he was done he stuffed a corner of the rag into the bottle and waved the arrangement under his nose. His nostrils didn't even tingle. And if a little ether leaked, he wasn't worried. It took a lot of anything to affect Ox Papineau. Every once in a great while, his size worked in his favor.

He tucked the beer bottle into his back pocket and checked his watch.

If that porch light didn't come on in the next five minutes, Glen told himself, Edgar Sawtelle was going for a ride.

Edgar

THEY CAME UP ALONG THE SOUTH FENCE AND CROSSED THE shallow swells of the field, with Essay, for once, content to stay near his side. The dry hay stroked his legs as he walked. A whippoorwill whistled from the woods. In the distance another sadly replied. They stopped at the birches and watched the yard. The truck was parked beside the milk house; the Impala, in the turnout by the porch. The yard light cast a yellow glow against the squat obelisk of the barn, leaving the back double doors in shadow. He saw no stripe of light glowing between or beneath the doors. Most important of all, the porch light was dark. Claude was in the house, then.

When they reached the barn, he paused and turned the latch on the back door and eased it open. Inside was darkness and the musky scent of the dogs intensified by enclosure and heat. Two dogs bayed a greeting, but before they could continue, he and Essay stepped inside. He switched on the aisle lights and walked along the runs, quieting the dogs, and when he finished, he went to the run where Finch and Pout stood and opened the door and let Essay glide in. She nosed her littermates and turned back. Edgar squatted in front of the pen door.

Last time, he signed. Just a little while longer.

He fetched a bucket from the workshop and carried it down the aisle, working from the front doors to the back, upending it and boosting himself up and unscrewing the light bulbs, all but the one nearest the back door, licking his fingers against their quick heat. The act familiar from those nights when his mother was housebound with pneumonia and he'd slept on the makeshift bed of bales. As he worked his way down the aisle, he planned where to search. There was no point looking in the mow. Claude hadn't thought the bottle was safe there; he wouldn't have put it back. It could be in the workshop or the medicine room or behind some loose board. It could also be in the Impala, but he doubted that. Nothing important would be in the Impala, not after Essay had appeared with a key. Seeing Claude rub his hands together and don gloves before touching the bottle made him think it wouldn't be in the house, either—he wouldn't have it nearer himself than absolutely necessary. But Edgar felt equally certain Claude wouldn't have thrown the bottle and its contents away. He could have done that months ago, but something in the way he'd handled it spoke of enthrallment as well as fear.

Edgar began with the medicine room. Half a dozen enameled white cabinets hung on the far wall. Only two contained medicine; the others held stacks of towels and scales and odds and ends rarely used. He sorted through each cabinet, opening the doors and peering in and lifting out the contents and replacing them before moving on, forcing himself to go slowly and look twice, despite his impulse to rush. He didn't want to doubt himself and have to check again. When he finished with the cabinets, he rifled the drawers beneath the counter, discovering as he went that he could run his hands through each drawer's contents without removing things and yet be certain that nothing as big as the bottle had been missed.

It wasn't there. At least not in the obvious places. To search for nooks and loose boards, he needed a flashlight. He walked to the workshop. Then he realized the flashlight was still in the mow, where he'd left it. He mounted the steps and, working almost entirely by feel, climbed the bales. The filament of the flashlight glowed like an ember when he pushed the switch, then darkened. He located a fresh set of batteries in the many-drawered chest on the workshop's far wall.

He walked back to the medicine room, engrossed in the problem of how to reach the boards between the ceiling beams. He could tap each one to see if it was loose. He could get the stepladder from the milk house or maybe stand on the floor and use a rake handle. He noticed, absently, the dogs all standing by their doors, worked up again by his running around. But they stayed quiet, as he had asked. After all, it wasn't so unusual for him to be working late at night in the barn. They would calm down soon enough.

He turned the corner into the medicine room, still in reverie. There was just time to register a whiff of something aromatic. From the corner of his eye he saw a figure standing off to the side. Then the barn whirled around him. A hand as big and solid as a steak pressed a wet cloth over his face. Instantly, his eyes began to water. He choked and then, despite himself, inhaled. It was as if someone had immersed his face in rotting flowers.

The odor was unmistakable.

Prestone. Ether.

The flashlight clattered to the floor. He dug the fingers of both his hands into the hand covering his face, but the wrist and arm holding it in place were thick and cable-muscled and he couldn't budge them, not even a fraction of an inch. The owner of the hand didn't attempt to move. He just stood and held the cloth against Edgar's face while he flailed.

"Just wait," the man said. "This'll only take a minute."

It was no surprise to hear Glen Papineau's voice. Only Glen had hands that big. Edgar gave up trying to pull the cloth away from his face and began instead to swing his fists backward, to no avail. Glen simply wrapped another arm around Edgar's chest and pinned his arms; in one of his hands he held a beer bottle with his thumb over the top.

Edgar held his breath, counted the racing beats of his heart.

"The longer you wait, the bigger your breath," Glen said, and tightened the pressure over his face. He was right, of course. After a time—an impossibly short time—Edgar began to suffocate, and he drew another breath of the nauseating stuff. And then, because his lungs were still burning, he needed to do it again, and again.

Everything grew quiet. They stood for a while and he heard only the huff of his own breath. He grew drowsy—just the way he'd imagined people might if they stared at the pocket watch he'd gotten for Christmas when he was little. Only the pocket watch hadn't worked, and this did, and it was the rhythm of his breathing and not the swinging of the fob. A detachment came over him, even drowning, as he was, in flowers. He stopped struggling. He began to float some distance from his body, just an inch or two above himself at first. The smell of ether slowly diminished. After a certain point he didn't float any farther away.

The walls of the room began to move. He felt the soles of his feet dragging against the floor. At the door to the medicine room, Glen paused, crouched slightly, and tightened his arm so Edgar was pinned against him more securely. Then they were moving along the kennel aisle. Edgar drifted back into his body again. One of his arms worked loose and dangled limply toward the floor.

When they reached the back doors, still latched, Glen lowered him to the cement. The cloth disappeared from his face momentarily and Glen's hand appeared, holding the beer bottle. He lifted his thumb and upended the bottle against the cloth.

It was difficult for Edgar to direct his eyes where he wanted, or even to focus. He stopped looking at Glen's hands. One of his eyes decided to close all by itself. Through the other, he saw a stack of flat, brown bags, blurred lumps. Then the cloth was over his face again.

Glen tightened his grip, prepared to stand. The brown lumps resolved into quicklime bags, stacked beside the back doors. The empty coffee can they used for a spreader protruded from a slit in the topmost sack.

Edgar's ribs bent as Glen hefted him to get a solid hold, then he was rising into the air. He saw his hand reach forward. The rim of the coffee can, jagged where the opener had punctured the metal, brushed his fingers, and then there was only powder against his palm, dry as moon dust. He'd tried and missed. Yet, when he could focus, the can was pinched between his fingers, his hand having somehow corrected the mistake on its own.

Glen was reaching for the door latch. Edgar closed his eyes and gripped the rim of the coffee can with all his might. It was only half full, but heavy as an anvil. All he could muster was a spastic, upward jerk. Then his hand fell back and the coffee can clattered to the floor.

A heavy layer of quicklime dropped onto his head and shoulders. He had remembered to squeeze his eyes shut, but his mouth must have been hanging open, slack from his effort and the effect of the ether. His tongue and throat were instantly coated with a bitter paste and he swallowed involuntarily and felt the heat in his mouth and retched.

Glen, too, began to cough. His arm loosened from around Edgar's chest and slipped away. For a long moment Edgar hung suspended in the air by nothing at all. He knew it was important that he collect his feet beneath him, but before he could get started the barn began to spin like a top with him at its center and the floor lunged forward and the fireworks above Scotia Lake burst all over again behind his closed eyes.

HE WOKE GAGGING. Even before he could open his eyes, he heard Glen Papineau's voice whispering his name.

"Edgar?" he said. "Edgar, are you there?" Then Glen muttered under his breath, "Oh Jesus." This was followed by the thump of something hitting the floor.

Edgar reached up and carefully drew his fingers across his eyelids. His lashes were caked with quicklime and it took all his concentration to make his hands brush it away. He cracked open one eye until a slit of light registered and then the other and he blinked and looked along the cement of the kennel floor. A cloud of quicklime dust swirled through the air, sifting and settling everywhere. Glen had staggered backward and fallen. He lay on his side, curly hair grayed, face thickly powdered. His eyes were closed and his expression was a painfully contracted grimace.

"Aw Jesus," Glen said again. He brought his hands to his face and pressed his fingers against his closed eyes. The cords in his neck stood out and he kicked at the floor—another thump. Then his hands began beating against his face open-palmed as if putting out a fire there. With great effort, he got control of them and lay panting.

"Edgar, are you there?" he repeated. His voice was hoarse but eerily calm. "Can you get me some water? I just meant to ask you a question. I wasn't going to hurt you, I swear. But right now I need water for my eyes. Oh Jesus. Edgar?"

But Edgar lay in a fugue, seeing everything as if through the wrong end of a pair of binoculars. When he tried to lift his head, the ache hit him at once and then the nausea. The florid smell of ether was everywhere now, nearly as strong as when the cloth was pressed against his face. He looked along the floor and spotted the beer bottle lying broken and liquid ether splashed around it in silver pools. Vapor shimmered in the air above it.

Edgar pushed to his knees. The rear barn doors were within arm's reach. He tried to stand, then sank back and dragged himself up the front of them until he could work his fingers into the metal hoop of the latch handle. When the leftmost of the double doors swung open, he stumbled drunkenly into the night along with it.

He began banging the door with the flat of his hand.

Glen turned his face toward the sound and rose on all fours.

"O god o god o god o god," he whispered. He crawled forward and stopped to wipe his face and eyes. Edgar pounded the door again and Glen started moving, then stopped a second time to beat the heels of his palms against his eyes. A shriek came out of him, high and incongruous, and then he pressed his face against the floor and ground it along, crying louder as he advanced.

"God, it burns! Oh, anything, *please*! Jesus God. Anything."

Edgar released his grip on the door and tried to step back, but he reeled and fell into the weeds. The dark mass of the barn towered over him, a great black swath cut out of a starry sky. He sat and shook his head, a mistake; the pain nearly blacked him out again. But the fresh night air was bringing him back from the ether and he could keep his eyes focused. In a minute he would be able to get his feet under him.

The dogs all stood in their pens, gazes fixed on the spectacle of Glen Papineau crawling down the aisle. It was the last thing Edgar wanted to see; he wanted the dogs out of the barn, away from those fumes. When Glen reached the threshold he worked his fingers along the bottom of the door then hoisted himself upright, pointing his face this way and that. When he tried again to pull one of his eyelids open, his body spasmed and he gave another hoarse and wordless cry and staggered past Edgar in a headlong rush.

And then Edgar got his wish, for the dogs wheeled and plunged through the passages to their outside runs. He watched as they dove through the canvas straps of their portals and disappeared, until all that remained inside the barn was the apparition of the ether fumes, quavering and rising under that single hot light bulb.

ONCE OUTSIDE, THE DOGS began to bark. Glen Papineau traced a broad circle in the south field, entering the light of the yard like an actor stepping onto a stage: enormous, thick-necked, head and shoulders powdered and tear-streaked, one hand clasped over his face as if to rip away a mask and the other hewing the air before him. He staggered up to Alice, parked beside the barn. When his blunt fingers touched her radiator, he stopped and traced the flanges of the grill, the peeling paint of the steering armature. He dropped to his knees and pressed his forehead against the close-set front tires.

"Aw, God," he said, "I can't see where I am. Is that a light? Can anyone hear me? Claude! Claude! They won't even open! Can't I please, *please* have some water for my *eyes*!"

Then Edgar heard his mother's voice calling from the back porch.

"Glen? Glen! What are you doing?"

Edgar looked into the barn. All the front pens were empty, but some of the dogs in the back runs, unable to see Glen or his mother, yet hearing their voices, had pushed back inside. Edgar stood, testing his balance. His mother was running across the yard.

He turned away and stumbled along the slope behind the barn, clapping his hands as loudly as he could. When he reached the pen doors, he hammered bare-handed on the timbers and wires, making every noise he could to draw the dogs out. One by one, they pushed through the canvas laps over their passageways and trotted out to him.

He was going down the line staying them when a light flashed from the rear barn doors, brilliant and blue. For a moment the birches in the south field stood icily illuminated, their shadows stretching behind them across the surf of hay. Then Edgar felt a pressure against his eardrums that slowly resolved itself into a sound, as if the sky above had been gripped at the corners and shaken out.

Trudy

S HE LAY WAITING AND LISTENING FOR THE SOUND OF EDGAR'S FOOT-steps on the porch. She didn't understand what he might be looking for in the barn and she didn't care. She was willing to humor him in any way required as long as he came to the house. It had been dark for a long time and he must be nearly done. She thought about how gaunt he'd looked. She thought about the expression on his face when she'd brought up Almondine.

The dogs began barking. Then, among the barks, a man's voice, moaning or crying. She sat bolt upright in bed.

"What's that?" she said. "Who's that?"

Trudy thought Claude was sleeping, but at the sound of the dogs he'd jerked as if stung, and now he was sitting up, too. He looked wide awake. He had a puzzled expression on his face, though it seemed somehow arranged that way, and beneath the puzzlement was a look of alarm.

"Don't get up," he said. "I'll check." He was already pulling on his thes. The man's voice rang out again. It was coming from the back-l. Trudy couldn't quite make out the words, but there was an unmis-le note of fear and pain in them.

"That sounds like Glen," she said.

"Oh Jesus. Howling drunk, I bet. He's been hitting the sauce lately. I ran into him last week, three sheets to the wind before sunset. I told him to come over if he ever needed to talk. I didn't think it would be in the middle of the night, though."

Trudy dressed hurriedly and ran to the back porch. Claude stood in the doorway, looking into the yard. The truck was parked where he'd left it that afternoon, facing the hitch end of the tractor. The dogs were flagging up and down their runs, barking and looking toward the south field. At first Trudy didn't see anything unusual there. Then the image registered: it *was* Glen. He was kneeling in front of the tractor with his forehead pressed against the close-set front tires, as if in supplication.

Claude seemed rooted to the porch. She pushed past him and ran across the lawn. Glen was sobbing. His hair and face and shoulders were powdered white. Behind him, the shadow of the barn was divided by a flickering light, and in it stood Edgar. The moment their gazes met, he turned and walked into the dark, staggering as he went. Trudy pulled up short, feeling as if she were splitting in two; one half of her cried, *Go to Edgar!* and the other half wanted only to distract Claude, close behind her, from the sight of him. The idea that Edgar might run away again was paramount in her mind. At first she didn't even connect Glen's presence with Edgar's. She only wanted to turn everyone around, get them facing the house.

"Glen," she said. "What's going on?"

"Trudy. Please. Get water," Glen said. "I need to wash out my eyes." His voice was quaking. He alternately clutched the front of the tractor and held his hands over his face, as if, by tremendous will, not touching his eyes. He sucked his breath through his teeth. Tear tracks cut through the white powder on his cheeks. By then Claude was there and he knelt beside Glen.

"All right, Hoss," he said. "We're cutting you off for the night." He worked his shoulder under Glen's thick arm and began to guide him to his feet.

"No," Trudy said. "Wait."

Claude looked at her, his face carefully composed into a mask of surprise. She ran her fingertip across Glen's cheek and brought it to her mouth. There was no mistaking the awful, chalky taste of quicklime and the burning sensation the moment it got wet. She looked into Glen's flour-white face.

"What were you doing here?"

"Ask him after we've got him in the house," Claude said. "That's quicklime."

"I know what it is," she said. "First he's going to explain what he was *doing here*."

These last words came out as a screech.

"I just wanted to ask him a question," Glen said. "Tell her, Claude! It was just to ask him a question."

She turned to Claude. He shook his head and shrugged as if to say it was the ranting of a drunk.

"Liar," she said.

Then, before she understood quite what she was doing, she'd twined her fingers into the curls atop Glen's head and yanked his face up. Her other palm caught him squarely on the flat of his cheek. Crack of skin against skin. Glen swayed and nearly collapsed, but instead he began to whimper and clutch at his eyes.

"You'll *wait*," she said, "until I know my son is safe."

She untangled her fingers from Glen's hair and stood. The dogs in the front runs pressed against their pen doors, barking and whining and straining to see what was happening. From behind the kennel, Trudy heard a rattling and banging. Pen doors being opened. She had taken only a few steps toward the sound when the first azure bubble of gas bellied out of the back doors. It crawled into the air, shifting from blue to yellow as it rose. It lit the field, then disappeared, bottom to top, halfway to the eaves. There was the low *huff* of vaporous ignition, the sound of a match tossed into a barbeque soaked with lighter fluid. Then a second belch of flame shot out of the doorway, more orange than the first, eating itself almost before it had a chance to rise. In the still night air, a thread of smoke began to seep from the top of the doorway. It tracked upward along the red siding and pooled under the eaves. With sickening rapidity, it broadened into a gray ribbon that spanned the doorway.

Trudy stopped, flatfooted, her thoughts momentarily logjammed. She jerked about in a circle, unable to decide in which direction to move first. A vast, soft explosion had erupted in the barn. Why? They didn't store flammables in there. Glen had been in there. He was covered with quicklime. Had Glen meant to burn down the barn? Had he doused the inside with gasoline? Why? Claude had Glen on his feet. They were walking toward the house, Glen's massive arm draped over Claude's shoulders. Had Claude not heard the sound? He was speaking urgently to Glen, but Trudy couldn't make out what he was saying. Then Glen stumbled and drove them both to the ground.

Not until Opal rounded the back corner of the barn and bolted past her did Trudy know for certain that Edgar had to be all right: he was releasing the dogs from their pens. She ran along the front pens, unlatching the doors and throwing them open, clapping and shouting, "Out! Come on! *Out!*" By the time she finished, two dozen dogs were loose; another twelve or fourteen were rounding the barn from the back. Packs formed and reformed and flowed into one another and split apart as they dashed behind the barn and across the yard and circled the house and garden. Claude had gotten Glen to his feet again, and the two men waded through the dogs that surrounded them.

"Get!" Claude shouted at the dogs, and "Come on, come *on*" to Glen.

"Call the fire department," Trudy shouted. "He's set the barn on fire!"

Claude stared back at her for a moment. Then he nodded and turned. With Glen's arm draped across his shoulders, they hobbled the rest of the way to the porch steps and he there guided the man down and ran past him into the house.

Two of the dogs began to snarl at each other. Trudy ran to the nearest and lifted it by its tail and wheeled it backward, shouting, "Go! Leave! *Get!*" to the other. She dropped the dog's tail and stepped quickly forward and shook it by the ruff. When she looked up, a pair of dogs were running through the orchard, close to the road. "You two," she called. "Come!" The dogs wheeled and began heading toward her but instead joined one of the packs circulating in the yard. She began methodically recalling and downing dogs, one by one, looking over her shoulder and waiting for Edgar to appear, and every time she looked again, more smoke streamed from the barn.

She was surprised, given the chaos of the moment, how many of the dogs held their stays, but every one looked as if it might bolt the moment she turned away; they craned their necks to watch the others plunging through the field and circling the house and charging up to the porch steps, where Glen Papineau sat cradling his face in his hands.

Edgar

FOURTEEN RUNS JUTTED INTO THE LONG NIGHT-SHADOW OF the barn. Edgar staggered along palming up the wooden latches and flinging open the doors without waiting for the dogs to emerge. The afterimage of the fire-flash twisted in the air before him like a violet snake. By the time he opened the last run, nearest the silo, the dogs were circling him in the dark, pawing one another and bucking in excited, foreshortened leaps. Then the sound of Glen Papineau's voice echoed from the front yard. Opal and Umbra stopped, cocked their heads, then turned and galloped side by side through the pack and rounded the stone belly of the silo.

Yes, he signed at the rest. He swept his hands along their sides to get them moving. *Go! Get!* They turned their heads to mouth his hands, then, one after another bolted past the silo until only Essay remained, seated in the grass. She was nosing the plush fur along the back of her hind leg. He knelt and pushed her muzzle away and ran his hand across singed fur. Brittle as wire. Another patch on her tail. The flash must have caught her on the way out, he thought, but the canvas flaps over the door had damped it. Essay nosed his hand aside impatiently and chewed at her leg and snorted to clear the scent from her nostrils. She scrambled to her feet and shook out.

Edgar gestured toward the silo. You too. Get.

She looked at him, blinking, then turned and bounded into the pale light, shadow out of shadow, a thing created mid-leap, her ears pricked forward, eyes wide, jaw agape, for the very first time wolflike to Edgar's eyes.

He ran to the rear of the barn. A band of smoke crawled past the lintel above the double doors and lifted skyward. How long had it taken to release the dogs? A minute? Two? How could that much smoke be pouring from the barn? From his vantage point he could see Glen sitting on the porch steps, hands to his face. A half-circle of dogs surrounded him with their heads cocked. Edgar's mother held a dozen or more dogs in quivering down-stays in the side yard and twice that number still ran wild, bunching up in packs and sailing through the orchard, splitting and joining in a chaotic ballet. As he watched, his mother halted a dog by name and walked to it and downed it using both hands. Then, noticing the gazes of the dogs, she turned. They began a simultaneous exchange of sign.

Are the pups with you?

Are you okay?

No.

Yes.

I'll get them.

Before she could sign anything else, he ran through the double doors. The interior of the barn was eerily hot. The bulb he'd left screwed into its socket flickered away and the smoke billowed and streamed past it along the ceiling and into the night. The air smelled of hickory and burning straw. Edgar came upon the remains of Glen's ether-soaked rag, an orange-fringed char. In two of the pens, he found straw still burning, the flames dispersed and yellow. He tore open the doors and kicked the straw until the embers were dark and he looked about. The plank walls were scorched in places. The timbers of the runs blackened. He found glowing, smoking piles of half-burnt straw in three other runs and he stomped them out. Overhead, the heavy crosswise beams were sooty but not aflame. Yet the smoke had not lessened. From outside, he could hear a shouted exchange between his mother and Claude. He ran down the aisle looking for the source of the smoke, but all he saw was a faint orange glow between two of the ceiling boards. When he looked again even that had gone black.

From the whelping room came a pair of high, yiking cries. The air inside was clearer. The solid walls of the whelping rooms had blocked all but a thin scum of smoke, but the two pups were panicked, almost hysterical. The moment he unlatched their pen door, they scrambled past, turned the corner, hindquarters skidding out from under them, and were gone. He followed them out. He wasn't groggy from the ether anymore, but his head throbbed. Once outside, he gasped the clear air into his lungs and raised his hand and pressed the lump where his head had struck the floor. What he felt wasn't even pain, just the black hand of unconsciousness passing before his eyes. His knees almost buckled and he yanked his fingers away.

The smoke pouring out of the doorway had doubled since he'd gone in, and blackened. He ran across the yard to where his mother stood among the dogs. The two pups were yapping and tumbling at her feet. She laid her hands on his shoulders and then on the sides of his face.

"Are you okay?"

He nodded.

"All the dogs are out?"

Yes.

"Then keep away from the barn. It's going to burn."

No. I put out all the flames I could find. Have you called the fire department?

She shook her head. "We can't get through."

What?

"When they put the extension in the barn, they routed the line there first. Claude just tried the house phone. The wires must have burnt or shorted already."

No. No. No. The lights are on in the barn. The phone there might still work.

"Edgar, listen to me. No one goes into the barn. Look at the smoke. Look at it. The barn is *gone*."

A glance was all it took to know she was right. Smoke had begun to seep from the eaves, rising and blacking out the stars in ebony rivulets. The sight of it pressed some tremendous weight down on Edgar. He knew very well how dry and brittle the wood in the barn was. He might have extinguished all the flames he could see, but something was smoldering inside the walls and ceiling. Even if they called that instant, it would take time for the Mellen Volunteer Fire Corps to arrive. Half an hour, maybe. And by then, the barn would be ablaze.

All at once the image of his father lying on the workshop floor flashed into his mind. Snow, seeping toward him. How he wouldn't look at Edgar. Wouldn't breathe. "These records are *it*," he'd once said. "Without those records, we wouldn't know what a dog *meant*."

When Edgar turned back, his mother was looking at the house. Glen sat slumped on the porch steps, towel pressed to his face. Claude was standing beside him, speaking in a low, urgent voice and trying to pull the towel away so he could flush Glen's eyes with a pan of water.

"Why would Glen do this?" his mother said. "God damn him."

He had ether. I knocked it out of his hand.

"What was he doing with ether?"

He had it in a bottle. He held a rag over my face.

She looked at the gray powder in Edgar's hair and on his clothes.

"You threw quicklime at him."

Yes.

"That flash was ether fumes."

Yes. I think the heat of the light bulb set it off.

"What did he mean to do?"

I don't know.

She was shaking her head. "It doesn't make sense," she said. "How did he even know you—"

Then her voice trailed off. She seemed to register for the first time that Glen Papineau was not in uniform. He was dressed in jeans and a checkered, short-sleeved shirt with its own bib of quicklime. Claude had coaxed him into setting aside the towel, and as they watched, he pulled back Glen's eyelids and tipped water across his broad face. When the liquid touched his eyes, Glen's back arched. He pushed Claude away with a sweep of his hand and hunched over again.

"How did he know?" she said. She took a tremulous breath. Tears spilled onto her cheeks. She began to walk toward the porch, hands fisted at her side. Then her strides lengthened and she was running and her voice rose to a wail, asking the same question over and over.

EDGAR FORCED HIMSELF TO turn away from the house, and away from the real, living dogs on the ground at his feet. Those dogs could take care of themselves for the few minutes it would take him to do what he had in mind. He ran to the front barn doors and rolled the heavy iron brace bar away and pulled the doors open. A billow of gray smoke engulfed him, carrying with it the smell of roasting straw and wood. He stepped back. After a minute the smoke leveled out around five feet above the barn floor.

If he stayed low, under the ceiling of smoke, he could easily reach the workshop door. The cabinets themselves would be impossible to move, but he could carry out individual files. The most valuable would be the newest, going back five generations. How many times could he go in? How many files each trip? They would get scrambled, but there would be time later to sort them out. He permitted himself a quick look at the porch steps. His mother stood facing Claude and Glen.

"How did you know, Glen?" she cried. "Tell me how you knew Edgar was here."

Claude was standing beside Glen on the steps. He leaned over and began to say something.

"Shut up, Claude. *Shut up*. I want to hear this from Glen."

But Glen sat silently rocking and grinding the towel against his face. Trudy knelt and put her hands on either side of Glen's massive head and wrenched it toward her.

If Edgar watched even a moment longer he thought he would run toward the house, toward Claude, and then there would be no hope. He began drawing the deepest breaths he could, and before the doubts and second-guesses could begin, he ran into the smoldering barn.

HOT SMOKE BILLOWED over his back. The sole light bulb, at the far end of the barn, flickered between folds of smoke. Walking, he might have crossed the distance to the workshop in a few seconds, but with his head down and peering about for flames, it took much longer. He touched the handle of the workshop door and rubbed his thumb over his fingertips, like a safecracker, to take the temperature. Warm, but no warmer than anything else in the barn. He swung the door open. Smoke sucked into the darkness and equalized between the aisle and the workshop.

His eyes began to itch and a stream of tears leaked onto his face. He scrambled through the doorway and flipped the light switch and the bulb in the ceiling fixture came on. He breathed a little sigh of relief. He knew the room so well he could find his way to the file cabinets in total darkness, but he wouldn't be able to locate the records he wanted just by feel, and there was no time to find the flashlight.

He opened the highest drawer of the rightmost file cabinet. A solid mass of paper, divided a hundred times, came toward him, the tab edges on the tops of the manila folders running in a long, ragged hump down the center and each penciled with a name. *Cotton. Vesta. Hoop. Frog.* He drove his hands into the mass, awkwardly lifting out a swath, and in the process scattering notes and photographs and paper clips. He left them and turned and scuttled through the doorway and down the aisle. The papers were heavy and they slid dryly against one another in his arms. Then he was in the yard, in the clear air. At the far edge of the lawn he stopped and bent and spilled the papers onto the ground.

And for the briefest instant, Edgar felt something new, something impossible and wholly out of place. A sense of elation. As if he'd somehow traveled back to the moment his father lay on the workshop floor and found the thing that could save him. Then, just as quickly, the sensation was gone. Something in him clamored for it again, at once. He ran to the barn and flailed heedlessly through the smoke and filled his arms with another pack of manila folders and all the papers and photographs inside them. He'd almost reached the double doors when the cement floor surged upward; he saw it tilting at him but there was no time to recover and he smashed shoulder-first into the hinges of the right-hand door, kicking as he fell and clutching the papers to his chest.

The impact brought him to his senses. He lay for a time half in and half out of the barn. After a few breaths of clear air he pushed to his feet and staggered into the grass. When he reached the folders he'd already rescued, he bent at his waist and let the papers flutter and splash to the ground.

Remember me.

Far in the distance, his mother's voice.

"Edgar! Stay out of there!"

She was standing by the porch. Glen had gripped her wrist in one giant hand like a straw in a vise. Edgar looked at her and shook his head. There was no time to argue. She couldn't feel what he felt or hear what he heard. She wouldn't understand the rightness of it. There were no words for the sensation that had washed through him.

His mother would have run forward to stop him, but she couldn't break Glen's grip. She whirled and began to beat at Glen's face with her free hand. It brought the enormous man to his feet. He was confused and in terrible pain and he stood thrashing his head side to side to avoid her blows. His stance was wide-legged and low. And then, in one fluid motion, he swept one of his thick legs under hers and folded her up in his arms and together they toppled onto the grass. By the time they came to rest, Glen had scissored his legs over hers.

"What's *happening*?" Glen said. His voice was filled with pain and fear but not the slightest hint of physical effort, as if all those wrestler's reflexes had come forward of their own volition to protect him. "Why won't anyone help me?" he cried. "Doesn't anyone understand *I can't see*?"

Edgar took a breath and turned away. The last thing he saw was the entwined figures of Glen Papineau and his mother, as she twisted and fought in his arms. And Claude, standing on the porch steps above them.

HE TROLLEYED ALONG PALM and knuckle into the workshop, careful now to stay below the strata of smoke, holding his breath as long as he could until it burst out of him. He was able to get the remainder of the first drawer's files. Coming out with his arms filled, it was much harder to stay low. His eyes teared and the light in the workshop became a greasy blur of yellow and gray. He had to be careful not to gulp the air. The crashing dizziness of his last attempt was warning enough. Even so, he felt smoke burning along his windpipe and in his lungs. Outside, he spilled the papers onto the ground and dropped to his knees. He supposed a normal person would have been coughing, but all he felt was a strange wooziness. He bent and forced himself through the motions, hacking and gasping to drive the smoke out of him.

He looked up to find Essay standing before him, tail flagging. Her ears were up high on her head, fully attentive, eyes gay and glittering. The same expression she'd worn parading around the cove after the tornado. She looked prepared to follow him into the barn. He took her ruff in his hands to shake her down, scare her away, then stopped himself. They were done with commands. He put his hand under her belly and drew her attention into him.

Away, he signed, pouring into the gesture all the force he could muster. *I know you understand. I know it's your choice. But please. Away!*

Essay backed up a step, eyes intent on him. She looked at the other dogs circling under the apple trees. Then she faced Edgar again and bucked a little and held his gaze.

Yes, he signed. Yes.

She bounded forward and swiped her tongue across his face and bolted into the mass of dogs, all of them up now and running, even the ones Edgar's mother had stayed. He wanted desperately to know if Essay had understood him, but short of giving up on the records and rushing after her, there was no way to be sure.

He turned back to the barn. He had almost passed through the wide double doors and into the smoky interior when he thought of the milk house and what he would find sitting inside it. He crossed along the front of the barn and when he reached the milk house door he flung it open.

The first time he saw a flame, he told himself, he would stop.

Claude

LET IT BURN, CLAUDE THOUGHT.

He was standing on the bottom porch step watching disaster unfold and trying to decide what to do. The disaster was not that the barn was going to burn; certainly not. The barn was insured, after all, and the dogs were outside and safe, even if they were running loose at the moment. At worst, losing the barn would make things inconvenient for a few months—they'd have to board the dogs somewhere, though finding families to look after them in the interim wouldn't be that hard—but, realistically, they'd have a better, more modern barn before snow fell. Nor was the disaster what had happened to Glen; though Claude had flushed Glen's eyes with water as soon as they'd reached the house, the quicklime had already done gruesome damage. It was hard to feel sorry for Glen. The man must have used enough Prestone out there to launch a rocket. Not what Claude had suggested at all.

No, the disaster was that Edgar kept running into the barn for those records, returning again and again to the workshop, and the filing cabinets, while smoke poured from the barn's eaves. Edgar had even fetched the wheelbarrow from the milk house and, as Claude watched, begun rolling it in a broad arc toward the barn doors.

If all that weren't strange enough, Glen had now taken Trudy in some sort of wrestler's hold. In a moment, Claude was going to have to say something or do something to make Glen release her, but he didn't know what that might be. The man had wrapped his huge limbs around Trudy and his embrace reminded Claude somehow of the tree roots at Angkor Wat, slowly crushing those ancient stone temples. The way Glen was acting, he might not stop unless he was unconscious. Yet Claude didn't want to step in until he was sure nothing could be done about the barn. The barn had to be a lost cause. That was why he'd told Trudy the telephone line was dead. By now, it probably *was* dead.

There was something enthralling about the sight of smoke rising from the barn, black into black, erasing such a broad swath of stars. It reminded Claude just how *big* that old barn was. When he'd first arrived home he'd been struck all over again by its size; then, quickly enough, it had become ordinary in his eyes, the way it had been when he was growing up, making other people's barns look like miniatures. The volume of smoke belching off the roof put things into perspective again and he marveled at the man who had originally built the place—what plans must he have had, to build a barn like that?

Better take a good look, Claude thought. He watched the smoke seeping from the gaps around the big mow door—the door Edgar had thrown open the night he'd pushed Papineau down the mow stairs; the door they had hauled six wagonloads of straw bales through, just two weeks earlier, in a long day of sweaty, exhausting effort. Strange: all that smoke rupturing outward, writhing and folding over itself, and yet, no sound, no flames. Claude knew enough about fire to understand that this was a phase, that the fire, or what was soon going to be a fire, was smoldering along the old timbers, probably in the straw as well, exploring hidden paths and alleyways in search of fuel and oxygen. He looked into the sky again. In the waxing moonlight, there was not a cloud to be seen.

Edgar appeared out of the smoke, pushing a wheelbarrow mounded with papers. The sight chilled Claude. Trudy, thrashing pointlessly, began shouting to Edgar to stay away from the barn. But Edgar wasn't in any immediate danger. Only a few steps lay between the workshop and the barn doors and unless the whole structure suddenly burst into flame there was little chance of his getting caught inside. Until then, at least on the surface of things, Edgar was doing right by salvaging the files. A help later. Not imperative, but good to have.

The problem was that bottle. In truth, Claude had lost his nerve—the bottle had already been well hidden in the mow, and he knew it, but when it looked like Edgar might be snooping up there Claude had panicked and dug it out. After that night with Benson, and that bizarre reenactment, he'd been certain Edgar had found it once already. He should have poured the bottle's contents into the creek the very next morning—he'd fantasized about doing that so many times—but he'd never answered the question of what would happen once he dumped the stuff. Would it just sink into the ground, disappear? Or would it trace some subterranean channel back to the house, to the well—to him? More important—and this was hard to admit—once whatever roiled inside that bottle was gone, it was gone for good, and the idea that it could solve his worst problems had become part of Claude's nature. The knowledge gave him confidence, the way some men drew confidence from a wad of money in the bank or a gun in the glove compartment of their car. It had become, at times, almost a living presence to him. *I exist for a reason.* And then the exhilaration and self-loathing when he'd listened. But, if he was careful now, that bottle would be incinerated and, along with it, the very worst part of him.

If he was careful. He'd already made one mistake. He'd carried the bottle out of the mow only to realize how few other places he trusted. There hadn't been time to think things through. Trudy could have walked in at any moment, and what, exactly, would he have said if she'd asked why he was carrying a bottle ribboned with Hangul lettering and with some liquid inside that looked like the purest, most distilled venom? Hiding it in the house was out of the question; it frightened him to be so near the stuff. He could barely stand to hold it in his work-gloved hands. After Gar, he'd showered until the hot water heater in his little rented apartment emptied, and when it filled, he'd emptied it all over again.

Once he'd taken that bottle out of the mow, there were few options left. The medicine room felt all wrong—Trudy went there sometimes: she might open a drawer, think, *What's this?*, twist the wax-sealed stopper, raise the bottle to her nose . . . So it had to be the workshop, where Trudy virtually never stepped foot except passing through on her way to the mow. He'd considered, briefly, putting it in plain sight, out on the shelves, as if it were nothing of value. With so many odds and ends there, one more bottle wouldn't stand out. But it *would* stand out to anyone looking for it; and his own gaze would always be drawn to it. So he'd wrapped up the bottle in an oily rag and buried it under a mass of old letters at the back of the bottom drawer of the oldest filing cabinet. No one but Edgar cared about the filing cabinets and even Edgar couldn't possibly care about a bunch of old letters. A good place, he'd been sure of it. And yet, the moment the bottle was safely hidden, a new worry came to him and he'd walked to the medicine room, selected a syringe from a cabinet, and worked it into the bundle of rags alongside the bottle.

Claude was still standing on the porch steps, watching the scene playing out before him. One of Glen's legs was thrown forward over Trudy's hips and he had tilted them both so they were lying on their sides, facing the barn. Claude could barely see Trudy over Glen's broad back. He sighed and stepped off the porch and onto the grass. Trudy had stopped struggling and lay enraptured, murmuring something like "no, no, not now," watching Edgar as he came running out of the barn pushing another batch of records. The dogs were scrambling every which way. Two of them raced over, paused to scent Trudy and Glen, then leapt away. Claude knelt behind Glen, reached over his shoulders, and tried to peel the man's enormous right hand away from where it was locked around his own left wrist.

"Glen, enough," he said, surprising himself with the evenness of his voice. "Let Trudy go. We can't help you unless you let Trudy go."

Glen didn't respond, but at the sound of her name, Trudy began to thrash. Though she was lithe and strong, it was no use. Glen dwarfed her. His shoulders bunched and his arms tightened until she stopped. She craned her neck to look at Claude. She was crying.

"Make Edgar stop. Please, Claude. Make Edgar stop going in there."

Claude just nodded. There was nothing to say in reply. He stood and began to cross the yard, mind racing. He didn't like having to make decisions that way; he needed time to think things through, but he could hardly sit and mull. Yes, he could stop Edgar, knock him down and hold him like Glen was holding Trudy until the fire was so advanced no one could go inside. To Trudy, it would look like he'd saved Edgar from madness, while inside, the bottle would crack and melt, its contents boil in the flames.

Afterward, there would be Glen to account for. The man was blind, his eyes etched globes. It was a testament to Glen's strength that he was conscious at all, even if half out of his mind with pain. The blindness would overwhelm him later on—all those late-night conversations had left Claude with no doubt about that. When that happened, Claude could insist that Glen, in his grief, had mistaken an innocent consolation over Page's death for something else entirely, and Trudy might believe that. Glen had, after all, tried to kidnap Edgar. And if that wasn't damning enough, after Trudy hit Glen he had reverted to this strange wrestling maneuver, moaning and rocking and refusing to release her.

But there would still be Edgar. The boy (it was hard to think of him that way, gray-haired from the quicklime, tall, whip-thin) might make some claims, though any real evidence would long have been dispersed in the clouds. In return, Claude could raise questions of his own. What had happened with Page in the mow, really? With luck, they might find the key to the Impala in Edgar's pocket, along with several hundred dollars. Would anyone be that surprised to find a runaway preparing to steal a car?

It could work, Claude thought. All he had to do was stop Edgar—save Edgar's life, in Trudy's eyes—and wait. Afterward, there would be a sense of release, a new beginning for all of them. The fire, and the reconstruction, would change everything. A turning point.

Claude was walking toward the barn, considering this, when he felt a blunt pressure against his thigh. He looked down. Essay stood before him. She'd pressed her nose into his leg, just above his knee, and his heart began to jangle, because for a moment Claude saw a syringe in the dog's mouth. But his eyes had been fooled. There was nothing in her mouth. He'd been thinking of the night Edgar played his trick in the kennel. Essay stood in front of him, gaze resolute, mouth agape, eyes glinting and mischievous, as if waiting to see his reaction from that distant night. Was it possible the boy was so single-minded that he'd come back to play this trick again?

All at once, Claude's certainty wavered. He hadn't been thinking clearly. It would *not* work. Not if all it took was the gaze of a dog to make his hands shake and the blood pound in his brain. He was kidding himself. Over and over again he would have to look Gar in the eye just that way.

No, not Gar—Edgar.

Why had he thought that? No sooner had he asked that question than he knew the answer: because Edgar, all softness stripped from his face, lit aslant by the yard light, hair grayed by quicklime, looked too much like his father. Because, carrying the files in his arms, the boy even walked with the same hunched-up step Gar had used cradling pups in and out of the whelping pens. Because some nights Claude couldn't sleep after the tick of a bug against the bedroom window made him start up in bed, adrenaline flooding his veins, heart leaping so ferociously he'd had to walk it off, and after that he couldn't lie down. Better to sit facing the night and take sleep that way, if it came at all. And because the look on Essay's face made him think of the morning he'd glanced up from the sink to discover Edgar outside the window in the apple tree—how, finally, he'd had to turn away.

When Claude looked down again, the dog had slipped away, rejoined one of the packs bounding through the yard. Claude walked to the double doors and entered, stooping. The air was breathable down by his waist, though it reeked in his nostrils and stung his eyes. He could see only a few feet ahead. When he reached the doorway of the workshop he made out the wheelbarrow, askew in the center of the workshop, and Edgar, yanking open the top drawer of a file cabinet, standing upright just long enough to scoop out the drawer's contents, then ducking again.

Edgar glanced over and spotted Claude in the doorway. He stopped for a moment and they looked at one another. Then Edgar turned and snatched another batch of files from the open drawer. The drawers of the file cabinets nearest the door hung half-open and empty—Edgar had been working from the newest records to the oldest. That explained why he hadn't already walked into the yard with the bottle in his hand.

Claude stepped past Edgar, to the last filing cabinet. He slid open the top drawer and began scooping armload after armload of records into the wheelbarrow, filling it as fast as he could, though it was already nearly overflowing. Edgar kept working on the bottom drawer of the adjacent file, turning and heaving papers. Some missed the wheelbarrow entirely and scattered toward the doorway. Then Edgar stood, took the handle-bars of the wheelbarrow, and disappeared into the smoke.

Edgar

H E COULD HAVE KICKED HIMSELF FOR NOT THINKING OF THE wheelbarrow sooner. It was possible to get everything this way, all of it, the whole history, outside and safe. Working frantically, he'd already pitched the contents of one complete file cabinet into the metal basin of the thing. The smoke in the workshop was bitter and thick, and he dropped to his knees to suck the clear air near the floor.

Now he rose again and plunged his hands into a drawer and turned and dumped an armload of papers. How swiftly his mind was spinning as he worked, how euphoric the sensation of deliverance that beat in him. He felt he'd struck another bargain, just as he had watching the apple trees in the winter, and he worked with great intensity. The part of him that loved order cried out at the wildness of what he was doing, the neat march of generations so quickly scrambled. But he couldn't stop. He'd meant to throw everything into this one final barrow load, but the papers had already begun to mound over the rim. Much more would just slide and spill as he rolled through the turn into the aisle and would be lost in the smoke.

He had glanced at the workshop door when Claude appeared, crouching low and squinting against the smoke. Claude's expression was a kind of perfect blankness, or rather, a mélange of expressions, any one of them fleeting and half made and out of registration with the next. Edgar thought that someone else, watching from another viewpoint, might see concern or apprehension there, or fear, or desire, or revulsion. But for Edgar, the result was something incomprehensible, unreadable, committing to nothing and summing to nothing. As it had always been with Claude. Edgar had not in the least forgotten what he'd seen in the mow, or that stream of memory that had passed through him in the rain. He had never had much of a plan for when he returned except to say what he knew was true and keep saying it, without evidence, without proof.

Then, before he had a chance to do anything, Claude was past him and had yanked open the topmost drawer of the last file cabinet and begun shoveling armloads of paper into the wheelbarrow. He didn't say anything or even hold Edgar's gaze. When Edgar understood what Claude was doing, he turned back to the files and they worked side by side. The wheelbarrow was quickly overfilled. There was no time to explain and no language for it. Edgar just grabbed the wheelbarrow's handles and ran through the doorway. Keeping low enough to breathe clear air was difficult and twice he had to halt to steady the mound of papers.

As soon as he was outside he dropped to his knees and forced another coughing fit; this time it tore at his throat. Then he stood and shoved the wheelbarrow into the grass and pitched it over and watched the papers scatter, sheets of white and cream everywhere, the writing on them like every language in the world, some ancient, others yet to be invented. Pictures and pedigrees and log sheets and notes, everywhere he looked. The story of forty generations. Fifty.

He looked toward the house. His mother lay bound up in Glen Papineau's arms. When she saw Edgar, she stopped struggling and turned her face to him.

"Let it go, Edgar! Let it go!"

I can't, he signed. Not yet.

He turned back to the smoldering kennel. His mother's cries, intertwined with Glen's moans, made an unnerving duet. The once-narrow ribbon of smoke had become an opaque mass that belched from the top half of the barn's entryway. He wondered if the straw in the mow had caught fire. Not even the tiniest lick of flame was visible, though plumes of black smoke poured from the roofline.

He understood what it meant to go back into the workshop. He did not believe Claude was there to help him. Yet every file he rescued restored some piece of a world that he thought had been lost forever. For so long he'd lived divided—from his father, from himself, now from Almondine. What he meant to do was not a question for him of wisdom or foolishness, courage or fearlessness, insight or ignorance. It was only that he could not split himself the way he once had; could not choose between imperatives. To resurrect or revenge. To fight or turn away.

Inside were two more cabinets filled with files and the letters from Brooks and the master litter book and *The New Webster Encyclopedic Dictionary of the English Language* with Alexander McQueen's essay on the significance of naming and page upon page of notes, markers of every dog Edgar had ever known. He pushed the wheelbarrow forward at a trot, and for the last time he passed through the double doors and into the barn. If he worked fast he could be in and out in three minutes. And if he needed more time, he had an idea that might clear the smoke long enough to get everything else.

An idea that had come to him long ago, in a dream.

Claude

THE MOMENT EDGAR DISAPPEARED THROUGH THE WORKSHOP door and into the smoke, Claude snatched open the bottom file drawer and dug the rag-wrapped bundle from beneath the mass of letters and newspaper clippings. The syringe, folded into the oily fabric, worked loose and fell into the drawer and he pawed through the chaos before his fingers touched the round plastic barrel. He retreated across photographs and pedigrees scattered over the floor like a lunatic's history of the kennel. When he reached the workbench, he turned his back to the room and knelt.

He wrapped the rag around his hand and grasped the bottle through it and worked the stopper loose and with great care set it on the floor away from himself, far back in the corner. He twisted the sheath off the needle. His motions were careful, but he was working in a rush, and by accident he jabbed the needle's point lightly into the flesh of his right palm. Before he even felt the sting, he'd jerked his hand away. The puncture was too small to release even a single drop of blood, but an infinitesimal red meniscus colored the needle's point.

When he looked at the bottle again, an iridescent rivulet had crept up the throat of the glass. He set the needle against the shear lip. To see the fluid wick so eagerly into that minute steel artery made his skin crawl. He needed only a drop but half a cc got into the barrel before he could put his thumb above the plunger and even then its insistent, upward force felt to him like some feral thing lunging from its cage. With effort, he pushed all but a fraction back into the bottle. When he drew the syringe away, a silver filament quivered in the air. He set the needle tip against the glass and turned it and withdrew it again, leaving a drop of clear oil that shivered and collapsed and slid down the inner curve of the bottle's neck. He left the bottle unstoppered and tossed away the rag and turned, holding the syringe at arm's length, and he waited.

The file cabinets opposite stood hazy and remote through the dense smoke. He wasn't sure Edgar meant to come back, but he could drop the syringe and be out of the barn in seconds if things suddenly felt unsafe. Fire didn't move *that* quickly, he thought. He looked at the bare bulb shining in its ceiling socket and wondered how long before the insulation on the wiring melted. The smoke carried a meaty, awful scent of roasted flesh. A nest of mice, he thought, or a bird in the eaves, overcome. All that smoke and still not a sound, not a flame. Outside, he could hear Trudy crying and calling out.

Then Edgar appeared, hunkered down behind the empty wheelbarrow, bent so low over the thing that the skids scraped the cement floor. He jammed it nose first into the space below the mow stairs and dropped to his knees and yanked open the bottommost drawer of the oldest cabinet—exactly where the bottle had been hidden—and began to heave out letters and papers. Claude stood. He remembered how the old herbalist had used a sharpened reed. How his withered hands had shaken with palsy afterward. Now that seemed like such a mild reaction, for Claude was suddenly conscious of all the mechanism of nerve and muscle and ligament that animated his fingers. The syringe began to tremble in his grip. With his free hand he squeezed his shaking wrist until the bones inside ground against one other.

He crossed the workshop.

The act itself took just an instant.

When it was done he backed away, reaching behind with one hand to swing the workshop door closed. All at once his teeth began chattering and he bit down so hard to make them stop that a groan escaped him. He had to get hold of himself, he thought. All he needed to do now was keep Edgar in the room and let time pass. But his heart threw itself against his ribs and the blood rushing through him felt as heavy as mercury. He pressed his back to the door and slid to the cement, and noticed for the first time that the syringe was still in his hand. With a convulsive jerk, he flung it away. As he had with Gar.

Edgar kept pitching files into the wheelbarrow as if nothing had happened. Then, abruptly, he sat back on his heels and looked over his head and behind, as if startled by a sound. He turned toward Claude, but his gaze hardly lingered. Then he stood and made his way across the workshop, working hand over hand along the shelves beneath the stairs, and he began looking for something in the corner, where the long-handled tools stood in a tangle.

When he turned, Edgar held a pitchfork in his hand.

Aw, God, Claude thought.

But Edgar wasn't looking at Claude. He walked to the center of the workshop, bent low to keep his face out of the thick mass of smoke. He crouched for a moment, squinting and wiping the tears from his eyes, and swaying as he fixed the position of something near the light fixture on the ceiling.

Then Edgar stood and drove the pitchfork straight up into the smoke.

Edgar

HIS FIRST THOUGHT WAS THAT SOMETHING HAD FALLEN ON him and dazzled a nerve, the way it happened when a person struck their elbow. A bolt of coldness in the back of his neck, nothing more. He had time to reach into the file drawer and press another handful of letters and papers between his palms and turn and dump them into the wheelbarrow, and then an icy wave radiated down his back and toward his limbs, settling in his crotch and knees and armpits and in the palms of his hands. Strange beyond words, the sensation. He reached back and touched his neck. He turned. Nothing had fallen. Claude had pushed the workshop door closed and now sat clumsily at the base of it, looking frightened and panting through his mouth.

Then, for no reason Edgar could see, the smoke suddenly tripled in thickness, until the walls of the room were barely visible. The ceiling light shrank to an orange, smoke-smeared crystal. He told himself he should cough and he bent down and put his elbows on his knees but the result was feeble. He needed to clear the smoke from the room; he was being overcome. He made his way to the implements leaning in the corner. Rakes. Hoes. Any of them would do, it didn't matter. The one that came into his hand was a pitchfork.

When he turned, the room careened around him. Ether, he thought, because that sense of detachment had come over him again, the same as when Glen had held the cloth over his face—the feeling that he was outside his body looking back at himself. But this was different, too. It came from that dazzled feeling that swept over him. He couldn't shake the idea that something had fallen on him. He touched his head. His fingers came away bloodless and dry.

He made his way to the center of the workshop, trying to keep his balance. It was impossible to see the ceiling through the smoke. Every time he drew a breath something scraped inside his lungs. He forced himself to concentrate. He tried to see in his mind where the hay hatch was positioned relative to that ceiling light. Twice he staggered off to the side and had to look at his feet in order to keep from falling.

At last, he took a guess. He lifted the pitchfork and drove it upward. The tines struck wood. When he pushed, there was solid, unyielding resistance. He yanked downward and the tines came free and he thrust up into the smoke again a foot to the right. This time something gave. He felt the hatch lift an inch, then catch, cockeyed in its slot. He shifted position and gave one final heave and felt the hatch clear the opening and slide along the mow floor above him.

Then the pitchfork clattered down. He found himself lying on his back, though he didn't remember falling. The air near the floor was blissfully clear. Smoke eddied and swirled about the hay hatch, a sweeping, tidal movement, like watching something alive. It had worked just the way he'd hoped, just the way it had happened in his dream that first morning after his father appeared in the rain. The sight filled him with exaltation and sadness. The smoke was rising into the mow, stretching when it came to the lip and tumbling upward. He could see nothing in the mow itself—no towering bales, no beams, no tackle, no bulbs among the rafters. Only a thousand layers of gray, lifting upward. He thought he might see flame, but it was nothing like that. Only the fluid rush of the smoke.

He'd meant to do something after he rolled this final barrow of records out of the barn, something important. He didn't blame Glen Papineau for doing what he'd done. He'd only wanted to ask Edgar a question, he'd said. But Edgar had something he'd wanted to say to Glen, and now he closed his eyes and imagined Glen standing there, and imagined himself saying the words so Glen could hear them.

I'm sorry, he said. He imagined it with all his might, with all the power of his mind. I'm sorry about your father.

He felt something recede inside him. A diminishment of barriers. He lay and watched the smoke crawl along the ceiling. After a time Almondine stepped out of some hidden place near the file cabinets. She walked to him and looked down at him and licked his face.

Get up, she said. Hurry. She panted. Her ears were cupped forward and drawn up tight, as they were when she was most fretful, though her movements were measured and calm. He was not surprised to hear her voice. It was just as he'd heard it in his mind all his life.

I thought I'd never see you again, he signed.

You were lost.

Yes. Lost.

You didn't need to come back. I would have found you.

No, I did. I understood some things while I was gone.

And you had to come back.

Yes.

What was it you understood.

What my grandfather was doing. Why people want Sawtelle dogs. Who should have them. What comes next.

You understood those things all along.

No. Not this way.

For a time they just looked at one another.

So many things happened, he signed.

Yes.

Sit here beside me. I want to tell you about someone. His name is Henry.

Get up, she said. Come outside.

I told him my name was Nathoo.

He laughed a little as he said this, knowing she would understand.

Mowgli's human name.

Yes.

Was that better.

He thought about her question.

At first. Later it didn't matter. I meant to tell him different, but I never got the chance.

Almondine sat and peered at him, brow knit, eyes like cherrywood polished to glass. It came to him then, a wholly new thought, that Nathoo was neither his name nor not his name; that even "Edgar" was a thing apart from his real name—the name Almondine had bestowed upon him in some distant past, long before he learned to carry ideas in time as memories, and whatever name that was had no expression in human words or gestures, nor could it exist beyond the curve and angle of her face, the shine of her eyes, the shape of her mouth when she looked at him.

Baboo and Tinder stayed with Henry.

Yes.

I shouldn't have turned away when I saw you with Claude that day. I don't know what happened to me.

You were lost.

I was lost.

Get up, she said one last time.

Come, he said. Lie here by me.

Almondine settled herself and leaned her chest against his side. Her face was near his face and she looked at him and followed his gaze up toward the ceiling.

He closed his eyes, then opened them again with a jerk, afraid that Almondine had gone, but there had been no need to worry. They lay on the floor and watched the smoke writhe across the ceiling. It was not so much like smoke at all anymore, but a river, broad and placid, beginning nowhere and ending nowhere, flowing on and on. The two of them lay on the bank of that river as it swept past like the creek in flood time.

Perhaps this river, too, had once been divided by a fence. But no more.

On the far side a figure appeared, distant but recognizable—someone he'd longed to see so often since that night the dogs had howled in the rain and the world had begun to turn on such a new and terrible axis. He'd meant to say something that night, the most important thing of all, it seemed to him now, but he'd cowered when the moment came and the chance was lost and afterward he'd been damned.

He set his fingers in the fur at the base of Almondine's throat. Breaths came into her and left, came and left. He closed his eyes, for how long he didn't know. When he opened them again the river was just the same but somehow the man had crossed to meet them. Or perhaps they had crossed. He couldn't be sure. Either way it made him happy. He felt he had a voice inside him for the first time and with it he could say what he'd meant to say all along. The man was close. There was no need to cry out the words. He could whisper, even, if he wanted.

He smiled.

"I love you," said Edgar Sawtelle.

Claude

H E SAT WITH HIS BACK TO THE WORKSHOP DOOR, WAITING and counting, watching Edgar lying in front of him. A vortex of smoke was rushing upward into the dark rectangle overhead. There had been one terrible moment when he'd thought, *it isn't working,* but he'd been mistaken. Instead of advancing on Claude, the boy had used the pitchfork to open the hay hatch. After he fell, he'd lain looking into the mow and working his hands over his chest in a stream of sign that Claude could not hope to read. That had gone on for a long time. Then, as if Edgar had come to some sort of decision, he draped one hand atop his chest, laid the other on the floor beside his leg, and hadn't moved since.

Claude thought of that rain-soaked alley in Pusan—what it had been like watching the old man drop the tip of his sharpened reed onto the crippled dog's withers—how gentle the motion—how the dog had paused from its lapping at the crock of soup and looked up and crumpled. There had been only an instant's delay. It seemed as if the contents of the bottle never acted the same way twice. Perhaps, over time, it had lost potency. Perhaps it drew on something different in each person. He would have liked to go back now and ask the old man to explain it. The bottle sat across the room, at the base of the workbench. He had to fight the desire to scramble over and twist the glass stopper into place—to seal it up again, at least for as long as he was confined to the same room with it. Only his dread of nearing the stuff stopped him. And if he touched it again, he couldn't be certain he would leave it behind.

He debated whether he should carry Edgar's body out. He could sling the boy over his shoulders in a fireman's carry and stagger into the yard. That way would be better for Trudy, he thought, and he would have done as she asked. Or he could tell Trudy the boy had grown confused and wandered into the smoky center of the barn, and though he'd searched and searched, he'd finally been driven out by the smoke, certain that Edgar must have emerged from the back doors. That was better—but only if it looked as if he had searched for a very long time—as long as humanly possible. Dangerously long. He forced himself to sit one minute more. He concentrated on stopping the jitter in his knees. It cost him nothing to wait, besides breathing a little smoke and having to look at the boy lying there. Claude could not fix his gaze on Edgar for long without a tremor rising from his insides, but that was foolish. If anything, the boy looked peaceful.

Then, from the mow, came a sound. A groan that rose in pitch to a squeal like shearing tin. Claude looked up. There was no change in the character of the smoke, and no flames glowed through the open hatch, but suddenly it felt dangerous to be in that barn for even a second longer. The boy had been right about one thing—opening the hatch had cleared much of the smoke from the workshop. But, Claude was deciding right then, it had been a less-than-great idea for other reasons, and the more he thought about it, the less desire he had to stay in the barn. Black, fluid smoke from under the door had begun to creep around either side of him.

Standing brought on a wave of dizziness. He stepped back from the door, taking care to avoid the boy's body. Standing hands to knees, he gasped breaths of the clear air. Then he twisted the knob on the workshop door. It was as if he'd swept aside a dam. The acrid smoke that poured in tore at his throat, forcing him back into the corner. He knelt and coughed and when he looked up again the smoke was rushing toward the open hay hatch. Not rising, *rushing*. And for the first time he saw the interior of the mow glowing orange through that curtain of gray.

And brightening.

He scrambled into the kennel aisle, hands on the floor. The atmosphere roiled in barrels around him. He was at the double doors, poised to step through, when something made him pause and drag the back of his knuckles across his tearing eyes. Precisely where the smoke belched into the light of the hooded lamp outside the doors stood the figure of a man. As Claude watched, the figure tattered and disappeared. Claude closed his eyes. When he opened them again, the figure had returned, not so much engulfed in the smoke as *made* of it. Through it, Claude saw the papers Edgar had retrieved, scattered across the grass of the lawn.

Glen, was his first thought. But Glen's voice echoed from out in the yard. And even at a glance, Claude recognized his brother's form.

This was hypoxia, hallucination, smoke rapture—what happened to oxygen-starved divers. He knelt and pressed his face against the cement floor to suck clear air into his lungs. As he stood again, the last ceiling light in the aisle winked out. Outside, the hooded lamp above the doors cast its light just long enough for Claude to see clearly that it *was* Gar, beyond any doubt.

And then it was dark. He stood for a moment trying to force himself forward, but in the end he turned to face the interior of the barn. Another pair of doors waited on the far end. He could traverse the length of the kennel and gain the clear summer night air that way—a few seconds' travel, if he hurried.

He navigated along in the darkness, imagining the arrangement of kennel runs on either side of him, the long straight aisle, the door to the whelping room ahead, the beams of the mow passing above one by one. He didn't break into a run until the timbers began to shriek far overhead, a twisting scream this time that made him sure the entire structure must be ready to collapse. And yet, that couldn't be happening. He'd barely seen a flame.

He stared up at the sound. Through a gap in the smoke, a thin pair of orange lines. Heat on his face.

He had taken only a step or two in full flight when an imageless blaze of white blossomed and dissipated before him. Then he was sitting on the cement. It took a moment for the pain to register, to understand he'd run into one of the posts lining the aisle. He reached out, felt it, sooty and warm, though he couldn't see it. His throat burned as if he'd swallowed acid. When he clambered to his feet, a coughing fit nearly drove him to the floor all over again.

The collision had turned him around. At first he couldn't tell which way he'd been heading. Over the sound of the timbers he thought he heard his name being called.

"What was that?" he shouted. "Who is it?"

But there was no reply—just his own voice, returning flatly through the smoke. He shouted again. Something about the shape of the echo gave him his bearings. To his left he made out a dim rectangle of light through the smoke. A doorway, but front or back? He turned away from it and began to walk, hands outstretched, moving in the straightest line he could.

His fingertips touched wood, then a hinge, then the wire of a pen door. He stepped back and corrected to the right. He had only to follow the perfectly straight line of the aisle to find the back doors. It should have been simple. He took another step into the blackness. Time and again his hands pressed against wire where there should have been open air. The aisle seemed to veer left, but when he moved left, it veered right, as though the sound in his ears was not the breaking strain of burning wood, but the agony of those great beams twisting.

At last a wind began to pass along the aisle, dragging smoke across his face like a streamer of hot silk. Now he had reason to panic, but to his surprise the sensation was exquisite, as if he had longed for it all his life. He stopped. Then even the sound of the timbers quieted and there was just the hollow roar of wind. He stood in the darkness, eyes closed, letting the smoke caress him. Then he lifted his hands and twined his fingers into the warm wire mesh he knew he would find waiting.

Trudy

FOR THE LONGEST TIME NEITHER CLAUDE NOR EDGAR APPEARED in the doorway of the barn. Trudy called until her throat grew raw, her voice a high and wordless lament, and her body thrashed and twisted in the cage of Glen's arms. In time, she fell silent. She began to think it wasn't Glen holding her at all but the black vine, grown now thick and strong and pressing its roots into the soil to draw the earth tight against her and outward then in all directions so that its tendrils pinched and grabbed at time itself and time, like a slowly scrolling stage backdrop, became entangled; and the black vine drew down that canvas to lie slack and unsprocketed beneath a great proscenium where upstage all manner of machinery and instruments nameless and never before seen lay roughly strewn.

And there Trudy found herself unable to look away from all those things she'd worked so hard not to see. When she'd viewed the canvas long enough, so that no part of it remained hidden from her and no part mistaken, the black vine relaxed its grip and time curled up upon its spindles again and rolled forward and Trudy was lying once more on the grass of the yard. Slowly, slowly, her face was turned until the light of the present world shone in the glassy lune of her eye.

And as she watched, flames began to eat through the long, shingled roof of the barn—not the tiny licks of orange that had so horribly fili- greed the eaves, but real fire now, living fire that burst forth into the air and disappeared and erupted again as if lunging in desperation to grasp the night and pull it in. A gout of flame flashed high above the barn's roof, twisting inside a pillar of smoke, a scarlet rose that blossomed and vanished. From inside the mammoth came a low, prolonged groan. The center beam of the roof sagged. Then the wreathing smoke shuddered and retreated into the barn, as if the structure had drawn its maiden breath, and the inferno began. As quickly as that: one moment, a mass of smoke; the next, all was flame. The wakening scorched Trudy's face. The light it cast painted the fields and woods all around them red.

As heat washed over them, Glen Papineau released Trudy and stood and put his hands in the air and began to slap at his face and chest and hair, throwing a nimbus of quicklime into the air around him.

Am I burning? he cried. Oh God! Have I caught fire?

But Trudy neither moved nor answered. She was not there. She did not know she was unbound. Glen Papineau staggered away, navigating by meridians of heat. Trudy lay on the grass, eyes fixed on the open doors of the barn and the flames that thrust through them like incandescent limbs.

And Glen Papineau plunged across the yard, a blinded bull, stum- bling, falling, rising again, bellowing over and over, What's happened? What's happened? For God sakes, what's happened?

The Sawtelle Dogs

THEY HAD MEASURED THEIR LIVES BY PROXIMITY TO THAT silent, inward creature, that dark-haired, sky-eyed boy who smoothed his hands along their flanks and legs and withers and muzzles, a boy they'd watched since the moment of their birth, a boy who appeared each morning carrying water and food and, every afternoon, a brush. Who pronounced names upon them from the leaves of a book. They had taught him while they watched him; they had learned by listening to Almondine. And though they had seldom seen it, they understood the meaning of fire: they looked at the flames soaring into the night sky and the sparks bursting from the timbers, flying upward, ever upward, and the bats flickering into the smoke and curling and plummeting and they knew they had no home.

They circled the fire until their chests belled and their tongues hung loose from their mouths. Embers settled on the pile of papers the boy had made and a few of these began to curl and rise flaming into the air. The flames leapt to the orchard trees by wind and sympathy, until only the house and the young maple and the elderly apple tree whose fingers brushed the house opposed them. Red beams beat across the trees. In the south field, the birches and the white crosses glowed like rubies. The shadows of the dogs, cast from the top of the hill, darkened the forests. Great drabs of tar flew sputtering from the barn roof until the whole structure became transparent, down to the glowing ribs. The wires of the pens pooled like water and boiled away. The fiberglass top of the truck crinkled and smoked and shrank inward, belching a nacreous yellow cloud. The wires strung between the house and barn lay snaked and smoking along the ground. In time, the tires of the truck swelled and burst like gunshots and the truck tipped its lee side toward the flames, lacking the sense to save itself. Far away, on the distant ledge of the world, a thunderhead glowed in response to the fire's call, but if those clouds came they would offer nothing but an inspection of the bones, charred and smoldering.

The woman lay sprawled on the heat-curled grass between the house and the fire, deaf to their calls, deaf to the cries of the blind man standing over her, ignorant and insensate, as though she had departed her body and left it heaving on the shores of the world. Those who understood saw that the time inside her had been boiled away by the heat of the fire and, if anything, thought she might rise transformed into a swan or a dove.

The heat grew. It drove them first toward the house, then to the garden behind the maple. Fire echoed between the now incandescent orchard and the cracked stone pedestal of the barn. Those dogs were not all equally good; some of them fought and others cowered and still others traced idiotic paths around the spectacle and harassed the blind man as he dragged the woman across the grass. Yet witnesses they were, one and all, trained and bred to watch, taught by their broody mothers to use their eyes, taught by the boy himself to wait for a gesture that put meaning into a world where none existed. Among them, the two pups whimpered and cried and pressed against whoever didn't snarl. One way or another, all oriented themselves against that hemisphere of fire. Some turned their faces into the night. Some sank to their bellies and rested their jaws on their forefeet, facing into the flames like Sphinxes into the sunset.

Essay ran down into the field then. A few of the other dogs followed, including her littermates and also the two pups, these last, slow and confused. When she reached the rock pile, Essay waited until all had stopped with her, then she circled back toward the yard, snarling at any who tried to follow. They milled and waited. She appeared again with half a dozen more dogs following, the rest unwilling to leave the aureole of heat. She trotted through the pack and along the edge of the field, her back reddened by the blaze. When they reached the old logging road, she passed the birches without hesitation and departed the field near the southwest corner, cutting crosswise through the forest. In the woods, they slowed their pace. The dogs spread out beside and behind her.

They passed through fence after fence. Some of the dogs fell away, lost or disheartened, but she did not stop or circle back. They would follow or they would not, she had only made the possibility clear. Night birds decried their passage. A ménage of deer sprang from their bedding grounds. She led the dogs along, checking her way, though it had been marked so obviously that some ran ahead. And then, realizing she'd lost the pups, she did stop and backtrack. She found them huddled near a fallen tree, whimpering and shaking in the moonlight. She lowered her muzzle and they licked at her face and swatted their tails through the bracken, and in return she mouthed their necks and nosed along their sides and feet and bellies, then turned and trotted away. So coaxed, they began to follow again.

The forest streamed round. The night passed. They tracked through marshes and forded creeks until the dark vault overhead gave way to a deep orange, the sky ignited by what they'd left behind. Presently, Essay emerged from the woods. Before her, a field sloped away, fallow for many seasons and dotted with scrub pine. The grass bent wet and heavy in the still morning. From behind her came the hoarse cry of the diaspora, bursting through the underbrush. When the sun broke over the treetops, all before her glittered.

To the west, across the field, Forte paced the tree line, his figure cutting back and forth on the thin fog that clung to the ground. To the east, where the field bottomed out, a scattering of lights twinkled among the trees and here and there the slanted rooftop of a house was visible. Essay could hear the earth breathing around her. If not for the white steeple that rose over the treetops and the headlights that flickered into view on a blacktop far away, she might have been looking on a scene from the beginning of the world. A thing like a song or a poem rang in her ears. There was Forte. There was the village. One by one, the Sawtelle dogs trotted from between the trunks of the trees and followed the forest's edge until they all stood together, Finch and Opal and Umbra and Pout and the two unnamed pups and all the others who had followed through the night. They traced Essay's gaze across the field, first east, then west, and shuffled about her and licked her muzzle, making their desires known, and then they waited.

Essay stepped into the grass. She stood, paw lifted to her chest, nose raised to scent the air, watching it all. For an instant, as the morning light brightened, everything in the field stood motionless. She looked behind her one last time, into the forest and along the way they'd come, and when she was sure all of them were together now and no others would appear, she turned and made her choice and began to cross.

Acknowledgments

This book has been a long time in the writing and consequently I owe thanks to a great many people. Eleanor Jackson, my literary agent, has been an unstinting champion, adviser, and friend; she is an idealist of the savviest kind. Lee Boudreaux, my editor at Ecco, worked like a dynamo to improve this book, challenging every line, every word, every preconception, yet somehow making me laugh in the process. The result is infinitely better for her efforts and she has my deepest gratitude. Abigail Holstein, also at Ecco, saw the manuscript through many travails and offered advice both timely and wise.

I am indebted to my teachers in the Warren Wilson MFA Program for Writers—Ehud Havazelet, Joan Silber, Margot Livesey, Richard Russo, and Wilton Barnhardt, as well as the rest of that remarkable faculty—for the confluence of ideas and talent they bring to Swannanoa each January and July. Richard Russo has been especially generous with his time and consideration. Thanks to Robert Boswell for a pivotal workshop in Aspen and the gracious advice that followed. Thanks also to Robert McBrearty, teaching at the University of Colorado and in ongoing workshops and innumerable lunches, for indispensable advice on writing and life. Finally, thanks to the Vermont Studio Center for a writing fellowship during which sections of Part Three were written.

The following people read drafts of this book and offered in return the great gift of their insight: Barbara Bohen, Carol Engelhardt, Charlene Finn, Nickole Ingram, Karen Lehmann, Cherie McCandless, Tim McCandless, Brad Reeves, Nancy Sullivan, Audrey Vernick, and Karen Wolfe. They pointed out, compassionately, each draft's weaknesses, which helped make this book better, and its strengths, which gave me hope. No writer could ask for a finer advisory council.

Factual information was provided to me by Maura Quinn-Padron at St. Joseph's Hospital in Marshfield, Wisconsin, on the basics of speech pathology; Peter Knox at the University of Colorado, on Latin; Jim Barnett, on Japanese; Rob Oberbreckling, on the nature of structure fires; Roger Sopher and Dr. William Burton, on the properties of ether; and Lisa Sabichi, DVM, who endured what are surely some of the strangest questions ever put to a veterinarian. I am grateful for her patient responses, as well as the extraordinary care she has given to two dogs I've been privileged to know. To suit my own purposes, I've twisted every fact these people supplied me; the resulting errors and inaccuracies are my fault alone.

There exists a wealth of literature on canine biology, cognition, and training methods. A list of sources consulted would be far too long for these notes, and inevitably incomplete, but anyone interested in the fictionalized training techniques employed by the Sawtelles might well begin with the essay "How to Say 'Fetch!'" by Vicki Hearne and work outward from there. I have also read, with great pleasure, *A Journey into Mellen*, a century's worth of Mellen newpaper articles, condensed and compiled by a committee of volunteers and edited by Joe Barabe. Last of all, from the two real authors of *Working Dogs*, Elliot Humphrey and Lucien Warner, I ask belated forgiveness for inventing a coauthor; John Sawtelle needed a friend who understood his project and from whom he could learn the lessons of the Fortunate Fields work.

Above all, this book owes its existence to Kimberly McClintock, an extraordinary artist, a loving and generous partner, my most ferocious advocate, my first, last, and most exacting reader. Her encouragement and wisdom suffuse every page of this book.

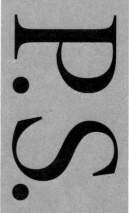

About the Author

About the Book

Insights,
Interviews
& More ...

Read On

Meet David Wroblewski

© 2008 Marion Ettlinger

DAVID WROBLEWSKI was born in 1959 in Oconomowoc, Wisconsin, a suburb of Milwaukee. When he was threes years old, his parents bought a small and somewhat ramshackle farm in rural central Wisconsin, determined to try their luck at dairy farming. Within two years, they'd sold their livestock and shut down the farm, and David's father had taken a job at a nearby machine shop to pay the bills. With an unused barn at her disposal, his mother began to raise dogs. David spent a good part of his childhood doing odd jobs around the kennel and honing his puppy-wrangling skills. In time, that barn and that land, transported one hundred miles to the north, would become the setting for *The Story of Edgar Sawtelle*.

In high school, David won a statewide arts competition with a short story about a pack of wolves. At the University of Wisconsin, he declared himself a theater major, imagining he would someday make a living as an actor; small stage roles in *Equus* and *West Side Story* convinced him otherwise. By the time he graduated, he had become fascinated with the practical and collaborative art of making software and took a degree in computer science. He has since developed software ranging from embedded controls in ring laser gyros, to artificial intelligence programs that analyze the meaning of English sentences, to websites that teach kids how to write essays. He is an active black-and-white landscape photographer and holds a creative writing degree from the Warren Wilson MFA Program for Writers.

Over the years, David has lived in La Crosse, Wisconsin; Minneapolis, Minnesota; and Austin, Texas. He currently makes his home in Colorado with the writer Kimberly McClintock; their dog, Lola; and their cat, Mitsou.

The Story of Edgar Sawtelle is his first novel. ∾

A Boy and His Dogs
Gil Adamson Interviews David Wroblewski

Gil Adamson, author of The Outlander, *interviewed David Wroblewski in the summer of 2008.*

David, you've been traveling, doing promotion for your book. A lot of it. How is that going?

Well, it's a relentless march of details that you have to make sure you get right. You know, normally the stakes are so low in my life. I only have to fumble my way from one thing to the next, and forget things and lose things and drop things and it doesn't really matter much. Now I have to be far more on the ball than usual.

It can also be exhausting talking endlessly about oneself, even talking about your book. You don't strike me as much of an egoist.

You know, if I did this at a party with my friends, they'd never invite me over again! But *Edgar* is so much about dogs that usually, you have this fairly regimented interview, and then afterwards people say, "Let me tell you about my dog." And we have this great discussion about their dog.

So you're home—for now anyway. Can you settle down and get back to writing?

That's the dream. I'll tell ya, it's never looked so good to just stay home and slog away at a first draft.

And you have an idea you are working on?

Yeah . . . but that doesn't count for much, right? All it's got to be is interesting or confusing or intriguing enough to get you in front of the keyboard. I don't know about you, but I got a number of questions on tour about "what are your writing habits like?" Fewer questions than I expected, but nevertheless, I had to make a moral judgment about whether to lie or tell the truth about just how undisciplined I am [laughs]. This is my first time writing a second novel, and I really don't know what to expect. I think back on the writing of *Edgar* when I thought it was fun writing a first draft, but things got *way* more fun in subsequent drafts.

Tinkering and fixing. It's fun, except when it's not fun.

When you go back over something because it's nagging at you—"this isn't right, this isn't right, something's missing here"—you may get no apparent good work done on that. But something else happens that is equally useful—at least sometimes—and that is that you prime ▶

5

A Boy and His Dogs *(continued)*

your attention, your imagination. Then you do whatever it is that you do with the rest of your life. And you pick up details that are relevant to whatever you are writing about. I've never been around the ocean much, but you see pictures of those fishing boats, and they have all this vast armature out, and there are nets hanging in every direction. You know they're going to drop those nets and drag them through the water and pick stuff up. I think of it along those lines. Your nets are deployed when you go out.

That's a great image.

You don't know what you're going to get from it. But time after time, for me, I'll work for a couple of days, and think, "Well, I didn't get much from that, I'm just going to move on." Then, a week later, something lands in front of me that was part of the solution to that problem. Maybe it's a detail or something on the radio or some other clue that helps me see how I can approach that material fresh.

Perhaps, if you hadn't had the question in your head in the first place, you might not have received that information or clue in the same way. You might not have been receptive at all. I've heard it said a different way: "Even when I'm not writing, I'm still writing." That's a statement that makes sense to most people— it's a nice way to explain the same weird process.

I don't know about you, but I'm addicted to metaphor, attracted to any activity that is highly metaphoric. For instance, I've spent all my professional life making software, which is just soaked in metaphor. There's no way to make software without engaging in metaphor-making and elaborating out of metaphor, because all software is a metaphor.

Give me an example of that.

Sure. The most obvious example is the desktop metaphor we're all familiar with. But what people outside of the software industry probably don't know is that every piece of software that's ever been developed is posed in terms of metaphor—all the algorithms and all the data structures are generally described in terms of some physical thing. For instance, there is a very common data structure called a "queue," a first-in-first-out list, that lines up hunks of data like people standing in line for something. Even the guts of programs with no visual manifestation—no graphic user interface at all—are described and documented for other programmers to appreciate and make sense of in highly metaphoric terms.

So you are already thinking metaphorically, and openly metaphorically, and it all has an ultimate use?

In the industrial world of software, it's just a practical way of making yourself clear. For instance, this program that draws a line is like a turtle crawling around that can only be told to turn left or right or go ahead or back up. That's the old programming language Logo. And once you understand it in terms of the metaphor, your understanding of the program comes along very quickly. Whereas if you just describe it in terms of *what it does*, you're generally asking for confusion and certainly misunderstanding. So, metaphor involves taking a complicated thing and reducing it somehow to something that's less complicated and that allows you to make sense of it. Which to me is very much . . . well, I do a lot of black-and-white photography, and that is visually metaphoric. You'll see a picture of, say, a gently lit pear, or something like that, and it'll look like a human body. Or you'll see a human body and it'll look like a pear [laughs].

And these days, the way we handle photographic images digitally, a black-and-white image is an image for which the color information has been removed. So it's been simplified. Now, your book is beautifully and obsessively about codes and information. Edgar is mute and uses sign language, but his way of signing is idiosyncratic; the way the family speaks to the dogs is idiosyncratic; even the breed of dog, the "Sawtelle dog," has been carefully bred not to produce ideal physical characteristics, ▶

A Boy and His Dogs *(continued)*

*but an ideal of intelligence, acumen, and—amazingly—
personality. I wonder how much of your lifelong interest in
codes and metaphor has got you thinking rather deeply about
that interface between dog and human, and generally about
codes and communication.*

Well, very much. This is a subject I *am* almost obsessively
interested in. I've worked a lot in research labs, and in particular
on software whose intention was to analyze written human
language and try to extract meaning from it, in one way or
another. Whether it's parsing out individual sentences and
breaking them down into grammatical components, or whether
it's statistical analysis of text, trying to understand larger chunks
of text based on, essentially, word frequency. It's always about
constructing meaning out of the partial information that you're
allowed to have about the world. And that's Edgar's dilemma
across the board. I mean, early in the book, he has to imagine
Schultz, the old farmer they bought the farm from. He will never
meet Schultz, he can never know Schultz, so he learns that if he's
going to answer this basic question, "Why did Schultz leave?" it's
going to come from inside him. It's going to be constructed out of
his imagination and whatever evidence he can find, pretty much at
random, around the farm. The only answer he's ever going to get
to that secret is the one he supplies.

*The ones he's supplied and that he's made through intuitive
connections. There's the old telegram confirming the sale of
the farm, and it's so old that words are falling off. He intuits by
these words falling off the tenuousness of that ownership. And so,
throughout the novel—and this may have to do with the presence
of animals in the book—there are these unusual intuitive flashes
and connections that strike the reader as being very true, and
quite fresh.*

There's a passage in the book that's always made me very happy,
when Trudy has told Edgar that Claude is going to move in, and
Edgar's very upset about it. He goes out to groom the dogs and to
think things over. He realizes he doesn't have a choice, that this is

going to happen whether he likes it or not. While he's grooming the dogs, this expression comes into his head that his mother is "taking up with a man." Which he immediately recognizes as a fussy expression. And he thinks about how having the words for a thing comes in the aftermath of understanding the thing—how words come later, as a sort of residue, if you know what I mean. And he knows that idea, of "taking up with a man," isn't what he's thinking *now*. What he's thinking *now* he doesn't have words for yet. And by the time he has words for that, he'll be off thinking something else. This is the idea you're touching on. Part of what's interesting to me about this book is trying to capture Edgar's way of thinking—especially those moments where dominos start to tip for him, and he suddenly understands, for instance, why they breed the dogs the way they do. Or he suddenly sees there's a way to maybe find an explanation for this thing he thinks he may know, and yet there's no way he'll ever get any evidence for it. He has these aha moments. Or he recognizes Henry having an "Aha" moment with the dogs.

And in many cases, the dogs knew something before the humans did. The people kind of follow the dogs in understanding a reality or a relationship.

Or the human beings understand finally in verbal terms what they've already known with their senses for quite a while. I don't know what it's like for you, but when I finally "understand" something, there's often a sense of déjà vu. I understood it before, but now I'm understanding it in a way that allows me to put it into words. And so there's a strange sense of . . . almost resonance. Like, oh yeah—*that's* why I've been feeling this way. That's been an interesting part of writing this book: trying to capture that cognitive experience, in Edgar's life, or in the lives of the people around him, through processing information—essentially their body knows something before their mind. Or their subconscious mind knows it before their conscious mind.

Several sections in this book are written from the point of view of the dogs, and these sections are very beautiful—and in the ▶

A Boy and His Dogs (*continued*)

sections from the perspective of Almondine, Edgar's companion dog, the writing verges on sublime. Was it a difficult decision for you step right up and write from inside the mind of a dog, or was it relatively easy?

Let's see. This project has been going on for so long that I lose track of what happened when. I know I'd been working on this novel for over two years, probably three years, before I wrote the first Almondine chapter. In the original conception of the book there were no Almondine chapters. I knew very broadly what the overall story arc was, and I knew I wanted it to be divided into five acts like a play. But I had originally imagined the entire book being written from Edgar's point of view—in first person, actually. The first half of the first draft was all in first person. In fact, I worked on this book all through the MFA program I was enrolled in; it was my thesis material, and all of that was first-person point of view. It wasn't pushed into third person until afterwards, when I'd lost steam on the project, then came back to it and said, I *will* finish this book one way or another—it may not be publishable, but I'll finish it. I think the reason I lost steam was that I knew I couldn't carry it through all the way in first person. I was too constrained in vocabulary and perspective.

And there are pretty clear pros and cons to each voice. So, when you moved the text into third person did you find that you were losing anything?

Not so much. I expected it to be a lot harder. What it really felt like was tremendous freedom. Because you now have this ability to zoom the camera in, or pull it way back, so that you're either getting a wide-angle view or a very interior view of a character. And until you're using that tool you're not really taking advantage of third person. In first person, I had felt constrained by Edgar's vocabulary. There were certain kinds of sentences I wanted to write, certain words I wanted to use, that his character, even written in retrospect, couldn't have used. It wouldn't sound right. And it was counter to my experience of Edgar, whom I view as a very stoic, inward character.

Yes. A very inward boy. There's a lot of attraction, for a writer, to get in there with him, in first person, but you'd lose the inwardness because most of what he's thinking would be transparent to you. I've done that before with a piece of fiction and it fascinates me, the little conundrums you encounter. It's like, to use a metaphor, finding your way around something that's in your path—how do you get to the same place using this completely different route?

What happened was, I'd been in this MFA program for two and a half years; I'd been working on *Edgar* for maybe a year before that. I got involved in the MFA program out of pure desperation because I did not know how to write a novel. I thought it would be a completely natural thing—I'd been reading them all my life. Then when I tried, it was so . . . just the whole idea of a novel and why it would work as a story suddenly became very unclear to me [laughs]. When you're three or four or five hundred pages along and you have to put the next sentence down, whatever it is, whatever comes to mind, why is that right or wrong? It seemed completely arbitrary. I'd written these opening chapters, and then as my final MFA thesis was coming due, I wrote the first Almondine chapter, which burst out of Edgar's point of view. When I look back on it now, I see that the narrative was erupting from the constraints I'd put on it. Here was this other character, Almondine, and the only way to understand her was to switch to her point of view.

And in the book as it is now, you do that with all kinds of other characters, including Schultz. Edgar never meets Schultz, but we get a glimpse into his thinking. There's a scene where he's falling asleep and remembers the sound of chains breaking on a logging truck and killing a man. You say in the book that no one knows exactly why he leaves the farm, he just goes . . . so you're talking about the mystery of knowing somebody. ▶

A Boy and His Dogs *(continued)*

Although Edgar does eventually imagine the reason.

He does. And we imagine it ourselves, too, because you've put enough into even that minor character to tell us why he might leave.

One of the unusual technical aspects about the beginning of this novel is that I wanted Edgar's mind and sensibility to suffuse the story even before he's born. So one thing you may have noticed about that section is that, even though Edgar isn't born yet, he keeps intruding on the story, all the way back to his grandfather's time and Schultz's time. I wanted him to exist, essentially, before he exists.

The way we all know our family past through stories.

Yeah, and in my family at least—I grew up on a farm very much like the one Edgar grows up on . . . in fact it is the farm I grew up on exactly. I thought, I know this ninety acres, and this house and this barn, and I don't see any reason why I can't use that as the stage for all this to play out on. For many years we didn't have a TV when I was a kid. And, you know, we'd sit around and play cards, and Mom and Dad would talk casually, about people . . . I mean there was nothing else to do. We were going to be quiet or they were going to tell stories. It wasn't like we had this grand storytelling tradition in our family. It's just we had nothing else to do!

Like the Sawtelles, your family ran a dog kennel for a time, didn't they? Sawtelle dogs are a breed specifically designed not for looks but for intelligence and personality, by Edgar's grandfather. And it drives his friend Brooks crazy because John Sawtelle's method seems to have no scientific basis. I think it's just a wonderful idea, to leave the notion of a physical breed behind and go for something else.

That's drawn from a couple of sources. The Fortunate Fields breeding program mentioned is a real project. It was the precursor to what we call the Seeing Eye program now. As far as I know, that was the first attempt to apply scientific principles to breeding dogs for behavior and not for physical conformation. And they wrote this wonderful book called *Working Dogs*—Elliott Humphrey and Lucien Warner are the real authors . . .

And you added Brooks . . .

As a third [laughs]. It was rude enough to usurp their book for my purposes, but to actually put words in their mouths seemed unforgivable. It was a more forgivable sin to add a third author, so that's what I did. And I also thought he [Brooks] was a lot of fun as a character because, through the letters he writes, the game was to portray this guy as envious of John Sawtelle for having the freedom to work in an artistic mode. Brooks had to reassure himself as he's writing these letters that, you know, "What I'm doing is valuable," even though he's green with envy, and you can see that.

And what does he say: you are the artist; I'm the factory man?

I'm the factory man. He says, that might make me sound like a dullard, and if you're buying cakes that might go bad, that's one thing; but if you're buying medicine, you'd rather have a dullard producing it.

And what the Fortunate Fields people were dealing with was medicine—they were dealing with dogs to help handicapped people. Am I correct in assuming that?

The Fortunate Fields program was not only for Seeing Eye dogs, they were interested in breeding dogs that would be helpers in a lot of areas—police dogs and other kinds of service. And the one thing that struck me, the one thing they did not particularly focus on, was companionship, which, to my mind, is the main occupation of dogs nowadays. The overwhelming majority of dogs that live with human beings do so specifically as companions. And I wanted John Sawtelle to take *that* job seriously, too. ▶

A Boy and His Dogs *(continued)*

The Sawtelles are very careful not to let other dogs, strays and so forth, anywhere near their own dogs for fear they'd pick up a bad attitude. And at one point, Trudy, I think it is, describes some other dogs as "idiot dogs." Which brings up the question: what constitutes a good dog, what constitutes a bad dog, or is there even such a thing?

I think that there are good relationships between people and their dogs. Good matches. Good chemistry. And so there is the canine equivalent of . . . love at first sight, your one true love, things like that. But I don't think it's a feature of the dog; it's a feature of the relationship that's built between the person and the dog.

Training must, especially for dogs, be a very important element in the comfort level of that relationship.

Exactly. There was another book that made a big impression on me, even before I started working on this novel, which was *Adam's Task* by Vicki Hearne. Her thesis in that book is that the process of training is only superficially about obedience; what it's really about is constructing a language in which you can have this conversation that will carry on for your entire life, a conversation about what matters and what doesn't matter. Does it matter if you come when I call you, or does it not matter? Does it matter that you wake me up in the morning, or bark at the doorbell? Or does it not matter? So, it seems to me—and this is true in my own life—that the training is the means to an end, and the end is not obedience. It's just better understanding, better communication.

And when we say training, we're at least in part talking about training of the owner.

Right. Another thing Hearne says in her book is that you earn the right to give commands by being obedient yourself.

And you use that in your novel. At a certain point, Edgar realizes that he's lost the right to give commands to one of the dogs who

14

has been out in the wild with him. And this is going back to what we said before: he understands it after it's already happened.

Yeah. He's already good with the dogs, he's sort of a natural, but part of his journey in this story is to reach a point where it's no longer a power thing, and he now wants to learn from them.

They're finished with their training. And early on in the book, you have Almondine realize that her training is over, and her job has begun: she is here to watch over this mute child.

Right. And Edgar, on the other hand, can go back after he has had this revelation that, if he's going to do this thing that he may be the best at, he has to leave the vestiges of his ego behind, he has to just follow the dogs. At least figuratively. I mean, it comes back again to language and what its limits are, even language to the degree that we have it with dogs. We have communication—we don't have what we would formally consider language. But we have tremendous communication. One of the things I like about Edgar, even now in retrospect, and that I worked hard on in this book, was constructing a character who just *reveres* language, because he's denied this certain aspect of it. To him, the most unforgivable thing you can do is to use language in a way that obscures the truth, or obscures communication, or obfuscates what is right.

Speaking of obscuring the truth, I wanted to talk about this wonderful character Claude. His experience starts the book— and that is one chilling little scene. He's not exactly a force for good—and yet you never give in to the urge to make him two-dimensional. A Snidely Whiplash. He even tries at times to be a stepfather to Edgar. Was it hard for you to extend this kind of compassion to a character this destructive?

Well, the idea for Claude is that he would be entirely opaque, at least from Edgar's point of view. Edgar, being the hyper-observant person that he is, runs into that one person that ▶

A Boy and His Dogs *(continued)*

I suppose everyone experiences in their life whose motives and motivations and way of thinking are just inexplicable, impenetrable. So that was the original idea for Claude—opacity. Part of why it was so important in that early chapter to have Edgar imagine Schultz, and why Schultz would leave the farm, is because Edgar's dilemma throughout this story is to be required to imagine things he cannot know. To imagine what happened between Gar and Claude.

It's necessary for him to know what's coming at him from Claude, and he can't.

Yeah. For whatever reason, Claude is a blind spot for him. And he knows it. He knows what he doesn't know.

Claude is a blind spot for everybody except perhaps for Edgar's father, Gar. He's the older brother who has been dealing with Claude's nonsense for all those decades.

Which, for a character like Claude, you can imagine might be intolerable. To have one person who knows what they are in their essence. And as you say, Claude's kind of a sociopath; he's a manipulator. But he's smart. The one thing that's true about Claude is that he's not a fool. And he's patient, because his motto is: you can get anything you want as long as you're willing to go slowly enough.

That's a chilling statement from someone who does not mean well.

Right. And he's smart enough to portray himself as transparent, to say things straight out that you wouldn't think he'd say, and to couch things as if they were superficially helpful. As a writer, in terms of developing characters in pairs, you look for—and I'd be real curious to know how it works for you—characters that are sort of twisted opposites. If that makes any sense? Not perfectly binary opposites. But if they're a little twisted in their opposition, there's all kinds of ambiguity to play with. So you have Edgar who is constrained in his language, but when he talks, he always says what he means, he speaks very directly. And we have Claude who is very verbal, and yet he never says what he's really after.

What's interesting about twisted opposites is not only how different they are but where they overlap. So in the case of Edgar and Claude, they are both good with the dogs. There's the casual scene where they both pat Almondine—the reader is in agony because we feel Claude shouldn't be touching her, but really it's the most natural thing in the world.

Yes. Edgar is a prodigy with the dogs, but so was Claude, in his day. It's a world he left behind and is coming back to. Edgar recognizes this and reluctantly admires Claude. Or at least that's implicit in the book.

This novel is wildly allusive, obviously to the play Hamlet, *but to many other texts. It's one of the pleasures of reading the book, to my mind. I think I know why it is that you don't enjoy reviewers' making too much of the* Hamlet *connection, but let me ask you, anyway. Why does that dissatisfy you?*

Actually, it doesn't dissatisfy me. I had always imagined that Edgar's story was going to draw heavily from *Hamlet*. But what is disturbing to me is when it is reduced to simply: It's *Hamlet*. Those two words. Because in fact when you take on something as well known and as iconic and such a cornerstone of Western literature as *Hamlet*, you're obligated to change it. To make a book simply *Hamlet*—that wouldn't interest me at all. To call it a retelling of *Hamlet* is going one step too far. I tried to subvert the story every step of the way, to look for, for instance, the dramatic white space of the stage play. Of course other writers have done this. Like [Stoppard's] *Rosencrantz and Guildenstern Are Dead*. And the way many other stories play off other stories, you look for the blank spaces in the original.

That's the nature of an allusion. You're under no obligation to put on a wretched little vaudeville act of the original. You're supposed to do something different with it. ▶

A Boy and His Dogs *(continued)*

[Laughs] I love that. Exactly. If you did a paint-by-numbers version, it would be wretched.

Was it hard for you to decide what parts of the plot you had to honor and what parts you could ignore?

What was frustrating was exactly the opposite. One way I was trying to subvert equivalence between the two stories was by looking more broadly than just at *Hamlet*. So, for instance, we could talk for a long time about how this story is a lot like *Romeo and Juliet*.

I was wondering—and I hope this isn't going to be on the test—is there a soothsayer in Hamlet*? Or is your soothsayer a reference to* Macbeth*?*

No. That harks to *Macbeth*.

What a wonderful treat, to think of these, as you say, cornerstones, as being available for you to play with. To be free with.

Yes. And there are the Mowgli stories from *The Jungle Book*, which are up front. For Edgar, the literary work that is most important has nothing to do with Hamlet or anybody else. It's to do with Mowgli, who has struggled with whether to live in the wild world or in the domestic world.

Whether to join the wolf pack or . . . what was it, the man pack?

Yeah. Because he's the man-cub [laughs]. So the only thing that was frustrating was that the material I was mining was so rich and connected. It had to do with the Elizabethan stage tradition, not a particular story, so there are devices that occur again and again. And I got to thinking, how is it that these old plays get to draw on these enormous emotions in a way that seems to be against the rules in a lot of contemporary literature. I mean, you can explore the extremes of human emotion. Jealousy and rage and revenge and sorrow, and all those things.

Whereas we're too cool to go at those things now.

Right. We take this ironic or cynical step back from those emotions and, for whatever reason, we embed it in humor, or in irony, or in what I call contemporary domestic realism, you know, where the seismometer on emotions is so subtle that the needle barely quivers . . . until the end, when it quivers a *little* more. Why are those [older] stories given license to have those gigantic, orchestral emotional moments in them? So part of the writing for me was just . . . envy. Of course, they're utterly artificial. No one looks at Shakespearean plays and says, "Ah, realism at its finest!" [Laughs] Right? And yet it doesn't matter.

That being said, your "Ophelia" is the first one I've ever really understood emotionally.

Thanks very much. I'm very proud to hear you say that. So I don't at all mind the *Hamlet* connection, but there's a larger context that is usually omitted in that discussion, which I think is too bad because if a reader comes to the novel with those two words, "It's Hamlet," then they're going to be disappointed.

Maybe it's our lack of experience with allusion that's the problem. It's not very common for modern American novels to be as allusive as The Story of Edgar Sawtelle *clearly is, so most people will simplify the idea down to a sound bite.*

You know what else is interesting is that *Hamlet* itself is a "retelling"—if I can use that word, even though I don't like it used for my book—is a retelling of a story that was older in Shakespeare's time than *Hamlet* is in our time. So *Hamlet* didn't emerge out of whole cloth; it's this other story that he adapted that is actually quite different from the story that we call *Hamlet* now.

As was Lear. *Now, you've got a background in theater, right?*

A very brief background. I was a theater major for one semester; it was my first semester in college. Actually, I have a longer ▶

background than that, but it's entirely imaginary because way, way back, like maybe third grade or so, I thought, *that's* what I'm going to do with my life: I'm going to be an actor. I guess it was in seventh grade, I actually staged a little play with my two best friends. We went from classroom to classroom, and it was just a talking play. So we'd just sit in chairs and talk. And it was adapted from a record I'd got for a ventriloquist's dummy. It was a routine meant for the guy and his dummy, you know, all those corny jokes. I couldn't do the ventriloquism at all, so I pitched the dummy into the corner, and sat down and wrote out everything that happened on the record, and I adapted it for three people rather than two: myself, my friend Brian, and my friend Lloyd. I don't remember how we talked the teachers into letting us do this; I think I just kind of insisted. We plunked our chairs down in front of our classmates, whom we were going to see in an hour on the playground . . . and they were probably going to beat the shit out of us for doing this. I kept forgetting my lines, I was terrible at it. I was too excited. My friends were not bad, though. I was never involved in theater when I was in high school, but when I finally tried it, I didn't like it.

You didn't like acting.

No!

Did you try any other jobs, like working backstage?

Oh I liked that even less. That was really awful. All the stagecraft and the lighting and having to paint the sets. Boy, I thought that was really pointless.

So it was the stories that attracted you in the first place?

Yeah. It was the stories. I'd gone through my high school years sensitized to the stories in these plays, like *Oedipus Rex* and *Romeo and Juliet*. But the one play I was in that I really, really loved was *West Side Story* . . . which is a retelling of *Romeo and Juliet*.

So we have three examples there, starting with the ventriloquist's dummy record. Over the years, I have to say, your referents have become more sophisticated.

But I still steal like crazy. ∿

Author's Picks:
Canine Classics

Fiction
The Call of the Wild, Jack London
Perhaps *the* classic tale of man and dog.
The beating heart of this story is the
bond that forms between John Thornton
and the dog, Buck, as they fight for
survival in the Yukon. For reasons
that escape me, this tale is sometimes
classified as children's literature. Don't
believe it.

So Long, See You Tomorrow,
William Maxwell
Read this autobiographical novel for its
achingly beautiful portrayal of jealousy,
murder, and familial loss in the 1920s
Midwest, and because it is about as close
to perfect as a novel can get. Along the
way, watch for a dog named Trixie,
Almondine's most direct literary
ancestor. One of my favorite novels
of all time.

The Jungle Book, Rudyard Kipling
It's hard to imagine a canine literary
world without "the wise little frog" of
Mowgli standing in the shadows, ready to
slip away into the jungle. If you haven't
read Kipling's wonderful stories, rush to
find them. And if you have, shouldn't you
spend some time with Bagheera, Baloo,
and the Seeonee Pack again?

Nonfiction

Dog Man, Martha Sherrill
The life story of Morie Sawataishi, responsible for rescuing the Akita breed from extinction in post–World War II Japan. In spare, lovely prose, Sherrill illustrates the sacrifices and rewards of a life devoted to dogs.

Adam's Task, Vicki Hearne
Hearne's wide-ranging treatise straddles philosophy and animal training, and in the process enlarges our understanding of what it means to belong to an animal. A remarkable book. Every dog owner should read the chapter entitled "How to Say 'Fetch.'"

Winterdance: The Fine Madness of Running the Iditarod, Gary Paulsen
In middle age, Gary Paulsen finds himself running the Iditarod with a homegrown team of dogs and a surplus of naïveté. By turns exciting, hilarious, and heartbreaking, this account of one man's adventure and obsession makes for great reading.

Animals in Translation, Temple Grandin and Catherine Johnson
Grandin, a professor of Animal Science at Colorado State University and a well-known autistic, first came to the public's attention after Oliver Sacks wrote about her in *An Anthropologist on Mars.* Here Grandin applies her professional and personal experience to summarizing the state of the art in understanding animal behavior. ▸

Author's Picks *(continued)*

If Dogs Could Talk, **Vilmos Csányi**
Outstandingly marshals what we know about canine evolution and cognition, interspersed with Csányi's observations of his own two dogs. Of particular note are the chapters describing how, through cleverly designed experiments, Csányi and others have isolated aspects of canine cognition, including the ability to reason about what information (such as the location of a highly desirable treat) people have or do not have, and change tactics accordingly. Fascinating from start to finish. ∾

D on't miss the next book by your favorite author. Sign up now for AuthorTracker by visiting www.AuthorTracker.com.